OVID'S
METAMORPHOSES

This PAUL DRY BOOKS *edition of*

OVID'S METAMORPHOSES

is dedicated to the memory of

JOHN FREDERICK NIMS

(1913–1999)

OVID'S
METAMORPHOSES

THE ARTHUR GOLDING TRANSLATION 1567

EDITED, WITH AN INTRODUCTION AND

NOTES, BY JOHN FREDERICK NIMS

WITH A NEW ESSAY, *SHAKESPEARE'S*

OVID, BY JONATHAN BATE

PAUL DRY BOOKS

Philadelphia   2000

First Paul Dry Books Edition, 2000

Paul Dry Books, Inc.
Philadelphia, Pennsylvania
www.pauldrybooks.com

Originally Published by The Macmillan Company
Reprinted by Scribner, An Imprint of Simon & Schuster, Inc.

3 5 7 9 10 8 6 4 2
Printed in the United States of America

Library of Congress Cataloging-in-Publication Data

Ovid, 43 B.C.–17 or 18 A.D.
    [Metamorphoses. English]
    Ovid's Metamorphoses : the Arthur Golding translation, 1567 / edited, with an introduction
and notes, by John Frederick Nims ; with a new essay, Shakespeare's Ovid, by Jonathan Bate. —
1st Paul Dry Books ed.
        p.   cm.
    Originally published: New York : Macmillan, 1965.
    ISBN 0-9664913-1-9 (pbk.)
    1. Fables, Latin Translations into English.   2. Metamorphosis—Mythology Poetry.
3. Mythology, Classical Poetry.   I. Golding, Arthur, 1536–1606.   II. Nims, John Frederick,
1913–   .   III. Bate, Jonathan.   IV. Title.
PA6522.M2G6 1999
873'.01—dc21

99-39904
CIP

ISBN 0-9664913-1-9

ACKNOWLEDGMENTS

The editor is grateful to the University of Illinois for its generous help, and particularly to Professor Robert W. Rogers, Head of the Department of English, and to Mary Kay Peer, secretary of the department, for their advice and assistance. And for coping with what Golding might have called an orpid queach of corsies, he is grateful to Mary Louise Robbins of the Department of English, who undertook to prepare a typescript from edited photostats of the black-letter original of 1567 and who in the course of her work made many helpful suggestions about the manuscript and the problems it raised.

ACKNOWLEDGMENTS

BOOK V

BOOK VI

BOOK VII

BOOK VIII

BOOK IX

BOOK X

BOOK XI

CONTENTS

BOOK XII

BOOK XIII

BOOK XIV

BOOK XV

INTRODUCTION

෨෨෨

OVID, GOLDING, AND THE
CRAFT OF POETRY

———————

"THE MOST BEAUTIFUL BOOK in the language"—so Ezra Pound salutes Arthur Golding's translation of Ovid's *Metamorphoses*. Not an offhand opinion either: in *Notes on Elizabethan Classicists* of 1915 or '16, Golding, "no inconsiderable poet," came in for high praise; Pound even found it necessary to specify that he was not saying "Golding is a greater poet than Milton." A 1929 footnote to the article says, "His *Metamorphoses* form possibly the most beautiful book in our language." By 1934, in the *ABC of Reading*, even the "possibly" is dropped; and by 1964, in *Confucius to Cummings*, an anthology of poetry edited by Pound and Marcella Spann, no writer except Browning is accorded such extensive representation: there are 28 pages of Golding to 24 of Shakespeare (and to less than three of Chapman's *Odyssey*); a note reminds us that it is "a volume that has been called 'the most beautiful book in our language.'"

But how carefully had Pound read Golding? He seems to have looked at the pages of Professor Rouse's edition of 1904, seen that the language was livelier than much translator's English, found a few bright passages, and exalted his discovery into a lifelong enthusiasm. There are signs of imperfect reading in the passages he quotes. He gives us, as from Golding, this line about Proserpina gathering flowers:

And while of Maidenly desire she fillde hir Haund and Lap . . .

But Golding's word was not "Haund"; it was "Maund." Pound apparently thought it a misprint, which he took on himself to correct. "Maund" means a wicker basket; Golding uses the word several times. Here it translates Ovid's "calathos." (In *Confucius to Cummings*, p.

xiii

56, the word is correctly glossed by one of the editors when it appears in VIII, 853.) "Haund," in any case, is an improbable spelling for "hand" in Golding, who wrote "hande" only ten lines above the line quoted. In the selection Pound calls "Address to Bacchus" he quotes Golding as writing

> . . . throngs of Fownes and Satyres on thee tend.

"Fownes" arouses our suspicion as an unlikely way to spell "Fawns," which is normally "Faunes" in Golding. What he wrote here was "Frowes," quite a common word in his translation. "Frow" (Dutch, *vrouw*) meant first a Dutch woman, later any woman; it was applied especially to the Bacchantes and in this passage translates "Bacchae." There are other misreadings in the lines Pound quotes; it is surprising that they still appear in *The Literary Essays of Ezra Pound,* published some forty years after the piece was written.

It is true that few critics have shared Pound's enthusiasm. C. S. Lewis, in *English Literature in the Sixteenth Century,* says that the poem, in "ugly fourteeners," "ought to be unendurable, and it almost is. . . ." A cooler judgment is that of F. O. Matthiessen, who, in his *Translation: An Elizabethan Art,* writes: "The barriers of meter are not easily crossed from one language into another, and it requires a poet to translate a poet. Such works as Golding's Ovid and Harington's Ariosto neither suggest the qualities of the original, nor possess exceptional poetic merit in compensation." My own opinion is that while Golding's work is not "beautiful"—if that word has any critical utility—it has other claims on our attention. It is certainly the most famous translation of Ovid into English. It was the English Ovid from the time of its publication in 1567 until about a decade after the death of Shakespeare in 1616—the Ovid, that is, for all who read him in English during the greatest period of our literature. And in its racy verve, its quirks and oddities, its rugged English gusto, it is still more enjoyable, more plain fun to read, than any other *Metamorphoses* in English.

An odd collaboration, that between the sophisticated darling of a dissolute society, the author of a scandalous handbook of seduction, and the respectable country gentleman and convinced Puritan who spent much of his life translating the sermons and commentaries of John Calvin. Hardly less striking than the metamorphoses the work dealt with.

Ovid—Publius Ovidius Naso—has given us his own autobiography in *Tristia*, IV, 10. He was born in 43 B.C., the year which closed the Ciceronian Age with the death of the great orator. The poets of that age had been Lucretius and Catullus, both dead about ten years when Ovid was born. Vergil, whom Ovid saw only once, was then about twenty-seven; Horace, whom he heard recite, about twenty-two. Propertius and Tibullus, who died long before Ovid, were in their childhood. He himself lived through the whole period of the Augustan Age: Augustus began to reign in 27 B.C., when Ovid was fifteen; he died in 14 A.D. Ovid, banished from Rome in 8 A.D., survived the emperor by four years—the only poet of the great age who lived on into the Christian era.

Like most of the Roman poets, he was born outside of the city itself, at Sulmo, now Sulmona, about 100 miles to the east. His family was prosperous if not affluent. His practical father, who once complained that not even Homer had left any money, sent him to Rome and later to Athens to be given the kind of education, largely rhetorical, that a prospective lawyer and public official should receive. Ovid's interests, however, lay elsewhere; poetry, he said, had always come naturally to him—though no poet has kept a craftier eye out for the artistic effect. At few times in the history of the world can an environment have been more congenial for poetry. The work of Vergil, Horace, Propertius, and Tibullus was beginning to circulate when Ovid was a young man; rich and powerful figures were willing to sponsor and encourage literary talent. Ovid's earliest work, the *Amores,* consists of rather lighthearted amorous elegiacs, which, especially in the translation of Christopher Marlowe, sound rather like the *Elegies* of the young John Donne. These were followed by the *Heroides,* a series of letters from "heroines" to their absent lovers. The *Ars Amatoria,* or *Art of Love,* a sort of tongue-in-cheek guide for philanderers, which some have seen as disenchanted or satiric, created something of a scandal; it may well have been one of the reasons why Ovid was banished by an emperor concerned about the morality of his people. There seems to have been a mysterious other reason too: Ovid refers to it sometimes as a mistake he made, sometimes as an inadvertence like that of Actaeon, who suddenly found himself staring on Diana while she bathed. Scholars have speculated ever since, often lewdly, on the exact reason for the banishment; John C. Thibault's *The Mystery of Ovid's Exile* (1964) finds none of some thirty-three theories satisfactory. The punishment was severe for a poet who loved Rome and its society: he was sent to Tomi on the shores of the

Black Sea, a savage outpost in a grim landscape of bitter winters, whose inhabitants spoke a barbarous dialect, and whose very survival was threatened by the wild tribesmen around them. Here he spent the ten years of life remaining, his poetry of complaint and appeal ignored by the authorities in Rome. Ovid was married three times; his only child, a daughter, was probably a wife at the time of his banishment.

Ovid's most famous English translator, Arthur Golding, was born in Essex in 1536 of a family of prosperous landowners whose name went back beyond the conquest. One of his sisters married John de Vere, 16th Earl of Oxford; she was later lady-in-waiting to the queen. Strongly Protestant, even Puritan, in his convictions, Golding probably dropped out of Cambridge when the Catholic Queen Mary came to the throne in 1553. But, in the university or out of it, he must have read the classics thoroughly as a young man. Translating from the Latin and the French became the chief work of his life. His *Preface* to Ovid explains why he could translate a poet so exuberantly pagan, and why at the same time he could be working on John Calvin's *Treatise on Offenses*, which he followed with several volumes of Calvin's sermons and commentaries. In all, Golding published over thirty volumes, most of them religious. But with them were a translation of Caesar's *Commentaries* (a work which Longfellow mentions as among the books Miles Standish owned), an account of a sensational London murder of 1573, later dramatized as *A Warning for Fair Women*, and an account of the London earthquake of 1580. Golding, who during the happiest period of his life was on speaking terms with many of his great contemporaries, was married and had eight children. From the time of his elder brother's death in 1575 until the end of his life he was harassed by a series of lawsuits over mortgaged property. For all of his famous friends and wealthy relatives, he spent a year or two in debtors' prison; when he died in 1606 he left debts so large that only a man once rich could have accumulated them.

When Ovid was ejected from Rome in 8 A.D., his most ambitious work, the *Metamorphoses* (Golding uses the singular *Metamorphosis* of some manuscripts) had not been given its final revision. Ovid, in despair, threw his own manuscript into the fire. Friends who had copies did not join him in this symbolic suicide, and before long he was sending back instructions for its publication. The fifteen books are a collection of some two hundred and fifty stories which involve the theme of transformation, though sometimes, as in the stories of Phaethon and Proserpina, the theme is incidental. The transformations are generally of men and women into something else—animal, vegetable, or even mineral. Sometimes the change is a means of escape, sometimes a reward, sometimes a punishment. Some stories are only a few lines long; some several hundred. There is an order roughly chronological from the change of original chaos into the universe up to the development of Rome from a humble village to world capital—and even on to the apotheosis of Julius Caesar as a star. There are many tones, from the homely sweetness of Philemon and Baucis to the frenzy of a girl's incestuous love for her father or her brother; from the little idyll of Pan and Syrinx to the rape, mutilation, and cannibalism of Tereus, Procne, and Philomela. The tales follow each other with marvellous rapidity—*senza tirar fiato,* says an Italian editor —and are connected in all sorts of ways, some so ingenious that Quintilian objected to the cleverness. Such compilations of *epyllia* (short narrative poems) had been made before; some had even dealt with the same theme or a more specialized one: transformation into birds, for example. How much Ovid borrowed from lost originals of course we do not know; we know that he did borrow, and we know that it was the custom for ancient poets (as for such modern ones as Pound and Eliot) to allude deliberately, even by quotation, to other literary works. Ovid's gallery of narrative exuberance has been called baroque, even "violently baroque," yet the language itself, for all of its rhetorical elegance, is simple and "classic." Ovid is a sensuous poet; he sees in pictures that have reminded some readers of those at Pompeii. Little wonder that in the Renaissance his book became a sort of "painter's bible," so that one can hardly go through a museum of Europe or America without seeing picture after picture of Ovidian inspiration. The sophisticated poet says elsewhere that such transformations as he describes are impossible. But if they were possible, he seems to say, this is how they would happen to such people as we know in such a world as that around us. "His book sings," says A. G. Lee, one of his recent editors, "of the manifold variety of life, telling us that the world is full of beauty and wonder, that life is good and to be enjoyed."

Mere escape literature, some might say. Yet perhaps the most delightful escape literature we have: off into an enchanted world very much like the one we know, except that sorcery and miracle are as real as gravitation. Any bird by the roadside may be the comrade or enemy of another day, encouraging or reproaching us; the tree in the yard may be last year's girl friend, the same sheen on the bright leaves as the golden hair had once.

Yet if not serious in the kaleidoscope of detail, the *Metamorphoses* have a serious philosophical undercurrent, brought to the surface in the long discussion of Pythagorean philosophy in XV, which sees change and growth as fundamental and eternal laws of the universe. As we know they are: over the years, if not before our faces, we have seen men turn into wolves or weasels, seen them turn to rocks of this kind or that. We have even seen them turn, last of all, into flowers and trees. Valéry is Ovidian when he writes:

> L'argile rouge a bu la blanche espèce,
> Le don de vivre a passé dans les fleurs!

Time is telescoped in Ovid: the girl is a tree in seconds, so that Apollo's palm on the warm bark can still feel the beating heart beneath. These transformations are like the time-lapse films of a flower developing—the process of weeks, perhaps, in a few seconds. Poets have always been fascinated by mutability; some have seen the meaning of life in passionate surrender to the spirit of change. We think of Goethe in *Dauer im Wechsel* or *Selige Sehnsucht*; of Rilke in the "Wolle die Wandlung" of the Sonnets to his Ovidian Orpheus—the phrase itself from a sonnet (II, 12) that ends with Daphne, now laurel, yearning for her pursuer to change into wind:

> Und die verwandelte Daphne
> will, seit sie lorbeern fühlt, dass du dich wandelst in Wind.

Lines like these remind us that in reading later poetry we cannot be quite sure we are not reading the classics, perhaps Ovid himself, metamorphosed. Goethe, in one of his noblest poems, the *Trilogie der Leidenschaft*, says that the hours went by like sisters, alike yet not identical:

> Die Stunden glichen sich in zartem Wandern
> Wie Schwestern zwar, doch keine ganz den andern.

We know he is thinking of Ovid's palace of the sun, where the engraved sea nymphs are described as having

> facies non omnibus una,
> non diuersa tamen, qualem decet esse sororum.

Goethe probably knew Ovid better than he knew any other poet. So, we suspect, did Dante, though he was obligated to take the more orthodox Vergil for his guide. So too did Shakespeare. One wonders if any other poet can claim so many devoted followers among the great?

It would be hard to come on a more striking illustration of Ovid's theme than the posthumous fate of the poet himself. Banished from pagan Rome for—we can almost say—immorality, he was enthusiastically gathered to the allegorical bosom of the Christian Middle Ages. Though earlier centuries had been hostile, the twelfth and thirteenth centuries have been called an Ovidian Age. In allegorized versions of his *Metamorphoses,* he became even a sort of Christian theologian. Extracts were made for convents: the goddesses were presented as nuns, the gods as their clergy. The amours Ovid described become their pious meetings. Although moralized versions of erotic stories were expressly banned by the Church, they remained long in vogue. In the most important, the endless *Ovide moralisé* of just after 1300, the whole of Christian morality is discovered in the *Metamorphoses.* Three-personed Diana, who was not only the huntress but also the Moon and Hecate, stood for the Trinity. Cupid, with halo, was the Infant Jesus. Ceres seeking Proserpina represented the Church looking for the strayed souls of sinners, her two torches the Old and New Testament. Another allegorizer took the story of the lewd nymph Salmacis, who flung off her clothes to leap into the water after the bathing Hermaphroditus, to be about the True Church soliciting Protestants to return to her ardent breast. Golding, in his *Epistle* and *Preface,* reprinted in this present edition after the fifteen books as an example of Ovid moralized, does not permit himself these absurdities. The Salmacis story for him merely shows that idleness encourages lust, which can be enervating. Golding is sensible in a century deluged by allegorical commentaries, which thinkers such as Rabelais derided. The allegorical tradition is alluded to in the books by Bolgar and Curtius (see Bibliography), but more fully treated by Jean Seznec in *The Survival of the Pagan Gods:*

. . . this pseudo science, which teaches us to hide, or to discover, the most serious precepts beneath the most frivolous outward appearance, offered a providential means of reconciling the pagan and the Christian worlds . . . basically, allegory is often sheer imposture, used to reconcile the irreconcilable—just as we have seen it lending decency to the manifestly indecent. . . .

But in Golding's two pieces, which may have been only a gesture toward his conscience and any censorious official eye, it is not the "dangerous fraud" Seznec calls it. Ovid, says Golding, is not merely telling stories; he is giving

> pitthye, apt and playne
> Instructions which import the prayse of vertues, and the shame
> Of vices, with the due rewardes of eyther of the same.

He proceeds to certain common-sense examples from each of the books, with some practical advice for the conduct of life. As the jingle on his title page insists, there is more here than meets the eye:

> With skill, heede, and judgement, this worke must be read,
> For else to the Reader it standes in small stead.

Ovid's importance in the Elizabethan Age can hardly be over-emphasized. In his *Mythology and the Renaissance Tradition in English Poetry*, Douglas Bush holds that "a history of mythology and the Renaissance tradition must be largely an account of the meta-morphoses of Ovid." And he finds Golding's translation "all-important" in England.

But, in these years of Shakespeare commemorations, we may wonder what Golding meant to the dramatist. We know what Ovid meant: L. P. Wilkinson, in the best book we have on Ovid, reminds us that Shakespeare echoes him about four times as often as he echoes Vergil, that he draws on every book of the *Metamorphoses*, and that there is scarcely a play untouched by his influence. Golding's transla-tion, through the many editions published during Shakespeare's life-time, was the standard Ovid in English. If Shakespeare read Ovid so, he read Golding.

It seems certain that he did. Yet for Professor Rouse to call his 1904 edition by the title of *Shakespeare's Ovid* is misleading in its implications. T. W. Baldwin (*William Shakspere's Small Latin and Lesse Greeke*) has brought his impressive knowledge to bear on this and other problems; his conclusion is that Shakespeare quite possibly used Golding in the Stratford school along with the Latin. This would account for the way Shakespeare now and then seems to blend the two together: "the evidence now seems to be conclusive that [he] habitually used both." Of one passage in Shakespeare Professor

Baldwin writes: "the nuclear greatness which Shakspere sees is in the original, not in Golding's awkwardly obscure translation." His general conclusion is that Shakespeare knew Ovid's stories and treatment, and that when he was working on a situation that recalled Ovid he would turn to the *Metamorphoses* for suggestions: "there is no indication that he does more than run through Golding's translation. . . ." Shakespeare's Ovid, we might say, was Ovid.

All writers on Golding and Shakespeare adduce Prospero's famous speech in *The Tempest,* which begins:

Ye elves of hills, brooks, standing lakes and groves . . .

and quote Golding's

Ye Ayres and windes: ye Elves of Hilles, of Brookes, of Woods alone,
Of standing Lakes . . .   (VII, 265)

Baldwin, after a close study, concludes that "at first sight the relation . . . appears a great deal stronger than it is." We can hardly claim that Shakespeare got his elves from Golding, since he had had elves of his own in the earlier plays. Baldwin points out that for the Elizabethans certain Roman minor gods (*dii*) were "elves," and he reminds us that if Golding and Shakespeare, looking at the same Latin text, had used the same Latin dictionary, they would have come up with the same English words. Pound may be overconfident when, after saying that Golding's work is "the most beautiful book in the language," he adds, "my opinion and I suspect it was Shakespeare's."

In the burlesque of the Pyramus and Thisbe story in *A Midsummer Night's Dream* (V, i), Shakespeare seems to be poking good-humored fun at Golding, whose version has one of the lovers thanking the wall for its "courtesie" in leaving the chink they can talk through (Ovid had said: "Nec sumus ingrati"), and has Thisbe ("thy Thisb") die with such lines as

This said, she tooke the sword yet warme with slaughter of hir love
And setting it beneath hir brest, did to hir heart it shove.   (IV, 196-7)

At the silly pitch of passion in the burlesque, it is curious that the lovers break into what are really Golding's fourteeners, complete with inversion and tautology, though in Shakespeare the line is printed as three short lines, made ridiculous by an overuse of rhyme:

Thy mantle good,/What stain'd with blood?/Approach, ye Furies fell!
O Fate, come come!/Cut thread and thrum;/Quail, crush, conclude, and
                                                                    quell.

Though Golding's translation of Ovid is the most enjoyable we have, the enjoyment is not, I think, in the poetry. Ovid was a great poet; Dante put him among the four greatest he knew. Golding was a respectable literary gentleman, with a thorough knowledge of Latin (he does not make the boners that Marlowe does), with a sharp eye for the life about him, and with a keen ear for racy English. But to read Golding with the original is to be in for continual disappointment. First, we notice how wordy Golding is. Latin is of course terser than English, but no difference between the languages can excuse Golding's writing twenty words for Ovid's three, or turning one line into two, three, or even four. Marlowe, a craftsman of genius, was able to render Ovid line for line; Golding adds over 2,500 lines to Ovid's 12,000. Ovid himself has been found long-winded, even if musically so, but the general effect of his writing is one of conciseness. Single lines and phrases have been ringing in the literary memory of Europe for two thousand years. He combines terse elements, with little reliance on modifiers; whereas he can introduce his Iron Age with "de durost ultima ferro," Golding has to write

> of yron is the last
> In no part good and tractable as former ages past.

Ovid calls gold the incentive to evil, "irritamenta malorum"; Golding, who tends to say things twice, calls it

> The spurres and stirrers unto vice, and foes to doing well.

Ovid says Lycaon is the very image of savagery, "eadem feritatis imagost"; Golding says

> and every kind of waye
> his cruell heart in outward shape doth well itself bewraye.

Even the simple "ibimus illac" ("we'll go there") becomes

> To make my passage that way then my cunning will I try.

Showpiece lines suffer the most. When Apollo warns his human son that he wants too much in asking to guide the solar chariot, he tells the boy that his state is mortal, what he asks is not

> Sors tua mortalis; non est mortale quod optas.

A line memorable in its phrasing and in its melancholy application to so much in our experience. But who would remember, or care to remember:

Thy state is mortall, weake and frayle, the thing thou doest desire
Is such, whereto no mortall man is able to aspire . . . ?

When the spiteful old hag Envy flies over Athens, she is said almost to weep because she sees nothing to weep at:

Vixque tenet lacrimas, quia nil lacrimabile cernit.

Perhaps the line is too clever. Golding, who loses the important word play of *lacrimas-lacrimabile,* makes it clumsy:

And forebicause she nothing saw that might provoke to weep,
It was a corsie to hir heart hir hatefull tears to keepe.

A last example, from thousands possible, of Ovid's polished conciseness and Golding's gangling diffusion, is in the dying words of Thisbe, who tells Pyramus that she—unfortunate!—will be called the cause and companion of his death:

letique miserrima dicar
causa comesque tui.

And wretched woman as I am, it shall of me be sed
That like as of thy death I was the only cause and blame,
So am I thy companion eke and partner in the same.

Golding has a special weakness for adjectives, the handiest means of stretching out a line metrically deficient. Ovid uses no adjectives when he has the wolf swimming among sheep in his great flood. Golding contributes three:

The grim and greedy Wolfe did swim among the siely sheepe.

Ovid first mentions Phaethon without an adjective; Golding contributes three overlapping ones: "a stalwart stripling strong and stout." Sometimes it seems that Golding—as Plato has Socrates say of a bad poet—seems to be trying to show in how many ways he can say the same thing, or how many synonyms he knows. Ovid: "pugnes"; Golding: "Strive, struggle, wrest, and writhe."

Golding, who in his prose can write perfectly natural English, in verse permits himself inversions that have never existed in our normal English speech patterns:

She staide without, for to the house in enter might she not . . .

or

. . . names that . . .
To thee O Liber wonted are to attributed bee.

The meter also forces him to patch out lines with such dull putty as "even so likewise," "howbeit yet of all this while," "conditionly that when that I," "by means whereof away without," and "immediately without delay." He uses "for" with the infinitive ("for to go"); says "the which" and "for because"; uses "the same" for "it." Pound defends one of his faults: "his constant use of 'did go,' 'did say' is not fustian and mannerism; it was contemporary speech, though in a present-day poet it is impotent affectation and definite lack of technique." But it was not contemporary speech; lack of technique is precisely what it was. Golding's prose is straightforward, without inversions, almost entirely without the *do*'s and *did*'s unless they are emphatic, as we still do use them. Here are some lines from his report of the earthquake, in modernized spelling: these, and not what we find too often in his verse, are the patterns of English speech.

Again, whereas in earthquakes that proceed of natural causes, certain signs and tokens are reported to go before them, as: a tempestuous working and raging of the sea, the weather being fair, temperate, and unwindy; calmness of the air matched with great cold; dimness of the sun for certain days afore; long and thin streaks of clouds appearing after the setting of the sun, the weather being otherwise clear; the troubledness of water even in the deepest wells, yielding moreover an infected and stinking savor; and lastly, great and terrible sounds in the earth, like the noise of groanings and thunderings, as well afore as after the quaking—we find that not any such foretoken happened against the coming of this earthquake. And therefore we may well conclude (though there were none other reason to move us) that this miracle proceeded not of the course of any natural cause, but of God's only determinate purpose, who maketh even the very foundations and pillars of the earth to shake, the mountains to melt like wax, and the seas to dry up and to become as a dry field, when he listeth to show the greatness of his glorious power, in uttering his heavy displeasure against sin.

This is English, and we can amuse ourselves by thinking how less English it would be if he had versified it:

> And whereas earthquakes, which that eke of causes naturall bee,
> Afore the same are signs thereof, and tokens for to see . . .

The rhythm was an old-fashioned one when Golding wrote. "To most sensitive contemporary ears," says T. S. Eliot, in writing of the Senecan translators of that decade, "the fourteener had had its day." It may seem curious to us now, who talk of poetry of "the fifties" or "the sixties," that Pound, so fond of making it new, should admire a behind-the-times translator. And yet who remembers if Catullus wrote in the manner of the 60's or the 70's B.C.? Villon in the manner of the 1460's or the '50's? And if Golding was behind the times, Chapman, in his translation of the *Iliad,* was even more so.

If Golding's fourteeners do not take us, with Chapman's, into the realms of gold, yet they have considerable narrative merit. Except for the wordiness and the inversions, they are clear and fast-moving— more readable than the lines of Studley and Jasper Heywood that Eliot quotes for their "vigorous vocabulary and swinging meter." For one thing, Golding's lines are not clotted with excessive alliteration: one finds almost never such a line as Heywood's

> Whose growing guttes the gnawing gripes and fylthy foules do fyll.

One of the merits of Golding as verse writer is the casualness with which he lets the syntactical pauses fall. The fourteener tends to break into two half-lines, one of four beats, one of three, with a strong pause after each. Richard Edwards' famous *Amantium Irae* begins:

> In goyng to my naked bedde, as one that would have slept,
> I heard a wife syng to her child, that long before had wept . . .

Every line in this eight-line stanza, almost every line in the five-stanza poem, has the pauses in exactly the same places. But in Golding, though his basic line is like Edwards', the pauses may come anywhere, as in Juno's complaint (II, 647–51):

> I have bereft hir womans shape, and at this present howre
> She is become a Goddesse. Loe this is the scourge so sowre
> Wherewith I strike mine enimies. Loe here is all the spight
> That I can do: this is the ende of all my wondrous might.
> No force. I would he should (for me) hir native shape restore . . .

Golding can so far disregard the end-stop as to have an "and" there:

> Here now I Arethusa dwell: here am I setled: and
> I humbly you beseche . . .

He can so far disregard the pause after the fourth beat that he can have a word straddling it:

> The horie Sallowes and the Poplars growing on the brim . . .

Equally carefree is his use of rhyme. He has no objection to drawing on unusual forms that happen to fit. "Breast" he generally spells "brest," but when he needs a rhyme for "fist" he is willing to spell it "brist." "Such" is his usual spelling, but as a rhyme for "whiche" it can turn to "syche." "Stand" is "stand" or "stande," but as a rhyme word for "pond" it can be "stond." "Like" and "well" become "lieke" and "weele" to go with "shrieke" and "keele." His normal form is "before," but to rhyme with "borne" he uses "beforne." No doubt these forms existed, but they are not the ones he uses naturally—say in mid-line, where no need for a rhyme affects his choice. No more natural are the archaic infinitives he uses only for rhyme, "to saine" for "to say"; "make me donne" for "make me do." Generally he rhymes in pairs, but often he uses triplets, and he feels quite free to run on to four or even five rhymes in a row.

Perhaps all Golding needed to write fourteeners well was a couple of sessions on meter and natural speech with so canny a teacher as Mr. Pound. His lines then might have sounded like Samuel Daniel's in *Ulysses and the Siren,* if we take the liberty of writing its four- and three-beat lines as one:

> Come, worthy Greek, Ulysses, come, possess these shores with me;
> The winds and seas are troublesome, and here we may be free.
> Here may we sit and view their toil that travail on the deep,
> And joy the day in mirth the while, and spend the night in sleep.

Here is something of the elegance so often ascribed to Ovid. As there is in the modern fourteeners that Yeats has occasionally written:

The old brown thorn-trees break in two high over Cummen Strand . . .

or

> "You but imagine lies all day, O murderer," I replied . . .

Golding's inability to dominate meter meant that most of his verse was not as well written as prose. If he failed in rather obvious matters, it is not surprising that he quite missed the kind of subtlety that Ovid tried for, and succeeded in, time after time. Examples are more interesting for the light they throw on poetic craftsmanship and the problems of translation than for what they tell us about what Golding failed to do.

Ovid, when writing about the Iron Age and its evils, mentions the frightful stepmothers mixing up their "lurid" poisons:

> Lurida terribiles miscent aconita nouercae.

"Lurida," transferred from the pale faces of the victims to the poison itself, its juxtaposition with "terribiles," and the suspense about what is "lurida" and what "terribiles" give the line its effect. This is entirely a matter of how words are put together. In Golding the eerie line comes to nothing except a couple of inversions and a wrong last word, for the rhyme:

> The stepdames fell their husbandes sonnes with poison do assayle.

In XIV the Sibyl tells Aeneas that nothing is impossible for human worth to achieve: "Invia virtuti nulla est via." The point is in the words: no *via* is *invia*. If one believes, with Goethe and Valéry, that what one wants from a translator of poetry is not mere paraphrase of thought but a rendering of equivalent effect, then one will not be satisfied with a translator who ignores such points, as Golding does with "No way to vertue is restreynd."

In VIII Ovid describes how Daedalus built the labyrinth, confusing its structure so deliberately that no one once in could find his way out. "It leads the eye into going astray by the riddle of its various ways," to give a loutish paraphrase of

> lumina . . .
> ducit in errorem variarum ambage viarum.

Variarum, viarum—these look so alike that one seems a blurred image of the other: the very diction dramatizes the confusions of the maze. Golding simply passes over such virtuosity. He even ignores a line as obvious as the one about the horses of the sun beating their hooves against the barriers in their eagerness to be away: "pedibusque repagula pulsant." Christopher Marlowe, faced with a similar problem in the *Amores*, did what he could by turning Ovid's four *p*'s into three *b*'s (the closest letter to *p* in effect) in translating

> Ite, piae volucres, et plangite pectora pinnis

as

> Go, godly birds, striking your breasts bewail . . .

Sometimes Ovid is indeed too clever. He was told so in his own time, and his ghost has been hearing it ever since. Should a translator then correct Ovid's taste, if indeed he offends in such passages as the one in which Jove is decreeing that mankind shall be destroyed by flood? The other gods lament the loss, the *iactura*. In the next three lines are heard the sounds -*tura*, -*turus*, and *tura*—not to speak of *terrae*, *terras*, and other echoes. The muffled repetition is supposed to represent the way the gods mutter among themselves, dwelling on the theme *iactura*. For the Roman ear, the effect may have succeeded or it may have failed. What is important is that Ovid, like most good poets, is well aware that it is not enough to express thoughts—that what the poet tries to do is somehow mimic, as far as possible in the medium of language, what he is saying, instead of *just* saying it. Ovid cares about this, and he is a poet; Golding does not—he is a good honest man.

Professor Bassett once decided that the most beautiful line in Homer was

$$\pi\grave{\alpha}\rho \ \pi o\tau\alpha\mu\grave{o}\nu \ \kappa\epsilon\lambda\acute{\alpha}\delta o\nu\tau\alpha, \ \pi\alpha\rho\grave{\alpha} \ \dot{\rho}o\delta\alpha\nu\grave{o}\nu \ \delta o\nu\alpha\kappa\tilde{\eta}\alpha$$

in the representation on the shield of Achilles of the cattle moving from barnyard to pasture "along the murmuring river, along the slender reed." Most of us might feel that a great line ought to have more human content; we want the rage of Achilles, the grief of Andromache, or at least the bright hair of Helen above the embattled walls. Bassett's line is a miniature abstraction in words; it has little reference to any reality beyond a musical one—though one can say, if he wishes, that he "hears" the ripple on the pebbles, the wind in the reeds. What we have here is a delicate musical pattern: the two halves of the line have almost—that important *almost!*—the same vowel pattern:

a   oao   eaoa
aa   oao   oaēa

A Hawaiian charm, if one singsongs it with the rhythm. This is a kind of effect that Ovid likes and works for. Describing the Golden Age, he says that there were rivers of milk, rivers of nectar, and that "golden honey was trickling from the green oak."

flumina iam lactis, iam flumina nectaris ibant,
flauaque de uiridi stillabant ilice mella.

Abundance is mimicked in the repetitions of the first line. The *fl*, twice associated with that abundance, is picked up in *flauaque*; the line begins in profusion. *Flaua* means *golden*; it modifies *mella* (*honey*) at the very end of the line. Honey is everywhere in this opulent world. But *flaua* is put next to *uiridi*, which means *green* and modifies *ilice* (*oak*), on the far side of the long word that means a continuous flowing. So we get gold against green, the pure idea of color, before we know what is gold, what is green. (Gold and green are the thematic colors used throughout *Fern Hill*, Dylan Thomas's poem of his own golden age.) The rich trickle begins in *stillabant*, with the *-bant* of continuity a bit more emphatic after the *ibant* of the line before. The liquid *ill* is sounded again in *ilice* and again—for the sound too trickles—slightly varied in the *ell* of *mella*. Of the eight central vowels, six are *i*'s, which, as Plato long ago observed in the *Cratylus*, is (as the quickest of the vowel sounds) "expressive of motion." Almost a patter of honey, gold on green. This, I suppose, is "beauty" in poetry, if anything is. (It is not the highest value; we can all think of lines in Dante or in Shakespeare far more piercing than these.) Golding gives us

Then streames ran milke, then streames ran wine, and yellow honey flowde
From ech greene tree whereon the rayes of firie Phebus glowde.

The first line is the better, though sibilant. Except for the long *e*'s of "greene tree" (whatever they stand for there), not much happens except bumbling in the second line. Golding loses the specific "oak" and gets in some unnecessary mythology with an obvious adjective. Ovid's line, without mentioning Phebus, is full of warmth and clarity. In I, 708, Ovid gets a similar effect when he describes how Pan, grasping for the nymph Syrinx, finds that she has turned into a sheaf of reeds, from which comes a "thin sound like one lamenting": " . . . sonum tenuem similemque querenti." Thin vowel sounds, many querulous nasals; the line itself is as *similem querenti* as sound can make it. Golding again only states: "which made a still and mourning noyse."

A parenthesis: thinking of such "trifles" when one composes, noticing them when one reads—all this seems, especially to those who do not write, to madness near allied. One can only say that the testimony of poets and the researches of their critics have shown that the poets have had such effects in mind, and have bent their expression in these directions when they had call to and could. No effort has been too great—provided it does not show. And no discipline has been too severe: Stravinsky in *Poetics of Music* approves of Baudelaire's "never have prosodies and rhetorics kept originality from fully manifesting itself. . . ." It is not only such poets as the magnificent Góngora who are craft-conscious in lines like

> le dejó por escondido
> o le perdonó por pobre . . .

but even—perhaps especially—such "spontaneous" poets as Catullus and Villon:

> litus ut longe resonante Eoa
> tunditur unda . . .

did not come about by chance. John Fox's recent book on Villon shows by example after example that "it would be quite wrong to think of him as the vagabond poet, dashing off his verse in careless fashion, without a thought for the finer points of versification" and other technical matters even more subtle. Ovid, like most good poets, was fascinated by such problems. Professor Bush quotes Gilbert Murray on Ovid: "He loved the actual technique of the verse." Which reminds us of the remark of Robert Frost to a lady who remonstrated that when he was writing his "beautiful poetry" ("beautiful" was a word he avoided) he surely wasn't thinking of technical problems, and he couldn't really like *those*. "Like 'em!" said Frost. "I revel in 'em."

The shape of sentences, for example. Frost also liked to say that to write poetry was to "go a-sentencing." It would be hard to find a poet who "sentences" more satisfactorily than Ovid does. Words are placed precisely where they will have the greatest effect; we are led through the suspensions and fulfillments of his syntax as through a Mozartean music. As one example of his precise placing, in VII he tells the sad but all too human tale of the love of Cephalus and Procris. Cephalus, after the heat and effort of the chase, calls out again and again for *aura*, for the fresh woodland breeze. His sighs are overheard and misunderstood; a zealous eavesdropper reports to Procris that her husband is meeting a certain Aura in the woods. Procris too misunderstands, and her misunderstanding is her death. The whole chain of circumstances depends on how the word *aura*, or *Aura*, occurs. Ovid places it carefully. When first used, it is separated from the *Et* that introduces it by a long *inciso* that keeps us waiting for the noun. Once uttered, it is repeated immediately; it is the first word of the next three lines, though varied by being never twice in the same case.

> repetebam frigus et umbras
> Et, quae de gelidis exibat uallibus, auram.
> Aura petebatur medio mihi lenis in aestu,
> auram exspectabam; requies erat illa labori.
> "Aura," (recordor enim) "uenias," cantare solebam . . .

Of the seven times Ovid uses the word, here and later, five times it is placed with special sensitivity. Golding uses his "Ayre" nine times, but he lets it fall where it happens to.

Why then read Golding, if, as Professor Bush says, he "often missed or blunted Ovidian points" and was only "moderately faithful"? At least for the stories, if not the poetry; stories translate when poetry does not. But Golding also has something very engaging of his own to give us.

He begins by metamorphosing Ovid: by turning the sophisticated Roman into a ruddy country gentleman with tremendous gusto, a sharp eye on the life around him, an ear for racy speech, and a gift for energetic doggerel. If the Latin mentions Midas's "tiara," Golding calls it a "purple nightcap." The exotic "harpé" of Perseus, the curved blade so special it had a special name, becomes a good English "wood-knife." The classical ilex, instead of being called a holm-oak, becomes the English "Sugarchest" tree. Instead of saying that Io sleeps on the ground, he says that what she lacks is a "good soft featherbed." When a skeptic sneers at the story that Perseus's father was Jove in a shower of gold, Golding has him call Jove the "forged Dad." He sees the ancient world in terms of his own. Instead of "nec supplex timebat/ Iudicis ora sui," he says, "There was no man would crouch or creepe to Judge with cap in hand." Mercury, on his way to kill Argus, does not merely drive "ut pastor, per deuia rura capellas"; he strides right into an Elizabethan countryside, and

Retayning nothing but his staffe, the which he closely helde
Betweene his elbowe and his side, and through the common fielde
Went plodding lyke some good plaine soule that had some flock to feede.

Golding does not translate quality or tone, but he infallibly "Englishes" the stories. When Jove has a council of the gods, Golding says that he summoned his "Court of Parliament." When the Cyclops arranges his hair, with rakes, in the hope of pleasing Galatea (or "Galat," as Golding calls her) he "marcussottes" it—which meant to leave Turkish mustachios, the kind that would be exotic in England, though what one might expect of a Cyclops, who was Sicilian anyway. More than once Golding modernizes military equipment, frankly turning an ancient siege engine into a gun. Even proper names may get their English equivalent. The Aegean Sea becomes the Goat Sea; Par-

thenium Nemus becomes Maiden Wood. Picus's wife, Canens, is
called "Singer." Hyllus becomes plain English "Hill," and Elis, "Ely."
He suggests in a marginal note that Vertumnus and Pomona might be
interpreted as "Turner" and "Applebee." When he doesn't translate
names, he declassicizes them with jaunty Elizabethan abbreviations.
Pentheus, Theseus, Orpheus, and others lose a few inches of their
heroic stature when they are called "Penthey," "Thesey," and "Or-
phey." Thisbe tells Pyramus she is his darling "Thisb." Augias is
"Augie." Morpheus loses all dignity when he turns into plain
"Morph."

Golding is at his best in describing places and people. Ovid, who
has some celebrated place descriptions himself, has of course given
the hints—I doubt anyone would say that Golding is doing it better.
But he is doing it freshly and with a view to his world and that of his
readers. Take the terrain of the great Calydonian boar hunt:

> A wood thick growen with trees which stoode unfelled to that day
> Beginning from a plaine . . . .
>   Now there was a hollow bottom by,
> To which the watershots of raine from all the high grounds drew.
> Within the compass of this pond great store of Osiers grew:
> And Sallowes lithe, and flackring Flags, and moorish Rushes eke,
> And lazie Reedes on little shankes, and other baggage like.
> From hence the Bore was rowzed out . . .
>   (VIII, 444–55)

All of this probably came home to the English reader as "Silua fre-
quens trabibus . . ." did not. Indeed, the whole boar hunt is well done
in Golding, whose rough-and-tumble verses often do well with scenes
of hubbub and uproar, into which he throws himself with the zest of
a sportscaster. (The ethical dative he is so fond of makes him the
participant of many a lively scene: "And with the like celeritie he cut
me Phorbas throte.") First a dog is the victim of what Golding might
have called a "jolly" mistake: the spear "through his guts did gore,/
And naild him to the earth." Then the fierce beast himself is hit:

> And while the Bore did play the fiend [*saevit*] and turned round agast,
> And grunting flang his fome about togither mixt with blood . . .

When Meleager, like a bullfighter, presents Atalanta with what cor-
responds to the ears and tail, the sons of Thestius (the "Thesties")
object and demand she drop them ("Pone age . . . femina . . ."):

> "Dame, come off, and lay us downe this geare."

The rowdy little scene below shows Golding at close to his best. It begins at V, 551, with Ceres wandering the whole earth looking for her daughter Proserpina:

> And being overwrought
> She caught a thirst: no liquor yet had come within hir throte.
> By chaunce she spied nere at hand a pelting thatched Cote
> Wyth peevish doores: she knockt thereat, and out there commes a trot.
> The Goddesse asked hir some drinke and she denide it not:
> But out she brought hir by and by a draught of merrie go downe
> And therewithall a Hotchpotch made of steeped Barlie browne
> And Flaxe and Coriander seede and other simples more
> The which she in an Earthen pot together sod before.
> While Ceres was a eating this, before hir gazing stood
> A hard-faced boy, a shrewde pert wag, that could no maners good:
> He laughed at hir and in scorne did call hir "Greedie gut."
> The Goddesse being wroth therewith, did on the Hotchpotch put
> The liquor ere that all was eate, and in his face it threw . . .

The translator gets the same opportunity for macabre verve in describing the witches' brew Medea cooks up:

> She put thereto the deaw that fell upon a Monday night:
> And flesh and feathers of a Witch, a cursed odious wight
> Which in the likenesse of an Owle abrode a nightes did flie,
> And Infants in their cradels chaunge or sucke them that they die.
>
> (VII, 349–52)

But probably the description of Philemon and Baucis, the good-hearted old country couple in their cottage, surrounded by all of their "homely gear," gives Golding the best scope for his talents. Dryden said he could fairly see Ovid's old couple, and Golding's is no less vivid: the old lady "busie as a Bee" stirring about with her skillet and her coleworts and her hoarded bacon and her "jolly lump of Butter" to bring everything "pyping from the fyre." The final effect of the well told episode is weakened by what may be an inadvertence or what may be a rather bad joke: as Philemon and Baucis, at the end of their lives, watch each other turn into boughs and foliage, Golding says they "did take their leave" of each other. He can joke: surely he is doing so at the end of Book I when Phaethon wants Clymene, his mother, to assure him that his father is really Apollo, not her husband Merops. He beseeches her

> as she lovde the lyfe
> Of Merops, and had kept hir selfe as undefiled wyfe . . .

The absurdity, or the mischief, is not in Ovid.

Sometimes his realism, charmingly enough, distorts to caricature, as in the vigorous personification of Hunger in VIII and of Envy in II. Golding likes to add detail: out of a mere list of names of nymphs provided by Ovid ("Nepheleque Hyaleque Rhanisque/ Et Psecas et Phiale . . ."), he makes:

> Then Niphe nete and cleene
> With Hiale glistring like the grass in beautie fresh and sheene,
> And Rhanis clearer of hir skin than are the rainie drops,
> And little bibling Phyale, and Pseke that pretie Mops . . .
>   (III, 200–3)

One suspects the details were suggested by the footnotes to his Latin text: *rhanis* means *raindrop; phiale, saucer,* etc. We know he incorporated such footnotes on other occasions.

What vivid and racy language this might all have been if Golding had not so often cramped and attenuated it to the meter! Even as it is, his strange, quirky, colloquial vocabulary is one of the chief delights of his translation. We notice immediately that he likes to translate a classical line into what must have had a jaunty swing in 1567. Certainly no one has translated so successfully *out* of Latin—or into so native an English. Ovid's "obscenique greges" becomes "roughts of filthie freaks"; his sleeper "alto sopore solutum" is "snorting bolt upright"; his girl "turbatis . . . capillis" becomes a "frizzletopped wench." Ovid's dancers, which duller translators might have "leading the festal chorus" ("festas duxere choreas"), and which in Ovid have something of the dignity of processions on Wedgwood, really kick up their heels in Golding:

>   Full oft
> The Woodnymphes underneath this tree did fetch theyr frisks aloft.

Golding is particularly good at taking a rather noncommittal line and giving it a startling immediacy. In one long gory battle scene

> Occidit et Celadon Mendesius; occidit Astreus,
> Matre Palaestina, dubio genitore creatus . . .

Or, as I am afraid the conventional translator might say:

> Then Celadon of Mendes fell, Astreus
> Of Palestinian mother, of dubious
> Progenitor begot . . .

Golding throws himself with vituperative gusto into the fight:

> There died also Celadon a Gipsie of the South:
> And so did bastard Astrey too, whose mother was a Jew . . .

When a crowd in Ovid calls out for "Arma, arma," Golding's mob comes to the point and howls "Kill, kill." In a couple of passages dealing with country people, he even falls into rural dialect. Sometimes he sounds curiously modern; he says "a body would have thought" and uses "latch" in the sense of "grab," as we use "latch on to" (modern dictionaries give this as "U.S. slang").

One fond of words will probably find himself poring over the footnotes to Golding's text.* He may even make out his own list of Golding-isms that ought to be revived, perhaps from among such as these:

woose: ooze
whewl: howl, whine
belk: throb
corsie: annoyance
throatboll: Adam's-apple
uppen: mention, bring up
quoath: faint
yesk: sob
awk: reversed, wrong
awkly: awkwardly
chank: chew (one chanks gobbets
    or collops)
sprink: sprinkle ("watering the
    grass" is "sprinking the clowers")
gnoor: snarl
toot: gaze at
parget: plaster
snudge: miser (Remark to gnoor at
    landlords: "Toot the parget,
                    snudge!")

gripple: what snudges are, greedy
coll: embrace, hug (Latin, *collum*,
                    neck)
queach: thicket, grove
ensue: follow ("Ensue me to the
                    queach," XIV, 966)
merry-go-down: strong drink
flacker: flutter, flap
orpid: fierce
overdreep: droop over
hittymissy: hit or miss
pooke: elf, demon
bugg: monster, boogieman
frosh: frog
woodspeck: woodpecker
leechcraft: medical science

Sometimes, with Golding's weird and piquant vocabulary, we feel we are in Lewis Carroll country, in a land where corsies whewl, where orpid buggs sty awkly in the queach, where froshes yesk, and flackering pookes ensue. None of this may be quite "beautiful," but it would be hard to deny it is rich in delights of its own.

* These footnotes explain unfamiliar words on their first occurrence. After a word has been glossed several times, it is not noticed thereafter.

⫶⫶⫶
THE TEXT

In 1565 William Seres published in London the first four books of
Golding's translation of the *Metamorphoses*. The title page reads:
THE FYRST FOWER BOOKES OF *P. Ouidius Nasos worke, in-
titled Metamorphoses, translated oute of Latin into Englishe meter
by Arthur Golding Gent. A woorke very pleasaunt and delectable.*
The complete translation was published two years later by the same
William Seres: THE XV BOOKES OF P. OUIDIUS NASO, EN-
TYTULED *Metamorphosis, translated oute of Latin into English
meeter, by Arthur Golding Gentleman. A worke very pleasaunt and
delectable.* A second edition appeared in 1575, and there had been six
more editions by the time of Shakespeare's death in 1616. Then there
were none until Professor Rouse's *Shakespeare's Ovid* in 1904, re-
printed in a facsimile edition by the Centaur Press (London) in 1961.

   This present edition is based on the copy of the first edition (1567)
now in the Library of the University of Illinois. Its purpose is simply
to present the pleasant and delectable work to a reader interested in
what must have been one of the favorite books of the young Shake-
speare, or to a reader who wonders if it is indeed, as Ezra Pound pro-
fessed, "the most beautiful book in English." It is not, then, primarily
a textual edition—one scrupulously based on a collation of many
copies of the first and later editions, with the laudable purpose of
arriving at a text scientifically as pure as possible—purer, in fact, than
any Elizabethan ever happened upon. The boy from Stratford, for
example, probably not long before 1580, would simply have picked
up a copy of the book; it would not have occurred to him to compare it
with other copies for variants in phrasing, spelling, punctuation,
most of these due to human accidents—to the extra tankard of beer
the compositor had at lunch, to the pretty girl who brushed by his
window and set his hand a-fumbling among the letters, to failing

light or weariness at the end of day. Yet, though altogether modest in
its bibliographical ambitions, this edition substantially reproduces the
text of one copy of the first edition. The arrangement differs from
Golding's in that his preliminary matter, a rather formidable obstacle
to come on at once, has been relegated to the end of the book. Both
Preface and *Epistle* deserve inclusion as examples of the moralizing
and allegorizing process to which Ovid was subjected: his most scan-
dalous stories, it seems, could be seen in a religious light, dim as that
light may seem to us.

The Elizabethan spelling has been almost everywhere retained.
Even if there were no other reasons for keeping it, considerations of
rhythm and rhyme, so essential to the vivacity of Golding's version,
would have been decisive. Generally, a difference is intended be-
tween *inclined* and *inclinde*: the first is pronounced *inclinèd* and has
three syllables; the second has two. To change the spelling is to cripple
the rhythm of many of the lines. Nor does a compromise seem possible
here: one cannot intersperse contemporary spelling with forms like
inclinde or, worse, *inclinèd*. With modern spelling, too, many of the
rhymes would go flat: we would have *always-day* (for his *alway-day*),
plow-enough (for his *plough-inough*), *know-grown* (for his *knowe-
igrowe*), *from-go* (for his *fro-go*).

The spelling has been retained, then, but with certain modifica-
tions. The letters *j, i, u, v* are used as they are today: *jest*, not *iest*;
over, not *ouer*. Abbreviations have been expanded: *that* for y^t,
wondrous for *wōdrous*, *quoth* for ⚡. Obvious misprints have been
corrected: *himself* is written for *hinself*, *it was* for *is was*. Turned
letters have been turned back: *such* is written for *snch*, *have* (*haue*)
for *hane*. Transposed letters have been set in order: *disdaine* for *dis-
diane*. Spelling has also been changed when the original (not fixed
anyway: Golding might spell the same word in different ways, or his
compositor might adjust the spelling to the space available) would
seem to modern readers to indicate a word which it is not. So *brute*
is changed to *bruit*, *of* to *off*, *neare*, to *ne'er*, *tone* to *t'one*, *parsonage*
to *personage*, *gased* to *gazed*, *vial* to *viol*, *travel* to *travail*. *Vade* is
changed to *fade*; *fat* to *vat*. Punctuation, while not modernized, has
been amended when clearly wrong (a period in what can only be the
middle of a sentence) or otherwise misleading.

Textual corruptions are more evident in a verse translation than
in other kinds of writing. Golding writes in inexorable fourteeners:
he never spares us the seven iambic feet, or their conventional varia-

tions, line after line after line, in a work that is longer than *Paradise Lost*. If his *ta-dum ta-dum ta-dum ta-dum* suddenly goes *ta-dum clump dum clump*, or otherwise misfires, we suspect that something is wrong with our text. We can also check by glancing at the Latin he is translating from—allowing for the fact that four centuries of labor by the classicists have not left us exactly the text he was working with. We know that *Cyllemus* and *Furilochus*, for example, must be misprints, since they stand for Ovid's *Cyllenius* and *Eurilochus*. Or if we are puzzled because one of the ingredients in Tisiphone's witches brew (IV, 615) is "the filthie fame of Cerberus"—for so it appears in all editions, up to the 1961 reprint—we can discover that what Ovid wrote is "Oris Cerberei spumas" (IV, 501)—the third word means *foam*, and what Golding must have written is *fome*, not *fame*, even though *fame* could mean "hunger."

But apart from such changes as these—and they probably do not affect more than a letter or two every dozen lines—the reader of this edition is looking on the same text that might have absorbed a young apprentice, jostling along between the stalls of a London street in 1580, or perhaps a country boy stretched out on the banks of the Avon.

SHAKESPEARE'S OVID

by Jonathan Bate

Ovid was Shakespeare's favorite classical poet. The first encounter between the English dramatist and the Roman poet probably occurred in the classroom of the grammar school at Stratford-upon-Avon. The boy William would have been drilled in extracts from Ovid's works in their original Latin—first brief passages in textbooks for the teaching of grammar and rhetoric, then more substantial sections of the poems themselves.

Ovid's love lyrics, the *Amores,* are among the key precedents for Shakespeare's sonnets: each poetic sequence is a set of variations on the moods of love, in which the narrative voice shifts rapidly between different poses and tones. His *Fasti,* which linked major events in Roman history and mythology to the calendrical year, was the principal source for Shakespeare's second narrative poem, *The Rape of Lucrece.* Though Shakespeare could have read the *Amores* in a translation by Christopher Marlowe, the *Fasti* were available only in Latin. This goes to show that when Ben Jonson wrote of Shakespeare's "small Latin," he was measuring with the yardstick of his own prodigious learning—by our modern standards, Shakespeare had perfectly adequate Latin.

One of the most popular texts in the Elizabethan classroom was the *Heroides,* Ovid's verse-epistles written from the point of view of women in mythology who are deserted by their lovers (Ariadne on Naxos, Dido after the departure of Aeneas from Carthage, and so on). A frequent exercise was to imitate them—"write a letter in the style of X or from the point of view of someone who has suffered Y"—and in this sense they would have helped the student Shakespeare to take his first steps in the art of dramatic impersonation. John Lyly and Christopher Marlowe, the two dramatists who most influenced him when he began writing plays himself, both made extensive use of the *Heroides* as models for the art of a character's self-examination at moments of emotional crisis —the art, that is to say, of soliloquy.

But the influence of all these works pales beside that of Ovid's magnum opus, the *Metamorphoses*. Scholars have calculated that about ninety percent of Shakespeare's allusions to classical mythology refer to stories included in this epic compendium of tales. We know that Shakespeare knew the book in both the original Latin and Arthur Golding's translation. We can demonstrate this by considering his most sustained passage of Ovidian imitation, Prospero's renunciation of his rough magic near the end of *The Tempest* (5.1.33–57). That Shakespeare borrowed in detail from the *Metamorphoses* so late in his career shows that his Ovidianism was no mere young man's affectation, as is sometimes supposed.

J. F. Nims touches on *The Tempest* passage in his Introduction to this edition of Golding's translation. Ovid's enchantress Medea begins "auraeque et venti montesque amnesque lacusque, / dique omnes nemorum, dique omnes noctis adeste," of which a literal translation might be "ye breezes and winds and mountains and rivers and lakes, and all ye gods of groves and of night, draw near." Golding translated this as "Ye Ayres and windes: ye Elves of Hilles, of Brookes, of Woods alone, / Of standing Lakes, and of the Night approche ye everychone." Shakespeare's Prospero begins his speech, "Ye elves of hills, brooks, standing lakes, and groves." Shakespeare surely got from Golding the notion of including those very English elves at this point (in Ovid, they are "gods" and are not associated with the hills), and he also followed the translator in amplifying "lacus" into "*standing* lakes." But later in the speech, where Ovid had "convulsaque robores" ("and rooted up oaks"), Golding did not specify the kind of tree ("and trees doe drawe"), so Shakespeare must have gone to the Latin for his "and rifted Jove's stout oak." Again, Golding lacks an equivalent for the ghosts actually coming out of their tombs: Prospero's "Graves at my command / Have waked their sleepers, oped, and let 'em forth" is a version of Ovid's "manesque *exire* sepulcris." Medea in Ovid says that she has made the sun go pale by means of her "song"; Golding has "Our Sorcerie dimmes the Morning faire"; Shakespeare neatly combines the song and the sorcery with Prospero's "By my so potent art," the art being that of both sorcerer and poet-singer. That the black arts of Medea are the source for Prospero's seemingly white magic reminds us of the complexity of the Shakespearean vision, the difficulty of assuming easy distinctions between good and evil in the world of his plays. Like Ovid, Shakespeare is interested in the mingled yarn of our human fabric. Both are writers who probe our humanity with great rigor, but ultimately do so in a spirit of sympathy for our frailties and indulgences, rather than stern judgement upon our faults. Prospero is a little too much the schoolmaster to be an exact analogue for his own creator.

Though Prospero's speech valuably demonstrates Shakespeare's continuing interest in the minutiae of Ovid's language even to the end of his career, it is exceptional in the detail of its borrowing. Shakespeare's more habitual use of the *Metamorphoses* was less specific. He would refer to the stories there as parallels, or paradigms, for the emotional turmoil of the characters in his plays. Where Ovid told of bodily metamorphoses wrought by extremes of passion, Shakespeare translated these into psychological transformations and vivid metaphors. In particular, he found in Ovid a great store of examples of female feeling—something that was notably lacking in many of his other models, such as the plays of Marlowe and the history books of Plutarch and Holinshed. What mattered to him most was Ovid's storytelling, and for that the Latin text was not necessary—in rereading Ovid for pleasure after he left school, Shakespeare seems mostly to have relied on Golding's English version.

Nims suggests that the Elizabethan translator turned "the sophisticated Roman into a ruddy country gentleman with tremendous gusto, a sharp eye on the life around him, an ear for racy speech, and a gift for energetic doggerel." The doggerel apart, is Golding's cumbersome "fourteener" being parodied in the lumbering verse of "Pyramus and Thisbe"? (Shakespeare took pleasure in this process of "Englishing.") After all, he himself was a countryman with a vivid eye for the running hare and the flower-filled meadow. Like Autolycus in *The Winter's Tale,* he was a snapper-up of unconsidered trifles: from Golding he filched such linguistic jewels as the bristles on the boar in *Venus and Adonis* and the "babbling" of the nymph Echo to whom Viola compares herself in *Twelfth Night*.

Shakespeare was most Ovidian at the beginning and at the end of his career. Both his narrative poems, written during the period in 1593–4 when the theaters were closed due to plague, are based on Ovidian sources. They are calling cards which announce his poetic sophistication, perhaps in response to Robert Greene's jibe about Shake-scene, the up-start crow, the jack-of-all-trades from the country. *Venus and Adonis* takes a one hundred line story from the third book of the *Metamorphoses* and expands it into more than a thousand lines of elegant artifice. Ovid provided the narrative framework: the comic idea of the lovely young Adonis's resistance to love, the dark twist of his boar-speared death, and the final release of floral transformation. Shakespeare wove into this structure elaborate arguments for and against the "use" of beauty. These were opportunities for him to show off his rhetorical skill, while also engaging with an issue much debated in Elizabethan times, namely, the relative value of courtly accomplishments and military ones. The success-ful courtier would have been equally adept in the arts of praise and chivalry. Shakespeare gives the chivalric skills to the hunter Adonis, then inverts the norm of man-praising-woman by having a woman—and not just any woman, but Venus the Queen of Love herself—praise a young man. For this, he pulled together different parts of Ovid: the witty per-suasions to love are in the manner of the *Amores* and the *Ars Amatoria*, while the figure of the vain youth has something of Narcissus and that of the froward woman more than a little of Salmacis, who in book four of the *Metamorphoses* seduces another gorgeous but self-absorbed boy, Hermaphroditus.

If *Venus and Adonis* and *The Rape of Lucrece* are poetic explorations of, respectively, the light and dark sides of desire, then *A Midsummer Night's Dream* (1595–6?) and *Titus Andronicus* (written or revised in 1594) are their dramatic equivalents. *Titus* is explicitly patterned on the story of the rape of Philomel in book seven of the *Metamorphoses* (the force of this horrid tale's influence upon Shakespeare is demonstrable from the fact that some fifteen years after *Titus*, he returned to it in *Cymbeline*, where Iachimo notices in Imogen's bedchamber that, "She hath been reading late / The tale of Tereus; here the leaf's turned down / Where Philomel gave up"). In perhaps the most self-consciously literary moment in all Shakespeare, a copy of Ovid's book is actually brought on stage in Act Four of *Titus* and used as a plot device for the revelation of the nature of the crime which has been committed. By pointing to the story of Philomel, raped in the secluded woods by her brother-in-law Tereus, Lavinia indicates that she too has been violated. Shakespeare then compounds the allusion by deploying one of his sophisticated inter-weavings of different sources: in Ovid, Tereus cuts out Philomel's tongue so that she cannot reveal his name, but she gets round her disability by sewing a sampler portraying her fate. The rapists in *Titus* forestall this course of action by cutting off Lavinia's hands as well as removing her tongue. She outwits them—and in so doing Shakespeare proves his wit—by going to another part of the *Metamorphoses,* namely the story of Io, in which a girl who has been transformed into a cow writes her name by scraping her hoof in the sand. So Lavinia writes her rapists' names upon the ground, holding a staff in her mouth, guiding it with her stumps. Titus then acts out his revenge in deliberate homage to that of Procne, Philomel's sister: "For worse than Philomel you used my daughter," he says to the murderers Chiron and Demetrius, "So worse than Procne I will be revenged"—Procne tricked Tereus into eating his own son, whereas Titus goes one better and bakes both Tamora's sons in a pie, which he takes pleasure in serving on stage to her and her husband.

The wood outside Athens in *A Midsummer Night's Dream* is a place of benign transformations in comparison with those of the Roman hunting grounds in *Titus.* But the comedy and the charm of the *Dream* depend on a certain fragility. Good comedy is tragedy narrowly averted, while fairy charm is only safe from sentimentality if attached to some potential for grotesquerie. Of course we laugh when Bottom wears the head of an ass and makes love to a queen, but the image deliberately courts the suggestion of bestiality. In Ovid, people are driven by bestial desires and are rewarded by being transformed into animals. In Shakespeare, the ass's head is worn in play—significantly, it is assumed during the rehearsal of a dramatic performance—but it remains the closest thing in the drama of the age to an actual animal metamorphosis on stage. As for the idea of near-tragedy, that is evoked by the staging on the part of Bottom and his friends of a comically bad dramatization of one of Ovid's most tragic stories of doomed love, the tale in book four of the ill-timed misadventures of Pyramus and Thisbe. Ovid's great theme is transformation, the inevitability of change. Book fifteen of the *Metamorphoses* offers a philosophical discourse on the subject, mediated via the philosophy of Pythagoras. From here Shakespeare got many of those images of transience that roll through the sonnets, but in the *Dream* he celebrates how something positive and potentially enduring may grow from change:

> But all the story of the night told over,
> And all their minds transfigured so together,
> More witnesseth than fancy's images,

And grows to something of great constancy;
But, howsoever, strange and admirable. (5.1.23–7)

Though no subsequent comedy has transformation woven so fully
into its texture as this, Ovid was of continued importance in Shake-
speare's later assays in the genre. At the climax of *The Merchant of Venice*
(1597?), Lorenzo and Jessica duet upon a sequence of Ovidian charac-
ters—Pyramus and Thisbe, Dido, Medea. All the lovers alluded to are
associated with the night. Shakespeare thus establishes the final act of
the play as a night of love. But the night-deeds evoked are dark and
bloody, another gesture towards the ease with which comedy can tumble
over the precipice into tragedy (something that Jessica's father Shylock
maybe knows all too well). Comedy can be as cruel as it is funny. Some-
times it goes a little too far, as with the gulling of Malvolio into near-
madness. Ovid provided Shakespeare with many a reminder that sexual
desire can lead men not only to foolishness, but to outright destruction.
Most famously, there was Actaeon, transformed into a hart and torn to
pieces by his own hounds as punishment for his lascivious gaze upon
the naked goddess Diana as she bathed in a pool. The horns of Herne
the Hunter, which Falstaff is made to wear at the end of *The Merry
Wives of Windsor* (1598?), render him a heavyweight but light-hearted
Actaeon; Malvolio, cursing the pack of knaves who have undone him,
is a little closer to the real thing. His undoing ensures that the end of
Twelfth Night (1601?) is not all celebration. Malvolio takes to an extreme
the tendency of nearly all the natives of Illyria to overindulge their pas-
sions—a motif suggested by the langorous Orsino's allusion to Actaeon
in the very first scene of the play:

That instant was I turned into a hart,
And my desires like fell and cruel hounds
Ere since pursue me. (1.1.20–22)

To interpret Actaeon's hounds as an image of his own desires is to
"moralise" Ovid in the exact manner of Golding's epistle prefacing his
translation.

Golding and his predecessors in the mediaeval tradition of "Ovide
moralisé" have often been explicitly or implicitly condemned for infidelity
to the style and temperament of their original. Was not Ovid the supreme
exemplar of style for style's sake, the great opposite of the moral Horace

and the imperial Virgil? Was he not the original poetic *immoralist,* who suffered exile to the icy shores of the Black Sea for the very reason that he penned a seducer's charter in the form of the *Ars Amatoria?* This might be the impression given by a play such as Ben Jonson's *Poetaster,* in which Ovid, Virgil, and Horace are rival characters on stage, but this impression greatly simplifies the truth of the matter. In the *Metamorphoses,* Ovid answers Virgil's *Aeneid* with his own version of Rome's mythical birth from the survivors of Troy. When the time is ripe, he knows how to flatter a Caesar. For all his reiterations of the precept that the only constant is change, he does establish—in the opening book of the poem—an image of the stable good life from which the bad times of the shifting present have declined. That image is the "Golden Age" before the scars of property ownership, legal codes, and empire building have sullied the pristine earth. Shakespeare and his contemporaries were haunted by this idea of a golden age of natural plenty in which man lived in harmony with fellow-man and with nature under the rule of Astraea, goddess of Justice. Late Elizabethan poets in pursuit of royal patronage often proclaimed the return of the Golden Age, sometimes by flattering Elizabeth herself with the analogy that she was Astraea returned to earth, on other occasions by celebrating the newfound colonies of the Americas as places of natural plenty which would offer both literal and metaphorical gold.

It is to Ovid's Golden Age that the lifestyle of the exiled courtiers in *As You Like It* (1599) is compared. Gonzalo, in *The Tempest* (1611), sums up the characteristics of that age in a speech in which Ovid is fused with a passage by another of Shakespeare's most-loved authors, Michel de Montaigne:

> All things in common nature should produce
> Without sweat or endeavour. Treason, felony,
> Sword, pike, knife, gun, or need of any engine,
> Would I not have; but nature should bring forth,
> Of its own kind all foison, all abundance,
> To feed my innocent people. (2.1.165–70)

Ovid, Montaigne, and Shakespeare are all committed to the claims of nature above those of empire. The sinister high politics of Shakespeare's mature tragedies—the treasons and felonies of *Hamlet, Othello, Macbeth,* and *Lear*—belong to Ovid's Age of Iron. In the final plays, the so-called romances of the period from about 1608 to his retirement around 1612, Shakespeare returns repeatedly to nature, working his plots towards the restoration of Golden Age wonders.

In both *Pericles* and *Cymbeline* (1608–9), the action moves from destructive, corrupt courts to places where nature exercises its healing force. *Pericles* works within the ancient romance tradition—a narrative form well known to Ovid—where a storm purifies old woes into new life. In *Cymbeline,* wholeness is restored in the fresh outdoor world of the Welsh mountains. Romance is the literary genre in which lost children are found and wonder is made familiar. Ovid presents an archetypal romance in book five, where he tells the story of Proserpina, daughter of Ceres, goddess of the harvest. Whilst out gathering flowers, she is abducted by Pluto (or Dis), god of the underworld, where she is forced to reside for half each year. Her departure below the earth signifies the onset of winter, her reappearance the return of spring. Another young woman, flowers in hand, compares herself to Proserpina in Shakespeare's *The Winter's Tale.* Her name, Perdita, "the lost one," evokes the mythic romance structure whereby we know that what is lost will eventually be found in a glad reunion. So, too, the play's title surely indicates that the drama will eventually move from Leontes' winter court, ruled by intrigue and jealousy, to the sunnier clime of the pastoral world, where a prince disguises himself in order to woo a shepherdess (who, it turns out, is really a princess herself). Florizel compares his mock-transformation of dress and rank to the disguises of the gods in the *Metamorphoses*:

> The gods themselves,
> Humbling their deities to love, have taken
> The shapes of beasts upon them. Jupiter
> Became a bull, and bellowed; the green Neptune
> A ram, and bleated; and the fire-robed god,
> Golden Apollo, a poor humble swain,
> As I seem now. (4.4.25–31)

The play's move from dark indoor court to the restorative air of the country follows the path of Shakespeare's principal source, Robert Greene's novella *Pandosto.* But in the source, the wronged queen does not return to life. The reanimation of what Leontes takes to be Hermione's statue is Shakespeare's invention. The wonder-filled final scene puts a seemingly life-giving art into the hands of Paulina. That art dramatizes the magical power of theater itself, so that we in the audience, like the characters on stage, awaken our faith. The many-layered quality of the illusion—a boy-actor pretending to be a female character, Hermione, who is herself pretending to be a statue—takes Shakespeare's art to an extreme level of self-consciousness. Fittingly, then, the scene is also an allusion to Ovid, the most self-conscious artist among Shakespeare's models.

In book ten of the *Metamorphoses,* the artist Pygmalion carves an ivory statue so realistic that it seems to be a real girl, so beautiful that he falls in love with it. He desperately wants to believe it is real, and there are moments when the perfection of the art is such that the statue does seem to be struggling into life. With a little assistance from the goddess Venus, a kiss then animates the statue in a striking reversal of the usual Ovidian metamorphic pattern in which people turn into things or animals. As Golding has it, "Shee felt the kisse, and blusht therat: and lifting fearefully / Hir eyelidds up, hir Lover and the light at once did spye." At a profound level, Pygmalion is a figure of Ovid himself: the artist who transforms mere words into living forms.

Shakespeare learned from Ovid's Pygmalion both an idea and a style. If you want something badly enough and you believe in it hard enough, you will eventually get it: though tragedy denies this possibility, comedy affirms it. This is the illusion that theater can foster. Ovid showed Shakespeare that the way to evoke this leap of faith is through pinpricks of sensation. The progression in the animation of Pygmalion's statue is both precise and sensuous: blood pulses through the veins, the lips respond, the ivory face flushes. Correspondingly, Leontes contrasts the warm life his queen once had with the coldness of the statue, but then he seems to see blood in the veins and warmth upon the lips. And when she descends and embraces him, she *is* warm.

Throughout his career Shakespeare metamorphosed Ovid's mythical metamorphoses into verbal and visual metaphors: Malvolio speaks and dresses like a Narcissus without actually becoming a flower; it is Othello's language and actions, not his body, that are reduced to bestiality; Lear's metaphor, "O, you are men of stones," replaces the literal metamorphosis of Niobe into stone. Now near the end of his career, Shakespeare reverses the process in *The Winter's Tale,* something he had previously done only in comedy (Bottom as ass, Falstaff as Actaeon). In Act One, Leontes freezes Hermione out of his life. Her body language with Polixenes is, he says, "Too hot, too hot!"—he wants her to be frigidly chaste (even though she is pregnant!). His jealous look is like that of the basilisk or the gorgon Medusa: he turns his wife to stone. In the final act, this metaphor becomes a metamorphosis, as Paulina conjures up the illusion of Hermione's depetrification. The transformation is triumphantly realized on stage both linguistically and visually. "Does not the stone rebuke me / For being more stone than it?" asks Leontes, when confronted with the statue. The hardened image of his wife forces him to turn his gaze inward upon his own hard heart. The play ends with the melting of that heart and the rekindling of love, with its concordant release of Hermione back into softness, warmth, and life.

We know in our heads that we are not really watching a statue coming to life. Yet in a good production, at the moment of awakening, we feel in our hearts that we are. The magic of the drama occurs in a strange but deeply satisfying space between the two poles of reality and illusion. Metamorphosis is a kind of translation which occurs in the passage from one state to another. Ovid's world shuttles between human passions and natural phenomena. Shakespeare, with the assistance of Arthur Golding, carried across the magic of that world into the medium of theater, where everything is illusion, but somehow—as he put it in the alternative title of another of his last plays, *Henry VIII*—"All is True."

JONATHAN BATE is Leverhulme Research Professor and King Alfred Professor of English Literature at the University of Liverpool.

The. xv. Bookes

of P. Ouidius Naso, entytuled
Metamorphosis, tranflated oute of
Latin into English meeter, by Ar-
thur Golding Gentleman,
A worke very pleafaunt
and delectable.

With skill, heede, and iudgement, this worke muft be read,
For elfe to the Reader it ftandes in fmall ftead.

Imprynted at London, by
Willyam Seres.

The title page of the first edition (1567)

THE FIRST BOOKE OF OVIDS METAMORPHOSIS,

TRANSLATED INTO ENGLYSHE METER

[*The Creation. The Four Ages. The Flood. Deucalion and Pyrrha. Apollo and Daphne. Jove and Io. Pan and Syrinx.*]

Of shapes transformde to bodies straunge, I purpose to entreate,
Ye gods vouchsafe (for you are they ywrought this wondrous
feate)
To further this mine enterprise. And from the world begunne,
Graunt that my verse may to my time, his course directly runne.
Before the Sea and Lande were made, and Heaven that all doth hide, ⁵
In all the worlde one onely face of nature did abide,
Which Chaos hight, a huge rude heape, and nothing else but even
A heavie lump and clottred clod of seedes togither driven,
Of things at strife among themselves, for want of order due.
No sunne as yet with lightsome beames the shapelesse world did
vew. ¹⁰
No Moone in growing did repayre hir hornes with borowed light.
Nor yet the earth amiddes the ayre did hang by wondrous slight
Just peysed by hir proper weight. Nor winding in and out
Did Amphitrytee with hir armes embrace the earth about.
For where was earth, was sea and ayre, so was the earth unstable. ¹⁵
The ayre all darke, the sea likewise to beare a ship unable.
No kinde of thing had proper shape, but ech confounded other.
For in one selfesame bodie strove the hote and colde togither,

⁷ *hight:* was called   ¹³ *peysed:* poised, balanced
⁸ *clottred:* clotted

3

The moist with drie, the soft with hard, the light with things of
weight.
This strife did God and Nature breake, and set in order streight.   20
The earth from heaven, the sea from earth, he parted orderly,
And from the thicke and foggie ayre, he tooke the lightsome skie.
Which when he once unfolded had, and severed from the blinde
And clodded heape, he setting eche from other did them binde
In endlesse friendship to agree. The fire most pure and bright,   25
The substance of the heaven it selfe, bicause it was so light
Did mount aloft, and set it selfe in highest place of all.
The second roume of right to ayre, for lightnesse did befall.
The earth more grosse drew down with it eche weighty kinde of
matter,
And set it selfe in lowest place. Againe, the waving water   30
Did lastly chalenge for his place, the utmost coast and bound,
Of all the compasse of the earth, to close the stedfast ground.
Now when he in this foresaid wise (what God so ere he was)
Had broke and into members put this rude confused masse,
Then first bicause in every part, the earth should equall bee,   35
He made it like a mighty ball, in compasse as we see.
And here and there he cast in seas, to whome he gave a lawe:
To swell with every blast of winde, and every stormie flawe.
And with their waves continually to beate upon the shore,
Of all the earth within their boundes enclosde by them afore.   40
Moreover, Springs and mighty Meeres and Lakes he did augment,
And flowing streames of crooked brookes in winding bankes he pent.
Of which the earth doth drinke up some, and some with restlesse race
Do seeke the sea: where finding scope of larger roume and space,
In steade of bankes, they beate on shores. He did commaund the
plaine   45
And champion groundes to stretch out wide: and valleys to remaine
Aye underneath: and eke the woods to hide them decently
With tender leaves: and stonie hilles to lift themselves on hie.
And as two Zones doe cut the Heaven upon the righter side,
And other twaine upon the left likewise the same devide,   50
The middle in outragious heat exceeding all the rest:
Even so likewise through great foresight to God it seemed best,
The earth encluded in the same should so devided bee,
As with the number of the Heaven, hir Zones might full agree.

---

46 *champion:* champaign, level and open   47 *eke:* also

Of which the middle Zone in heate, the utmost twaine in colde   55
Exceede so farre, that there to dwell no creature dare be bolde.
Betweene these two so great extremes, two other Zones are fixt,
Where temprature of heate and colde indifferently is mixt.
Now over this doth hang the Ayre, which as it is more fleightie
Than earth or water: so againe than fire it is more weightie.   60
There hath he placed mist and cloudes, and for to feare mens mindes,
The thunder and the lightning eke, with colde and blustring windes.
But yet the maker of the worlde permitteth not alway
The windes to use the ayre at will. For at this present day,
Though ech from other placed be in sundry coasts aside,   65
The violence of their boystrous blasts, things scarsly can abide.
They so turmoyle as though they would the world in pieces rende,
So cruell is those brothers wrath when that they doe contende.
And therefore to the morning graye, the Realme of Nabathie,
To Persis and to other lands and countries that doe lie   70
Farre underneath the Morning starre, did Eurus take his flight.
Likewise the setting of the Sunne, and shutting in of night
Belong to Zephyr. And the blasts of blustring Boreas raigne,
In Scythia and in other landes set under Charles his waine.
And unto Auster doth belong the coast of all the South,   75
Who beareth shoures and rotten mistes, continuall in his mouth.
Above all these he set aloft the cleare and lightsome skie,
Without all dregs of earthly filth or grossenesse utterlie.
The boundes of things were scarsly yet by him thus pointed out,
But that appeared in the heaven, starres glistring all about,   80
Which in the said confused heape had hidden bene before,
And to th'intent with lively things eche Region for to store,
The heavenly soyle, to Gods and Starres and Planets first he gave.
The waters next both fresh and salt he let the fishes have.
The suttle ayre to flickring fowles and birdes he hath assignde. 85
The earth to beasts both wilde and tame of sundrie sort and kinde.
Howbeit yet of all this while, the creature wanting was,
Farre more devine, of nobler minde, which should the residue passe
In depth of knowledge, reason, wit, and high capacitie,
And which of all the residue should the Lord and ruler bee.   90
Then eyther he that made the worlde, and things in order set,
Of heavenly seede engendred Man: or else the earth as yet
Yong, lustie, fresh, and in hir floures, and parted from the skie,

---

⁶⁷ *turmoyle:* be agitated   ⁷⁴ *Charles his waine:* the Big Dipper

But late before, the seede thereof as yet held inwardlie.
The which Prometheus tempring straight with water of the spring,   95
Did make in likenesse to the Gods that governe everie thing.
And where all other beasts behold the ground with groveling eie,
He gave to Man a stately looke replete with majestie.
And willde him to behold the Heaven wyth countnance cast on hie,
To marke and understand what things were in the starrie skie.   100
And thus the earth which late before had neyther shape nor hew,
Did take the noble shape of man, and was transformed new.
        Then sprang up first the golden age, which of it selfe maintainde
        The truth and right of every thing unforct and unconstrainde.
There was no feare of punishment, there was no threatning lawe   105
In brazen tables nayled up, to keepe the folke in awe.
There was no man would crouch or creepe to Judge with cap in hand,
They lived safe without a Judge, in everie Realme and lande.
The loftie Pynetree was not hewen from mountaines where it stood,
In seeking straunge and forren landes, to rove upon the flood.   110
Men knew none other countries yet, than where themselves did keepe:
There was no towne enclosed yet, with walles and diches deepe.
No horne nor trumpet was in use, no sword nor helmet worne,
The worlde was such, that souldiers helpe might easly be forborne.
The fertile earth as yet was free, untoucht of spade or plough,   115
And yet it yeelded of it selfe of every things inough.
And men themselves contented well with plaine and simple foode,
That on the earth of natures gift without their travail stoode,
Did live by Raspis, heppes and hawes, by cornelles, plummes and
                                                        cherries,
By sloes and apples, nuttes and peares, and lothsome bramble
                                                        berries,   120
And by the acornes dropt on ground, from Joves brode tree in fielde.
The Springtime lasted all the yeare, and Zephyr with his milde
And gentle blast did cherish things that grew of owne accorde,
The ground untilde, all kinde of fruits did plenteously afforde.
No mucke nor tillage was bestowde on leane and barren land,   125
To make the corne of better head, and ranker for to stand.
Then streames ran milke, then streames ran wine, and yellow honny
                                                        flowde

---

[119] *Raspis:* raspberries; *heppes:* hips, fruit of   [120] *sloes:* fruit of blackthorn
      wild rose; *hawes:* fruit of hawthorn;
      cornelles: fruit of cornels (cornelian
      cherry tree)

From ech greene tree whereon the rayes of firie Phebus glowde.
 But when that into Lymbo once Saturnus being thrust,
  The rule and charge of all the worlde was under Jove unjust, 130
And that the silver age came in, more somewhat base than golde,
More precious yet than freckled brasse, immediatly the olde
And auncient Spring did Jove abridge, and made therof anon,
Foure seasons: Winter, Sommer, Spring, and Autumne off and on:
Then first of all began the ayre with fervent heate to swelt. 135
Then Isycles hung roping downe: then for the colde was felt
Men gan to shroud themselves in house. Their houses were the
              thickes,
And bushie queaches, hollow caves, or hardels made of stickes.
Then first of all were furrowes drawne, and corne was cast in ground.
The simple Oxe with sorie sighes, to heavie yoke was bound. 140
 Next after this succeded streight, the third and brazen age:
 More hard of nature, somewhat bent to cruell warres and rage.
But yet not wholy past all grace. Of yron is the last
In no part good and tractable as former ages past.
For when that of this wicked Age once opened was the veyne 145
Therein all mischief rushed forth: then Fayth and Truth were faine
And honest shame to hide their heades: for whom crept stoutly in,
Craft, Treason, Violence, Envie, Pride and wicked Lust to win.
The shipman hoyst his sailes to wind, whose names he did not knowe:
And shippes that erst in toppes of hilles and mountaines had
             ygrowe, 150
Did leape and daunce on uncouth waves: and men began to bound
With dowles and diches drawen in length the free and fertile ground,
Which was as common as the Ayre and light of Sunne before.
Not onely corne and other fruites, for sustnance and for store,
Were now exacted of the Earth: but eft they gan to digge, 155
And in the bowels of the ground unsaciably to rigge,
For Riches coucht and hidden deepe, in places nere to Hell,
The spurres and stirrers unto vice, and foes to doing well.
Then hurtfull yron came abrode, then came forth yellow golde,
More hurtfull than the yron farre, then came forth battle bolde, 160
That feightes with bothe, and shakes his sword in cruell bloudy hand.
Men live by ravine and by stelth: the wandring guest doth stand

---

135 *swelt:* swelter
137 *thickes:* thickets
138 *queaches:* dense growths of bushes, thickets; *hardels:* hurdles, wattles, woven huts

151 *uncouth:* unknown, strange
152 *dowles:* dools, boundry marks of stone, wood, etc.
155 *eft:* after
156 *rigge:* search, ransack

In daunger of his host: the host in daunger of his guest:
And fathers of their sonne in lawes: yea seldome time doth rest,
Betweene borne brothers such accord and love as ought to bee.   165
The goodman seekes the goodwifes death, and his againe seeks shee.
The stepdames fell their husbandes sonnes with poyson do assayle.
To see their fathers live so long the children doe bewayle.
All godlynesse lies under foote. And Ladie Astrey, last
Of heavenly vertues, from this earth in slaughter drowned past.   170
    And to th'intent the earth alone thus should not be opprest,
    And heaven above in slouthfull ease and carelesse quiet rest,
Men say that Giantes went about the Realme of Heaven to win
To place themselves to raigne as Gods and lawlesse Lordes therein.
And hill on hill they heaped up aloft into the skie,   175
Till God almighty from the Heaven did let his thunder flie,
The dint whereof the ayrie tops of high Olympus brake,
And pressed Pelion violently from under Ossa strake.
When whelmed in their wicked worke those cursed Caitives lay,
The Earth their mother tooke their bloud yet warme and (as they
                say)   180
Did give it life. And for bicause some ympes should still remaine
Of that same stocke, she gave it shape and limmes of men againe.
This offspring eke against the Gods did beare a native spight,
In slaughter and in doing wrong was all their whole delight.
Their deedes declared them of bloud engendred for to bee.   185
The which as soone as Saturns sonne from Heaven aloft did see,
He fetcht a sigh, and therwithall revolving in his thought
The shamefull act which at a feast Lycaon late had wrought,
As yet unknowne or blowne abrode: He gan thereat to storme
And stomacke like an angry Jove. And therfore to reforme   190
Such haynous actes, he sommonde streight his Court of Parliament,
Whereto resorted all the Gods that had their sommons sent.
Highe in the Welkin is a way apparant to the sight
In starrie nights, which of his passing whitenesse Milkie hight:
It is the streete that to the Court and Princely Pallace leades,   195
Of mightie Jove whose thunderclaps eche living creature dreades.
On both the sides of this same waye do stand in stately port
The sumptuous houses of the Peeres. For all the common sort

---

[166] *goodman:* husband, head of household;
    goodwife: wife, lady of the house
[167] *fell:* fierce, cruel
[170] *past:* passed
[178] *strake:* struck

[179] *Caitives:* wretches
[181] *ympes:* shoots, scions, offspring
[190] *stomacke:* take offense, resent
[197] *port:* style

Dwell scattring here and there abrode: the face of all the skie
The houses of the chiefe estates and Princes doe supplie.   200
And sure and if I may be bolde to speake my fancie free
I take this place of all the Heaven the Pallace for to bee.
Now when the Goddes assembled were, and eche had tane his place,
Jove standing up aloft and leaning on his yvorie Mace,
Right dreadfully his bushie lockes did thrise or four times shake,   205
Wherewith he made both Sea and Land and Heaven it self to quake,
And afterward in wrathfull wordes his angrie minde thus brake:
    I never was in greater care nor more perplexitie,
    How to maintaine my soveraigne state and Princelie royaltie,
When with their hundreth handes apiece the Adderfooted rout,   210
Did practise for to conquere Heaven and for to cast us out.
For though it were a cruell foe: yet did that warre depende
Upon one ground, and in one stocke it had his finall ende.
But now as farre as any sea about the worlde doth winde,
I must destroy both man and beast and all the mortall kinde.   215
I sweare by Styxes hideous streames that run within the ground,
All other meanes must first be sought: but when there can be found
No helpe to heale a festred sore, it must away be cut,
Lest that the partes that yet are sound, in daunger should be put.
We have a number in the worlde that mans estate surmount,   220
Of such whom for their private Gods the countrie folkes account,
As Satyres, Faunes, and sundry Nymphes, with Silvanes eke beside,
That in the woods and hillie grounds continually abide.
Whome into Heaven since that as yet we vouch not safe to take,
And of the honour of this place copartners for to make,   225
Such landes as to inhabite in, we erst to them assignde,
That they should still enjoye the same, it is my will and minde.
But can you thinke that they in rest and safetie shall remaine
When proud Lycaon laye in waite by secret meanes and traine
To have confounded me your Lorde, who in my hand doe beare   230
The dreadfull thunder, and of whom even you doe stand in feare?
    The house was moved at his words and earnestly requirde,
    The man that had so traiterously against their Lord conspirde.
Even so when Rebels did arise to stroy the Romane name,
By shedding of our Cesars bloud, the horror of the same   235
Did pierce the heartes of all mankinde, and made the world to quake.

---

210 *Adderfooted rout:* the Giants
222 *Silvanes:* wood-spirits or deities
224 *vouch not safe:* do not vouchsafe

229 *traine:* stratagem, trap
232 *requirde:* inquire
234 *stroy:* destroy

Whose fervent zeale in thy behalfe (O August) thou did take,
As thankfully as Jove doth heare the loving care of his,
Who beckning to them with his hand, forbiddeth them to hisse.
And therewithall through all the house attentive silence is.   240
As soone as that his majestie all muttring had alayde,
He brake the silence once againe, and thus unto them sayde:
    Let passe this carefull thought of yours: for he that did offende,
    Hath dearely bought the wicked Act, the which he did entende.
Yet shall you heare what was his fault and vengeance for the same.   245
A foule report and infamie unto our hearing came
Of mischiefe used in those times: which wishing all untrew
I did descend in shape of man, th'infamed Earth to vew.
It were a processe overlong to tell you of the sinne,
That did abound in every place where as I entred in.   250
The bruit was lesser than the truth, and partiall in report.
The dreadfull dennes of Menalus where savage beastes resort
And Cyllen had I overpast, with all the Pynetrees hie
Of cold Lyceus, and from thence I entred by and by
The herbroughlesse and cruell house of late th'Arcadian King,   255
Such time as twilight on the Earth dim darknesse gan to bring.
I gave a signe that God was come, and streight the common sort
Devoutly prayde, whereat Lycaon first did make a sport
And after said: By open proufe, ere long I minde to see,
If that this wight a mighty God or mortall creature bee.   260
The truth shall trie it selfe: he ment (the sequele did declare)
To steale upon me in the night, and kyll me unbeware.
And yet he was not so content: but went and cut the throte,
Of one that laye in hostage there, which was an Epyrote:
And part of him he did to rost, and part he did to stewe.   265
Which when it came upon the borde, forthwith I overthrew
The house with just revenging fire upon the owners hed,
Who seeing that, slipt out of doores amazde for feare, and fled
Into the wilde and desert woods, where being all alone,
As he endevorde (but in vaine) to speake and make his mone,   270
He fell a howling: wherewithall for verie rage and moode
He ran me quite out of his wits and waxed furious woode.
Still practising his wonted lust of slaughter on the poore

244 *bought:* paid for
248 *infamed:* accused, made infamous
251 *bruit:* report

255 *herbroughlesse:* harborless, inhospitable
271 *moode:* anger
272 *me:* cf. I, 988; *woode:* insane, enraged

And sielie cattle, thirsting still for bloud as heretofore,
His garments turnde to shackie haire, his armes to rugged pawes: 275
So is he made a ravening Wolfe: whose shape expressely drawes
To that the which he was before: his skinne is horie graye,
His looke still grim with glaring eyes, and every kinde of waye
His cruell heart in outward shape doth well it selfe bewraye.
Thus was one house destroyed quite, but that one house alone   280
Deserveth not to be destroyde: in all the Earth is none,
But that such vice doth raigne therein, as that ye would beleve,
That all had sworne and solde themselves to mischiefe us to greve.
And therefore as they all offende: so am I fully bent,
That all forthwith (as they deserve) shall have due punishment.   285
    These wordes of Jove some of the Gods did openly approve,
    And with their sayings more to wrath his angry courage move.
And some did give assent by signes. Yet did it grieve them all
That such destruction utterly on all mankinde should fall,
Demaunding what he purposed with all the Earth to doe,   290
When that he had all mortall men so cleane destroyde, and whoe
On holie Altars afterward should offer frankinsence,
And whother that he were in minde to leave the Earth fro thence
To savage beastes to wast and spoyle, bicause of mans offence.
    The king of Gods bade cease their thought and questions in that
                                                                case,   295
    And cast the care thereof on him. Within a little space
He promist for to frame a newe, an other kinde of men
By wondrous meanes, unlike the first to fill the world agen.
And now his lightning had he thought on all the earth to throw,
But that he feared lest the flames perhaps so hie should grow   300
As for to set the Heaven on fire, and burne up all the skie.
He did remember furthermore how that by destinie
A certaine time should one day come, wherein both Sea and Lond
And Heaven it selfe shoulde feele the force of Vulcans scorching
                                                                brond,
So that the huge and goodly worke of all the worlde so wide   305
Should go to wrecke, for doubt whereof forthwith he laide aside
His weapons that the Cyclops made, intending to correct
Mans trespasse by a punishment contrary in effect.
And namely with incessant showres from heaven ypoured downe,
He did determine with himselfe the mortall kinde to drowne.   310

---

274 *sielie:* poor, simple, helpless   279 *bewraye:* reveal
275 *shackie:* shaggy   304 *brond:* torch

In Aeolus prison by and by he fettred Boreas fast,
With al such winds as chase the cloudes or breake them with
                                                    their blast,
And set at large the Southerne winde: who straight with watry wings
And dreadfull face as blacke as pitch, forth out of prison flings.
His beard hung full of hideous stormes, all dankish was his head,   315
With water streaming downe his haire that on his shoulders shead.
His ugly forehead wrinkled was with foggie mistes full thicke,
And on his fethers and his breast a stilling dew did sticke.
As soone as he betweene his hands the hanging cloudes had crusht,
With ratling noyse adowne from heaven the raine full sadly gusht.   320
The Rainbow, Junos messenger, bedect in sundrie hue,
To maintaine moysture in the cloudes, great waters thither drue:
The corne was beaten to the grounde, the Tilmans hope of gaine,
For which he toyled all the yeare, lay drowned in the raine.
Joves indignation and his wrath began to grow so hot   325
That for to quench the rage thereof, his Heaven suffised not.
His brother Neptune with his waves was faine to doe him ease:
Who straight assembling all the streames that fall into the seas,
Said to them standing in his house: Sirs get you home apace,
(You must not looke to have me use long preaching in this case.)   330
Poure out your force (for so is neede) your heads ech one unpende,
And from your open springs, your streames with flowing waters sende.
He had no sooner said the word, but that returning backe,
Eche one of them unlosde his spring, and let his waters slacke.
And to the Sea with flowing streames yswolne above their bankes,   335
One rolling in anothers necke, they rushed forth by rankes.
Himselfe with his threetyned Mace, did lend the earth a blow,
That made it shake and open wayes for waters forth to flow.
The flouds at randon where they list, through all the fields did stray,
Men, beastes, trees, corne, and with their gods were Churches washt
                                                    away.   340
If any house were built so strong, against their force to stonde
Yet did the water hide the top: and turrets in that ponde
Were overwhelmde: no difference was betweene the sea and ground,
For all was sea: there was no shore nor landing to be found.
Some climbed up to tops of hils, and some rowde to and fro   345
In Botes, where they not long before, to plough and Cart did go,
One over corne and tops of townes, whome waves did overwhelme,

---

323 *Tilmans:* tiller's   334 *slacke:* flow freely
331 *heads:* sources   339 *randon:* random

Doth saile in ship, an other sittes a fishing in an Elme.
In meddowes greene were Anchors cast (so fortune did provide)
And crooked ships did shadow vynes, the which the floud did hide. 350
And where but tother day before did feede the hungry Gote,
The ugly Seales and Porkepisces now to and fro did flote.
The Sea nymphes wondred under waves the townes and groves to see,
And Dolphines playd among the tops and boughes of every tree.
The grim and greedy Wolfe did swim among the siely sheepe, 355
The Lion and the Tyger fierce were borne upon the deepe.
It booted not the foming Boare his crooked tuskes to whet,
The running Hart coulde in the streame by swiftnesse nothing get.
The fleeting fowles long having sought for land to rest upon,
Into the Sea with werie wings were driven to fall anon. 360
Th'outragious swelling of the Sea the lesser hillockes drownde,
Unwonted waves on highest tops of mountaines did rebownde.
The greatest part of men were drownde, and such as scapte the floode,
Forlorne with fasting overlong did die for want of foode.
Against the fieldes of Aonie and Atticke lies a lande 365
That Phocis hight, a fertile ground while that it was a lande:
But at that time a part of Sea, and even a champion fielde
Of sodaine waters which the floud by forced rage did yeelde,
Where as a hill with forked top the which Parnasus hight,
Doth pierce the cloudes and to the starres doth raise his head
                                                      upright. 370
When at this hill (for yet the Sea had whelmed all beside)
Deucalion and his bedfellow, without all other guide,
Arrived in a little Barke immediatly they went,
And to the Nymphes of Corycus with full devout intent
Did honor due, and to the Gods to whome that famous hill 375
Was sacred, and to Themis eke in whose most holie will
Consisted then the Oracles. In all the world so rounde
A better nor more righteous man could never yet be founde
Than was Deucalion, nor againe a woman, mayde nor wife,
That feared God so much as shee, nor led so good a life. 380
    When Jove behelde how all the worlde stoode lyke a plash of
                                                      raine,
    And of so many thousand men and women did remaine
But one of eche, howbeit those both just and both devout,

---

352 *Porkepisces:* porpoises
357 *booted:* helped

371 *whelmed:* overwhelmed
381 *plash:* pool, splash

He brake the Cloudes, and did commaund that Boreas with his stout
And sturdie blasts should chase the floud, that Earth might see the
skie   385
And Heaven the Earth: the Seas also began immediatly
Their raging furie for to cease. Their ruler laide awaye
His dreadfull Mace, and with his wordes their woodnesse did alaye.
He called Tryton to him straight, his trumpetter, who stoode
In purple robe on shoulder cast, aloft upon the floode,   390
And bade him take his sounding Trumpe and out of hand to blow
Retreat, that all the streames might heare, and cease from thence to
flow.
He tooke his Trumpet in his hand, hys Trumpet was a shell
Of some great Whelke or other fishe, in facion like a Bell
That gathered narrow to the mouth, and as it did descende   395
Did waxe more wide and writhen still, downe to the nether ende:
When that this Trumpe amid the Sea was set to Trytons mouth,
He blew so loude that all the streames both East, West, North and
South,
Might easly heare him blow retreate, and all that heard the sounde
Immediatly began to ebbe and draw within their bounde.   400
Then gan the Sea to have a shore, and brookes to finde a banke,
And swelling streames of flowing flouds within hir chanels sanke.
Then hils did rise above the waves that had them overflow,
And as the waters did decrease the ground did seeme to grow.
And after long and tedious time the trees did shew their tops   405
All bare, save that upon the boughes the mud did hang in knops.
The worlde restored was againe, which though Deucalion joyde
Then to beholde: yet forbicause he saw the earth was voyde
And silent like a wildernesse, with sad and weeping eyes
And ruthfull voyce he then did speake to Pyrrha in this wise: 410
    O sister, O my loving spouse, O sielie woman left,
    As onely remnant of thy sexe that water hath bereft,
Whome Nature first by right of birth hath linked to me fast
In that we brothers children bene: and secondly the chast
And stedfast bond of lawfull bed: and lastly now of all,   415
The present perils of the time that latelye did befall.
On all the Earth from East to West where Phebus shewes his face
There is no moe but thou and I of all the mortall race.

388 *woodnesse:* madness, rage   402 *hir:* their
391 *out of hand:* immediately   406 *knops:* knobs
396 *writhen:* twisted, coiled

The Sea hath swallowed all the rest: and scarsly are we sure,
That our two lives from dreadfull death in safetie shall endure.   420
For even as yet the duskie cloudes doe make my heart adrad.
Alas poore wretched sielie soule, what heart wouldst thou have had
To beare these heavie happes, if chaunce had let thee scape alone?
Who should have bene thy consort then: who should have rewd thy
                                                                mone?
Now trust me truly, loving wife, had thou as now bene drownde,   425
I would have followde after thee and in the sea bene fownde.
Would God I could my fathers Arte, of claye to facion men
And give them life that people might frequent the world agen.
Mankinde (alas) doth onely now wythin us two consist,
As mouldes whereby to facion men. For so the Gods doe lyst.   430
      And with these words the bitter teares did trickle down their
                                                                cheeke,
      Untill at length betweene themselves they did agree to seeke
To God by prayer for his grace, and to demaund his ayde
By aunswere of his Oracle. Wherein they nothing stayde,
But to Cephisus sadly went, whose streame as at that time   435
Began to run within his bankes though thicke with muddie slime,
Whose sacred liquor straight they tooke and sprinkled with the same
Their heads and clothes: and afterward to Themis chappell came,
The roofe whereof with cindrie mosse was almost overgrowne.
For since the time the raging floud the worlde had overflowne,   440
No creature came within the Churche: so that the Altars stood
Without one sparke of holie fyre or any sticke of wood.
As soon as that this couple came within the chappell doore,
They fell downe flat upon the ground, and trembling kist the floore.
And sayde: If prayer that proceedes from humble heart and
                                                                minde   445
May in the presence of the Gods, such grace and favor finde
As to appease their worthie wrath, then vouch thou safe to tell
(O gentle Themis) how the losse that on our kinde befell,
May now eftsoones recovered be, and helpe us to repaire
The world, which drowned under waves doth lie in great
                                                                dispaire. 450
The Goddesse moved with their sute, this answere did them make:
Depart you hence: Go hille your heads, and let your garmentes slake,

---

427 *could:* knew   449 *eftsoones:* again, soon
430 *the Gods doe lyst:* it pleases the gods   452 *hille:* cover; *slake:* hang loose

And both of you your Graundames bones behind your shoulders cast.
They stoode amazed at these wordes, tyll Pyrrha at the last,
Refusing to obey the hest the which the Goddesse gave,   455
Brake silence, and with trembling cheere did meekely pardon crave.
For sure she saide she was afraide hir Graundames ghost to hurt
By taking up hir buried bones to throw them in the durt.
And with the aunswere here upon eftsoones in hand they go,
The doubtfull wordes wherof they scan and canvas to and fro.   460
Which done, Prometheus sonne began by counsell wise and sage
His cousin germanes fearfulnesse thus gently to asswage:
Well, eyther in these doubtfull words is hid some misterie,
Whereof the Gods permit us not the meaning to espie,
Or questionlesse and if the sence of inward sentence deeme   465
Like as the tenour of the words apparantly doe seeme,
It is no breach of godlynesse to doe as God doth bid.
I take our Graundame for the earth, the stones within hir hid
I take for bones, these are the bones the which are meaned here.
Though Titans daughter at this wise conjecture of hir fere   470
Were somewhat movde, yet none of both did stedfast credit geve,
So hardly could they in their heartes the heavenly hestes beleve.
But what and if they made a proufe? what harme could come thereby?
They went their wayes and heild their heades, and did their cotes
                                                                              untie.
And at their backes did throw the stones by name of bones
                                                                    foretolde.   475
The stones (who would beleve the thing, but that the time of olde
Reportes it for a stedfast truth?) of nature tough and harde,
Began to warre both soft and smothe: and shortly afterwarde
To winne therwith a better shape: and as they did encrease,
A mylder nature in them grew, and rudenesse gan to cease.   480
For at the first their shape was such, as in a certaine sort
Resembled man, but of the right and perfect shape came short.
Even like to Marble ymages new drawne and roughly wrought,
Before the Carver by his Arte to purpose hath them brought.
Such partes of them where any juice or moysture did abound,   485
Or else were earthie, turned to flesh: and such as were so sound,
And harde as would not bow nor bende did turne to bones: againe
The part that was a veyne before, doth still his name retaine.

455 *hest:* bidding, command   465 *sentence:* significance, meaning
456 *cheere:* countenance, expression   470 *fere:* mate
460 *canvas:* scrutinize, discuss   478 *warre:* wear, gradually become

Thus by the mightie powre of God ere lenger time was past,
The mankinde was restorde by stones, the which a man did cast.   490
And likewise also by the stones the which a woman threw,
The womankinde repayred was and made againe of new.
Of these are we the crooked ympes, and stonie race in deede,
Bewraying by our toyling life, from whence we doe proceede.
    The lustie earth of owne accorde soone after forth did bring   495
    According to their sundrie shapes eche other living thing,
As soone as that the moysture once caught heate against the Sunne,
And that the fat and slimie mud in moorish groundes begunne
To swell through warmth of Phebus beames, and that the fruitfull
                                                              seede
Of things well cherisht in the fat and lively soyle in deede,   500
As in their mothers wombe, began in length of time to grow,
To one or other kinde of shape wherein themselves to show.
Even so when that seven mouthed Nile the watrie fieldes forsooke,
And to his auncient channel eft his bridled streames betooke,
So that the Sunne did heate the mud, the which he left behinde,   505
The husbandmen that tilde the ground, among the cloddes did finde
Of sundrie creatures sundrie shapes: of which they spied some,
Even in the instant of their birth but newly then begonne,
And some unperfect, wanting brest or shoulders in such wise,
That in one bodie oftentimes appeared to the eyes   510
One halfe thereof alive to be, and all the rest beside
Both voyde of life and seemely shape, starke earth to still abide.
For when that moysture with the heate is tempred equally,
They doe conceyve: and of them twaine engender by and by
All kinde of things. For though that fire with water aye debateth   515
Yet moysture mixt with equall heate all living things createth.
And so those discordes in their kinde, one striving with the other,
In generation doe agree and make one perfect mother.
And therfore when the mirie earth bespred with slimie mud,
Brought over all but late before by violence of the flud,   520
Caught heate by warmnesse of the Sunne, and calmenesse of the skie,
Things out of number in the worlde, forthwith it did applie.
Whereof in part the like before in former times had bene,
And some so straunge and ougly shapes as never erst were sene.
In that she did such Monsters breede, was greatly to hir woe,   525
But yet thou, ougly Python, wert engendred by hir thoe.

498 *moorish:* boggy, swampy   526 *thoe:* then

A terror to the new made folke, which never erst had knowne
So foule a Dragon in their life, so monstrously foregrowne,
So great a ground thy poyson paunch did underneath thee hide.
The God of shooting who no where before that present tide   530
Those kinde of weapons put in ure, but at the speckled Deere,
Or at the Does so wight of foote, a thousand shaftes well neare
Did on that hideous serpent spende, of which there was not one,
But forced forth the venimd bloud along his sides to gone.
So that his quiver almost voyde, he nailde him to the grounde,   535
And did him nobly at the last by force of shot confounde.
And lest that time might of this worke deface the worthy fame,
He did ordeyne in minde thereof a great and solemne game,
Which of the serpent that he slue of Pythians bare the name,
Where who so could the maistrie winne in feates of strength, or
                                                       sleight   540
Of hande or foote or rolling wheele, might claime to have of right
An Oken garland fresh and brave. There was not any wheare
As yet a Bay, by meanes whereof was Phebus faine to weare
The leaves of every pleasant tree about his golden heare.
        Peneian Daphne was the first where Phebus set his love,   545
        Which not blind chaunce but Cupids fierce and cruel wrath did
                                                              move.
The Delian God but late before surprisde with passing pride:
For killing of the monstrous worme, the God of love espide,
With bowe in hand already bent and letting arrowes go:
To whome he sayd: And what hast thou, thou wanton baby, so   550
With warlike weapons for to toy? It were a better sight,
Too see this kind of furniture on our two shoulders bright:
Who when we list with stedfast hand both man and beast can wound,
Who tother day wyth arrowes keene, have nayled to the ground
The serpent Python so forswolne, whose filthie wombe did hide   555
So many acres of the grounde in which he did abide.
Content thy selfe, sonne, sorie loves to kindle with thy brand,
For these our prayses to attaine thou must not take in hand.
To him quoth Venus sonne againe: Well Phebus I agree
Thy bow to shoote at every beast, and so shall mine at thee.   560
And looke how far that under God eche beast is put by kinde,
So much thy glorie lesse than ours in shooting shalt thou finde.

---

528 *foregrowne:* overgrown
531 *ure:* use
532 *wight:* swift
547 *surprisde with:* seized by

550 *wanton:* spoiled
552 *furniture:* equipment
553 *list:* like
555 *forswolne:* greatly swollen

This saide, with drift of fethered wings in broken ayre he flue,
And to the forkt and shadie top of Mount Parnasus drue.
There from hys quiver full of shafts two arrowes did he take   565
Of sundrie workes: t'one causeth Love, the tother doth it slake.
That causeth love, is all of golde with point full sharpe and bright,
That chaseth love is blunt, whose stele with leaden head is dight.
The God this fired in the Nymph Peneis for the nones:
The tother perst Apollos heart and overraft his bones.   570
Immediatly in smoldring heate of Love the t'one did swelt,
Againe the tother in hir heart no sparke nor motion felt.
In woods and forrests is hir joy, the savage beasts to chase,
And as the price of all hir paine to take the skinne and case.
Unwedded Phebe doth she haunt and follow as hir guide,   575
Unordred doe hir tresses wave scarce in a fillet tide.
Full many a wooer sought hir love, she lothing all the rout,
Impacient and without a man walkes all the woods about.
And as for Hymen, or for love, and wedlocke often sought
She tooke no care, they were the furthest end of all hir thought.   580
Hir father many a time and oft would saye: My daughter deere,
Thow owest me a sonneinlaw to be thy lawfull feere.
Hir father many a time and oft would say: My daughter deere,
Of Nephewes thou my debtour art, their Graundsires heart to cheere.
She hating as a haynous crime the bonde of bridely bed   585
Demurely casting downe hir eyes, and blushing somwhat red,
Did folde about hir fathers necke with fauning armes: and sed:
Deare father, graunt me while I live my maidenhead for to have,
As to Diana here tofore hir father freely gave.
Thy father (Daphne) could consent to that thou doest require,   590
But that thy beautie and thy forme impugne thy chaste desire:
So that thy will and his consent are nothing in this case,
By reason of the beautie bright that shineth in thy face.
Apollo loves and longs to have this Daphne to his Feere,
And as he longs he hopes, but his foredoomes doe fayle him
                                                              there.   595
And as light hame when corne is reapt, or hedges burne with brandes,
That passers by when day drawes neere throwe loosely fro their
                                                              handes,
So into flames the God is gone and burneth in his brest

---

568 *stele:* shaft; *dight:* equipped
569 *for the nones:* expressly
570 *overraft:* tore or cleft

577 *rout:* crowd
595 *foredoomes:* destinies
596 *hame:* haulm, stubble

And feedes his vaine and barraine love in hoping for the best.
Hir haire unkembd about hir necke downe flaring did he see,   600
O Lord and were they trimd (quoth he) how seemely would she bee?
He sees hir eyes as bright as fire the starres to represent,
He sees hir mouth which to have seene he holdes him not content.
Hir lillie armes mid part and more above the elbow bare,
Hir handes, hir fingers and hir wrystes, him thought of beautie rare.⁶⁰⁵
And sure he thought such other parts as garments then did hyde,
Excelled greatly all the rest the which he had espyde.
But swifter than the whyrling winde shee flees and will not stay,
To give the hearing to these wordes the which he had to say:
    I pray thee Nymph Penaeis stay, I chase not as a fo: 610
    Stay Nymph: the Lambes so flee the Wolves, the Stags the
                                        Lions so.
With flittring feathers sielie Doves so from the Gossehauke flie,
And every creature from his foe. Love is the cause that I
Do followe thee: alas alas how would it grieve my heart,
To see thee fall among the briers, and that the bloud should start   615
Out of thy tender legges, I, wretch, the causer of thy smart.
The place is rough to which thou runst, take leysure I thee pray,
Abate thy flight, and I my selfe my running pace will stay.
Yet would I wishe thee take advise, and wisely for to viewe
What one he is that for thy grace in humble wise doth sewe.   620
I am not one that dwelles among the hilles and stonie rockes,
I am no sheepehearde with a Curre, attending on the flockes:
I am no Carle nor countrie Clowne, nor neathearde taking charge
Of cattle grazing here and there within this Forrest large.
Thou doest not know, poore simple soule, God wote thou dost not
                                        knowe,   625
From whome thou fleest. For if thou knew, thou wouldste not
                                        flee me so.
In Delphos is my chiefe abode, my Temples also stande
At Glaros and at Patara within the Lycian lande.
And in the Ile of Tenedos the people honour mee.
The king of Gods himselfe is knowne my father for to bee.   630
By me is knowne that was, that is, and that that shall ensue,
By mee men learne to sundrie tunes to frame sweete ditties true.
In shooting have I stedfast hand, but surer hand had hee

---

⁶⁰⁰ *flaring:* spreading, waving
⁶²³ *Carle:* farmer, churl; *neathearde:* cow-
  herd

⁶²⁵ *wote:* knows
⁶³¹ *that was:* that which was

600 *flaring:* spreading, waving   625 *wote:* knows
623 *Carle:* farmer, churl; *neathearde:* cow-   631 *that was:* that which was
    herd

That made this wound within my heart that heretofore was free.
Of Phisicke and of surgerie I found the Artes for neede,   635
The powre of everie herbe and plant doth of my gift proceede.
Nowe wo is me that nere an herbe can heale the hurt of love
And that the Artes that others helpe their Lord doth helpelesse prove.
    As Phoebus would have spoken more, away Penaeis stale
    With fearefull steppes, and left him in the midst of all his tale. 640
And as she ran the meeting windes hir garments backewarde blue,
So that hir naked skinne apearde behinde hir as she flue,
Hir goodly yellowe golden haire that hanged loose and slacke,
With every puffe of ayre did wave and tosse behinde hir backe.
Hir running made hir seeme more fayre, the youthfull God therefore 645
Coulde not abyde to waste his wordes in dalyance any more.
But as his love advysed him he gan to mende his pace,
And with the better foote before, the fleeing Nymph to chace.
And even as when the greedie Grewnde doth course the sielie Hare,
Amiddes the plaine and champion fielde without all covert bare,   650
Both twaine of them doe straine themselves and lay on footemanship,
Who may best runne with all his force the tother to outstrip,
The t'one for safetie of his lyfe, the tother for his pray,
The Grewnde aye prest with open mouth to beare the Hare away,
Thrusts forth his snoute and gyrdeth out and at hir loynes doth
                                    snatch,   655
As though he would at everie stride betweene his teeth hir latch:
Againe in doubt of being caught the Hare aye shrinking slips
Upon the sodaine from his Jawes, and from betweene his lips:
So farde Apollo and the Mayde: hope made Apollo swift,
And feare did make the Mayden fleete devising how to shift.   660
Howebeit he that did pursue of both the swifter went,
As furthred by the feathred wings that Cupid had him lent,
So that he would not let hir rest, but preased at hir heele
So neere that through hir scattred haire she might his breathing feele.
But when she sawe hir breath was gone and strength began to fayle,   665
The colour faded in hir cheekes, and ginning for to quayle,
Shee looked to Penaeus streame and sayde: Nowe Father dere,
And if yon streames have powre of Gods then help your daughter here.
O let the earth devour me quicke, on which I seeme too fayre,

638 *prove:* try
649 *Grewnde:* greyhound
655 *gyrdeth:* darts, moves
656 *latch:* seize

660 *shift:* make shift, manage
663 *preased:* pressed
666 *quayle:* weaken

Or else this shape which is my harme by chaunging straight appayre. 670
This piteous prayer scarsly sed: hir sinewes waxed starke,
And therewithall about hir breast did grow a tender barke.
Hir haire was turned into leaves, hir armes in boughes did growe,
Hir feete that were ere while so swift, now rooted were as slowe.
Hir crowne became the toppe, and thus of that she earst had beene, 675
Remayned nothing in the worlde, but beautie fresh and greene.
Which when that Phoebus did beholde (affection did so move)
The tree to which his love was turnde he coulde no lesse but love,
And as he softly layde his hande upon the tender plant,
Within the barke newe overgrowne he felt hir heart yet pant. 680
And in his armes embracing fast hir boughes and braunches lythe,
He proferde kisses to the tree, the tree did from him writhe.
Well (quoth Apollo) though my Feere and spouse thou can not bee,
Assuredly from this tyme forth yet shalt thou be my tree.
Thou shalt adorne my golden lockes, and eke my pleasant Harpe, 685
Thou shalt adorne my Quyver full of shaftes and arrowes sharpe.
Thou shalt adorne the valiant knyghts and royall Emperours:
When for their noble feates of armes like mightie conquerours,
Triumphantly with stately pompe up to the Capitoll,
They shall ascende with solemne traine that doe their deedes extoll. 690
Before Augustus Pallace doore full duely shalt thou warde,
The Oke amid the Pallace yarde aye faythfully to garde,
And as my heade is never poulde nor never more without
A seemely bushe of youthfull haire that spreadeth rounde about,
Even so this honour give I thee continually to have 695
Thy braunches clad from time to tyme with leaves both fresh and brave.
Now when that Pean of this talke had fully made an ende,
The Lawrell to his just request did seeme to condescende,
By bowing of hir newe made boughs and tender braunches downe,
And wagging of hir seemely toppe, as if it were hir crowne. 700
    There is a lande in Thessalie enclosd on every syde
    With wooddie hilles, that Timpe hight, through mid whereof
                                                   doth glide
Penaeus gushing full of froth from foote of Pindus hye,
Which with his headlong falling downe doth cast up violently
A mistie streame lyke flakes of smoke, besprinckling all about 705
The toppes of trees on eyther side, and makes a roaring out

---

670 *appayre:* impair   691 *warde:* keep guard
671 *starke:* stiff   693 *poulde:* polled, shorn
680 *pant:* throb   705 *flakes:* fleecy streaks or tufts

That may be heard a great way off. This is the fixed seate,
This is the house and dwelling place and chamber of the greate
And mightie Ryver: Here he sittes in Court of Peeble stone,
And ministers justice to the waves and to the Nymphes eche one,　710
That in the Brookes and waters dwell. Now hither did resorte
(Not knowing if they might rejoyce and unto mirth exhort
Or comfort him) his Countrie Brookes, Sperchius well beseene
With sedgie heade and shadie bankes of Poplars fresh and greene,
Enipeus restlesse, swift and quicke, olde father Apidane,　715
Amphrisus with his gentle streame, and Aeas clad with cane:
With dyvers other Ryvers moe, which having runne their race,
Into the Sea their wearie waves doe lead with restlesse pace.
From hence the carefull Inachus absentes him selfe alone,
Who in a corner of his cave with doolefull teares and mone,　720
Augments the waters of his streame, bewayling piteously
His daughter Io lately lost. He knewe not certainly
And if she were alive or deade. But for he had hir sought
And coulde not finde hir any where, assuredly he thought
She did not live above the molde, ne drewe the vitall breath:　725
Misgiving worser in his minde, if ought be worse than death.
　　It fortunde on a certaine day that Jove espide this Mayde
　　Come running from hir fathers streame alone: to whome he sayde:
O Damsell worthie Jove himselfe, like one day for to make
Some happie person whome thou list unto thy bed to take,　730
I pray thee let us shroude our selves in shadowe here togither,
Of this or that (he poynted both) it makes no matter whither,
Untill the hotest of the day and Noone be overpast.
And if for feare of savage beastes perchaunce thou be agast
To wander in the Woods alone, thou shalt not neede to feare,　735
A God shall bee thy guide to save thee harmelesse every where.
And not a God of meaner sort, but even the same that hath
The heavenly scepter in his hande, who in my dreadfull wrath,
Do dart downe thunder wandringly: and therefore make no hast
To runne away. She ranne apace, and had alreadie past　740
The Fen of Lerna and the field of Lincey set with trees:
When Jove intending now in vaine no lenger tyme to leese,
Upon the Countrie all about did bring a foggie mist,
And caught the Mayden whome poore foole he used as he list.
　　Queene Juno looking downe that while upon the open field,　745

713 *beseene:* appearing　　　　726 *Misgiving:* suspecting
725 *ne:* nor

When in so fayre a day such mistes and darkenesse she behelde,
Dyd marvell much, for well she knewe those mistes ascended not
From any Ryver, moorishe ground, or other dankishe plot.
She lookt about hir for hir Jove as one that was acquainted
With such escapes and with the deede had often him attainted.   750
Whome when she founde not in the heaven: Onlesse I gesse amisse,
Some wrong agaynst me (quoth she) now my husbande working is.
And with that worde she left the Heaven, and downe to earth shee
                                                                  came,
Commaunding all the mistes away. But Jove foresees the same,
And to a Cow as white as milke his Leman he convayes.   755
She was a goodly Heifer sure: and Juno did hir prayse,
Although (God wot) she thought it not, and curiously she sought,
Where she was bred, whose Cow she was, who had hir thither broughte
As though she had not knowne the truth. Hir husband by and by
(Bycause she should not search too neare) devisde a cleanly lie,   760
And tolde hir that the Cow was bred even nowe out of the grounde.
Then Juno who hir husbands shift at fingers endes had founde,
Desirde to have the Cow of gift. What should he doe as tho?
Great cruelnesse it were to yeelde his Lover to hir so.
And not to give would breede mistrust. As fast as shame provoked,   765
So fast agayne a tother side his Love his minde revoked.
So much that Love was at the poynt to put all shame to flight.
But that he feared if he should denie a gift so light
As was a Cowe to hir that was his sister and his wyfe,
Might make hir thinke it was no Cow, and breede perchaunce
                                                            some strife. 770
    Now when that Juno had by gift hir husbands Leman got,
    Yet altogether out of feare and carelesse was she not.
She had him in a jelousie and thoughtfull was she still
For doubt he should invent some meanes to steale hir from hir: till
To Argus, olde Aristors sonne, she put hir for to keepe.   775
This Argus had an hundreth eyes: of which by turne did sleepe
Alwayes a couple, and the rest did duely watch and warde,
And of the charge they tooke in hande had ever good regarde,
What way so ever Argus stood with face, with backe, or side,
To Io warde, before his eyes did Io still abide.   780

---

750 *attainted:* dishonored
755 *Leman:* sweetheart, mistress; *convayes:*
   secretly changes
760 *cleanly:* pure, outright
762 *shift:* trick
763 *as tho:* then
780 *to Io warde:* toward Io

All day he let hir graze abroade, the Sunne once under ground
He shut hir up and by the necke with wrythen Withe hir bound.
With croppes of trees and bitter weedes now was she dayly fed,
And in the stead of costly couch and good soft featherbed,
She sate a nightes upon the ground, and on such ground whereas   785
Was not sometime so much as grasse: and oftentymes she was
Compeld to drinke of muddie pittes: and when she did devise
To Argus for to lift hir handes in meeke and humble wise,
She sawe she had no handes at all: and when she did assay
To make complaint, she lowed out, which did hir so affray,   790
That oft she started at the noyse, and would have runne away.
Unto hir father Inachs banckes she also did resorte,
Where many a tyme and oft before she had beene wont to sporte.
Now when she looked in the streame, and sawe hir horned hed,
She was agast and from hir selfe would all in hast have fled.   795
The Nymphes hir sisters knewe hir not nor yet hir owne deare father,
Yet followed she both him and them, and suffred them the rather
To touch and stroke hir where they list, as one that preaced still
To set hir selfe to wonder at and gaze upon their fill.
The good old Inach puls up grasse and to hir straight it beares.   800
She as she kyst and lickt his handes did shed forth dreerie teares.
And had she had hir speach at will to utter forth hir thought,
She would have tolde hir name and chaunce and him of helpe besought.
But for bicause she could not speake, she printed in the sande,
Two letters with hir foote, whereby was given to understande   805
The sorrowfull chaunging of hir shape. Which seene straight cryed out
Hir father Inach, Wo is me, and clasping hir about
Hir white and seemely Heifers necke and christal hornes both twaine,
He shricked out full piteously: Now wo is me, again.
Alas art thou my daughter deare, whome through the worlde I sought   810
And could not finde, and now by chaunce art to my presence brought?
My sorrow certesse lesser farre a thousande folde had beene
If never had I seene thee more, than thus to have thee seene.
Thou standst as dombe and to my wordes no answere can thou give,
But from the bottom of thy heart full sorie sighes dost drive   815
As tokens of thine inwarde griefe, and doolefully dost mooe
Unto my talke, the onely thing leaft in thy powre to dooe.
But I mistrusting nothing lesse than this so great mischaunce,
By some great mariage earnestly did seeke thee to advaunce,

---

783 *croppes:* croppings   812 *certesse:* certes, assuredly
790 *affray:* frighten

In hope some yssue to have seene betweene my sonne and thee. 820
But now thou must a husband have among the Heirds I see,
And eke thine issue must be such as other cattels bee.
Oh that I were a mortall wight as other creatures are,
For then might death in length of time quite rid mee of this care,
But now bycause I am a God, and fate doth death denie, 825
There is no helpe but that my griefe must last eternallie.

    As Inach made this piteous mone quicke sighted Argus drave
    His daughter into further fieldes to which he could not have
Accesse, and he himselfe aloof did get him to a hill,
From whence he sitting at his ease viewd everie way at will. 830
Now could no lenger Jove abide his Lover so forlorne,
And thereupon he cald his sonne that Maia had him borne,
Commaunding Argus should be kild. He made no long abod,
But tyde his feathers to his feete, and tooke his charmed rod.
(With which he bringeth things asleepe, and fetcheth soules from
        Hell) 835
And put his Hat upon his head: and when that all was well
He leaped from his fathers towres, and downe to earth he flue
And there both Hat and winges also he lightly from him thrue,
Retayning nothing but his staffe, the which he closely helde
Betweene his elbowe and his side, and through the common fielde 840
Went plodding lyke some good plaine soule that had some flocke to
        feede.

And as he went he pyped still upon an Oten Reede.
Queene Junos Heirdman farre in love with this straunge melodie
Bespake him thus: Good fellow mine, I pray thee heartely
Come sitte downe by me on this hill, for better feede I knowe 845
Thou shalt not finde in all these fieldes, and (as the thing doth showe)
It is a coole and shadowie plot, for sheepeheirds verie fitte.
Downe by his elbow by and by did Atlas nephew sit.
And for to passe the tyme withall for seeming overlong,
He helde him talke of this and that, and now and than among 850
He playd upon his merrie Pipe to cause his watching eyes
To fall asleepe. Poore Argus did the best he could devise
To overcome the pleasant nappes: and though that some did sleepe,
Yet of his eyes the greater part he made their watch to keepe.
And after other talke he askt (for lately was it founde) 855
Who was the founder of that Pype that did so sweetely sounde.

833 *abod:* delay   850 *among:* at the same time

Then sayde the God: There dwelt sometime a Nymph of noble
fame

Among the hilles of Arcadie, that Syrinx had to name.
Of all the Nymphes of Nonacris and Fairie farre and neere,
In beautie and in personage thys Ladie had no peere.   860
Full often had she given the slippe both to the Satyrs quicke
And other Gods that dwell in Woods, and in the Forrests thicke,
Or in the fruitfull fieldes abrode: It was hir whole desire
To follow chaste Dianas guise in Maydenhead and attire,
Whome she did counterfaite so nighe, that such as did hir see   865
Might at a blush have taken hir Diana for to bee,
But that the Nymph did in hir hande a bowe of Cornell holde,
Whereas Diana evermore did beare a bowe of golde.
And yet she did deceyve folke so. Upon a certaine day
God Pan with garland on his heade of Pinetree, sawe hir stray   870
From Mount Lyceus all alone, and thus to hir did say:
Unto a Gods request, O Nymph, voucesafe thou to agree
That doth desire thy wedded spouse and husband for to bee.

There was yet more behinde to tell: as how that Syrinx fled,
Through waylesse woods and gave no eare to that that Pan had
sed,   875

Untill she to the gentle streame of sandie Ladon came,
Where, for bicause it was so deepe, she could not passe the same,
She piteously to chaunge hir shape the water Nymphes besought:
And how when Pan betweene his armes, to catch the Nymph had
thought,

In steade of hir he caught the Reedes newe growne upon the brooke, 880
And as he sighed, with his breath the Reedes he softly shooke
Which made a still and mourning noyse, with straungnesse of the which
And sweetenesse of the feeble sounde the God delighted mich,
Saide: Certesse, Syrinx, for thy sake it is my full intent,
To make my comfort of these Reedes wherein thou doest lament: 885
And how that there of sundrie Reedes with wax together knit,
He made the Pipe which of hir name the Greekes call Syrinx yet.

But as Cyllenius would have tolde this tale, he cast his sight
On Argus, and beholde his eyes had bid him all good night.
There was not one that did not sleepe, and fast he gan to nodde,   890
Immediately he ceast his talke, and with his charmed rodde,
So stroked all his heavie eyes that earnestly they slept.

---

858 *to name:* as name   884 *Certesse:* certainly
883 *mich:* much

Then with his Woodknife by and by he lightly to him stept,
And lent him such a perlous blowe, where as the shoulders grue
Unto the necke, that straight his heade quite from the bodie flue.   895
Then tombling downe the headlong hill his bloudie coarse he sent,
That all the way by which he rolde was stayned and besprent.
There lyest thou Argus under foote, with all thy hundreth lights,
And all the light is cleane extinct that was within those sights.
One endelesse night thy hundred eyes hath nowe bereft for aye,   900
Yet would not Juno suffer so hir Heirdmans eyes decay:
But in hir painted Peacocks tayle and feathers did them set,
Where they remayne lyke precious stones and glaring eyes as yet.
      She tooke his death in great dispight and as hir rage did move,
      Determinde for to wreeke hir wrath upon hir husbandes Love.   905
Forthwith she cast before hir eyes right straunge and ugly sightes,
Compelling hir to thinke she sawe some Fiendes or wicked sprightes.
And in hir heart such secret prickes and piercing stings she gave hir,
As through the worlde from place to place with restlesse sorrow
                                                            drave hir.
Thou Nylus wert assignd to stay hir paynes and travails past,   910
To which as soone as Io came with much adoe at last,
With wearie knockles on thy brim she kneeled sadly downe,
And stretching foorth hir faire long necke and christall horned crowne,
Such kinde of countnaunce as she had she lifted to the skie,
And there with sighing sobbes and teares and lowing doolefully   915
Did seeme to make hir mone to Jove, desiring him to make
Some ende of those hir troublous stormes endured for his sake.
He tooke his wife about the necke, and sweetely kissing prayde,
That Ios penance yet at length might by hir graunt be stayde.
Thou shalt not neede to feare (quoth he) that ever she shall grieve
                                                            thee   920
From this day forth. And in this case the better to beleve mee,
The Stygian waters of my wordes unparciall witnesse beene.
      As soone as Juno was appeasde, immediately was seene
      That Io tooke hir native shape in which she first was borne,
      And eke became the selfesame thing the which she was beforne.   925
For by and by she cast away hir rough and hairie hyde,
Insteede whereof a soft smouth skinne with tender fleshe did byde.
Hir hornes sank down, hir eies and mouth were brought in lesser roome,
Hir handes, hir shoulders, and hir armes in place againe did come.

---

894 *perlous:* perilous, terrible   898 *lights:* eyes
897 *besprent:* bespattered   912 *knockles:* joints

Hir cloven Clees to fingers five againe reduced were,
On which the nayles lyke pollisht Gemmes did shine full bright and
                                                                clere.

In fine, no likenesse of a Cow save whitenesse did remaine
So pure and perfect as no snow was able it to staine.
She vaunst hir selfe upon hir feete which then was brought to two.
And though she gladly would have spoke: yet durst she not so do,   935
Without good heede, for feare she should have lowed like a Cow.
And therefore softly with hir selfe she gan to practise how
Distinctly to pronounce hir wordes that intermitted were.
Now, as a Goddesse, is she had in honour everie where
Among the folke that dwell by Nyle yclad in linnen weede.   940
Of her in tyme came Epaphus begotten of the seede
Of myghtie Jove. This noble ympe nowe joyntly with his mother,
Through all the Cities of that lande have temples t'one with toother.
     There was his match in heart and yeares, the lustie Phaeton,
     A stalworth stripling strong and stout, the golden Phoebus
                                                                sonne. 945
Whome making proude and stately vauntes of his so noble race,
And unto him in that respect in nothing giving place,
The sonne of Io coulde not beare: but sayde unto him thus:
No marvell though thou be so proude and full of wordes ywus.
For everie fonde and trifling tale the which thy mother makes,   950
Thy gyddie wit and hairebrainde heade forthwith for gospell takes.
Well, vaunt thy selfe of Phoebus still, for when the truth is seene,
Thou shalt perceyve that fathers name a forged thing to beene.
At this reproch did Phaeton wax as red as any fire:
Howbeit for the present tyme did shame represse his ire.   955
Unto his mother Clymen straight he goeth to detect
The spitefull wordes that Epaphus against him did object.
Yes mother (quoth he) and which ought your greater griefe to bee,
I who at other tymes of talke was wont to be so free
And stoute, had neere a worde to say, I was ashamde to take   960
So fowle a foyle: the more because I could none answere make.
But if I be of heavenly race exacted as ye say,
Then shewe some token of that highe and noble byrth I pray.
And vouche me for to be of heaven. With that he gently cast

930 *Clees:* hooves
934 *vaunst hir selfe:* got up
938 *intermitted:* discontinued for a time
940 *weede:* garment

949 *ywus:* iwis, certainly
950 *fonde:* foolish
956 *detect:* expose
961 *foyle:* setback

His armes about his mothers necke, and clasping hir full fast,   965
Besought hir as she lovde his life, and as she lovde the lyfe
Of Merops, and had kept hir selfe as undefiled wyfe,
And as she wished welthily his sisters to bestowe,
She would some token give whereby his rightfull Sire to knowe.
It is a doubtful matter whither Clymen moved more   970
With this hir Phaetons earnest sute, exacting it so sore,
Or with the slaunder of the bruit layde to hir charge before,
Did holde up both hir handes to heaven, and looking on the Sunne,
My right deare childe I safely sweare (quoth she to Phaeton)
That of this starre the which so bright doth glister in thine eye: 975
Of this same Sunne that cheares the world with light indifferently
Wert thou begot: and if I fayne, then with my heart I pray,
That never may I see him more unto my dying day.
But if thou have so great desire thy father for to knowe,
Thou shalt not neede in that behalfe much labour to bestowe.   980
The place from whence he doth arise adjoyneth to our lande.
And if thou thinke thy heart will serve, then go and understande
The truth of him. When Phaeton heard his mother saying so,
He gan to leape and skip for joye. He fed his fansie tho,
Upon the Heaven and heavenly things: and so with willing minde,   985
From Aethiop first his native home, and afterwarde through Inde
Set underneath the morning starre he went so long, till as
He founde me where his fathers house and dayly rising was.

FINIS PRIMI LIBRI.

988 *me:* Golding makes frequent use of this "ethical dative," which indicates that although he is not personally involved in the events he is describing, he is taking a keen personal interest in them.

THE SECONDE BOOKE

OF OVIDS METAMORPHOSIS.

[Phaethon. Jove and Callisto. Coronis and Apollo. Ocyrhoe. Mercury and Battus. Mercury and Herse. Aglauros. Jove and Europa.]

The Princely Pallace of the Sunne stood gorgeous to beholde
　　On stately Pillars builded high of yellow burnisht golde,
Beset with sparckling Carbuncles that like to fire did shine.
The roofe was framed curiously of Ivorie pure and fine.
The two doore leaves of silver cleare a radiant light did cast:　　　5
But yet the cunning workemanship of things therein farre past
The stuffe wherof the doores were made. For there a perfect plat
Had Vulcane drawne of all the worlde: Both of the sourges that
Embrace the earth with winding waves, and of the stedfast ground,
And of the heaven it selfe also that both encloseth round.　　　10
And first and formest in the Sea the Gods thereof did stande:
Loude sounding Tryton with his shirle and writhen Trumpe in hande:
Unstable Protew chaunging aye his figure and his hue,
From shape to shape a thousande sithes as list him to renue:
Aegeon leaning boystrously on backes of mightie Whales　　　15
And Doris with hir daughters all: of which some cut the wales
With splaied armes, some sate on rockes and dride their goodly haire,
And some did ryde uppon the backes of fishes here and theare.
Not one in all poyntes fully lyke an other coulde ye see,
Nor verie farre unlike, but such as sisters ought to bee.　　　20
The Earth had townes, men, beasts and Woods with sundrie trees
　　　　　　　　　　　　　　　　　　　　and rods,

---

7 *plat:* map
11 *formest:* foremost
12 *shirle:* shrill; *writhen:* twisted, coiled

14 *sithes:* times; *list:* pleased
16 *wales:* waves
17 *splaied:* extended

31

And running Ryvers with their Nymphes and other countrie Gods.
Directly over all these same the plat of heaven was pight,
Upon the two doore leaves, the signes of all the Zodiak bright,
Indifferently six on the left and six upon the right.   25
When Clymens sonne had climbed up at length with weerie pace,
And set his foote within his doubted fathers dwelling place,
Immediately he preaced forth to put him selfe in sight,
And stoode aloofe. For neere at hande he could not bide the light.
In purple Robe and royall Throne of Emeraudes freshe and greene   30
Did Phoebus sitte, and on eche hande stoode wayting well beseene,
Dayes, Monthes, yeares, ages, seasons, times, and eke the equall houres.
There stoode the springtime with a crowne of fresh and fragrant floures.
There wayted Sommer naked starke all save a wheaten Hat:
And Autumne smerde with treading grapes late at the pressing Vat.   35
And lastly quaking for the colde, stood Winter all forlorne,
With rugged heade as white as Dove, and garments all to torne,
Forladen with the Isycles that dangled up and downe
Uppon his gray and hoarie bearde and snowie frozen crowne.
The Sunne thus sitting in the middes did cast his piercing eye,   40
(With which full lightly when he list he all thinges doth espye)
Upon his childe that stood aloofe, agast and trembling sore
At sight of such unwonted things, and thus bespake him thore:
O noble ympe, O Phaeton which art not such (I see)
Of whome thy father should have cause ashamed for to bee: 45
Why hast thou traveld to my court? what is thy will with mee?
Then answerde he: Of all the worlde O onely perfect light,
O Father Phoebus, (if I may usurpe that name of right,
And that my mother for to save hir selfe from worldely shame,
Hyde not hir fault with false pretence and colour of thy name)   50
Some signe apparant graunt whereby I may be knowne thy Sonne,
And let mee hang no more in doubt. He had no sooner donne,
But that his father putting off the bright and fierie beames
That glistred rounde about his heade like cleare and golden streames,
Commaunded him to draw him neere, and him embracing sayde: 55
To take mee for thy rightfull Sire thou neede not be afrayde.
Thy mother Clymen of a truth from falshood standeth free.
And for to put thee out of doubt aske what thou wilt of mee,

---

23 *pight:* placed   38 *Forladen:* heavily laden
28 *preaced:* pressed   43 *thore:* there
31 *beseene:* appearing   44 *ympe:* scion, child
32 *eke:* also   50 *colour:* outward show, pretense
37 *to torne:* much torn, torn in pieces

And I will give thee thy desire, the Lake whereby of olde
We Gods do sweare (the which mine eyes did never yet beeholde)   60
Beare witnesse with thee of my graunt. He scarce this tale had tolde,
But that the foolish Phaeton straight for a day did crave
The guyding of his winged Steedes, and Chariot for to have.
Then did his Father by and by forethinke him of his oth.
And shaking twentie tymes his heade, as one that was full wroth,   65
Bespake him thus: Thy wordes have made me rashly to consent
To that which shortly both of us (I feare mee) shall repent.
Oh that I might retract my graunt, my sonne I doe protest
I would denie thee nothing else save this thy fond request.
I may disswade, there lyes herein more perill than thou weene: 70
The things the which thou doest desire of great importance beene:
More than thy weakenesse well can wielde, a charge (as well appeares)
Of greater weight, than may agree with these thy tender yeares.
Thy state is mortall, weake and frayle, the thing thou doest desire
Is such, whereto no mortall man is able to aspire.   75
Yea, foolish boy, thou doest desire (and all for want of wit)
A greater charge than any God coulde ever have as yet.
For were there any of them all so overseene and blinde,
To take upon him this my charge, full quickly should he finde
That none but I could sit upon the fierie Axeltree.   80
No not even he that rules this wast and endlesse space we see,
Not he that darts with dreadfull hande the thunder from the Skie,
Shall drive this chare. And yet what thing in all the world perdie
Is able to compare with Jove? Now first the morning way
Lyes steepe upright, so that the steedes in coolest of the day   85
And beeing fresh have much adoe to climbe against the Hyll.
Amiddes the heaven the gastly heigth augmenteth terror still.
My heart doth waxe as colde as yse full many a tyme and oft
For feare to see the Sea and land from that same place aloft.
The Evening way doth fall plump downe requiring strength to guide,   90
That Tethis who doth harbrowgh mee within hir sourges wide
Doth stand in feare lest from the heaven I headlong down should slide.
Besides all this the Heaven aye swimmes and wheeles about full swift
And with his rolling dryves the starres their proper course to shift.
Yet doe I keepe my native course against this brunt so stout,   95
Not giving place as others doe: but boldely bearing out

---

64 *by and by:* immediately; *forethinke him*   78 *overseene:* deluded, rash
  of: regret   83 *chare:* car, chariot; *perdie:* by god, verily
70 *weene:* think, suppose   91 *harbrowgh:* harbor

The force and swiftnesse of that heaven that whyrleth so about.
Admit thou had my winged Steedes and Chariot in thine hande:
What couldste thou doe? dost thinke thy selfe well able to withstande
The swiftnesse of the whyrled Poles, but that their brunt and sway 100
(Yea doe the best and worst thou can) shall beare thee quite away?
Perchaunce thou dost imagine there some townes of Gods to finde,
With groves and Temples richt with giftes as is among mankinde.
Thou art deceyved utterly: thou shalt not finde it so.
By blinde bywayes and ugly shapes of monsters must thou go. 105
And though thou knewe the way so well as that thou could not stray,
Betweene the dreadful bulles sharp hornes yet must thou make thy way.
Agaynst the cruell Bowe the which the Aemonian archer drawes:
Against the ramping Lyon armde with greedie teeth and pawes:
Against the Scorpion stretching farre his fell and venymd clawes: 110
And eke the Crab that casteth forth his crooked clees awrie
Not in such sort as th'other doth, and yet as dreadfully.
Againe thou neyther hast the powre nor yet the skill I knowe
My lustie coursers for to guide that from their nostrilles throwe
And from their mouthes the fierie breath that breedeth in their brest. 115
For scarcely will they suffer mee who knowes their nature best
When that their cruell courages begin to catch a heate,
That hardely should I deale with them, but that I know the feate.
But lest my gift should to thy griefe and utter perill tend
My Sonne beware and (whyle thou mayst) thy fonde request amend. 120
Bycause thou woulde be knowne to bee my childe thou seemst to crave
A certaine signe: what surer signe I pray thee canst thou have
Than this my feare so fatherly the which I have of thee
Which proveth me most certainly thy father for to bee?
Beholde and marke my countenaunce. O would to God thy sight 125
Could pierce within my wofull brest, to see the heavie plight,
And heapes of cares within my heart. Looke through the worlde so
round
Of all the wealth and goodes therein: if ought there may be found
In Heaven or Earth or in the Sea, aske what thou lykest best,
And sure it shall not be denide. This onely one request 130
That thou hast made I heartely beseech thee to relent,
Which for to tearme the thing aright is even a punishment,
And not an honour as thou thinkest: my Phaeton thou dost crave
In stead of honour even a scourge and punishment for to have.

110 *fell:* fierce, cruel   120 *fonde:* foolish
111 *clees:* claws   131 *relent:* abandon

Thou fondling thou, what dost thou meane with fawning armes about [135]
My necke thus flattringly to hang? Thou needest not to dout.
I have alreadie sworne by Styx, aske what thou wilt of mee
And thou shalt have. Yet let thy next wish somewhat wiser bee.
　　Thus ended his advertisment: and yet the wilfull Lad
　　Withstood his counsell urging still the promisse that he had,   [140]
Desiring for to have the chare as if he had been mad.
His father having made delay as long as he could shift,
Did lead him where his Chariot stood, which was of Vulcans gift.
The Axeltree was massie golde, the Bucke was massie golde,
The utmost fellies of the wheeles, and where the tree was rolde.   [145]
The spokes were all of sylver bright, the Chrysolites and Gemmes
That stood uppon the Collars, Trace, and hounces in their hemmes
Did cast a sheere and glimmering light, as Phoebus shone thereon.
Now while the lustie Phaeton stood gazing here upon,
And wondered at the workemanship of everie thing: beeholde   [150]
The earely morning in the East beegan mee to unfolde
Hir purple Gates, and shewde hir house bedeckt with Roses red.
The twinckling starres withdrew which by the morning star are led:
Who as the Captaine of that Host that hath no peere nor match,
Dooth leave his standing last of all within that heavenly watch.   [155]
Now when his Father sawe the worlde thus glister red and trim,
And that his waning sisters hornes began to waxen dim,
He had the fetherfooted howres go harnesse in his horse.
The Goddesses with might and mayne themselves thereto enforce.
His fierifoming Steedes full fed with juice of Ambrosie   [160]
They take from Maunger trimly dight: and to their heades doe tie
Strong reyned bits: and to the Charyot doe them well appoint.
Then Phoebus did with heavenly salve his Phaetons heade annoint,
That scorching fire coulde nothing hurt: which done, upon his haire
He put the fresh and golden rayes himselfe was wont to weare.   [165]
And then as one whose heart misgave the sorrowes drawing fast,
With sorie sighes he thus bespake his retchlesse sonne at last:
　　(And if thou canst) at least yet this thy fathers lore obay:
　　Sonne, spare the whip, and reyne them hard, they run so swift
　　　　　　　　　　　　　　　　　　　　　　　　　　　away

[135] *fondling:* foolish one
[139] *advertisment:* admonition
[142] *shift:* manage
[144] *Bucke:* body, or here perhaps tongue, of cart
[145] *fellies:* felloes, rims

[147] *hounces:* ornaments on collar of horse; *hemmes:* edges
[161] *dight:* equipped, made ready
[162] *appoint:* fix, fasten
[166] *misgave:* was apprehensive of
[167] *retchlesse:* reckless

As that thou shalt have much adoe their fleeing course to stay.   170
Directly through the Zones all five beware thou doe not ride,
A brode byway cut out askew that bendeth on the side
Contaynde within the bondes of three the midmost Zones doth lie:
Which from the grisely Northren beare, and Southren Pole doth flie.
Keepe on this way: my Charyot rakes thou plainely shalt espie   175
And to th'intent that heaven and earth may well the heate endure,
Drive neyther over high nor yet too lowe. For be thou sure,
And if thou mount above thy boundes, the starres thou burnest cleane.
Againe beneath thou burnst the Earth: most safetie is the meane.
And least perchaunce thou overmuch the right hand way should take,   180
And so misfortune should thee drive upon the writhen Snake,
Or else by taking overmuche upon the lefter hand
Unto the Aultar thou be driven that doth against it stand:
Indifferently betweene them both I wish thee for to ride.
The rest I put to fortunes will, who be thy friendly guide,   185
And better for thee than thy selfe as in this case provide.
Whiles that I prattle here with thee, behold the dankish night
Beyond all Spaine hir utmost bound is passed out of sight.
We may no lenger tariance make: my wonted light is cald,
The Morning with hir countnance cleare the darknesse hath appald.   190
Take raine in hand, or if thy minde by counsell altred bee,
Refuse to meddle with my Wayne: and while thou yet art free,
And doste at ease within my house in safegarde well remaine,
Of this thine unadvised wish not feeling yet the paine,
Let me alone with giving still the world his wonted light,   195
And thou thereof as heretofore enjoy the harmelesse sight.
        Thus much in vaine: for Phaeton both yong in yeares and wit,
        Into the Chariot lightly lept, and vauncing him in it
Was not a little proud that he the brydle gotten had.
He thankt his father whom it grievde to see his childe so mad.   200
While Phebus and his rechelesse sonne were entertalking this,
Aeous, Aethon, Phlegon, and the firie Pyrois,
The restlesse horses of the Sunne, began to ney so hie
Wyth flaming breath, that all the heaven might heare them perfectly.
And with their hoves they mainly beate upon the lattisde grate.   205
The which when Tethis (knowing nought of this hir cousins fate)
Had put aside, and given the steedes the free and open scope
Of all the compasse of the Skie within the heavenly Cope:

175 *rakes:* paths, ruts   198 *vauncing him in:* getting up into
192 *Wayne:* chariot   205 *mainly:* strongly

They girded forth, and cutting through the Cloudes that let their race,
With splayed wings they overflew the Easterne winde apace.   210
The burthen was so lyght as that the Genets felt it not.
The wonted weight was from the Waine, the which they well did wot.
For like as ships amids the Seas that scant of ballace have,
Doe reele and totter with the wynde, and yeeld to every wave:
Even so the Waine for want of weight it erst was wont to beare,   215
Did hoyse aloft and scayle and reele, as though it empty were.
Which when the Cartware did perceyve, they left the beaten way
And taking bridle in the teeth began to run astray.
The rider was so sore agast, he knew no use of Rayne,
Nor yet his way: and though he had, yet had it ben in vayne,   220
Because he wanted powre to rule the horses and the Wayne.
      Then first did sweat cold Charles his Wain through force of
                                                Phebus rayes
      And in the Sea forbidden him, to dive in vaine assayes.
The Serpent at the frozen Pole both colde and slow by kinde,
Through heat waxt wroth, and stird about a cooler place to finde.   225
And thou Bootes though thou be but slow of footemanship,
Yet wert thou faine (as Fame reports) about thy Waine to skip.
Now when unhappy Phaeton from top of all the Skie
Behelde the Earth that underneath a great way off did lie,
He waxed pale for sodaine feare, his joynts and sinewes quooke,   230
The greatnesse of the glistring light his eyesight from him tooke.
Now wisht he that he never had his fathers horses see:
It yrkt him that he thus had sought to learne his piedegre.
It grievde him that he had prevailde in gaining his request.
To have bene counted Merops sonne he thought it now the best.   235
Thus thinking was he headlong driven, as when a ship is borne
By blustring windes, hir saileclothes rent, hir sterne in pieces torne,
And tacling brust, the which the Pilote trusting all to prayre
Abandons wholy to the Sea and fortune of the ayre.
What should he doe? much of the heaven he passed had behinde   240
And more he saw before: both whiche he measurde in his minde,
Eft looking forward to the West which to approch as then
Might not betide, and to the East eft looking backe agen.

209 *girded:* rushed, sprung; *let:* impeded,   217 *Cartware:* team of horses
    hindered   222 *Charles his Wain:* the Big Dipper
211 *Genets:* jennets, horses   224 *by kinde:* naturally
212 *from:* out of; *wot:* know   238 *brust:* burst
213 *scant of ballace:* lack of ballast   242 *Eft:* again, after
215 *erst:* before   243 *betide:* happen
216 *hoyse:* rise; *scayle:* climb

He wist not what was best to doe, his wittes were ravisht so.
For neither could he hold the Reynes, nor yet durst let them go.   245
And of his horses names was none that he remembred tho.
Straunge uncoth Monsters did he see dispersed here and there
And dreadfull shapes of ugly beasts that in the Welkin were.
There is a certaine place in which the hidious Scorpion throwes
His armes in compasse far abrode, much like a couple of bowes,   250
With writhen tayle and clasping cles, whose poyson limmes doe stretch
On every side, that of two signes they full the roume doe retch,
Whome when the Lad beheld all moyst with blacke and lothly swet,
With sharpe and nedlepointed sting as though he seemde to thret,
He was so sore astraught for feare, he let the bridels slacke,   255
Which when the horses felt lie lose upon their sweating backe,
At rovers straight throughout the Ayre by wayes unknowne they ran
Whereas they never came before since that the worlde began.
For looke what way their lawlesse rage by chaunce and fortune drue
Without controlment or restraint that way they freely flue   260
Among the starres that fixed are within the firmament
They snatcht the Chariot here and there. One while they coursing went
Upon the top of all the skie: anon againe full round
They troll me downe to lower wayes and nearer to the ground,
So that the Moone was in a Maze to see hir brothers Waine   265
Run under hirs: the singed cloudes began to smoke amaine.
Eche ground the higher that it was and nearer to the Skie
The sooner was it set on fire, and made therewith so drie
That every where it gan to chinke. The Medes and Pastures greene
Did seare away: and with the leaves, the trees were burned cleene.   270
The parched corne did yeelde wherewith to worke his owne decaie.
Tushe, these are trifles. Mightie townes did perish that same daie.
          Whose countries with their folke were burnt: and forests ful
                                                            of wood
          Were turnde to ashes with the rocks and mountains where they
                                                            stood.
Then Athe, Cilician, Taure and Tmole and Oeta flamed hie,   275
And Ide erst full of flowing springs was then made utter drie.
The learned virgins daily haunt, the sacred Helicon,
And Thracian Hemus (not as yet surnamde Oeagrion,)

---

244 *wist:* knew
246 *tho:* then
247 *uncoth:* unknown, repellent
248 *Welkin:* sky

255 *astraught:* distraught, distracted; *slacke:*
          hang loose
257 *At rovers:* at random, haphazard
264 *troll:* roll, whirl

Did smoke both twaine: and Aetna hote of nature aye before,
Encreast by force of Phebus flame now raged ten times more.   280
The forkt Parnasus, Eryx, Cynth, and Othrys then did swelt
And all the snow of Rhodope did at that present melt.
The like outrage Mount Dindymus, and Mime and Micale felt.
Cytheron borne to sacred use with Osse, and Pindus hie
And Olymp greater than them both did burne excessively.   285
The passing colde that Scithie had defended not the same
But that the barren Caucasus was partner of this flame.
And so were eke the Airie Alpes and Appennyne beside,
For all the Cloudes continually their snowie tops doe hide.
Then wheresoever Phaeton did chaunce to cast his vew,   290
The world was all on flaming fire. The breath the which he drew,
Came smoking from his scalding mouth as from a seething pot.
His Chariot also under him began to waxe red hot.
He could no lenger dure the sparkes and cinder flyeng out,
Againe the culme and smouldring smoke did wrap him round about, 295
The pitchie darkenesse of the which so wholy had him hent
As that he wist not where he was nor yet which way he went.
The winged horses forcibly did draw him where they wolde.
The Aethiopians at that time (as men for truth upholde)
(The bloud by force of that same heate drawne to the outer part   300
And there adust from that time forth) became so blacke and swart.
The moysture was so dried up in Lybie land that time
That altogither drie and scorcht continueth yet that Clyme.
The Nymphes with haire about their eares bewayld their springs and
                                                         lakes.
Beotia for hir Dyrces losse great lamentation makes.   305
For Amimone Argos wept, and Corinth for the spring
Pyrene, at whose sacred streame the Muses usde to sing.
The Rivers further from the place were not in better case,
For Tanais in his deepest streame did boyle and steme apace,
Old Penew and Caycus of the countrie Teuthranie,   310
And swift Ismenos in their bankes by like misfortune frie.
Then burnde the Psophian Erymanth: and (which should burne
                                                         ageine)
The Trojan Xanthus and Lycormas with his yellow veine,

279 *aye:* always   295 *culme:* soot, smut
281 *swelt:* swelter   296 *hent:* caught
282 *present:* time   301 *adust:* scorched
294 *dure:* endure

Meander playing in his bankes aye winding to and fro,
Migdonian Melas with his waves as blacke as any slo.   315
Eurotas running by the foote of Tenare boyled tho.
Then sod Euphrates cutting through the middes of Babilon.
Then sod Orontes, and the Scithian swift Thermodoon.
Then Ganges, Colchian Phasis, and the noble Istre
Alpheus and Sperchius bankes with flaming fire did glistre.   320
The golde that Tagus streame did beare did in the chanell melt.
Amid Cayster of this fire the raging heat was felt
Among the quieres of singing Swannes that with their pleasant lay
Along the bankes of Lidian brakes from place to place did stray.
And Nyle for feare did run away into the furthest Clyme   325
Of all the world, and hid his heade, which to this present tyme
Is yet unfound: his mouthes all seven cleane voyde of water beene,
Like seven great valleys where (save dust) could nothing else be seene.
By like misfortune Hebrus dride and Strymon, both of Thrace.
The Westerne Rivers Rhine and Rhone and Po were in like case: 330
And Tyber unto whome the Goddes a faithfull promise gave
Of all the world the Monarchie and soveraigne state to have.
The ground did cranie everie where and light did pierce to hell
And made afraide the King and Queene that in that Realme doe dwell.
The Sea did shrinke and where as waves did late before remaine,   335
Became a Champion field of dust and even a sandy plaine.
The hilles erst hid farre under waves like Ilelandes did appeare
So that the scattred Cyclades for the time augmented were.
The fishes drew them to the deepes: the Dolphines durst not play
Above the water as before, the Seales and Porkpis lay   340
With bellies upward on the waves starke dead: and fame doth go
That Nereus with his wife and daughters all were faine as tho
To dive within the scalding waves. Thrise Neptune did advaunce
His armes above the scalding Sea with sturdy countenaunce:
And thrise for hotenesse of the Ayre, was faine himselfe to hide.   345
But yet the Earth the Nurce of things enclosde on every side
(Betweene the waters of the Sea and Springs that now had hidden
Themselves within their Mothers wombe) for all the paine abidden,
Up to the necke put forth hir head and casting up hir hand,
Betweene hir forehead and the sunne as panting she did stand   350
With dreadfull quaking, all that was she fearfully did shake,

315 *slo:* fruit of blackthorn
316 *tho:* then
317 *sod:* seethed

336 *Champion:* champaign, level and open
340 *Porkpis:* porpoises
348 *abidden:* endured

And shrinking somewhat lower downe with sacred voyce thus spake:
    O king of Gods and if this be thy will and my desart,
    Why doste thou stay with deadly dint thy thunder downe to dart?
And if that needes I perish must through force of firie flame,   355
Let thy celestiall fire O God I pray thee doe the same.
A comfort shall it be to have thee Author of my death.
I scarce have powre to speak these words (the smoke had stopt hir
               breath).
Behold my singed haire: behold my dim and bleared eye,
See how about my scorched face the scalding embers flie.   360
Is this the guerdon wherewithall ye quite my fruitfulnesse?
Is this the honor that ye gave me for my plenteousnesse
And dutie done with true intent? for suffring of the plough
To draw deepe woundes upon my backe and rakes to rend me through?
For that I over all the yeare continually am wrought?   365
For giving foder to the beasts and cattell all for nought?
For yeelding corne and other foode wherewith to keepe mankinde?
And that to honor you withall sweete frankinsence I finde?
But put the case that my desert destruction duely crave,
What hath thy brother? what the Seas deserved for to have?   370
Why doe the Seas, his lotted part, thus ebbe and fall so low,
Withdrawing from thy Skie to which it ought most neare to grow?
But if thou neyther doste regarde thy brother, neyther mee,
At least have mercy on thy heaven, looke round about and see
How both the Poles begin to smoke which if the fire appall   375
To utter ruine (be thou sure) thy pallace needes must fall.
Behold how Atlas ginnes to faint. His shoulders though full strong,
Unneth are able to uphold the sparkling Extree long.
If Sea and Land doe go to wrecke, and heaven it selfe doe burne
To olde confused Chaos then of force we must returne.   380
Put to thy helping hand therfore to save the little left
If ought remaine before that all be quite and cleane bereft.
    When ended was this piteous plaint, the Earth did hold hir peace.
    She could no lenger dure the heate but was compelde to cease.
Into hir bosome by and by she shrunke hir cinged heade   385
More nearer to the Stygian caves, and ghostes of persones deade.
The Sire of Heaven protesting all the Gods and him also

---

353 *desart:* deserving
354 *stay:* refrain
361 *quite:* reward, requite
365 *wrought:* worked

378*Unneth:* hardly; *Extree:* axle-tree, axis
380 *of force:* necessarily
387 *protesting:* calling to witness

That lent the Chariot to his child, that all of force must go
To havocke if he helped not, went to the highest part
And top of all the Heaven from whence his custome was to dart   390
His thunder and his lightning downe. But neyther did remaine
A Cloude wherewith to shade the Earth, nor yet a showre of raine.
Then with a dreadfull thunderclap up to his eare he bent
His fist, and at the Wagoner a flash of lightning sent,
Which strake his bodie from the life and threw it over wheele   395
And so with fire he quenched fire. The Steedes did also reele
Upon their knees, and starting up sprang violently, one here,
And there another, that they brast in pieces all their gere.
They threw the Collars from their neckes, and breaking quite asunder
The Trace and Harnesse flang away: here lay the bridles: yonder   400
The Extree plucked from the Naves: and in another place
The shevered spokes of broken wheeles: and so at every pace
The pieces of the Chariot torne lay strowed here and there.
But Phaeton (fire yet blasing stil among his yellow haire)
Shot headlong downe, and glid along the Region of the Ayre   405
Like to a starre in Winter nights (the wether cleare and fayre)
Which though it doe not fall in deede, yet falleth to our sight,
Whome almost in another world and from his countrie quite
The River Padus did receyve, and quencht his burning head.
The water Nymphes of Italie did take his carkasse dead   410
And buried it yet smoking still, with Joves threeforked flame,
And wrate this Epitaph in the stone that lay upon the same:
Here lies the lusty Phaeton which tooke in hand to guide
His fathers Chariot, from the which although he chaunst to slide:
Yet that he gave a proud attempt it cannot be denide.   415
        Wyth ruthfull cheere and heavie heart his father made great mone
        And would not shew himselfe abrode, but mournd at home alone.
And if it be to be beleved, as bruited is by fame
A day did passe without the Sunne. The brightnesse of the flame
Gave light: and so unto some kinde of use that mischiefe came.   420
But Clymen having spoke, as much as mothers usually
Are wonted in such wretched case, discomfortablely,
And halfe beside hir selfe for wo, with torne and scratched brest,
Sercht through the universall world, from East to furthest West,
First seeking for hir sonnes dead coarse, and after for his bones.   425
She found them by a forren streame, entumbled under stones.

---

398 *brast:* burst   416 *cheere:* expression
413 *tooke in hand:* undertook

There fell she groveling on his grave, and reading there his name,
Shed teares thereon, and layd hir breast all bare upon the same.
The daughters also of the Sunne no lesse than did their mother,
Bewaild in vaine with flouds of teares, the fortune of their brother: 430
And beating piteously their breasts, incessantly did call
The buried Phaeton day and night, who heard them not at all,
About whose tumbe they prostrate lay. Foure times the Moone had filde
The Circle of hir joyned hornes, and yet the sisters hilde
Their custome of lamenting still: (for now continuall use 435
Had made it custome.) Of the which the eldest, Phaetuse,
About to kneele upon the ground, complaynde hir feete were nom.
To whome as fayre Lampetie was rising for to com,
Hir feete were held with sodaine rootes. The third about to teare
Hir ruffled lockes, filde both hir handes with leaves in steade of heare. 440
One wept to see hir legges made wood: another did repine
To see hir armes become long boughes. And shortly to define,
While thus they wondred at themselves, a tender barke began
To grow about their thighes and loynes, which shortly overran
Their bellies, brestes, and shoulders eke, and hands successively, 445
That nothing (save their mouthes) remainde, aye calling piteously
Upon the wofull mothers helpe. What could the mother doe
But runne now here now there, as force of nature drue hir to
And deale hir kisses while she might? She was not so content:
But tare their tender braunches downe: and from the slivers went 450
Red drops of bloud as from a wound. The daughter that was rent
Cride: Spare us mother spare I pray, for in the shape of tree
The bodies and the flesh of us your daughters wounded bee.
And now farewell. That word once said, the barke grew over all.
Now from these trees flow gummy teares that Amber men doe call, 455
Which hardened with the heate of sunne as from the boughs they fal
The trickling River doth receyve, and sendes as things of price
To decke the daintie Dames of Rome and make them fine and nice.
  Now present at this monstruous hap was Cygnus, Stenels son,
  Who being by the mothers side akinne to Phaeton 460
Was in condicion more akinne. He leaving up his charge
(For in the land of Ligurie his Kingdome stretched large)
Went mourning all along the bankes and pleasant streame of Po
Among the trees encreased by the sisters late ago.
Annon his voyce became more small and shrill than for a man. 465
Gray fethers muffled in his face: his necke in length began

---

442 *define*: describe, bring to end   459 *hap*: happening

Far from his shoulders for to stretche: and furthermore there goes
A fine red string acrosse the joyntes in knitting of his toes:
With fethers closed are his sides: and on his mouth there grew
A brode blunt byll: and finally was Cygnus made a new   470
And uncoth fowle that hight a Swan, who neither to the winde,
The Ayre, nor Jove betakes himselfe, as one that bare in minde
The wrongfull fire sent late against his cousin Phaeton.
In Lakes and Rivers is his joy: the fire he aye doth shon,
And chooseth him the contrary continually to won.   475
        Forlorne and altogether voyde of that same bodie shene
        Was Phaetons father in that while which erst had in him bene,
Like as he looketh in Th'eclypse. He hates the yrkesome light,
He hates him selfe, he hates the day, and settes his whole delight
In making sorrow for his sonne, and in his griefe doth storme   480
And chaufe denying to the worlde his dutie to performe.
My lot (quoth he) hath had inough of this unquiet state
From first beginning of the worlde. It yrkes me (though too late)
Of restlesse toyles and thankelesse paines. Let who so will for me
Go drive the Chariot in the which the light should caried be.   485
If none dare take the charge in hand, and all the Gods persist
As insufficient, he himselfe go drive it if he list,
That at the least by venturing our bridles for to guide
His lightning making childlesse Sires he once may lay aside.
By that time that he hath assayde the unappalled force   490
That doth remaine and rest within my firiefooted horse,
I trow he shall by tried proufe be able for to tell
How that he did not merit death that could not rule them well.
The Goddes stoode all about the Sunne thus storming in his rage
Beseching him in humble wise his sorrow to asswage.   495
And that he would not on the world continuall darkenesse bring,
Jove eke excusde him of the fire the which he chaunst to sling,
And with entreatance mingled threates as did become a King.
Then Phebus gathered up his steedes that yet for feare did run
Like flaighted fiendes, and in his moode without respect begun   500
To beate his whipstocke on their pates and lash them on the sides.
It was no neede to bid him chaufe; for ever as he rides
He still upbraides them with his sonne, and layes them on the hides.
        And Jove almighty went about the walles of heaven to trie

471 *hight:* is called   492 *trow:* trust, think
475 *won:* wone, live in   500 *flaighted:* fleeing, frightened; *moode:*
476 *shene:* bright, beautiful   anger

If ought were perisht with the fire, which when he did espie   505
Continuing in their former state, all strong and safe and sound,
He went to vew the workes of men, and things upon the ground.
Yet for his land of Arcadie he tooke most care and charge.
The Springs and streames that durst not run he set againe at large.
He clad the earth with grasse, the trees with leaves both fresh and
                                                                            greene   510
Commaunding woods to spring againe that erst had burned bene.
Now as he often went and came it was his chaunce to light
Upon a Nymph of Nonacris whose forme and beautie bright
Did set his heart on flaming fire. She used not to spinne
Nor yet to curle hir frisled haire with bodkin or with pinne.   515
A garment with a buckled belt fast girded did she weare
And in a white and slender Call slight trussed was hir heare.
Sometimes a dart sometime a bow she used for to beare.
She was a knight of Phebes troope. There came not at the mount
Of Menalus of whome Diana made so great account.   520
But favor never lasteth long. The Sunne had gone that day
A good way past the poynt of Noone: when werie of hir way
She drue to shadowe in a wood that never had bene cut.
Here off hir shoulder by and by hir quiver did she put,
And hung hir bow unbent aside, and coucht hir on the ground,   525
Hir quiver underneth hir head. Whom when that Jove had found
Alone and wearie: Sure (he said) my wife shall never know
Of this escape, and if she do, I know the worst I trow.
She can but chide, shall feare of chiding make me to forslow?
He counterfeiteth Phebe streight in countnance and aray.   530
And says: O virgine of my troope, where didst thou hunt to day?
The Damsell started from the ground and said: Hayle Goddesse deare,
Of greater worth than Jove (I thinke) though Jove himselfe did heare.
Jove heard hir well and smylde thereat, it made his heart rejoyce
To heare the Nymph preferre him thus before himselfe in choyce.   535
He fell to kissing: which was such as out of square might seeme,
And in such sort as that a mayde coulde nothing lesse beseeme.
And as she would have told what woods she ranged had for game,
He tooke hir fast betweene his armes, and not without his shame,
Bewrayed plainly what he was and wherefore that he came.   540
The wench against him strove as much as any woman could:

517 *Call:* caul, snood   537 *beseeme:* become, suit
529 *forslow:* be slow   540 *Bewrayed:* exposed, betrayed
536 *out of square:* out of order

I would that Juno had it seene. For then I know thou would
Not take the deede so heynously: with all hir might she strove.
But what poore wench or who alive could vanquish mighty Jove?
Jove having sped flue straight to heaven. She hateth in hir hart   545
The guiltlesse fields and wood where Jove had playd that naughty part,
Alwaye she goes in such a griefe as that she had welnie
Forgot hir quiver with hir shaftes and bow that hanged by.
Dictynna, garded with hir traine and proude of killing Deere,
In raunging over Menalus, espying, cald hir neere.   550
The Damsell hearing Phebe call did run away amaine,
She feared lest in Phebes shape that Jove had come againe,
But when she saw the troope of Nymphes that garded hir about,
She thought there was no more deceyt, and came among the rout.
Oh Lord how hard a matter ist for guiltie hearts to shift   555
And kepe their countnance? from the ground hir eyes scarce durst she
lift.
She prankes not by hir mistresse side, she preases not to bee
The foremost of the companie, as when she erst was free.
She standeth muet: and by chaunging of hir colour ay
The treading of hir shooe awrie she plainely doth bewray,   560
Diana might have founde the fault but that she was a May.
A thousand tokens did appeare apparant to the eye,
By which the Nymphes themselves (they say) hir fault did well espie.
Nine times the Moone full to the worlde had shewde hir horned face
When fainting through hir brothers flames and hunting in the chace,   565
She found a coole and shadie lawnde through midst whereof she spide
A shallow brooke with trickling streame on gravell bottom glide.
And liking well the pleasant place, upon the upper brim
She dipt hir foote, and finding there the water coole and trim,
Away (she sayd) with standers by: and let us bath us here.   570
Then Parrhasis cast downe hir head with sad and bashfull chere.
The rest did strip them to their skinnes. She only sought delay,
Untill that would or would she not hir clothes were pluckt away.
Then with hir naked body straight hir crime was brought to light.
Which yll ashamde as with hir hands she would have hid from sight,   575
Fie beast (quoth Cynthia) get thee hence, thou shalt not here defile
This sacred Spring, and from hir traine she did hir quite exile.
    The Matrone of the thundring Jove had inckling of the fact,
    Delaying till convenient time the punishment to exact.

545 *sped:* succeeded   557 *prankes:* capers, displays herself
554 *rout:* crowd   561 *May:* maiden

There is no cause of further stay. To spight hir heart withall, 580
Hir husbands Leman bare a boy that Arcas men did call.
On whome she casting lowring looke with fell and cruell minde
Saide: Was there, arrant strumpet thou, none other shift to finde
But that thou needes must be with barne? that all the world must see
My husbandes open shame and thine in doing wrong to mee? 585
But neyther unto heaven nor hell this trespasse shalt thou beare.
I will bereve thee of thy shape through pride whereof thou were
So hardy to entyce my Feere. Immediatly with that
She raught hir by the foretop fast and fiercely threw hir flat
Against the grounde. The wretched wench hir armes up mekely cast, 590
Hir armes began with griesly haire to waxe all rugged fast.
Hir handes gan warpe and into pawes ylfavordly to grow,
And for to serve in stede of feete. The lippes that late ago
Did like the mightie Jove so well, with side and flaring flaps
Became a wide deformed mouth. And further lest perhaps 595
Hir prayers and hir humble wordes might cause hir to relent:
She did bereve hir of hir speach. In steade whereof there went
An yreful, horce, and dreadfull voyce out from a threatning throte:
But yet the selfesame minde that was before she turnde hir cote,
Was in hir still in shape of Beare. The griefe whereof she showes 600
By thrusting forth continuall sighes, and up she gastly throwes
Such kinde of handes as then remainde unto the starrie Skie.
And forbicause she could not speake she thought Jove inwardly
To be unthankfull. Oh how oft she daring not abide
Alone among the desert woods, full many a time and tide 605
Would stalke before hir house in grounds that were hir owne erewhile?
How oft oh did she in the hilles the barking houndes beguile
And in the lawndes where she hir selfe had chased erst hir game,
Now flie hirselfe to save hir life when hunters sought the same?
Full oft at sight of other beastes she hid hir head for feare, 610
Forgetting what she was hir selfe. For though she were a Beare,
Yet when she spied other Beares she quooke for verie paine:
And feared Wolves although hir Sire among them did remaine.
    Beholde Lycaons daughters sonne that Archas had to name
    About the age of fiftene yeares within the forrest came 615
Of Erymanth, not knowing ought of this his mothers case.
There after pitching of his toyles, as he the stagges did chase,

583 *shift:* trick, expedient
584 *barne:* bairn, child
588 *Feere:* mate
589 *raught:* reached, grasped
594 *like:* please
614 *to name:* as name

Upon his mother sodenly it was his chaunce to light,
Who for desire to see hir sonne did stay hirselfe from flight.
And wistly on him cast hir looke as one that did him know.   620
But he not knowing what she was began his heeles to show.
And when he saw hir still persist in staring on his face,
He was afrayde, and from hir sight withdrew himselfe apace,
But when he coulde not so be rid, he tooke an armed pike,
In full intent hir through the heart with deadly wound to strike.   625
But God almighty held his hand, and lifting both away
Did disapoint the wicked Act. For straight he did convay
Them through the Ayre with whirling windes to top of all the skie,
And there did make them neighbour starres about the Pole on hie.

    When Juno shining in the heaven hir husbands minion found,   630
    She swelde for spight: and downe she comes to watry Tethys round
And unto olde Oceanus, whome even the Gods aloft
Did reverence for their just deserts full many a time and oft,
To whome demaunding hir the cause: And aske ye (quoth she) why
That I which am the Queene of Goddes come hither from the sky?   635
Good cause there is I warrant you. Another holdes my roome.
For never trust me while I live, if when the night is coome,
And overcasteth all the world with shadie darknesse whole,
Ye see not in the heigth of heaven hard by the Northren Pole
Whereas the utmost circle runnes about the Axeltree   640
In shortest circuit, gloriously enstalled for to bee
In shape of starres the stinging woundes that make me yll apayde.
Now is there (trow ye) any cause why folke should be afrayde
To do to Juno what they list, or dread hir wrathfull mood,
Which only by my working harme doe turne my foes to good?   645
O what a mightie act is done? How passing is my powre!
I have bereft hir womans shape, and at this present howre
She is become a Goddesse. Loe this is the scourge so sowre
Wherewith I strike mine enimies. Loe here is all the spight
That I can doe: this is the ende of all my wondrous might,   650
No force. I would he should (for me) hir native shape restore,
And take away hir brutish shape, like as he hath before
Done by his other Paramour, that fine and proper piece
Of Argos whom he made a Cow, I meane Phononeus Niece.
Why makes he not a full devorce from me, and in my stead   655

---

620 *wistly:* intently, wistfully   642 *apayde:* satisfied, repaid
627 *disapoint:* thwart   644 *list:* like
630 *minion:* darling, mistress   651 *No force:* no matter

Straight take his Sweetheart to his wife, and coll hir in my bed?
He can not doe a better deede (I thinke) than for to take
Lycaon to his fatherinlaw. But if that you doe make
Accompt of me your foster childe, then graunt that for my sake,
The Oxen and the wicked Waine of starres in number seven,   660
For whoredome sake but late ago receyved into heaven,
May never dive within your waves. Ne let that strumpet vyle
By bathing of hir filthie limmes your waters pure defile.
    The Gods did graunt hir hir request: and straight to heaven she
               flue,
  In handsome Chariot through the Ayre, which painted peacocks
               drue   665
As well beset with blasing eyes late tane from Argus hed,
As thou thou prating Raven white by nature being bred,
Hadst on thy fethers justly late a coly colour spred.
For this same birde in auncient time had fethers faire and whight
As ever was the driven snow, or silver cleare and bright.   670
He might have well comparde himself in beautie with the Doves
That have no blemish, or the Swan that running water loves:
Or with the Geese that afterward should with their gagling out
Preserve the Romaine Capitoll beset with foes about.
His tongue was cause of all his harme, his tatling tongue did make   675
His colour which before was white, become so foule and blake.
Coronis of Larissa was the fairest maide of face,
In all the land of Thessalie. Shee stoode in Phebus grace
As long as that she kept hir chast, or at the least as long
As that she scaped unespide in doing Phebus wrong.   680
But at the last Apollos birde hir privie packing spide,
Whome no entreatance could persuade but that he swiftly hide
Him to his maister, to bewray the doings of his love.
Now as he flue, the pratling Crow hir wings apace did move:
And overtaking fell in talke and was inquisitive   685
For what intent and to what place he did so swiftly drive.
And when she heard the cause thereof, she said: Now trust me sure,
This message on the whiche thou goste no goodnesse will procure.
And therefore hearken what I say: disdaine thou not at all,
To take some warning by thy friende in things that may befall.   690
Consider what I erst have bene and what thou seest me now:

656 *coll*: hug
659 *Accompt*: account

680 *scaped*: escaped
681 *packing*: intrigue

And what hath bene the ground hereof. I boldly dare avow,
That thou shalt finde my faithfulnesse imputed for a crime.
For Pallas in a wicker chest had hid upon a time
A childe calde Ericthonius, whome never woman bare,   695
And tooke it unto Maidens three that Cecrops daughters were,
Not telling them what was within, but gave them charge to keepe
The Casket shut, and for no cause within the same to peepe.
I standing close among the leaves upon an Elme on hie,
Did marke their doings and their wordes, and there I did espie   700
How Pandrosos and Herse kept their promise faithfully.
Aglauros calles them Cowardes both, and makes no more adoe,
But takes the Casket in hir hand and doth the knots undooe.
And there they saw a childe whose partes beneath were like a snake.
Straight to the Goddesse of this deede a just report I make.   705
For which she gave me this reward that never might I more
Accompt hir for my Lady and my Mistresse as before.
And in my roume she put the fowle that flies not but by night,
A warning unto other birdes my lucke should be of right
To holde their tongues for being shent. But you will say perchaunce   710
I came unsentfor of my selfe, she did me not advaunce.
I dare well say though Pallas now my heavie Mistresse stand
Yet if perhaps ye should demaund the question at hir hand,
As sore displeased as she is, she would not this denie:
But that she chose me first hir selfe to beare hir companie.   715
For (well I know) my father was a Prince of noble fame,
Of Phocis King by long discent, Coronew was his name:
I was his darling and his joy, and many a welthie Piere
(I would not have you thinke disdaine) did seeke me for their Fere.
My forme and beautie did me hurt. For as I leysurely   720
Went jetting up and downe the shore upon the gravell drie,
As yet I customably doe, the God that rules the Seas
Espying me fell straight in love. And when he saw none ease
In sute, but losse of wordes and time, he offred violence,
And after me he runnes apace. I skudde as fast fro thence,   725
From sand to shore from shore to sand, still playing Foxe to hole,
Untill I was so tirde that he had almost got the gole.
Then cald I out on God and man. But (as it did appeare)
There was no man so neare at hand that could my crying heare.

692 *ground:* reason   722 *customably:* customarily
710 *shent:* reproached, punished   725 *skudde:* scudded, hurried, **went quickly**
721 *jetting:* strolling, parading

A Virgin Goddesse pitied me bicause I was a mayde: 730
And at the utter plunge and pinche did send me present ayde.
I cast mine armes to heaven, mine armes waxt light with fethers black,
I went about to cast in hast my garments from my back,
And all was fethers. In my skinne the rooted fethers stack.
I was about with violent hand to strike my naked breast,   735
But nether had I hand nor breast that naked more did reast.
I ran, but of my feete as erst remained not the print.
Me thought I glided on the ground. Anon with sodaine dint,
I rose and hovered in the Ayre. And from that instant time
Did wait on Pallas faithfully without offence or crime.   740
But what availes all this to me, and if that in my place
The wicked wretch Nyctyminee (who late for lacke of grace
Was turned to an odious birde) to honor called bee?
I pray thee didst thou never heare how false Nyctyminee
(A thing all over Lesbos knowne) defilde hir fathers couch?   745
The beast is now become a birde, whose lewdnesse doth so touch
And pricke hir guiltie conscience that she dares not come in sight,
Nor shewe hirselfe abrode a dayes, but fleeteth in the night
For shame lest folke should see hir fault: and every other birde
Doth in the Ayre and Ivie toddes with wondring at hir girde.   750
A mischiefe take thy tatling tongue, the Raven answerde tho.
Thy vaine forspeaking moves me not. And so he forth did go
And tels his Lorde Apollo how he saw Coronis lie
Wyth Isthyis, a Gentleman that dwelt in Thessalie.
    When Phebus heard his lovers fault, he fiersly gan to frowne,   755
    And cast his garlond from his head, and threw his violl downe.
His colour chaungde, his face lookt pale, and as the rage of yre
That boyled in his belking breast had set his heart on fyre,
He caught me up his wonted tooles, and bent his golden bow
And by and by with deadly stripe of unavoyded blow   760
Strake through the breast the which his owne had toucht so oft afore.
She wounded gave a piteous shrike, and (drawing from the sore
The deadly Dart the which the bloud pursuing after fast
Upon hir white and tender limmes a scarlet colour cast)
Saide: Phebus, well, thou might have wreakt this trespasse on my
                                                               head   765
And yet forborne me till the time I had bene brought abed.

731 *plunge:* crisis; *pinche:* exigency   758 *belking:* throbbing
738 *dint:* force   760 *stripe:* wound
750 *toddes:* clusters; *girde:* sneer, scoff   766 *forborne:* spared
752 *forspeaking:* forbidding

Now in one body by thy meanes a couple shall be dead.
Thus muche she saide: and with the bloud hir life did fade away.
The bodie being voyde of soule became as colde as clay.
Than all too late, alas too late gan Phebus to repent   770
That of his lover he had tane so cruell punishment.
He blames himselfe for giving eare so unadvisedly.
He blames himselfe in that he tooke it so outragiously.
He hates and bannes his faithfull birde bicause he did enforme
Him of his lovers naughtinesse that made him so to storme.   775
He hates his bow, he hates his shaft that rashly from it went:
And eke he hates his hasty hands by whom the bow was bent.
He takes hir up betweene his armes endevoring all too late
By plaister made of precious herbes to stay hir helplesse fate.
But when he saw there was no shift: but that she needes must burne,   780
And that the solemne sacred fire was prest to serve the turne,
Then from the bottome of his heart full sorie sighes he fet,
(For heavenly powres with watrie teares their cheekes may never wet)
In case as when a Cow beholdes the cruell butcher stand
With launching Axe embrewd with bloud and lifting up his hand   785
Aloft to snatch hir sucking Calfe that hangeth by the heeles
And of the Axe the deadly dint upon his forehead feeles.
Howbeit after sweete perfumes bestowde upon hir corse
And much embracing, having sore bewailde hir wrong divorse,
He followed to the place assignde hir bodie for to burne.   790
There coulde he not abide to see his seede to ashes turne.
But tooke the baby from hir wombe and from the firie flame,
And unto double Chyrons den conveyed straight the same.
The Raven hoping for his truth to be rewarded well,
He maketh blacke, forbidding him with whiter birdes to dwell.   795
     The Centaure Chyron in the while was glad of Phebus boy,
     And as the burthen brought some care the honor brought him joy.
Upon a time with golden lockes about hir shoulders spread,
A daughter of the Centaurs (whome a certaine Nymph had bred
About the brooke Caycus bankes) that hight Ocyroe   800
Came thither. This same fayre yong Nymph could not contented be
To learne the craft of Surgerie as perfect as hir Sire,
But that to learne the secret doomes of Fate she must aspire.
And therfore when the furious rage of frenzie had hir cought,
And that the spright of Prophecie enflamed had hir thought,   805

774 *bannes:* curses   782 *fet:* fetched
781 *prest:* ready   800 *hight:* was called

She lookt upon the childe and saide: Sweete babe the Gods thee make
A man. For all the world shall fare the better for thy sake.
All sores and sicknesse shalt thou cure: thy powre shall eke be syche,
To make the dead alive again. For doing of the whiche
Against the pleasure of the Gods, thy Graundsire shall thee strike   810
So with his fire, that never more thou shalt performe the like.
And of a God a bludlesse corse, and of a corse (full straunge)
Thou shalt become a God againe, and twice thy nature chaunge.
And thou my father liefe and deare, who now by destinie,
Art borne to live for evermore and never for to die,   815
Shalt suffer such outragious paine throughout thy members all,
By wounding of a venimde dart that on thy foote shall fall,
That oft thou shalt desire to die, and in the latter end
The fatall'dames shall breake thy threede and thy desire thee send.
There was yet more behinde to tell, when sodenly she fet   820
A sore deepe sigh, and downe hir cheekes the teares did trickle wet.
Mine owne misfortune (quoth she) now hath overtake me sure.
I cannot utter any more, for words waxe out of ure.
My cunning was not worth so much as that it should procure
The wrath of God. I feele by proufe far better had it bene: 825
If that the chaunce of things to come I never had foreseene.
For now my native shape withdrawes. Me thinkes I have delight
To feede on grasse and fling in fieldes: I feele my selfe so light.
I am transformed to a Mare like other of my kinne.
But wherfore should this brutish shape all over wholy winne?   830
Considering that although both horse and man my father bee:
Yet is his better part a man as plainly is to see.
The latter ende of this complaint was fumbled in such wise,
As what she meant the standers by could scarcely well devise.
Anon she neyther semde to speake nor fully for to ney,   835
But like to one that counterfeites in sport the Mare to play.
Within a while she neyed plaine, and downe hir armes were pight
Upon the ground all clad with haire, and bare hir bodie right.
Hir fingers joyned all in one, at ende wherof did grow
In stede of nayles a round tough hoofe of welked horne bylow.   840
Hir head and necke shot forth in length, hir kirtle trayne became
A faire long taile. Hir flaring haire was made a hanging Mane.
And as hir native shape and voyce most monstrously did passe,

808 *syche:* such   840 *welked:* ridged, rough
814 *liefe:* beloved   842 *flaring:* spreading, waving
823 *ure:* use

So by the uncoth name of Mare she after termed was.
    The Centaure Chyron wept hereat: and piteously dismaide   845
    Did call on thee (although in vaine) thou Deipnian God for ayde.
For neyther lay it in thy hande to breake Joves mighty hest,
And though it had, yet in thy state as then thou did not rest.
In Elis did thou then abide and in Messene lande.
It was the time when under shape of shepehierde with a wande   850
Of Olyve and a pipe of reedes thou kept Admetus sheepe.
Now in this time that (save of Love) thou tooke none other keepe,
And madste thee merrie with thy pipe, the glistring Maias sonne
By chaunce abrode the fields of Pyle spide certaine cattle runne
Without a hierde, the which he stole and closely did them hide   855
Among the woods. This pretie slight no earthly creature spide,
Save one old churle that Battus hight. This Battus had the charge
Of welthie Neleus feeding groundes, and all his pastures large,
And kept a race of goodly Mares. Of him he was afraide.
And lest by him his privie theft should chaunce to be bewraide,   860
He tooke a bribe to stop his mouth, and thus unto him saide:
My friend I pray thee if perchaunce that any man enquire
This cattell say thou saw them not. And take thou for thy hire
This faire yong Bullocke. Tother tooke the Bullocke at his hand,
And shewing him a certaine stone that lay upon the lande,   865
Sayd, go thy way: Assoone this stone thy doings shall bewray,
As I shall doe. So Mercurie did seeme to go his way.
Annon he commes me backe againe, and altred both in speche
And outward shape, saide: Countrieman Ich heartely bezeche,
And if thou zawest any kie come royling through this grounde,   870
Or driven away, tell what he was and where they may be vownde.
And I chill gethee vor thy paine an Hecfar and hir match.
The Carle perceyving double gaine, and greedy for to catch,
Sayde: Under yon same hill they were, and under yon same hill
Cham zure they are, and with his hand he poynted thereuntill.   875
At that Mercurius laughing saide: False knave: and doste bewray
Me to my selfe? doste thou bewray me to my selfe I say?
And with that word strayt to a stone he turnde his double heart,
In which the slaunder yet remaines without the stones desart.

847 *hest:* command
852 *keepe:* heed, notice
855 *hierde:* herdsman
869 *Ich:* I. In the rustic dialect of the lines
that follow, *s*'s change to *z*'s, *f*'s to *v*'s.
Cf. XI, 409 ff.

870 *kie:* cow; *royling:* roving
872 *chill gethee:* I'll give thee
875 *Cham zure:* I'm sure

The Bearer of the charmed Rod, the suttle Mercurie,   880
This done, arose with waving wings and from that place did flie.
And as he hovered in the Ayre he viewde the fieldes bylow
Of Atticke and the towne it selfe with all the trees that grow
In Lycey where the learned Clarkes did wholsome preceptes show.
By chaunce the verie selfesame day the virgins of the towne   885
Of olde and auncient custome bare in baskets on their crowne
Beset with garlands fresh and gay and strowde with flowres sweete
To Pallas towre such sacrifice as was of custome meete.
The winged God beholding them returning in a troupe
Continued not directly forth, but gan me downe to stoupe,   890
And fetch a wyndlasse round about. And as the hungry kite
Beholding unto sacrifice a Bullocke redie dight,
Doth sore about his wished pray desirous for to snatche
But that he dareth not for such as stand about and watch:
So Mercurie with nimble wings doth keepe a lower gate   895
About Minervas loftie towres in round and wheeling rate.
   As far as doth the Morning starre in cleare and streaming light
   Excell all other starres in heaven: as far also as bright
Dame Phebe dimmes the Morning starre, so far did Herses face
Staine all the Ladies of hir troupe: she was the verie grace   900
And beautie of that solemne pompe, and all that traine so fayre.
Joves sonne was ravisht with the sight, and hanging in the ayre
Began to swelt within himselfe, in case as when the poulder
Hath driven the Pellet from the Gunne, the Pellet ginnes to smoulder:
And in his flying waxe more hote. In smoking brest he shrowdes   905
His flames not brought from heaven above but caught beneath the
                            clouds.
He leaves his jorney toward heaven and takes another race
Not minding any lenger time to hide his present case.
So great a trust and confidence his beautie to him gave
Which though it seemed of it selfe sufficient force to have,   910
Yet was he curious for to make himselfe more fine and brave.
He kembd his head and strokt his beard, and pried on every side
To see that in his furniture no wrinkle might be spide.
And forbicause his Cloke was fringde and garded brode with golde,
He cast it on his shoulder up most seemely to beholde.   915
He takes in hand his charmed rod that bringeth things asleepe

891 *fetch a wyndlasse:* make a circuit   911 *curious:* careful
896 *rate:* manner   912 *pried:* peered
903 *poulder:* powder   913 *furniture:* apparel

And wakes them when he list againe. And lastly taketh keepe
That on his faire welformed feete his golden shooes sit cleene,
And that all other things therto well correspondent beene.
  In Cecrops Court were Chambers three set far from all resort 920
  With yvorie beddes all furnished in far most royall sort.
Of which Aglauros had the left and Pandrose had the right,
And Herse had the middlemost. She that Aglauros hight
First markt the comming of the God, and asking him his name
Demaunded him for what entent and cause he thither came. 925
Pleiones Nephew, Maias sonne, did make hir aunswere thus:
I am my fathers messenger, his pleasure to discusse
To mortall folke and hellish fiendes as list him to commaund.
My father is the mightie Jove. To that thou doste demaund
I will not feyne a false excuse. I aske no more but graunt 930
To keepe thy sisters counsell close, and for to be the Aunt
Of such the issue as on hir my chaunce shalbe to get.
Thy sister Herse is the cause that hath me hither fet.
I pray thee beare thou with my love that is so firmely set.
Aglauros cast on Mercurie hir scornfull eyes aside, 935
With which against Minervas will hir secretes late she spide,
Demaunding him in recompence a mighty masse of Golde:
And would not let him enter in until the same were tolde.
The warlike Goddesse cast on hir a sterne and cruell looke,
And fetched such a cutting sigh that forcibly it shooke 940
Both brest and brestplate, wherewithall it came unto hir thought
How that Aglauros late ago against hir will had wrought
In looking on the Lemman childe contrarie to hir othe,
The whiche she tooke hir in the chest, for which she waxed wrothe.
Againe she saw hir cancred heart maliciously repine 945
Against hir sister and the God. And furthermore in fine
How that the golde which Mercurie had given hir for hir meede,
Would make hir both in welth and pride all others to exceede.
  She goes me straight to Envies house, a foule and irksome cave,
  Replete with blacke and lothly filth and stinking like a grave. 950
It standeth in a hollow dale where neyther light of Sunne
Nor blast of any winde or Ayre may for the deepenesse come.
A dreyrie sad and dolefull den ay full of slouthfull colde
As which ay dimd with smoldring smoke doth never fire beholde,
When Pallas, that same manly Maide, approched nere this plot, 955

---

938 *tolde:* counted
943 *Lemman childe:* sweetheart's child
945 *cancred:* corrupt, spiteful
947 *meede:* reward, payment

She staide without, for to the house in enter might she not,
And with hir Javelin point did give a push against the doore.
The doore flue open by and by and fell me in the floore.
There saw she Envie sit within fast gnawing on the flesh
Of Snakes and Todes, the filthie foode that keepes hir vices fresh.   960
It lothde hir to beholde the sight. Anon the Elfe arose
And left the gnawed Adders flesh, and slouthfully she goes
With lumpish laysure like a Snayle, and when she saw the face
Of Pallas and hir faire attire adournde with heavenly grace,
She gave a sigh, a sorie sigh, from bottome of hir heart.   965
Hir lippes were pale, hir cheekes were wan, and all hir face was swart:
Hir bodie leane as any Rake. She looked eke askew.
Hir teeth were furde with filth and drosse, hir gums were waryish blew.
The working of hir festered gall had made hir stomacke greene.
And all bevenimde was hir tongue. No sleepe hir eyes had seene.   970
Continuall Carke and cankred care did keepe hir waking still:
Of laughter (save at others harmes) the Helhound can no skill.
It is against hir will that men have any good successe,
And if they have, she frettes and fumes within hir minde no lesse
Than if hir selfe had taken harme. In seeking to annoy   975
And worke distresse to other folke, hir selfe she doth destroy.
Thus is she torment to hir selfe. Though Pallas did hir hate,
Yet spake she briefly these few wordes to hir without hir gate:
Infect thou with thy venim one of Cecrops daughters three,
It is Aglauros whome I meane, for so it needes must bee.   980
This said, she pight hir speare in ground, and tooke hir rise thereon.
And winding from that wicked wight did take hir flight anon.
  The Caitife cast hir eye aside, and seeing Pallas gon,
  Began to mumble with hir selfe the Divels Paternoster,
  And fretting at hir good successe, began to blow and bluster.   985
She takes a crooked staffe in hand bewreathde with knubbed prickes,
And covered with a coly cloude, where ever that she stickes
Hir filthie feete, she tramples downe and seares both grasse and corne:
That all the fresh and fragrant fieldes seeme utterly forlorne.
And with hir staffe she tippeth off the highest poppie heades.   990
Such poyson also every where ungraciously she sheades,
That every Cottage where she comes and every Towne and Citie
Doe take infection at hir breath. At length (the more is pitie)

958 *in:* on
963 *lumpish:* dull, clumsy
968 *waryish:* unwholesome looking

971 *Carke:* anxiety, worry
972 *can:* knows
984 *Divels Paternoster:* a muttered curse

She found the faire Athenian towne that flowed freshly then
In feastfull peace and joyfull welth and learned witts of men. 995
And forbicause she nothing saw that might provoke to weepe,
It was a corsie to hir heart hir hatefull teares to keepe.
Now when she came within the Court, she went without delay
Directly to the lodgings where King Cecrops daughters lay,
There did she as Minerva bad. She laide hir scurvie fist 1000
Besmerde with venim and with filth upon Aglauros brist,
The whiche she filde with hooked thornes: and breathing on hir face
Did shead the poyson in hir bones: which spred it selfe apace,
As blacke as ever virgin pitch through Lungs and Lights and all.
And to th'intent that cause of griefe abundantly should fall, 1005
She placed ay before hir eyes hir sisters happie chaunce
In being wedded to the God, and made the God to glaunce
Continually in heavenly shape before hir wounded thought.
And all these things she painted out, which in conclusion wrought
Such corsies in Aglauros brest that sighing day and night 1010
She gnawde and fretted in hir selfe for very cancred spight.
And like a wretche she wastes hir selfe with restlesse care and pine
Like as the yse whereon the Sunne with glimering light doth shine.
Hir sister Herses good successe doth make hir heart to yerne,
In case as when that fire is put to greenefeld wood or fearne 1015
Whych giveth neyther light nor heate, but smulders quite away:
Sometime she minded to hir Sire hir sister to bewray,
Who (well she knew) would yll abide so lewde a part to play.
And oft she thought with wilfull hande to brust hir fatall threede,
Bicause she woulde not see the thing that made hir heart to bleede. 1020
At last she sate hir in the doore and leaned to a post
To let the God from entring in. To whome now having lost
Much talke and gentle wordes in vayne, she said: Sir, leave I pray
For hence I will not (be you sure) onlesse you go away.
I take thee at thy word (quoth he) and therewithall he pusht 1025
His rod against the barred doore, and wide it open rusht.
She making proffer for to rise, did feele so great a waight
Through all hir limmes, that for hir life she could not stretch hir straight.
She strove to set hirself upright: but striving booted not.
Hir hamstrings and hir knees were stiffe, a chilling colde had got 1030
In at hir nayles, through all hir limmes. And eke hir veynes began

997 *corsie:* grievance
1004 *Lights:* lungs
1022 *let:* keep
1029 *booted not:* did no good

For want of bloud and lively heate, to waxe both pale and wan.
And as the freting Fistula forgrowne and past all cure
Runnes in the flesh from place to place, and makes the sound and pure
As bad or worser than the rest, even so the cold of death 1035
Strake to hir heart, and closde hir veines, and lastly stopt hir breath:
She made no profer for to speake, and though she had done so
It had bene vaine. For way was none for language forth to go.
Hir throte congealed into stone: hir mouth became hard stone,
And like an image sate she still, hir bloud was clearely gone, 1040
The which the venim of hir heart so fowly did infect,
That ever after all the stone with freckled spots was spect.
    When Mercurie had punisht thus Aglauros spightfull tung
    And cancred heart, immediatly from Pallas towne he flung.
And flying up with flittering wings did pierce to heaven above. 1045
His father calde him straight aside (but shewing not his love)
Said: Sonne, my trustie messenger and worker of my will,
Make no delay but out of hand flie downe in hast untill
The land that on the left side lookes upon thy mothers light,
Yon same where standeth on the coast the towne that Sidon hight. 1050
The King hath there a heirde of Neate that on the Mountaines feede,
Go take and drive them to the sea with all convenient speede.
He had no sooner said the word but that the heirde begun
Driven from the mountaine to the shore appointed for to run,
Whereas the daughter of the King was wonted to resort 1055
With other Ladies of the Court there for to play and sport.
Betweene the state of Majestie and love is set such oddes,
As that they can not dwell in one. The Sire and King of Goddes
Whose hand is armd with triplefire, who only with his frowne
Makes Sea and Land and Heaven to quake, doth lay his scepter
                                     downe 1060

With all the grave and stately port belonging thereunto:
And putting on the shape of Bull (as other cattell doe)
Goes lowing gently up and downe among them in the field
The fairest beast to looke upon that ever man beheld.
For why? his colour was as white as any winters snow 1065
Before that eyther trampling feete or Southerne winde it thow.
His necke was brawnd with rolles of flesh, and from his chest before
A dangling dewlap hung me downe good halfe a foote and more.
His hornes were small, but yet so fine as that ye would have thought

1048 _untill:_ to   1066 _thow:_ thaw
1051 _heirde of Neate:_ herd of cattle

They had bene made by cunning hand or out of waxe bene wrought. ¹⁰⁷⁰
More cleare they were a hundreth fold than is the Christall stone,
In all his forehead fearfull frowne or wrinkle there was none.
No fierce, no grim, nor griesly looke as other cattle have,
But altogether so demure as friendship seemde to crave.
Agenors daughter marveld much so tame a beast to see,   1075
But yet to touche him at the first too bolde she durst not bee.
Annon she reaches to his mouth hir hand with herbes and flowres.
The loving beast was glad thereof and neither frownes nor lowres.
But till the hoped joy might come with glad and fauning cheare
He lickes hir hands and scarce ah scarce the resdue he forbeare.   1080
Sometime he friskes and skippes about and showes hir sport at hand
Annon he layes his snowie side against the golden sand.
So feare by little driven away, he offred eft his brest
To stroke and coy, and eft his hornes with flowers to be drest.
At last Europa knowing not (for so the Maide was calde)   1085
On whome she venturde for to ride, was nerawhit appalde
To set hir selfe upon his backe. Then by and by the God
From maine drie land to maine moyst Sea gan leysurly to plod.
At first he did but dip his feete within the outmost wave,
And backe againe, then further in another plunge he gave.   1090
And so still further till at the last he had his wished pray
Amid the deepe where was no meanes to scape with life away.
The Ladie quaking all for feare with rufull countnance cast
Ay toward shore from whence she came, held with hir righthand fast
One of his hornes: and with the left did stay upon his backe.   1095
The weather flaskt and whisked up hir garments being slacke.

FINIS SECUNDI LIBRI.

¹⁰⁸⁴ *coy:* caress   ¹⁰⁹⁶ *flaskt:* flapped, fluttered

꧁꧁꧁

THE THIRD BOOKE

OF OVIDS METAMORPHOSIS.

[*Cadmus. Actaeon. Jove and Semele. Echo and Narcissus. Pentheus and Bacchus.*]

The God now having laide aside his borrowed shape of Bull
    Had in his likenesse shewde himself: and with his pretie trull
Tane landing in the Ile of Crete. When in that while hir Sire
Not knowing where she was become, sent after to enquire
Hir brother Cadmus, charging him his sister home to bring,   5
Or never for to come againe: wherein he did a thing,
For which he might both justly kinde and cruell called bee.
When Cadmus over all the world had sought, (for who is hee
That can detect the thefts of Jove?) and no where could hir see,
Then as an outlaw (to avoyde his fathers wrongfull yre)   10
He went to Phebus Oracle most humbly to desire
His heavenly counsell, where he would assigne him place to dwell.
An Heifer all alone in field (quoth Phebus) marke hir well,
Which never bare the pinching yoke, nor drew the plough as yit,
Shall meete thee. Follow after hir, and where thou seest hir sit, 15
There builde a towne, and let thereof Beotia be the name.
Downe from Parnasus stately top scarce fully Cadmus came,
When royling softly in the vale before the herde alone
He saw an Heifer on whose necke of servage print was none.
He followde after leysurly as hir that was his guide,   20
And thanked Phebus in his heart that did so well provide.
Now had he past Cephisus forde, and eke the pleasant groundes
About the Citie Panope conteinde within those boundes.

2 *trull:* wench   19 *servage:* servitude
18 *royling:* roving   22 *eke:* also

61

The Heifer staide, and lifting up hir forehead to the skie
Full seemely for to looke upon with hornes like braunches hie   25
Did with hir lowing fill the Ayre: and casting backe hir eie
Upon the rest that came aloofe, as softly as she could
Kneelde downe and laide hir hairie side against the grassie mould.
Then Cadmus gave Apollo thankes, and falling flat bylow
Did kisse the ground and haile the fields which yet he did not know.   30
He was about to sacrifice to Jove the Heavenly King,
And bad his servants goe and fetch him water of the spring.
     An olde forgrowne unfelled wood stoode neare at hand thereby,
     And in the middes a queachie plot with Sedge and Osiers hie,
Where courbde about with peble stone in likenesse of a bow   35
There was a spring with silver streames that forth thereof did flow.
Here lurked in his lowring den God Mars his griesly Snake
With golden scales and firie eyes beswolne with poyson blake.
Three spirting tongues, three rowes of teeth within his head did sticke.
No sooner had the Tirian folke set foote within this thicke   40
And queachie plot, and deped downe their bucket in the well,
But that to buscle in his den began this Serpent fell,
And peering with a marble head right horribly to hisse.
The Tirians let their pitchers slip for sodaine feare of this,
And waxing pale as any clay, like folke amazde and flaight,   45
Stoode trembling like an Aspen leafe. The specled serpent straight
Commes trailing out in waving linkes, and knottie rolles of scales,
And bending into bunchie boughts his bodie forth he hales.
/And lifting up above the wast himselfe unto the Skie,
He overlooketh all the wood, as huge and big welnie   50
As is the Snake that in the Heaven about the Nordren Pole
Devides the Beares. He makes no stay but deales his dreadfull dole
Among the Tirians. Whether they did take them to their tooles,
Or to their heeles, or that their feare did make them stand like fooles,
And helpe themselves by none of both, he snapt up some alive,   55
And swept in others with his taile, and some he did deprive
Of life with rankenesse of his breath, and other some againe
He stings and poysons unto death till all at last were slaine.
     Now when the Sunne was at his heigth and shadowes waxed short,
     And Cadmus saw his companie make tarience in that sort,   60

33 *forgrowne:* overgrown, grown wild
34 *queachie:* swampy
35 *courbde:* curved
42 *fell:* fierce, cruel

45 *flaight:* frightened
48 *boughts:* loops
52 *dole:* grief, cause of grief
53 *tooles:* weapons

He marveld what should be their let, and went to seeke them out.
His harnesse was a Lions skin that wrapped him about.
His weapons were a long strong speare with head of yron tride,
And eke a light and piercing Dart. And thereunto beside
Worth all the weapons in the world a stout and valiant hart.   65
When Cadmus came within the wood and saw about that part
His men lie slaine upon the ground, and eke their cruell fo
Of bodie huge stand over them, and licking with his blo
And blasting tongue their sorie woundes: Well trustie friendes
                                                    (quoth he)
I eyther of your piteous deathes will streight revenger be,   70
Or else will die my selfe therefore. With that he raughting fast
A mightie Milstone, at the Snake with all his might it cast.
The stone with such exceding force and violence forth was driven,
As of a fort the bulwarkes strong and walles it would have riven.
And yet it did the Snake no harme: his scales as hard and tough   75
As if they had bene plates of mayle did fence him well inough,
So that the stone rebounded backe against his freckled slough.
But yet his hardnesse savde him not against the piercing dart.
For hitting right betweene the scales that yeelded in that part
Whereas the joynts doe knit the backe, it thirled through the skin,   80
And pierced to his filthy mawe and greedy guts within.
He fierce with wrath wrings backe his head, and looking on the stripe,
The Javeling steale that sticked out, betwene his teeth doth gripe.
The which with wresting to and fro at length he forth did winde,
Save that he left the head therof among his bones behinde.   85
When of his courage through the wound more kindled was the ire,
His throteboll swelde with puffed veines, his eyes gan sparkle fire.
There stoode about his smeared chaps a lothly foming froth.
His skaled brest ploughes up the ground, the stinking breath that goth
Out from his blacke and hellish mouth infectes the herbes full fowle.   90
Sometime he windes himselfe in knots as round as any Bowle.
Sometime he stretcheth out in length as straight as any beame.
Anon againe with violent brunt he rusheth like a streame
Encreast by rage of latefalne raine, and with his mightie sway
Beares downe the wood before his breast that standeth in his way.   95
Agenors sonne retiring backe doth with his Lions spoyle

61 *let:* hindrance
62 *harnesse:* protection
68 *blo:* blue
71 *raughting:* reaching, seizing
77 *slough:* skin

80 *thirled:* pierced
82 *stripe:* wound
87 *throteboll:* Adam's-apple
91 *Bowle:* ball

Defend him from his fierce assaults, and makes him to recoyle
Aye holding at the weapons point. The Serpent waxing wood
Doth crashe the steele betwene his teeth, and bites it till the blood,
Dropt mixt with poyson from his mouth, did die the greene grasse
                                                    blacke,   100
But yet the wound was verie light bicause he writhed backe
And puld his head still from the stroke: and made the stripe to die
By giving way, untill that Cadmus following irefully
The stroke, with all his powre and might did through the throte him
                                                    rive,
And naylde him to an Oke behind the which he eke did clive.   105
The Serpents waight did make the tree to bend. It grievde the tree
His bodie of the Serpents taile thus scourged for to bee.
        While Cadmus wondred at the hugenesse of the vanquisht foe
        Upon the sodaine came a voyce: from whence he could not know,
But sure he was he heard the voyce. Which said: Agenors sonne,   110
What gazest thus upon this Snake? the time will one day come
That thou thy selfe shalt be a Snake. He pale and wan for feare,
Had lost his speach: and ruffled up stiffe staring stood his heare.
Behold (mans helper at his neede) Dame Pallas gliding through
The vacant Ayre was straight at hand, and bade him take a plough   115
And cast the Serpents teeth in ground, as of the which should spring
Another people out of hand. He did in every thing
As Pallas bade, he tooke a plough, and earde a furrow low
And sowde the Serpents teeth whereof the foresaid folke should grow.
Anon (a wondrous thing to tell) the clods began to move,   120
And from the furrow first of all the pikes appearde above,
Next rose up helmes with fethered crests, and then the Poldrens bright,
Successively the Curets whole, and all the armor right.
Thus grew up men like corne in field in rankes of battle ray
With shields and weapons in their hands to feight the field that day. 125
Even so when stages are attirde against some solemne game,
With clothes of Arras gorgeously, in drawing up the same
The faces of the ymages doe first of all them showe,
And then by peecemeale all the rest in order seemes to grow,
Untill at last they stand out full upon their feete bylow.   130
        Afrighted at this new found foes gan Cadmus for to take
        Him to his weapons by and by resistance for to make.

---

98 *Aye:* always; *wood:* enraged   118 *earde:* plowed
111 *What:* why   122 *Poldrens:* shoulder-plates
113 *staring:* standing on end   123 *Curets:* cuirasses
117 *out of hand:* immediately   132 *by and by:* immediately

Stay, stay thy selfe (cride one of them that late before were bred
Out of the ground) and meddle not with civill warres. This sed,
One of the brothers of that brood with launcing sworde he slue. 135
Another sent a dart at him, the which him overthrue.
The third did straight as much for him and made him yeelde the breath,
(The which he had receyvde but now) by stroke of forced death.
Likewise outraged all the rest untill that one by one
By mutuall stroke of civill warre dispatched everychone, 140
This broode of brothers all behewen and weltred in their blood,
Lay sprawling on their mothers womb, the ground where erst they
stood,
Save only five that did remaine. Of whom Echion led
By Pallas counsell, threw away the helmet from his head,
And with his brothers gan to treat attonement for to make. 145
The which at length (by Pallas helpe) so good successe did take,
That faithfull friendship was confirmd and hand in hand was plight.
These afterward did well assist the noble Tyrian knight,
In building of the famous towne that Phebus had behight.
     Now Thebes stoode in good estate, now Cadmus might thou say 150
     That when thy father banisht thee it was a luckie day.
To joyne aliance both with Mars and Venus was thy chaunce,
Whose daughter thou hadst tane to wife, who did thee much advaunce,
Not only through hir high renowne, but through a noble race
Of sonnes and daughters that she bare: whose children in like case 155
It was thy fortune for to see all men and women growne.
But ay the ende of every thing must marked be and knowne.
For none the name of blessednesse deserveth for to have
Onlesse the tenor of his life last blessed to his grave.
Among so many prosprous happes that flowde with good successe, 160
Thine eldest Nephew was a cause of care and sore distresse.
Whose head was armde with palmed hornes, whose own hounds in the
wood
Did pull their master to the ground and fill them with his bloud.
But if you sift the matter well, ye shall not finde desart
But cruell fortune to have bene the cause of this his smart. 165
For who could doe with oversight? Great slaughter had bene made
Of sundrie sortes of savage beastes one morning: and the shade

139 *outraged:* raged
140 *everychone:* everyone
145 *attonement:* reconciliation
149 *behight:* promised

160 *happes:* happenings
162 *palmed:* flattened
164 *desart:* deserving

Of things was waxed verie short. It was the time of day
That mid betweene the East and West the Sunne doth seeme to stay.
When as the Thebane stripling thus bespake his companie,   170
Still raunging in the waylesse woods some further game to spie:
Our weapons and our toyles are moist and staind with bloud of Deere:
This day hath done inough as by our quarrie may appeare.
As soone as with hir scarlet wheeles next morning bringeth light,
We will about our worke againe. But now Hiperion bright   175
Is in the middes of Heaven, and seares the fieldes with firie rayes.
Take up your toyles, and cease your worke, and let us go our wayes.
They did even so, and ceast their worke. There was a valley thicke
With Pinaple and Cipresse trees that armed be with pricke.
Gargaphie hight this shadie plot, it was a sacred place   180
To chast Diana and the Nymphes that wayted on hir grace.
Within the furthest end thereof there was a pleasant Bowre
So vaulted with the leavie trees the Sunne had there no powre:
Not made by hand nor mans devise: and yet no man alive,
A trimmer piece of worke than that could for his life contrive.   185
With flint and Pommy was it wallde by nature halfe about,
And on the right side of the same full freshly flowed out
A lively spring with Christall streame: whereof the upper brim
Was greene with grasse and matted herbes that smelled verie trim.
When Phebe felt hir selfe waxe faint, of following of hir game,   190
It was hir custome for to come and bath hir in the same.
That day she, having timely left hir hunting in the chace,
Was entred with hir troupe of Nymphes within this pleasant place.
She tooke hir quiver and hir bow the which she had unbent,
And eke hir Javelin to a Nymph that served that intent.   195
Another Nymph to take hir clothes among hir traine she chose,
Two losde hir buskins from hir legges and pulled off hir hose.
The Thebane Ladie Crocale more cunning than the rest
Did trusse hir tresses handsomly which hung behind undrest.
And yet hir owne hung waving still. Then Niphe nete and cleene   200
With Hiale glistring like the grass in beautie fresh and sheene,
And Rhanis clearer of hir skin than are the rainie drops,
And little bibling Phyale, and Pseke that pretie Mops
Powrde water into vessels large to washe their Ladie with.
Now while she keepes this wont, behold, by wandring in the frith   205

186 *Pommy:* pumice   203 *bibling:* drinking; *Mops:* moppet
197 *buskins:* boots   205 *wont:* custom; *frith:* wood
201 *sheene:* bright

He wist not whither (having staid his pastime till the morrow)
Comes Cadmus Nephew to this thicke: and entring in with sorrow
(Such was his cursed cruell fate) saw Phebe where she washt.
The Damsels at the sight of man quite out of countnance dasht,
(Bicause they everichone were bare and naked to the quicke)   210
Did beate their handes against their breasts, and cast out such a shricke,
That all the wood did ring thereof: and clinging to their dame
Did all they could to hide both hir and eke themselves fro shame.
But Phebe was of personage so comly and so tall,
That by the middle of hir necke she overpeerd them all.   215
Such colour as appeares in Heaven by Phebus broken rayes
Directly shining on the Cloudes, or such as is always
The colour of the Morning Cloudes before the Sunne doth show,
Such sanguine colour in the face of Phoebe gan to glowe
There standing naked in his sight. Who though she had hir gard   220
Of Nymphes about hir: yet she turnde hir bodie from him ward.
And casting back an angrie looke, like as she would have sent
An arrow at him had she had hir bow there readie bent,
So raught she water in hir hande and for to wreake the spight
Besprinckled all the heade and face of this unluckie knight,   225.
And thus forespake the heavie lot that should upon him light:
Now make thy vaunt among thy Mates, thou sawste Diana bare.
Tell if thou can: I give thee leave: tell hardily: doe not spare.
This done she makes no further threates, but by and by doth spread
A payre of lively olde Harts hornes upon his sprinckled head.   230
She sharpes his eares, she makes his necke both slender, long and lanke.
She turnes his fingers into feete, his armes to spindle shanke.
She wrappes him in a hairie hyde beset with speckled spottes,
And planteth in him fearefulnesse. And so away he trottes,
Full greatly wondring to him selfe what made him in that cace   235
To be so wight and swift of foote. But when he saw his face
And horned temples in the brooke, he would have cryde Alas,
But as for then no kinde of speach out of his lippes could passe.
He sighde and brayde: for that was then the speach that did remaine,
And downe the eyes that were not his, his bitter teares did raine.   240
No part remayned (save his minde) of that he earst had beene.
What should he doe? turne home againe to Cadmus and the Queene?
Or hyde himselfe among the Woods? Of this he was afrayd,

---

206 *wist:* knew
207 *thicke:* thicket
221 *from him ward:* away from him

224 *wreake the spight:* revenge the injury
236 *wight:* swift

And of the tother ill ashamde. While doubting thus he stayd.
   His houndes espyde him where he was, and Blackfoote first of
                                                                    all 245
   And Stalker speciall good of scent began aloud to call.
This latter was a hounde of Crete, the other was of Spart.
Then all the kenell fell in round, and everie for his part,
Dyd follow freshly in the chase more swifter than the winde,
Spy, Eateal, Scalecliffe, three good houndes comne all of Arcas
                                                                    kinde, 250
Strong Bilbucke, currish Savage, Spring, and Hunter fresh of smell,
And Lightfoote who to lead a chase did beare away the bell,
Fierce Woodman hurte not long ago in hunting of a Bore,
And Shepeheird woont to follow sheepe and neate to fielde afore.
And Laund, a fell and eger bitch that had a Wolfe to Syre: 255
Another brach callde Greedigut with two hir Puppies by her.
And Ladon gant as any Greewnd, a hownd in Sycion bred,
Blab, Fleetewood, Patch whose flecked skin with sundrie spots was
                                                                    spred:
Wight, Bowman, Royster, Beautie faire and white as winters snow,
And Tawnie full of duskie haires that over all did grow,   260
With lustie Ruffler passing all the resdue there in strength,
And Tempest best of footemanshipe in holding out at length.
And Cole and Swift, and little Woolfe, as wight as any other,
Accompanide with a Ciprian hound that was his native brother,
And Snatch amid whose forehead stoode a starre as white as snowe, 265
The resdue being all as blacke and slicke as any Crowe.
And shaggie Rugge with other twaine that had a Syre of Crete,
And Dam of Sparta: T'one of them callde Jollyboy, a great
And large flewd hound: the tother Chorle who ever gnoorring went,
And Kingwood with a shyrle loude mouth the which he freely spent, 270
With divers mo whose names to tell it were but losse of tyme.
This fellowes over hill and dale in hope of pray doe clyme.
Through thicke and thin and craggie cliffes where was no way to go,
He flyes through groundes where oftentymes he chased had ere tho.
Even from his owne folke is he faine (alas) to flee away.   275
He strayned oftentymes to speake, and was about to say:
I am Acteon: know your Lorde and Mayster, sirs, I pray.

---

250 *Arcas:* Arcadian
252 *beare away the bell:* take the prize
254 *neate:* cattle
256 *brach:* hound, hound-bitch
257 *Greewnd:* greyhound

269 *gnoorring:* snarling
270 *shyrle:* shrill
274 *tho:* then
275 *faine:* disposed, obliged, glad

But use of wordes and speach did want to utter forth his minde.
Their crie did ring through all the Wood redoubled with the winde,
First Slo did pinch him by the haunch, and next came Kildeere in,   280
And Hylbred fastned on his shoulder, bote him through the skinne.
These cam forth later than the rest, but coasting thwart a hill,
They did gainecope him as he came, and helde their Master still
Untill that all the rest came in, and fastned on him too.
No part of him was free from wound. He could none other do   285
But sigh, and in the shape of Hart with voyce as Hartes are woont,
(For voyce of man was none now left to helpe him at the brunt)
By braying shew his secret grief among the Mountaynes hie,
And kneeling sadly on his knees with dreerie teares in eye,
As one by humbling of himselfe that mercy seemde to crave,   290
With piteous looke in stead of handes his head about to wave.
Not knowing that it was their Lord, the huntsmen cheere their hounds
With wonted noyse and for Acteon looke about the grounds.
They hallow who could lowdest crie still calling him by name,
As though he were not there, and much his absence they do blame   295
In that he came not to the fall, but slackt to see the game.
As often as they named him he sadly shooke his head,
And faine he would have beene away thence in some other stead.
But there he was. And well he could have found in heart to see
His dogges fell deedes, so that to feele in place he had not bee.   300
They hem him in on everie side, and in the shape of Stagge,
With greedie teeth and griping pawes their Lord in peeces dragge.
So fierce was cruell Phoebes wrath, it could not be alayde,
Till of his fault by bitter death the raunsome he had payde.
     Much muttring was upon this fact. Some thought there was
                                                  extended   305
     A great deale more extremitie than neded. Some commended
Dianas doing: saying that it was but worthely
For safegarde of hir womanhod. Eche partie did applie
Good reasons to defende their case. Alone the wife of Jove,
Of lyking or misliking it not all so greatly strove,   310
As secretly rejoyst in heart that such a plague was light
On Cadmus linage: turning all the malice and the spight
Conceyved earst against the wench that Jove had fet fro Tyre,
Upon the kinred of the wench, and for to fierce hir ire,

---

283 *gainecope:* catch up with, encounter   298 *stead:* place
287 *brunt:* attack   313 *fet:* fetched

Another thing cleane overthwart there commeth in the nicke: 315
The Ladie Semell great with childe by Jove as then was quicke.
Hereat she gan to fret and fume, and for to ease hir heart,
Which else would burst, she fell in hande with scolding out hir part:
    And what a goodyeare have I woon by scolding erst? (she sed)
    It is that arrant queane hir selfe, against whose wicked hed   320
I must assay to give assault: and if (as men me call)
I be that Juno who in heaven beare greatest swing of all,
If in my hande I worthie bee to holde the royall Mace,
And if I be the Queene of heaven and soveraigne of this place,
Or wife and 'sister unto Jove, (his sister well I know: 325
But as for wife that name is vayne, I serve but for a show,
To cover other privie skapes) I will confound that Whore.
Now (with a mischiefe) is she bagd and beareth out before
Hir open shame to all the world, and shortly hopes to bee
The mother of a sonne by Jove, the which hath hapt to mee   330
Not passing once in all my time, so sore she doth presume
Upon hir beautie. But I trowe hir hope shall soone consume.
For never let me counted be for Saturns daughter more,
If by hir owne deare darling Jove on whome she trustes so sore,
I sende hir not to Styxes streame. This ended up she rose   335
And covered in golden cloud to Semelles house she goes.
And ere she sent away the cloud, she takes an olde wyves shape
With hoarie haire and riveled skinne, with slow and crooked gate.
As though she had the Palsey had, hir feeble limmes did shake,
And eke she foltred in the mouth as often as she spake.   340
She seemde olde Beldame Beroe of Epidaure to bee,
This Ladie Semelles Nourse as right as though it had beene shee.
    So when that after mickle talke of purpose ministred
    Joves name was upned: by and by she gave a sigh and sed:
I wish with all my heart that Jove bee cause to thee of this.   345
But daughter deare I dreade the worst, I feare it be amisse.
For manie Varlets under name of Gods to serve their lust,
Have into undefiled beddes themselves full often thrust.
And though it bene the mightie Jove yet doth not that suffise,
Onlesse he also make the same apparant to our eyes.   350
And if it be even verie hee, I say it doth behove,

<hr>

315 *overthwart:* amiss, vexing
319 *what a goodyeare:* what in the world;
    erst: before
322 *swing:* sway
327 *skapes:* transgressions

328 *bagd:* big with child
338 *riveled:* wrinkled
343 *mickle:* much
344 *upned:* mentioned
351 *doth behove:* is fitting

He prove it by some open signe and token of his love.
And therefore pray him for to graunt that, looke, in what degree,
What order, fashion, sort and state he use to companie
With mightie Juno, in the same in everie poynt and cace,   355
To all intents and purposes he thee likewise embrace,
And that he also bring with him his bright threeforked Mace.
    With such instructions Juno had enformed Cadmus Neece:
    And she poore sielie simple soule immediately on this
Requested Jove to graunt a boone the which she did not name.   360
Aske what thou wilt sweete heart (quoth he) thou shalt not misse the
                                                                  same,
And for to make thee sure hereof, the grisely Stygian Lake,
Which is the feare and God of Gods beare witnesse for thy sake.
She joying in hir owne mischaunce, not having any powre
To rule hir selfe, but making speede to hast hir fatall howre,   365
In which she through hir Lovers helpe should worke hir owne decay,
Sayd: Such as Juno findeth you when you and she doe play
The games of Venus, such I pray thee shew thy selfe to mee
In everie case. The God would faine have stopt hir mouth. But shee
Had made such hast that out it was. Which made him sigh full sore,   370
For neyther she could then unwish the thing she wisht before,
Nor he revoke his solemne oth. Wherefore with sorie heart
And heavie countnance by and by to Heaven he doth depart,
And makes to follow after him with looke full grim and stoure
The flakie clouds all grisly blacke, as when they threat a shoure.   375
To which he added mixt with winde a fierce and flashing flame,
With drie and dreadfull thunderclaps and lightning to the same
Of deadly unavoyded dynt. And yet as much as may
He goes about his vehement force and fiercenesse to allay.
He doth not arme him with the fire with which he did remove   380
The Giant with the hundreth handes, Typhoeus, from above:
It was too cruell and too sore to use against his Love.
The Cyclops made an other kinde of lightning farre more light,
Wherein they put much lesse of fire, lesse fierceness, lesser might.
It hight in Heaven the seconde Mace. Jove armes himselfe with this   385
And enters into Cadmus house where Semelles chamber is.
She being mortall was too weake and feeble to withstande
Such troublous tumultes of the Heavens: and therefore out of hande
Was burned in hir Lovers armes. But yet he tooke away

---

359 *sielie:* poor, simple   378 *dynt:* force
374 *stoure:* fierce   385 *hight:* is called

His infant from the mothers wombe unperfect as it lay,   390
And (if a man may credit it) did in his thigh it sowe,
Where byding out the mothers tyme it did to ripenesse growe.
And when the time of birth was come his Aunt the Ladie Ine
Did nourse him for a while by stealth and kept him trym and fine.
The Nymphes of Nysa afterwarde did in their bowres him hide,   395
And brought him up with Milke till tyme he might abrode be spyde.
    Now while these things were done on earth, and that by fatal
           doome
    The twice borne Bacchus had a tyme to mannes estate to come,
They say that Jove disposde to myrth as he and Juno sate
A drinking Nectar after meate in sport and pleasant rate,   400
Did fall a jeasting with his wife, and saide: A greater pleasure
In Venus games ye women have than men beyonde all measure.
She answerde no. To trie the truth, they both of them agree
The wise Tyresias in this case indifferent Judge to bee,
Who both the man and womans joyes by tryall understood.   405
For finding once two mightie Snakes engendring in a Wood,
He strake them overthwart the backs, by meanes whereof beholde
(As straunge a thing to be of truth as ever yet was tolde)
He being made a woman straight, seven winter lived so.
The eight he finding them againe did say unto them tho: 410
And if to strike ye have such powre as for to turne their shape
That are the givers of the stripe, before you hence escape,
One stripe now will I lende you more. He strake them as beforne
And straight returnd his former shape in which he first was borne.
Tyresias therefore being tane to judge this jesting strife,   415
Gave sentence on the side of Jove. The which the Queene his wife
Did take a great deale more to heart than needed, and in spight
To wreake hir teene upon hir Judge, bereft him of his sight.
But Jove (for to the Gods it is unleefull to undoe
The things which other of the Gods by any meanes have doe)   420
Did give him sight in things to come for losse of sight of eye,
And so his grievous punishment with honour did supplie.
By meanes whereof within a while in Citie, fielde, and towne
Through all the coast of Aony was bruited his renowne.
And folke to have their fortunes read that dayly did resorte   425
Were aunswerde so as none of them could give him misreporte.
    The first that of his soothfast wordes had proufe in all the Realme

₄₀₀ *rate:* manner   ₄₁₉ *unleefull:* unlawful
₄₁₈ *teene:* anger, annoyance

Was freckled Lyriop, whom sometime surprised in his streame
The floud Cephisus did enforce. This Lady bare a sonne
Whose beautie at his verie birth might justly love have wonne. 430
Narcissus did she call his name. Of whome the Prophet sage,
Demaunded if the childe should live to many yeares of age,
Made aunswere: Yea full long, so that him selfe he doe not know.
The Soothsayers wordes seemde long but vaine, untill the end did show
His saying to be true in deede by straungenesse of the rage, 435
And straungenesse of the kinde of death that did abridge his age.
For when yeares three times five and one he fully lyved had,
So that he seemde to stande beetwene the state of man and Lad,
The hearts of dyvers trim yong men his beautie gan to move
And many a Ladie fresh and faire was taken in his love. 440
But in that grace of Natures gift such passing pride did raigne,
That to be toucht of man or Mayde he wholy did disdaine.
A babling Nymph that Echo hight, who hearing others talke,
By no meanes can restraine hir tongue but that it needes must walke,
Nor of hir selfe hath powre to ginne to speake to any wight, 445
Espyde him dryving into toyles the fearefull stagges of flight.
This Echo was a body then and not an onely voyce.
Yet of hir speach she had that time no more than now the choyce,
That is to say, of many wordes the latter to repeate.
The cause thereof was Junos wrath. For when that with the feate 450
She might have often taken Jove in daliance with his Dames,
And that by stealth and unbewares in middes of all his games,
This elfe would with hir tatling talke deteine hir by the way,
Untill that Jove had wrought his will and they were fled away.
The which when Juno did perceyve, she said with wrathfull mood: 455
This tongue that hath deluded me shall doe thee little good,
For of thy speach but simple use hereafter shalt thou have.
The deede it selfe did straight confirme the threatnings that she gave.
Yet Echo of the former talke doth double oft the ende
And backe againe with just report the wordes earst spoken sende. 460
 Now when she sawe Narcissus stray about the Forrest wyde,
 She waxed warme and step for step fast after him she hyde.
The more she followed after him and neerer that she came,
The hoter ever did she waxe as neerer to hir flame.
Lyke as the lively Brimstone doth which dipt about a match, 465
And put but softly to the fire, the flame doth lightly catch.

450 *feate:* act

O Lord how often woulde she faine (if nature would have let)
Entreated him with gentle wordes some favour for to get?
But nature would not suffer hir nor give hir leave to ginne.
Yet (so farre forth as she by graunt at natures hande could winne)   470
As readie with attentive eare she harkens for some sounde,
Whereto she might replie hir wordes, from which she is not bounde.
By chaunce the stripling being strayde from all his companie,
Sayde: Is there any body nie? Straight Echo answerde: I.
Amazde he castes his eye aside, and looketh round about,   475
And Come (that all the Forrest roong) aloud he calleth out.
And Come (sayth she:) he looketh backe, and seeing no man followe,
Why fliste, he cryeth once againe: and she the same doth hallowe.
He still persistes and wondring much what kinde of thing it was
From which that answering voyce by turne so duely seemde to passe,   480
Said: Let us joyne. She (by hir will desirous to have said
In fayth with none more willingly at any time or stead)
Said: Let us joyne. And standing somewhat in hir owne conceit,
Upon these wordes she left the Wood, and forth she yeedeth streit,
To coll the lovely necke for which she longed had so much,   485
He runnes his way and will not be imbraced of no such,
And sayth: I first will die ere thou shalt take of me thy pleasure.
She aunswerde nothing else thereto, but Take of me thy pleasure.
Now when she saw hir selfe thus mockt, she gate hir to the Woods,
And hid hir head for verie shame among the leaves and buddes.   490
And ever sence she lyves alone in dennes and hollow Caves,
Yet stacke hir love still to hir heart, through which she dayly raves
The more for sorrowe of repulse. Through restlesse carke and care
Hir bodie pynes to skinne and bone, and waxeth wonderous bare.
The bloud doth vanish into ayre from out of all hir veynes,   495
And nought is left but voyce and bones: the voyce yet still remaynes:
Hir bones they say were turnde to stones. From thence she lurking still
In Woods, will never shewe hir head in field nor yet on hill.
Yet is she heard of every man: it is hir only sound,
And nothing else that doth remayne alive above the ground.   500
Thus had he mockt this wretched Nymph and many mo beside,
That in the waters, Woods and groves, or Mountaynes did abyde.
Thus had he mocked many men. Of which one miscontent
To see himselfe deluded so, his handes to Heaven up bent,
And sayd: I pray to God he may once feele fierce Cupids fire   505

482 *stead:* place   485 *coll:* hug
484 *yeedeth:* went   493 *carke:* anxiety, care

As I doe now, and yet not joy the things he doth desire.
The Goddesse Ramnuse (who doth wreake on wicked people take)
Assented to his just request for ruth and pities sake.
    There was a spring withouten mudde as silver cleare and still,
    Which neyther sheepeheirds, nor the Goates that fed upon the
                                           hill,   510
Nor other cattell troubled had, nor savage beast had styrd,
Nor braunch nor sticke, nor leafe of tree, nor any soule nor byrd.
The moysture fed and kept aye fresh the grasse that grew about,
And with their leaves the trees did keepe the heate of Phoebus out.
The stripling wearie with the heate and hunting in the chace,   515
And much delighted with the spring and coolenesse of the place,
Did lay him downe upon the brim: and as he stooped lowe
To staunche his thurst, another thurst of worse effect did growe.
For as he dranke, he chaunst to spie the Image of his face,
The which he did immediately with fervent love embrace.   520
He feedes a hope without cause why. For like a foolishe noddie
He thinkes the shadow that he sees, to be a lively boddie.
Astraughted like an ymage made of Marble stone he lyes,
There gazing on his shadowe still with fixed staring eyes.
Stretcht all along upon the ground, it doth him good to see   525
His ardant eyes which like two starres full bright and shyning bee,
And eke his fingars, fingars such as Bacchus might beseeme,
And haire that one might worthely Apollos haire it deeme,
His beardlesse chinne and yvorie necke, and eke the perfect grace
Of white and red indifferently bepainted in his face.   530
All these he woondreth to beholde, for which (as I doe gather)
Himselfe was to be woondred at, or to be pitied rather.
He is enamored of himselfe for want of taking heede,
And where he lykes another thing, he lykes himselfe in deede.
He is the partie whome he wooes, and suter that doth wooe,   535
He is the flame that settes on fire, and thing that burneth tooe.
O Lord how often did he kisse that false deceitfull thing?
How often did he thrust his armes midway into the spring
To have embraste the necke he saw and could not catch himselfe?
He knowes not what it was he sawe. And yet the foolish elfe   540
Doth burne in ardent love thereof. The verie selfsame thing
That doth bewitch and blinde his eyes, encreaseth all his sting.

---

506 *joy:* enjoy   523 *Astraughted:* distraught, distracted
507 *wreake:* revenge   527 *beseeme:* become, suit
521 *noddie:* simpleton

Thou fondling thou, why doest thou raught the fickle image so?
The thing thou seekest is not there. And if aside thou go,
The thing thou lovest straight is gone. It is none other matter   545
That thou doest see, than of thy selfe the shadow in the water.
The thing is nothing of it selfe: with thee it doth abide,
With thee it would departe if thou withdrew thy selfe aside.
     No care of meate could draw him thence, nor yet desire of rest.
     But lying flat against the ground, and leaning on his brest,   550
With greedie eyes he gazeth still uppon the falced face,
And through his sight is wrought his bane. Yet for a little space
He turnes and settes himselfe upright, and holding up his hands
With piteous voyce unto the wood that round about him stands,
Cryes out and ses: Alas ye Woods, and was there ever any   555
That loovde so cruelly as I? you know: for unto many
A place of harbrough have you beene, and fort of refuge strong.
Can you remember any one in all your tyme so long
That hath so pinde away as I? I see and am full faine,
Howbeit that I like and see I can not yet attaine: 560
So great a blindnesse in my heart through doting love doth raigne.
And for to spight me more withall, it is no journey farre,
No drenching Sea, no Mountaine hie, no wall, no locke, no barre,
It is but even a little droppe that keepes us two asunder.
He would be had. For looke how oft I kisse the water under,   565
So oft againe with upwarde mouth he riseth towarde mee.
A man would thinke to touch at least I should yet able bee.
It is a trifle in respect that lettes us of our love.
What wight soever that thou art come hither up above.
O pierlesse piece, why dost thou mee thy lover thus delude?   570
Or whither fliste thou of thy friende thus earnestly pursude?
Iwis I neyther am so fowle nor yet so growne in yeares
That in this wise thou shouldst me shoon. To have me to their Feeres,
The Nymphes themselves have sude ere this. And yet (as should
                                                  appeere)
Thou dost pretende some kinde of hope of friendship by thy cheere.   575
For when I stretch mine armes to thee, thou stretchest thine likewise.
And if I smile thou smilest too: and when that from mine eyes
The teares doe drop, I well perceyve the water stands in thine.

543 *fondling:* foolish person   569 *wight:* man
552 *bane:* harm   572 *Iwis:* certainly
557 *harbrough:* harbor   573 *shoon:* shun; *Feeres:* companions
560 *that:* that which   575 *cheere:* expression
568 *lettes:* hinders

Like gesture also dost thou make to everie becke of mine.
And as by moving of thy sweete and lovely lippes I weene, 580
Thou speakest words although mine eares conceive not what they beene,
It is my selfe I well perceyve, it is mine Image sure,
That in this sort deluding me, this furie doth procure.
I am inamored of my selfe, I doe both set on fire,
And am the same that swelteth too, through impotent desire. 585
What shall I doe? be woode or woo? whome shall I woo therefore?
The thing I seeke is in my selfe, my plentie makes me poore.
I would to God I for a while might from my bodie part.
This wish is straunge to heare, a Lover wrapped all in smart
To wish away the thing the which he loveth as his heart. 590
My sorrowe takes away my strength. I have not long to live,
But in the floure of youth must die. To die it doth not grieve.
For that by death shall come the ende of all my griefe and paine
I would this yongling whome I love might lenger life obtaine:
For in one soule shall now decay we stedfast Lovers twaine. 595
    This saide in rage he turnes againe unto the forsaide shade,
    And rores the water with the teares and sloubring that he made,
That through his troubling of the Well his ymage gan to fade.
Which when he sawe to vanish so: Oh whither dost thou flie?
Abide I pray thee heartely, aloud he gan to crie. 600
Forsake me not so cruelly that loveth thee so deere,
But give me leave a little while my dazled eyes to cheere
With sight of that which for to touch is utterly denide,
Thereby to feede my wretched rage and furie for a tide.
As in this wise he made his mone, he stripped off his cote 605
And with his fist outragiously his naked stomacke smote.
A ruddie colour where he smote rose on his stomacke sheere,
Lyke Apples which doe partly white and striped red appeere,
Or as the clusters ere the grapes to ripenesse fully come:
An Orient purple here and there beginnes to grow on some. 610
Which things as soon as in the spring he did beholde againe,
He could no longer beare it out. But fainting straight for paine,
As lith and supple waxe doth melt against the burning flame,
Or morning dewe against the Sunne that glareth on the same:
Even so by piecemale being spent and wasted through desire, 615
Did he consume and melt away with Cupids secret fire.
His lively hue of white and red, his cheerefulnesse and strength

585 *swelteth:* swelters   607 *sheere:* clear, bright
597 *rores:* troubles

And all the things that lyked him did wanze away at length.
So that in fine remayned not the bodie which of late
The wretched Echo loved so. Who when she sawe his state,   620
Although in heart she angrie were, and mindefull of his pride,
Yet ruing his unhappie case, as often as he cride
Alas, she cride, Alas likewise with shirle redoubled sound.
And when he beate his breast, or strake his feete against the ground,
She made like noyse of clapping too. These are the woordes that last 625
Out of his lippes beholding still his woonted ymage past:
Alas sweete boy belovde in vaine, farewell. And by and by
With sighing sound the selfesame wordes the Echo did reply.
With that he layde his wearie head against the grassie place
And death did cloze his gazing eyes that woondred at the grace   630
And beautie which did late adorne their Masters heavenly face.
And afterward when into Hell receyved was his spright
He goes me to the Well of Styx, and there both day and night
Standes tooting on his shadow still as fondely as before.
The water Nymphes, his sisters, wept and wayled for him sore   635
And on his bodie strowde their haire clipt off and shorne therefore.
The Wood nymphes also did lament. And Echo did rebound
To every sorrowfull noyse of theirs with like lamenting sound.
The fire was made to burne the corse, and waxen Tapers light.
A Herce to lay the bodie on with solemne pompe was dight.   640
But as for bodie none remaind: in stead thereof they found
A yellow floure with milke white leaves new sprong upon the ground.
    This matter all Achaia through did spreade the Prophets fame:
    That every where of just desert renowned was his name.
But Penthey, olde Echions sonne (who proudely did disdaine   645
Both God and man) did laughe to scorne the Prophets words as vaine,
Upbrading him most spitefully with loosing of his sight,
And with the fact for which he lost fruition of this light.
The good olde father (for these wordes his pacience much did move)
Saide: O how happie shouldest thou be and blessed from above,   650
If thou wert blinde as well as I, so that thou might not see
The sacred rytes of Bacchus band. For sure the time will bee,
And that full shortely (as I gesse) that hither shall resort
Another Bacchus, Semelles sonne, whome if thou not support
With pompe and honour like a God, thy carcasse shall be tattred,   655

---

618 *wanze:* waste   640 *dight:* prepared, arrayed
634 *tooting:* gazing

And in a thousand places eke about the Woods be scattred.
And for to reade thee what they are that shall perfourme the deede,
It is thy mother and thine Auntes that thus shall make thee bleede.
I know it shall so come to passe, for why thou shalt disdaine,
To honour Bacchus as a God: and then thou shalt with paine   660
Feele how that blinded as I am I sawe for thee too much.
As olde Tiresias did pronounce these wordes and other such,
Echions sonne did trouble him. His wordes prove true in deede,
For as the Prophet did forespeake so fell it out with speede.
Anon this newefound Bacchus commes: the woods and fieldes
                                        rebound   665
With noyse of shouts and howling out, and such confused sound.
The folke runne flocking out by heapes, men, Mayds and wives togither
The noble men and rascall sorte ran gadding also thither,
The Orgies of this unknowne God full fondely to performe,
The which when Penthey did perceyve, he gan to rage and storme.   670
    And sayde unto them: O ye ympes of Mars his snake by kinde
    What ayleth you? what fiend of hell doth thus enrage your minde?
Hath tinking sound of pottes and pannes, hath noyse of crooked horne,
Have fonde illusions such a force that them whome heretoforne
No arming sworde, no bloudie trumpe, no men in battail ray   675
Could cause to shrinke, no sheepish shriekes of simple women fray,
And dronken woodnesse wrought by wine and roughts of filthie freakes
And sound of toying timpanes dauntes, and quite their courage breakes?
Shall I at you, yee auncient men which from the towne of Tyre
To bring your housholde Gods by Sea, in safetie did aspyre,   680
And setled them within this place the which ye nowe doe yeelde
In bondage quite without all force and fighting in the fielde,
Or woonder at you yonger sorte approching unto mee
More neare in courage and in yeares? whome meete it were to see
With speare and not with thirse in hande, with glittring helme on
                                        hed,   685
And not with leaves. Now call to minde of whome ye all are bred,
And take the stomackes of that Snake, which being one alone,
Right stoutly in his owne defence confounded many one.
He for his harbrough and his spring his lyfe did nobly spend.
Doe you no more but take a heart your Countrie to defende.   690

659 *for why:* because
665 *rebound:* reecho, resound
671 *ympes:* offspring
675 *ray:* array
676 *fray:* frighten

677 *roughts:* routs, noisy crowds
685 *thirse:* thyrsus, decorated staff associated
    with Dionysius. Cf. IV, 8.
687 *stomackes:* spirit, courage

He put to death right valeant knightes. Your battaile is with such
As are but Meicocks in effect: and yet ye doe so much
In conquering them, that by the deede the olde renowne ye save,
Which from your fathers by discent this present time ye have.
If fatall destnies doe forbid that Thebae long shall stande,   695
Would God that men with Canon shot might raze it out of hande.
Would God the noyse of fire and sworde did in our hearing sound.
For then in this our wretchednesse there could no fault be found.
Then might we justly waile our case that all the world might see
We should not neede of sheading teares ashamed for to bee.   700
But now our towne is taken by a naked beardelesse boy,
Who doth not in the feates of armes nor horse nor armour joy,
But for to moyste his haire with Mirrhe, and put on garlands gay,
And in soft Purple silke and golde his bodie to aray.
But put to you your helping hand and straight without delay   705
I will compell him poynt by poynt his lewdnesse to bewray,
Both in usurping Joves high name in making him his sonne
And forging of these Ceremonies lately now begonne.
Hath King Atrisius heart inough this fondling for to hate
That makes himselfe to be a God? and for to shut the gate   710
Of Argus at his comming there? and shall this rover make
King Penthey and the noble towne of Thebae thus to quake?
Go quickly sirs (these wordes he spake unto his servaunts) go
And bring the Captaine hither bound with speede. Why stay ye so?
His Grandsire Cadmus, Athamas and others of his kinne   715
Reproved him by gentle meanes but nothing could they winne:
The more intreatance that they made the fiercer was he still:
The more his friendes did go about to breake him of his will,
The more they did provoke his wrath, and set his rage on fire:
They made him worse in that they sought to bridle his desire.   720
So have I seene a brooke ere this, where nothing let the streame,
Runne smooth with little noyse or none, but where as any beame
Or cragged stones did let his course, and make him for to stay:
It went more fiercely from the stoppe with fomie wroth away.
Beholde all bloudie come his men, and straight he them demaunded 725
Where Bacchus was, and why they had not done as he commaunded.
Sir (aunswerde they) we saw him not, but this same fellow heere
A chiefe companion in his traine and worker in this geere,
Wee tooke by force: and therewithall presented to their Lord

692 *Meicocks:* cowards, weaklings   721 *let:* hindered
706 *bewray:* expose   728 *this geere:* these doings

A certaine man of Tirrhene lande, his handes fast bound with cord, 730
Whome they, frequenting Bacchus rites had found but late before.
A grim and cruell looke which yre did make to seeme more sore,
Did Penthey cast upon the man. And though he scarcely stayd
From putting him to tormentes strait, O wretched man (he sayde)
Who by thy worthie death shalt be a sample unto other,   735
Declare to me the names of thee, thy father and thy mother,
And in what Countrie thou wert borne, and what hath caused thee,
Of these straunge rites and sacrifice, a follower for to bee.
          He voyd of feare made aunswere thus: Acetis is my name:
          Of Parentes but of lowe degree in Lidy land I came.   740
No ground for painfull Oxe to till, no sheepe to beare me wooll
My father left me: no nor horse, nor Asse, nor Cow nor Booll.
God wote he was but poore himselfe. With line and bayted hooke
The frisking fishes in the pooles upon his Reede he tooke.
His handes did serve in steade of landes, his substance was his craft. 745
Nowe have I made you true accompt of all that he me laft,
As well of ryches as of trades, in which I was his heire
And successour. For when that death bereft him use of aire,
Save water he me nothing left. It is the thing alone
Which for my lawfull heritage I clayme, and other none.   750
Soone after I (bicause that loth I was to ay abide
In that poore state) did learne a ship by cunning hande to guide,
And for to know the raynie signe, that hight th'Olenien Gote
Which with hir milke did nourish Jove. And also I did note
The Pleiads and the Hiads moyst, and eke the siely Plough   755
With all the dwellings of the winds that make the Seas so rough.
And eke such Havens as are meete to harbrough vessels in:
With everie starre and heavenly signe that guides to shipmen bin.
Now as by chaunce I late ago did toward Dilos sayle,
I came on coast of Scios Ile, and seeing day to fayle,   760
Tooke harbrough there and went alande. As soone as that the night
Was spent, and morning gan to peere with ruddie glaring light,
I rose and bad my companie fresh water fetch aboord.
And pointing them the way that led directly to the foorde,
I went me to a little hill, and viewed round about   765
To see what weather we were lyke to have ere setting out.
Which done, I cald my watermen and all my Mates togither,
And willde them all to go aboord my selfe first going thither.

---

743 *wote:* knows   767 *watermen:* sailors
746 *accompt:* account

Loe here we are (Opheltes sayd) (he was the Maysters Mate)
And (as he thought) a bootie found in desert fields alate,   770
He dragd a boy upon his hande that for his beautie sheene
A mayden rather than a boy appeared for to beene.
This childe, as one forelade with wine, and dreint with drousie sleepe
Did reele, as though he scarcely coulde himselfe from falling keepe.
I markt his countnance, weede and pace, no inckling could I see,   775
By which I might conjecture him a mortall wight to bee.
I thought, and to my fellowes sayd: What God I can not tell
But in this bodie that we see some Godhead sure doth dwell.
What God so ever that thou art, thy favour to us showe,
And in our labours us assist, and pardone these also.   780
Pray for thy selfe and not for us (quoth Dictys by and by).
A nimbler fellow for to climbe upon the Mast on hie
And by the Cable downe to slide, there was not in our keele.
Swart Melanth patrone of the shippe did like his saying weele.
So also did Alcimedon: and so did Libys too,   785
And blacke Epopeus eke whose charge it did belong unto
To see the Rowers at their tymes their dueties duely do.
And so did all the rest of them: so sore mennes eyes were blinded
Where covetousenesse of filthie gaine is more than reason minded.
Well sirs (quoth I) but by your leave ye shall not have it so,   790
I will not suffer sacriledge within this shippe to go.
For I have here the most to doe. And with that worde I stept
Uppon the Hatches, all the rest from entrance to have kept.
The rankest Ruffian of the rout that Lycab had to name,
(Who for a murder being late driven out of Tuscane came   795
To me for succor) waxed woode, and with his sturdie fist
Did give me such a churlish blow bycause I did resist,
That over boord he had me sent, but that with much ado
I caught the tackling in my hand and helde me fast thereto:
The wicked Varlets had a sport to see me handled so.   800
Then Bacchus (for it Bacchus was) as though he had but tho
Bene waked with their noyse from sleepe, and that his drousie braine
Discharged of the wine, begon to gather sence againe,
Said: What adoe? what noyse is this? how came I here I pray?
Sirs tell me whether you doe meane to carie me away.   805
Feare not my boy (the Patrone sayd) no more but tell me where
Thou doest desire to go alande, and we will set thee there.

---

773 *forelade:* overladen; *dreint:* drenched   794 *to name:* as name
775 *weede:* clothing

To Naxus ward (quoth Bacchus tho) set ship upon the fome.
There would I have yow harbrough take, for Naxus is my home.
Like perjurde Caitifs by the Sea and all the Gods thereof,   810
They falsly sware it should be so, and therewithall in scoffe
They bade me hoyse up saile and go. Upon the righter hand
I cast about to fetch the winde, for so did Naxus stand.
What meanst? art mad? Opheltes cride, and therewithall begun
A feare of loosing of their pray through every man to run.   815
The greater part with head and hand a signe did to me make,
And some did whisper in mine eare the left hand way to take.
I was amazde and said: Take charge henceforth who will for me:
For of your craft and wickednesse I will no furthrer be.
Then fell they to reviling me, and all the rout gan grudge: 820
Of which Ethalion said in scorne: By like in you Sir snudge
Consistes the savegard of us all. And wyth that word he takes
My roume, and leaving Naxus quite to other countries makes.
The God then dalying with these mates, as though he had at last
Begon to smell their suttle craft, out of the foredecke cast   825
His eye upon the Sea: and then as though he seemde to weepe,
Sayd: Sirs, to bring me on this coast ye doe not promise keepe.
I see that this is not the land the which I did request.
For what occasion in this sort deserve I to be drest?
What commendation can you win, or praise thereby receyve,   830
If men a Lad, if many one ye compasse to deceyve?
I wept and sobbed all this while, the wicked villaines laught,
And rowed forth with might and maine, as though they had bene
                                                         straught.

Now even by him (for sure than he in all the worlde so wide
There is no God more neare at hand at every time and tide)   835
I sweare unto you that the things the which I shall declare,
Like as they seeme incredible, even so most true they are.
The ship stoode still amid the Sea as in a dustie docke.
They wondring at this miracle, and making but a mocke,
Persist in beating with their Ores, and on with all their sayles.   840
To make their Galley to remove, no Art nor labor fayles.
But Ivie troubled so their Ores that forth they could not row:
And both with Beries and with leaves their sailes did overgrow.
And he himselfe with clustred grapes about his temples round,

808 *To . . . ward:* toward
810 *Caitifs:* wretches, villains
812 *hoyse:* raise
818 *for me:* for all I care

821 *By like:* probably; *snudge:* niggard
829 *drest:* treated
833 *straught:* distraught, crazy

Did shake a Javeling in his hand that round about was bound   845
With leaves of Vines: and at his feete there seemed for to couch
Of Tygers, Lynx, and Panthers shapes most ougly for to touch.
I cannot tell you whether feare or woodnesse were the cause,
But every person leapeth up and from his labor drawes.
And there one Medon first of all began to waxen blacke,   850
And having lost his former shape did take a courbed backe.
What Monster shall we have of thee (quoth Licab) and with that
This Licabs chappes did waxen wide, his nosetrils waxed flat,
His skin waxt tough, and scales thereon began anon to grow.
And Libis as he went about the Ores away to throw,   855
Perceived how his hands did shrinke and were become so short,
That now for finnes and not for hands he might them well report.
Another as he would have claspt his arme about the corde:
Had nere an arme, and so bemaimd in bodie, over boord
He leapeth downe among the waves, and forked is his tayle   860
As are the hornes of Phebes face when halfe hir light doth fayle.
They leape about and sprinkle up much water on the ship,
One while they swim above, and downe againe anon they slip.
They fetch their friskes as in a daunce, and wantonly they writhe
Now here now there among the waves their bodies bane and lithe.   865
And with their wide and hollow nose the water in they snuffe,
And by their noses out againe as fast they doe it puffe.
Of twentie persons (for our ship so many men did beare)
I only did remaine nigh straught and trembling still for feare.
The God could scarce recomfort me, and yet he said: Go too,   870
Feare not but saile to Dia ward. His will I gladly doe.
And so as soone as I came there with right devout intent,
His Chaplaine I became. And thus his Orgies I frequent.
     Thou makste a processe verie long (quoth Penthey) to th'intent
     That (choler being coolde by time) mine anger might relent.   875
But Sirs (he spake it to his men) go take him by and by,
With cruell torments out of hand goe cause him for to die.
Immediately they led away Acetes out of sight,
And put him into prison strong from which there was no flight.
But while the cruell instruments of death as sword and fire   880
Were in preparing wherewithall t'accomplish Pentheys yre,
It is reported that the doores did of their owne accorde
Burst open and his chaines fall off. And yet this cruell Lorde
Persisteth fiercer than before, not bidding others go

---

864 *wantonly:* playfully   865 *bane:* limber

But goes himselfe unto the hill Cytheron, which as tho
To Bacchus being consecrate did ring of chaunted songs,
And other loud confused sounds of Bacchus drunken throngs.
And even as when the bloudie Trumpe doth to the battell sound,
The lustie horse streight neying out bestirres him on the ground,
And taketh courage thereupon t'assaile his emnie proud: 890
Even so when Penthey heard afarre the noyse and howling loud
That Bacchus franticke folke did make, it set his heart on fire,
And kindled fiercer than before the sparks of settled ire.
    There is a goodly plaine about the middle of the hill,
    Environd in with Woods, where men may view eche way at will. 895
Here looking on these holie rites with lewde prophaned eyes
King Pentheys mother first of all hir foresaid sonne espies,
And like a Bedlem first of all she doth upon him runne,
And with hir Javeling furiously she first doth wound hir sonne.
Come hither sisters come, she cries, here is that mighty Bore,   900
Here is the Bore that stroyes our fieldes, him will I strike therefore.
With that they fall upon him all as though they had bene mad,
And clustring all upon a heape fast after him they gad.
He quakes and shakes: his words are now become more meeke and
                                                      colde:
He now condemnes his owne default, and sayes he was too bolde.   905
And wounded as he was he cries: Helpe, Aunt Autonoe,
Now for Acteons blessed soule some mercie show to me.
She wist not who Acteon was, but rent without delay
His right hand off: and Ino tare his tother hand away.
To lift unto his mother tho the wretch had nere an arme: 910
But shewing hir his maimed corse, and woundes yet bleeding warme,
O mother see, he sayes: with that Agaue howleth out:
And writhed with hir necke awrie, and shooke hir haire about.
And holding from his bodie torne his head in bloudie hands,
She cries: O fellowes in this deede our noble conquest stands.   915
No sooner could the winde have blowen the rotten leaves from trees,
When Winters frost hath bitten them, then did the hands of these
Most wicked women Pentheys limmes from one another teare.
The Thebanes being now by this example brought in feare,
Frequent this newfound sacrifice, and with sweete frankinsence   920
God Bacchus Altars lode with gifts in every place doe cense.
                FINIS TERTII LIBRI.

890 *emnie:* enemy   901 *stroyes:* destroys
898 *Bedlem:* lunatic   921 *lode:* laden

THE FOURTH BOOKE

OF OVIDS METAMORPHOSIS.

[*Pyramus and Thisbe. Mars and Venus. Apollo, Leucothoe, and Clytie.
Salmacis and Hermaphroditus. Athamas and Ino. Perseus and Andro-
meda.*]

Yet would not stout Alcithoe, Duke Mineus daughter, bow
   The Orgies of this newfound God in conscience to allow
But still she stiffly doth denie that Bacchus is the sonne
Of Jove: and in this heresie hir sisters with hir runne.
The Priest had bidden holiday, and that as well the Maide   5
As Mistresse (for the time aside all other businesse layde)
In Buckskin cotes, with tresses loose, and garlondes on their heare,
Should in their hands the leavie speares (surnamed Thyrsis) beare,
Foretelling them that if they did the Goddes commaundement breake,
He would with sore and grievous plagues his wrath upon them wreake. 10
The women straight both yong and olde doe thereunto obay.
Their yarne, their baskets, and their flax unsponne aside they lay,
And burne to Bacchus frankinsence. Whome solemly they call
By all the names and titles high that may to him befall:
As Bromius, and Lyeus eke, begotten of the flame,   15
Twice borne, the sole and only childe that of two mothers came,
Unshorne Thyoney, Niseus, Leneus, and the setter
Of Wines, whose pleasant liquor makes all tables fare the better,
Nyctileus and th'Elelean Sire, Iacchus, Evan eke,
With divers other glorious names that through the land of Greke   20
To thee O Liber wonted are to attributed bee.
Thy youthfull yeares can never wast: there dwelleth ay in thee

---

8 *Thyrsis:* thyrsus, decorated staff associated   10 *wreake:* vent, express
   with Dionysius. Cf. III, 685.   15 *eke:* also

A childhod tender, fresh and faire: in Heaven we doe thee see
Surmounting every other thing in beautie and in grace
And when thou standste without thy hornes thou hast a Maidens face. 25
To thee obeyeth all the East as far as Ganges goes,
Which doth the scorched land of Inde with tawnie folke enclose.
Lycurgus with his twibill sharpe, and Penthey who of pride
Thy Godhead and thy mightie power rebelliously denide,
Thou right redowted didst confounde: thou into Sea didst send   30
The Tyrrhene shipmen. Thou with bittes the sturdy neckes doste bend
Of spotted Lynxes: throngs of Frowes and Satyres on thee tend,
And that olde Hag that with a staffe his staggering limmes doth stay
Scarce able on his Asse to sit for reeling every way.
Thou commest not in any place but that is hearde the noyse   35
Of gagling womens tatling tongues and showting out of boyes,
With sound of Timbrels, Tabors, Pipes, and Brazen pannes and pots
Confusedly among the rout that in thine Orgies trots.
The Thebane women for thy grace and favour humbly sue,
And (as the Priest did bid) frequent thy rites with reverence due.   40
Alonly Mineus daughters bent of wilfulnesse, with working
Quite out of time to breake the feast, are in their houses lurking:
And there doe fall to spinning yarne, or weaving in the frame,
And kepe their maidens to their worke. Of which one pleasant dame
As she with nimble hand did draw hir slender threede and fine,   45
Said: Whyle that others idelly doe serve the God of wine,
Let us that serve a better Sainct Minerva, finde some talke
To ease our labor while our handes about our profite walke.
And for to make the time seeme shorte, let eche of us recite,
(As every bodies turne shall come) some tale that may delight.   50
Hir saying likte the rest so well that all consent therein,
And thereupon they pray that first the eldest would begin.
She had such store and choyce of tales she wist not which to tell.
She doubted if she might declare the fortune that befell
To Dircetes of Babilon whome now with scaly hide   55
In altred shape the Philistine beleveth to abide
In watrie Pooles: or rather how hir daughter taking wings
In shape of Dove on toppes of towres in age now sadly sings:
Or how a certaine water Nymph by witchcraft and by charmes
Converted into fishes dumbe of yongmen many swarmes,   60

---

28 *twibill:* double-bladed battle-ax
32 *Frowes:* women
33 *Hag:* ugly old creature

36 *gagling:* gabbling
51 *likte:* pleased
53 *wist:* knew

Untill that of the selfesame sauce hir selfe did tast at last:
Or how the tree that usde to beare fruite white in ages past,
Doth now beare fruite in manner blacke, by sprincling up of blood.
This tale (because it was not stale nor common) seemed good
To hir to tell: and thereupon she in this wise begun,   65
Hir busie hand still drawing out the flaxen threede she spun:
    Within the towne (of whose huge walles so monstrous high and
                                                       thicke
    The fame is given Semyramis for making them of bricke)
Dwelt hard together two yong folke in houses joynde so nere
That under all one roofe well nie both twaine conveyed were.   70
The name of him was Pyramus, and Thisbe calde was she.
So faire a man in all the East was none alive as he,
Nor nere a woman, maide nor wife in beautie like to hir.
This neighbrod bred acquaintance first, this neyghbrod first did stirre
The secret sparkes, this neighbrod first an entrance in did showe,   75
For love to come to that to which it afterward did growe.
And if that right had taken place they had bene man and wife,
But still their Parents went about to let which (for their life)
They could not let. For both their heartes with equall flame did burne.
No man was privie to their thoughts. And for to serve their turne   80
In steade of talke they used signes. The closelier they supprest
The fire of love, the fiercer still it raged in their brest.
The wall that parted house from house had riven therein a crany
Which shronke at making of the wall. This fault not markt of any
Of many hundred yeares before (what doth not love espie)   85
These lovers first of all found out, and made a way whereby
To talke togither secretly, and through the same did goe
Their loving whisprings verie light and safely to and fro.
Now as at one side Pyramus and Thisbe on the tother
Stoode often drawing one of them the pleasant breath from other: 90
O thou envious wall (they sayd) why letst thou lovers thus?
What matter were it if that thou permitted both of us
In armes eche other to embrace? Or if thou thinke that this
Were overmuch, yet mightest thou at least make roume to kisse.
And yet thou shalt not finde us churles: we thinke our selves in det   95
For this same piece of courtesie, in vouching safe to let
Our sayings to our friendly eares thus freely come and goe.
Thus having where they stoode in vaine complayned of their woe,

---

74 *neighbrod:* neighborhood   96 *vouching safe:* vouchsafing
78 *let:* prevent

When night drew nere, they bade adew and eche gave kisses sweete
Unto the parget on their side, the which did never meete.   100
Next morning with hir cherefull light had driven the starres aside
And Phebus with his burning beames the dewie grasse had dride.
These lovers at their wonted place by foreappointment met.
Where after much complaint and mone they covenanted to get
Away from such as watched them and in the Evening late   105
To steale out of their fathers house and eke the Citie gate.
And to th'intent that in the fieldes they strayde not up and downe
They did agree at Ninus Tumb to meete without the towne,
And tarie underneath a tree that by the same did grow
Which was a faire high Mulberie with fruite as white as snow,   110
Hard by a coole and trickling spring. This bargaine pleasde them both
And so daylight (which to their thought away but slowly goth)
Did in the Ocean fall to rest, and night from thence doth rise.
As soone as darkenesse once was come, straight Thisbe did devise
A shift to wind hir out of doores, that none that were within   115
Perceyved hir: and muffling hir with clothes about hir chin,
That no man might discerne hir face, to Ninus Tumb she came
Unto the tree, and sat hir downe there underneath the same.
Love made hir bold. But see the chaunce, there comes besmerde with
                   blood
About the chappes a Lionesse all foming from the wood   120
From slaughter lately made of kine to staunch hir bloudie thurst
With water of the foresaid spring. Whome Thisbe spying furst,
Afarre by moonelight, thereupon with fearfull steppes gan flie,
And in a darke and yrkesome cave did hide hirselfe thereby.
And as she fled away for hast she let hir mantle fall   125
The whych for feare she left behind not looking backe at all.
Now when the cruell Lionesse hir thurst had stanched well,
In going to the Wood she found the slender weede that fell
From Thisbe, which with bloudie teeth in pieces she did teare.
The night was somewhat further spent ere Pyramus came there   130
Who seeing in the suttle sande the print of Lions paw,
Waxt pale for feare. But when also the bloudie cloke he saw
All rent and torne: One night (he sayd) shall lovers two confounde,
Of which long life deserved she of all that live on ground.
My soule deserves of this mischaunce the perill for to beare.   135

---

100 *parget:* plaster   124 *yrkesome:* loathsome
115 *shift:* trick; *wind hir:* escape   128 *weede:* dress

I, wretch, have bene the death of thee, which to this place of feare
Did cause thee in the night to come, and came not here before.
My wicked limmes and wretched guttes with cruell teeth therfore
Devour ye, O ye Lions all that in this rocke doe dwell.
But Cowardes use to wish for death. The slender weede that fell   140
From Thisbe up he takes, and streight doth beare it to the tree,
Which was appointed erst the place of meeting for to bee.
And when he had bewept and kist the garment which he knew,
Receyve thou my bloud too (quoth he) and therewithall he drew
His sworde, the which among his guttes he thrust, and by and by   145
Did draw it from the bleeding wound beginning for to die,
And cast himselfe upon his backe, the bloud did spin on hie
As when a Conduite pipe is crackt, the water bursting out
Doth shote it selfe a great way off and pierce the Ayre about.
The leaves that were upon the tree besprincled with his blood   150
Were died blacke. The roote also bestained as it stoode,
A deepe darke purple colour straight upon the Berries cast.
Anon scarce ridded of hir feare with which she was agast,
For doubt of disapointing him commes Thisbe forth in hast,
And for hir lover lookes about, rejoycing for to tell   155
How hardly she had scapt that night the daunger that befell.
And as she knew right well the place and facion of the tree
(As whych she saw so late before): even so when she did see
The colour of the Berries turnde, she was uncertaine whither
It were the tree at which they both agreed to meete togither.   160
While in this doubtfull stounde she stoode, she cast hir eye aside
And there beweltred in his bloud hir lover she espide
Lie sprawling with his dying limmes: at which she started backe,
And looked pale as any Box, a shuddring through hir stracke,
Even like the Sea which sodenly with whissing noyse doth move,   165
When with a little blast of winde it is but toucht above.
But when approching nearer him she knew it was hir love,
She beate hir brest, she shricked out, she tare hir golden heares,
And taking him betweene hir armes did wash his wounds with teares,
She meynt hir weeping with his bloud, and kissing all his face   170
(Which now became as colde as yse) she cride in wofull case:
Alas what chaunce, my Pyramus, hath parted thee and mee?
Make aunswere O my Pyramus: it is thy Thisb', even shee
Whome thou doste love most heartely, that speaketh unto thee.

142 *erst:* before   164 *Box:* boxwood
161 *stounde:* amazement, stupor   170 *meynt:* mingled

Give eare and rayse thy heavie heade. He hearing Thisbes name,   175
Lift up his dying eyes and having seene hir closde the same.
But when she knew hir mantle there and saw his scabberd lie
Without the swoorde: Unhappy man thy love hath made thee die:
Thy love (she said) hath made thee sley thy selfe. This hand of mine
Is strong inough to doe the like. My love no lesse than thine   180
Shall give me force to worke my wound. I will pursue the dead.
And wretched woman as I am, it shall of me be sed
That like as of thy death I was the only cause and blame,
So am I thy companion eke and partner in the same,
For death which only coulde alas asunder part us twaine,   185
Shall never so dissever us but we will meete againe.
And you the Parentes of us both, most wretched folke alyve,
Let this request that I shall make in both our names bylive
Entreate you to permit that we whome chaste and stedfast love
And whome even death hath joynde in one, may as it doth behove   190
In one grave be together layd. And thou unhappie tree
Which shroudest now the corse of one, and shalt anon through mee
Shroude two, of this same slaughter holde the sicker signes for ay,
Blacke be the colour of thy fruite and mourning like alway,
Such as the murder of us twaine may evermore bewray.   195
This said, she tooke the sword yet warme with slaughter of hir love
And setting it beneath hir brest, did to hir heart it shove.
Hir prayer with the Gods and with their Parentes tooke effect.
For when the frute is throughly ripe, the Berrie is bespect
With colour tending to a blacke. And that which after fire   200
Remained, rested in one Tumbe as Thisbe did desire.

  This tale thus tolde a little space of pawsing was betwist,
  And then began Leucothoe thus, hir sisters being whist:
This Sunne that with his streaming light al worldly things doth cheare
Was tane in love. Of Phebus loves now list and you shall heare.   205
It is reported that this God did first of all espie,
(For everie thing in Heaven and Earth is open to his eie)
How Venus with the warlike Mars advoutrie did commit.
It grieved him to see the fact and so discovered it,
He shewed hir husband Junos sonne th'advoutrie and the place   210
In which this privie scape was done. Who was in such a case
That heart and hand and all did faile in working for a space.

---

188 *bylive:* immediately, eagerly   203 *whist:* hushed
193 *sicker:* certain; *ay:* ever   208 *advoutrie:* adultery
195 *bewray:* reveal   211 *scape:* transgression

Anon he featly forgde a net of Wire so fine and slight,
That neyther knot nor nooze therein apparant was to sight.
This piece of worke was much more fine than any handwarpe oofe   215
Or that whereby the Spider hanges in sliding from the roofe.
And furthermore the suttlenesse and slight thereof was such,
It followed every little pull and closde with every touch,
And so he set it handsomly about the haunted couch.
Now when that Venus and hir mate were met in bed togither   220
Hir husband by his newfound snare before convayed thither
Did snarle them both togither fast in middes of all theyr play
And setting ope the Ivorie doores, callde all the Gods streight way
To see them: they with shame inough fast lockt togither lay.
A certaine God among the rest disposed for to sport   225
Did wish that he himselfe also were shamed in that sort.
The resdue laught and so in heaven there was no talke a while,
But of this Pageant how the Smith the lovers did beguile.
     Dame Venus highly stomacking this great displeasure, thought
     To be revenged on the part by whome the spight was wrought.   230
And like as he hir secret loves and meetings had bewrayd,
So she with wound of raging love his guerdon to him payd.
What now avayles (Hyperions sonne) thy forme and beautie bright?
What now avayle thy glistring eyes with cleare and piercing sight?
For thou that with thy gleames art wont all countries for to burne,   235
Art burnt thy selfe with other gleames that serve not for thy turne.
And thou that oughtst thy cherefull looke on all things for to shew
Alonly on Leucothoe doste now the same bestow.
Thou fastnest on that Maide alone the eyes that thou doste owe
To all the worlde. Sometime more rathe thou risest in the East,   240
Sometime againe thou makste it late before thou fall to reast.
And for desire to looke on hir, thou often doste prolong
Our winter nightes. And in thy light thou faylest eke among.
The fancie of thy faultie minde infectes thy feeble sight,
And so thou makste mens hearts afrayde by daunting of thy light,   245
Thou looxte not pale bycause the globe of Phebe is betweene
The Earth and thee: but love doth cause this colour to be seene.
Thou lovest this Leucothoe so far above all other,
That neyther now for Clymene, for Rhodos, nor the mother

---

213 *featly:* cleverly
215 *handwarpe:* handywarp, a sixteenth-
    century cloth; *oofe:* woof
219 *haunted:* frequented
229 *stomacking:* resenting
240 *rathe:* early
245 *daunting:* subduing

Of Circe, nor for Clytie (who at that present tyde
Rejected from thy companie did for thy love abide
Most grievous torments in hir heart) thou seemest for to care.
Thou mindest hir so much that all the rest forgotten are.
Hir mother was Eurynome of all the fragrant clime
Of Arabie esteemde the flowre of beautie in hir time.
But when hir daughter came to age the daughter past the mother
As far in beautie, as before the mother past all other.
Hir father was king Orchamus and rulde the publike weale
Of Persey, counted by descent the seventh from auncient Bele.
Far underneath the Westerne clyme of Hesperus doe runne
The pastures of the firie steedes that draw the golden Sunne.
There are they fed with Ambrosie in stead of grasse all night
Which doth refresh their werie limmes and keepeth them in plight
To beare their dailie labor out: now while the steedes there take
Their heavenly foode and night by turne his timely course doth make,
The God disguised in the shape of Queene Eurynome
Doth prease within the chamber doore of faire Leucothoe
His lover, whome amid twelve Maides he found by candlelight
Yet spinning on hir little Rocke, and went me to hir right.
And kissing hir as mothers use to kisse their daughters deare,
Saide: Maydes, withdraw your selves a while and sit not listning here.
I have a secret thing to talke. The Maides avoyde eche one,
The God then being with his love in chamber all alone,
Said: I am he that metes the yeare, that all things doe beholde,
By whome the Earth doth all things see, the Eye of all the worlde.
Trust me I am in love with thee. The Ladie was so nipt
With sodaine feare that from hir hands both rocke and spindle slipt.
Hir feare became hir wondrous well. He made no mo delayes,
But turned to his proper shape and tooke hys glistring rayes.
The damsell being sore abasht at this so straunge a sight,
And overcome with sodaine feare to see the God so bright,
Did make no outcrie nor no noyse, but helde hir pacience still,
And suffred him by forced powre his pleasure to fulfill.
    Hereat did Clytie sore repine. For she beyond all measure
    Was then enamoured of the Sunne: and stung with this
                           displeasure
That he another Leman had, for verie spight and yre

250 *tyde:* time
263 *plight:* condition
267 *prease:* press

269 *Rocke:* distaff
272 *avoyde:* withdraw

She playes the blab, and doth defame Leucothoe to hir Syre.
He cruell and unmercifull would no excuse accept,
But holding up hir handes to heaven when tenderly she wept,
And said it was the Sunne that did the deede against hir will: 290
Yet like a savage beast full bent his daughter for to spill,
He put hir deepe in delved ground, and on hir bodie laide
A huge great heape of heavie sand. The Sunne full yll appaide
Did with his beames disperse the sand and made an open way
To bring thy buried face to light, but such a weight there lay   295
Upon thee, that thou couldst not raise thine hand aloft againe,
And so a corse both voide of bloud and life thou didst remaine.
There never chaunst since Phaetons fire a thing that grievde so sore
The ruler of the winged steedes as this did. And therfore
He did attempt if by the force and vertue of his ray   300
He might againe to lively heate hir frozen limmes convay.
But forasmuch as destenie so great attempts denies,
He sprincles both the corse it selfe and place wherein it lyes
With fragrant Nectar. And therewith bewayling much his chaunce
Sayd: Yet above the starrie skie thou shalt thy selfe advaunce.   305
Anon the body in this heavenly liquor steeped well
Did melt, and moisted all the earth with sweete and pleasant smell.
And by and by first taking roote among the cloddes within
By little and by little did with growing top begin
A pretie spirke of Frankinsence above the Tumbe to win.   310
        Although that Clytie might excuse hir sorrow by hir love
        And seeme that so to play the blab hir sorrow did hir move,
Yet would the Author of the light resort to hir no more
But did withholde the pleasant sportes of Venus usde before.
The Nymph not able of hir selfe the franticke fume to stay,   315
With restlesse care and pensivenesse did pine hir selfe away.
Bareheaded on the bare cold ground with flaring haire unkempt
She sate abrode both night and day: and clearly did exempt
Hirselfe by space of thrise three dayes from sustnance and repast
Save only dewe and save hir teares with which she brake hir fast.   320
And in that while she never rose but stared on the Sunne
And ever turnde hir face to his as he his corse did runne.
Hir limmes stacke fast within the ground, and all hir upper part
Did to a pale ashcolourd herbe cleane voyde of bloud convart.

291 *spill:* kill
293 *appaide:* satisfied
298 *chaunst:* happened

310 *spirke:* sprout, shoot
317 *flaring:* spreading, waving

The floure whereof part red part white beshadowed with a blew   325
Most like a Violet in the shape hir countnance overgrew.
And now (though fastned with a roote) she turnes hir to the Sunne
And keepes (in shape of herbe) the love with which she first begunne.
    She made an ende: and at hir tale all wondred: some denide
    Hir saying to be possible: and other some replide   330
That such as are in deede true Gods may all things worke at will:
But Bacchus is not any such. Thys arguing once made still,
To tell hir tale as others had Alcithoes turne was come.
Who with hir shettle shooting through hir web within the Loome,
Said: Of the shepeheird Daphnyes love of Ida whom erewhile   335
A jealouse Nymph (bicause he did with Lemans hir beguile)
For anger turned to a stone (such furie love doth sende:)
I will not speake: it is to knowe: ne yet I doe entende
To tell how Scython variably digressing from his kinde,
Was sometime woman, sometime man, as liked best his minde.   340
And Celmus also wyll I passe, who for bicause he cloong
Most faithfully to Jupiter when Jupiter was yoong,
Is now become an Adamant. So will I passe this howre
To shew you how the Curets were engendred of a showre:
Or how that Crocus and his love faire Smylax turned were   345
To little flowres. With pleasant newes your mindes now will I chere.
Learne why the fountaine Salmacis diffamed is of yore,
Why with his waters overstrong it weakeneth men so sore
That whoso bathes him there commes thence a perfect man no more.
The operation of this Well is knowne to every wight.   350
But few can tell the cause thereof, the which I will recite.
    The waternymphes did nurce a sonne of Mercuries in Ide
    Begot on Venus, in whose face such beautie did abide,
As well therein his father both and mother might be knowne,
Of whome he also tooke his name. As soone as he was growne   355
To fiftene yeares of age, he left the Countrie where he dwelt
And Ida that had fostered him. The pleasure that he felt
To travell Countries, and to see straunge rivers with the state
Of forren landes, all painfulnesse of travell did abate.
He travelde through the lande of Lycie to Carie that doth bound   360
Next unto Lycia. There he saw a Poole which to the ground
Was Christall cleare. No fennie sedge, no barren reeke, no reede
Nor rush with pricking poynt was there, nor other moorish weede.

338 *ne:* nor
343 *Adamant:* steel, diamond, magnet
361 *ground:* bottom

362 *reeke:* wrack, seaweed
363 *moorish:* marshy

The water was so pure and shere a man might well have seene
And numbred all the gravell stones that in the bottome beene.   365
The utmost borders from the brim environd were with clowres
Beclad with herbes ay fresh and greene and pleasant smelling flowres.
A Nymph did haunt this goodly Poole: but such a Nymph as neyther
To hunt, to run, nor yet to shoote, had any kinde of pleasure.
Of all the Waterfairies she alonly was unknowne   370
To swift Diana. As the bruit of fame abrode hath blowne,
Hir sisters oftentimes would say: take lightsome Dart or bow,
And in some painefull exercise thine ydle time bestow.
But never could they hir persuade to runne, to shoote or hunt,
Or any other exercise as Phebes knightes are wont.   375
Sometime hir faire welformed limbes she batheth in hir spring:
Sometime she downe hir golden haire with Boxen combe doth bring.
And at the water as a glasse she taketh counsell ay
How every thing becommeth hir. Erewhile in fine aray
On soft sweete hearbes or soft greene leaves hir selfe she nicely layes: 380
Erewhile againe a gathering flowres from place to place she strayes.
And (as it chaunst) the selfesame time she was a sorting gayes
To make a Poisie, when she first the yongman did espie,
And in beholding him desirde to have his companie.
But though she thought she stoode on thornes untill she went to him: 385
Yet went she not before she had bedect hir neat and trim,
And pride and peerd upon hir clothes that nothing sat awrie,
And framde hir countnance as might seeme most amrous to the eie.
    Which done she thus begon: O childe most worthie for to bee
    Estemde and taken for a God, if (as thou seemste to mee)   390
Thou be a God, to Cupids name thy beautie doth agree.
Or if thou be a mortall wight, right happie folke are they,
By whome thou camste into this worlde, right happy is (I say)
Thy mother and thy sister too (if any bee): good hap
That woman had that was thy Nurce and gave thy mouth hir pap.   395
But farre above all other, far more blist than these is shee
Whome thou vouchsafest for thy wife and bedfellow for to bee.
Now if thou have alredy one, let me by stelth obtaine
That which shall pleasure both of us. Or if thou doe remaine
A Maiden free from wedlocke bonde, let me then be thy spouse,   400

366 *clowres:* sward, grassy ground
373 *painefull:* arduous
382 *gayes:* gay flowers
383 *Poisie:* posy, bouquet
387 *pride:* looked closely

389 *childe:* well-born youth
392 *wight:* man
394 *hap:* fortune
400 *Maiden:* unmarried person

And let us in the bridelie bed our selves togither rouse.
    This sed, the Nymph did hold hir peace, and therewithall the boy
    Waxt red: he wist not what love was: and sure it was a joy
To see it how exceeding well his blushing him became.
For in his face the colour fresh appeared like the same   405
That is in Apples which doe hang upon the Sunnie side:
Or Ivorie shadowed with a red: or such as is espide
Of white and scarlet colours mixt appearing in the Moone
When folke in vaine with sounding brasse would ease unto hir done.
When at the last the Nymph desirde most instantly but this,   410
As to his sister brotherly to give hir there a kisse,
And therewithall was clasping him about the Ivorie necke:
Leave off (quoth he) or I am gone and leave thee at a becke
With all thy trickes. Then Salmacis began to be afraide,
And, To your pleasure leave I free this place, my friend, she sayde.   415
Wyth that she turnes hir backe as though she would have gone hir way:
But evermore she looketh backe, and (closely as she may)
She hides hir in a bushie queach, where kneeling on hir knee
She alwayes hath hir eye on him. He as a childe and free,
And thinking not that any wight had watched what he did   420
Romes up and downe the pleasant Mede: and by and by amid
The flattring waves he dippes his feete, no more but first the sole
And to the ancles afterward both feete he plungeth whole.
And for to make the matter short, he tooke so great delight
In coolenesse of the pleasant spring, that streight he stripped quight   425
His garments from his tender skin. When Salmacis behilde
His naked beautie, such strong pangs so ardently hir hilde,
That utterly she was astraught. And even as Phebus beames
Against a myrrour pure and clere rebound with broken gleames:
Even so hir eys did sparcle fire. Scarce could she tarience make: 430
Scarce could she any time delay hir pleasure for to take:
She wolde have run, and in hir armes embraced him streight way:
She was so far beside hir selfe, that scarsly could she stay.
He clapping with his hollow hands against his naked sides,
Into the water lithe and baine with armes displayed glydes.   435
And rowing with his hands and legges swimmes in the water cleare:
Through which his bodie faire and white doth glistringly appeare,
As if a man an Ivorie Image or a Lillie white

---

401 *rouse:* (1) excite, (2) rest
409 *done:* do
413 *at a becke:* in a flash

418 *queach:* thicket
428 *astraught:* distraught, distracted
435 *baine:* limber; *displayed:* extended

Should overlay or close with glasse that were most pure and bright.
    The prize is won (cride Salmacis aloud) he is mine owne.   440
    And therewithall in all post hast she having lightly throwne
Hir garments off, flew to the Poole and cast hir thereinto
And caught him fast between hir armes, for ought that he could doe:
Yea maugre all his wrestling and his struggling to and fro,
She held him still, and kissed him a hundred times and mo.   445
And willde he nillde he with hir handes she toucht his naked brest:
And now on this side now on that (for all he did resist
And strive to wrest him from hir gripes) she clung unto him fast:
And wound about him like a Snake which snatched up in hast
And being by the Prince of Birdes borne lightly up aloft,   450
Doth writhe hir selfe about his necke and griping talants oft:
And cast hir taile about his wings displayed in the winde:
Or like as Ivie runnes on trees about the utter rinde:
Or as the Crabfish having caught his enmy in the Seas,
Doth claspe him in on every side with all his crooked cleas.   455
    But Atlas Nephew still persistes, and utterly denies
    The Nymph to have hir hoped sport: she urges him likewise.
And pressing him with all hir weight, fast cleaving to him still,
Strive, struggle, wrest and writhe (she said) thou froward boy thy fill:
Doe what thou canst thou shalt not scape. Ye Goddes of Heaven agree 460
That this same wilfull boy and I may never parted bee.
The Gods were pliant to hir boone. The bodies of them twaine
Were mixt and joyned both in one. To both them did remaine
One countnance: like as if a man should in one barke beholde
Two twigges both growing into one and still togither holde.   465
Even so when through hir hugging and hir grasping of the tother
The members of them mingled were and fastned both togither,
They were not any lenger two: but (as it were) a toy
Of double shape. Ye could not say it was a perfect boy
Nor perfect wench: it seemed both and none of both to beene.   470
Now when Hermaphroditus saw how in the water sheene
To which he entred in a man, his limmes were weakened so
That out fro thence but halfe a man he was compelde to go,
He lifteth up his hands and said (but not with manly reere):
O noble father Mercurie, and Venus mother deere,   475
This one petition graunt your son which both your names doth beare,

444 *maugre:* in spite of   468 *toy:* curiosity
455 *cleas:* claws   471 *sheene:* bright
462 *boone:* prayer   474 *reere:* sound

That whoso commes within this Well may so be weakened there,
That of a man but halfe a man he may fro thence retire.
Both Parentes moved with the chaunce did stablish this desire
The which their doubleshaped sonne had made: and thereupon   480
Infected with an unknowne strength the sacred spring anon.
    Their tales did ende and Mineus daughters still their businesse plie
    In spight of Bacchus whose high feast they breake contemptuously.
When on the sodaine (seeing nought) they heard about them round
Of tubbish Timbrels perfectly a hoarse and jarring sound,   485
With shraming shalmes and gingling belles, and furthermore they felt
A cent of Saffron and of Myrrhe that verie hotly smelt.
And (which a man would ill beleve) the web they had begun
Immediatly waxt fresh and greene, the flaxe the which they spun
Did flourish full of Ivie leaves. And part thereof did run   490
Abrode in Vines. The threede it selfe in braunches forth did spring.
Yong burgeons full of clustred grapes their Distaves forth did bring.
And as the web they wrought was dide a deepe darke purple hew,
Even so upon the painted grapes the selfesame colour grew.
The day was spent, and now was come the time which neyther night 495
Nor day, but even the bound of both a man may terme of right.
The house at sodaine seemde to shake, and all about it shine
With burning lampes, and glittering fires to flash before their eyen,
And Likenesses of ougly beastes with gastfull noyses yeld.
For feare whereof in smokie holes the sisters were compeld   500
To hide their heades, one here and there another, for to shun
The glistring light. And while they thus in corners blindly run,
Upon their little pretie limmes a fine crispe filme there goes,
And slender finnes in stead of handes their shortned armes enclose.
But how they lost their former shape of certaintie to know   505
The darknesse would not suffer them. No feathers on them grow,
And yet with shere and velume wings they hover from the ground
And when they goe about to speake they make but little sound,
According as their bodies give, bewayling their despight
By chirping shirlly to themselves. In houses they delight   510
And not in woods: detesting day they flitter towards night:
Wherethrough they of the Evening late in Latin take their name,
And we in English language Backes or Reermice call the same.
    Then Bacchus name was reverenced through all the Theban coast,

486 *shraming:* screaming; *shalmes:* shawmes,   507 *velume:* vellum, fine parchment
   oboe-like instruments   510 *shirlly:* shrilly
499 *gastfull:* dreadful   513 *Backes:* bats; *Reermice:* bats

And Ino of hir Nephewes powre made every where great boast. 515
Of Cadmus daughters she alone no sorowes tasted had,
Save only that hir sisters haps perchaunce had made hir sad.
Now Juno noting how she waxt both proud and full of scorne,
As well by reason of the sonnes and daughters she had borne,
As also that she was advaunst by mariage in that towne   520
To Athamas, King Aeolus sonne, a Prince of great renowne,
But chiefly that hir sisters sonne who nourced was by hir
Was then exalted for a God: began thereat to stir,
And freating at it in hirselfe said: Coulde this harlots burd
Transforme the Lydian watermen, and drowne them in the foord? 525
And make the mother teare the guttes in pieces of hir sonne?
And Mineus al three daughters clad with wings, bicause they sponne
Whiles others howling up and down like frantick folke did ronne?
And can I Juno nothing else save sundrie woes bewaile?
Is that sufficient? can my powre no more than so availe?   530
He teaches me what way to worke. A man may take (I see)
Example at his enmies hand the wiser for to bee.
He shewes inough and overmuch the force of furious wrath
By Pentheys death: why should not Ine be taught to tread the path
The which hir sisters heretofore and kinred troden hath?   535
    There is a steepe and irksome way obscure with shadow fell
    Of balefull yewgh, all sad and still, that leadeth downe to hell.
The foggie Styx doth breath up mistes: and downe this way doe wave
The ghostes of persons lately dead and buried in the grave.
Continuall colde and gastly feare possesse this queachie plot   540
On eyther side: the siely Ghost new parted knoweth not
The way that doth directly leade him to the Stygian Citie
Or where blacke Pluto keepes his Court that never sheweth pitie.
A thousand wayes, a thousand gates that always open stand,
This Citie hath: and as the Sea the streames of all the lande   545
Doth swallow in his gredie gulfe, and yet is never full:
Even so that place devoureth still and hideth in his gull
The soules and ghostes of all the world: and though that nere so many
Come thither, yet the place is voyd as if there were not any.
The ghostes without flesh, bloud, or bones, there wander to and fro, 550
Of which some haunt the judgement place: and other come and go
To Plutos Court: and some frequent the former trades and Artes

---

517 *haps:* fortunes   541 *siely:* poor, helpless
524 *burd:* young girl   547 *gull:* gullet
525 *watermen:* sailors

The which they used in their life: and some abide the smartes
And torments for their wickednesse and other yll desartes.
  So cruell hate and spightfull wrath did boyle in Junos brest, 555
  That in the high and noble Court of Heaven she coulde not rest:
But that she needes must hither come: whose feet no sooner toucht
The thresholde, but it gan to quake. And Cerberus erst coucht
Start sternely up with three fell heades which barked all togither.
She callde the daughters of the night, the cruell furies, thither: 560
They sate a kembing foule blacke Snakes from off their filthie heare
Before the dungeon doore, the place where Caitives punisht were,
The which was made of Adamant. When in the darke in part
They knew Queene Juno, by and by upon their feete they start.
There Titius stretched out (at least) nine acres full in length, 565
Did with his bowels feede a Grype that tare them out by strength.
The water fled from Tantalus that toucht his neather lip,
And Apples hanging over him did ever from him slip.
There also laborde Sisyphus that drave against the hill
A rolling stone that from the top came tumbling downeward still. 570
Ixion on his restlesse wheele to which his limmes were bound
Did flie and follow both at once in turning ever round.
And Danaus daughters forbicause they did their cousins kill,
Drew water into running tubbes which evermore did spill.
  When Juno with a louring looke had vewde them all through-
                  out, 575
  And on Ixion specially before the other rout,
She turnes from him to Sisyphus, and with an angry cheere
Sayes: Wherefore should this man endure continuall penance here,
And Athamas his brother reigne in welth and pleasure free
Who through his pride hath ay disdainde my husband Jove and mee? 580
And therewithall she poured out th'occasion of hir hate,
And why she came and what she would. She would that Cadmus state
Should with the ruine of his house be brought to swyft decay,
And that to mischiefe Athamas the Fiendes should force some way.
She biddes, she prayes, she promises, and all is with a breth, 585
And moves the furies earnestly: and as these things she seth,
The hatefull Hag Tisiphone with horie ruffled heare,
Removing from hir face the Snakes that loosely dangled there,
Sayd thus: Madame there is no neede long circumstance to make.

---

554 *desartes:* deservings   576 *rout:* crowd
562 *Caitives:* wretches   577 *cheere:* expression
566 *Grype:* vulture

Suppose your will already done. This lothsome place forsake,   590
And to the holsome Ayre of heaven your selfe agayne retire.
Queene Juno went right glad away with graunt of hir desire.
And as she woulde have entred heaven, the Ladie Iris came
And purged hir with streaming drops. Anon upon the same
The furious Fiende Tisiphone doth cloth hir out of hand   595
In garment streaming gorie bloud, and taketh in hir hand
A burning Cresset steepte in bloud, and girdeth hir about
With wreathed Snakes and so goes forth. And at hir going out,
Feare, terror, grief and pensivenesse for companie she tooke,
And also madnesse with his flaight, and gastly staring looke.   600
        Within the house of Athamas no sooner foote she set,
        But that the postes began to quake and doores looke blacke as Jet.
The sonne withdrew him, Athamas and eke his wife were cast
With ougly sightes in such a feare, that out of doores agast
They would have fled. There stoode the Fiend, and stopt their passage
                                                                out,   605
And splaying forth hir filthie armes beknit with Snakes about,
Did tosse and wave hir hatefull head. The swarme of scaled snakes
Did make an irksome noyse to heare as she hir tresses shakes.
About hir shoulders some did craule: some trayling downe hir brest
Did hisse and spit out poyson greene, and spirt with tongues infest.   610
        Then from amyd hir haire two snakes with venymd hand she drew
        Of which shee one at Athamas and one at Ino threw.
The snakes did craule about their breasts, inspiring in their heart
Most grievous motions of the minde: the bodie had no smart
Of any wound: it was the minde that felt the cruell stings.   615
A poyson made in Syrup wise, shee also with hir brings.
The filthie fome of Cerberus, the casting of the Snake
Echidna, bred among the Fennes about the Stygian Lake:
Desire of gadding foorth abroad: forgetfulnesse of minde:
Delight in mischiefe: woodnesse: teares: and purpose whole inclinde   620
To cruell murther: all the which shee did together grinde:
And mingling them with new shed bloud had boyled them in brasse,
And stird them with a Hemblock stalke. Now whyle that Athamas
And Ino stood and quakte for feare, this poyson ranke and fell
Shee tourned into both their breastes and made their heartes to swell. 625
Then whisking often round about hir head hir balefull brand,

595 *out of hand:* immediately   610 *infest:* hostile
600 *flaight:* fright   620 *woodnesse:* rage, insanity
606 *splaying:* stretching   626 *brand:* torch

She made it soone by gathering winde to kindle in hir hand.
Thus as it were in triumph wise accomplishing hir hest,
To Duskie Plutos emptie Realme shee gettes hir home to rest,
And putteth off the snarled Snakes that girded in hir brest.   630
        Immediatly King Aeolus sonne starke madde comes crying out
        Through all the court: What meane yee Sirs? why go yee not about
To pitch our toyles within this chace? I saw even nowe here ran
A Lyon with hir two yong whelpes. And there withall he gan
To chase his wyfe as if in deede shee had a Lyon beene   635
And lyke a Bedlem boystouslie he snatcheth from betweene
The mothers armes his little babe Loearchus smyling on him
And reaching foorth his preatie armes, and floong him fiercely from him
A twice or thrice as from a slyng: and dasht his tender head
Against a hard and rugged stone until he sawe him dead.   640
The wretched mother (whither griefe did move hir thereunto
Or that the poyson spred within did force hir so to doe)
Howld out and frantikly with scattered haire about hir eares
And with hir little Melicert whome hastely shee beares
In naked armes she cryeth out, Hoe Bacchus. At the name   645
Of Bacchus Juno gan to laugh and scorning sayde in game:
This guerden loe thy foster child requiteth for the same.
There hangs a rocke about the Sea the foote whereof is eate
So hollow with the saltish waves which on the same doe beate,
That like a house it keepeth off the moysting showers of rayne.   650
The toppe is rough and shootes his front amiddes the open mayne.
Dame Ino (madnesse made hir strong) did climb this cliffe anon
And headlong downe (without regarde of hurt that hoong thereon)
Did throwe hir burden and hir selfe, the water where shee dasht
In sprincling upwarde glisterd red. But Venus sore abasht   655
At this hir Neeces great mischaunce without offence or fault,
Hir Uncle gently thus bespake: O ruler of the hault
And swelling Seas, O noble Neptune whose dominion large
Extendeth to the Heaven, whereof the mightie Jove hath charge,
The thing is great for which I sue. But shewe thou for my sake   660
Some mercie on my wretched friends whome in thine endlesse lake
Thou seest tossed to and fro. Admit thou them among
The Goddes. Of right even here to mee some favour doth belong
At least wise if amid the Sea engendred erst I were
Of Froth, as of the which yet still my pleasaunt name I beare.   665

628 *hest:* command   636 *Bedlem:* lunatic
630 *girded:* started, sprung   657 *hault:* haughty

Neptunus graunted hir request, and by and by bereft them
Of all that ever mortall was. Insted wherof he left them
A hault and stately majestie: and altring them in hew
With shape and names most meete for Goddes he did them both endew.
Leucothoe was the mothers name, Palemon was the sonne.   670
     The Thebane Ladies following hir as fast as they could runne,
     Did of hir feete perceive the print upon the utter stone.
And taking it for certaine signe that both were dead and gone,
In making mone for Cadmus house, they wrang their hands and tare
Their haire, and rent their clothes, and railde on Juno out of square,   675
As nothing just, but more outragious farre than did behove
In so revenging of hir selfe upon hir husbands love.
The Goddesse Juno could not beare their railing. And in faith:
You also will I make to be as witnesses (she sayth)
Of my outragious crueltie. And so shee did in deede.   680
For shee that loved Ino best was following hir with speede
Into the Sea. But as shee would hir selfe have downeward cast,
She could not stirre, but to the rock as nailed sticked fast.
The second as shee knockt hir breast, did feele hir armes wax stiffe.
Another as shee stretched out hir hands upon the cliffe,   685
Was made a stone, and there stoode still ay stretching forth hir hands
Into the water as before. And as an other standes
A tearing of hir ruffled lockes, hir fingers hardened were
And fastned to hir frisled toppe still tearing of hir heare,
And looke what gesture eche of them was taken in that tide,   690
Even in the same transformde to stones, they fastned did abide.
And some were altered into birds which Cadmies called bee
And in that goolfe with flittering wings still to and fro doe flee.
     Nought knoweth Cadmus that his daughter and hir little childe
     Admitted were among the Goddes that rule the surges wilde.   695
Compellde with griefe and great mishappes that had ensewd togither,
And straunge foretokens often seene since first his comming thither,
He utterly forsakes his towne the which he builded had,
As though the fortune of the place so hardly him bestad,
And not his owne. And fleeting long like pilgrims, at the last   700
Upon the coast of Illirie his wife and he were cast.
Where ny forpind with cares and yeares, while of the chaunces past
Upon their house, and of their toyles and former travails tane

675 *out of square:* out of order   699 *bestad:* availed, beset
692 *Cadmies:* descendants of Cadmus   702 *forpind:* pined away

They sadly talkt betweene themselves: Was my speare head the bane
Of that same ougly Snake of Mars (quoth Cadmus) when I fled   705
From Sidon? or did I his teeth in ploughed pasture spred?
If for the death of him the Goddes so cruell vengeaunce take,
Drawen out in length upon my wombe then traile I like a snake.
He had no sooner sayde the worde but that he gan to glide
Upon his belly like a Snake. And on his hardened side   710
He felt the scales new budding out, the which was wholy fret
With speccled droppes of blacke and gray as thicke as could be set.
He falleth groveling on his breast, and both his shankes doe growe
In one round spindle Bodkinwise with sharpned point below.
His armes as yet remayned still: his armes that did remayne,   715
He stretched out, and sayde with teares that plentuously did raine
Adowne his face, which yet did keepe the native fashion sownd:
Come hither wyfe, come hither wight most wretched on the ground,
And whyle that ought of mee remaynes vouchsafe to touche the same.
Come take mee by the hand as long as hand may have his name,   720
Before this snakish shape doe whole my body over runne.
He would have spoken more when sodainely his tongue begunne
To split in two and speache did fayle: and as he did attempt
To make his mone, he hist: for nature now had cleane exempt
All other speach. His wretched wyfe hir naked stomack beete   725
And cryde: What meaneth this? deare Cadmus, where are now thy
                                                            feete?
Where are thy shoulders and thy handes? thy hew and manly face?
With all the other things that did thy princely person grace
Which nowe I overpasse? But why yee Goddes doe you delay
My bodie into lyke misshape of Serpent to convay?   730
When this was spoken, Cadmus lickt his wyfe about the lippes:
And (as a place with which he was acquaynted well) he slippes
Into hir boosome, lovingly embracing hir, and cast
Himselfe about hir necke, as oft he had in tyme forepast.
Such as were there (their folke were there) were flaighted at the sight, 735
For by and by they sawe their neckes did glister slicke and bright.
And on their snakish heades grew crests: and finally they both
Were into verie Dragons tournd, and foorth together goth
T'one trayling by the tothers side, untill they gaynd a wood,
The which direct against the place where as they were then stood. 740
And now remembring what they were themselves in tymes forepast,

704 *bane:* destruction   724 *exempt:* taken away
711 *fret:* variegated   735 *flaighted:* frightened

They neyther shonne nor hurten men with stinging nor with blast.
 But yet a comfort to them both in this their altred hew
 Became that noble impe of theirs that Indie did subdew,
Whom al Achaia worshipped with temples builded new.   745
All only Acrise, Abas sonne, (though of the selfesame stocke)
Remaind, who out of Argos walles unkindly did him locke,
And moved wilfull warre against his Godhead: thinking that
There was not any race of Goddes, for he beleved not
That Persey was the sonne of Jove: or that he was conceyved   750
By Danae of golden shower through which shee was deceived.
But yet ere long (such present force hath truth) he doth repent
As well his great impietie against God Bacchus meant,
As also that he did disdaine his Nephew for to knowe.
But Bacchus now full gloriously himselfe in Heaven doth showe.   755
And Persey bearing in his hand the monster Gorgons head,
That famous spoyle which here and there with snakish haire was spread,
Doth beat the ayre with wavyng wings. And as he overflew
The Lybicke sandes, the droppes of bloud that from the head did sew
Of Gorgon being new cut off, upon the ground did fal.   760
Which taking them (and as it were conceyving therwithall)
Engendred sundrie Snakes and wormes: by meanes wherof that clyme
Did swarme with Serpents ever since, even to this present tyme.
 From thence he lyke a watrie cloud was caried with the weather,
 Through all the heaven, now here, now there as light as any
                feather.   765
And from aloft he viewes the earth that underneath doth lie,
And swiftly over all the worlde doth in conclusion flie,
Three times the chilling Beares, three times the Crabbes fel cleas he saw:
Oft times to Weast, oftimes to East did drive him many a flaw.
Now at such time as unto rest the sonne began to drawe,   770
Bicause he did not thinke it good to be abroad all night,
Within King Atlas western Realme he ceased from his flight,
Requesting that a little space of rest enjoy he might,
Untill such tyme as Lucifer should bring the morning gray,
And morning bring the lightsome Sunne that guides the cherefull
                 day.   775
This Atlas, Japets Nephewe, was a man that did excell
In stature everie other wight that in the worlde did dwell.
The utmost coast of all the earth and all that Sea wherein

---

744 *impe:* offspring   768 *fel:* fierce, cruel
759 *sew:* drain, ooze

The tyred steedes and wearied Wayne of Phoebus dived bin,
Were in subjection to this King. A thousande flockes of sheepe, 780
A thousand heirdes of Rother beastes he in his fields did keepe:
And not a neighbor did anoy his ground by dwelling nie.
To him the wandring Persey thus his language did applie:
If high renowne of royall race thy noble heart may move,
I am the sonne of Jove himselfe: or if thou more approve 785
The valiant deedes and hault exploytes, thou shalt perceive in mee
Such doings as deserve with prayse extolled for to bee.
I pray thee of thy courtesie receive mee as thy guest,
And let mee only for this night within thy palace rest.
King Atlas called straight to minde an auncient prophesie 790
Made by Parnassian Themys, which this sentence did implie:
The time shall one day, Atlas, come in which thy golden tree
Shall of hir fayre and precious fruite dispoyld and robbed bee.
And he shall be the sonne of Jove that shall enjoy the pray.
For feare hereof he did enclose his Orchard everie way 795
With mightie hilles, and put an ougly Dragon in the same
To keepe it. Further he forbad that any straunger came
Within his Realme, and to this knight he sayde presumtuouslie:
Avoyd my land, onlesse thou wilt by utter perill trie
That all thy glorious actes whereof thou doest so loudly lie 800
And Jove thy father be too farre to helpe thee at thy neede.
To these his wordes he added force, and went about in deede
To drive him out by strength of hand. To speake was losse of winde
For neyther could intreating faire nor stoutnesse tourne his minde.
Well then (quoth Persey) sith thou doest mine honour set so light, 805
Take here a present: and with that he turnes away his sight,
And from his left side drewe mee out Medusas lothly head.
As huge and big as Atlas was he tourned in that stead
Into a mountaine: into trees his beard and locks did passe:
His hands and shoulders made the ridge: that part which lately was 810
His head, became the highest top of all the hill: his bones
Were turnd to stones: and therewithall he grew mee all at once
Beyond all measure up in heighth (for so God thought it best)
So farre that Heaven with all the starres did on his shoulders rest.
    In endlesse prison by that time had Aeolus lockt the wind 815
    And now the cheerely morning starre that putteth folke in mind
To rise about their daylie worke shone brightly in the skie.

779 *Wayne:* chariot   808 *stead:* place
781 *Rother:* of the ox family

Then Persey unto both his feete did streight his feathers tie
And girt his Woodknife to his side, and from the earth did stie.
And leaving nations nomberlesse beneath him everie way   820
At last upon King Cepheyes fields in Aethiop did he stay.
Where cleane against all right and law by Joves commaundement
Andromad for hir mothers tongue did suffer punishment.
Whome to a rocke by both the armes when fastned hee had seene,
He would have thought of Marble stone shee had some image beene, 825
But that hir tresses to and fro the whisking winde did blowe,
And trickling teares warme from hir eyes adowne hir cheeks did flow,
Unwares hereat gan secret sparkes within his breast to glow.
His wits were straught at sight thereof and ravisht in such wise,
That how to hover with his wings he scarsly could devise.   830
As soone as he had stayd himselfe: O Ladie faire (quoth hee)
Not worthie of such bands as these, but such wherewith we see
Togither knit in lawfull bed the earnest lovers bee,
I pray thee tell mee what thy selfe and what this lande is named
And wherefore thou dost weare these Chains. The Ladie ill ashamed 835
Was at the sodaine striken domb: and lyke a fearfull maid
Shee durst not speake unto a man. Had not hir handes beene staid
She would have hid hir bashfull face. Howbeit as she might
With great abundance of hir teares shee stopped up hir sight
But when that Persey oftentimes was earnestly in hand   840
To learne this matter, for bicause shee would not seeme to stand
In stubborne silence of hir faultes, shee tolde him what the land
And what she hight: and how hir mother for hir beauties sake
Through pride did unadvisedly too much upon hir take.
And ere shee full had made an ende, the water gan to rore: 845
An ougly monster from the deepe was making to the shore
Which bare the Sea before his breast. The Virgin shrieked out.
Hir father and hir mother both stood mourning thereabout,
In wretched ease both twaine, but not so wretched as the maid
Who wrongly for hir mothers fault the bitter raunsome paid.   850
They brought not with them any help: but (as the time and cace
Requird) they wept and wrang their hands, and streightly did embrace
Hir bodie fastened to the rock. Then Persey them bespake,
And sayde: The time may serve too long this sorrow for to make:
But time of helpe must eyther now or never else be take.   855
Now if I, Persey, sonne of hir whome in hir fathers towre

819 *stie:* rise   843 *hight:* was called
829 *straught:* distraught

The mightie Jove begat with childe in shape of golden showre,
Who cut off ougly Gorgons head bespred with snakish heare,
And in the ayre durst trust these winges my body for to beare,
Perchaunce should save your daughters life, I think ye should as then 860
Accept mee for your sonne in lawe before all other men.
To these great thewes (by the help of God) I purpose for to adde
A just desert in helping hir that is so hard bestadde.
I covenaunt with you by my force and manhod for to save hir,
Conditionly that to my wife in recompence I have hir.   865
    Hir parents tooke his offer streight: for who would sticke thereat?
    And praid him faire, and promisde him that for performing that
They would endow him with the ryght of al their Realme beeside.
Like as a Gally with hir nose doth cut the waters wide,
Enforced by the sweating armes of Rowers wyth the tide   870
Even so the monster with his brest did beare the waves aside,
And was now come as neere the rocke as well a man myght fling
Amid the pure and vacant aire a pellet from a sling.
When on the sodaine Persey pusht his foote against the ground,
And stied upward to the clouds his shadow did rebound   875
Upon the sea: the beast ran fierce upon the passing shade.
And as an Egle when he sees a Dragon in a glade
Lie beaking of his blewish backe against the sunnie rayes,
Doth seize upon him unbeware, and with his talants layes
Sure holde upon his scalie necke lest writhing back his head   880
His cruell teeth might doe him harme: so Persey in that stead
Discending downe the ayre amaine with all his force and might
Did seize upon the monsters backe: and underneath the right
Finne hard unto the verie hilt his hooked sworde did smight.
The monster being wounded sore did sometime leape aloft,   885
And sometime under water dive, bestirring him full oft
As doth a chaufed Boare beset with barking Dogges about.
But Persey with his lightsome wings still keeping him without
The monsters reach, with hooked sword doth sometime hew his back
Where as the hollow scales give way: and sometime he doth hacke   890
The ribbes on both his maled sides: and sometime he doth wound
His spindle tayle where into fish it growes most smal and round.
The Whale at Persey from his mouth such waves of water cast,
Bemixed with the purple bloud, that all bedreint at last

---

862 *thewes:* endowments, attributes   878 *beaking:* projecting
863 *bestadde:* beset   894 *bedreint:* bedrenched
865 *Conditionly:* on condition

His feathers verie heavie were: and doubting any more   895
To trust his wings now waxing wet, he straight began to sore
Up to a rocke which in the calme above the water stood:
But in the tempest evermore was hidden with the flood.
And leaning thereunto and with his left hand holding just
The top thereof a dozen times his weapon he did thrust   900
Among his guttes. The joyfull noyse and clapping of their hands
The which were made for loosening of Andromad from hir bands,
Filde all the coast and heaven it selfe. The parents of the Maide
Cassiope and Cepheus were glad and well appayde:
And calling him their sonne in law confessed him to bee   905
The helpe and savegarde of their house. Andromade the fee
And cause of Perseys enterprise from bondes now beyng free,
He washed his victorious hands. And lest the Snakie heade
With lying on the gravell hard should catch some harme, he spred
Soft leaves and certaine tender twigs that in the water grew,   910
And laid Medusas head thereon: the twigs yet being new
And quicke and full of juicie pith full lightly to them drew
The nature of this monstrous head. For both the leafe and bough
Full straungely at the touch thereof became both hard and tough.
The Sea nymphes tride this wondrous fact in divers other roddes   915
And were full glad to see the chaunge, bicause there was no oddes
Of leaves or twigs or of the seedes new shaken from the coddes.
For still like nature ever since is in our Corall founde:
That looke how soone it toucheth Ayre it waxeth hard and sounde,
And that which under water was a sticke, above is stone.   920
Three altars to as many Gods he makes of Turfe anon:
Upon the left hand Mercuries: Minervas on the right:
And in the middle Jupiters: to Pallas he did dight
A Cow: a Calfe to Mercurie: a Bull to royall Jove.
Forthwith he tooke Andromade the price for which he strove   925
Endowed with hir fathers Realme. For now the God of Love
And Hymen unto mariage his minde in hast did move.
Great fires were made of sweete perfumes, and curious garlandes hung
About the house, which every where of mirthful musicke rung
The gladsome signe of merie mindes. The Pallace gates were set   930
Wide open. None from comming in were by the Porters let.
All Noblemen and Gentlemen that were of any port

916 *oddes:* difference
917 *coddes:* husks, pods
923 *dight:* prepare, ordain

931 *let:* prevented
932 *port:* station, status

To this same great and royall feast of Cephey did resort.
    When having taken their repast as well of meate as wine
    Their hearts began to pleasant mirth by leysure to encline,   935
The valiant Persey of the folke and facions of the land
Began to be inquisitive. One Lincide out of hand
The rites and manners of the folke did doe him t'understand.
Which done he sayd: O worthie knight I pray thee tell us by
What force or wile thou gotst the head with haires of Adders slie.   940
Then Persey tolde how underneath colde Atlas lay a plaine
So fenced in on every side with mountaines high, that vaine
Were any force to win the same. In entrance of the which
Two daughters of King Phorcis dwelt whose chaunce and hap was such
That one eye served both their turnes: whereof by wilie slight   945
And stealth in putting forth his hand he did bereve them quight,
As they from t'one to tother were delivering of the same.
From whence by long blind crooked wayes unhandsomly he came
Through gastly groves by ragged cliffes unto the drerie place
Whereas the Gorgons dwelt: and there he saw (a wretched case)   950
The shapes as well of men as beasts lie scattered everie where
In open fields and common wayes, the which transformed were
From living things to stones at sight of foule Medusas heare,
But yet that he through brightnesse of his monstrous brazen shield
The which he in his left hand bare, Medusas face beheld.   955
And while that in a sound dead sleepe were all hir Snakes and she,
He softly pared off hir head: and how that he did see
Swift Pegasus the winged horse and eke his brother grow
Out of their mothers new shed bloud. Moreover he did show
A long discourse of all his happes and not so long as trew: 960
As namely of what Seas and landes the coasts he overflew,
And eke what starres with stying wings he in the while did vew.
But yet his tale was at an ende ere any lookt therefore.
    Upon occasion by and by of wordes reherst before
    There was a certaine noble man demaunded him wherefore   965
Shee only of the sisters three haire mixt with Adders bore.
Sir (aunswerde Persey) sith you aske a matter worth report
I graunt to tell you your demaunde. She both in comly port
And beautie, every other wight surmounted in such sort,
That many suters unto hir did earnestly resort.   970
And though that whole from top to toe most bewtifull she were,

938 *doe:* make   968 *port:* bearing
967 *sith:* since

In all hir bodie was no part more goodly than hir heare.
I know some parties yet alive, that say they did hir see.
It is reported how she should abusde by Neptune bee
In Pallas Church: from which fowle facte Joves daughter turnde hir
                                                eye,   975

And with hir Target hid hir face from such a villanie.
And lest it should unpunisht be, she turnde hir seemely heare
To lothly Snakes: the which (the more to put hir foes in feare)
Before hir brest continually she in her shield doth beare.

FINIS QUARTI LIBRI.

⧉⧉⧉

THE FYFT BOOKE

OF OVIDS METAMORPHOSIS.

---

*[Perseus and Phineus. Pallas, the Muses, and the Pierides. Proserpina
and Ceres. Arethusa.]*

Now while that Danaes noble sonne was telling of these things
    Amid a throng of Cepheys Lordes, through al the Pallace rings
A noyse of people nothing like the sound of such as sing
At wedding feastes, but like the rore of such as tidings bring
Of cruell warre. This sodaine chaunge from feasting unto fray   5
Might well be likened to the Sea: whych standing at a stay
The woodnesse of the windes makes rough by raising of the wave.
King Cepheys brother Phyney was the man that rashly gave
The first occasion of this fray. Who shaking in hys hand
A Dart of Ash with head of steele, sayd: Loe: loe here I stand   10
To chalenge thee that wrongfully my ravisht spouse doste holde.
Thy wings nor yet thy forged Dad in shape of feyned golde
Shall now not save thee from my handes. As with that word he bent
His arme aloft, the foresaid Dart at Persey to have sent,
What doste thou brother (Cephey cride) what madnesse moves thy
                                      minde   15
To doe so foule a deede? is this the friendship he shall finde
Among us for his good deserts? And wilt thou needes requite
The saving of thy Neeces life with such a foule despight?
Whome Persey hath not from thee tane: but (if thou be advisde)
But Neptunes heavie wrath bicause his Sea nymphes were despisde: 20
But horned Hammon: but the beast which from the Sea arrived
On my deare bowels for to feede. That time wert thou deprived
Of thy betroothed, when hir life upon the losing stoode:

---

⁷ *woodnesse:* rage

113

Onlesse perchaunce to see hir lost it woulde have done thee good,
And easde thy heart to see me sad. And may it not suffice   25
That thou didst see hir to the rocke fast bound before thine eyes
And didst not helpe hir beyng both hir husband and hir Eame?
Onlesse thou grudge that any man should come within my Realme
To save hir life, and seeke to rob him of his just rewarde?
Which if thou thinke to be so great, thou shouldst have had regarde   30
Before, to fetch it from the rocke to which thou sawste it bound.
I pray thee, brother, seeing that by him the meanes is found
That in mine age without my childe I go not to the grounde,
Permit him to enjoy the price for which we did compounde,
And which he hath by due desert of purchace deerely bought.   35
For brother, let it never sinke nor enter in thy thought
That I set more by him than thee: but this may well be sed
I rather had to give hir him than see my daughter dead.
He gave him not a worde againe: but looked eft on him,
And eft on Persey irefully with countnance stoure and grim,   40
Not knowing which were best to hit: and after little stay
He shooke his Dart, and flung it forth with all the powre and sway
That Anger gave at Perseys head. But harme it did him none,
It sticked in the Bedsteddes head that Persey sate upon.
        Then Persey sternely starting up and pulling out the Dart   45
        Did throw it at his foe agayne, and therewithall his hart
Had cliven asunder, had he not behinde an Altar start.
The Altar (more the pitie was) did save the wicked wight.
Yet threw he not the Dart in vaine: it hit one Rhetus right
Amid the foreheade: who therewith sanke downe, and when the steele   50
Was plucked out, he sprawlde about and spurned with his heele,
And all berayd the boorde with bloud. Then all the other rout
As fierce as fire flang Dartes: and some there were that cried out
That Cephey with his sonne in lawe was worthy for to die.
But he had wound him out of doores protesting solemly   55
As he was just and faithfull Prince, and swearing eke by all
The Gods of Hospitalitie, that that same broyle did fall
Full sore against his will. At hand was warlie Pallas streight
And shadowed Persey with hir shielde, and gave him heart in feight.
There was one Atys borne in Inde, (of faire Lymniace   60

27 *Eame:* uncle
39 *eft:* again, after
40 *stoure:* fierce
48 *wight:* man
51 *spurned:* struck, kicked

52 *berayd:* defiled
55 *wound him:* made his way
56 *eke:* also
58 *warlie:* warlike

The River Ganges daughter thought the issue for to be),
Of passing beautie which with rich aray he did augment.
He ware that day a scarlet Cloke, about the which there went
A garde of golde: a cheyne of golde he ware about his necke:
And eke his haire perfumde with Myrrhe a costly crowne did decke. 65
Full sixtene yeares he was of age: such cunning skill he coulde
In darting, as to hit his marke farre distant when he would.
Yet how to handle Bow and shaftes much better did he know.
Now as he was about that time to bende his horned Bowe,
    A firebrand Persey raught that did upon the Aultar smoke,   70
    And dasht him overtwhart the face with such a violent stroke,
That all bebattred was his head, the bones asunder broke.
When Lycabas of Assur lande, his moste assured friend
And deare companion, being no dissembler of his miend,
Which most entierly did him love, behelde him on the ground   75
Lie weltring with disfigurde face, and through that grievous wound
Now gasping out his parting ghost, his death he did lament,
And taking hastly up the Bow that Atys erst had bent:
Encounter thou with me (he saide) thou shalt not long enjoy
Thy triumphing in braverie thus, for killing of this boy,   80
By which thou getst more spight than praise. All this was scarsly sed,
But that the arrow from the string went streyned to the head.
Howbeit Persey (as it hapt) so warely did it shunne,
As that it in his coteplights hung. Then to him did he runne
With Harpe in his hand bestaind with grim Medusas blood,   85
And thrust him through the brest therwith. He quothing as he stood
Did looke about where Atys lay with dim and dazeling eyes,
Now waving under endlesse night: and downe by him he lies,
And for to comfort him withall togither with him dies.
Behold through gredie haste to feight one Phorbas, Methions son,   90
A Swevite: and of Lybie lande one callde Amphimedon
By fortune sliding in the blood with which the ground was wet,
Fell downe: and as they woulde have rose, Perseus fauchon met
With both of them. Amphimedon upon the ribbes he smote,
And with the like celeritie he cut me Phorbas throte.   95
But unto Erith, Actors sonne, that in his hand did holde

64 *garde:* border
66 *coulde:* knew
70 *raught:* seized
82 *streyned:* pulled back (to the arrowhead)
84 *coteplights:* folds of garments

85 *Harpe:* Latin *harpe,* Perseus's sickle-
    shaped sword
86 *quothing:* fainting
93 *fauchon:* falchion, curved sword

A brode browne Bill, with his short sword he durst not be too bolde
To make approch. With both his handes a great and massie cup
Embost with cunning portrayture aloft he taketh up,
And sendes it at him. He spewes up red bloud: and falling downe   100
Upon his backe, against the ground doth knocke his dying crowne.
Then downe he Polydemon throwes, extract of royall race,
And Abaris the Scithian, and Clytus in like case,
And Elice with his unshorne lockes, and also Phlegias,
And Lycet, olde Sperchesies sonne, with divers other mo,   105
That on the heapes of corses slaine he treades as he doth go.
      And Phyney daring not presume to meet his foe at hand,
      Did cast a Dart: which hapt to light on Idas who did stand
Aloofe as neuter (though in vaine) not medling with the Fray.
Who casting backe a frowning looke at Phyney, thus did say: 110
Sith whether that I will or no compeld I am perforce
To take a part, have Phyney here him whome thou doste enforce
To be thy foe, and with this wound my wrongfull wound requite.
But as he from his body pullde the Dart, with all his might
To throw it at his foe againe, his limmes so feebled were   115
With losse of bloud, that downe he fell and could not after steare.
There also lay Odites slaine the chiefe in all the land
Next to King Cephey, put to death by force of Clymens hand.
Protenor was by Hypsey killde, and Lyncide did as much
For Hypsey. In the throng there was an auncient man and such   120
A one as loved righteousnesse and greatly feared God:
Emathion called was his name: whome sith his yeares forbad
To put on armes, he feights with tongue, inveying earnestly
Against that wicked war the which he banned bitterly.
As on the Altar he himselfe with quivering handes did stay,   125
One Cromis tipped off his head: his head cut off streight way
Upon the Altar fell, and there his tongue not fully dead
Did bable still the banning wordes the which it erst had sed,
And breathed forth his fainting ghost among the burning brandes.
      Then Brote and Hammon brothers, twins, stout champions of their
                                                            hands   130
      In wrestling Pierlesse (if so be that wrestling could sustaine
The furious force of slicing swordes) were both by Phyney slaine.
And so was Alphit, Ceres Priest, that ware upon his crowne

---

⁹⁷ *browne Bill:* brown-bill, halberd painted   ¹¹⁶ *steare:* stir
   brown   ¹²⁴ *banned:* cursed
¹⁰⁹ *neuter:* neutral   ¹²⁶ *tipped:* struck
¹¹¹ *Sith:* since

A stately Miter faire and white with Tables hanging downe.
Thou also Japets sonne for such affaires as these unmeete   135
But meete to tune thine instrument with voyce and Ditie sweete,
The worke of peace, wert thither callde th'assemblie to rejoyce
And for to set the mariage forth with pleasant singing voyce.
As with his Violl in his hand he stoode a good way off,
There commeth to him Petalus and sayes in way of scoffe: 140
Go sing the resdue to the ghostes about the Stygian Lake,
And in the left side of his heade his dagger poynt he strake.
He sanke downe deade with fingers still yet warbling on the string
And so mischaunce knit up with wo the song that he did sing.
But fierce Lycormas could not beare to see him murdred so   145
Without revengement. Up he caught a mightie Leaver tho
That wonted was to barre the doore a right side of the house
And therewithall to Petalus he lendeth such a souse
Full in the noddle of the necke, that like a snetched Oxe
Streight tumbling downe, against the ground his groveling face he
                                                              knox.   150

And Pelates, a Garamant, attempted to have caught
The left doore barre: but as thereat with stretched hand he raught,
One Coryt, sonne of Marmarus did with a Javelin stricke
Him through the hand, that to the wood fast nayled did it sticke.
As Pelates stoode fastned thus, one Abas goard his side: 155
He could not fall, but hanging still upon the poste there dide
Fast nayled by the hand. And there was overthrowne a Knight
Of Perseyes band callde Melaney, and one that Dorill hight,
A man of greatest landes in all the Realme of Nasamone.
That occupide so large a grounde as Dorill was there none,   160
Nor none that had such store of corne. There came a Dart askew
And lighted in his Coddes, the place where present death doth sew.
When Alcion of Barcey, he that gave this deadly wound,
Beheld him yesking forth his ghost and falling to the ground
With watrie eyes the white turnde up: Content thy selfe, he said,   165
With that same litle plot of grounde whereon thy corse is layde,
In steade of all the large fat fieldes which late thou didst possesse.
And with that word he left him dead. Perseus to redresse

---

134 *Tables:* flat inscribed decorations (?). The   148 *souse:* blow
    word may be misprinted: the second   149 *noddle:* back; *snetched:* slaughtered
    edition has *Labelles,* which can mean   158 *hight:* was called
    ribbons.   162 *Coddes:* testicles; *sew:* ensue
144 *knit up:* concluded   164 *yesking:* sobbing
146 *tho:* then

This slaughter and this spightfull taunt, streight snatched out the Dart
That sticked in the fresh warme wound, and with an angrie hart   170
Did send it at the throwers head: the Dart did split his nose
Even in the middes, and at his necke againe the head out goes:
So that it peered both the wayes. Whiles fortune doth support
And further Persey thus, he killes (but yet in sundrie sort)
Two brothers by the mother: t'one callde Clytie, tother Dane.   175
For on a Dart through both his thighes did Clytie take his bane:
And Danus with another Dart was striken in the mouth.
There died also Celadon, a Gypsie of the South:
And so did bastard Astrey too, whose mother was a Jew:
And sage Ethion well foreseene in things that should ensew,   180
But utterly beguilde as then by Birdes that aukly flew.
King Cepheyes harnessebearer callde Thoactes lost his life,
And Agyrt whom for murdring late his father with a knife
The worlde spake shame of. Nathelesse much more remainde behinde
Than was dispatched out of hand: for all were full in minde   185
To murder one. The wicked throng had sworne to spend their blood
Against the right, and such a man as had deserved good.
A tother side (although in vaine) of mere affection stood
The Father and the Motherinlaw, and eke the heavie bride,
Who filled with their piteous playnt the Court on everie side.   190
But now the clattring of the swordes and harnesse at that tide
With grievous grones and sighes of such as wounded were or dide,
Did raise up such a cruell rore that nothing could be heard.
For fierce Bellona so renewde the battell afterward,
That all the house did swim in blood. Duke Phyney with a rout   195
Of moe than of a thousand men environd round about
The valiant Persey all alone. The Dartes of Phyneys bande
Came thicker than the Winters hayle doth fall upon the lande,
By both his sides, his eyes and eares. He warely thereupon
Withdrawes, and leanes his backe against a huge great arche of
                                    stone: 200
And being safe behind, he settes his face against his foe
Withstanding all their fierce assaultes. There did assaile him thoe
Upon the left side Molpheus, a Prince of Choanie,
And on the right Ethemon, borne hard by in Arabie.
Like as the Tyger when he heares the lowing out of Neate   205

---

176 *bane:* destruction   185 *out of hand:* immediately
180 *foreseene:* having foresight   191 *tide:* time
181 *aukly:* awkwardly, unluckily   205 *Neate:* cattle

In sundrie Medes, enforced sore through abstinence from meate,
Would faine be doing with them both, and can not tell at which
Were best to give adventure first: so Persey who did itch
To be at host with both of them, and doubtfull whether side
To turne him on, the right or left, upon advantage spide   210
Did wound me Molphey on the leg, and from him quight him drave.
He was contented with his flight: for why Ethemon gave
No respite to him to pursue: but like a franticke man
Through egernesse to wounde his necke, without regarding whan
Or how to strike for haste, he burst his brittle sworde in twaine   215
Against the Arche: the poynt whereof rebounding backe againe,
Did hit himselfe upon the throte. Howbeit that same wound
Was unsufficient for to sende Ethemon to the ground.
He trembled holding up his handes for mercie, but in vaine,
For Persey thrust him through the heart with Hermes hooked skaine. 220
      But when he saw that valiantnesse no lenger could avayle,
      By reason of the multitude that did him still assayle:
Sith you your selves me force to call mine enmie to mine ayde,
I will do so: if any friend of mine be here (he sayd)
Sirs, turne your faces all away: and therewithall he drew   225
Out Gorgons head. One Thessalus streight raging to him flew,
And sayd: Go seeke some other man whome thou mayst make abasht
With these thy foolish juggling toyes. And as he would have dasht
His Javeling in him with that worde to kill him out of hand,
With gesture throwing forth his Dart all Marble did he stand.   230
His sworde through Lyncids noble heart had Amphix thought to shove:
His hand was stone, and neyther one nor other way could move:
But Niley who did vaunt himselfe to be the Rivers sonne
That through the boundes of Aegypt land in channels seven doth
                                                          runne,
And in his shielde had graven part of silver, part of golde   235
The said seven channels of the Nile, sayd: Persey here beholde
From whence we fetch our piedegree: it may rejoyce thy hart
To die of such a noble hand as mine. The latter part
Of these his words could scarce be heard: the dint therof was drownde:
Ye would have thought him speaking still with open mouth: but
                                                          sound   240
Did none forth passe: there was for speache no passage to be found.
Rebuking them cries Eryx: Sirs, it is not Gorgons face,

209 *at host with:* at home with, close to   239 *dint:* force
220 *skaine:* short sword

It is your owne faint heartes that make you stonie in this case.
Come let us on this fellow run and to the ground him beare
That feightes by witchcraft: as with that his feete forth stepping
                                                          were,   245
They stacke still fastened to the floore: he could not move aside,
An armed image all of stone he speachlesse did abide.
All these were justly punished. But one there was a knight
Of Perseys band, in whose defence as Acont stoode to feight,
He waxed overgrowne with stone at ugly Gorgons sight.   250
Whome still as yet Astyages supposing for to live,
Did with a long sharpe arming sworde a washing blow him give.
The sword did clinke against the stone and out the sparcles drive.
While all amazde Astyages stoode wondring at the thing,
The selfesame nature on himselfe the Gorgons head did bring.   255
And in his visage which was stone a countnance did remaine
Of wondring still. A wearie worke it were to tell you plaine
The names of all the common sort. Two hundred from that fray
Did scape unslaine: but none of them did go alive away.
The whole two hundred every one at sight of Gorgons heare   260
Were turned into stockes of stone. Then at the length for feare
Did Phyney of his wrongfull war forthinke himselfe full sore.
But now (alas) what remedie? he saw there stand before
His face, his men like Images in sundrie shapes all stone.
He knew them well, and by their names did call them everychone: 265
Desiring them to succor him: and trusting not his sight
He feeles the bodies that were next, and all were Marble quight.
He turnes himselfe from Persey ward and humbly as he standes
He wries his armes behind his backe: and holding up his handes,
O noble Persey, thou hast got the upper hand, he sed.   270
Put up that monstruous shield of thine: put up that Gorgons head
That into stones transformeth men: put up, I thee desire.
Not hatred, nor bicause to reigne as King I did aspire,
Have moved me to make this fray. The only force of love
In seeking my betrothed spouse, did hereunto me move.   275
The better title seemeth thine bicause of thy desert:
And mine by former promise made. It irkes me at the heart
In that I did not give the place. None other thing I crave
O worthie knight, but that thou graunt this life of mine to save.

---

250 *overgrowne:* grown over   265 *everychone:* everyone
252 *washing:* swashing   268 *from Persey ward:* away from Perseus
262 *forthinke himselfe:* repent   269 *wries:* twists

Let all things else beside be thine. As he thus humbly spake   280
Nor daring looke at him to whome he did entreatance make,
The thing (quoth Persey) which to graunt both I can finde in heart,
And is no little courtesie to shewe without desert
Upon a Coward, I will graunt, O fearfull Duke, to thee.
Set feare aside: thou shalt not hurt with any weapon bee.   285
I will moreover so provide as that thou shalt remaine
An everlasting monument of this dayes toyle and paine.
The pallace of my Fathrinlaw shall henceforth be thy shrine
Where thou shalt stand continually before my spouses eyen,
That of hir husband having ay the Image in hir sight,   290
She may from time to time receyve some comfort and delight.
He had no sooner sayd these wordes but that he turnde his shielde
With Gorgons heade to that same part where Phyney with a mielde
And fearfull countnance set his face. Then also as he wride
His eyes away, his necke waxt stiffe, his teares to stone were dride.   295
A countnance in the stonie stocke of feare did still appeare
With humble looke and yeelding handes and gastly ruthfull cheare.
        With conquest and a noble wife doth Persey home repaire
        And in revengement of the right against the wrongfull heyre,
As in his Graundsires just defence, he falles in hand with Prete   300
Who like no brother but a foe did late before defeate
King Acrise of his townes by warre and of his royall seate.
But neyther could his men of warre nor fortresse won by wrong
Defend him from the griesly looke of grim Medusa long.
And yet thee, foolish Polydect of little Seriph King,   305
Such rooted rancor inwardly continually did sting,
That neyther Perseys prowesse tride in such a sort of broyles
Nor yet the perils he endurde, nor all his troublous toyles
Could cause thy stomacke to relent. Within thy stonie brest
Workes such a kinde of festred hate as cannot be represt.   310
Thy wrongfull malice hath none ende. Moreover thou of spite
Repining at his worthy praise, his doings doste backbite:
Upholding that Medusas death was but a forged lie:
So long till Persey for to shewe the truth apparantly,
Desiring such as were his friendes to turne away their eye,   315
Drue out Medusas ougly head. At sight whereof anon
The hatefull Tyran Polydect was turned to a stone.

---

283 *desert:* merit   307 *broyles:* tumults, quarrels
290 *ay:* always   317 *Tyran:* tyrant
297 *ruthfull cheare:* pitiful expression

The Goddesse Pallas all this while did keepe continually
Hir brother Persey companie, till now that she did stie
From Seriph in a hollow cloud, and leaving on the right   320
The Iles of Scyre and Gyaros, she made from thence hir flight
Directly over that same Sea as neare as eye could ame
To Thebe and Mount Helicon, and when she thither came,
She stayde hir selfe, and thus bespake the learned sisters nine:
A rumor of an uncouth spring did pierce these eares of mine   325
The which the winged stede should make by stamping with his hoofe.
This is the cause of my repaire: I would for certaine proofe
Be glad to see the wondrous thing. For present there I stoode
And saw the selfesame Pegasus spring of his mothers blood.
Dame Uranie did entertaine and aunswere Pallas thus: 330
What cause so ever moves your grace to come and visit us,
Most heartely you welcome are: and certaine is the fame
Of this our Spring, that Pegasus was causer of the same.
And with that worde she led hir forth to see the sacred spring.
Who musing greatly with hir selfe at straungenesse of the thing,   335
Surveyde the Woodes and groves about of auncient stately port.
And when she saw the Bowres to which the Muses did resort,
And pleasant fields beclad with herbes of sundrie hew and sort,
She said that for their studies sake they were in happie cace
And also that to serve their turne they had so trim a place.   340
Then one of them replied thus: O noble Ladie who
(But that your vertue greater workes than these are calles you to)
Should else have bene of this our troupe, your saying is full true.
To this our trade of life and place is commendation due.
And sure we have a luckie lot and if the world were such   345
As that we might in safetie live, but lewdnesse reignes so much
That all things make us Maides afraide. Me thinkes I yet do see
The wicked Tyran Pyren still: my heart is yet scarce free
From that same feare with which it hapt us flighted for to bee.
This cruell Pyren was of Thrace and with his men of war   350
The land of Phocis had subdude, and from this place not far
Within the Citie Dawlis reignde by force of wrongfull hand,
One day to Phebus Temples warde that on Parnasus stand
As we were going, in our way he met us courteously,
And by the name of Goddesses saluting reverently   355

319 *stie:* rise   336 *port:* appearance
325 *uncouth:* unknown, strange   349 *flighted:* frightened
327 *repaire:* coming   353 *to . . . warde:* toward
332 *fame:* report

Said: O ye Dames of Meonie (for why he knew us well)
I pray you stay and take my house untill this storme (there fell
That time a tempest and a showre) be past: the Gods aloft
Have entred smaller sheddes than mine full many a time and oft.
The rainie wether and hys wordes so moved us, that wee   360
To go into an outer house of his did all agree.
As soone as that the showre was past and heaven was voyded cleare
Of all the Cloudes which late before did every where appeare,
Until that Boreas had subdude the rainie Southerne winde,
We woulde have by and by bene gone. He shet the doores in minde   365
To ravish us: but we with wings escaped from his hands.
He purposing to follow us, upon a Turret stands,
And sayth he needes will after us the same way we did flie.
And with that worde full frantickly he leapeth downe from hie,
And pitching evelong on his face the bones asunder crasht,   370
And dying, all abrode the ground his wicked bloud bedasht.
        Now as the Muse was telling this, they heard a noyse of wings
        And from the leavie boughes aloft a sound of greeting rings.
Minerva looking up thereat demaunded whence the sounde
Of tongues that so distinctly spake did come so plaine and rounde? 375
She thought some woman or some man had greeted hir that stounde.
It was a flight of Birdes. Nyne Pies bewailing their mischaunce
In counterfetting everie thing from bough to bough did daunce.
As Pallas wondred at the sight, the Muse spake thus in summe:
These also being late ago in chalenge overcome,   380
Made one kinde more of Birdes than was of auncient time beforne.
In Macedone they were about the Citie Pella borne
Of Pierus, a great riche Chuffe, and Euip, who by ayde
Of strong Lucina travailing nine times, nine times was laide
Of daughters in hir childbed safe. This fond and foolish rout   385
Of doltish sisters taking pride and waxing verie stout,
Bicause they were in number nine came flocking all togither
Through all the townes of Thessalie and all Achaia hither,
And us with these or such like wordes to combate did provoke.
Cease off, ye Thespian Goddesses, to mocke the simple folke   390
With fondnesse of your Melodie. And if ye thinke in deede
Ye can doe ought, contend with us and see how you shall speede.
I warrant you ye passe us not in cunning nor in voyce.

356 *for why:* because   377 *Pies:* magpies
365 *by and by:* immediately   383 *Chuffe:* lout
370 *evelong:* evenlong, straight 386 *stout:* bold
376 *stounde:* time

Ye are here nine, and so are we. We put you to the choyce,
That eyther we will vanquish you and set you quight beside   395
Your fountaine made by Pegasus which is your chiefest pride,
And Aganippe too: or else confounde you us, and we
Of all the woods of Macedone will dispossessed be
As farre as snowie Peonie: and let the Nymphes be Judges.
Now in good sooth it was a shame to cope with suchie Drudges,   400
But yet more shame it was to yeeld. The chosen Nymphes did sweare
By Styx, and sate them downe on seates of stone that growed there.
Then streight without commission or election of the rest,
The formost of them preasing forth undecently, profest
The chalenge to performe: and song the battels of the Goddes.   405
She gave the Giants all the praise, the honor and the oddes,
Abasing sore the worthie deedes of all the Gods. She telles
How Typhon issuing from the earth and from the deepest helles,
Made all the Gods above afraide, so greatly that they fled
And never staide till Aegypt land and Nile whose streame is shed   410
In channels seven, received them forwearied all togither:
And how the Helhound Typhon did pursue them also thither.
By meanes wherof the Gods eche one were faine themselves to hide
In forged shapes. She saide that Jove the Prince of Gods was wride
In shape of Ram: which is the cause that at this present tide   415
Joves ymage which the Lybian folke by name of Hammon serve,
Is made with crooked welked hornes that inward still doe terve:
That Phebus in a Raven lurkt, and Bacchus in a Geate,
And Phebus sister in a Cat, and Juno in a Neate,
And Venus in the shape of Fish, and how that last of all   420
Mercurius hid him in a Bird which Ibis men doe call.
This was the summe of all the tale which she with rolling tung
And yelling throteboll to hir harpe before us rudely sung.
    Our turne is also come to speake, but that perchaunce your grace
    To give the hearing to our song hath now no time nor space.   425
Yes yes (quoth Pallas) tell on forth in order all your tale:
And downe she sate among the trees which gave a pleasant swale.
The Muse made aunswere thus: To one Calliope here by name
This chalenge we committed have and ordring of the same.
Then rose up faire Calliope with goodly bush of heare   430

---

395 *set . . . beside:* take from
400 *suchie:* such; *Drudges:* hacks
404 *preasing:* pressing
417 *welked:* twisted; *terve:* bend

418 *Geate:* goat
419 *Neate:* cow
423 *throteboll:* Adam's-apple
427 *swale:* shade

Trim wreathed up with yvie leaves, and with hir thumbe gan steare
The quivering strings, to trie them if they were in tune or no.
Which done, she playde upon hir Lute and song hir Ditie so:
    Dame Ceres first to breake the Earth with plough the maner found,
    She first made corne and stover soft to grow upon the ground,   435
She first made lawes: for all these things we are to Ceres bound.
Of hir must I as now intreate: would God I could resound
Hir worthie laude: she doubtlesse is a Goddesse worthie praise.
Bicause the Giant Typhon gave presumptuously assayes
To conquer Heaven, the howgie Ile of Trinacris is layd   440
Upon his limmes, by weight whereof perforce he downe is weyde.
He strives and strugles for to rise full many a time and oft.
But on his right hand toward Rome Pelorus standes aloft:
Pachynnus standes upon his left: his legs with Lilybie
Are pressed downe: his monstrous head doth under Aetna lie.   445
From whence he lying bolt upright with wrathfull mouth doth spit
Out flames of fire. He wrestleth oft and walloweth for to wit
And if he can remove the weight of all that mightie land
Or tumble downe the townes and hilles that on his bodie stand.
By meanes whereof it commes to passe that oft the Earth doth shake: 450
And even the King of Ghostes himselfe for verie feare doth quake,
Misdoubting lest the Earth should clive so wide that light of day
Might by the same pierce downe to Hell and there the Ghostes affray.
Forecasting this, the Prince of Fiendes forsooke his darksome hole,
And in a Chariot drawen with Steedes as blacke as any cole   455
The whole foundation of the Ile of Sicill warely vewde.
When throughly he had sercht eche place that harme had none
                                 ensewde,
As carelessly he raungde abrode, he chaunced to be seene
Of Venus sitting on hir hill: who taking streight betweene
Hir armes hir winged Cupid, said: My sonne, mine only stay,   460
My hand, mine honor and my might, go take without delay
Those tooles which all wightes do subdue, and strike them in the hart
Of that same God that of the world enjoyes the lowest part.
The Gods of Heaven, and Jove himselfe, the powre of Sea and Land
And he that rules the powres on Earth obey thy mightie hand: 465
And wherefore then should only Hell still unsubdued stand?
Thy mothers Empire and thine own why doste thou not advaunce?

---

435 *stover:* fodder   447 *wit:* know
437 *intreate:* treat   462 *tooles:* weapons
440 *howgie:* huge

The third part of al the world now hangs in doubtful chaunce.
And yet in heaven too now, their deedes thou seest me faine to beare.
We are despisde: the strength of love with me away doth weare.   470
Seeste not the Darter Diane and dame Pallas have already
Exempted them from my behestes? and now of late so heady
Is Ceres daughter too, that if we let hir have hir will,
She will continue all hir life a Maid unwedded still.
For that is all hir hope, and marke whereat she mindes to shoote.   475
But thou (if ought this gracious turne our honor may promote,
Or ought our Empire beautifie which joyntly we doe holde,)
This Damsell to hir uncle joyne. No sooner had she tolde
These wordes, but Cupid opening streight his quiver chose therefro
One arrow (as his mother bade) among a thousand mo.   480
But such a one it was, as none more sharper was than it,
Nor none went streighter from the Bow the amed marke to hit.
He set his knee against his Bow and bent it out of hande,
And made his forked arrowes steale in Plutos heart to stande.
   Neare Enna walles there standes a Lake: Pergusa is the name.   485
   Cayster heareth not mo songs of Swannes than doth the same.
A wood environs everie side the water round about,
And with his leaves as with a veyle doth keepe the Sunne heate out.
The boughes doe yeelde a coole fresh Ayre: the moystnesse of the
                                                        grounde
Yeeldes sundrie flowres: continuall spring is all the yeare there
                                                        founde.   490
While in this garden Proserpine was taking hir pastime,
In gathering eyther Violets blew, or Lillies white as Lime,
And while of Maidenly desire she fillde hir Maund and Lap,
Endevoring to outgather hir companions there, by hap
Dis spide hir: lovde hir: caught hir up: and all at once well nere,   495
So hastie, hote, and swift a thing is Love as may appeare.
The Ladie with a wailing voyce afright did often call
Hir Mother and hir waiting Maides, but Mother most of all.
And as she from the upper part hir garment would have rent,
By chaunce she let hir lap slip downe, and out hir flowres went.   500
And such a sillie simplenesse hir childish age yet beares,
That even the verie losse of them did move hir more to teares.
The Catcher drives his Chariot forth, and calling every horse
By name, to make away apace he doth them still enforce:

472 *behestes:* commands   493 *Maund:* woven basket
484 *steale:* stele, shaft

And shakes about their neckes and Manes their rustie bridle reynes ⁵⁰⁵
And through the deepest of the Lake perforce he them constreynes.
And through the Palik pooles, the which from broken ground doe boyle
And smell of Brimstone verie ranke: and also by the soyle
Where as the Bacchies, folke of Corinth with the double Seas,
Betweene unequall Havons twaine did reere a towne for ease. ⁵¹⁰
     Betweene the fountaines of Cyane and Arethuse of Pise
      An arme of Sea that meetes enclosde with narrow hornes there lies.
Of this the Poole callde Cyane which beareth greatest fame
Among the Nymphes of Sicilie did algates take the name.
Who vauncing hir unto the waste amid hir Poole did know ⁵¹⁵
Dame Proserpine, and said to Dis: Ye shall no further go:
You cannot Ceres sonneinlawe be, will she so or no.
You should have sought hir courteously and not enforst hir so.
And if I may with great estates my simple things compare,
Anapus was in love with me: but yet he did not fare ⁵²⁰
As you doe now with Proserpine. He was content to woo
And I unforst and unconstreind consented him untoo.
This said, she spreaded forth hir armes and stopt him of his way.
His hastie wrath Saturnus sonne no lenger then could stay.
But chearing up his dreadfull Steedes did smight his royall mace ⁵²⁵
With violence in the bottome of the Poole in that same place.
The ground streight yeelded to his stroke and made him way to Hell,
And downe the open gap both horse and Chariot headlong fell.
Dame Cyan taking sore to heart as well the ravishment
Of Proserpine against hir will, as also the contempt ⁵³⁰
Against hir fountaines priviledge, did shrowde in secret hart
An inward corsie comfortlesse, which never did depart
Untill she melting into teares consumde away with smart.
The selfesame waters of the which she was but late ago
The mighty Goddesse, now she pines and wastes hirselfe into. ⁵³⁵
Ye might have seene hir limmes wex lithe, ye might have bent hir bones.
Hir nayles wext soft: and first of all did melt the smallest ones:
As haire and fingars, legges and feete: for these same slender parts
Doe quickly into water turne, and afterward converts
To water, shoulder, backe, brest, side: and finally in stead ⁵⁴⁰
Of lively bloud, within hir veynes corrupted there was spred
Thinne water: so that nothing now remained whereupon
Ye might take holde, to water all consumed was anon.

⁵¹⁴ *algates:* at any rate   ⁵³² *corsie:* grievance
⁵¹⁵ *vauncing hir:* raising herself

The carefull mother in the while did seeke hir daughter deare
Through all the world both Sea and Land, and yet was nere the
                                                        neare.   545
The Morning with hir deawy haire hir slugging never found,
Nor yet the Evening star that brings the night upon the ground.
Two seasoned Pynetrees at the mount of Aetna did she light
And bare them restlesse in hir handes through all the dankish night.
Againe as soone as chierfull day did dim the starres, she sought   550
Hir daughter still from East to West. And being overwrought
She caught a thirst: no liquor yet had come within hir throte.
By chaunce she spied nere at hand a pelting thatched Cote
Wyth peevish doores: she knockt thereat, and out there commes a trot.
The Goddesse asked hir some drinke and she denide it not: 555
But out she brought hir by and by a draught of merrie go downe
And therewithall a Hotchpotch made of steeped Barlie browne
And Flaxe and Coriander seede and other simples more
The which she in an Earthen pot together sod before.
While Ceres was a eating this, before hir gazing stood   560
A hard faaste boy, a shrewde pert wag, that could no maners good:
He laughed at hir and in scorne did call hir greedie gut.
The Goddesse being wroth therewith, did on the Hotchpotch put
The liquor ere that all was eate, and in his face it threw.
Immediatly the skinne thereof became of speckled hew,   565
And into legs his armes did turne: and in his altred hide
A wrigling tayle streight to his limmes was added more beside.
And to th'intent he should not have much powre to worken scathe,
His bodie in a little roume togither knit she hathe.
For as with pretie Lucerts he in facion doth agree: 570
So than the Lucert somewhat lesse in every poynt is he.
The poore old woman was amazde: and bitterly she wept:
She durst not touche the uncouth worme, who into corners crept.
And of the flecked spottes like starres that on his hide are set
A name agreeing thereunto in Latine doth he get.   575
It is our Swift whose skinne with gray and yellow specks is fret.
    What Lands and Seas the Goddesse sought it were too long to
                                                        saine.

[544] *carefull:* full of care   [559] *sod:* seethed
[545] *neare:* nearer   [561] *faaste:* faced; *could:* knew
[546] *slugging:* lazing   [568] *scathe:* harm
[553] *pelting:* paltry, mean; *Cote:* cottage   [570] *Lucerts:* lizards
[554] *peevish:* narrow, low, etc.; *trot:* hag   [573] *uncouth:* strange, repellent
[556] *merrie go downe:* strong ale   [576] *Swift:* eft, small lizard; *fret:* variegated
[557] *Hotchpotch:* mixed dish   [577] *saine:* say

The worlde did want. And so she went to Sicill backe againe.
And as in going every where she serched busily,
She also came to Cyane: who would assuredly   580
Have tolde hir all things, had she not transformed bene before.
But mouth and tongue for uttrance now would serve hir turne no more.
Howbeit a token manifest she gave hir for to know
What was become of Proserpine. Her girdle she did show
Still hovering on hir holie poole, which slightly from hir fell   585
As she that way did passe: and that hir mother knew too well.
For when she saw it, by and by as though she had but than
Bene new advertisde of hir chaunce, she piteously began
To rend hir ruffled haire, and beate hir handes against hir brest.
As yet she knew not where she was. But yet with rage opprest,   590
She curst all landes, and said they were unthankfull everychone,
Yea and unworthy of the fruites bestowed them upon.
But bitterly above the rest she banned Sicilie,
In which the mention of hir losse she plainely did espie.
And therefore there with cruell hand the earing ploughes she brake,   595
And man and beast that tilde the grounde to death in anger strake.
She marrde the seede, and eke forbade the fieldes to yeelde their frute.
The plenteousnesse of that same Ile of which there went suche bruit
Through all the world, lay dead: the corne was killed in the blade:
Now too much drought, now too much wet did make it for to fade.   600
The starres and blasting windes did hurt, the hungry foules did eate
The corne in ground: the Tines and Briars did overgow the Wheate.
And other wicked weedes the corne continually annoy,
Which neyther tylth nor toyle of man was able to destroy.
        Then Arethuse, floud Alpheys love, lifts from hir Elean waves   605
        Hir head, and shedding to hir eares hir deawy haire that waves
About hir foreheade sayde: O thou that art the mother deare
Both of the Maiden sought through all the world both far and neare,
And eke of all the earthly fruites, forbeare thine endlesse toyle,
And be not wroth without a cause with this thy faithfull soyle: 610
The Lande deserves no punishment. Unwillingly, God wote,
She opened to the Ravisher that violently hir smote.
It is not sure my native soyle for which I thus entreate.
I am but here a sojourner, my native soyle and seate
Is Pisa and from Ely towne I fetch my first discent.   615
I dwell but as a straunger here: but sure to my intent

585 *slightly:* lightly, carelessly   602 *Tines:* wild vetch or tares
595 *earing:* plowing   611 *wote:* knows

This Countrie likes me better farre than any other land.
Here now I Arethusa dwell: here am I setled: and
I humbly you beseche extend your favour to the same.
A time will one day come when you to mirth may better frame,   620
And have your heart more free from care, which better serve me may
To tell you why I from my place so great a space doe stray,
And unto Ortygie am brought through so great Seas and waves.
The ground doth give me passage free, and by the lowest caves
Of all the Earth I make my way, and here I raise my heade,   625
And looke upon the starres agayne neare out of knowledge fled.
Now while I underneath the Earth the Lake of Styx did passe,
I saw your daughter Proserpine with these same eyes. She was
Not merrie, neyther rid of feare as seemed by hir cheere.
But yet a Queene, but yet of great God Dis the stately Feere: 630
But yet of that same droupie Realme the chiefe and sovereigne Peere.
    Hir mother stoode as starke as stone, when she these newes did
                                                                heare,
        And long she was like one that in another worlde had beene.
But when hir great amazednesse by greatnesse of hir teene
Was put aside, she gettes hir to hir Chariot by and by   635
And up to heaven in all post haste immediately doth stie.
And there beslowbred all hir face: hir haire about hir eares,
To royall Jove in way of plaint this spightfull tale she beares:
As well for thy bloud as for mine a suter unto thee
I hither come. If no regard may of the mother bee   640
Yet let the childe hir father move, and have not lesser care
Of hir (I pray) bicause that I hir in my bodie bare.
Behold our daughter whome I sought so long is found at last:
If finding you it terme, when of recoverie meanes is past.
Or if you finding do it call to have a knowledge where   645
She is become. Hir ravishment we might consent to beare,
So restitution might be made. And though there were to me
No interest in hir at all, yet forasmuche as she
Is yours, it is unmeete she be bestowde upon a theefe.
Jove aunswerde thus: My daughter is a Jewell deare and leefe: 650
A collup of mine owne flesh cut as well as out of thine.
But if we in our heartes can finde things rightly to define,
This is not spight but love. And yet Madame in faith I see

617 *likes:* pleases   631 *droupie:* despondent
620 *frame:* fit   634 *teene:* grief
629 *cheere:* expression   650 *leefe:* beloved
630 *Feere:* mate   651 *collup:* piece of flesh

No cause of such a sonne in law ashamed for to bee,
So you contented were therewith. For put the case that hee 655
Were destitute of all things else, how greate a matter ist
Joves brother for to be? but sure in him is nothing mist.
Nor he inferior is to me save only that by lot
The Heavens to me, the Helles to him the destnies did allot.
But if you have so sore desire your daughter to divorce, 660
Though she againe to Heaven repayre I doe not greatly force.
But yet conditionly that she have tasted there no foode:
For so the destnies have decreed. He ceaste: and Ceres stoode
Full bent to fetch hir daughter out: but destnies hir withstoode,
Bicause the Maide had broke hir fast. For as she hapt one day 665
In Plutos Ortyard rechlessely from place to place to stray,
She gathering from a bowing tree a ripe Pownegarnet, tooke
Seven kernels out and sucked them. None chaunst hereon to looke,
Save onely one Ascalaphus whome Orphne, erst a Dame
Among the other Elves of Hell not of the basest fame, 670
Bare to hir husbande Acheron within hir duskie den.
He sawe it, and by blabbing it ungraciously as then,
Did let hir from returning thence. A grievous sigh the Queene
Of Hell did fetch, and of that wight that had a witnesse beene
Against hir made a cursed Birde. Upon his face she shead 675
The water of the Phlegeton: and by and by his head
Was nothing else but Beake and Downe, and mightie glaring eyes.
Quight altred from himselfe betweene two yellow wings he flies.
He groweth chiefly into head and hooked talants long
And much adoe he hath to flaske his lazie wings among. 680
The messenger of Morning was he made, a filthie fowle,
A signe of mischiefe unto men, the sluggish skreching Owle.
    This person for his lavish tongue and telling tales might seeme
    To have deserved punishment. But what should men esteeme
To be the verie cause why you, Acheloes daughters, weare 685
Both feete and feathers like to Birdes, considering that you beare
The upper partes of Maidens still? And commes it so to passe
Bicause when Ladie Proserpine a gathering flowers was,
Ye Meremaides kept hir companie? Whome after you had sought
Through all the Earth in vaine, anon of purpose that your thought 690
Might also to the Seas be knowen, ye wished that ye might
Upon the waves with hovering wings at pleasure rule your flight,

---

661 *force:* care   673 *let:* prevent
667 *Pownegarnet:* pomegranate   680 *flaske:* flap

And had the Goddes to your request so pliant, that ye found
With yellow feathers out of hand your bodies clothed round:
Yet lest that pleasant tune of yours ordeyned to delight   695
The hearing, and so high a gift of Musicke perish might
For want of uttrance, humaine voyce to utter things at will
And countnance of virginitie remained to you still.
But meane betweene his brother and his heavie sister goth
God Jove, and parteth equally the yeare betweene them both.   700
And now the Goddesse Proserpine indifferently doth reigne
Above and underneath the Earth, and so doth she remaine
One halfe yeare with hir mother and the resdue with hir Feere.
Immediatly she altred is as well in outwarde cheere
As inwarde minde. For where hir looke might late before appeere   705
Sad even to Dis, hir countnance now is full of mirth and grace
Even like as Phebus having put the watrie cloudes to chace,
Doth shew himselfe a Conqueror with bright and shining face.
      Then fruitfull Ceres voide of care in that she did recover
      Hir daughter, prayde thee, Arethuse, the storie to discover,   710
What caused thee to fleete so farre and wherefore thou became
A sacred spring? The waters whist. The Goddesse of the same
Did from the bottome of the Well hir goodly head up reare.
And having dried with hir hand hir faire greene hanging heare,
The River Alpheys auncient loves she thus began to tell.   715
      I was (quoth she) a Nymph of them that in Achaia dwell.
      There was not one that earnester the Lawndes and forests sought
Or pitcht hir toyles more handsomly. And though that of my thought
It was no part, to seeke the fame of beautie: though I were
All courage: yet the pricke and prise of beautie I did beare.   720
My overmuch commended face was unto me a spight.
This gift of bodie in the which another would delight,
I, rudesbye, was ashamed of: me thought it was a crime
To be belikte. I beare it well in minde that on a time
In comming wearie from the chase of Stymphalus, the heate   725
Was fervent, and my traveling had made it twice as great.
I founde a water neyther deepe nor shallow which did glide
Without all noyse, so calme that scarce the moving might be spide.
And throughly to the very ground it was so crispe and cleare,
That every little stone therein did plaine aloft appeere.   730
The horie Sallowes and the Poplars growing on the brim

712 *whist:* became silent   723 *rudesbye:* insolent one
720 *pricke:* mark aimed at (in archery)   729 *ground:* bottom

Unset, upon the shoring bankes did cast a shadow trim.
I entred in, and first of all I deeped but my feete:
And after to my knees. And not content to wade so fleete,
I put off all my clothes, and hung them on a Sallow by   735
And threw my selfe amid the streame, which as I dallyingly
Did beate and draw, and with my selfe a thousand maistries trie,
In casting of mine armes abrode and swimming wantonly:
I felt a bubling in the streame I wist not how nor what,
And on the Rivers nearest brim I stept for feare. With that,   740
O Arethusa, whither runst? and whither runst thou, cride
Floud Alphey from his waves againe with hollow voyce. I hide
Away unclothed as I was. For on the further side
My clothes hung still. So much more hote and eger then was he,
And for I naked was, I seemde the readier for to be.   745
My running and his fierce pursuite was like as when ye se
The sillie Doves with quivering wings before the Gossehauke stie,
The Gossehauke sweeping after them as fast as he can flie.
To Orchomen, and Psophy land, and Cyllen I did holde
Out well, and thence to Menalus and Erymanth the colde,   750
And so to Ely. All this way no ground of me he wonne.
But being not so strong as he, this restlesse race to runne
I could not long endure, and he could hold it out at length.
Yet over plaines and wooddie hilles (as long as lasted strength)
And stones, and rockes, and desert groundes I still maintaind my race. 755
The Sunne was full upon my backe. I saw before my face
A lazie shadow: were it not that feare did make me see't.
But certenly he feared me with trampling of his feete:
And of his mouth the boystous breath upon my hairlace blew.
Forwearied with the toyle of flight: Helpe, Diane, I thy true   760
And trustie Squire (I said) who oft have caried after thee
Thy bow and arrowes, now am like attached for to bee.
The Goddesse moved, tooke a cloude of such as scattred were
And cast upon me. Hidden thus in mistie darkenesse there
The River poard upon me still and hunted round about   765
The hollow cloude, for feare perchaunce I should have scaped out.
And twice not knowing what to doe he stalkt about the cloude
Where Diane had me hid, and twice he called out aloude:
Hoe Arethuse, hoe Arethuse. What heart had I poore wretch then?

734 *fleete:* shallow   739 *wist:* knew
737 *maistries:* feats, tricks   765 *poard upon:* searched for
738 *wantonly:* sportively

Even such as hath the sillie Lambe that dares not stirre nor quetch
                when   770
He heares the howling of the Wolfe about or neare the foldes,
Or such as hath the squatted Hare that in hir foorme beholdes
The hunting houndes on every side, and dares not move a whit,
He would not thence, for why he saw no footing out as yit.
And therefore watcht he narrowly the cloud and eke the place.   775
A chill colde sweat my sieged limmes opprest, and downe apace
From all my bodie steaming drops did fall of watrie hew.
Which way so ere I stird my foote the place was like a stew.
The deaw ran trickling from my haire. In halfe the while I then
Was turnde to water, that I now have tolde the tale agen.   780
His loved waters Alphey knew, and putting off the shape
Of man the which he tooke before bicause I should not scape,
Returned to his proper shape of water by and by
Of purpose for to joyne with me and have my companie.
But Delia brake the ground, at which I sinking into blinde   785
Bycorners, up againe my selfe at Ortigie doe winde,
Right deare to me bicause it doth Dianas surname beare,
And for bicause to light againe I first was raysed there.
  Thus far did Arethusa speake: and then the fruitfull Dame
  Two Dragons to hir Chariot put, and reyning hard the same,   790
Midway beweene the Heaven and Earth she in the Ayer went,
And unto Prince Triptolemus hir lightsome Chariot sent
To Pallas Citie lode with corne, commaunding him to sowe
Some part in ground new broken up, and some thereof to strow
In ground long tillde before. Anon the yong man up did stie   795
And flying over Europe and the Realme of Asias hie,
Alighted in the Scithian land. There reyned in that coast
A King callde Lyncus, to whose house he entred for to host.
And being there demaunded how and why he thither came,
And also of his native soyle and of his proper name,   800
I hight (quoth he) Triptolemus and borne was in the towne
Of Athens in the land of Greece, that place of high renowne.
I neyther came by Sea nor Lande, but through the open Aire
I bring with me Dame Ceres giftes which being sowne in faire
And fertile fields may fruitfull Harvests yeelde and finer fare.   805
The savage King had spight, and to th'intent that of so rare

---

770 *quetch:* stir   798 *host:* be a guest
786 *Bycorners:* out-of-the-way corners   801 *hight:* am called
793 *lode:* laden

And gracious gifts himselfe might seeme first founder for to be,
He entertainde him in his house, and when asleepe was he,
He came upon him with a sword: but as he would have killde him,
Dame Ceres turnde him to a Lynx, and waking tother willde him   810
His sacred Teemeware through the Ayre to drive abrode agen.
      The chiefe of us had ended this hir learned song, and then
      The Nymphes with one consent did judge that we the Goddesses
Of Helicon had wonne the day. But when I sawe that these
Unnurtred Damsels overcome began to fall a scolding,   815
I sayd: so little sith to us you thinke your selves beholding,
For bearing with your malapertnesse in making chalenge, that
Besides your former fault, ye eke doe fall to rayling flat,
Abusing thus our gentlenesse: we will from hence proceede
The punishment, and of our wrath the rightfull humor feede.   820
Euippyes daughters grinnd and jeerde and set our threatnings light.
But as they were about to prate, and bent their fistes to smight
Theyr wicked handes with hideous noyse, they saw the stumps of quilles
New budding at their nayles, and how their armes soft feather hilles.
Eche saw how others mouth did purse and harden into Bill,   825
And so becomming uncouth Birdes to haunt the woods at will.
For as they would have clapt their handes their wings did up them
                                                            heave,
And hanging in the Ayre the scoldes of woods did Pies them leave.
Now also being turnde to Birdes they are as eloquent
As ere they were, as chattring still, as much to babling bent.   830

FINIS QUINTI LIBRI.

THE SIXT BOOKE

OF OVIDS METAMORPHOSIS.

[*Arachne. Niobe. Marsyas. Tereus, Procne, and Philomela. Boreas and Orithyia.*]

Tritonia unto all these wordes attentive hearing bendes,
    And both the Muses learned song and rightfull wrath commendes.
And thereupon within hir selfe this fancie did arise:
It is no matter for to prayse: but let our selfe devise
Some thing to be commended for: and let us not permit   5
Our Majestie to be despisde without revenging it.
And therewithall she purposed to put the Lydian Maide
Arachne to hir neckeverse who (as had to hir bene saide)
Presumed to prefer hir selfe before hir noble grace
In making cloth. This Damsell was not famous for the place   10
In which she dwelt, nor for hir stocke, but for hir Arte. Hir Sier
Was Idmon, one of Colophon, a pelting Purple Dier.
Hir mother was deceast: but she was of the baser sort,
And egall to hir Make in birth, in living, and in port.
But though this Maide were meanly borne, and dwelt but in a shed 15
At little Hypep: yet hir trade hir fame abrode did spred
Even all the Lydian Cities through. To see hir wondrous worke
The Nymphes that underneath the Vines of shadie Tmolus lurke
Their Vineyards oftentimes forsooke. So did the Nymphes also
About Pactolus oftentimes their golden streames forgo.   20
And evermore it did them good not only for to see
Hir clothes already made, but while they eke a making bee

---

8 *neckeverse:* Latin verse shown to a defendant who claimed benefit of clergy; ability to read it would save him from hanging.

12 *pelting:* paltry
14 *Make:* mate; *port:* social position

Such grace was in hir workmanship. For were it so that shee
The newshorne fleeces from the sheepe in bundels deftly makes,
Or afterward doth kemb the same, and drawes it out in flakes   25
Along like cloudes, or on the Rocke doth spinne the handwarpe woofe,
Or else embroydreth, certenly ye might perceive by proofe
She was of Pallas bringing up, which thing she nathelesse
Denyeth, and disdaining such a Mistresse to confesse,
Let hir contend with me, she saide: and if she me amend   30
I will refuse no punishment the which she shall extend.
     Minerva tooke an olde wives shape and made hir haire seeme gray,
     And with a staffe hir febled limmes pretended for to stay.
Which done, she thus began to speake: Not all that age doth bring
We ought to shonne. Experience doth of long continuance spring.   35
Despise not mine admonishment. Seeke fame and chiefe report
For making cloth, and Arras worke, among the mortall sort.
But humbly give the Goddesse place: and pardon of hir crave
For these thine unadvised wordes. I warrant thou shalt have
Forgivenesse, if thou aske it hir. Arachne bent hir brewes   40
And lowring on hir, left hir worke: and hardly she eschewes
From flying in the Ladies face. Hir countnance did bewray
Hir moodie minde: which bursting forth in words she thus did say:
Thou commest like a doting foole: thy wit is spent with yeares:
Thy life hath lasted over long as by thy talke appeares.   45
And if thou any daughter have, or any daughtrinlawe,
I would she heard these wordes of mine: I am not such a Daw,
But that without thy teaching I can well ynough advise
My selfe. And lest thou shouldest thinke thy words in any wise
Availe, the selfesame minde I keepe with which I first begonne.   50
Why commes she not hirselfe I say? this matche why doth she shonne?
Then said the Goddesse: Here she is. And therewithall she cast
Hir oldewives riveled shape away, and shewde hir selfe at last
Minerva like. The Nymphes did streight adore hir Majestie.
So did the yong newmaried wives that were of Migdonie.   55
The Maiden only unabasht woulde nought at all relent.
But yet she blusht and sodenly a ruddynesse besprent
Hir cheekes which wanzd away againe, even like as doth the Skie
Looke sanguine at the breake of day, and turneth by and by

26 *Rocke:* distaff; *handwarpe:* handywarpe,   42 *bewray:* reveal
   a sixteenth-century cloth   47 *Daw:* simpleton
30 *amend:* surpass   53 *riveled:* wrinkled
40 *brewes:* brows   58 *wanzd:* faded

To white at rising of the Sunne. As hote as any fire   60
She sticketh to hir tackling still. And through a fond desire
Of glorie, to hir owne decay all headlong forth she runnes.
For Pallas now no lenger warnes, ne now no lenger shunnes
Ne seekes the chalenge to delay. Immediatly they came
And tooke their places severally, and in a severall frame   65
Eche streynde a web, the warpe whereof was fine. The web was tide
Upon a Beame. Betweene the warpe a stay of reede did slide.
The woofe on sharpened pinnes was put betwixt the warp, and wrought
With fingars. And as oft as they had through the warpe it brought,
They strake it with a Boxen combe. Both twayne of them made hast: 70
And girding close for handsomnesse their garments to their wast
Bestirde their cunning handes apace. Their earnestnesse was such
As made them never thinke of paine. They weaved verie much
Fine Purple that was dide in Tyre, and colours set so trim
That eche in shadowing other seemde the very same with him.   75
Even like as after showres of raine when Phebus broken beames
Doe strike upon the Cloudes, appeares a compast bow of gleames
Which bendeth over all the Heaven: wherein although there shine
A thousand sundry colours, yet the shadowing is so fine,
That looke men nere so wistly, yet beguileth it their eyes: 80
So like and even the selfsame thing eche colour seemes to rise
Whereas they meete, which further off doe differ more and more.
Of glittring golde with silken threede was weaved there good store.
And stories put in portrayture of things done long afore.
      Minerva painted Athens towne and Marsis rocke therein,   85
      And all the strife betweene hirselfe and Neptune, who should win
The honor for to give the name to that same noble towne.
In loftie thrones on eyther side of Jove were settled downe
Six Peeres of Heaven with countnance grave and full of Majestie,
And every of them by his face discerned well might be.   90
The Image of the mightie Jove was Kinglike. She had made
Neptunus standing striking with his long thre tyned blade
Upon the ragged Rocke: and from the middle of the clift
She portrayd issuing out a horse, which was the noble gift
For which he chalengde to himselfe the naming of the towne.   95
She picturde out hirselfe with shielde and Morion on hir crowne

---

61 *tackling:* undertaking   77 *compast:* curved, arched
63 *ne:* nor   80 *wistly:* intently
66 *streynde:* stretched   93 *clift:* cleft
71 *handsomnesse:* handiness, dexterity 96 *Morion:* helmet

With Curet on hir brest, and Speare in hand with sharpened ende.
She makes the Earth (the which hir Speare doth seeme to strike)
                                to sende
An Olyf tree with fruite thereon: and that the Gods thereat
Did wonder: and with victorie she finisht up that plat.   100
    Yet to th'intent examples olde might make it to be knowne
    To hir that for desire of praise so stoutly helde hir owne,
What guerdon she shoulde hope to have for hir attempt so madde,
Foure like contentions in the foure last corners she did adde.
The Thracians Heme and Rodope the formost corner hadde: 105
Who being sometime mortall folke usurpt to them the name
Of Jove and Juno, and were turnde to mountaines for the same.
A Pigmie womans piteous chaunce the second corner shewde,
Whome Juno turned to a Crane (bicause she was so lewde
As for to stand at strife with hir for beautie) charging hir   110
Against hir native countriefolke continuall war to stir.
The thirde had proude Antigone, who durst of pride contende
In beautie with the wife of Jove: by whome she in the ende
Was turned to a Storke. No whit availed hir the towne
Of Troy, or that Laomedon hir father ware a crowne,   115
But that she, clad in feathers white, hir lazie wings must flap.
And with a bobbed Bill bewayle the cause of hir missehap.
The last had chyldelesse Cinyras: who being turnde to stone,
Was picturde prostrate on the grounde, and weeping all alone,
And culling fast betweene his armes a Temples greeces fine   120
To which his daughters bodies were transformde by wrath divine.
The utmost borders had a wreath of Olyf round about,
And this is all the worke the which Minerva portrayd out.
For with the tree that she hirselfe had made but late afore
She bounded in hir Arras cloth, and then did worke no more.   125
    The Lydian maiden in hir web did portray to the full
    How Europe was by royall Jove beguilde in shape of Bull.
A swimming Bull, a swelling Sea, so lively had she wrought,
That Bull and Sea in very deede ye might them well have thought.
The Ladie seemed looking backe to landwarde and to crie   130
Upon hir women, and to feare the water sprinkling hie,
And shrinking up hir fearfull feete. She portrayd also there

---

97 *Curet:* cuirass
100 *plat:* design
109 *lewde:* ignorant

117 *bobbed:* rapped, tapped
120 *culling:* hugging; *greeces:* steps, flight of
    steps

Asteriee struggling with an Erne which did away hir beare.
And over Leda she had made a Swan his wings to splay.
She added also how by Jove in shape of Satyr gaye   135
The faire Antiope with a paire of children was besped:
And how he tooke Amphitrios shape when in Alcmenas bed
He gate the worthie Hercules: and how he also came
To Danae like a shoure of golde, to Aegine like a flame,
A sheepeherd to Mnemosyne, and like a Serpent sly   140
To Proserpine. She also made Neptunus leaping by
Upon a Maide of Aeolus race in likenesse of a Bull,
And in the streame Enipeus shape begetting on a trull
The Giants Othe and Ephialt, and in the shape of Ram
Begetting one Theophane Bisalties ympe with Lam,   145
And in a lustie Stalions shape she made him covering there
Dame Ceres with the yellow lockes, and hir whose golden heare
Was turnde to crawling Snakes: on whome he gate the winged horse.
She made him in a Dolphins shape Melantho to enforce.
Of all these things she missed not their proper shapes, nor yit   150
The full and just resemblance of their places for to hit.
In likenesse of a Countrie cloyne was Phebus picturde there,
And how he now ware Gossehaukes wings, and now a Lions heare.
And how he in a shepeherdes shape was practising a wile
The daughter of one Macarie, dame Issa, to beguile.   155
And how the faire Erygone by chaunce did suffer rape
By Bacchus who deceyved hir in likenesse of a grape.
And how that Saturne in the shape of Genet did beget
The double Chiron. Round about the utmost Verdge was set
A narrow Traile of pretie floures with leaves of Ivie fret.   160
        Not Pallas, no, nor spight it selfe could any quarrell picke
        To this hir worke: and that did touch Minerva to the quicke.
Who thereupon did rende the cloth in pieces every whit,
Bicause the lewdnesse of the Gods was blased so in it.
And with an Arras weavers combe of Box she fiercely smit   165
Arachne on the forehead full a dozen times and more.
The Maide impacient in hir heart, did stomacke this so sore,
That by and by she hung hirselfe. Howbeit as she hing,
Dame Pallas pitying hir estate, did stay hir in the string
From death, and said: Lewde Callet live: but hang thou still for mee.   170

133 *Erne:* eagle   152 *cloyne:* clown, boor
134 *splay:* spread   158 *Genet:* horse
136 *besped:* provided   167 *stomacke:* resent
148 *gate:* begot   170 *Callet:* trull

And lest hereafter from this curse that time may set thee free,
I will that this same punishment enacted firmely bee,
As well on thy posteritie for ever as on thee.
And after when she should depart, with juice of Hecats flowre
She sprinkled hir: and by and by the poyson had such powre,   175
That with the touch thereof hir haire, hir eares, and nose did fade:
And verie small it both hir heade and all hir bodie made.
In steade of legs, to both hir sides sticke fingars long and fine:
The rest is bellie. From the which she nerethelesse doth twine
A slender threede, and practiseth in shape of Spider still   180
The Spinners and the Websters crafts of which she erst had skill.
    All Lydia did repine hereat, and of this deede the fame
    Through Phrygie ran, and through the world was talking of the
                                same.
Before hir mariage Niobe had knowen hir verie well,
When yet a Maide in Meonie and Sipyle she did dwell.   185
And yet Arachnes punishment at home before hir eyes,
To use discreter kinde of talke it could hir not advise,
Nor (as behoveth) to the Gods to yeelde in humble wise.
For many things did make hir proud. But neyther did the towne
The which hir husband builded had, nor houses of renowne   190
Of which they both descended were, nor yet the puissance
Of that great Realme wherein they reignde so much hir minde enhaunce
(Although the liking of them all did greatly hir delight)
As did the offspring of hir selfe. And certenly she might
Have bene of mothers counted well most happie, had she not   195
So thought hir selfe. For she whome sage Tyresias had begot,
The Prophet Manto, through instinct of heavenly powre, did say
These kinde of wordes in open strete: Ye Thebanes go your way
Apace, and unto Laton and to Latons children pray,
And offer godly Frankinsence, and wreath your haire with Bay.   200
Latona by the mouth of me commaundes you so to do.
The Thebane women by and by obeying thereunto,
Deckt all their heades with Laurell leaves as Manto did require,
And praying with devout intent threw incense in the fire.
    Beholde out commeth Niobe environde with a garde   205
    Of servaunts and a solemne traine that followed afterward.
She was hirselfe in raiment made of costly cloth of golde
Of Phrygia facion verie brave and gorgeous to beholde.
And of hir selfe she was right faire and beautifull of face,

But that hir wrathfull stomake then did somewhat staine hir grace.   210
She moving with hir portly heade hir haire the which as then
Did hang on both hir shoulders loose, did pawse a while, and when
Wyth loftie looke hir stately eyes she rolled had about:
    What madnesse is it (quoth she) to prefer the heavenly rout
    Of whome ye doe but heare, to such as daily are in sight?   215
Or why should Laton honored be with Altars? Never wight
To my most sacred Majestie did offer incense. Yit
My Father was that Tantalus whome only as most fit
The Gods among them at their boordes admitted for to sit.
A sister of the Pleyades is my mother. Finally   220
My Graundsire on the mothers side is that same Atlas hie
That on his shoulders beareth up the heavenly Axeltree.
Againe my other Graundfather is Jove, and (as you see)
He also is my Fathrinlawe, wherein I glorie may.
The Realme of Phrygia here at hand doth unto me obay.   225
In Cadmus pallace I thereof the Ladie doe remaine
And joyntly with my husbande I as peerlesse Princesse reigne
Both over this same towne whose walles my husbands harpe did frame,
And also over all the folke and people in the same.
In what soever corner of my house I cast mine eye,   230
A worlde of riches and of goods I everywhere espie.
Moreover for the beautie, shape, and favor growen in me,
Right well I know I doe deserve a Goddesse for to be.
Besides all this, seven sonnes I have and daughters seven likewise,
By whome shall shortly sonneinlawes and daughtrinlawes arise.   235
Judge you now if that I have cause of statelynesse or no.
How dare ye then prefer to me Latona that same fro
The Titan Ceus ympe, to whome then readie downe to lie
The hugy Earth a little plot to childe on did denie?
From Heaven, from Earth, and from the Sea your Goddesse banisht
                                               was,   240
And as an outcast through the world from place to place did passe,
Untill that Delos pitying hir, sayde Thou doste fleete on land
And I on Sea, and thereupon did lende hir out of hand
A place unstable. Of two twinnes there brought abed was she:
And this is but the seventh part of the issue borne by me.   245
Right happie am I. Who can this denie? and shall so still

210 *stomake:* temper, pride   236 *no:* not
211 *portly:* stately   237 *fro:* woman
214 *rout:* crowd   242 *fleete:* float, drift

Continue. Who doth doubt of that? Abundance hath and will
Preserve me. I am greater than that frowarde fortune may
Empeache me. For although she should pull many things away,
Yet should she leave me many more. My state is out of feare.   250
Of thys my huge and populous race surmise you that it were
Possible some of them should misse: yet can I never be
So spoyled that no mo than two shall tarie styll with me.
Leave quickly thys lewde sacrifice, and put me off this Bay
That on your heads is wreathed thus. They laide it streight away   255
And left their holie rites undone, and closely as they may
With secret whispring to themselves to Laton they dyd pray.
        How much from utter barrennesse the Goddesse was: so much
        Disdeind she more: and in the top of Cynthus framed such
Complaint as this to both hir twinnes. Lo I your mother deare,   260
Who in my bodie once you twaine with painefull travail beare,
Loe I whose courage is so stout as for to yeelde to none
Of all the other Goddesses except Joves wife alone,
Am lately doubted whether I a Goddesse be or no.
And if you helpe not, children mine, the case now standeth so   265
That I the honor must from hence of Altars quight forgo.
But this is not mine only griefe. Besides hir wicked fact
Most railing words hath Niobe to my defacing rackt.
She durst prefer hir Barnes to you. And as for me, she naamde
Me barren in respect of hir, and was no whit ashaamde   270
To shewe hir fathers wicked tongue which she by birth doth take.
This said: Latona was about entreatance for to make.
Cease off (quoth Phebus) long complaint is nothing but delay
Of punishment, and the selfesame wordes did Phebe also say.
And by and by they through the Ayre both gliding swiftly downe,   275
On Cadmus pallace hid in cloudes did light in Thebe towne.
        A fielde was underneath the wall both levell, large and wide,
        Betrampled every day with horse that men therin did ride,
Where store of Carres and Horses hoves the cloddes to dust had trode.
A couple of Amphions sonnes on lustie coursers rode   280
In this same place. Their horses faire Coperisons did weare
Of scarlet: and their bridles brave with golde bedecked were.
Of whome as Niobs eldest sonne Ismenos hapt to bring
His horse about, and reynde him in to make him keepe the ring,

---

248 *frowarde:* adverse
253 *spoyled:* despoiled
268 *rackt:* stretched, strained

269 *Barnes:* children
281 *Coperisons:* caparisons, ornamental coverings

He cride alas: and in his brest with that an arrow stacke   285
And by and by hys dying hand did let the bridle slacke.
And on the right side of the horse he slipped to the ground.
The second brother Sipylus did chaunce to heare the sound
Of Quivers clattring in the Ayre, and giving streight the reyne
And spur togither to his horse, began to flie amayne: 290
As doth the master of a ship: who when he sees a shoure
Approching, by some mistie cloud that ginnes to gloume and loure
Doth clap on all his sayles bicause no winde should scape him by
Though nere so small. Howbeit as he turned for to flie,
He was not able for to scape the Arrow which did stricke   295
Him through the necke. The nocke thereof did shaking upward sticke,
The head appeared at his throte. And as he forward gave
Himselfe in flying: so to ground he groveling also drave,
And toppled by the horses mane and feete amid his race,
And with his warme newshedded bloud berayed all the place.   300
But Phedimus, and Tantalus, the heir of the name
Of Tantalus, his Graundfather, who customably came
From other dailie exercise to wrestling, had begun
To close, and eache at other now with brest to brest to run,
When Phebus Arrow being sent with force from streyned string   305
Did strike through both of them as they did fast togither cling.
And so they sighed both at once, and both at once for paine
Fell downe to ground, and both of them at once their eyes did streine
To see their latest light, and both at once their ghostes did yeelde.
Alphenor this mischaunce of theirs with heavie heart behelde,   310
And scratcht and beate his wofull brest: and therewith flying out
To take them up betweene his armes, was as he went about
This worke of kindly pitie, killde. For Phebus with a Dart
Of deadly dint did rive him through the Bulke and brake his hart.
And when the steale was plucked out, a percell of his liver   315
Did hang upon the hooked heade: and so he did deliver
His life and bloud into the Ayre departing both togither.
But Damasicthon (on whose heade came never scissor) felt
Mo woundes than one. It was his chaunce to have a grievous pelt
Upon the verie place at which the leg is first begun   320
And where the hamstrings by the joynt with supple sinewes run

286 *slacke:* hang loose   300 *berayed:* stained
290 *amayne:* at full speed   314 *Bulke:* trunk
293 *bicause:* so that   315 *percell:* part
296 *nocke:* notch   319 *pelt:* wound

And while to draw this arrow out he with his hand assaide,
Another through his wezant went, and at the feathers staide.
The bloud did drive out this againe, and spinning high did spout
A great way off, and pierst the Ayre with sprinkling all about.   325
The last of all Ilionie with streched handes, and speche
Most humble (but in vaine) did say: O Gods I you beseche
Of mercie all in generall. He wist not what he saide
Ne how that unto all of them he ought not to have praide.
The God that helde the Bow in hande was moved: but as then   330
The Arrow was alredie gone so farre, that backe agen
He could not call it. Neerthelesse the wound was verie small
Of which he dide, for why his heart it did but lightly gall.
       The rumor of the mischiefe selfe, and mone of people, and
       The weeping of hir servants gave the mother t'understand   335
The sodaine stroke of this mischaunce. She wondred verie much
And stormed also that the Gods were able to doe such
A deede, or durst attempt it, yea she thought it more than right
That any of them over hir should have so mickle might.
Amphion had fordone himselfe alreadie with a knife,   340
And ended all his sorrowes quite togither with his life.
Alas, alas how greatly doth this Niobe differ here
From tother Niobe who alate disdaining any Pere
Did from Latonas Altars drive hir folke, and through the towne
With haultie looke and stately gate went pranking up and downe,   345
Then spighted at among hir owne, but piteous now to those:
That heretofore for hir deserts had bene hir greatest foes.
She falleth on the corses colde, and taking no regard,
Bestowde hir kysses on hir sonnes as whome she afterwarde
Did know she never more shoulde kisse. From whome she lifting thoe 350
Hir blew and broosed armes to heaven sayd: O thou cruell foe
Latona, feede, yea feede thy selfe I say upon my woe
And overgorge thy stomacke, yea and glut thy cruell hart
With these my present painefull pangs of bitter griping smart.
In corses seven I seven times deade am caried to my grave.   355
Rejoyce thou foe and triumph now in that thou seemste to have
The upper hande. What? upper hand? no no it is not so.
As wretched as my case doth seeme, yet have I left me mo

323 *wezant:* windpipe   345 *pranking:* parading
333 *gall:* injure   346 *spighted at:* regarded spitefully
339 *mickle:* much   348 *corses:* corpses
340 *fordone:* killed   350 *thoe:* then

Than thou for all thy happinesse canst of thine owne account.
Even after all these corses yet I still doe thee surmount.   360
Upon the ende of these same wordes the twanging of the string
In letting of the Arrow flie was clearly heard: which thing
Made every one save Niobe afraide. Hir heart was so
With sorrowe hardned, that she grew more bolde. Hir daughters tho
Were standing all with mourning weede and hanging haire before 365
Their brothers coffins. One of them in pulling from the sore
An Arrow sticking in his heart, sanke downe upon hir brother
With mouth to mouth, and so did yeelde hir fleeting ghost. Another
In comforting the wretched case and sorrow of hir mother
Upon the sodaine helde hir peace. She stricken was within   370
With double wound: which caused hir hir talking for to blin
And shut hir mouth: but first hir ghost was gone. One all in vaine
Attempting for to scape by flight was in hir flying slaine.
Another on hir sisters corse doth tumble downe starke dead.
This quakes and trembles piteously, and she doth hide hir head.   375
And when that sixe with sundrye woundes dispatched were and gone,
At last as yet remained one: and for to save that one,
Hir mother with hir bodie whole did cling about hir fast,
And wrying hir did over hir hir garments wholy cast:
And cried out: O leave me one: this little one yet save: 380
Of many but this only one the least of all I crave.
But while she prayd, for whome she prayd was kild. Then down she sate
Bereft of all hir children quite, and drawing to hir fate,
Among hir daughters and hir sonnes and husband newly dead.
Hir cheekes waxt hard, the Ayre could stirre no haire upon hir head. 385
The colour of hir face was dim and clearly voide of blood,
And sadly under open lids hir eyes unmoved stood.
In all hir bodie was no life. For even hir verie tung
And palat of hir mouth was hard, and eche to other clung.
Hir Pulses ceased for to beate, hir necke did cease to bow,   390
Hir armes to stir, hir feete to go, all powre forwent as now.
And into stone hir verie wombe and bowels also bind.
But yet she wept: and being hoyst by force of whirling wind
Was caried into Phrygie. There upon a mountaines top
She weepeth still in stone. From stone the drerie teares do drop.   395
    Then all both men and women fearde Latonas open ire

---

365 *weede:* garment
371 *blin:* stop
379 *wrying:* twisting, contorting

391 *forwent:* passed away
393 *hoyst:* lifted up

    And far with greater sumptuousnesse and earnester desire
Did worship the great majestie of this their Goddesse who
Did beare at once both Phebus and his sister Phebe too.
And through occasion of this chaunce, (as men are wont to do   400
In cases like) the people fell to telling things of old
Of whome a man among the rest this tale ensuing told.
    The auncient folke that in the fieldes of fruitfull Lycia dwelt
    Due penance also for their spight to this same Goddesse felt.
The basenesse of the parties makes the thing it selfe obscure.   405
Yet is the matter wonderfull. My selfe I you assure
Did presently beholde the Pond, and saw the very place
In which this wondrous thing was done. My father then in case,
Not able for to travell well by reason of his age,
To fetch home certaine Oxen thence made me to be his page,   410
Appointing me a countryman of Lycia to my guide.
With whome as I went plodding in the pasture groundes, I spide
Amids a certaine Pond an olde square Aultar colourd blacke
With cinder of the sacrifice that still upon it stacke.
About it round grew wavering Reedes. My guide anon did stay: 415
And softly, O be good to me, he in himselfe did say.
And I with like soft whispering did say, Be good to mee.
And then I askt him whether that the Altar wee did see
Belonged to the Waternymphes, or Faunes or other God
Peculiar to the place it selfe upon the which we yod.   420
He made me aunswere thus: My guest, no God of countrie race
Is in this Altar worshipped. That Goddesse claymes this place,
From whome the wife of mightie Jove did all the world forfend:
When wandring restlesse here and there full hardly in the end
Unsetled Delos did receyve then floting on the wave,   425
As tide and weather to and fro the swimming Iland drave.
There maugre Juno (who with might and main against hir strave)
Latona staying by a Date and Olyf tree that sted
In travail, of a paire of twinnes was safely brought abed.
And after hir delivrance folke report that she for feare   430
Of Junos wrath did flie from hence, and in hir armes did beare
Hir babes which afterwarde became two Gods. In which hir travell
In Sommer when the scorching Sunne is wont to burne the gravell
Of Lycie countrie where the fell Chymera hath his place,

408 *case:* condition
414 *stacke:* stuck
420 *yod:* went

423 *forfend:* forbid
427 *maugre:* in spite of
428 *sted:* help

The Goddesse wearie with the long continuance of hir race,   435
Waxt thirstie by the meanes of drought with going in the Sunne.
Hir babes had also suckt hir brestes as long as milke wold runne.
By chaunce she spide this little Pond of water here bylow.
And countrie Carles were gathering there these Osier twigs that grow
So thicke upon a shrubbie stalke: and of these rushes greene: 440
And flags that in these moorish plots so rife of growing beene.
She comming hither kneeled downe the water up to take
To coole hir thirst. The churlish cloynes forfended hir the Lake.
Then gently said the Goddesse: Sirs, why doe you me forfend
The water? Nature doth to all in common water send.   445
For neither Sunne, nor Ayre, nor yet the Water private bee,
I seeke but that which natures gift hath made to all things free.
And yet I humbly crave of you to graunt it unto mee.
I did not go about to wash my werie limmes and skin,
I would but only quench my thirst. My throte is scalt within   450
For want of moysture: and my chappes and lippes are parching drie:
And scarsly is there way for wordes to issue out thereby.
A draught of water will to me be heavenly Nectar now.
And sure I will confesse I have received life of you.
Yea in your giving of a drop of water unto mee,   455
The case so standeth as you shall preserve the lives of three.
Alas let these same sillie soules that in my bosome stretch
Their little armes (by chaunce hir babes their pretie dolles did retch)
To pitie move you. What is he so hard that would not yeeld
To this the gentle Goddesses entreatance meeke and meeld?   460
Yet they for all the humble wordes she could devise to say,
Continued in their willfull moode of churlish saying nay,
And threatned for to sende hir thence onlesse she went away,
Reviling hir most spightfully. And not contented so,
With handes and feete the standing Poole they troubled to and fro,   465
Until with trampling up and downe maliciously, the soft
And slimie mud that lay beneath was raised up aloft.
With that the Goddesse was so wroth that thirst was quight forgot.
And unto such unworthie Carles hirselfe she humbleth not:
Ne speaketh meaner wordes than might beseeme a Goddesse well.   470
But holding up hir handes to heaven: For ever mought you dwell
In this same Pond, she said: hir wish did take effect with speede.

---

439 *Carles:* fellows, churls   451 *chappes:* jaws
441 *moorish:* swampy   458 *dolles:* palms; *retch:* reach, stretch
450 *scalt:* parched

For underneath the water they delight to be in deede.
Now dive they to the bottome downe, now up their heades they pop,
Another while with sprawling legs they swim upon the top.   475
And oftentimes upon the bankes they have a minde to stond,
And oftentimes from thence againe to leape into the Pond.
And there they now doe practise still their filthy tongues to scold
And shamelessely (though underneath the water) they doe hold
Their former wont of brawling still amid the water cold.   480
Their voices stil are hoarse and harsh, their throtes have puffed goles,
Their chappes with brawling widened are, their hammer headed Jowls
Are joyned to their shoulders just, the neckes of them doe seeme
Cut off, the ridgebone of their backe stickes up of colour greene.
Their paunch which is the greatest part of all their trunck is gray,   485
And so they up and downe the Pond made newly Frogges doe play.
      When one of Lyce (I wote not who) had spoken in this sort,
      Another of a Satyr streight began to make report,
Whome Phebus overcomming on a pipe (made late ago
By Pallas) put to punishment. Why flayest thou me so,   490
Alas, he cride, it irketh me. Alas a sorie pipe
Deserveth not so cruelly my skin from me to stripe.
For all his crying ore his eares quight pulled was his skin.
Nought else he was than one whole wounde. The griesly bloud did spin
From every part, the sinewes lay discovered to the eye,   495
The quivering veynes without a skin lay beating nakedly.
The panting bowels in his bulke ye might have numbred well,
And in his brest the shere small strings a man might easly tell.
The Countrie Faunes, the Gods of Woods, the Satyrs of his kin,
The Mount Olympus whose renowne did ere that time begin,   500
And all the Nymphes, and all that in those mountaines kept their
                                      sheepe,
Or grazed cattell thereabouts, did for this Satyr weepe.
The fruitfull earth waxt moyst therewith, and moysted did receyve
Their teares, and in hir bowels deepe did of the same conceyve.
And when that she had turned them to water, by and by   505
She sent them forth againe aloft to see the open Skie.
The River that doth rise thereof beginning there his race,
In verie deepe and shoring bankes to Seaward runnes apace
Through Phrygie, and according as the Satyr, so the streame
Is called Marsias, of the brookes the clearest in that Realme.   510

481 *goles:* gullets

With such examples as these same the common folke returnde
To present things, and every man through all the Citie moornde
For that Amphion was destroyde with all his issue so.
But all the fault and blame was laide upon the mother tho.
For hir alonly Pelops mournde (as men report) and hee   515
In opening of his clothes did shewe that everie man might see
His shoulder on the left side bare of Ivorie for to bee.
This shoulder at his birth was like his tother both in hue
And flesh, untill his fathers handes most wickedly him slue,
And that the Gods when they his limmes againe togither drue,   520
To joyne them in their proper place and forme by nature due,
Did finde out all the other partes, save only that which grue
Betwene the throteboll and the arme, which when they could not get
This other made of Ivorie white in place therof they set
And by that meanes was Pelops made againe both whole and sound. 525
    The neyghbor Princes thither came, and all the Cities round
    About besought their Kings to go and comfort Thebe: as Arge
And Sparta, and Mycene which was under Pelops charge,
And Calydon unhated of the frowning Phebe yit,
The welthie towne Orchomenos, and Corinth which in it   530
Had famous men for workmanship in mettals: and the stout
Messene which full twentie yeares did hold besiegers out.
And Patre, and the lowly towne Cleona, Nelies Pyle,
And Troyzen not surnamed yet Pittheia for a while.
And all the other Borough townes and Cities which doe stand   535
Within the narrow balke at which two Seas doe meete at hand,
Or which do bound upon the balke without in maine firme land.
Alonly Athens (who would thinke?) did neither come nor send.
Warre barred them from courtesie the which they did entend.
The King of Pontus with an host of savage people lay   540
In siege before their famous walles and curstly did them fray.
Untill that Tereus, King of Thrace, approching to their ayde,
Did vanquish him, and with renowne was for his labor payde.
And sith he was so puissant in men and ready coyne,
And came of mightie Marsis race, Pandion sought to joyne   545
Aliance with him by and by, and gave him to his Feere
His daughter Progne. At this match (as after will appeare)
Was neyther Juno, President of mariage wont to bee,

523 *throteboll:* Adam's-apple
536 *balke:* isthmus
537 *bound:* border

541 *fray:* frighten
546 *to his Feere:* for his mate
548 *President of:* presiding over

Nor Hymen, no nor any one of all the graces three.
The Furies snatching Tapers up that on some Herce did stande   550
Did light them, and before the Bride did beare them in their hande.
The Furies made the Bridegroomes bed. And on the house did rucke
A cursed Owle the messenger of yll successe and lucke.
And all the night time while that they were lying in their beds,
She sate upon the bedsteds top right over both their heds.   555
Such handsell Progne had the day that Tereus did hir wed.
Such handsell had they when that she was brought of childe abed.
All Thracia did rejoyce at them, and thankt their Gods, and willd
That both the day of Prognes match with Tereus should be hild
For feastfull, and the day likewise that Itys first was borne: 560
So little know we what behoves. The Sunne had now outworne
Five Harvests, and by course five times had run his yearly race,
When Progne flattring Tereus saide: If any love or grace
Betweene us be, send eyther me my sister for to see,
Or finde the meanes that hither she may come to visit mee.   565
You may assure your Fathrinlaw she shall againe returne
Within a while. Ye doe to me the highest great good turne
That can be, if you bring to passe I may my sister see.
Immediatly the King commaundes his shippes aflote to bee.
And shortly after, what with sayle and what with force of **Ores**,   570
In Athens haven he arrives and landes at Pyrey shores.
As soone as of his fathrinlaw the presence he obtainde,
And had of him bene courteously and friendly entertainde,
Unhappie handsell entred with their talking first togither.
The errandes of his wife, the cause of his then comming thither,   575
He had but new begon to tell, and promised that when
She had hir sister seene, she should with speede be sent agen:
When (see the chaunce) came Philomele in raiment very rich,
And yet in beautie farre more rich, even like the Fairies which
Reported are the pleasant woods and water springs to haunt,   580
So that the like apparell and attire to them you graunt.
King Tereus at the sight of hir did burne in his desire,
As if a man should chaunce to set a gulfe of corne on fire,
Or burne a stacke of hay. Hir face in deede deserved love.
But as for him, to fleshly lust even nature did him move.   585
For of those countries commonly the people are above

---

550 *Herce:* hearse, bier
552 *rucke:* huddle
556 *handsell:* omen

583 *gulfe:* goaf—as much corn as could be
held in the bay of a barn

All measure prone to lecherie. And therefore both by kinde
His flame encreast, and by his owne default of vicious minde.
He purposde fully to corrupt hir servants with reward:
Or for to bribe hir Nurce, that she should slenderly regarde   590
Hir dutie to hir mistresseward. And rather than to fayle,
The Ladie even hirselfe with gifts he minded to assayle,
And all his kingdome for to spend, or else by force of hand
To take hir, and in maintenance thereof by sword to stand.
There was not under heaven the thing but that he durst it prove,   595
So far unable was he now to stay his lawlesse love.
Delay was deadly. Backe againe with greedie minde he came
Of Prognes errands for to talke: and underneath the same
He workes his owne ungraciousnesse. Love gave him power to frame
His talke at will. As oft as he demaunded out of square,   600
Upon his wives importunate desire himselfe he bare.
He also wept: as though his wife had willed that likewise.
O God, what blindnesse doth the heartes of mortall men disguise?
By working mischiefe Tereus gets him credit for to seeme
A loving man, and winneth praise by wickednesse extreeme.   605
Yea and the foolish Philomele the selfesame thing desires.
Who hanging on hir fathers necke with flattring armes, requires
Against hir life and for hir life his licence for to go
To see hir sister. Tereus beholdes hir wistly tho,
And in beholding handles hir with heart. For when he saw   610
Hir kisse hir father, and about his necke hir armes to draw,
They all were spurres to pricke him forth, and wood to feede his fire,
And foode of forcing nourishment to further his desire.
As oft as she hir father did betweene hir armes embrace,
So often wished he himselfe hir father in that case.   615
For nought at all should that in him have wrought the greater grace.
Hir father could not say them nay, they lay at him so sore.
Right glad thereof was Philomele and thanked him therefore.
And wretched wench she thinkes she had obtained such a thing,
As both to Progne and hir selfe should joy and comfort bring,   620
When both of them in verie deede should afterward it rew.
To endward of his daily race and travell Phebus drew,
And on the shoring side of Heaven his horses downeward flew.
A princely supper was prepaarde, and wine in golde was set:

---

587 *kinde:* nature
600 *out of square:* out of order, wrongly

609 *wistly:* intently
617 *lay at:* urged

And after meate to take their rest the Princes did them get. 625
But though the King of Thrace that while were absent from hir sight,
Yet swelted he: and in his minde revolving all the night
Hir face, hir gesture, and hir hands, imaginde all the rest
(The which as yet he had not seene) as likte his fancie best.
He feedes his flames himselfe. No winke could come within his eyes, 630
For thinking ay on hir. As soone as day was in the skies,
Pandion holding in his hand the hand of Tereus prest
To go his way, and sheading teares betooke him thus his guest:
Deare sonneinlaw I give thee here (sith godly cause constraines)
This Damsell. By the faith that in thy Princely heart remaines, 635
And for our late aliance sake, and by the Gods above,
I humbly thee beseche that as a Father thou doe love
And maintaine hir, and that as soone as may be (all delay
Will unto me seeme over long) thou let hir come away,
The comfort of my carefull age on whome my life doth stay. 640
And thou my daughter Philomele (it is inough ywis
That from hir father set so farre thy sister Progne is)
If any sparke of nature doe within thy heart remayne,
With all the haaste and speede thou canst returne to me againe.
In giving charge he kissed hir: and downe his cheekes did raine 645
The tender teares, and as a pledge of faith he tooke the right
Handes of them both, and joyning them did eche to other plight,
Desiring them to beare in minde his commendations to
His daughter and hir little sonne. And then with much adoe
For sobbing, at the last he bad adew as one dismaid. 650
The foremisgiving of his minde did make him sore afraid.
    As soone as Tereus and the Maide togither were aboord,
    And that their ship from land with Ores was haled on the foord,
The fielde is ours, he cride aloude, I have the thing I sought
And up he skipt, so barbrous and so beastly was his thought, 655
That scarce even there he could forbeare his pleasure to have wrought.
His eye went never off of hir: as when the scarefull Erne
With hooked talants trussing up a Hare among the Ferne,
Hath laid hir in his nest, from whence the prisoner can not scape,
The ravening fowle with greedie eyes upon his pray doth gape. 660
Now was their journey come to ende: now were they gone aland
In Thracia, when that Tereus tooke the Ladie by the hand,

---

627 *swelted:* burned
633 *betooke him:* entrusted to him
640 *carefull:* full of care

641 *ywis:* indeed
653 *foord:* sea

And led hir to a pelting graunge that peakishly did stand
In woods forgrowen. There waxing pale and trembling sore for feare,
And dreading all things, and with teares demaunding sadly where   665
Hir sister was, he shet hir up: and therewithall bewraide
His wicked lust, and so by force bicause she was a Maide
And all alone he vanquisht hir. It booted nought at all
That she on sister, or on Sire, or on the Gods did call.
She quaketh like the wounded Lambe which from the Wolves hore
                                                    teeth   670
New shaken thinkes hir selfe not safe: or as the Dove that seeth
Hir fethers with hir owne bloud staynde, who shuddring still doth feare
The greedie Hauke that did hir late with griping talants teare.
        Anon when that this mazednesse was somewhat overpast,
    She rent hir haire, and beate hir brest, and up to heavenward cast   675
Hir hands in mourningwise, and said: O cankerd Carle, O fell
And cruell Tyrant, neyther could the godly teares that fell
Adowne my fathers cheekes when he did give thee charge of mee,
Ne of my sister that regarde that ought to be in thee,
Nor yet my chaaste virginitie, nor conscience of the lawe   680
Of wedlocke, from this villanie thy barbrous heart withdraw?
Behold thou hast confounded all. My sister thorough mee
Is made a Cucqueane: and thy selfe through this offence of thee
Art made a husband to us both, and unto me a foe,
A just deserved punishment for lewdly doing so.   685
But to th'intent, O perjurde wretch, no mischiefe may remaine
Unwrought by thee, why doest thou from murdring me refraine?
Would God thou had it done before this wicked rape. From hence
Then should my soule most blessedly have gone without offence.
But if the Gods doe see this deede, and if the Gods, I say,   690
Be ought, and in this wicked worlde beare any kinde of sway
And if with me all other things decay not, sure the day
Will come that for this wickednesse full dearly thou shalt pay.
Yea I my selfe rejecting shame thy doings will bewray.
And if I may have power to come abrode, them blase I will   695
In open face of all the world. Or if thou keepe me still
As prisoner in these woods, my voyce the verie woods shall fill,
And make the stones to understand. Let Heaven to this give eare
And all the Gods and powers therein if any God be there.

---

663 *peakishly:* steep-roofed   670 *hore:* white, gray
666 *bewraide:* revealed   676 *cankerd:* corrupt
668 *booted:* helped   682 *Cucqueane:* female cuckold

The cruell tyrant being chaaft and also put in feare   700
With these and other such hir wordes, both causes so him stung,
That drawing out his naked sworde that at his girdle hung,
He tooke hir rudely by the haire, and wrung hir hands behind hir,
Compelling hir to holde them there while he himselfe did bind hir.
When Philomela sawe the sworde, she hoapt she should have dide,   705
And for the same hir naked throte she gladly did provide.
But as she yirnde and called ay upon hir fathers name,
And strived to have spoken still, the cruell tyrant came
And with a paire of pinsons fast did catch hir by the tung,
And with his sword did cut it off. The stumpe whereon it hung   710
Did patter still. The tip fell downe and quivering on the ground
As though that it had murmured it made a certaine sound.
And as an Adders tayle cut off doth skip a while: even so
The tip of Philomelaas tongue did wriggle to and fro,
And nearer to hir mistresseward in dying still did go.   715
And after this most cruell act, for certaine men report
That he (I scarcely dare beleve) did oftentimes resort
To maymed Philomela and abusde hir at his will:
Yet after all this wickednesse he keeping countnance still,
Durst unto Progne home repaire. And she immediatly   720
Demaunded where hir sister was. He sighing feynedly
Did tell hir falsly she was dead: and with his suttle teares
He maketh all his tale to seeme of credit in hir eares.
Hir garments glittring all with golde she from hir shoulders teares
And puts on blacke, and setteth up an emptie Herce, and keepes   725
A solemne obite for hir soule, and piteously she weepes
And waileth for hir sisters fate who was not in such wise
As that was, for to be bewailde. The Sunne had in the Skies
Past through the twelve celestiall signes, and finisht full a yeare.
But what should Philomela doe? She watched was so neare   730
That start she could not for hir life. The walles of that same graunge
Were made so high of maine hard stone, that out she could not raunge.
Againe hir tunglesse mouth did want the utterance of the fact.
Great is the wit of pensivenesse, and when the head is rakt
With hard misfortune, sharpe forecast of practise entereth in.   735
A warpe of white upon a frame of Thracia she did pin,
And weaved purple letters in betweene it, which bewraide

---

700 *chaaft:* angered
709 *pinsons:* pincers

726 *obite:* service in commemoration of the dead
732 *maine:* solid

The wicked deede of Tereus. And having done, she praide
A certaine woman by hir signes to beare them to hir mistresse.
She bare them and deliverde them not knowing nerethelesse   740
What was in them. The Tyrants wife unfolded all the clout,
And of hir wretched fortune red the processe whole throughout.
She held hir peace (a wondrous thing it is she should so doe)
But sorrow tide hir tongue, and wordes agreeable unto
Hir great displeasure were not at commaundment at that stound.   745
And weepe she could not. Ryght and wrong she reckeneth to confound,
And on revengement of the deede hir heart doth wholy ground.
      It was the time that wives of Thrace were wont to celebrate
The three yeare rites of Bacchus which were done a nighttimes late.
A nighttimes soundeth Rhodope of tincling pannes and pots: 750
A nighttimes giving up hir house abrode Queene Progne trots
Disguisde like Bacchus other froes and armed to the proofe
With all the frenticke furniture that serves for that behoofe.
Hir head was covered with a vine. About hir loose was tuckt
A Reddeeres skin, a lightsome Launce upon hir shoulder ruckt.   755
In post gaddes terrible Progne through the woods, and at hir heeles
A flocke of froes. And where the sting of sorrow which she feeles
Enforceth hir to furiousnesse, she feynes it to proceede
Of Bacchus motion. At the length she finding out in deede
The outset Graunge howlde out, and cride, Now well, and open brake   760
The gates, and streight hir sister thence by force of hand did take,
And veyling hir in like attire of Bacchus, hid hir head
With Ivie leaves, and home to Court hir sore amazed led.
      As soone as Philomela wist she set hir foote within
      That cursed house, the wretched soule to shudther did begin,   765
And all hir face waxt pale. Anon hir sister getting place
Did pull off Bacchus mad attire, and making bare hir face
Embraced hir betweene hir armes. But she considering that
Queene Progne was a Cucqueane made by meanes of hir, durst nat
Once raise hir eyes: but on the ground fast fixed helde the same.   770
And where she woulde have taken God to witnesse that the shame
And villanie was wrought to hir by violence, she was fayne
To use hir hand in stead of speache. Then Progne chaaft amaine,
And was not able in hir selfe hir choler to restraine.
But blaming Philomela for hir weeping, said these wordes: 775

---

741 *clout:* cloth   753 *furniture:* furnishings, apparel; *behoofe:*
745 *stound:* time   use, duty
                                      755 *ruckt:* leaned

Thou must not deale in this behalfe with weeping, but with swordes:
Or with some thing of greater force than swords. For my part, I
Am readie, yea and fully bent all mischiefe for to trie.
This pallace will I eyther set on fire, and in the same
Bestow the cursed Tereus the worker of our shame: 780
Or pull away his tongue: or put out both his eyes: or cut
Away those members which have thee to such dishonor put:
Or with a thousand woundes expulse that sinfull soule of his.
The thing that I doe purpose on is great, what ere it is.
I know not what it may be yet. While Progne hereunto 785
Did set hir minde, came Itys in, who taught hir what to doe.
She staring on him cruelly, said: Ah, how like thou art
Thy wicked father, and without moe wordes a sorowfull part
She purposed, such inward ire was boyling in hir heart.
But notwithstanding when hir sonne approched to hir neare, 790
And lovingly had greeted hir by name of mother deare,
And with his pretie armes about the necke had hugde hir fast,
And flattring wordes with childish toyes in kissing forth had cast,
The mothers heart of hirs was then constreyned to relent,
Asswaged wholy was the rage to which she erst was bent, 795
And from hir eyes against hir will the teares enforced went.
But when she saw how pitie did compell hir heart to yeelde,
She turned to hir sisters face from Itys, and behelde
Now t'one, now tother earnestly and said: Why tattles he
And she sittes dumbe bereft of tongue? as well why calles not she 800
Me sister, as this boy doth call me mother? Seest thou not,
Thou daughter of Pandion, what a husband thou hast got?
Thou growest wholy out of kinde. To such a husband as
Is Tereus, pitie is a sinne. No more delay there was.
She dragged Itys after hir, as when it happes in Inde 805
A Tyger gets a little Calfe that suckes upon a Hynde
And drags him through the shadie woods. And when that they had
                                        found
A place within the house far off and far above the ground,
Then Progne strake him with a sword now plainly seeing whother
He should, and holding up his handes, and crying mother, mother, 810
And flying to hir necke: even where the brest and side doe bounde,
And never turnde away hir face. Inough had bene that wound
Alone to bring him to his ende. The tother sister slit

793 *toyes:* caresses   809 *whother:* whither

His throte. And while some life and soule was in his members yit,
In gobbits they them rent: whereof were some in Pipkins boyld,   815
And other some on hissing spits against the fire were broyld,
And with the gellied bloud of him was all the chamber foyld.

    To this same banquet Progne bade hir husband knowing nought
    Nor nought mistrusting of the harme and lewdnesse she had
                         wrought.

And feyning a solemnitie according to the guise   820
Of Athens, at the which there might be none in any wise
Besides hir husband and hir selfe, she banisht from the same
Hir householde folke and sojourners, and such as guestwise came.
King Tereus sitting in the throne of his forefathers, fed
And swallowed downe the selfesame flesh that of his bowels bred.   825
And he (so blinded was his heart) Fetch Itys hither, sed.
No lenger hir most cruell joy dissemble could the Queene.
But of hir murther coveting the messenger to beene,
She said: The thing thou askest for, thou hast within. About
He looked round, and asked where? To put him out of dout,   830
As he was yet demaunding where, and calling for him: out
Lept Philomele with scattred haire aflaight like one that fled
Had from some fray where slaughter was, and threw the bloudy head
Of Itys in his fathers face. And never more was shee
Desirous to have had hir speache, that able she might be   835
Hir inward joy with worthie wordes to witnesse franke and free.
The tyrant with a hideous noyse away the table shoves:
And reeres the fiends from Hell. One while with yawning mouth he
                         proves
To perbrake up his meate againe, and cast his bowels out.
Another while with wringing handes he weeping goes about.   840
And of his sonne he termes himselfe the wretched grave. Anon
With naked sword and furious heart he followeth fierce upon
Pandions daughters. He that had bene present would have deemde
Their bodies to have hovered up with fethers. As they seemde,
So hovered they with wings in deede. Of whome the one away   845
To woodward flies, the other still about the house doth stay.
And of their murther from their brestes not yet the token goth,
For even still yet are stainde with bloud the fethers of them both.

---

815 *gobbits:* pieces of flesh; *Pipkins:* pots   832 *aflaight:* flying
817 *foyld:* fouled   838 *reeres:* raises, rouses; *proves:* tries
819 *lewdnesse:* wickedness   839 *perbrake:* vomit

And he through sorrow and desire of vengeance waxing wight,
Became a Bird upon whose top a tuft of feathers light   850
In likenesse of a Helmets crest doth trimly stand upright.
In stead of his long sword, his bill shootes out a passing space:
A Lapwing named is this Bird, all armed seemes his face.
The sorrow of this great mischaunce did stop Pandions breath
Before his time, and long ere age determinde had his death.   855
Erecthey reigning after him the government did take:
A Prince of such a worthinesse as no man well can make
Resolution, if he more in armes or justice did excell.
Foure sonnes, and daughters foure he had. Of which a couple well
Did eche in beautie other match. The one of these whose name   860
Was Procris unto Cephalus, King Aeolus sonne, became
A happie wife. The Thracians and King Tereus were a let
To Boreas: so that long it was before the God could get
His dearbeloved Orithya, while trifling he did stand
With faire entreatance rather than did use the force of hand.   865
But when he saw he no reliefe by gentle meanes could finde,
Then turning unto boystous wrath (which unto that same winde
Is too familiar and too much accustomed by kinde)
He said: I served am but well: for why laid I apart
My proper weapons, fiercenesse, force, and ire, and cruell hart?   870
And fell to fauning like a foole, which did me but disgrace?
For me is violence meete. Through this the pestred cloudes I chace.
Through this I tosse the Seas. Through this I turne up knottie Okes,
And harden Snow, and beate the ground in hayle with sturdie strokes,
When I my brothers chaunce to get in open Ayre and Skie.   875
(For that is my fielde in the which my maisteries I doe trie)
I charge upon them with such brunt, that of our meeting smart
The Heaven betweene us soundes, and from the hollow Cloudes doth
                                                           start
Enforced fire. And when I come in holes of hollow ground,
And fiersly in those emptie caves doe rouse my backe up round,   880
I trouble even the ghostes, and make the verie world to quake.
This helpe in wooing of my wife (to speede) I should have take.
Erecthey should not have bene prayde my Fatherinlaw to bee:
He should have bene compelde thereto by stout extremitie.
In speaking these or other wordes as sturdie, Boreas gan   885

---

849 *wight:* agile, swift   876 *maisteries:* feats
862 *let:* hindrance   882 *take:* taken
872 *pestred:* troubled

    To flaske his wings. With waving of the which he raysed than
So great a gale, that all the earth was blasted therewithall,
And troubled was the maine brode Sea. And as he traylde his pall
Bedusted over highest tops of things, he swept the ground.
And having now in smokie cloudes himselfe enclosed round,   890
Betweene his duskie wings he caught Orithya straught for feare,
And like a lover, verie soft and easly did hir beare.
And as he flew, the flames of love enkindled more and more
By meanes of stirring. Neither did he stay his flight before
He came within the land and towne of Cicons with his pray.   895
And there soone after being made his wife she hapt to lay
Hir belly, and a paire of boyes she at a burthen brings,
Who else in all resembled full their mother, save in wings
The which they of their father tooke. Howbeit (by report)
They were not borne with wings upon their bodies in this sort.   900
While Calais and Zetes had no beard upon their chin,
They both were callow. But as soone as haire did once begin
In likenesse of a yellow Downe upon their cheekes to sprout,
Then (even as comes to passe in Birdes) the feathers budded out
Togither on their pinyons too, and spreaded round about   905
On both their sides. And finally when childhod once was spent
And youth come on, togither they with other Minyes went
To Colchos in the Galley that was first devisde in Greece,
Upon a sea as then unknowen, to fetch the golden fleece.

FINIS SEXTI LIBRI.

886 *flaske:* flap   891 *straught:* distraught

THE SEVENTH BOOKE

OF OVIDS METAMORPHOSIS.

[Jason and Medea. The Myrmidons. Cephalus and Procris.]

And now in ship of Pagasa the Mynies cut the seas.
And leading under endlesse night his age in great disease
Of scarcitie was Phiney seene, and Boreas sonnes had chaste
Away the Maidenfaced foules that did his victels waste.
And after suffring many things in noble Jasons band,   5
In muddie Phasis gushing streame at last they went aland.
There while they going to the King demaund the golden fleece
Brought thither certaine yeares before by Phryxus out of Greece,
And of their dreadfull labors wait an answere to receive:
Aeetas daughter in hir heart doth mightie flames conceyve.   10
And after struling verie long, when reason could not win
The upper hand of rage: she thus did in hir selfe begin:
    In vaine, Medea, doste thou strive: some God what ere he is
    Against thee bendes his force. For what a wondrous thing is this?
Is any thing like this which men doe terme by name of Love?   15
For why should I my fathers hestes esteeme so hard above
All measure? sure in very deede they are too hard and sore.
Why feare I lest yon straunger whome I never saw before
Should perish? what should be the cause of this my feare so great?
Unhappie wench (and if thou canst) suppresse this uncouth heat   20
That burneth in thy tender brest: and if so be I coulde,
A happie turne it were, and more at ease then be I shoulde.
But now an uncouth maladie perforce against my will
Doth hale me. Love persuades me one, another thing my skill.

16 *hestes:* commands   24 *skill:* reason
20 *uncouth:* unfamiliar, improper

The best I see and like: the worst I follow headlong still.   25
Why being of the royall bloud so fondly doste thou rave,
Upon a straunger thus to dote, desiring for to have
An husband of another world? at home thou mightest finde
A lover meete for thine estate on whome to set thy minde.
And yet it is but even a chaunce if he shall live or no: 30
God graunt him for to live. I may without offence pray so,
Although I lovde him not: for what hath Jason trespast me?
Who woulde not pitie Jasons youth onlesse they cruell be?
What creature is there but his birth and prowesse might him move?
And setting all the rest asyde, who woulde not be in love   35
With Jasons goodlie personage? my heart assuredly
Is toucht therewith. But if that I provide not remedie,
With burning breath of blasting Bulles needes sindged must he bee.
Of seedes that he himselfe must sow a harvest shall he see
Of armed men in battell ray upon the ground up grow   40
Against the which it hoveth him his manhode for to show.
And as a pray he must be set against the Dragon fell.
If I these things let come to passe, I may confesse right well
That of a Tyger I was bred: and that within my brest
A heart more harde than any steele or stonie rocke doth rest.   45
Why rather doe I not his death with wrathfull eyes beholde?
And joy with others seeing him to utter perill solde?
Why doe I not enforce the Bulles against him? Why, I say,
Exhort I not the cruell men which shall in battell ray
Arise against him from the ground? and that same Dragon too   50
Within whose eyes came never sleepe? God shield I so should doo.
But prayer smally bootes, except I put to helping hand.
And shall I like a Caytife then betray my fathers land?
Shall I a straunger save whome we nor none of ours doth know?
That he by me preserved may without me homeward row?   55
And take another to his wife, and leave me, wretched wight,
To torments? If I wist that he coulde worke me such a spight,
Or could in any others love than only mine delight,
The Churle should die for me. But sure he beareth not the face
Like one that wold doe so. His birth, his courage, and his grace   60
Doe put me clearly out of doubt he will not me deceyve,

40 *ray:* array   52 *bootes:* helps
41 *hoveth:* behoveth   53 *Caytife:* wretch, villain
51 *shield:* forbid

No nor forget the great good turnes he shall by me receyve.
Yet shall he to me first his faith for more assurance plight
And solemly he shall be sworne to keepe the covenant right.
Why fearste thou now without a cause? step to it out of hand: 65
And doe not any lenger time thus lingring fondly stand.
For ay shall Jason thinke himselfe beholding unto thee:
And shall thee marrie solemly: yea honored shalt thou bee
Of all the Mothers great and small throughout the townes of Greece
For saving of their sonnes that come to fetch the golden fleece.   70
And shall I then leave brother, sister, father, kith and kin?
And household Gods, and native soyle, and all that is therein?
And saile I know not whither with a straunger? Yea: why not?
My father surely cruell is, my Countrie rude God wot:
My brother yet a verie babe: my sister I dare say   75
Contented is with all hir heart that I should go away:
The greatest God is in my selfe: the things I doe forsake
Are trifles in comparison of those that I shall take.
For saving of the Greekish ship renoumed shall I bee.
A better place I shall enjoy with Cities riche and free,   80
Whose fame doth florish fresh even here, and people that excell
In civill life and all good Artes: and whome I would not sell
For all the goods within the worlde, Duke Aesons noble sonne.
Whome had I to my lawfull Feere assuredly once wonne,
Most happie yea and blest of God I might my selfe account,   85
And with my head above the starres to heaven I should surmount.
But men report that certaine rockes (I know not what) doe meete
Amid the waves, and monstrously againe asunder fleete:
And how Charybdis, utter foe to ships that passe thereby,
Now sowpeth in, now speweth out the Sea incessantly: 90
And ravening Scylla being hemde with cruell dogs about,
Amids the gulfe of Sicilie doth make a barking out.
What skilleth that? As long as I enjoy the thing I love,
And hang about my Jasons necke, it shall no whit me move
To saile the daungerous Seas: as long as him I may embrace   95
I cannot surely be afraide in any kinde of case.
Or if I chaunce to be afraide, my feare shall only tende
But for my husband. Callste thou him thy husband? Doste pretende
Gay titles to thy foule offence, Medea? nay not so:

79 *renoumed:* renowned   90 *sowpeth:* soaks, sips
84 *Feere:* mate   93 *skilleth:* makes a difference, matters
88 *fleete:* drift, slip away

But rather looke about how great a lewdnesse thou doste go,   100
And shun the mischiefe while thou mayst. She had no sooner said
These wordes, but right and godlinesse and shamefastnesse were staid
Before hir eyes, and frantick love did flie away dismaid.
    She went me to an Altar that was dedicate of olde
    To Perseys daughter Hecate (of whome the witches holde   105
As of their Goddesse) standing in a thicke and secrete wood
So close it coulde not well be spide: and now the raging mood
Of furious love was well alaide and clearely put to flight:
When spying Aesons sonne, the flame that seemed quenched quight
Did kindle out of hand againe. Hir cheekes began to glowe,   110
And flushing over all hir face the scarlet bloud did flowe.
And even as when a little sparke that was in ashes hid,
Uncovered with the whisking windes is from the ashes rid,
Eftsoones it taketh nourishment and kindleth in such wise,
That to his former strength againe and flaming it doth rise: 115
Even so hir quailed love which late ye would have thought had quight
Bene vanisht out of minde, as soone as Jason came in sight
Did kindle to his former force in vewing of the grace
With which he did avaunce himselfe then comming there in place.
And (as it chaunced) farre more faire and beautifull of face   120
She thought him then than ever erst, but sure it doth behove
Hir judgement should be borne withall bicause she was in love.
She gapte and gazed in his face with fixed staring eyen
As though she never had him seene before that instant time.
So farre she was beside hir selfe she thought it should not bee   125
The face of any worldly wight the which she then did see.
She was not able for hir life to turne hir eyes away,
But when he tooke hir by the hand and speaking gan to pray
Hir softly for to succor him, and promisde faithfully
To take hir to his wedded wife, she falling by and by   130
A weeping, said: Sir, what I doe I see apparantly.
Not want of knowledge of the truth but love shall me deceive.
You shalbe saved by my meanes. And now I must receive
A faithfull promise at your hand for saving of your life.
He made a solemne vow, and sware to take hir to his wife,   135
By triple Hecates holie rites, and by what other power
So ever else had residence within that secret bower,
And by the Sire of him that should his Fathrinlaw become
Who all things doth behold, and as he hopte to overcome

100 *lewdnesse:* wickedness

The dreadfull daungers which he had soone after to assay.   140
Duke Jason being credited receivde of hir streight way
Enchaunted herbes: and having learnde the usage of the same,
Departed thence with merrie heart, and to his lodging came.
  Next Morne had chaste the streaming stars: and folke by heapes
                                                  did flocke
To Marsis sacred field, and there stoode thronging in a shocke,   145
To see the straunge pastimes. The King most stately to beholde
With yvorie Mace above them all did sit in throne of golde.
Anon the brazenhoved Bulles from stonie nostrils cast
Out flakes of fire: their scalding breath the growing grasse did blast.
And looke what noise a chimney full of burning fewell makes,   150
Or Flint in softning in the Kell when first the fire it takes
By sprincling water thereupon: such noyse their boyling brests
Turmoyling with the firie flames enclosed in their chests,
Such noise their scorched throtebolles make. Yet stoutly Jason went
To meete them. They their dreadfull eyes against him grimly bent, 155
And eke their hornes with yron tipt: and strake the dust about
In stamping with their cloven clees: and with their belowing out
Set all the fielde upon a smoke. The Mynies seeing that
Were past their wits with sodaine feare, but Jason feeled nat
So much as any breath of theirs: such strength hath sorcerie.   160
Their dangling Dewlaps with his hand he coyd unfearfully.
And putting yokes upon their neckes he forced them to draw
The heavie burthen of the plough which erst they never saw,
And for to breake the fielde which erst had never felt the share.
The men of Colchos seeing this, like men amazed fare.   165
The Mynies with their shouting out their mazednesse augment,
And unto Jason therewithall give more encouragement.
Then in a souldiers cap of steele a Vipers teeth he takes,
And sowes them in the new plowde fielde. The ground then soking
                                                  makes
The seede foresteepte in poyson strong, both supple lithe and soft, 170
And of these teeth a right straunge graine there growes anon aloft.
For even as in the mothers wombe an infant doth begin
To take the lively shape of man, and formed is within
To due proportion piece by piece in every limme, and when
Full ripe he is, he takes the use of Aire with other men: 175
So when that of the Vipers teeth the perfect shape of man

145 *shocke:* crowd   157 *clees:* claws
151 *Kell:* kiln   161 *coyd:* caressed

Within the bowels of the earth was formed, they began
To rise togither orderly upon the fruitefull fielde:
And (which a greater wonder is) immediatly they wielde
Their weapons growing up with them, whom when the Greekes
                                                    behilde   180
Preparing for to push their Pikes (which sharply headed were)
In Jasons face, downe went their heades, their heartes did faint for
                                                    feare:
And also she that made him safe began abasht to bee.
For when against one naked man so huge an armie shee
Beheld of armed enmies bent, hir colour did abate   185
And sodainly both voyd of bloud and livelie heate she sate.
And lest the chaunted weedes the which she had him given before
Should faile at neede, a helping charme she whispred overmore,
And practisde other secret Artes the which she kept in store.
He casting streight a mightie stone amid his thickest foes,   190
Doth voyde the battell from him selfe and turnes it unto those.
These earthbred brothers by and by did one another wound
And never ceased till that all lay dead upon the ground.
The Greekes were glad, and in their armes did clasp their Champion
                                                    stout,
And clinging to him earnestly embraced him about.   195
And thou O fond Medea too couldst well have found in hart
The Champion for to have embraste, but that withheld thou wart
By shamefastnesse, and yet thou hadst embraced him, if dread
Of stayning of thine honor had not staid thee in that stead.
But yet as far forth as thou maist, thou doste in heart rejoyce,   200
And secretly (although without expressing it in voyce)
Doste thanke thy charmes and eke the Gods as Authors of the same.
       Now was remaining as the last conclusion of this game,
By force of chaunted herbes to make the watchfull Dragon sleepe
Within whose eyes came never winke: who had in charge to keepe   205
The goodly tree upon the which the golden fleeces hung.
With crested head, and hooked pawes, and triple spirting tung,
Right ougly was he to beholde. When Jason had besprent
Him with the juice of certaine herbes from Lethey River sent,
And thrice had mumbled certaine wordes which are of force to cast 210
So sound a sleepe on things that even as dead a time they last,

187 *chaunted:* enchanted   199 *stead:* (1) place, (2) time
191 *voyde:* avert   208 *besprent:* sprinkled
198 *shamefastnesse:* modesty, bashfulness

Which make the raging surges calme and flowing Rivers stay,
The dreadfull Dragon by and by (whose eyes before that day
Wist never erst what sleeping ment) did fall so fast asleepe
That Jason safely tooke the fleece of golde that he did keepe.   215
Of which his bootie being proud, he led with him away
The Author of his good successe another fairer pray:
And so with conquest and a wife he loosde from Colchos strand,
And in Larissa haven safe did go againe aland.
  The auncient men of Thessalie togither with their wives   220
  To Church with offrings gone for saving of their childrens lives.
Great heapes of fuming frankincense were fryed in the flame
And vowed Bulles to sacrifice with hornes faire gilded came.
But from this great solemnitie Duke Aeson was away,
Now at deathes door and spent with yeares. Then Jason thus gan   225
              say:

O wife to whome I doe confesse I owe my life in deede,
Though al things thou to me hast given, and thy deserts exceede
Beleife: yet if enchauntment can, (for what so hard appeares
Which strong enchauntment can not doe?) abate thou from my yeares,   230
And add them to my fathers life. As he these wordes did speake,
The teares were standing in his eyes. His godly sute did breake
Medeas heart: who therewithall bethought hir of hir Sire
In leaving whome she had exprest a far unlike desire.
But yet bewraying not hir thoughts, she said: O Husband fie,
What wickednesse hath scapt your mouth? Suppose you then that I   235
Am able of your life the terme where I will to bestow?
Let Hecat never suffer that. Your sute (as well you know)
Against all right and reason is. But I will put in proofe
A greater gift than you require and more for your behoofe.
I will assay your father's life by cunning to prolong,   240
And not with your yeares for to make him yong againe and strong:
So our threeformed Goddesse graunt with present helpe to stand
A furthrer of the great attempt the which I take in hand.
  Before the Moone should circlewise close both hir hornes in one
  Three nightes were yet as then to come. As soon as that she   245
             shone
Most full of light, and did behold the earth with fulsome face,
Medea with hir haire not trust so much as in a lace,

---

221 *gone:* go
229 *abate:* deduct
234 *bewraying:* revealing

239 *behoofe:* benefit
246 *fulsome:* full
247 *trust:* trussed

But flaring on hir shoulders twaine, and barefoote, with hir gowne
Ungirded, gate hir out of doores and wandred up and downe
Alone the dead time of the night. Both Man, and Beast, and Bird   250
Were fast asleepe: the Serpents slie in trayling forward stird
So softly as ye would have thought they still asleepe had bene.
The moysting Ayre was whist. No leafe ye could have moving sene.
The starres alonly faire and bright did in the welkin shine
To which she lifting up hir handes did thrise hirselfe encline: 255
And thrice with water of the brooke hir haire besprincled shee:
And gasping thrise she opte hir mouth: and bowing downe hir knee
Upon the bare hard ground, she said: O trustie time of night
Most faithfull unto privities, O golden starres whose light
Doth jointly with the Moone succeede the beames that blaze by day   260
And thou three headed Hecate who knowest best the way
To compasse this our great attempt and art our chiefest stay:
Ye Charmes and Witchcrafts, and thou Earth which both with herbe
                                                        and weed
Of mightie working furnishest the Wizardes at their neede:
Ye Ayres and windes: ye Elves of Hilles, of Brookes, of Woods alone, 265
Of standing Lakes, and of the Night approche ye everychone.
Through helpe of whom (the crooked bankes much wondring at the
                                                        thing)
I have compelled streames to run cleane backward to their spring.
By charmes I make the calme Seas rough, and make the rough Seas
                                                        plaine,
And cover all the Skie with Cloudes and chase them thence againe.   270
By charmes I raise and lay the windes, and burst the Vipers jaw.
And from the bowels of the Earth both stones and trees doe draw.
Whole woods and Forestes I remove: I make the Mountaines shake,
And even the Earth it selfe to grone and fearfully to quake.
I call up dead men from their graves: and thee O lightsome Moone   275
I darken oft, though beaten brasse abate thy perill soone.
Our Sorcerie dimmes the Morning faire, and darkes the Sun at Noone.
The flaming breath of firie Bulles ye quenched for my sake
And caused their unwieldie neckes the bended yoke to take.
Among the Earthbred brothers you a mortall war did set   280
And brought asleepe the Dragon fell whose eyes were never shet.
By meanes whereof deceiving him that had the golden fleece
In charge to keepe, you sent it thence by Jason into Greece.

253 *whist:* silent   259 *privities:* secrets

Now have I neede of herbes that can by vertue of their juice
To flowring prime of lustie youth old withred age reduce. 285
I am assurde ye will it graunt. For not in vaine have shone
These twincling starres, ne yet in vaine this Chariot all alone
By drought of Dragons hither comes. With that was fro the Skie
A Chariot softly glaunced downe, and stayed hard thereby.
    As soone as she had gotten up, and with hir hand had coyd 290
    The Dragons reined neckes, and with their bridles somewhat toyd,
They mounted with hir in the Ayre, whence looking downe she saw
The pleasant Temp of Thessalie, and made hir Dragons draw
To places further from resort: and there she tooke the view
What herbes on high mount Pelion, and what on Ossa grew, 295
And what on mountaine Othris and on Pyndus growing were,
And what Olympus (greater than mount Pyndus far) did beare.
Such herbes of them as liked hir she pullde up roote and rinde
Or cropt them with a hooked knife. And many she did finde
Upon the bankes of Apidane agreeing to hir minde: 300
And many at Amphrisus foords: and thou Enipeus eke
Didst yeelde hir many pretie weedes of which she well did like.
Peneus and Sperchius streames contributarie were,
And so were Boebes rushie bankes of such as growed there.
About Anthedon which against the Ile Euboea standes, 305
A certaine kind of lively grasse she gathered with her handes,
The name whereof was scarsly knowen or what the herbe could doe
Untill that Glaucus afterward was chaunged thereinto.
Nine dayes with winged Dragons drawen, nine nights in Chariot swift
She searching everie field and frith from place to place did shift. 310
She was no sooner home returnde but that the Dragons fell
Which lightly of hir gathered herbes had taken but the smell,
Did cast their sloughes and with their sloughes their riveled age forgo.
She would none other house than heaven to hide hir head as tho:
But kept hir still without the doores: and as for man was none 315
That once might touch hir. Altars twayne of Turfe she builded: one
Upon hir left hand unto Youth, another on the right
To tryple Hecat. Both the which as soone as she had dight
With Vervain and with other shrubbes that on the fieldes doe rise,
Not farre from thence she digde two pits: and making sacrifice 320
Did cut a couple of blacke Rams throtes and filled with their blood

288 _was . . ./. . . glaunced:_ had slid, veered   313 _sloughes:_ old skins; _riveled:_ wrinkled
310 _frith:_ wood   318 _dight:_ arrayed
311 _fell:_ hide

The open pits, on which she pourde of warme milke pure and good
A boll full, and another boll of honie clarifide.
And babling to hir selfe therewith full bitterly she cride
On Pluto and his ravisht wife the sovereigne states of Hell,   325
And all the Elves and Gods that on or in the Earth doe dwell,
To spare olde Aesons life a while, and not in hast deprive
His limmes of that same aged soule which kept them yet alive.
Whome when she had sufficiently with mumbling long besought,
She bade that Aesons feebled corse should out of doores be brought   330
Before the Altars. Then with charmes she cast him in so deepe
A slumber, that upon the herbes he lay for dead asleepe.
Which done she willed Jason thence a great way off to go
And likewise all the Ministers that served hir as tho:
And not presume those secretes with unhallowed eyes to see.   335
They did as she commaunded them. When all were voyded, shee
With scattred haire about hir eares like one of Bacchus froes
Devoutly by and by about the burning Altars goes:
And dipping in the pits of bloud a sort of clifted brandes
Upon the Altars kindled them that were on both hir handes.   340
And thrise with brimstone, thrise with fire, and thrise with water pure
She purged Aesons aged corse that slept and slumbred sure.
    The medicine seething all the while a wallop in a pan
    Of brasse, to spirt and leape aloft and gather froth began.
There boyled she the rootes, seedes, flowres, leaves, stalkes and juice
                                   togither   345
Which from the fieldes of Thessalie she late had gathered thither.
She cast in also precious stones fetcht from the furthest East
And, which the ebbing Ocean washt, fine gravell from the West.
She put thereto the deaw that fell upon a Monday night:
And flesh and feathers of a Witch, a cursed odious wight   350
Which in the likenesse of an Owle abrode a nightes did flie,
And Infants in their cradels chaunge or sucke them that they die.
The singles also of a Wolfe which when he list could take
The shape of man, and when he list the same againe forsake.
And from the River Cyniphis which is in Lybie lande   355
She had the fine sheere scaled filmes of water snayles at hand.
And of an endlesselived hart the liver had she got,

---

325 *states:* rulers, dignitaries   339 *clifted:* cleft
336 *were voyded:* had gone out   343 *wallop:* noisy boiling
337 *froes:* women   353 *singles:* entrails

To which she added of a Crowe that then had lived not
So little as nine hundred yeares the head and Bill also.
    Now when Medea had with these and with a thousand mo   360
    Such other kinde of namelesse things bestead hir purpose through
For lengthning of the old mans life, she tooke a withered bough
Cut lately from an Olyf tree, and jumbling all togither
Did raise the bottome to the brim: and as she stirred hither
And thither with the withered sticke, behold it waxed greene.   365
Anon the leaves came budding out: and sodenly were seene
As many berries dangling downe as well the bough could beare.
And where the fire had from the pan the scumming cast, or where
The scalding drops did fall, the ground did springlike florish there,
And flowres with fodder fine and soft immediatly arose.   370
    Which when Medea did behold, with naked knife she goes
    And cuttes the olde mans throte: and letting all his old bloud go
Supplies it with the boyled juice: the which when Aeson tho
Had at his mouth or at his wounde receyved in, his heare
As well of head as beard from gray to coleblacke turned were.   375
His leane, pale, hore, and withered corse grew fulsome, faire and fresh:
His furrowed wrincles were fulfilde with yong and lustie flesh.
His limmes waxt frolicke, baine and lithe: at which he wondring much,
Remembred that at fortie yeares he was the same or such.
And as from dull unwieldsome age to youth he backward drew: 380
Even so a lively youthfull spright did in his heart renew.
    The wonder of this monstrous act had Bacchus seene from hie,
    And finding that to youthfull yeares his Nurses might thereby
Restored bee, did at hir hand receive it as a gift.
And lest deceitfull guile should cease, Medea found a shift   385
To feyne that Jason and hir selfe were falne at oddes in wroth:
And thereupon in humble wise to Pelias Court she goth.
Where forbicause the King himselfe was feebled sore with age,
His daughters entertainde hir, whome Medea, being sage,
Within a while through false pretence of feyned friendship brought 390
To take hir baite. For as she tolde what pleasures she had wrought
For Jason, and among the rest as greatest sadly tolde
How she had made his father yong that withred was and olde,
And taried long upon that point: they hoped glad and faine
That their olde father might likewise his youthful yeares regaine. 395
And this they craving instantly did proffer for hir paine

361 *bestead:* helped   378 *baine:* limber
370 *fodder:* herbage   392 *sadly:* seriously

What recompence she would desire. She helde hir peace a while
As though she doubted what to doe: and with hir suttle guile
Of counterfetted gravitie more eger did them make.
As soone as she had promisde them to doe it for their sake,   400
For more assurance of my graunt, your selves (quoth she) shall see
The oldest Ram in all your flocke a Lambe streight made to bee
By force of my confections strong. Immediatly a Ram
So olde that no man thereabouts remembred him a Lam
Was thither by his warped hornes which turned inward to   405
His hollow Temples, drawne: whose withred throte she slit in two.
And when she cleane had drayned out that little bloud that was,
Upon the fire with herbes of strength she set a pan of brasse,
And cast his carcasse thereinto. The Medcine did abate
The largenesse of his limmes and seard his dossers from his pate,   410
And with his hornes abridgde his yeares. Anon was plainly heard
The bleating of a new yeand Lambe from mid the Ketleward.
And as they wondred for to heare the bleating, streight the Lam
Leapt out, and frisking ran to seeke the udder of some Dam.
King Pelias daughters were amazde. And when they did beholde   415
Hir promise come to such effect, they were a thousand folde
More earnest at hir than before. Thrise Phoebus having pluckt
The Collars from his horses neckes, in Iber had them duckt.
And now in Heaven the streaming starres the fourth night shined
                                                                     cleare:
When false Medea on the fire had hanged water shere,   420
With herbes that had no powre at all. The King and all his garde
Which had the charge that night about his person for to warde
Were through hir nightspels and hir charmes in deadly sleepe all cast.
And Pelias daughters with the Witch which eggde them forward, past
Into his chamber by the watch, and compast in his bed.   425
Then: Wherefore stand ye doubting thus like fooles, Medea sed.
On: draw your swordes: and let ye out his old bloud, that I may
Fill up his emptie veynes againe with youthfull bloud streight way.
Your fathers life is in your handes: it lieth now in you
To have him olde and withred still or yong and lustie. Now   430
If any nature in ye be, and that ye doe not feede
A fruitelesse hope, your dutie to your father doe with speede.
Expulse his age by sword, and let the filthy matter out.

---

410 *dossers:* horns   420 *shere:* pure
412 *yeand:* born   425 *compast in:* surrounded

Through these persuasions which of them so ever went about
To shewe hirselfe most naturall, became the first that wrought   435
Against all nature: and for feare she should be wicked thought,
She executes the wickednesse which most to shun she sought.
Yet was not any one of them so bolde that durst abide
To looke upon their father when she strake, but wride aside
Hir eyes: and so their cruell handes not marking where they hit   440
With faces turnde another way at all aventure smit.
He all beweltred in his bloud awaked with the smart,
And maimde and mangled as he was did give a sodeyne start
Endevoring to have risen up. But when he did beholde
Himselfe among so many swordes, he lifting up his olde   445
Pale waryish armes, said: Daughters mine what doe ye? who hath put
These wicked weapons in your hands your fathers throte to cut?
With that their heartes and handes did faint. And as he talked yet,
Medea breaking off his wordes, his windpipe quickly slit,
And in the scalding liquor torne did drowne him by and by.   450
        But had she not with winged wormes streight mounted in the skie
        She had not scaped punishment, but stying up on hie
She over shadie Pelion flew where Chyron erst did dwell,
And over Othrys and the grounds renoumde for that befell
To auncient Ceramb: who such time as old Deucalions flood   455
Upon the face of all the Earth like one maine water stood,
By helpe of Nymphes with fethered wings was in the Ayer lift,
And so escaped from the floud undrowned by the shift.
She left Aeolian Pytanie upon hir left hand: and
The Serpent that became a stone upon the Lesbian sand.   460
And Ida woods where Bacchus hid a Bullocke (as is sayd)
In shape of Stag the which his sonne had theevishly convayde.
And where the Sire of Corytus lies buried in the dust.
The fieldes which Meras (when he first did into barking brust)
Affraide with straungenesse of the noyse. And eke Eurypils towne   465
In which the wives of Cos had hornes like Oxen on their crowne
Such time as Hercles with his hoste departed from the Ile,
And Rhodes to Phoebus consecrate: and Ialyse where ere while
The Telchines with their noysome sight did every thing bewitch.
At which their hainous wickednesse Jove taking rightfull pritch,   470

---

439 *wride:* twisted
441 *at all aventure:* at random
446 *waryish:* unwholesome looking
451 *wormes:* dragons

452 *stying:* rising
458 *shift:* device, trick
464 *brust:* burst
470 *pritch:* offense

Did drowne them in his brothers waves. Moreover she did passe
By Ceos and olde Carthey walles where Sir Alcidamas
Did wonder how his daughter should be turned to a Dove.
The Swannie Temp and Hyries Poole she viewed from above,
The which a sodeine Swan did haunt. For Phyllie there for love   475
Of Hyries sonne did at his bidding Birdes and Lions tame,
And being willde to breake a Bull performed streight the same:
Till wrothfull that his love so oft so streightly should him use,
When for his last reward he askt the Bull, he did refuse
To give it him. The boy displeasde, said: Well: thou wilt anon   480
Repent thou gave it not: and leapt downe headlong from a stone.
They all supposde he had bene falne: but being made a Swan
With snowie feathers in the Ayre to flacker he began.
His mother Hyrie knowing not he was preserved so,
Resolved into melting teares for pensivenesse and wo,   485
And made the Poole that beares hir name. Not far from hence doth
                                                                stand
The Citie Brauron, where sometime by mounting from the land
With waving pinions Ophyes ympe, dame Combe, did eschue
Hir children which with naked swordes to slea hir did pursue.
Anon she kend Calaurie fieldes which did sometime pertaine   490
To chast Diana where a King and eke his wife both twaine
Were turnde to Birdes. Cyllene hill upon hir right hand stood,
In which Menephron like a beast of wilde and savage moode
To force his mother did attempt. Far thence she spide where sad
Cephisus mourned for his Neece whome Phebus turned had   495
To ugly shape of swelling Seale: and Eumelles pallace faire
Lamenting for his sonnes mischaunce with whewling in the Aire.
At Corinth with hir winged Snakes at length she did arrive.
Here men (so auncient fathers said that were as then alive)
Did breede of deawie Mushrommes. But after that hir teene   500
With burning of hir husbands bride by witchcraft wreakt had beene
And that King Creons pallace she on blasing fire had seene,
And in hir owne deare childrens bloud had bathde hir wicked knife
Not like a mother but a beast bereving them of life:
Lest Jason should have punisht hir she tooke hir winged Snakes,   505
And flying thence againe in haste to Pallas Citie makes,
Which saw the auncient Periphas and rightuous Phiney too

478 *streightly:* rigorously   490 *kend:* saw
483 *flacker:* flutter, flap   497 *whewling:* howling, whining
488 *ympe:* child   500 *teene:* grief

Togither flying, and the Neece of Polypemon who
Was fastened to a paire of wings as well as t'other two.
   Aegeus enterteined hir wherein he was to blame   510
   Although he had no further gone but staid upon the same.
He thought it not to be inough to use hir as his guest
Onlesse he tooke hir to his wife. And now was Thesey prest,
Unknowne unto his father yet, who by his knightly force
Had set from robbers cleare the balke that makes the streight divorce 515
Betweene the seas Ionian and Aegean. To have killde
This worthie knight, Medea had a Goblet readie fillde
With juice of Flintwoort venemous the which she long ago
Had out of Scythie with hir brought. The common bruit is so
That of the teeth of Cerberus this Flintwoort first did grow.   520
There is a cave that gapeth wide with darksome entrie low,
There goes a way slope downe by which with triple cheyne made new
Of strong and sturdie Adamant the valiant Hercle drew
The currish Helhounde Cerberus: who dragging arsward still
And writhing backe his scowling eyes bicause he had no skill   525
To see the Sunne and open day, for verie moodie wroth
Three barkings yelled out at once, and spit his slavering froth
Upon the greenish grasse. This froth (as men suppose) tooke roote
And thriving in the batling soyle in burgeons forth did shoote,
To bane and mischiefe men withall: and forbicause the same   530
Did grow upon the bare hard Flints, folke gave the foresaid name
Of Flintwoort thereunto. The King by egging of his Queene
Did reach his sonne this bane as if he had his enmie beene.
And Thesey of this treason wrought not knowing ought had tane
The Goblet at his fathers hand which helde his deadly bane: 535
When sodenly by the Ivorie hilts that were upon his sword
Aegeus knew he was his sonne: and rising from the borde
Did strike the mischiefe from his mouth. Medea with a charme
Did cast a mist and so scapte death deserved for the harme
Entended. Now albeit that Aegeus were right glad   540
That in the saving of his sonne so happy chaunce he had,
Yet grieved it his heart full sore that such a wicked wight
With treason wrought against his sonne should scape so cleare and
                                      quight.
     Then fell he unto kindling fire on Altars everie where

515 *balke:* isthmus
518 *Flintwoort:* aconite
525 *skill:* ability

529 *batling:* rich
543 *quight:* free, acquitted

And glutted all the Gods with gifts. The thicke neckt Oxen were ⁵⁴⁵
With garlands wreathd about their hornes knockt downe for sacrifice.
A day of more solemnitie than this did never rise
Before on Athens (by report). The auncients of the Towne
Made feastes: so did the meaner sort, and every common clowne.
And as the wine did sharpe their wits, they sung this song: O knight ⁵⁵⁰
Of peerlesse prowesse Theseus, thy manhod and thy might
Through all the coast of Marathon with worthie honor soundes,
For killing of the Cretish Bull that wasted those same groundes.
The folke of Cremyon thinke themselves beholden unto thee.
For that without disquieting their fieldes may tilled be.   ⁵⁵⁵
By thee the land of Epidaure behelde the clubbish sonne
Of Vulcane dead. By thee likewise the countrie that doth runne
Along Cephisus bankes behelde the fell Procrustes slaine.
The dwelling place of Ceres, our Eleusis glad and faine,
Beheld the death of Cercyon. That orpid Sinis who   ⁵⁶⁰
Abusde his strength in bending trees and tying folke thereto,
Their limmes asunder for to teare when loosened from the stops
The trees unto their proper place did trice their streyned tops,
Was killde by thee. Thou made the way that leadeth to the towne
Alcathoe in Beotia cleare by putting Scyron downe.   ⁵⁶⁵
To this same outlawes scattred bones the land denied rest,
And likewise did the Sea refuse to harbrough such a guest:
Till after floting to and fro long while as men doe say
At length they hardened into stones: and at this present day
The stones are called Scyrons cliffes. Now if we should account   ⁵⁷⁰
Thy deedes togither with thy yeares, thy deedes would far surmount
Thy yeares. For thee, most valiant Prince, these publike vowes we keepe
For thee with cherefull heartes we quaffe these bolles of wine so deepe.
The Pallace also of the noyse and shouting did resounde
The which the people made for joy. There was not to be founde   ⁵⁷⁵
In all the Citie any place of sadnesse. Nathelesse
(So hard it is of perfect joy to find so great excesse,
But that some sorrow therewithall is medled more or lesse),
Aegeus had not in his sonnes recoverie such delight,
But that there followed in the necke a piece of fortunes spight.   ⁵⁸⁰
     King Minos was preparing war, who though he had great store
     Of ships and souldiers yet the wrath the which he had before

---

⁵⁵⁶ *clubbish:* armed with a club   ⁵⁶⁷ *harbrough:* harbor
⁵⁶⁰ *orpid:* fierce   ⁵⁷⁸ *medled:* mingled
⁵⁶³ *trice:* snatch, haul   ⁵⁸⁰ *necke:* nick

Conceyved in his fathers brest for murthring of his sonne
Androgeus made him farre more strong and fiercer for to ronne
To rightfull battell to revenge the great displeasure donne. 585
Howbeit he thought it best ere he his warfare did begin
To finde the meanes of forreine aides some friendship for to win.
And thereupon with flying fleete where passage did permit
He went to visit all the Iles that in those seas doe sit.
Anon the Iles Astypaley and Anaphey both twaine 590
The first constreynde for feare of war, the last in hope of gaine,
Tooke part with him. Low Myconey did also with him hold
So did the chalkie Cymoley, and Syphney which of olde
Was verie riche with veynes of golde, and Scyros full of bolde
And valiant men, and Seryphey the smooth or rather fell, 595
And Parey which for Marblestone doth beare away the bell.
And Sythney which a wicked wench callde Arne did betray
For mony: who upon receit thereof without delay
Was turned to a birde which yet of golde is gripple still,
And is as blacke as any cole, both fethers, feete and bill. 600
A Cadowe is the name of hir. But yet Olyarey,
And Didymey, and Andrey eke, and Tene, and Gyarey,
And Pepareth where Olive trees most plenteously doe grow,
In no wise would agree their helpe on Minos to bestow.
     Then Minos turning lefthandwise did sayle to Oenope 605
     Where reignde that time King Aeacus. This Ile had called be
Of old by name of Oenope: but Aeacus turnde the name
And after of his mothers name Aegina callde the same.
The common folke ran out by heapes desirous for to see
A man of such renowne as Minos bruited was to bee. 610
The Kings three sonnes Duke Telamon, Duke Peley, and the yong
Duke Phocus went to meete with him. Old Aeacus also clung
With age, came after leysurely, and asked him the cause
Of his repaire. The ruler of the hundred Shires gan pause:
And musing on the inward griefe that nipt him at the hart, 615
Did shape him aunswere thus: O Prince vouchsafe to take my part
In this same godly warre of mine: assist me in the just
Revengement of my murthred sonne that sleepeth in the dust.
I crave your comfort for his death. Aeginas sonne replide:
Thy suite is vaine: and of my Realme perforce must be denide. 620

596 *beare away the bell:* take first place   601 *Cadowe:* jackdaw
599 *gripple:* gripping, greedy   612 *clung:* shrunken

For unto Athens is no lande more sure than this alide:
Such leagues betweene us are which shall infringde for me abide.
Away went Minos sad: and said: full dearly shalt thou bie
Thy leagues. He thought it for to be a better pollicie
To threaten war than war to make, and there to spend his store   625
And strength which in his other needes might much availe him more.
　　As yet might from Oenopia walles the Cretish fleete be kend.
　　When thitherward with puffed sayles and wind at will did tend
A ship from Athens, which anon arriving at the strand
Set Cephal with Ambassade from his Countrimen aland.   630
The Kings three sonnes though long it were since last they had him
　　　　　　　　　　　　　　　　　　　　　　　　　　　seene,
Yet knew they him. And after olde acquaintance eft had beene
Renewde by shaking hands, to Court they did him streight convay.
This Prince which did allure the eyes of all men by the way,
As in whose stately person still remained to be seene   635
The markes of beautie which in flowre of former yeares had beene,
Went holding out an Olife braunch that grew in Atticke lande
And for the reverence of his age there went on eyther hand
A Nobleman of yonger yeares. Sir Clytus on the right
And Butes on the left, the sonnes of one that Pallas hight.   640
When greeting first had past betweene these Nobles and the King,
Then Cephal setting streight abroche the message he did bring,
Desired aide: and shewde what leagues stoode then in force betweene
His countrie and the Aeginites, and also what had beene
Decreed betwixt their aunceters, concluding in the ende   645
That under colour of this war which Minos did pretende
To only Athens, he in deede the conquest did intende
Of all Achaia. When he thus by helpe of learned skill
His countrie message furthred had, King Aeacus leaning still
His left hand on his scepter, saide: My Lordes, I would not have   650
Your state of Athens seeme so straunge as succor here to crave.
I pray commaund. For be ye sure that what this Ile can make
Is yours. Yea all that ere I have shall hazard for your sake.
I want no strength. I have such store of souldiers, that I may
Both vex my foes and also keepe my Realme in quiet stay.   655
And now I thinke me blest of God that time doth serve to showe
Without excuse the great good will that I to Athens owe.
God holde it sir (quoth Cephalus) God make the number grow

---

622 *infringde:* uninfringed   651 *straunge:* reserved
623 *bie:* aby, pay for

Of people in this towne of yours: it did me good alate
When such a goodly sort of youth of all one age and rate   660
Did meete me in the streete. But yet me thinkes that many misse
Which at my former being here I have beheld ere this.
     At that the King did sigh, and thus with plaintfull voice did say:
     A sad beginning afterward in better lucke did stay.
I would I plainly could the same before your faces lay.   665
Howbeit I will disorderly repeate it as I may.
And lest I seeme to wearie you with overlong delay,
The men that you so mindefully enquire for lie in ground
And nought of them save bones and dust remayneth to be found.
But as it hapt what losse thereby did unto me redound?   670
A cruell plague through Junos wrath who dreadfully did hate
This Land that of hir husbands Love did take the name alate,
Upon my people fell: as long as that the maladie
None other seemde than such as haunts mans nature usually,
And of so great mortalitie the hurtfull cause was hid,   675
We strove by Phisicke of the same the Pacients for to rid.
The mischief overmaistred Art: yea Phisick was to seeke
To doe it selfe good. First the Aire with foggie stinking reeke
Did daily overdreepe the earth: and close culme Clouds did make
The wether faint: and while the Moone foure times hir light did take 680
And fillde hir emptie hornes therewith, and did as often slake:
The warme South windes with deadly heate continually did blow.
Infected were the Springs, and Ponds, and streames that ebbe and flow.
And swarmes of Serpents crawld about the fieldes that lay untillde
Which with their poison even the brookes and running water fillde.   685
     In sodaine dropping downe of Dogs, of Horses, Sheepe and Kine,
     Of Birds and Beasts both wild and tame as Oxen, Wolves, and
                        Swine,
The mischiefe of this secret sore first outwardly appeeres.
The wretched Plowman was amazde to see his sturdie Steeres
Amid the furrow sinking downe ere halfe his worke was donne.   690
Whole flocks of sheepe did faintly bleate, and therewithall begonne
Their fleeces for to fall away and leave the naked skin,
And all their bodies with the rot attainted were within.
The lustie Horse that erst was fierce in field renowne to win
Against his kinde grew cowardly: and now forgetting quight   695

660 *rate*: class, kind
679 *overdreepe*: drip or droop over; *culme*:
   calm, motionless (though OED gives no

instance of this spelling. The noun
   means soot or smut)
695 *kinde*: nature

The auncient honor which he preast so oft to get in fight,
Stoode sighing sadly at the Racke as wayting for to yeelde
His wearie life without renowne of combat in the fielde.
The Boare to chafe, the Hinde to runne, the cruell Beare to fall
Upon the herdes of Rother beastes had now no lust at all.   700
A languishing was falne on all. In wayes, in woods, in plaines,
The filthie carions lay, whose stinche, the Ayre it selfe distaines.
(A wondrous thing to tell) not Dogges, not ravening Foules, nor yit
Horecoted Wolves would once attempt to tast of them a bit.
Looke, where they fell, there rotted they: and with their savor bred   705
More harme, and further still abrode the foule infection spred.
        With losse that touched yet more nere, on Husbandmen it crept,
        And ragingly within the walles of this great Citie stept.
It tooke men first with swelting heate that scalt their guts within:
The signes whereof were steaming breath and firie colourde skin.   710
The tongue was harsh and swolne, the mouth through drought of
                                                              burning veines
Lay gaping up to hale in breath, and as the pacient streines
To draw it in, he suckes therewith corrupted Aire beside.
No bed, no clothes though nere so thinne the pacients could abide.
But laide their hardened stomackes flat against the bare colde ground   715
Yet no abatement of the heate therein their bodies found:
But het the earth, and as for Leache was none that helpe could hight.
The Surgians and Phisitions too were in the selfesame plight.
Their curelesse cunning hurt themselves. The nerer any man
Approcheth his diseased friend, and doth the best he can   720
To succor him most faithfully, the sooner did he catch
His bane. All hope of health was gone. No easment nor dispatch
Of this disease except in death and buriall did they finde.
Looke, whereunto that eche mans minde and fancie was enclinde,
That followed he. He never past what was for his behoofe.   725
For why? that nought could doe them good was felt too much by proofe.
In everie place without respect of shame or honestie
At Wels, at brookes, at ponds, at pits, by swarmes they thronging lie:
But sooner might they quench their life than staunch their thirst
                                                              thereby.
And therewithall so heavie and unwieldie they become,   730

697 *Racke:* manger
700 *Rother:* of the ox family
702 *distaines:* defiles

717 *het:* heated; *Leache:* physician; *hight:*
      promise, provide
725 *past:* cared for; *behoofe:* use, advantage

That wanting power to rise againe, they died there. Yet some
The selfesame waters guzled still without regard of feare,
So weary of their lothsome beds the wretched people were,
That out they lept: or if to stand their feeble force denide,
They wallowed downe and out of doores immediatly them hide: 735
It was a death to every man his owne house to abide.
And for they did not know the cause whereof the sicknesse came,
The place (bicause they did it know) was blamed for the same.
Ye should have seene some halfe fordead go plundring here and there
By highways sides while that their legges were able them to beare. 740
And some,lie weeping on the ground or rolling piteously
Their wearie eyes which afterwards should never see the Skie:
Or stretching out their limmes to Heaven that overhangs on hie,
Some here, some there, and yonder some, in what so ever coste
Death finding them enforced them to yeelde their fainting Ghoste. 745
    What heart had I, suppose you, then, or ought I then to have?
    In faith I might have lothde my life, and wisht me in my grave
As other of my people were. I could not cast mine eie
In any place, but that dead folke there strowed I did spie
Even like as from a shaken twig when rotten Apples drop, 750
Or Mast from Beches, Holmes or Okes when Poales doe scare their top.
Yon stately Church with greeces long against our Court you see:
It is the shrine of Jupiter. What Wight was he or shee
That on those Altars burned not their frankincense in vaine?
How oft, yet even with Frankincense that partly did remaine 755
Still unconsumed in their hands, did die both man and wife,
As ech of them with mutuall care did pray for others life?
How often dyde the mother there in suing for hir sonne,
Unheard upon the Altarstone, hir prayer scarce begonne?
How often at the Temple doore even while the Priest did bid 760
His Beades, and poure pure wine betwene their hornes, at sodaine slid
The Oxen downe without stroke given? Yea once when I had thought
My selfe by offring sacrifice Joves favor to have sought,
For me, my Realme, and these three ymps, the Oxe with grievous grone
Upon the sodaine sunke me downe: and little bloud or none 765
Did issue scarce to staine the knife with which they slit his throte.
The sickly inwardes eke had lost the signes whereby we note
What things the Gods for certaintie would warne us of before:
For even the verie bowels were attainted with the sore.

735 *hide:* hied   752 *greeces:* steps
751 *Mast:* acorns, etc.

Before the holie Temple doores, and (that the death might bee   770
The more dispitefull) even before the Altars did I see
The stinking corses scattred. Some with haltars stopt their winde,
By death expulsing feare of death: and of a wilfull minde
Did haste their ende, which of it selfe was coming on apace.
The bodies which the plague had slaine were (O most wretched case)   775
Not caried forth to buriall now. For why such store there was
That scarce the gates were wyde inough for Coffins forth to passe.
So eyther lothly on the ground unburied did they lie,
Or else without solemnitie were burnt in bonfires hie.
No reverence nor regard was had. Men fell togither by   780
The eares for firing. In the fire that was prepared for one
Another straungers corse was burnt. And lastly few or none
Were left to mourne. The sillie soules of Mothers with their small
And tender babes, and age with youth as Fortune did befall
Went wandring gastly up and downe unmourned for at all.   785
In fine so farre outrageously this helpelesse Murren raves,
There was not wood inough for fire, nor ground inough for graves.
        Astonied at the stourenesse of so stout a storme of ills
        I said: O father Jupiter whose mightie power fulfills
Both Heaven and Earth, if flying fame report thee not amisse   790
In vouching that thou didst embrace in way of Love ere this
The River Asops daughter, faire Aegina even by name,
And that to take me for thy sonne thou count it not a shame:
Restore thou me my folke againe, or kill thou me likewise.
He gave a signe by sodaine flash of lightning from the Skies,   795
And double peale of Thundercracks. I take this same (quoth I)
And as I take it for a true and certaine signe whereby
Thou doest confirme me for thy sonne: so also let it be
A hansell of some happie lucke thou mindest unto me.
Hard by us as it hapt that time, there was an Oken tree   800
With spreaded armes as bare of boughes as lightly one shall see.
This tree (as all the rest of Okes) was sacred unto Jove
And sprouted of an Acorne which was fet from Dodon grove.
Here markt we how the pretie Ants, the gatherers up of graine,
One following other all along in order of a traine,   805
Great burthens in their little mouthes did painfully sustaine:
And nimbly up the rugged barke their beaten path maintaine.

---

776 *For why:* because
783 *sillie:* poor, helpless
786 *Murren:* murrain, plague

788 *stourenesse:* harshness, violence
799 *hansell:* omen
801 *lightly:* easily

As wondring at the swarme I stoode, I said: O father deere
As many people give thou me, as Ants are creeping heere.
And fill mine empty walles againe. Anon the Oke did quake,   810
And unconstreynde of any blast, his loftie braunches shake,
The which did yeeld a certaine sound. With that for dreadfull feare
A shuddring through my bodie strake and up stoode stiffe my heare.
But yet I kissed reverently the ground and eke the tree.
Howbeit I durst not be so bolde of hope acknowne to bee.   815
Yet hoped I: and in my heart did shroude my secret hope.
Anon came night: and sleepe upon my carefull carcasse crope.
Me thought I saw the selfesame Oke with all his boughes and twigs,
And all the Pismeres creeping still upon his tawnts and sprigs,
Which trembling with a sodaine brayd these Harvest folke off threw   820
And shed them on the ground about, who on the sodaine grew
In bignesse more and more, and from the earth themselves did lift:
And stoode upright against the tree: and therewithall did shift
Their maygernesse, and coleblacke hue, and number of their feete:
And clad their limmes with shape of man. Away my sleepe did fleete.   825
And when I wooke, misliking of my dreame I made my mone
That in the Gods I did perceive but slender helpe or none.
But straight much trampling up and downe and shuffling did I heare,
And (which to me that present time did verie straunge appeare)
Of people talking in my house me thought I heard the reare.   830
Now while I musing on the same supposde it to have been
Some fancie of the foolish dreame which lately I had seen,
Behold, in comes me Telamon in hast, and thrusting ope
My Chamber doore, said: Sir, a sight of things surmounting hope
And credit shall you have: come forth. Forth came I by and by   835
And even such men for all the world there standing did I spie
As in my sleepe I dreamed of, and knew them for the same.
They comming to me greeted me, their sovereigne Lord, by name.
And I (my vowes to Jove performde) my Citie did devide
Among my new inhabiters: and gave them land beside   840
Which by decease of such as were late owners of the same
Lay wast. And in remembrance of the race whereof they came,
The name of Emets I them gave. Their persons you have seen:
Their disposition is the same that erst in them hath been.
They are a sparing kinde of folke, on labor wholy set,   845

---

815 *acknowne:* aware, acknowledged
817 *crope:* crept
819 *tawnts:* branches, twigs

820 *brayd:* start, sudden movement
830 *reare:* noise
843 *Emets:* ants

A gatherer, and a hoorder up of such as they doe get.
These fellowes being like in yeares and courage of the minde,
Shall go a warfare ny as soone as that the Easterne winde
Which brought you hither luckely, (the Easterne winde was it
That brought them thither) turning, to the Southerne coast doe flit.   850
    With this and other such like talke they brought the day to ende.
    The Even in feasting, and the night in sleeping they did spende.
The Sunne next Morrow in the heaven with golden beames did burne,
And still the Easterne winde did blow and hold them from returne.
Sir Pallas sonnes to Cephal came (for he their elder was)   855
And he and they to Aeacus Court togither forth did passe.
The King as yet was fast asleepe. Duke Phocus at the gate
Did meete them, and receyved them according to their state.
For Telamon and Peleus alreadie forth were gone,
To muster Souldiers for the warres. So Phocus all alone   860
Did leade them to an inner roume, where goodly Parlours were,
And caused them to sit them downe. As he was also there
Now sitting with them, he beheld a Dart in Cephals hand
With golden head, the stele whereof he well might understand
Was of some straunge and unknowne tree. When certain talke had   865

                              past

A while of other matters there, I am (quoth he) at last
A man that hath delight in woods and loves to follow game
And yet I am not able sure by any meanes to ame
What wood your Javeling stele is of. Of Ash it can not bee.
For then the colour should be browne. And if of Cornell tree,   870
It would be full of knubbed knots. I know not what it is:
But sure mine eies did never see a fairer Dart than this.
    The one of those same brethren twaine replying to him said:
    Nay then the speciall propertie will make you more dismaid,
Than doth the beautie of this Dart. It hitteth whatsoever   875
He throwes it at. The stroke thereof by Chaunce is ruled never.
For having done his feate, it flies all bloudie backe agen
Without the helpe of any hand. The Prince was earnest then
To know the truth of all: as whence so riche a present came,
Who gave it him, and whereupon the partie gave the same.   880
Duke Cephal answerde his demaund in all points (one except)
The which (as knowne apparantly) for shame he overlept:
His beautie namely, for the which he did receive the Dart.

---

864 *stele:* shaft   871 *knubbed:* knobby

And for the losse of his deare wife right pensive at the hart,
He thus began with weeping eies: This Dart, O Goddesse sonne,   885
(Ye ill would thinke it) makes me yirne, and long shall make me donne,
If long the Gods doe give me life. This weapon hath undonne
My deare beloved wife and me. O would to God this same
Had never unto me bene given. There was a noble Dame
That Procris hight (but you perchaunce have oftner heard the name 890
Of great Orythia whose renowne was bruited so by fame,
That blustring Boreas ravisht hir.) To this Orythia shee
Was sister. If a bodie should compare in ech degree
The face and natures of them both, he could none other deeme
But Procris worthier of the twaine of ravishment should seeme.   895
Hir father and our mutuall love did make us man and wife.
Men said I had (and so I had in deede) a happie life.
Howbeit Gods will was otherwise, for had it pleased him
Of all this while, and even still yet in pleasure should I swim.
The second Month that she and I by band of lawfull bed   900
Had joynde togither bene, as I my masking Toyles did spred,
To overthrow the horned Stags, the early Morning gray
Then newly having chased night and gun to breake the day,
From Mount Hymettus highest tops that freshly flourish ay,
Espide me, and against my will conveyde me quight away.   905
I trust the Goddesse will not be offended that I say
The troth of hir. Although it would delight one to beholde
Hir ruddie cheekes: although of day and night the bounds she holde:
Although on juice of Ambrosie continually she feede:
Yet Procris was the only Wight that I did love in deede.   910
On Procris only was my heart: none other word had I
But Procris only in my mouth: still Procris did I crie.
I upned what a holy thing was wedlocke: and how late
It was ago since she and I were coupled in that state.
Which band (and specially so soone) it were a shame to breake.   915
The Goddesse being moved at the words that I did speake,
Said: Cease thy plaint, thou Carle, and keepe thy Procris still for me.
But (if my minde deceyve me not) the time will shortly be
That wish thou wilt thou had hir not. And so in anger she
To Procris sent me backe againe. In going homeward as   920
Upon the Goddesse sayings with my selfe I musing was,

886 *donne:* do   913 *upned:* mentioned
901 *Toyles:* nets   917 *Carle:* churl; *for me:* for all I care

I gan to dreade bad measures lest my wife had made some scape.
Hir youthfull yeares begarnished with beautie, grace and shape,
In maner made me to beleve the deede already done.
Againe hir maners did forbid mistrusting over soone.   925
But I had bene away: but even the same from whom I came
A shrewde example gave how lightly wives doe run in blame:
But we poore Lovers are afraide of all things. Hereupon
I thought to practise feates: which thing repented me anon:
And shall repent me while I live. The purpose of my drifts   930
Was for t'assault hir honestie with great rewards and gifts.
The Morning fooding this my feare, to further my device,
My shape (which thing me thought I felt) had altered with a trice.
By meanes whereof anon unknowne to Pallas towne I came,
And entred so my house: the house was clearely voide of blame: 935
And shewed signes of chastitie in mourning ever sith
Their maister had bene rapt away. A thousand meanes wherewith
To come to Procris speach had I devisde: and scarce at last
Obteinde I it. As soone as I mine eie upon hir cast,
My wits were ravisht in such wise that nigh I had forgot   940
The purposde triall of hir troth. Right much adoe God wot
I had to holde mine owne that I the truth bewrayed not.
To keepe my selfe from kissing hir full much adoe I had
As reason was I should have done. She looked verie sad.
And yet as sadly as she lookte, no Wight alive can show   945
A better countenance than did she. Hir heart did inward glow
In longing for hir absent spouse. How beautifull a face
Thinke you, Sir Phocus, was in hir whome sorrow so did grace?
What should I make report how oft hir chast behaviour strave
And overcame most constantly the great assaults I gave?   950
Or tell how oft she shet me up with these same words? To one
(Where ere he is) I keepe my selfe, and none but he alone
Shall sure enjoy the use of me. What creature having his
Wits perfect would not be content with such a proofe as this
Of hir most stedfast chastitie? I could not be content: 955
But still to purchase to my selfe more wo I further went.
At last by profering endlesse welth, and heaping gifts on gifts,
In overlading hir with wordes I drave hir to hir shifts.

922 *scape:* transgression   942 *bewrayed:* revealed
929 *feates:* tricks   958 *shifts:* waverings
932 *fooding:* foding, encouraging, confirm-
    ing

Then cride I out: Thine evill heart my selfe I tardie take.
Where of a straunge advouterer the countenance I did make,   960
I am in deede thy husband. O unfaithfull woman thou,
Even I my selfe can testifie thy lewde behavior now.
She made none answere to my words, but being stricken dum
And with the sorrow of hir heart alonly overcum,
Forsaketh hir entangling house, and naughtie husband quight: 965
And hating all the sort of men by reason of the spight
That I had wrought hir, straide abrode among the Mountaines hie,
And exercisde Dianas feates. Then kindled by and by
A fiercer fire within my bones than ever was before,
When she had thus forsaken me by whome I set such store.   970
I prayde hir she woulde pardon me, and did confesse my fault.
Affirming that my selfe likewise with such a great assault
Of richesse might right well have bene enforst to yeelde to blame,
The rather if performance had ensewed of the same.
When I had this submission made, and she sufficiently   975
Revengde hir wronged chastitie, she then immediatly
Was reconcilde: and afterward we lived many a yeare
In joy and never any jarre betweene us did appeare.
Besides all this (as though hir love had bene too small a gift)
She gave me eke a goodly Grewnd which was of foote so swift,   980
That when Diana gave him hir, she said he should outgo
All others, and with this same Grewnd she gave this Dart also
The which you see I hold in hand. Perchaunce ye faine would know
What fortune to the Grewnd befell. I will unto you show
A wondrous case. The straungenesse of the matter will you move.   985
The krinkes of certaine Prophesies surmounting farre above
The reach of auncient wits to read, the Brookenymphes did expound:
And mindlesse of hir owne darke doubts Dame Themis being found,
Was as a rechelesse Prophetisse throwne flat against the ground.
For which presumptuous deede of theirs she tooke just punishment.   990
    To Thebes in Baeotia streight a cruell beast she sent,
    Which wrought the bane of many a Wight. The countryfolk did
                                                            feed
Him with their cattell and themselves, untill (as was agreed)
That all we youthfull Gentlemen that dwelled there about
Assembling pitcht our corded toyles the champion fields throughout.   995

960 *advouterer:* adulterer   986 *krinkes:* cranks, twists
978 *jarre:* quarrel   989 *rechelesse:* uncaring
980 *Grewnd:* greyhound   995 *champion:* champaign, level and open

But Net ne toyle was none so hie that could his wightnesse stop,
He mounted over at his ease the highest of the top.
Then everie man let slip their Grewnds, but he them all outstript
And even as nimbly as a birde in daliance from them whipt.
Then all the field desired me to let my Laelaps go: 1000
(The Grewnd that Procris unto me did give was named so)
Who strugling for to wrest his necke already from the band
Did stretch his collar. Scarsly had we let him off of hand
But that where Laelaps was become we could not understand.
The print remained of his feete upon the parched sand,   1005
But he was clearly out of sight. Was never Dart I trow,
Nor Pellet from enforced Sling, nor shaft from Cretish bow,
That flew more swift than he did runne. There was not farre fro thence
About the middle of the Laund a rising ground, from whence
A man might overlooke the fieldes. I gate me to the knap   1010
Of this same hill, and there beheld of this straunge course the hap
In which the beast seemes one while caught, and ere a man would think,
Doth quickly give the Grewnd the slip, and from his bighting shrink:
And like a wilie Foxe he runnes not forth directly out,
Nor makes a windlasse over all the champion fieldes about,   1015
But doubling and indenting still avoydes his enmies lips,
And turning short, as swift about as spinning wheele he whips,
To disapoint the snatch. The Grewnd pursuing at an inch
Doth cote him, never losing ground: but likely still to pinch
Is at the sodaine shifted off. Continually he snatches   1020
In vaine: for nothing in his mouth save only Aire he latches.
Then thought I for to trie what helpe my Dart at neede could show.
Which as I charged in my hand by levell aime to throw,
And set my fingars to the thongs, I lifting from bylow
Mine eies, did looke right forth againe, and straight amids the field 1025
(A wondrous thing) two Images of Marble I beheld:
Of which ye would have thought the t'one had fled on still apace
And that with open barking mouth the tother did him chase.
In faith it was the will of God (at least if any Goddes
Had care of them) that in their pace there should be found none
                                                  oddes.   1030
       Thus farre: and then he held his peace. But tell us ere we part
       (Quoth Phocus) what offence or fault committed hath your Dart?

996 *wightnesse:* agility
1009 *Laund:* glade, pasture
1010 *knap:* summit
1015 *windlasse:* circuit

1016 *indenting:* zigzagging
1019 *cote:* overtake
1030 *none oddes:* no difference

His Darts offence he thus declarde: My Lorde, the ground of all
My grief was joy. Those joyes of mine remember first I shall.
It doth me good even yet to thinke upon that blissfull time 1035
(I meane the fresh and lustie yeares of pleasant youthfull Prime)
When I a happie man enjoyde so faire and good a wife,
And she with such a loving make did lead a happie life.
The care was like of both of us, the mutuall love all one.
She would not to have line with Jove my presence have forgone. 1040
Ne was there any Wight that could of me have wonne the love,
No though Dame Venus had hir selfe descended from above.
The glowing brands of love did burne in both our brests alike.
Such time as first with crased beames the Sunne is wont to strike
The tops of Towres and mountaines high, according to the wont 1045
Of youthfull men, in woodie Parkes I went abrode to hunt.
But neither horse nor Hounds to make pursuit upon the scent.
Nor Servingman, nor knottie toyle before or after went,
For I was safe with this same Dart. When wearie waxt mine arme
With striking Deere, and that the day did make me somewhat
warme, 1050
Withdrawing for to coole my selfe I sought among the shades
For Aire that from the valleyes colde came breathing in at glades.
The more excessive was my heate the more for Aire I sought.
I waited for the gentle Aire: the Aire was that that brought
Refreshing to my wearie limmes. And (well I bear't in thought) 1055
Come Aire I wonted was to sing, come ease the paine of me
Within my bosom lodge thy selfe most welcome unto me,
And as thou heretofore art wont abate my burning heate.
By chaunce (such was my destinie) proceeding to repeate
Mo words of daliance like to these, I used for to say 1060
Great pleasure doe I take in thee: for thou from day to day
Doste both refresh and nourish me. Thou makest me delight
In woods and solitarie grounds. Now would to God I might
Receive continuall at my mouth this pleasant breath of thine.
Some man (I wote not who) did heare these doubtfull words of
mine, 1065
And taking them amisse supposde that this same name of Aire
The which I callde so oft upon, had bene some Ladie faire:
He thought that I had lovde some Nymph. And thereupon streight way
He runnes me like a Harebrainde blab to Procris, to bewray

1038 *make:* mate   1044 *crased:* weak, oblique
1040 *line:* lain

This fault as he surmised it: and there with lavish tung   1070
Reported all the wanton words that he had heard me sung.
A thing of light beliefe is love. She (as I since have harde)
For sodeine sorrow swounded downe: and when long afterwarde
She came againe unto hir selfe, she said she was accurst
And borne to cruell destinie: and me she blamed wurst   1075
For breaking faith: and freating at a vaine surmised shame
She dreaded that which nothing was: she fearde a headlesse name.
She wist not what to say or thinke. The wretch did greatly feare
Deceit: yet could she not beleve the tales that talked were.
Onlesse she saw hir husbands fault apparant to hir eie,   1080
She thought she would not him condemne of any villanie.
Next day as soone as Morning light had driven the night away,
I went abrode to hunt againe: and speeding, as I lay
Upon the grasse, I said: Come, Aire, and ease my painfull heate.
And on the sodaine as I spake there seemed for to beate   1085
A certaine sighing in mine eares of what I could not gesse.
But ceasing not for that I still proceeded nathelesse:
And said, O come, most pleasant Aire. With that I heard a sound
Of russling softly in the leaves that lay upon the ground.
And thinking it had bene some beast I threw my flying Dart.   1090
It was my wife. Who being now sore wounded at the hart,
Cride out, Alas. As soone as I perceyved by the shrieke
It was my faithfull spouse, I ran me to the voiceward lieke
A madman that had lost his wits. There found I hir halfe dead,
Hir scattred garments staining in the bloud that she had bled,   1095
And (wretched creature as I am) yet drawing from the wound
The gift that she hir selfe had given. Then softly from the ground
I lifted up that bodie of hirs of which I was more chare
Than of mine owne, and from hir brest hir clothes in hast I tare.
And binding up hir cruell wound I strived for to stay   1100
The bloud, and prayd she would not thus by passing so away
Forsake me as a murtherer: she waxing weake at length
And drawing to hir death apace, enforced all hir strength
To utter these few wordes at last: I pray thee humbly by
Our bond of wedlocke, by the Gods as well above the Skie   1105
As those to whome I now must passe, as ever I have ought
Deserved well by thee, and by the Love which having brought
Me to my death doth even in death unfaded still remaine,
To nestle in thy bed and mine let never Aire obtaine.

1093 *lieke:* like   1098 *chare:* chary, careful

This sed, she held hir peace, and I perceyved by the same   1110
And tolde hir also how she was beguiled in the name.
But what avayled telling then? she quoathde: and with hir bloud
Hir little strength did fade. Howbeit as long as that she coud
See ought, she stared in my face and gasping still on me
Even in my mouth she breathed forth hir wretched ghost. But she   1115
Did seeme with better cheare to die for that hir conscience was
Discharged quight and cleare of doubtes. Now in conclusion as
Duke Cephal weeping told this tale to Phocus and the rest
Whose eyes were also moyst with teares to heare the pitious gest,
Behold King Aeacus and with him his eldest sonnes both twaine   1120
Did enter in and after them there followed in a traine
Of well appointed men of warre new levied: which the King
Delivered unto Cephalus to Athens towne to bring.

FINIS SEPTIMI LIBRI.

1112 *quoathde:* lost consciousness   1119 *gest:* tale
1117 *quight:* free

THE EIGHT BOOKE

OF OVIDS METAMORPHOSIS.

[Minos and Scylla. Daedalus and Icarus. The Boar of Calydon. Meleager and Althaea. Philemon and Baucis. Erysichthon.]

The day starre now beginning to disclose the Morning bright
And for to clense the droupie Skie from darkenesse of the night,
The Easterne wind went downe and flakes of foggie Clouds gan show,
And from the South a merrie gale on Cephals sayles did blow.
The which did hold so fresh and large, that he and all his men   5
Before that he was looked for arrived safe agen
In wished Haven. In that while King Minos with his fleete
Did waste the cost of Megara. And first he thought it meete
To make a triall of the force and courage of his men
Against the towne Alcathoe where Nisus reigned then.   10
Among whose honorable haire that was of colour gray,
One scarlet haire did grow upon his crowne, whereon the stay
Of all his Kingdome did depende. Sixe times did Phoebe fill
Hir hornes with borrowed light, and yet the warre hung wavering still
In fickle fortunes doubtfull scaales: and long with fleeting wings   15
Betwene them both flew victorie. A Turret of the Kings
Stood hard adjoyning to the Wall which being touched rings,
For Phoebus (so men say) did lay his golden Violl there,
And so the stones the sound thereof did ever after beare.
King Nisus daughter oftentimes resorted to this Wall   20
And strake it with a little stone to raise the sound withall,
In time of peace. And in the warre she many a time and oft

2 *droupie:* gloomy

Behelde the sturdie stormes of Mars from that same place aloft.
And by continuance of the siege the Captaines names she knew,
Their armes, horse, armor and aray in everie band and crew.   25
But specially above the rest she noted Minos face.
She knew inough and more than was inough as stoode the case.
For were it that he hid his head in Helme with fethered crest,
To hir opinion in his Helme he stayned all the rest.
Or were it that he tooke in hand of steele his target bright,   30
She thought in weelding of his shielde he was a comly Knight.
Or were it that he raisde his arme to throw the piercing Dart,
The Ladie did commend his force and manhode joynde with Art.
Or drew he with his arrow nockt his bended Bow in hand
She sware that so in all respectes was Phoebus wont to stand.   35
But when he shewde his visage bare, his Helmet laid aside,
And on a Milke white Steede brave trapt, in Purple Robe did ride,
She scarce was Mistresse of hir selfe, hir wits were almost straught.
A happie Dart she thought it was that he in fingars caught,
And happie called she those reynes that he in hand had raught.   40
And if she might have had hir will, she could have founde in hart,
Among the enmies to have gone. She could have found in hart,
From downe the highest Turret there hir bodie to have throwne,
Among the thickest of the Tents of Gnossus to have flowne,
Or for to ope the brazen gates and let the enmie in,   45
Or whatsoever else she thought might Minos favor win.
And as she sate beholding still the King of Candies tent,
    She said: I doubt me whether that I rather may lament
    Or of this wofull warre be glad. It grieves me at the hart
That thou O Minos unto me thy Lover enmie art.   50
But had not this same warfare bene, I never had him knowne.
Yet might he leave this cruell warre, and take me as his owne.
A wife, a feere, a pledge for peace he might receive of me.
O flowre of beautie, O thou Prince most pearlesse: if that she
That bare thee in hir wombe were like in beautie unto thee,   55
A right good cause had Jove on hir enamored for to bee.
Oh happie were I if with wings I through the Aire might glide
And safely to King Minos Tent from this same Turret slide.
Then would I utter who I am, and how the firie flame

---

30 *target:* round shield   38 *straught:* distraught, distracted
34 *nockt:* notched   40 *raught:* taken, seized
37 *trapt:* adorned   53 *feere:* mate

Of Cupid burned in my brest, desiring him to name   60
What dowrie he would aske with me in loan of his love,
Save only of my Fathers Realme no question he should move.
For rather than by traitrous meanes my purpose should take place,
Adue, desire of hoped Love. Yet oftentimes such grace
Hath from the gentle Conqueror proceeded erst, that they   65
Which tooke the foyle have found the same their profit and their stay.
Assuredly the warre is just that Minos takes in hand,
As in revengement of his sonne late murthered in this land.
And as his quarrell seemeth just, even so it cannot faile,
But rightfull warre against the wrong must (I beleve) prevaile.   70
Now if this Citie in the ende must needes be taken, why
Should his owne sworde and not my Love be meanes to win it by?
It were yet better he should speede by gentle meanes without
The slaughter of his people, yea and (as it may fall out)
With spending of his owne bloud too. For sure I have a care   75
O Minos lest some Souldier wound thee ere he be aware.
For who is he in all the world that hath so hard a hart
That wittingly against thy head would aime his cruell Dart?
I like well this devise, and on this purpose will I stand:
To yeelde my selfe endowed with this Citie to the hand   80
Of Minos: and in doing so to bring this warre to ende.
But smally it availeth me the matter to intende.
The gates and yssues of this towne are kept with watch and warde,
And of the Keyes continually my Father hath the garde.
My Father only is the man of whome I stand in dreede,   85
My Father only hindreth me of my desired speede.
Would God that I were Fatherlesse. Tush, everie Wight may bee
A God as in their owne behalfe, and if their hearts be free
From fearefulnesse. For fortune works against the fond desire
Of such as through faint heartednesse attempt not to aspire.   90
Some other feeling in hir heart such flames of Cupids fire
Already would have put in proofe some practise to destroy
What thing so ever of hir Love the furtherance might anoy
And why should any woman have a bolder heart than I?
Through fire and sword I boldly durst adventure for to flie.   95
And yet in this behalfe at all there needes no sword nor fire,
There needeth but my fathers haire to accomplish my desire.

---

[66] *foyle:* setback   [83] *yssues:* exits
[73] *speede:* succeed

That Purple haire of his to me more precious were than golde:
That Purple haire of his would make me blest a thousand folde:
That haire would compasse my desire and set my heart at rest.   100
  Night (chiefest Nurce of thoughts to such as are with care opprest)
  Approched while she spake these words, and darknesse did
                                                        encrease
Hir boldnesse. At such time as folke are wont to finde release
Of cares that all the day before were working in their heds,
By sleepe which falleth first of all upon them in their beds,   105
Hir fathers chamber secretly she entered: where (alasse
That ever Maiden should so farre the bounds of Nature passe)
She robde hir Father of the haire upon the which the fate
Depended both of life and death and of his royall state.
And joying in hir wicked prey, she beares it with hir so   110
As if it were some lawfull spoyle acquired of the fo.
And passing through a posterne gate she marched through the mid
Of all hir enmies (such a trust she had in that she did)
Untill she came before the King, whom troubled with the sight
She thus bespake: Enforst, O King, by love against all right   115
I Scylla, Nisus daughter, doe present unto thee heere
My native soyle, my household Gods, and all that else is deere
For this my gift none other thing in recompence I crave
Than of thy person which I love, fruition for to have.
And in assurance of my love receyve thou here of mee   120.
My fathers Purple haire: and thinke I give not unto thee
A haire but even my fathers head. And as these words she spake,
The cursed gift with wicked hand she profered him to take.
But Minos did abhorre hir gift: and troubled in his minde
With straungenesse of the heynous act so sore against hir kinde,   125
He aunswerde: O thou slaunder of our age, the Gods expell
Thee out of all this world of theirs and let thee no where dwell.
Let rest on neither Sea nor Land be graunted unto thee.
Assure thy selfe that as for me I never will agree
That Candie, Joves owne foster place (as long as I there raigne),   130
Shall unto such a monstruous Wight a Harbrow place remaine.
    This said, he like a righteous Judge among his vanquisht foes
    Set order under paine of death. Which done he willed those
That served him to go aboorde and Anchors up to wey.

131 *Harbrow:* harbor

When Scylla saw the Candian fleete aflote to go away,   135
And that the Captaine yeelded not so good reward as shee
Had for hir lewdnesse looked for: and when in fine she see
That no entreatance could prevaile, then bursting out in ire
With stretched hands and scattred haire, as furious as the fire
She shraming cryed out aloud: And whither doste thou flie   140
Rejecting me, the only meanes that thou hast conquerde by?
O cankerde Churle preferde before my native soyle, preferd
Before my father, whither flyste, O Carle of heart most hard?
Whose conquest as it is my sinne, so doth it well deserve
Reward of thee, for that my fault so well thy turne did serve.   145
Doth neither thee the gift I gave, nor yet my faithfull love,
Nor yet that all my hope on thee alonly rested, move?
For whither shall I now resort forsaken thus of thee?
To Megara the wretched soyle of my nativitie?
Behold it lieth vanquished and troden under foote.   150
But put the case it flourisht still: yet could it nothing boote.
I have foreclosde it to my selfe through treason when I gave
My fathers head to thee. Whereby my countriefolke I drave
To hate me justly for my crime. And all the Realmes about
My lewde example doe abhorre. Thus have I shet me out   155
Of all the world that only Crete might take me in, which if
Thou like a Churle denie, and cast me up without relief,
The Ladie Europ surely was not mother unto thee:
But one of Affricke Sirts where none but Serpents fostred bee,
But even some cruell Tiger bred in Armen or in Inde,   160
Or else the Gulfe Charybdis raisde with rage of Southerne winde.
Thou wert not got by Jove: ne yet thy mother was beguilde
In shape of Bull: of this thy birth the tale is false compilde.
But rather some unwieldie Bull even altogither wilde
That never lowed after Cow was out of doubt thy Sire.   165
O father Nisus, put thou me to penance for my hire.
Rejoyce thou in my punishment, thou towne by me betrayd.
I have deserved (I confesse) most justly to be payd
With death. But let some one of them that through my lewdnesse smart
Destroy me, why doste thou that by my crime a gainer art,   170
Commit like crime thy selfe? Admit this wicked act of me

137 *lewdnesse:* wickedness   143 *Carle:* churl
140 *shraming:* shreaming, screaming 151 *boote:* help
142 *cankerde:* corrupt   166 *hire:* payment

As to my land and Fatherward in deede most hainous be.
Yet oughtest thou to take it as a friendship unto thee.
But she was meete to be thy wife, that in a Cow of tree
Could play the Harlot with a Bull, and in hir wombe could beare   175
A Barne, in whome the shapes of man and beasts confounded were.
How sayst thou, Carle? compell not these my words thine eares to glow?
Or doe the windes that drive thy shyps, in vaine my sayings blow?
In faith it is no wonder though thy wife Pasiphae
Preferrde a Bull to thee, for thou more cruell wert than he.   180
Now wo is me. To make more hast it standeth me in hand.
The water sounds with Ores, and hales from me and from my land.
In vaine thou striveth, O thou Churle, forgetfull quight of my
Desertes: for even in spight of thee pursue thee still will I.
Upon thy courbed Keele will I take holde: and hanging so   185
Be drawen along the Sea with thee where ever thou do go.
        She scarce had said these words, but that she leaped on the wave
        And getting to the ships by force of strength that Love hir gave
Upon the King of Candies Keele in spight of him she clave.
Whome when hir father spide (for now he hovered in the aire,   190
And being made a Hobby Hauke did soare between a paire
Of nimble wings of yron Mayle) he soused downe amaine
To seaze upon hir as she hung, and would have torne hir faine
With bowing Beake. But she for feare did let the Caricke go:
And as she was about to fall, the lightsome Aire did so   195
Uphold hir that she could not touch the Sea as seemed tho.
Anon all fethers she became, and forth away did flie
Transformed to a pretie Bird that stieth to the Skie.
And for bicause like clipped haire hir head doth beare a marke,
The Greekes it Cyris call, and we doe name the same a Larke.   200
        As soone as Minos came aland in Crete, he by and by
        Performde his vowes to Jupiter in causing for to die
A hundred Bulles for sacrifice. And then he did adorne
His Pallace with the enmies spoyles by conquest wonne beforne.
The slaunder of his house encreast: and now appeared more   205
The mothers filthie whoredome by the monster that she bore
Of double shape, an ugly thing. This shamefull infamie,

174 *tree:* wood
176 *Barne:* child
185 *courbed:* curved
191 *Hobby Hauke:* small falcon

192 *soused:* swooped
194 *bowing:* bent; *Caricke:* large ship
198 *stieth:* rises

This monster borne him by his wife he mindes by pollicie
To put away, and in a house with many nookes and krinks
From all mens sights and speach of folke to shet it up he thinks.   210
Immediatly one Daedalus renowmed in that lande
For fine devise and workmanship in building, went in hand
To make it. He confounds his worke with sodaine stops and stayes,
And with the great uncertaintie of sundrie winding wayes
Leades in and out, and to and fro, at divers doores astray.   215
And as with trickling streame the Brooke Maeander seemes to play
In Phrygia, and with doubtfull race runnes counter to and fro,
And meeting with himselfe doth looke if all his streame or no
Come after, and retiring eft cleane backward to his spring
And marching eft to open Sea as streight as any string,   220
Indenteth with reversed streame: even so of winding wayes
Unnumerable Daedalus within his worke convayes.
Yea scarce himselfe could find the meanes to winde himselfe well out:
So busie and so intricate the house was all about.
          Within this Maze did Minos shet the Monster that did beare   225
          The shape of man and Bull. And when he twise had fed him there
With bloud of Atticke Princes sonnes that given for tribute were,
The third time at the ninth yeares end the lot did chaunce to light
On Theseus, King Aegaeus sonne: who like a valiant Knight
Did overcome the Minotaur: and by the pollicie   230
Of Minos eldest daughter (who had taught him for to tie
A clew of Linnen at the doore to guide himselfe thereby)
As busie as the turnings were, his way he out did finde,
Which never man had done before. And streight he having winde,
With Minos daughter sailde away to Dia: where (unkinde   235
And cruell creature that he was) he left hir post alone
Upon the shore. Thus desolate and making dolefull mone
God Bacchus did both comfort hir and take hir to his bed.
And with an everlasting starre the more hir fame to spred,
He tooke the Chaplet from hir head, and up to Heaven it threw.   240
The Chaplet thirled through the Aire: and as it gliding flew,
The precious stones were turnd to starres which blased cleare and bright,
And tooke their place (continuing like a Chaplet still to sight)

208 *pollicie:* cunning, trickery
209 *krinks:* twists
213 *stops and stayes:* obstacles
219 *eft:* after, now

221 *Indenteth:* zigzags
223 *winde . . . out:* make way out
232 *clew:* ball of yarn, thread
241 *thirled:* pierced

Amid betweene the Kneeler Downe and him that gripes the Snake.
 Now in this while gan Daedalus a wearinesse to take 245
 Of living like a banisht man and prisoner such a time
In Crete, and longed in his heart to see his native Clime.
But Seas enclosed him as if he had in prison be.
Then thought he: though both Sea and Land King Minos stop fro me,
I am assurde he cannot stop the Aire and open Skie. 250
To make my passage that way then my cunning will I trie.
Although that Minos like a Lord held all the world beside:
Yet doth the Aire from Minos yoke for all men free abide.
This sed: to uncoth Arts he bent the force of all his wits
To alter natures course by craft. And orderly he knits 255
A rowe of fethers one by one, beginning with the short,
And overmatching still eche quill with one of longer sort,
That on the shoring of a hill a man would thinke them grow.
Even so the countrie Organpipes of Oten reedes in row
Ech higher than another rise. Then fastned he with Flax 260
The middle quilles, and joyned in the lowest sort with Wax.
And when he thus had finisht them, a little he them bent
In compasse, that the verie Birdes they full might represent.
There stoode me by him Icarus, his sonne, a pretie Lad.
Who knowing not that he in handes his owne destruction had, 265
With smiling mouth did one while blow the fethers to and fro
Which in the Aire on wings of Birds did flask not long ago:
And with his thumbes another while he chafes the yelow Wax
And lets his fathers wondrous worke with childish toyes and knacks.
As soon as that the worke was done, the workman by and by 270
Did peyse his bodie on his wings, and in the Aire on hie
Hung wavering: and did teach his sonne how he should also flie.
I warne thee (quoth he), Icarus, a middle race to keepe.
For if thou hold too low a gate, the dankenesse of the deepe
Will overlade thy wings with wet. And if thou mount too hie, 275
The Sunne will sindge them. Therfore see betweene them both thou
             flie.
I bid thee not behold the Starre Bootes in the Skie.
Nor looke upon the bigger Beare to make thy course thereby,
Nor yet on Orions naked sword. But ever have an eie

244 *Kneeler Downe:* the constellation Her-
 cules
254 *uncoth:* unknown, strange
267 *flask:* flap, flutter

269 *lets:* hinders
271 *peyse:* balance
274 *gate:* course

To keepe the race that I doe keepe, and I will guide thee right.   280
In giving counsell to his sonne to order well his flight,
He fastned to his shoulders twaine a paire of uncoth wings.
And as he was in doing it and warning him of things,
His aged cheekes were wet, his hands did quake, in fine he gave
His sonne a kisse the last that he alive should ever have.   285
And then he mounting up aloft before him tooke his way
Right fearfull for his followers sake: as is the Bird the day
That first she tolleth from hir nest among the braunches hie
Hir tender yong ones in the Aire to teach them for to flie.
So heartens he his little sonne to follow teaching him   290
A hurtfull Art. His owne two wings he waveth verie trim,
And looketh backward still upon his sonnes. The fishermen
Then standing angling by the Sea, and shepeherdes leaning then
On sheepehookes, and the Ploughmen on the handles of their Plough,
Beholding them, amazed were: and thought that they that through   295
The Aire could flie were Gods. And now did on their left side stand
The Iles of Paros and of Dele and Samos, Junos land:
And on their right, Lebinthos and the faire Calydna fraught
With store of honie: when the Boy a frolicke courage caught
To flie at randon. Whereupon forsaking quight his guide,   300
Of fond desire to flie to Heaven, above his boundes he stide.
And there the nerenesse of the Sunne which burnd more hote aloft,
Did make the Wax (with which his wings were glewed) lithe and soft.
As soone as that the Wax was molt, his naked armes he shakes,
And wanting wherewithall to wave no helpe of Aire he takes.   305
But calling on his father loud he drowned in the wave:
And by this chaunce of his those Seas his name for ever have.
His wretched Father (but as then no father) cride in feare:
O Icarus, O Icarus, where art thou? tell me where
That I may finde thee, Icarus. He saw the fethers swim   310
Upon the waves, and curst his Art that so had spighted him.
At last he tooke his bodie up and laid it in a grave,
And to the Ile the name of him then buried in it gave.
    And as he of his wretched sonne the corse in ground did hide,
    The cackling Partrich from a thicke and leavie thorne him
                                                                  spide,   315

284 *in fine:* finally   300 *randon:* random
288 *tolleth:* lures, pulls   304 *molt:* melted
299 *frolicke:* merry, sportive

And clapping with his wings for joy aloud to call began.
There was of that same kinde of Birde no mo but he as than.
In times forepast had none bene seene. It was but late anew
Since he was made a bird: and that thou, Daedalus, mayst rew:
For whyle the world doth last thy shame shall thereupon ensew.   320
For why thy sister, ignorant of that which after hapt,
Did put him to thee to be taught full twelve yeares old and apt
To take instruction. He did marke the middle bone that goes
Through fishes, and according to the paterne tane of those
He filed teeth upon a piece of yron one by one   325
And so devised first the Saw where erst was never none.
Moreover he two yron shankes so joynde in one round head,
That opening an indifferent space, the one point downe shall tread,
And tother draw a circle round. The finding of these things,
The spightfull heart of Daedalus with such a malice stings,   330
That headlong from the holy towre of Pallas downe he thrue
His Nephew, feyning him to fall by chaunce, which was not true.
But Pallas (who doth favour wits) did stay him in his fall
And chaunging him into a Bird did clad him over all
With fethers soft amid the Aire. The quicknesse of his wit   335
(Which erst was swift) did shed it selfe among his wings and feete.
And as he Partrich hight before, so hights he Partrich still.
Yet mounteth not this Bird aloft ne seemes to have a will
To build hir nest in tops of trees among the boughes on hie
But flecketh nere the ground and layes hir egges in hedges drie. 340
And forbicause hir former fall she ay in minde doth beare,
She ever since all lofty things doth warely shun for feare.
　　　And now forwearied Daedalus alighted in the land
　　　Within the which the burning hilles of firie Aetna stand.
To save whose life King Cocalus did weapon take in hand,   345
For which men thought him merciful. And now with high renowne
Had Theseus ceast the wofull pay of tribute in the towne
Of Athens. Temples decked were with garlands every where,
And supplications made to Jove and warlicke Pallas were,
And all the other Gods, to whome more honor for to show,   350
Gifts, blud of beasts, and frankincense the people did bestow
As in performance of their vowes. The right redoubted name
Of Theseus through the lande of Greece was spred by flying fame.

And now the folke that in the land of rich Achaia dwelt,
Praid him of succor in the harmes and perils that they felt.   355
Although the land of Calydon had then Meleager:
Yet was it faine in humble wise to Theseus to prefer
A supplication for the aide of him. The cause wherfore
They made such humble suit to him was this. There was a Bore
The which Diana for to wreake hir wrath conceyvde before   360
Had thither as hir servant sent the countrie for to waast.
For men report that Oenie when he had in storehouse plaast
The full encrease of former yeare, to Ceres did assigne
The firstlings of his corne and fruits: to Bacchus, of the Wine:
And unto Pallas Olife oyle. This honoring of the Gods   365
Of graine and fruits who put their help to toyling in the clods,
Ambitiously to all, even those that dwell in heaven did clime.
Dianas Altars (as it hapt) alonly at that time
Without reward of Frankincense were overskipt (they say).
Even Gods are subject unto wrath. He shall not scape away   370
Unpunisht, though unworshipped he passed me wyth spight:
He shall not make his vaunt he scapt me unrevenged quight,
Quoth Phoebe. And anon she sent a Bore to Oenies ground
Of such a hugenesse as no Bull could ever yet be found,
In Epyre: but in Sicilie are Bulles much lesse than hee.   375
His eies did glister blud and fire: right dreadfull was to see
His brawned necke, right dredfull was his haire which grew as thicke
With pricking points as one of them could well by other sticke.
And like a front of armed Pikes set close in battell ray
The sturdie bristles on his back stoode staring up alway.   380
The scalding fome with gnashing hoarse which he did cast aside,
Upon his large and brawned shield did white as Curdes abide.
Among the greatest Oliphants in all the land of Inde,
A greater tush than had this Boare, ye shall not lightly finde.
Such lightning flashed from his chappes, as seared up the grasse.   385
Now trampled he the spindling corne to ground where he did passe,
Now ramping up their riped hope he made the Plowmen weepe.
And chankt the kernell in the eare. In vaine their floores they sweepe:
In vaine their Barnes for Harvest long, the likely store they keepe.

---

377 *brawned:* muscular
380 *staring:* standing on end
382 *shield:* tough side-skin
384 *tush:* tusk; *lightly:* easily

386 *spindling:* slender
387 *ramping:* tearing
388 *chankt:* champed, chewed

The spreaded Vines with clustred Grapes to ground he rudely sent, 390
And full of Berries loden boughes from Olife trees he rent.
On cattell also did he rage. The shepeherd nor his dog,
Nor yet the Bulles could save the herdes from outrage of this Hog.
The folke themselves were faine to flie. And yet they thought them not
In safetie when they had themselves within the Citie got. 395
Untill their Prince Meleager, and with their Prince a knot
Of Lords and lustie gentlemen of hand and courage stout,
With chosen fellowes for the nonce of all the Lands about,
Inflamed were to win renowne. The chiefe that thither came
Were both the twinnes of Tyndarus of great renowne and fame, 400
The one in all activitie of manhode, strength and force,
The other for his cunning skill in handling of a horse.
And Jason he that first of all the Gallie did invent:
And Theseus with Pirithous betwene which two there went
A happie leage of amitie: And two of Thesties race: 405
And Lynce, the sonne of Apharie and Idas, swift of pace.
And fierce Leucyppus and the brave Acastus with his Dart
In handling of the which he had the perfect skill and Art.
And Caeny who by birth a wench, the shape of man had wonne
And Drias and Hippothous: and Phoenix eke the sonne 410
Of olde Amyntor: and a paire of Actors ympes: and Phyle
Who came from Elis. Telamon was also there that while:
And so was also Peleus, the great Achilles Sire:
And Pherets sonne: and Iolay, the Thebane who with fire
Helpt Hercules the monstruous heades of Hydra off to seare. 415
The lively Lad Eurytion and Echion who did beare
The pricke and prise for footemanship, were present also there.
And Lelex of Narytium too. And Panopie beside:
And Hyle: and cruell Hippasus: and Naestor who that tide
Was in the Prime of lustie youth: moreover thither went 420
Three children of Hippocoon from old Amicle sent.
And he that of Penelope the fathrinlaw became.
And eke the sonne of Parrhasus, Ancaeus cald by name.
There was the sonne of Ampycus of great forecasting wit:
And Oeclies sonne who of his wife was unbetrayed yit. 425
And from the Citie Tegea there came the Paragone

³⁹⁸ *nonce:* occasion   ⁴¹⁷ *pricke:* acme, apex
⁴⁰³ *Gallie:* ship   ⁴¹⁹ *tide:* time

Of Lycey forrest, Atalant, a goodly Ladie, one
Of Schoenyes daughters, then a Maide. The garment she did weare
A brayded button fastned at hir gorget. All hir heare
Untrimmed in one only knot was trussed. From hir left   430
Side hanging on hir shoulder was an Ivorie quiver deft:
Which being full of arrowes, made a clattring as she went.
And in hir right hand she did beare a Bow already bent.
Hir furniture was such as this. Hir countnance and hir grace
Was such as in a Boy might well be cald a Wenches face,   435
And in a Wench be cald a Boyes. The Prince of Calydon
No sooner cast his eie on hir, but being caught anon
In love, he wisht hir to his wife. But unto this desire
God Cupid gave not his consent. The secret flames of fire
He haling inward still did say: O happy man is he   440
Whom this same Ladie shall vouchsave hir Husband for to be.
The shortnesse of the time and shame would give him leave to say
No more: a worke of greater weight did draw him then away.
  A wood thick growen with trees which stoode unfelled to that day
  Beginning from a plaine, had thence a large prospect
                                        throughout   445
The falling grounds that every way did muster round about.
As soone as that the men came there, some pitched up the toyles,
Some tooke the couples from the Dogs, and some pursude the foyles
In places where the Swine had tract: desiring for to spie
Their owne destruction. Now there was a hollow bottom by,   450
To which the watershots of raine from all the high grounds drew.
Within the compasse of this pond great store of Osiers grew:
And Sallowes lithe, and flackring Flags, and moorish Rushes eke,
And lazie Reedes on little shankes, and other baggage like.
From hence the Bore was rowzed out, and fiersly forth he flies   455
Among the thickest of his foes like thunder from the Skies,
When Clouds in meeting force the fire to burst by violence out.
He beares the trees before him downe, and all the wood about
Doth sound of crashing. All the youth with hideous noyse and shout
Against him bend their Boarspeare points with hand and courage
                                        stout.   460

429 *gorget:* collar
434 *furniture:* furnishings, apparel
440 *haling:* drawing
446 *muster:* appear, make a fine appearance
448 *foyles:* tracks

451 *watershots:* overflows of water
453 *Sallowes:* willows; *flackring:* fluttering;
     moorish: marshy
454 *baggage like:* such growth

He rushes forth among the Dogs that held him at a bay,
And now on this side now on that, as any come in way,
He rippes their skinnes and splitteth them, and chaseth them away,
Echion first of all the rout a Dart at him did throw,
Which mist and in a Maple tree did give a little blow.   465
The next (if he that threw the same had used lesser might),
The backe at which he aimed it was likely for to smight.
It overflew him. Jason was the man that cast the Dart.
With that the sonne of Ampycus sayd: Phoebus (if with hart
I have and still doe worship thee) now graunt me for to hit   470
The thing that I doe levell at. Apollo graunts him it
As much as lay in him to graunt. He hit the Swine in deede.
But neyther entred he his hide nor caused him to bleede.
For why Diana (as the Dart was flying) tooke away
The head of it: and so the Dart could headlesse beare no sway.   475
But yet the moodie beast thereby was set the more on fire
And chafing like the lightning swift he uttreth forth his ire.
The fire did sparkle from his eyes: and from his boyling brest
He breathed flaming flakes of fire conceyved in his chest.
And looke with what a violent brunt a mightie Bullet goes   480
From engines bent against a wall, or bulwarks full of foes:
With even such violence rusht the Swine among the Hunts amayne,
And overthrew Eupalamon and Pelagon both twaine
That in the right wing placed were. Their fellowes stepping to
And drawing them away, did save their lives with much ado.   485
But as for poore Enesimus, Hippocoons sonne had not
The lucke to scape the deadly dint. He would away have got,
And trembling turnde his backe for feare. The Swine him overtooke,
And cut his hamstrings, so that streight his going him forsooke.
And Naestor to have lost his life was like by fortune ere   490
The siege of Troie, but that he tooke his rist upon his speare:
And leaping quickly up upon a tree that stoode hard by,
Did safely from the place behold his foe whome he did flie.
The Boare then whetting sharpe his tuskes against the Oken wood
To mischiefe did prepare himselfe with fierce and cruell mood.   495
And trusting to his weapons which he sharpened had anew,
In great Orithyas thigh a wound with hooked groyne he drew.

475 *sway:* force   497 *groyne:* snout
482 *amayne:* at full speed

The valiant brothers, those same twinnes of Tyndarus (not yet
Celestiall signes), did both of them on goodly coursers sit
As white as snow: and ech of them had shaking in his fist   500
A lightsome Dart with head of steele to throw it where he lyst.
And for to wound the bristled Bore they surely had not mist
But that he still recovered so the coverts of the wood,
That neyther horse could follow him, nor Dart doe any good.
Still after followed Telamon, whom taking to his feete   505
No heede at all for egernesse, a Maple roote did meete,
Which tripped up his heeles, and flat against the ground him laid.
And while his brother Peleus relieved him, the Maid
Of Tegea tooke an arrow swift, and shot it from hir bow.
The arrow lighting underneath the havers eare bylow,   510
And somewhat rasing of the skin, did make the bloud to show.
The Maid hirselfe not gladder was to see that luckie blow,
Than was the Prince Meleager. He was the first that saw,
And first that shewed to his Mates the blud that she did draw:
And said: For this thy valiant act due honor shalt thou have.   515
The men did blush, and chearing up ech other courage gave
With shouting, and disorderly their Darts by heaps they threw.
The number of them hindred them, not suffring to ensew
That any lighted on the marke at which they all did ame.
Behold, enragde against his ende the hardie Knight that came   520
From Arcadie, rusht rashly with a Pollax in his fist
And said: You yonglings learne of me what difference is betwist
A wenches weapons and a mans: and all of you give place
To my redoubted force. For though Diana in this ✓hase
Should with hir owne shield him defend, yet should this hand of mine 525
Even maugre Dame Dianas heart confound this orped Swine.
Such boasting words as these through pride presumptuously he crakes:
And streyning out himselfe upon his tiptoes streight he takes
His Pollax up with both his hands. But as this bragger ment
To fetch his blow, the cruell beast his malice did prevent: 530
And in his coddes (the speeding place of death) his tusshes puts,

---

501 *lyst:* wanted
510 *havers:*(?) the word, which translates
    Ovid's *ferus,* means beast. Not in OED,
    except in the sense gelded deer. *Aver*
    means animal, though generally do-
    mestic.

521 *Pollax:* pole-axe, battle-axe
526 *maugre:* in spite of; *orped:* fierce
527 *crakes:* brags
531 *coddes:* testicles

And rippeth up his paunche. Downe falles Ancaeus and his guts
Come tumbling out besmearde with bloud, and foyled all the plot.
Pirithous, Ixions sonne, at that abashed not:
But shaking in his valiant hand his hunting staffe did goe   535
Still stoutly forward face to face t'encounter with his foe
To whome Duke Theseus cride afarre: O dearer unto mee
Than is my selfe, my soule I say, stay: lawfull we it see
For valiant men to keepe aloofe. The over hardie hart
In rash adventring of him selfe hath made Ancaeus smart.   540
This sed, he threw a weightie Dart of Cornell with a head
Of brasse: which being leveld well was likely to have sped,
But that a bough of Chestnut tree thick leaved by the way
Did latch it, and by meanes therof the dint of it did stay.
Another Dart that Jason threw, by fortune mist the Bore,   545
And light betwene a Mastifes chaps, and through his guts did gore,
And naild him to the earth. The hand of Prince Meleager
Plaid hittymissie. Of two Darts his first did flie too far,
And lighted in the ground: the next amid his backe stickt fast.
And while the Bore did play the fiend and turned round agast,   550
And grunting flang his fome about togither mixt with blood,
The giver of the wound (the more to stirre his enmies mood,)
Stept in, and underneath the shield did thrust his Boarspeare through.
Then all the Hunters shouting out demeaned joy inough.
And glad was he that first might come to take him by the hand.   555
About the ugly beast they all with gladnesse gazing stand
And wondring what a field of ground his carcasse did possesse,
There durst not any be so bolde to touch him. Nerethelesse,
They every of them with his bloud their hunting staves made red.
Then stepped forth Meleager, and treading on his hed   560
Said thus: O Ladie Atalant, receive thou here my fee,
And of my glorie vouch thou safe partaker for to bee.
Immediatly the ugly head with both the tusshes brave
And eke the skin with bristles stur right griesly, he hir gave.
The Ladie for the givers sake, was in hir heart as glad   565
As for the gift. The rest repinde that she such honor had.
Through all the rout was murmuring. Of whom with roring reare
And armes displayd that all the field might easly see and heare,

533 *foyled:* defiled; *plot:* place   554 *demeaned:* expressed
544 *latch:* catch; *dint:* force   564 *stur:* stiff
548 *hittymissie:* hit or miss   567 *reare:* noise, shout

The Thesties cried: Dame, come off and lay us downe this geare.
And thou a woman offer not us men so great a shame,   570
As we to toyle and thou to take the honor of our game.
Ne let that faire smooth face of thine beguile thee, lest that hee
That being doted in thy love did give thee this our fee,
Be over farre to rescow thee. And with that word they tooke
The gift from hir, and right of gift from him. He could not brooke   575
This wrong: but gnashing with his teeth for anger that did boyle
Within, said fiersly: learne ye you that other folkes dispoyle
Of honor given, what diffrence is betweene your threats, and deedes.
And therewithall Plexippus brest (who no such matter dreedes)
With wicked weapon he did pierce. As Toxey doubting stood   580
What way to take, desiring both t'advenge his brothers blood,
And fearing to be murthered as his brother was before,
Meleager (to dispatch all doubts of musing any more)
Did heate his sword for companie in bloud of him againe,
Before Plexippus bloud was cold that did thereon remaine.   585
        Althaea going toward Church with presents for to yild
        Due thankes and worship to the Gods that for hir sonne had kild
The Boare, beheld hir brothers brought home dead: and by and by
She beate hir brest, and filde the towne with shrieking piteously,
And shifting all hir rich aray, did put on mourning weede   590
But when she understoode what man was doer of the deede,
She left all mourning, and from teares to vengeance did proceede.
There was a certaine firebrand which when Oenies wife did lie
In childebed of Meleager, she chaunced to espie
The Destnies putting in the fire: and in the putting in,   595
She heard them speake these words, as they his fatall threede did spin:
O lately borne, like time we give to thee and to this brand.
And when they so had spoken, they departed out of hand.
Immediatly the mother caught the blazing bough away,
And quenched it. This bough she kept full charely many a day: 600
And in the keeping of the same she kept hir sonne alive.
But now intending of his life him clearly to deprive,
She brought it forth, and causing all the coales and shivers to
Be layed by, she like a foe did kindle fire thereto.
Fowre times she was about to cast the firebrand in the flame: 605

---

575 *brooke:* endure   600 *charely:* carefully
590 *weede:* garb   603 *shivers:* splinters

Fowre times she pulled backe hir hand from doing of the same.
As mother and as sister both she strove what way to go:
The divers names drew diversly hir stomacke to and fro.
Hir face waxt often pale for feare of mischiefe to ensue:
And often red about the eies through heate of ire she grew.   610
One while hir looke resembled one that threatned cruelnesse:
Another while ye would have thought she minded pitiousnesse.
And though the cruell burning of hir heart did drie hir teares,
Yet burst out some. And as a Boate which tide contrarie beares
Against the winde, feeles double force, and is compeld to yeelde   615
To both, so Thesties daughter now unable for to weelde
Hir doubtful passions, diversly is caried off and on,
And chaungeably she waxes calme, and stormes againe anon.
But better sister ginneth she than mother for to be.
And to th'intent hir brothers ghostes with bloud to honor, she   620
In meaning to be one way kinde, doth worke another way
Against kinde. When the plagie fire waxt strong she thus did say:
Let this same fire my bowels burne. And as in cursed hands
The fatall wood she holding at the Hellish Altar stands:
She said: Ye triple Goddesses of wreake, ye Helhounds three   625
Beholde ye all this furious fact and sacrifice of mee.
I wreake, and do against all right: with death must death be payde:
In mischiefe mischiefe must be heapt: on corse must corse be laide.
Confounded let this wicked house with heaped sorrowes bee.
Shall Oenie joy his happy sonne in honor for to see   630
And Thestie mourne bereft of his? Nay: better yet it were,
That eche with other companie in mourning you should beare.
Ye brothers Ghostes and soules new dead I wish no more, but you
To feele the solemne obsequies which I prepare as now:
And that mine offring you accept, which dearly I have bought   635
The yssue of my wretched wombe. Alas, alas what thought
I for to doe? O brothers, I besech you beare with me.
I am his mother: so to doe my hands unable be.
His trespasse I confesse deserves the stopping of his breath:
But yet I doe not like that I be Author of his death.   640
And shall he then with life and limme, and honor too, scape free?
And vaunting in his good successe the King of Calidon bee?
And you deare soules lie raked up but in a little dust?

---

608 *stomacke:* spirit, desire   625 *wreake:* revenge
622 *kinde:* nature   626 *fact:* action, deed

I will not surely suffer it. But let the villaine trust
That he shall die, and draw with him to ruine and decay   645
His Kingdome, Countrie and his Sire that doth upon him stay.
Why where is now the mothers heart and pitie that should raigne
In Parents? and the ten Monthes paines that once I did sustaine?
O would to God thou burned had a babie in this brand,
And that I had not tane it out and quencht it with my hand.   650
That all this while thou lived hast, my goodnesse is the cause.
And now most justly unto death thine owne desert thee drawes.
Receive the guerdon of thy deede: and render thou agen
Thy twice given life, by bearing first, and secondarly when
I caught this firebrand from the flame: or else come deale with me   655
As with my brothers, and with them let me entumbed be.
I would, and cannot. What then shall I stand to in this case?
One while my brothers corses seeme to prease before my face
With lively Image of their deaths. Another while my minde
Doth yeelde to pitie, and the name of mother doth me blinde.   660
Now wo is me. To let you have the upper hand is sinne:
But nerethelesse the upper hand O brothers doe you win.
Condicionly that when that I to comfort you withall
Have wrought this feate, my selfe to you resort in person shall.
        This sed, she turnde away hir face, and with a trembling hand   665
        Did cast the deathfull brand amid the burning fire. The brand
Did eyther sigh, or seeme to sigh in burning in the flame,
Which sorie and unwilling was to fasten on the same.
Meleager being absent and not knowing ought at all
Was burned with this flame: and felt his bowels to appall   670
With secret fire. He bare out long the paine with courage stout.
But yet it grieved him to die so cowardly without
The shedding of his bloud. He thought Anceus for to be
A happie man that dide of wound. With sighing called he
Upon his aged father, and his sisters, and his brother,   675
And lastly on his wife too, and by chaunce upon his mother.
His paine encreased with the fire, and fell therewith againe:
And at the selfe same instant quight extinguisht were both twaine.
And as the ashes soft and hore by leysure overgrew
The glowing coales: so leysurly his spirit from him drew.   680

658 *while:* time   679 *hore:* grayish-white
670 *appall:* fail, weaken

Then drouped stately Calydon. Both yong and olde did mourne,
The Lords and Commons did lament, and maried wives with torne
And tattred haire did crie alas. His father did beray
His horie head and face with dust, and on the earth flat lay,
Lamenting that he lived had to see that wofull day   685
For now his mothers giltie hand had for that cursed crime
Done execution on hir selfe by sword before hir time.
If God to me a hundred mouthes with sounding tongues should send,
And reason able to conceyve, and thereunto should lend
Me all the grace of eloquence that ere the Muses had,   690
I could not shew the wo wherewith his sisters were bestad.
Unmindfull of their high estate, their naked brests they smit,
Untill they made them blacke and blew. And while his bodie yit
Remained, they did cherish it, and cherish it againe.
They kist his bodie: yea they kist the chist that did containe   695
His corse. And after that the corse was burnt to ashes, they
Did presse his ashes with their brests: and downe along they lay
Upon his tumb, and there embraste his name upon the stone,
And filde the letters of the same with teares that from them gone.
At length Diana satisfide with slaughter brought upon   700
The house of Oenie, lifts them up with fethers everichone,
(Save Gorgee and the daughtrinlaw of noble Alcmene) and
Makes wings to stretch along their sides, and horned nebs to stand
Upon their mouthes. And finally she altring quight their faire
And native shape, in shape of Birds dooth sent them through the Aire.   705
    The noble Theseus in this while with others having donne
    His part in killing of the Boare, to Athens ward begonne
To take his way. But Acheloy then being swolne with raine
Did stay him of his journey, and from passage him restraine.
Of Athens valiant knight (quoth he) come underneath my roofe,   710
And for to passe my raging streame as yet attempt no proofe.
This brooke is wont whole trees to beare and evelong stones to carry
With hideous roring down his streame. I oft have seene him harry
Whole Shepcotes standing nere his banks, with flocks of sheepe therin.
Nought booted buls their strength: nought steedes by swiftnes there
                                                        could win.   715
Yea many lustie men this brooke hath swallowed, when the snow

683 *beray:* stain, soil   712 *evelong:* straight along
691 *bestad:* beset   715 *booted:* availed, helped
703 *nebs:* beaks

From mountaines molten, caused him his banks to overflow.
The best is for you for to rest untill the River fall
Within his boundes: and runne ageine within his chanell small.
Content (quoth Theseus): Acheloy, I will not sure refuse   720
Thy counsell nor thy house. And so he both of them did use.
Of Pommy hollowed diversly and ragged Pebble stone
The walles were made. The floore with Mosse was soft to tread upon.
The roofe thereof was checkerwise with shelles of Purple wrought
And Perle. The Sunne then full two parts of day to end had brought, 725
And Theseus downe to table sate with such as late before
Had friendly borne him companie at killing of the Bore.
At one side sate Ixions sonne, and on the other sate
The Prince of Troyzen, Lelex, with a thin hearde horie pate.
And then such other as the brooke of Acarnania did   730
Vouchsafe the honor to his boord and table for to bid,
Who was right glad of such a guest. Immediatly there came
Barefooted Nymphes who brought in meate. And when that of the same
The Lords had taken their repast, the meate away they tooke,
And set downe wine in precious stones. Then Theseus who did looke 735
Upon the Sea that underneath did lie within their sight,
Said: tell us what is yon same place, (and with his fingar right
Hee poynted thereunto) I pray, and what that Iland hight,
Although it seemeth mo than one. The River answerd thus,
It is not one mayne land alone that kenned is of us.   740
There are uppon a fyve of them. The distaunce of the place,
Dooth hinder to discerne betweene eche Ile the perfect space.
And that the lesse yee woonder may at Phoebees act alate,
To such as had neglected her uppon contempt or hate,
Theis Iles were sumtyme Waternimphes: who having killed Neate,   745
Twyce fyve, and called to theyr feast the Country Gods to eate,
Forgetting mee kept frolicke cheere. At that gan I to swell,
And ran more large than ever erst, and being over fell
In stomacke and in streame, I rent the wood from wood, and feeld
From feeld, and with the ground the Nymphes as then with stomacks
                                                          meeld 750
Remembring mee, I tumbled to the Sea. The waves of mee
And of the sea the ground that erst all whole was woont to bee
Did rend asunder into all the Iles you yonder see,

717 *molten:* melted   745 *Neate:* cattle
722 *Pommy:* pumice   749 *stomacke:* temper, pride
729 *hearde:* haired

And made a way for waters now to passe betweene them free.
They now of Urchins have theyr name. But of theis Ilands, one   755
A great way off (behold yee) stands a great way off alone,
As you may see. The Mariners doo call it Perimell.
With her (shee was as then a Nymph) so farre in love I fell,
That of her maydenhod I her spoyld: which thing displeasd so sore
Her father Sir Hippodamas, that from the craggy shore   760
He threw her headlong downe to drowne her in the sea. But I
Did latch her streight, and bearing her aflote did lowd thus crie:
O Neptune with thy threetynde Mace who hast by lot the charge
Of all the waters wylde that bound uppon the earth at large,
To whom wee holy streames doo runne, in whome wee take our end,   765
Draw neere, and gently to my boone effectually attend.
This Ladie whome I beare aflote myselfe hath hurt. Bee meeke
And upright. If Hippodamas perchaunce were fatherleeke,
Or if that he extremitie through outrage did not seeke,
He oughted to have pitied her and for to beare with mee.   770
Now help us Neptune, I thee pray, and condescend that shee
Whom from the land her fathers wrath and cruelnesse dooth chace
Who through her fathers cruelnesse is drownd: may find the grace
To have a place: or rather let hirselfe become a place.
And I will still embrace the same. The King of Seas did move   775
His head, and as a token that he did my sute approve,
He made his surges all to shake. The Nymph was sore afrayd.
Howbee't shee swam, and as she swam, my hand I softly layd
Upon her brest which quivered still. And whyle I toucht the same,
I sensibly did feele how all her body hard became: 780
And how the earth did overgrow her bulk. And as I spake,
New earth enclosde hir swimming limbes, which by and by did take
Another shape, and grew into a mighty Ile. With that
The River ceast and all men there did woonder much thereat.
    Pirithous being over hault of mynde and such a one   785
    As did despyse bothe God and man, did laugh them everychone
To scorne for giving credit, and sayd thus: The woords thou spaakst
Are feyned fancies, Acheloy: and overstrong thou maakst
The Gods: to say that they can give and take way shapes. This scoffe
Did make the heerers all amazde, for none did like thereof.   790
And Lelex of them all the man most rype in yeeres and wit,
Sayd thus: Unmeasurable is the powre of heaven, and it
Can have none end. And looke what God dooth mynd to bring about,

---

⁷⁶⁸ *fatherleeke:* fatherly   ⁷⁸⁵ *hault:* haughty

Must take effect. And in this case to put yee out of dout,
  Upon the hilles of Phrygie neere a Teyle there stands a tree   795
  Of Oke enclosed with a wall. Myself the place did see.
For Pithey untoo Pelops feelds did send mee where his father
Did sumtyme reigne. Not farre fro thence there is a poole which rather
Had bene dry ground inhabited. But now it is a meare
And Moorecocks, Cootes, and Cormorants doo breede and nestle
                                                    there.   800
The mightie Jove and Mercurie his sonne in shape of men
Resorted thither on a tyme. A thousand houses when
For roome to lodge in they had sought, a thousand houses bard
Theyr doores against them. Nerethelesse one Cotage afterward
Receyved them, and that was but a pelting one in deede.   805
The roofe therof was thatched all with straw and fennish reede.
Howbee't two honest auncient folke, (of whom she Baucis hight
And he Philemon) in that Cote theyr fayth in youth had plight:
And in that Cote had spent theyr age. And for they paciently
Did beare theyr simple povertie, they made it light thereby,   810
And shewed it no thing to bee repyned at at all.
It skilles not whether there for Hyndes or Maister you doo call,
For all the houshold were but two: and both of them obeyde,
And both commaunded. When the Gods at this same Cotage staid,
And ducking downe their heads, within the low made Wicket came,   815
Philemon bringing ech a stoole, bade rest upon the same
Their limmes: and busie Baucis brought them cuishons homely geere.
Which done, the embers on the harth she gan abrode to steere,
And laid the coales togither that were raakt up over night,
And with the brands and dried leaves did make them gather might,   820
And with the blowing of hir mouth did make them kindle bright.
Then from an inner house she fetcht seare sticks and clifted brands,
And put them broken underneath a Skillet with hir hands.
Hir Husband from their Gardenplot fetcht Coleworts. Of the which
She shreaded small the leaves, and with a Forke tooke downe a flitch   825
Of restie Bacon from the Balke made blacke with smoke, and cut
A peece thereof, and in the pan to boyling did it put.
And while this meate a seething was, the time in talke they spent,

795 *Teyle:* linden
798 *rather:* earlier
805 *pelting:* paltry, little
812 *skilles:* matters
815 *Wicket:* small door
817 *geere:* equipment, furnishings

818 *steere:* stir
822 *clifted:* cleft
824 *Coleworts:* cabbage or cabbage-like
        plants, kale
826 *restie:* rancid; *Balke:* beam

By meanes whereof away without much tedousnesse it went.
There hung a Boawle of Beeche upon a spirget by a ring. 830
The same with warmed water filld the two old folke did bring
To bathe their guests foule feete therein. Amid the house there stood
A Couch whose bottom sides and feete were all of Sallow wood,
And on the same a Mat of Sedge. They cast upon this bed
A covering which was never wont upon it to be spred 835
Except it were at solemne feastes: and yet the same was olde
And of the coursest, with a bed of sallow meete to holde.
The Gods sate downe. The aged wife right chare and busie as
A Bee, set out a table, of the which the thirde foote was
A little shorter than the rest. A tylesherd made it even 840
And tooke away the shoringnesse: and when they had it driven
To stand up levell, with greene Mintes they by and by it wipte.
Then set they on it Pallas fruite with double colour stripte.
And Cornels kept in pickle moyst, and Endive, and a roote
Of Radish, and a jolly lump of Butter fresh and soote, 845
And Egges reare rosted. All these Cates in earthen dishes came.
Then set they downe a graven cup made also of the same
Selfe kinde of Plate, and Mazers made of Beech whose inner syde
Was rubd with yellow wax. And when they pawsed had a tyde,
Hot meate came pyping from the fyre. And shortly thereupon 850
A cup of greene hedg wyne was brought. This tane away, anon
Came in the latter course, which was of Nuts, Dates, dryed figges,
Sweete smelling Apples in a Mawnd made flat of Osier twigges,
And Prunes and Plums and Purple grapes cut newly from the tree,
And in the middes a honnycomb new taken from the Bee. 855
Besydes all this there did ensew good countnance overmore,
With will not poore nor nigardly. Now all the whyle before,
As ofen as Philemon and Dame Baucis did perceyve
The emptie Cup to fill alone, and wyne to still receyve,
Amazed at the straungenesse of the thing, they gan streyght way 860
With fearfull harts and hands hilld up to frame themselves to pray.
Desyring for theyr slender cheere and fare to pardoned bee.
They had but one poore Goose which kept theyr little Tennantree,
And this to offer to the Gods theyr guestes they did intend.

830 *spirget:* peg   848 *Mazers:* bowls
838 *chare:* careful   851 *hedg wyne:* cheap wine
840 *tylesherd:* a shard, piece of tile   853 *Mawnd:* woven basket
841 *shoringnesse:* unevenness, slantingness   856 *overmore:* moreover
845 *soote:* sweet   861 *frame:* set, prepare
846 *reare:* slightly, underdone

The Gander wyght of wing did make the slow old folke to spend   865
Theyr paynes in vayne, and mokt them long. At length he seemd to flye
For succor to the Gods themselves, who bade he should not dye.
For wee bee Gods (quoth they) and all this wicked towneship shall
Abye their gylt. On you alone this mischeef shall not fall.
No more but give you up your house, and follow up this hill   870
Togither, and upon the top therof abyde our will.
They bothe obeyd. And as the Gods did lead the way before,
They lagged slowly after with theyr staves, and labored sore
Ageinst the rysing of the hill. They were not mickle more
Than full a flyghtshot from the top, when looking backe they saw   875
How all the towne was drowned save their lyttle shed of straw.
And as they wondred at the thing and did bewayle the case
Of those that had theyr neyghbours beene, the old poore Cote so base
Whereof they had beene owners erst, became a Church. The proppes
Were turned into pillars huge. The straw uppon the toppes   880
Was yellow, so that all the roof did seeme of burnisht gold:
The floore with Marble paved was. The doores on eyther fold
Were graven. At the sight hereof Philemon and his make
Began to pray in feare. Then Jove thus gently them bespake:
Declare thou ryghtuowse man, and thou O woman meete to have   885
A ryghtuowse howsband, what yee would most cheefly wish or crave.
Philemon taking conference a little with his wyfe,
Declared bothe theyr meenings thus: We covet during lyfe,
Your Chapleynes for to bee to keepe your Temple. And bycause
Our yeeres in concord wee have spent, I pray when death neere
                                    drawes,   890
Let bothe of us togither leave our lives: that neyther I
Behold my wyves deceace, nor shee see myne when I doo dye.
Theyr wish had sequele to theyr will. As long as lyfe did last,
They kept the Church. And beeing spent with age of yeares forepast,
By chaunce as standing on a tyme without the Temple doore   895
They told the fortune of the place, Philemon old and poore
Saw Baucis floorish greene with leaves, and Baucis saw likewyse
Philemon braunching out in boughes and twigs before hir eyes.
And as the Bark did overgrow the heades of both, eche spake
To other whyle they myght. At last they eche of them did take   900
Theyr leave of other bothe at once, and therewithall the bark

865 *wyght:* fast   875 *flyghtshot:* bow-shot
874 *mickle:* much

Did hyde theyr faces both at once. The Phrygians in that park
Doo at this present day still shew the trees that shaped were
Of theyr two bodies, growing yit togither joyntly there.
Theis things did auncient men report of credit verie good.   905
For why there was no cause why they should lye. As I there stood
I saw the garlands hanging on the boughes, and adding new
I sayd: Let them whom God dooth love be Gods, and honor dew
Bee given to such as honor him with feare and reverence trew.
    He hilld his peace, and bothe the thing and he that did it tell   910
    Did move them all, but Theseus most. Whom being mynded well
To heere of woondrous things, the brooke of Calydon thus bespake:
There are, O valiant knyght, sum folke that had the powre to take
Straunge shape for once, and all their lyves continewed in the same.
And other sum to sundrie shapes have power themselves to frame,   915
As thou, O Protew, dwelling in the sea that cleepes the land.
For now a yoonker, now a boare, anon a Lyon, and
Streyght way thou didst become a Snake, and by and by a Bull
That people were afrayd of thee to see thy horned skull.
And oftentymes thou seemde a stone, and now and then a tree,   920
And counterfetting water sheere thou seemedst oft to bee
A River: and another whyle contrarie thereunto
Thou wart a fyre. No lesser power than also thus to doo
Had Erisicthons daughter whom Awtolychus tooke to wyfe.
Her father was a person that despysed all his lyfe   925
The powre of Gods, and never did vouchsauf them sacrifyse.
He also is reported to have heawen in wicked wyse
The grove of Ceres, and to fell her holy woods which ay
Had undiminisht and unhackt continewed to that day.
There stood in it a warrie Oke which was a wood alone.   930
Uppon it round hung fillets, crownes, and tables, many one,
The vowes of such as had obteynd theyr hearts desyre. Full oft
The Woodnymphes underneath this tree did fetch theyr frisks aloft
And oftentymes with hand in hand they daunced in a round
About the Trunk, whose bignesse was of timber good and sound   935
Full fifteene fadom. All the trees within the wood besyde,
Were unto this, as weedes to them: so farre it did them hyde.
Yit could not this move Triops sonne his axe therefro to hold,
But bade his servants cut it downe. And when he did behold

---

912 *bespake:* addressed   921 *sheere:* pure
916 *cleepes:* embraces   930 *warrie:* knotty
917 *yoonker:* young man   931 *tables:* tablets, plaques

218 OVID'S METAMORPHOSES

Them stunting at his hest, he snatcht an axe with furious mood 940
From one of them, and wickedly sayd thus: Although thys wood
Not only were the derling of the Goddesse, but also
The Goddesse even herself: yet would I make it ere I go
To kisse the clowers with her top that pranks with braunches so.
This spoken, as he sweakt his axe asyde to fetch his blow, 945
The manast Oke did quake and sygh, the Acornes that did grow
Thereon togither with the leaves to wex full pale began,
And shrinking in for feare the boughes and braunches looked wan.
As soone as that his cursed hand had wounded once the tree,
The blood came spinning from the carf, as freshly as yee see 950
It issue from a Bullocks necke whose throte is newly cut
Before the Altar, when his flesh to sacrifyse is put.
They were amazed everychone. And one among them all
To let the wicked act, durst from the tree his hatchet call.
The lewd Thessalian facing him sayd: Take thou heere to thee 955
The guerdon of thy godlynesse, and turning from the tree,
He chopped off the fellowes head. Which done, he went agen
And heawed on the Oke. Streight from amid the tree as then
There issued such a sound as this: Within this tree dwell I
A Nymph to Ceres very deere, who now before I dye 960
In comfort of my death doo give thee warning thou shalt bye
Thy dooing deere within a whyle. He goeth wilfully
Still thorrough with his wickednesse, untill at length the Oke
Pulld partly by the force of ropes, and cut with axis stroke,
Did fall, and with his weyght bare downe of under wood great store. 965
The Wood nymphes with the losses of the woods and theyrs ryght sore
Amazed, gathered on a knot, and all in mourning weede
Went sad to Ceres, praying her to wreake that wicked deede
Of Erisicthons. Ceres was content it should bee so.
And with the moving of her head in nodding to and fro, 970
Shee shooke the feeldes which laden were with frutefull Harvest tho,
And therewithall a punishment most piteous shee proceedes
To put in practyse: were it not that his most heynous deedes
No pitie did deserve to have at any bodies hand.
With helpelesse hungar him to pyne, in purpose shee did stand. 975

940 *stunting:* stinting, holding back; *hest:* command
944 *clowers:* sward, grassy ground; *pranks:* shows self off
945 *sweakt:* swung
946 *manast:* menaced
950 *carf:* cut
954 *let:* prevent
955 *lewd:* wicked
961 *bye:* aby, pay for
968 *wreake:* revenge
975 *pyne:* starve

And forasmuch as shee herself and Famin myght not meete
(For fate forbiddeth Famin to abyde within the leete
Where plentie is) shee thus bespake a fayrie of the hill:
There lyeth in the utmost bounds of Tartarie the chill
A Dreerie place, a wretched soyle, a barreine plot: no grayne,   980
No frute, no tree, is growing there: but there dooth ay remayne
Unweeldsome cold, with trembling feare, and palenesse white as clowt,
And foodlesse Famin. Will thou her immediatly withowt
Delay to shed herself into the stomacke of the wretch,
And let no plentie staunch her force but let her working stretch   985
Above the powre of mee. And lest the longnesse of the way
May make thee wearie, take thou heere my charyot: take I say
My draggons for to beare thee through the aire. In saying so
She gave hir them. The Nymph mounts up, and flying thence as tho
Alyghts in Scythy land, and up the cragged top of hye   990
Mount Caucasus did cause hir Snakes with much adoo to stye.
Where seeking long for Famin, shee the gaptoothd elfe did spye
Amid a barreine stony feeld a ramping up the grasse
With ougly nayles and chanking it. Her face pale colourd was.
Hir heare was harsh and shirle, her eyes were sunken in her head.   995
Her lyppes were hore with filth, her teeth were furd and rusty red.
Her skinne was starched, and so sheere a man myght well espye
The verie bowels in her bulk how every one did lye.
And eke above her courbed loynes her withered hippes were seene.
In stead of belly was a space where belly should have beene.   1000
Her brest did hang so sagging downe as that a man would weene
That scarcely to her ridgebone had hir ribbes beene fastened well.
Her leannesse made her joynts bolne big, and kneepannes for to swell.
And with exceeding mighty knubs her heeles behynd boynd out.
Now when the Nymph behild this elfe afarre, (she was in dout   1005
To come too neere her:) shee declarde her Ladies message. And
In that same little whyle although the Nymph aloof did stand,
And though shee were but newly come, yit seemed shee to feele
The force of Famin. Wheruppon shee turning backe her wheele
Did reyne her dragons up aloft: who streyght with courage free   1010
Conveyd her into Thessaly. Although that Famin bee
Ay contrarye to Ceres woork, yit did shee then agree

977 *leete:* district
982 *Unweeldsome:* inert; *clowt:* cloth
994 *chanking:* champing, chewing
995 *shirle:* rough

997 *starched:* stark, hard; *sheere:* thin
1003 *bolne:* swollen
1004 *knubs:* knobs; *bonyd:* were swollen

To do her will and glyding through the Ayre supported by
The wynd, she found th'appoynted house: and entring by and by
The caytifs chamber where he slept (it was in tyme of nyght)   1015
Shee hugged him betweene her armes there snorting bolt upryght,
And breathing her into him, blew uppon his face and brest,
That hungar in his emptie veynes myght woorke as hee did rest.
And when she had accomplished her charge, shee then forsooke
The frutefull Clymates of the world, and home ageine betooke   1020
Herself untoo her frutelesse feeldes and former dwelling place.
The gentle sleepe did all this whyle with fethers soft embrace
The wretched Erisicthons corse. Who dreaming streight of meate
Did stirre his hungry jawes in vayne as though he had to eate
And chanking tooth on tooth apace he gryndes them in his head,   1025
And occupies his emptie throte with swallowing, and in stead
Of food devoures the lither ayre. But when that sleepe with nyght
Was shaken off, immediatly a furious appetite
Of feeding gan to rage in him, which in his greedy gummes
And in his meatlesse maw dooth reigne unstauncht. Anon there
                                        cummes   1030
Before him whatsoever lives on sea, in aire or land:
And yit he crieth still for more. And though the platters stand
Before his face full furnished, yit dooth he still complayne
Of hungar, craving meate at meale. The food that would susteine
Whole householdes, Towneships, Shyres and Realmes suffyce not him
                                        alone.   1035
The more his pampred paunch consumes, the more it maketh mone
And as the sea receyves the brookes of all the worldly Realmes,
And yit is never satisfyde for all the forreine streames,
And as the fell and ravening fyre refuseth never wood,
But burneth faggots numberlesse, and with a furious mood   1040
The more it hath, the more it still desyreth evermore,
Encreacing in devouring through encreasement of the store:
So wicked Erisicthons mouth in swallowing of his meate
Was ever hungry more and more, and longed ay to eate.
Meate tolld in meate: and as he ate the place was empty still.   1045
The hungar of his brinklesse Maw, the gulf that nowght might fill,
Had brought his fathers goods to nowght. But yit continewed ay
His cursed hungar unappeasd: and nothing could alay

1015 *caytifs:* villains   1027 *lither:* light, supple
1016 *snorting bolt upryght:* snoring on his   1045 *tolld:* summoned, drew in
        back

The flaming of his starved throte. At length when all was spent,
And into his unfilled Maw bothe goods and lands were sent,   1050
An only daughter did remayne unworthy to have had
So lewd a father. Hir he sold, so hard he was bestad.
But shee of gentle courage could no bondage well abyde.
And therfore stretching out her hands to seaward there besyde,
Now save mee, quoth shee, from the yoke of bondage I thee pray,   1055
O thou that my virginitie enjoyest as a pray.
Neptunus had it. Who to this her prayer did consent.
And though her maister looking backe (for after him shee went)
Had newly seene her: yit he turnd hir shape and made hir man,
And gave her looke of fisherman. Her mayster looking than   1060
Upon her, sayd: Good fellow, thou that on the shore doost stand
With angling rod and bayted hooke and hanging lyne in hand,
I pray thee as thou doost desyre the Sea ay calme to thee,
And fishes for to byght thy bayt, and striken still to bee,
Tell where the frizzletopped wench in course and sluttish geere   1065
That stoode right now uppon this shore (for well I wote that heere
I saw her standing) is become. For further than this place
No footestep is appeering. Shee perceyving by the cace
That Neptunes gift made well with her, and beeing glad to see
Herself enquyrd for of herself, sayd thus: Who ere you bee   1070
I pray you for to pardon mee. I turned not myne eye
A t'one syde ne a toother from this place, but did apply
My labor hard. And that you may the lesser stand in dowt,
So Neptune further still the Art and craft I go abowt,
As now a whyle no living Wyght uppon this levell sand   1075
(Myself excepted) neyther man nor woman heere did stand.
Her maister did beleeve her words: and turning backward went
His way beguyld: and streight to her her native shape was sent.
But when her father did perceyve his daughter for to have
A bodye so transformable, he oftentymes her gave   1080
For monny. But the damzell still escaped, now a Mare
And now a Cow, and now a Bird, a Hart, a Hynd, or Hare,
And ever fed her hungry Syre with undeserved fare.
But after that the maladie had wasted all the meates
As well of store as that which shee had purchast by her feates: 1085
Most cursed keytife as he was, with bighting hee did rend
His flesh, and by diminishing his bodye did intend

1065 *geere:* clothes   1086 *keytife:* caitiff, wretch

To feede his bodye, till that death did speede his fatall end.
But what meene I to busye mee in forreine matters thus?
To alter shapes within precinct is lawfull even to us,   1090
My Lords. For sumtime I am such as you do now mee see,
Sumtyme I wynd mee in a Snake: and oft I seeme to bee
A Capteine of the herd with hornes. For taking hornes on mee
I lost a tyne which heeretofore did arme mee as the print
Dooth playnly shew. With that same word he syghed and did stint.   1095

FINIS OCTAVI LIBRI.

1094 *tyne:* point, prong

THE NINTH BOOKE

OF OVIDS METAMORPHOSIS.

[*Achelous and Hercules. Hercules, Dejanira, and Nessus. Alcmena.*
Dryope. Byblis and Caunus. Iphis and Ianthe.]

What ayleth thee (quoth Theseus) to sygh so sore? and how
Befell it thee to get this mayme that is uppon thy brow?
The noble streame of Calydon made answer, who did weare
A Garland made of reedes and flags upon his sedgie heare:
A greeveus pennance you enjoyne. For who would gladly show   5
The combats in the which himself did take the overthrow?
Yit will I make a just report in order of the same.
For why? to have the woorser hand was not so great a shame,
As was the honor such a match to undertake. And much
It comforts mee that he who did mee overcome, was such   10
A valiant champion. If perchaunce you erst have heard the name
Of Deyanyre, the fayrest Mayd that ever God did frame
Shee was in myne opinion. And the hope to win her love
Did mickle envy and debate among hir wooers move.
With whome I entring to the house of him that should have bee   15
My fathrilaw: Parthaons sonne (I sayd) accept thou mee
Thy Sonnylaw. And Hercules in selfsame sort did woo.
And all the other suters streight gave place unto us two.
He vaunted of his father Jove, and of his famous deedes,
And how ageinst his stepdames spyght his prowesse still proceedes.   20
And I ageine a toother syde sayd thus: It is a shame
That God should yeeld to man. (This stryfe was long ere he became
A God). Thou seeist mee a Lord of waters in thy Realme

---

² *mayme:* injury   ¹⁴ *mickle:* much

223

Where I in wyde and wynding banks doo beare my flowing streame.
No straunger shalt thou have of mee sent farre from forreine land: 25
But one of household, or at least a neyghbour heere at hand.
Alonly let it bee to mee no hindrance that the wyfe
Of Jove abhorres mee not, ne that upon the paine of lyfe
Shee sets mee not to talk. For where thou bostest thee to bee
Alcmenas sonne, Jove eyther is not father unto thee: 30
Or if he bee it is by sin. In making Jove thy father,
Thou maakst thy mother but a whore. Now choose thee whither rather
Thou had to graunt this tale of Jove surmised for to bee,
Or else thy selfe begot in shame and borne in bastardee.
    At that he grimly bendes his browes, and much adoo he hath   35
    To hold his hands, so sore his hart inflamed is with wrath.
He said no more but thus: My hand dooth serve mee better than
My toong. Content I am (so I in feighting vanquish can)
That thou shalt overcome in wordes. And therewithall he gan
Mee feercely to assaile. Mee thought it was a shame for mee   40
That had even now so stoutly talkt, in dooings faint to bee.
I casting off my greenish cloke thrust stifly out at length
Mine armes and streynd my pawing armes to hold him out by strength,
And framed every limme to cope. With both his hollow hands
He caught up dust and sprincked mee: and I likewise with sands   45
Made him all yelow too. One whyle hee at my necke dooth snatch
Another whyle my cleere crisp legges he striveth for to catch,
Or trippes at mee: and everywhere the vauntage he dooth watch.
My weightinesse defended mee, and cleerly did disfeate
His stoute assaults as when a wave with hideous noyse dooth beate   50
Against a Rocke, the Rocke dooth still both sauf and sound abyde
By reason of his massinesse. Wee drew a whyle asyde.
And then incountring fresh ageine, wee kept our places stowt
Full minded not to yeeld an inch, but for to hold it owt.
Now were wee stonding foote to foote. And I with all my brest   55
Was leaning forward, and with head ageinst his head did rest,
And with my gryping fingars I ageinst his fingars thrust.
So have I seene two myghtie Bulles togither feercely just
In seeking as their pryse to have the fayrest Cow in all
The feeld to bee their make, and all the herd bothe greate and small   60
Stand gazing on them fearfully not knowing unto which

33 *surmised:* supposed, imagined   49 *disfeate:* defeat
45 *sprincked:* sprinkled   58 *just:* fight
47 *crisp:* smooth, shining   60 *make:* mate
48 *vauntage:* advantage, opportunity

The conquest of so greate a gayne shall fall. Three tymes a twich
Gave Hercules and could not wrinch my leaning brest him fro
But at the fourth he shooke mee off and made mee to let go
My hold: and with a push (I will tell truthe) he had a knacke   65
To turne me off, and heavily he hung upon my backe.
And if I may beleeved bee (as sure I meene not I
To vaunt my selfe vayngloriusly by telling of a lye,)
Mee thought a mountaine whelmed me. But yit with much adoo
I wrested in my sweating armes, and hardly did undoo   70
His griping hands. He following still his vauntage, suffred not
Mee once to breath or gather strength, but by and by he got
Mee by the necke. Then was I fayne to sinke with knee to ground,
And kisse the dust. Now when in strength too weake myself I found,
I tooke mee to my slights, and slipt in shape of Snake away   75
Of wondrous length. And when that I of purpose him to fray
Did bend myself in swelling rolles, and made a hideous noyse
Of hissing with my forked toong, he smyling at my toyes,
And laughing them to scorne sayd thus: It is my Cradle game
To vanquish Snakes, O Acheloy. Admit thou overcame   80
All other Snakes, yet what art thou compared to the Snake
Of Lerna, who by cutting off did still encreasement take?
For of a hundred heades not one so soone was paarde away,
But that uppon the stump therof there budded other tway.
This sprouting Snake whose braunching heads by slaughter did revive 85
And grow by cropping, I subdewd, and made it could not thryve.
And thinkest thou (who being none wouldst seeme a Snake) to scape?
Who doost with foorged weapons feyght and under borowed shape?
This sayd, his fingars of my necke he fastned in the nape.
Mee thought he graand my throte as though he did with pinsons nip.   90
I struggled from his churlish thumbes my pinched chappes to slip
But doo the best and worst I could he overcame mee so.
Then thirdly did remayne the shape of Bull, and quickly tho
I turning to the shape of Bull rebelld ageinst my fo.
He stepping to my left syde cloce, did fold his armes about   95
My wattled necke, and following mee then running maynely out
Did drag mee backe, and made mee pitch my hornes against the ground,
And in the deepest of the sand he overthrew mee round.

---

75 *slights:* tricks
78 *toyes:* trifles, vanities

90 *graand:* graned, choked, strangled; *pin-
sons:* pincers
96 *maynely:* rapidly

And yit not so content, such hold his cruell hand did take
Uppon my welked horne, that he asunder quight it brake,   100
And pulld it from my maymed brew. The waterfayries came
And filling it with frute and flowres did consecrate the same,
And so my horne the Tresory of plenteousnesse became.
    As soone as Acheloy had told this tale a wayting Mayd
    With flaring heare that lay on both hir shoulders and arrayd   105
Like one of Dame Dianas Nymphes with solemne grace forth came
And brought that rich and precious horne, and heaped in the same
All kynd of frutes that Harvest sendes, and specially such frute
As serves for latter course at meales of every sort and sute.
    As soone as daylight came ageine, and that the Sunny rayes   110
    Did shyne upon the tops of things, the Princes went their wayes.
They would not tarry till the floud were altogither falne
And that the River in his banks ran low ageine and calme.
Then Acheloy amid his waves his Crabtree face did hyde
And head disarmed of a horne. And though he did abyde   115
In all parts else bothe sauf and sound, yit this deformitye
Did cut his comb: and for to hyde this blemish from the eye
He hydes his hurt with Sallow leaves, or else with sedge and reede.
    But of the selfsame Mayd the love killd thee, feerce Nesse, in
                                           deede,
    When percing swiftly through thy back an arrow made thee
                                          bleede.   120
For as Joves issue with his wyfe was onward on his way
In going to his countryward, enforst he was to stay
At swift Euenus bank, bycause the streame was risen sore
Above his bounds through rage of rayne that fell but late before.
Agein so full of whoorlpooles and of gulles the channell was,   125
That scarce a man could any where fynd place of passage. As
Not caring for himself but for his wyfe he there did stand,
This Nessus came unto him (who was strong of body and
Knew well the foordes), and sayd: Use thou thy strength, O Hercules,
In swimming. I will fynd the meanes this Ladie shall with ease   130
Bee set uppon the further bank. So Hercules betooke
His wyfe to Nessus. Shee for feare of him and of the brooke
Lookte pale. Her husband as he had his quiver by his syde
Of arrowes full, and on his backe his heavy Lyons hyde,

---

100 *welked:* ridged, rough, twisted   118 *Sallow:* willow
101 *brew:* brow   125 *gulles:* gullies, channels
109 *sute:* kind

(For to the further bank he erst his club and bow had cast) 135
Said: Sith I have begonne, this brooke bothe must and shalbee past.
He never casteth further doubts, nor seekes the calmest place,
But through the roughest of the streame he cuts his way apace.
Now as he on the furthersyde was taking up his bow,
His heard his wedlocke shreeking out, and did hir calling know: 140
And cryde to Nesse (who went about to deale unfaythfully
In running with his charge away): Whoa, whither doost thou fly,
Thou Royster thou, uppon vaine hope by swiftnesse to escape
My hands? I say give eare thou Nesse for all thy double shape,
And meddle not with that thats myne. Though no regard of mee 145
Might move thee to refrayne from rape, thy father yit might bee
A warning, who for offring shame to Juno now dooth feele
Continuall torment in his limbes by turning on a wheele.
For all that thou hast horses feete which doo so bolde thee make,
Yit shalt thou not escape my hands. I will thee overtake 150
With wound and not with feete. He did according as he spake.
For with an arrow as he fled he strake him through the backe,
And out before his brist ageine the hooked iron stacke.
And when the same was pulled out, the blood amayne ensewd
At both the holes with poyson foule of Lerna Snake embrewd: 155
This blood did Nessus take, and said within himselfe: Well: sith
I needes must dye, yet will I not dye unrevendgd. And with
The same he staynd a shirt, and gave it unto Dyanyre,
Assuring hir it had the powre to kindle Cupids fyre.
    A greate whyle after when the deedes of worthy Hercules 160
    Were such as filled all the world, and also did appease
The hatred of his stepmother, as he uppon a day
With conquest from Oechalia came, and was abowt to pay
His vowes to Jove uppon the Mount of Cenye, tatling fame
(Who in reporting things of truth delyghts to sauce the same 165
With tales, and of a thing of nowght dooth ever greater grow
Through false and newly forged lyes that shee hirself dooth sow)
Told Dyanyre that Hercules did cast a liking to
A Ladie called Iolee. And Dyanyra (whoo
Was jealous over Hercules,) gave credit to the same. 170
And when that of a Leman first the tidings to hir came,
She being striken to the hart, did fall to teares alone,

---

140 *wedlocke:* wife   153 *stacke:* stuck
143 *Royster:* swaggerer, braggart   171 *Leman:* sweetheart

And in a lamentable wise did make most wofull mone.
  Anon she said: what meene theis teares thus gushing from myne
                                                              eyen?
  My husbands Leman will rejoyce at theis same teares of myne.   175
Nay, sith she is to come, the best it were to shonne delay,
And for to woork sum new devyce and practyse whyle I may,
Before that in my bed her limbes the filthy strumpet lay.
And shall I then complayne? or shall I hold my toong with skill?
Shall I returne to Calydon? or shall I tarry still?   180
Or shall I get me out of doores, and let them have their will?
What if that I (Meleager) remembring mee to bee
Thy suster, to attempt sum act notorious did agree?
And in a harlots death did shew (that all the world myght see)
What greef can cause the womankynd to enterpryse among?   185
And specially when thereunto they forced are by wrong.
  With wavering thoughts ryght violently her mynd was tossed long.
  At last shee did preferre before all others, for to send
The shirt bestayned with the blood of Nessus to the end
To quicken up the quayling love. And so not knowing what   190
She gave, she gave her owne remorse and greef to Lychas that
Did know as little as herself: and wretched woman, shee
Desyrd him gently to her Lord presented it to see.
The noble Prince receyving it without mistrust therein,
Did weare the poyson of the Snake of Lerna next his skin.   195
  To offer incense and to pray to Jove he did begin,
  And on the Marble Altar he full boawles of wyne did shed,
When as the poyson with the heate resolving, largely spred
Through all the limbes of Hercules. As long as ere he could,
The stoutnesse of his hart was such, that sygh no whit he would. 200
But when the mischeef grew so great all pacience to surmount,
He thrust the altar from him streight, and filled all the mount
Of Oeta with his roring out. He went about to teare
The deathfull garment from his backe, but where he pulled, there
He pulld away the skin: and (which is lothsum to report)   205
It eyther cleaved to his limbes and members in such sort
As that he could not pull it off, or else it tare away
The flesh, that bare his myghty bones and grisly sinewes lay.
The scalding venim boyling in his blood, did make it hisse,

---

¹⁷⁷ *practyse:* scheme, trick   ¹⁹⁰ *quayling:* failing, lessening

As when a gad of steel red hot in water quenched is.   210
There was no measure of his paine. The frying venim hent
His inwards, and a purple swet from all his body went.
His sindged sinewes shrinking crakt, and with a secret strength
The poyson even within his bones the Maree melts at length.
And holding up his hands to heaven, he sayd, with hideous reere: 215
      O Saturnes daughter, feede thy selfe on my distresses heere.
      Yea feede, and, cruell wyght, this plage behold thou from above
And glut thy savage hart therewith. Or if thy fo may move
Thee unto pitie, (for to thee I am an utter fo)
Bereeve mee of my hatefull soule distrest with helplesse wo,   220
And borne to endlesse toyle. For death shall unto mee bee sweete,
And for a cruell stepmother is death a gift most meete.
And is it I that did destroy Busiris, who did foyle
His temple floores with straungers blood? Ist I that did dispoyle
Antaeus of his mothers help? Ist I that could not bee   225
Abashed at the Spanyard who in one had bodies three?
Nor at the trypleheaded shape, O Cerberus, of thee?
Are you the hands that by the hornes the Bull of Candie drew?
Did you king Augies stable clenze whom afterward yee slew?
Are you the same by whom the fowles were scaard from Stymphaly?   230
Caught you the Stag in Maydenwood which did not runne but fly?
Are you the hands whose puissance receyved for your pay
The golden belt of Thermodon? Did you convey away
The Apples from the Dragon fell that waked nyght and day?
Ageinst the force of mee, defence the Centaures could not make,   235
Nor yit the Boare of Arcadie: nor yit the ougly Snake
Of Lerna, who by losse did grow and dooble force still take.
What? is it I that did behold the pampyred Jades of Thrace
With Maungers full of flesh of men on which they fed apace?
Ist I that downe at syght thereof theyr greazy Maungers threw,   240
And bothe the fatted Jades themselves and eke their mayster slew?
The Nemean Lyon by theis armes lyes dead uppon the ground.
Theis armes the monstruous Giant Cake by Tyber did confound.
Uppon theis shoulders have I borne the weyght of all the skie.
Joves cruell wyfe is weerye of commaunding mee. Yit I   245

210 *gad:* bar, spike   217 *plage:* calamity, seizure
211 *hent:* seized   223 *foyle:* defile
214 *Maree:* marrow   238 *Jades:* horses
215 *reere:* shout

Unweerie am of dooing still. But now on mee is lyght
An uncoth plage, which neyther force of hand, nor vertues myght,
Nor Arte is able to resist. Like wasting fyre it spreedes
Among myne inwards, and through out on all my body feedes.
But all this whyle Eurysthye lives in health. And sum men may   250
Beeleve there bee sum Goddes in deede. Thus much did Hercule say.
      And wounded over Oeta hygh, he stalking gan to stray,
      As when a Bull in maymed bulk a deadly dart dooth beare,
And that the dooer of the deede is shrunke asyde for feare.
Oft syghing myght you him have seene, oft trembling, oft about   255
To teare the garment with his hands from top to toe throughout,
And throwing downe the myghtye trees, and chaufing with the hilles,
Or casting up his handes to heaven where Jove his father dwelles.
Behold as Lychas trembling in a hollow rock did lurk,
He spyed him. And as his greef did all in furie woork,   260
He sayd: Art thou, syr Lychas, he that broughtest unto mee
This plagye present? of my death must thou the woorker bee?
Hee quaakt and shaakt, and looked pale, and fearfully gan make
Excuse. But as with humbled hands hee kneeling to him spake,
The furious Hercule caught him up, and swindging him about   265
His head a halfe a doozen tymes or more, he floong him out
Into th'Euboyan sea with force surmounting any sling.
He hardened into peble stone as in the ayre he hing.
And even as rayne conjeald by wynd is sayd to turne to snowe,
And of the snow round rolled up a thicker masse to growe,   270
Which falleth downe in hayle: so men in auncient tyme report,
That Lychas beeing swindgd about by violence in that sort,
(His blood then beeing drayned out, and having left at all
No moysture,) into peble stone was turned in his fall.
Now also in th'Euboyan sea appeeres a hygh short rocke   275
In shape of man ageinst the which the shipmen shun to knocke,
As though it could them feele, and they doo call it by the name
Of Lychas still. But thou Joves imp of great renowme and fame,
Didst fell the trees of Oeta high, and making of the same
A pyle, didst give to Poeans sonne thy quiver and thy bow,   280
And arrowes which should help agein Troy towne to overthrow.
He put to fyre, and as the same was kindling in the pyle,
Thy selfe didst spred thy Lyons skin upon the wood the whyle,
And leaning with thy head ageinst thy Club, thou laydst thee downe

257 *chaufing:* raging   265 *swindging:* brandishing, swinging

As cheerfully, as if with flowres and garlonds on thy crowne   285
Thou hadst beene set a banquetting among full cups of wyne.
Anon on every syde about those carelesse limbes of thyne
The fyre began to gather strength, and crackling noyse did make,
Assayling him whose noble hart for daliance did it take.
        The Goddes for this defender of the earth were sore afrayd   290
        To whom with cheerefull countnance Jove perceyving it thus
                                                                sayd:

This feare of yours is my delyght, and gladly even with all
My hart I doo rejoyce, O Gods, that mortall folk mee call
Their king and father, thinking mee ay myndfull of their weale,
And that myne offspring should doo well your selves doo show such
                                                                zeale.   295

For though that you doo attribute your favor to desert,
Considring his most woondrous acts: yit I too for my part
Am bound unto you. Nerethelesse, for that I would not have
Your faythfull harts without just cause in fearfull passions wave,
I would not have you of the flames in Oeta make account.   300
For as he hath all other things, so shall he them surmount.
Save only on that part that he hath taken of his mother,
The fyre shall have no power at all. Eternall is the tother,
The which he takes of mee, and cannot dye, ne yeeld to fyre.
When this is rid of earthly drosse, then will I lift it hygher,   305
And take it unto heaven: and I beleeve this deede of myne
Will gladsome bee to all the Gods. If any doo repyne,
If any doo repyne, I say, that Hercule should become
A God, repyne he still for mee, and looke he sowre and glum.
But let him know that Hercules deserveth this reward,   310
And that he shall ageinst his will alow it afterward.
The Gods assented everychone. And Juno seemd to make
No evill countnance to the rest, untill hir husband spake
The last. For then her looke was such as well they might perceyve,
Shee did her husbands noting her in evil part conceyve.   315
        Whyle Jove was talking with the Gods, as much as fyre could waste
        So much had fyre consumde. And now, O Hercules, thou haste
No carkesse for to know thee by. That part is quyght bereft
Which of thy mother thou didst take. Alonly now is left
The likenesse that thou tookst of Jove. And as the Serpent slye   320
In casting of his withered slough, renewes his yeeres thereby,

---

289 *daliance:* sport   315 *in evil part:* with hostility
309 *for mee:* as far as I am concerned

And wexeth lustyer than before, and looketh crisp and bryght
With scoured scales: so Hercules as soone as that his spryght
Had left his mortall limbes, gan in his better part to thryve,
And for to seeme a greater thing than when he was alyve,   325
And with a stately majestie ryght reverend to appeere.
His myghty father tooke him up above the cloudy spheere,
And in a charyot placed him among the streaming starres.
Huge Atlas felt the weyght thereof. But nothing this disbarres
Eurysthyes malice. Cruelly he prosecutes the hate   330
Uppon the offspring, which he bare ageinst the father late.
      But yit to make her mone unto and wayle her miserie
      And tell her sonnes great woorkes, which all the world could
                                                            testifie,
Old Alcmen had Dame Iolee. By Hercules last will
In wedlocke and in hartie love shee joyned was to Hill,   335
By whome shee then was big with chyld: when thus Alcmena sayd:
The Gods at least bee mercifull and send thee then theyr ayd,
And short thy labor, when the fruite the which thou goste withall
Now beeing rype enforceth thee wyth fearfull voyce to call
Uppon Ilithya, president of chyldbirthes, whom the ire   340
Of Juno at my travailing made deaf to my desire.
For when the Sun through twyce fyve signes his course had fully run,
And that the paynfull day of birth approched of my sonne,
My burthen strayned out my wombe, and that that I did beare
Became so greate, that of so huge a masse yee well myght sweare   345
That Jove was father. Neyther was I able to endure
The travail any lenger tyme. Even now I you assure
In telling it a shuddring cold through all my limbes dooth strike,
And partly it renewes my peynes to thinke upon the like.
I beeing in most cruell throwes nyghts seven and dayes eke seven,   350
And tyred with continuall pangs, did lift my hands to heaven,
And crying out aloud did call Lucina to myne ayd,
To loose the burthen from my wombe. Shee came as I had prayd:
But so corrupted long before by Juno my most fo,
That for to martir mee to death with peyne she purposde tho.   355
For when shee heard my piteous plaints and gronings, downe shee sate
On yon same altar which you see there standing at my gate.
Upon her left knee shee had pitcht her right ham, and besyde
Shee stayd the birth with fingars one within another tyde
In lattiswyse. And secretly she whisperde witching spells   360

340 *president of:* that presides over   358 *ham:* back of upper leg

Which hindred my deliverance more than all her dooings ells.
I labord still: and forst by payne and torments of my Fitts,
I rayld on Jove (although in vayne) as one besyde her witts.
And ay I wished for to dye. The woords that I did speake,
Were such as even the hardest stones of very flint myght breake. 365
The wyves of Thebee beeing there, for sauf deliverance prayd
And giving cheerfull woords, did bid I should not bee dismayd.
Among the other women there that to my labor came,
There was an honest yeomans wyfe, Galantis was her name.
Her heare was yellow as the gold, she was a jolly Dame. 370
And stoutly served mee, and I did love her for the same.
This wyfe (I know not how) did smell some packing gone about
On Junos part. And as she oft was passing in and out,
Shee spyde Lucina set uppon the altar holding fast
Her armes togither on her knees, and with her fingars cast 375
Within ech other on a knot, and sayd unto her thus:
I pray you who so ere you bee, rejoyce you now with us,
My Lady Alcmen hath her wish, and sauf is brought abed.
Lucina leaped up amazde at that that shee had sed,
And let her hands asunder slip. And I immediatly 380
With loosening of the knot, had sauf deliverance by and by.
They say that in deceyving Dame Lucina Galant laught.
And therfore by the yellow locks the Goddesse wroth hir caught,
And dragged her. And as she would have risen from the ground,
She kept her downe, and into legges her armes shee did confound. 385
Her former stoutnesse still remaynes: her backe dooth keepe the hew
That erst was in her heare: her shape is only altered new.
And for with lying mouth shee helpt a woman laboring, shee
Dooth kindle also at her mouth. And now she haunteth free
Our houses as shee did before, a Weasle as wee see. 390
     With that shee syghes to think uppon her servants hap, and then
     Her daughtrinlaw immediatly replied thus agen:
But mother, shee whose altred shape dooth move your hart so sore,
Was neyther kith nor kin to you. What will you say therefore,
If of myne owne deere suster I the woondrous fortune show, 395
Although my sorrow and the teares that from myne eyes doo flow,
Doo hinder mee, and stop my speeche? Her mother (you must know
My father by another wyfe had mee) bare never mo
But this same Ladie Dryopee, the fayrest Ladye tho

---

372 *packing:* intrigue   389 *kindle:* give birth
386 *stoutnesse:* courage

In all the land of Oechalye. Whom beeing then no mayd   400
(For why the God of Delos and of Delphos had her frayd)
Andraemon taketh to hys wyfe, and thinkes him well apayd.
There is a certaine leaning Lake whose bowing banks doo show
A likenesse of the salt sea shore. Uppon the brim doo grow
All round about it Mirtletrees. My suster thither goes   405
Unwares what was her destinie, and (which you may suppose
Was more to bee disdeyned at) the cause of comming there
Was to the fayries of the Lake fresh garlonds for to beare.
And in her armes a babye her sweete burthen shee did hold.
Who sucking on her brest was yit not full a twelvemoonth old.   410
Not farre from this same pond did grow a Lote tree florisht gay
With purple flowres and beries sweete, and leaves as greene as Bay.
Of theis same flowres to please her boy my suster gathered sum,
And I had thought to doo so too, for I was thither cum.
I saw how from the slivered flowres red drops of blood did fall,   415
And how that shuddring horribly the braunches quaakt withall.
You must perceyve that (as too late the Countryfolk declare)
A Nymph cald Lotos flying from fowle Pryaps filthy ware,
Was turned into this same tree reserving still her name.
My suster did not know so much, who when shee backward came   420
Afrayd at that that shee had seene, and having sadly prayd
The Nymphes of pardon, to have gone her way agen assayd:
Her feete were fastned downe with rootes. Shee stryved all she myght
To plucke them up, but they so sure within the earth were pyght,
That nothing save her upper partes shee could that present move.   425
A tender barke growes from beneath up leysurly above,
And softly overspreddes her loynes, which when shee saw, shee went
About to teare her heare, and full of leaves her hand shee hent.
Her head was overgrowen with leaves. And little Amphise (so
Had Eurytus his Graundsyre naamd her sonne not long ago)   430
Did feele his mothers dugges wex hard. And as he still them drew
In sucking, not a whit of milke nor moysture did ensew.
I standing by thee did behold thy cruell chaunce: but nought
I could releeve thee, suster myne. Yit to my powre I wrought
To stay the growing of thy trunk and of thy braunches by   435

---

401 *frayd:* attacked   415 *slivered:* cut
402 *apayd:* satisfied   418 *ware:* stuff, stock in trade
403 *leaning:* with sloping banks   424 *pyght:* thrust, fixed
407 *bee disdeyned at:* be indignant at   425 *present:* moment, time
411 *Lote:* lotus

Embracing thee. Yea I protest I would ryght willingly
Have in the selfesame barke with thee bene closed up. Behold,
Her husband, good Andraemon, and her wretched father, old
Sir Eurytus came thither and enquyrd for Dryopee.
And as they askt for Dryopee, I shewd them Lote the tree.   440
They kist the wood which yit was warme, and falling downe bylow,
Did hug the rootes of that their tree. My suster now could show
No part which was not wood except her face. A deawe of teares
Did stand uppon the wretched leaves late formed of her heares.
And whyle she might, and whyle her mouth did give her way to
                                 speake,   445
With such complaynt as this, her mynd shee last of all did breake:
If credit may bee given to such as are in wretchednesse,
I sweare by God I never yit deserved this distresse.
I suffer peyne without desert. My lyfe hath guiltlesse beene.
And if I lye, I would theis boughes of mine which now are greene,   450
Myght withered bee, and I heawen downe and burned in the fyre.
This infant from his mothers wombe remove you I desyre:
And put him forth to nurce, and cause him underneath my tree
Oft tymes to sucke, and oftentymes to play. And when that hee
Is able for to speake I pray you let him greete mee heere,   455
And sadly say: in this same trunk is hid my mother deere.
But lerne him for to shun all ponds and pulling flowres from trees,
And let him in his heart beleeve that all the shrubs he sees,
Are bodyes of the Goddesses. Adew deere husband now,
Adew deere father, and adew deere suster. And in yow   460
If any love of mee remayne, defend my boughes I pray
From wound of cutting hooke and ax, and bite of beast for ay.
And for I cannot stoope to you, rayse you yourselves to mee,
And come and kisse mee whyle I may yit toucht and kissed bee.
And lift mee up my little boy. I can no lenger talke,   465
For now about my lillye necke as if it were a stalke
The tender rynd beginnes to creepe, and overgrowes my top.
Remove your fingars from my face. The spreading barke dooth stop
My dying eyes without your help. Shee had no sooner left
Her talking, but her lyfe therewith togither was bereft.   470
But yit a goodwhyle after that her native shape did fade,
Her newmade boughes continewed warme. Now whyle that Iole made
Report of this same woondrous tale, and whyle Alcmena (who

---

⁴⁴⁶ *breake:* reveal, utter

Did weepe) was drying up the teares of Iole weeping too,
By putting to her thomb: there hapt a sodeine thing so straunge,   475
That unto mirth from heavinesse theyr harts it streight did chaunge.
    For at the doore in manner even a very boy as then
    With short soft Downe about his chin, revoked backe agen
To youthfull yeares, stood Iolay with countnance smooth and trim.
Dame Hebee, Junos daughter, had bestowde this gift on him,   480
Entreated at his earnest sute. Whom mynding fully there
The giving of like gift ageine to any to forsweare,
Dame Themis would not suffer. For (quoth shee) this present howre
Is cruell warre in Thebee towne, and none but Jove hath powre
To vanquish stately Canapey. The brothers shall alike   485
Wound eyther other. And alyve a Prophet shall go seeke
His owne quicke ghoste among the dead, the earth him swallowing in.
The sonne by taking vengeance for his fathers death shall win
The name of kynd and wicked man, in one and selfsame cace.
And flayght with mischeefes, from his wits and from his native place   490
The furies and his mothers ghoste shall restlessely him chace,
Untill his wyfe demaund of him the fatall gold for meede,
And that his cousin Phegies swoord doo make his sydes to bleede.
Then shall the fayre Callirrhoee, Achelous daughter, pray
The myghty Jove in humble wyse to graunt her children may   495
Retyre ageine to youthfull yeeres, and that he will not see
The death of him that did revenge unvenged for to bee.
Jove moved at her sute shall cause his daughtrinlaw to give
Like gift, and backe from age to youth Callirrhoes children drive.
    When Themis through foresyght had spoke theis woords of
                                        prophesie,   500
    The Gods began among themselves vayne talke to multiplie,
They mooyld why others myght not give like gift as well as shee.
First Pallants daughter grudged that her husband old should bee.
The gentle Ceres murmurde that her Iasions heare was hore.
And Vulcane would have calld ageine the yeeres long spent before   505
By Ericthonius. And the nyce Dame Venus having care
Of tyme to come, the making yong of old Anchises sware.
So every God had one to whom he speciall favor bare.
And through this partiall love of theyrs seditiously increast
A hurlyburly, till the time that Jove among them preast,   510

490 *flayght:* frightened   506 *nyce:* wanton, tender, hard to please
502 *mooyld:* fretted, raged

And sayd: So smally doo you stand in awe of mee this howre,
As thus too rage? Thinkes any of you himself to have such powre,
As for to alter destinye? I tell you Iolay
Recovered hath by destinye his yeeres erst past away,
Callirrhoes children must returne to youth by destiny, 515
And not by force of armes, or sute susteynd ambitiously.
And to th'entent with meelder myndes yee may this matter beare,
Even I myself by destinyes am rulde. Which if I were
Of power to alter, thinke you that our Aeacus should stoope
By reason of his feeble age? or Radamanth should droope? 520
Or Minos, who by reason of his age is now disdeynd,
And lives not in so sure a state as heretofore he reygnd?
   The woords of Jove so movd the Gods that none of them
                                              complaynd,
   Sith Radamanth and Aeacus were both with age constreynd:
And Minos also: who (as long as lusty youth did last,) 525
Did even with terror of his name make myghty Realmes agast.
But then was Minos weakened sore, and greatly stood in feare
Of Milet, one of Deyons race: who proudly did him beare
Uppon his father Phoebus and the stoutnesse of his youth.
And though he feard he would rebell: yit durst he not his mouth 530
Once open for to banish him his Realme: untill at last
Departing of his owne accord, Miletus swiftly past
The Gotesea and did build a towne uppon the Asian ground,
Which still reteynes the name of him that first the same did found.
And there the daughter of the brooke Maeander which dooth go 535
So often backward, Cyane, a Nymph of body so
Exceeding comly as the lyke was seldome heard of, as
Shee by her fathers wynding bankes for pleasure walking was,
Was knowen by Milet: unto whom a payre of twinnes shee brought,
And of the twinnes the names were Caune and Byblis. Byblis ought 540
To bee a mirror unto Maydes in lawfull wyse to love.
   This Byblis cast a mynd to Caune, but not as did behove
   A suster to her brotherward. When first of all the fyre
Did kindle, shee perceyvd it not. Shee thought in her desyre
Of kissing him so oftentymes no sin, ne yit no harme 545
In cleeping him about the necke so often with her arme.
The glittering glosse of godlynesse beguyld her long. Her love
Began from evill unto woorse by little too remove.

---

524 *Sith:* since   546 *cleeping:* embracing
533 *Gotesea:* the Aegean Sea

Shee commes to see her brother deckt in brave and trim attyre,
And for to seeme exceeding fayre it was her whole desyre.   550
And if that any fayrer were in all the flocke than shee,
It spyghts her. In what case she was as yit shee did not see.
Her heate exceeded not so farre as for to vow: and yit
Shee suffred in her troubled brist full many a burning fit.
Now calleth shee him mayster, now shee utter hateth all   555
The names of kin. Shee rather had he should her Byblis call
Than suster. Yit no filthy hope shee durst permit to creepe
Within her mynd awake. But as shee lay in quiet sleepe,
Shee oft behild her love: and oft she thought her brother came
And lay with her, and (though asleepe) shee blushed at the same.   560
When sleepe was gone, she long lay dumb still musing on the syght,
And said with wavering mynd: Now wo is mee, most wretched wyght.
What meenes the image of this dreame that I have seene this nyght?
I would not wish it should bee trew. Why dreamed I then so?
Sure hee is fayre although hee should bee judged by his fo.   565
He likes mee well, and were he not my brother, I myght set
My love on him, and he were mee ryght woorthy for to get,
But unto this same match the name of kinred is a let.
Well, so that I awake doo still mee undefylde keepe,
Let come as often as they will such dreamings in my sleepe.   570
In sleepe there is no witnesse by. In sleepe yit may I take
As greate a pleasure (in a sort) as if I were awake.
Oh Venus and thy tender sonne, Sir Cupid, what delyght,
How present feeling of your sport hath touched mee this nyght.
How lay I as it were resolvd both maree, flesh, and bone.   575
How gladdes it mee to thinke thereon. Alas too soone was gone
That pleasure, and too hastye and despyghtfull was the nyght
In breaking of my joyes. O Lord, if name of kinred myght
Betweene us two removed bee, how well it would agree,
O Caune, that of thy father I the daughtrinlaw should bee.   580
How fitly myght my father have a sonneinlaw of thee.
Would God that all save auncesters were common to us twayne.
I would thou were of nobler stocke than I. I cannot sayne,
O perle of beautie, what shee is whom thou shalt make a mother.
Alas how ill befalles it mee that I could have none other   585
Than those same parents which are thyne. So only still my brother

---

568 *let:* hindrance   575 *resolvd:* dissolved

And not my husband mayst thou bee. The thing that hurts us bothe
Is one, and that betweene us ay inseparably gothe.
What meene my dreames then? what effect have dreames? and may
there bee
Effect in dreames? The Gods are farre in better case than wee. 590
For why? the Gods have matched with theyr susters as wee see.
So Saturne did alie with Ops, the neerest of his blood.
So Tethys with Oceanus: So Jove did think it good
To take his suster Juno to his wyfe. What then? the Goddes
Have lawes and charters by themselves. And sith there is such oddes 595
Betweene the state of us and them, why should I sample take,
Our worldly matters equall with the heavenly things to make?
This wicked love shall eyther from my hart be driven away,
Or if it can not bee expulst, God graunt I perish may,
And that my brother kisse me, layd on Herce to go to grave. 600
But my desyre the full consent of both of us dooth crave.
Admit the matter liketh me. He will for sin it take.
But yit the sonnes of Aeolus no scrupulousnesse did make
In going to theyr susters beds. And how come I to know
The feates of them? To what intent theis samples doo I show? 605
Ah whither am I headlong driven? avaunt foule filthy fyre:
And let mee not in otherwyse than susterlyke desyre
My brothers love. Yit if that he were first in love with mee,
His fondnesse to inclyne unto perchaunce I could agree.
Shall I therefore who would not have rejected him if hee 610
Had sude to mee, go sue to him? and canst thou speake in deede?
And canst thou utter forth thy mynd? and tell him of thy neede?
My love will make mee speake. I can. Or if that shame doo stay
My toong, a sealed letter shall my secret love bewray.
    This likes her best. Uppon this poynt now restes her doubtful
mynd. 615

So raysing up herself uppon her leftsyde shee enclynd,
And leaning on her elbow sayd: Let him advyse him what
To doo, for I my franticke love will utter playne and flat.
Alas to what ungraciousnesse intend I for to fall?
What furie raging in my hart my senses dooth appall? 620
In thinking so, with trembling hand shee framed her to wryght
The matter that her troubled mynd in musing did indyght.
Her ryght hand holdes the pen, her left dooth hold the empty wax.

614 *bewray:* reveal   621 *framed:* prepared

She ginnes. Shee doutes, shee wryghtes: shee in the tables findeth lacks.
She notes, she blurres, dislikes, and likes: and chaungeth this for that. 625
Shee layes away the booke, and takes it up. Shee wotes not what
She would herself. What ever thing shee myndeth for to doo
Misliketh her. A shamefastnesse with boldenesse mixt thereto
Was in her countnance. Shee had once writ Suster: Out agen
The name of Suster for to raze shee thought it best. And then   630
She snatcht the tables up, and did theis following woords ingrave:
    The health which if thou give her not shee is not like to have
    Thy lover wisheth unto thee. I dare not ah for shame
I dare not tell thee who I am, nor let thee heare my name.
And if thou doo demaund of mee what thing I doo desyre,   635
Would God that namelesse I myght pleade the matter I requyre,
And that I were unknowen to thee by name of Byblis, till
Assurance of my sute were wrought according to my will.
As tokens of my wounded hart myght theis to thee appeere:
My colour pale, my body leane, my heavy mirthlesse cheere,   640
My watry eyes, my sighes without apparent causes why,
My oft embracing of thee: and such kisses (if perdye
Thou marked them) as very well thou might have felt and found
Not for to have beene Susterlike. But though with greevous wound
I then were striken to the hart, although the raging flame   645
Did burne within: yit take I God to witnesse of the same,
I did as much as lay in mee this outrage for to tame.
And long I stryved (wretched wench) to scape the violent Dart
Of Cupid. More I have endurde of hardnesse and of smart,
Than any wench (a man would think) were able to abyde.   650
Force forceth mee to shew my case which faine I still would hyde,
And mercy at thy gentle hand in fearfull wyse to crave.
Thou only mayst the lyfe of mee thy lover spill or save.
Choose which thou wilt. No enmy craves this thing: but such a one
As though shee bee alyde so sure as surer can bee none,   655
Yit covets shee more surely yit alyed for to bee,
And with a neerer kynd of band to link her selfe to thee.
Let aged folkes have skill in law: to age it dooth belong
To keepe the rigor of the lawes and search out ryght from wrong.
Such youthfull yeeres as ours are yit rash folly dooth beseeme.   660
Wee know not what is lawfull yit. And therefore wee may deeme
That all is lawfull that wee list: ensewing in the same

---

642 *perdye:* by God, indeed   660 *beseeme:* become, suit
653 *spill:* kill   662 *ensewing:* following, imitating

The dooings of the myghtye Goddes. Not dread of worldly shame
Nor yit our fathers roughnesse, no nor fearfulnesse should let
Our purpose. Only let all feare asyde be wholy set. 665
Wee underneath the name of kin our pleasant scapes may hyde.
Thou knowest I have libertie to talke with thee asyde,
And openly wee kysse and cull. And what is all the rest
That wants? Have mercy on mee now, who playnly have exprest
My case: which thing I had not done, but that the utter rage 670
Of love constreynes mee thereunto the which I cannot swage.
Deserve not on my tumb thy name subscribed for to have,
That thou art he whose cruelnesse did bring mee to my grave.
    Thus much shee wrate in vayne, and wax did want her to indyght,
    And in the margent she was fayne the latter verse to wryght. 675
Immediatly to seale her shame shee takes a precious stone,
The which shee moystes with teares: from tung the moysture quight
                                                    was gone.
She calld a servant shamefastly, and after certaine fayre
And gentle woords: My trusty man, I pray thee beare this payre
Of tables (quoth shee) to my (and a great whyle afterward 680
Shee added) brother. Now through chaunce or want of good regard
The table slipped downe to ground in reaching to him ward.
The handsell troubled sore her mynd. But yit shee sent them. And
Her servant spying tyme did put them into Caunyes hand.
Maeanders nephew sodeinly in anger floong away 685
The tables ere he half had red, (scarce able for to stay
His fistocke from the servants face who quaakt) and thus did say:
Avaunt, thou baudye ribawd, whyle thou mayst. For were it not
For shame I should have killed thee. Away afrayd he got,
And told his mistresse of the feerce and cruell answer made 690
By Caunye. By and by the hew of Byblis gan to fade,
And all her body was benumd with Icie colde for feare
To heere of this repulse. Assoone as that her senses were
Returnd ageine, her furious flames returned with her witts.
And thus shee sayd so soft that scarce hir toong the ayer hitts: 695
    And woorthely. For why was I so rash as to discover
    By hasty wryghting this my wound which most I ought to cover?

---

666 *scapes:* transgressions
668 *cull:* hug
671 *swage:* assuage
674 *want:* was lacking

683 *handsell:* omen
687 *fistocke:* fist
688 *ribawd:* base or wicked person
691 *By and by:* at once

I should with dowtfull glauncing woords have felt his humor furst,
And made a trayne to trye him if pursue or no he durst.
I should have vewed first the coast, to see the weather cleere,   700
And then I myght have launched sauf and boldly from the peere.
But now I hoyst up all my sayles before I tryde the wynd:
And therfore am I driven uppon the rockes against my mynd,
And all the sea dooth overwhelme mee. Neyther may I fynd
The meanes to get to harbrough, or from daunger to retyre.   705
Why did not open tokens warne to bridle my desyre,
Then when the tables falling in delivering them declaard
My hope was vaine? And ought not I then eyther to have spaard
From sending them as that day? or have chaunged whole my mynd?
Nay rather shifted of the day? For had I not beene blynd   710
Even God himself by soothfast signes the sequele seemd to hit.
Yea rather than to wryghting thus my secrets to commit,
I should have gone and spoke myself, and presently have showde
My fervent love. He should have seene how teares had from mee flowde.
Hee should have seene my piteous looke ryght loverlike. I could   715
Have spoken more than into those my tables enter would.
About his necke against his will, myne armes I myght have wound
And had he shaakt me off, I myght have seemed for to swound.
I humbly myght have kist his feete, and kneeling on the ground
Besought him for to save my lyfe. All theis I myght have proved,   720
Wherof although no one alone his stomacke could have moved,
Yit all togither myght have made his hardened hart relent.
Perchaunce there was some fault in him that was of message sent.
He stept unto him bluntly (I beleeve) and did not watch
Convenient tyme, in merrie kew at leysure him to catch.   725
Theis are the things that hindred mee. For certeinly I knowe
No sturdy stone nor massy steele dooth in his stomacke grow.
He is not made of Adamant. He is no Tygers whelp.
He never sucked Lyonesse. He myght with little help
Bee vanquisht. Let us give fresh charge uppon him. Whyle I live   730
Without obteyning victorie I will not over give.
For firstly (if it lay in mee my dooings to revoke)
I should not have begonne at all. But seeing that the stroke
Is given, the second poynt is now to give the push to win.

699 *trayne:* trick, trap   720 *proved:* tried
701 *sauf:* safe   721 *stomacke:* desire, temper
718 *swound:* faint   725 *kew:* frame of mind, sign

For neyther he (although that I myne enterpryse should blin)   735
Can ever whyle he lives forget my deede. And sith I shrink,
My love was lyght, or else I meant to trap him, he shall think.
Or at the least he may suppose that this my rage of love
Which broyleth so within my brest, proceedes not from above
By Cupids stroke, but of some foule and filthy lust. In fyne   740
I cannot but to wickednesse now more and more inclyne.
By wryghting is my sute commenst: my meening dooth appeere:
And though I cease: yit can I not accounted bee for cleere.
Now that that dooth remayne behynd is much as in respect
My fond desyre to satisfy: and little in effect   745
To aggravate my fault withall. Thus much shee sayd. And so
Unconstant was her wavering mynd still floting to and fro,
That though it irkt her for to have attempted, yit proceedes
Shee in the selfsame purpose of attempting, and exceedes
All measure, and, unhappy wench, shee takes from day to day   750
Repulse upon repulse, and yit shee hath not grace to stay.
    Soone after when her brother saw there was with her no end,
    He fled his countrie forbycause he would not so offend,
And in a forreine land did buyld a Citie. Then men say
That Byblis through despayre and thought all wholy did dismay.   755
Shee tare her garments from her brest, and furiously shee wroong
Her hands, and beete her armes, and like a bedlem with her toong
Confessed her unlawfull love. But beeing of the same
Dispoynted, shee forsooke her land and hatefull house for shame,
And followed after flying Caune. And as the Froes of Thrace   760
In dooing of the three yeere rites of Bacchus: in lyke cace
The maryed wyves of Bubasie saw Byblis howling out
Through all theyr champion feeldes, the which shee leaving, ran about
In Caria to the Lelegs who are men in battell stout,
And so to Lycia. Shee had past Crag, Limyre, and the brooke   765
Of Xanthus, and the countrie where Chymaera that same pooke
Hath Goatish body, Lions head and brist, and Dragons tayle,
When woods did want: and Byblis now beginning for to quayle
Through weerynesse in following Caune, sank down and layd her hed
Ageinst the ground, and kist the leaves that wynd from trees had
                              shed.   770

735 *blin:* stop
757 *bedlem:* lunatic
760 *Froes:* women

763 *champion:* champaign, level and open
766 *pooke:* demon, goblin

The Nymphes of Caria went about in tender armes to take
Her often up. They oftentymes perswaded her to slake
Her love. And woords of comfort to her deafe eard mynd they spake.
Shee still lay dumbe: and with her nayles the greenish herbes shee hild,
And moysted with a streame of teares the grasse upon the feeld.   775
The waternymphes (so folk report) put under her a spring,
Whych never myght be dryde: and could they give a greater thing?
Immediatly even like as when yee wound a pitchtree rynd,
The gum dooth issue out in droppes: or as the westerne wynd
With gentle blast toogither with the warmth of Sunne, unbynd   780
The yce: or as the clammy kynd of cement which they call
Bitumen issueth from the ground full fraughted therewithall:
So Phoebus neece, Dame Byblis, then consuming with her teares,
Was turned to a fountaine, which in those same vallyes beares
The tytle of the founder still, and gusheth freshly out   785
From underneath a Sugarchest as if it were a spowt.
        The fame of this same wondrous thing perhappes had filled all
        The hundred Townes of Candye had a greater not befall
More neerer home by Iphys meanes transformed late before.
For in the shyre of Phestos hard by Gnossus dwelt of yore   790
A yeoman of the meaner sort that Lyctus had to name.
His stocke was simple, and his welth according to the same.
Howbee't his lyfe so upryght was, as no man could it blame.
He came unto his wyfe then big and ready downe to lye,
And sayd: Two things I wish thee. T'one, that when thou out shalt
                                          crye,   795
Thou mayst dispatch with little payne: the other that thou have
A Boay. For Gyrles to bring them up a greater cost doo crave.
And I have no abilitie. And therefore if thou bring
A wench (it goes ageinst my heart to thinke uppon the thing)
Although ageinst my will, I charge it streyght destroyed bee.   800
The bond of nature needes must beare in this behalf with mee.
This sed, both wept exceedingly, as well the husband who
Did give commaundement, as the wyfe that was commaunded too.
Yit Telethusa earnestly at Lyct her husband lay,
(Although in vayne) to have good hope, and of himselfe more stay.   805
But he was full determined. Within a whyle, the day
Approched that the frute was rype, and shee did looke to lay

786 *Sugarchest:* any of various hardwood   798 *abilitie:* resources
   trees   804 *at . . . lay:* urged
791 *to name:* as name   805 *stay:* reliance, support

Her belly every mynute: when at midnyght in her rest
Stood by her (or did seeme to stand) the Goddesse Isis, drest
And trayned with the solemne pomp of all her rytes. Two hornes 810
Uppon her forehead lyke the moone, with eares of rypened cornes
Stood glistring as the burnisht gold. Moreover shee did weare
A rich and stately diademe. Attendant on her were
The barking bug Anubis, and the saint of Bubast, and
The pydecote Apis, and the God that gives to understand 815
By fingar holden to his lippes that men should silence keepe,
And Lybian wormes whose strnging dooth enforce continuall sleepe,
And thou, Osyris, whom the folk of Aegypt ever seeke,
And never can have sought inough, and Rittlerattles eke.
Then even as though that Telethuse had fully beene awake, 820
And seene theis things with open eyes, thus Isis to her spake:
My servant Telethusa, cease this care, and breake the charge
Of Lyct. And when Lucina shall have let thy frute at large,
Bring up the same what ere it bee. I am a Goddesse who
Delyghts in helping folke at neede. I hither come to doo 825
Thee good. Thou shalt not have a cause hereafter to complayne
Of serving of a Goddesse that is thanklesse for thy payne.
When Isis had this comfort given, shee went her way agayne.
    A joyfull wyght rose Telethuse, and lifting to the sky
Her hardened hands, did pray hir dreame myght woorke
                                                    effectually. 830
Her throwes increast, and forth alone anon the burthen came,
A wench was borne to Lyctus who knew nothing of the same.
The mother making him beleeve it was a boay, did bring
It up, and none but shee and nurce were privie to the thing.
The father thanking God did give the chyld the Graundsyres name, 835
The which was Iphys. Joyfull was the moother of the same,
Bycause the name did serve alike to man and woman bothe,
And so the lye through godly guile forth unperceyved gothe.
The garments of it were a boayes. The face of it was such
As eyther in a boay or gyrle of beawtie uttered much. 840
When Iphys was of thirteene yeeres, her father did insure
The browne Ianthee unto her, a wench of looke demure,
Commended for her favor and her person more than all
The Maydes of Phestos: Telest, men her fathers name did call.

---

810 *trayned:* attended   819 *Rittlerattles:* rattles, sistrums
814 *bug:* bugbear, bogy   841 *insure:* guarantee, promise
815 *pydecote:* dressed in many colors

He dwelt in Dyctis. They were bothe of age and favor leeke,   845
And under both one schoolemayster they did for nurture seeke.
And hereupon the hartes of both, the dart of Love did streeke,
And wounded both of them aleeke. But unlike was theyr hope.
Both longed for the wedding day togither for to cope.
For whom Ianthee thinkes to bee a man, shee hopes to see   850
Her husband. Iphys loves whereof shee thinkes shee may not bee
Partaker, and the selfesame thing augmenteth still her flame.
Herself a Mayden with a Mayd (ryght straunge) in love became.
        Shee scarce could stay her teares. What end remaynes for mee
                                          (quoth shee)
        How straunge a love? how uncoth? how prodigious reygnes in
                                                mee?   855
If that the Gods did favor mee, they should destroy mee quyght.
Of if they would not mee destroy, at least wyse yit they myght
Have given mee such a maladie as myght with nature stond,
Or nature were acquainted with. A Cow is never fond
Uppon a Cow, nor Mare on Mare. The Ram delyghts the Eawe,   860
The Stag the Hynde, the Cocke the Hen. But never men could shew,
That female yit was tane in love with female kynd. O would
To God I never had beene borne. Yit least that Candy should
Not bring foorth all that monstruous were, the daughter of the Sonne
Did love a Bull. Howbee't there was a Male to dote uppon.   865
My love is furiouser than hers, if truthe confessed bee.
For shee was fond of such a lust as myght bee compast. Shee
Was served by a Bull beguyld by Art in Cow of tree.
And one there was for her with whom advowtrie to commit.
If all the conning in the worlde and slyghts of suttle wit   870
Were heere, or if that Daedalus himselfe with uncowth wing
Of Wax should hither fly againe, what comfort should he bring?
Could he with all his conning crafts now make a boay of mee?
Or could he, O Ianthee, chaunge the native shape of thee?
Nay rather, Iphys, settle thou thy mynd and call thy witts   875
Abowt thee: shake thou off theis flames that foolishly by fitts
Without all reason reigne. Thou seest what Nature hathe thee made
(Onlesse thow wilt deceyve thy selfe.) So farre foorth wysely wade,
As ryght and reason may support, and love as women ought.

845 *leeke:* like   868 *tree:* wood
847 *streeke:* strike   869 *advowtrie:* adultery
849 *cope:* meet   878 *wade:* go
855 *uncoth:* strange, improper

Hope is the thing that breedes desyre, hope feedes the amorous
thought. 880
This hope thy sex denieth thee. Not watching doth restreyne
Thee from embracing of the thing wherof thou art so fayne.
Nor yit the Husbands jealowsie, nor rowghnesse of her Syre,
Nor yit the coynesse of the Wench dooth hinder thy desyre.
And yit thou canst not her enjoy. No, though that God and man 885
Should labor to their uttermost and doo the best they can
In thy behalfe, they could not make a happy wyght of thee.
I cannot wish the thing but that I have it. Frank and free
The Goddes have given mee what they could. As I will, so will hee
That must become my fathrinlaw. So willes my father, too. 890
But nature stronger than them all consenteth not thereto.
This hindreth mee, and nothing else. Behold the blisfull tyme,
The day of Mariage is at hand. Ianthee shalbee myne,
And yit I shall not her enjoy. Amid the water wee
Shall thirst. O Juno, president of mariage, why with thee 895
Comes Hymen to this wedding where no brydegroome you shall see,
But bothe are Brydes that must that day togither coupled bee?
    This spoken, shee did hold hir peace. And now the tother mayd
    Did burne as hote in love as shee. And earnestly shee prayd
The brydale day myght come with speede. The thing for which shee
longd 900

Dame Telethusa fearing sore, from day to day prolongd
The tyme, oft feyning siknesse, oft pretending shee had seene
Ill tokens of successe. At length all shifts consumed beene.
The wedding day so oft delayd was now at hand. The day
Before it, taking from her head the kercheef quyght away, 905
And from her daughters head likewyse, with scattred heare she layd
Her handes upon the Altar, and with humble voyce thus prayd:
    O Isis, who doost haunt the towne of Paretonie, and
    The feeldes by Maraeotis lake, and Pharos which dooth stand
By Alexandria, and the Nyle divided into seven 910
Great channels, comfort thou my feare, and send mee help from heaven,
Thyself, O Goddesse, even thyself, and theis thy relikes I
Did once behold and knew them all: as well thy company
As eke thy sounding rattles, and thy cressets burning by,
And myndfully I marked what commaundement thou didst give. 915
That I escape unpunished, that this same wench dooth live,

903 *shifts:* subterfuges
908 *haunt:* resort to often, frequent
914 *cressets:* torches

Thy counsell and thy hest it is. Have mercy now on twayne,
And help us. With that word the teares ran downe her cheekes amayne.
The Goddesse seemed for to move her Altar: and in deede
She moved it. The temple doores did tremble like a reede.   920
And hornes in likenesse to the Moone about the Church did shyne.
And Rattles made a raughtish noyse. At this same luckie signe,
Although not wholy carelesse, yit ryght glad shee went away.
And Iphys followed after her with larger pace than ay
Shee was accustomd. And her face continued not so whyght.   925
Her strength encreased, and her looke more sharper was to syght.
Her heare grew shorter, and shee had a much more lively spryght,
Than when shee was a wench. For thou, O Iphys, who ryght now
A modther wert, art now a boay. With offrings both of yow
To Church retyre, and there rejoyce with fayth unfearfull. They   930
With offrings went to Church ageine, and there theyr vowes did pay.
They also set a table up, which this breef meeter had:
The vowes that Iphys vowd a wench he hath performd a Lad.
Next morrow over all the world did shine with lightsome flame,
When Juno, and Dame Venus, and Sir Hymen joyntly came   935
To Iphys mariage, who as then transformed to a boay
Did take Ianthee to his wyfe, and so her love enjoy.

FINIS NONI LIBRI.

917 *hest:* command
922 *raughtish:* harsh
923 *carelesse:* carefree

929 *modther:* mauther, young girl (apparently not related to *mother*)
932 *meeter:* poem

THE TENTH BOOKE

OF OVIDS METAMORPHOSIS.

[Orpheus and Eurydice. Hyacinth. Pygmalion. Myrrha and Cinyras.
Venus and Adonis. Atalanta.]

From thence in saffron colourd robe flew Hymen through the ayre,
And into Thracia beeing called by Orphy did repayre.
He came in deede at Orphyes call: but neyther did he sing
The woordes of that solemnitie, nor merry countnance bring,
Nor any handsell of good lucke. His torch with drizling smoke   5
Was dim: the same to burne out cleere, no stirring could provoke.
The end was woorser than the signe. For as the Bryde did rome
Abrode accompanyde with a trayne of Nymphes to bring her home,
A serpent lurking in the grasse did sting her in the ancle:
Whereof shee dyde incontinent, so swift the bane did rancle.   10
Whom when the Thracian Poet had bewayld sufficiently
On earth, the Ghostes departed hence he minding for to trie,
Downe at the gate of Taenarus did go to Limbo lake.
And thence by gastly folk and soules late buried he did take
His journey to Persephonee and to the king of Ghosts   15
That like a Lordly tyran reignes in those unpleasant coasts.
And playing on his tuned harp he thus began to sound:
    O you, the Sovereines of the world set underneath the ground,
    To whome wee all (what ever thing is made of mortall kynd)
Repayre, if by your leave I now may freely speake my mynd,   20
I come not hither as a spye the shady Hell to see:
Nor yet the foule three headed Curre whose heares all Adders bee
To tye in cheynes. The cause of this my vyage is my wyfe

5 *handsell:* omen, sign   10 *incontinent:* immediately

Whose foote a Viper stinging did abridge her youthfull lyfe.
I would have borne it paciently: and so to doo I strave,   25
But Love surmounted powre. This God is knowen great force to have
Above on earth. And whether he reigne heere or no I dowt.
But I beleeve hee reignes heere too. If fame that flies abowt
Of former rape report not wrong, Love coupled also yow.
By theis same places full of feare: by this huge Chaos now,   30
And by the stilnesse of this waste and emptye Kingdome, I
Beseech yee of Eurydicee unreele the destinye
That was so swiftly reeled up. All things to you belong.
And though wee lingring for a whyle our pageants do prolong,
Yit soone or late wee all to one abyding place doo rome: 35
Wee haste us hither all: this place becomes our latest home:
And you doo over humaine kynd reigne longest tyme. Now when
This woman shall have lived full her tyme, shee shall agen
Become your owne. The use of her but for a whyle I crave.
And if the Destnyes for my wyfe denye mee for to have   40
Releace, I fully am resolvd for ever heere to dwell.
Rejoyce you in the death of both. As he this tale did tell,
          And played on his instrument, the bloodlesse ghostes shed teares:
          To tyre on Titius growing hart the greedy Grype forbeares:
The shunning water Tantalus endevereth not to drink: 45
And Danaus daughters ceast to fill theyr tubbes that have no brink.
Ixions wheele stood still: and downe sate Sisyphus uppon
His rolling stone. Then first of all (so fame for truth hath gone)
The Furies beeing striken there with pitie at his song
Did weepe. And neyther Pluto nor his Ladie were so strong   50
And hard of stomacke to withhold his just petition long.
They called foorth Eurydicee who was as yit among
The newcome Ghosts, and limped of her wound. Her husband tooke
Her with condicion that he should not backe uppon her looke,
Untill the tyme that hee were past the bounds of Limbo quyght: 55
Or else to lose his gyft. They tooke a path that steepe upryght
Rose darke and full of foggye mist. And now they were within
A kenning of the upper earth, when Orphye did begin
To dowt him lest shee followed not, and through an eager love
Desyrous for to see her he his eyes did backward move.   60
Immediatly shee slipped backe. He retching out his hands,

----

25 *strave:* strove   58 *kenning:* sight
44 *tyre:* tear at meat, prey upon; *Grype:*
     vulture

Desyrous to bee caught and for to ketch her grasping stands.
But nothing save the slippry aire (unhappy man) he caught.
Shee dying now the second tyme complaynd of Orphye naught.
For why what had shee to complayne, onlesse it were of love   65
Which made her husband backe agen his eyes uppon her move?
Her last farewell shee spake so soft, that scarce he heard the sound,
And then revolted to the place in which he had her found.
      This double dying of his wife set Orphye in a stound,
      No lesse than him who at the syght of Plutos dreadfull Hound   70
That on the middle necke of three dooth beare an iron cheyne,
Was striken in a sodein feare and could it not restreyne,
Untill the tyme his former shape and nature beeing gone,
His body quyght was overgrowne, and turned into stone.
Or than the foolish Olenus, who on himself did take   75
Anothers fault, and giltlesse needes himself would giltie make,
Togither with his wretched wyfe Lethaea, for whose pryde
They both becomming stones, doo stand even yit on watry Ide.
He would have gone to Hell ageine, and earnest sute did make:
But Charon would not suffer him to passe the Stygian lake.   80
Seven dayes he sate forlorne uppon the bank and never eate
A bit of bread. Care, teares, and thought, and sorrow were his meate
And crying out uppon the Gods of Hell as cruell, hee
Withdrew to lofty Rhodopee and Heme which beaten bee
With Northern wynds. Three tymes the Sunne had passed through the
                                                      sheere   85
And watry signe of Pisces and had finisht full the yeere,
And Orphye (were it that his ill successe hee still did rew,
Or that he vowed so to doo) did utterly eschew
The womankynd. Yit many a one desyrous were to match
With him, but he them with repulse did all alike dispatch.   90
He also taught the Thracian folke a stewes of Males to make
And of the flowring pryme of boayes the pleasure for to take.
      There was a hyll, and on the hyll a verie levell plot,
      Fayre greene with grasse. But as for shade or covert was there not.
As soone as that this Poet borne of Goddes, in that same place   95
Sate downe and toucht his tuned strings, a shadow came apace.
There wanted neyther Chaons tree, nor yit the trees to which
Fresh Phaetons susters turned were, nor Beeche, nor Holme, nor Wich,

---

68 *revolted:* turned back   98 *Wich:* name for various kinds of trees
69 *stound:* state of stupefaction   with pliant branches
91 *stewes:* brothel

Nor gentle Asp, nor wyvelesse Bay, nor lofty Chestnuttree.
Nor Hazle spalt, nor Ash wherof the shafts of speares made bee.   100
Nor knotlesse Firre, nor cheerfull Plane, nor Maple flecked grayne.
Nor Lote, nor Sallow which delights by waters to remayne.
Nor slender twigged Tamarisk, nor Box ay greene of hew.
Nor Figtrees loden with theyr frute of colours browne and blew.
Nor double colourd Myrtletrees. Moreover thither came   105
The wrything Ivye, and the Vyne that runnes uppon a frame,
Elmes clad with Vynes, and Ashes wyld and Pitchtrees blacke as cole,
And full of trees with goodly frute red stryped, Ortyards whole.
And Palmetrees lythe which in reward of conquest men doo beare,
And Pynapple with tufted top and harsh and prickling heare,   110
The tree to Cybele, mother of the Goddes, most deere. For why?
Her minion Atys putting off the shape of man, did dye,
And hardened into this same tree. Among this companee
Was present with a pyked top the Cypresse, now a tree,
Sumtime a boay beloved of the God that with a string   115
Dooth arme his bow, and with a string in tune his Violl bring.
For hallowed to the Nymphes that in the feeldes of Carthye were
There was a goodly myghty Stag whose hornes such bredth did beare,
As that they shadowed all his head. His hornes of gold did shyne,
And downe his brest hung from his necke, a cheyne with jewels fyne. 120
Amid his frunt with prettie strings a tablet beeing tyde,
Did waver as he went: and from his eares on eyther syde
Hung perles of all one growth about his hollow temples bryght.
This goodly Spitter beeing voyd of dread, as having quyght
Forgot his native fearefulnesse, did haunt mens houses, and   125
Would suffer folk (yea though unknowen) to coy him with theyr hand.
But more than unto all folke else he deerer was to thee
O Cyparisse, the fayrest Wyght that ever man did see
In Coea. Thou to pastures, thou to water springs him led,
Thou wreathedst sundry flowres betweene his hornes uppon his hed. 130
Sumtyme a horsman thou his backe for pleasure didst bestryde,
And haltring him with silken bit from place to place didst ryde.
In summer tyme about hygh noone when Titan with his heate
Did make the hollow crabbed cleas of Cancer for to sweate,
Unweeting Cyparissus with a Dart did strike this Hart   135

---

100 *spalt:* brittle
102 *Lote:* lotus; *Sallow:* willow
107 *Pitchtrees:* pitch-pines
121 *tablet:* medallion

124 *Spitter:* young deer
126 *coy:* caress
134 *cleas:* claws

Quyght through. And when that of the wound he saw he must depart,
He purposd for to die himself. What woords of comfort spake
Not Phoebus to him? willing him the matter lyght to take
And not more sorrow for it than was requisite to make.
But still the Lad did sygh and sob, and as his last request   140
Desyred God he myght thenceforth from moorning never rest.
Anon through weeping overmuch his blood was drayned quyght:
His limbes wext greene: his heare which hung upon his forehead
                                                                    whyght
Began to bee a bristled bush: and taking by and by
A stiffnesse, with a sharpened top did face the starrie skye.   145
The God did sigh, and sadly sayd: Myselfe shall moorne for thee,
And thou for others: and ay one in moorning thou shalt bee.
Such wood as this had Orphye drawen about him as among
The herdes of beasts, and flocks of Birds he sate amyds the throng.
And when his thumbe sufficiently had tryed every string,   150
And found that though they severally in sundry sounds did ring,
Yit made they all one Harmonie, he thus began to sing:
      O Muse my mother, frame my song of Jove, for every thing
      Is subject unto royall Jove. Of Jove the heavenly King
I oft have shewed the glorious power. I erst in graver verse   155
The Gyants slayne in Phlaegra feeldes with thunder, did reherse.
But now I neede a meelder style to tell of prettie boyes
That were the derlings of the Gods: and of unlawfull joyes
That burned in the brests of Girles, who for theyr wicked lust
According as they did deserve, receyved penance just.   160
The King of Goddes did burne erewhyle in love of Ganymed
The Phrygian and the thing was found which Jupiter that sted
Had rather bee than that he was. Yit could he not beteeme
The shape of any other Bird than Aegle for to seeme
And so he soring in the ayre with borrowed wings trust up   165
The Trojane boay who still in heaven even yit dooth beare his cup,
And brings him Nectar though against Dame Junos will it bee.
      And thou Amyclys sonne (had not thy heavy destinee
      Abridged thee before thy tyme) hadst also placed beene
By Phoebus in the firmament. How bee it (as is seene)   170
Thou art eternall so farre forth as may bee. For as oft
As watrie Piscis giveth place to Aries that the soft
And gentle springtyde dooth succeede the winter sharp and stowre:

162 *sted:* time   173 *stowre:* fierce, harsh
163 *beteeme:* think fit

So often thou renewest thyself, and on the fayre greene clowre
Doost shoote out flowres. My father bare a speciall love to thee   175
Above all others. So that whyle the God went oft to see
Eurotas and unwalled Spart, he left his noble towne
Of Delphos (which amid the world is situate in renowne)
Without a sovereigne. Neyther Harp nor Bow regarded were.
Unmyndfull of his Godhead he refused not to beare   180
The nets, nor for to hold the hounds, nor as a peynfull mate
To travell over cragged hilles, through which continuall gate
His flames augmented more and more. And now the sunne did stand
Well neere midway beetweene the nyghts last past and next at hand.
They stript themselves and noynted them with oyle of Olyfe fat.   185
And fell to throwing of a Sledge that was ryght huge and flat.
Fyrst Phoebus peysing it did throw it from him with such strength,
As that the weyght drave downe the clouds in flying. And at length
It fell upon substantiall ground, where plainly it did show
As well the cunning as the force of him that did it throw.   190
Immediatly upon desyre himself the sport to trie,
The Spartane lad made haste to take up unadvisedly
The Sledge before it still did lye. But as he was in hand
To catch it, it rebounding up ageinst the hardened land,
Did hit him full upon the face. The God himselfe did looke   195
As pale as did the lad, and up his swounding body tooke.
Now culles he him, now wypes he from the wound the blood away,
Anotherwhyle his fading lyfe he stryves with herbes to stay.
Nought booted Leechcraft. Helplesse was the wound. And like as one
Broosd violet stalkes or Poppie stalkes or Lillies growing on   200
Browne spindles, streight they withering droope with heavy heads and
                                                                                                             are
Not able for to hold them up, but with their tops doo stare
Uppon the ground, so Hyacinth in yeelding of his breath
Chopt downe his head. His necke bereft of strength by meanes of death
Was even a burthen to itself, and downe did loosely wrythe   205
On both his shoulders, now a t'one and now a toother lythe.
Thou faadst away, my Hyacinth, defrauded of the pryme
Of youth (quoth Phoebus) and I see thy wound my heynous cryme.

---

174 *clowre:* sward, grassy ground
181 *peynfull:* painstaking, laborious
182 *gate:* going, course
187 *peysing:* poising, balancing
196 *swounding:* swooning

197 *culles:* embraces
199 *booted:* helped; *Leechcraft:* medical
      science
204 *Chopt:* drooped heavily

Thou art my sorrow and my fault: this hand of myne hath wrought
Thy death: I like a murtherer have to thy grave thee brought.   210
But what have I offended thow? onlesse that to have playd,
Or if that to have loved, an offence it may be sayd.
Would God I render myght my lyfe with and instead of thee.
To which syth fatall destinee denyeth to agree,
Both in my mynd and in my mouth thou evermore shalt bee.   215
My Violl striken with my hand, my songs shall sound of thee,
And in a newmade flowre thou shalt with letters represent
Our syghings. And the tyme shall come ere many yeeres bee spent,
That in thy flowre a valeant Prince shall joyne himself with thee,
And leave his name uppon the leaves for men to reede and see.   220
Whyle Phoebus thus did prophesie, behold the blood of him
Which dyde the grasse, ceast blood to bee, and up there sprang a trim
And goodly flowre, more orient than the Purple cloth ingrayne,
In shape a Lillye, were it not that Lillyes doo remayne
Of sylver colour, whereas theis of purple hew are seene.   225
Although that Phoebus had the cause of this greate honor beene,
Yit thought he not the same ynough. And therfore did he wryght
His syghes uppon the leaves thereof: and so in colour bryght
The flowre hath a ι writ theron, which letters are of greef.
So small the Spartanes thought the birth of Hyacinth repreef   230
Unto them, that they woorship him from that day unto this.
And as their fathers did before, so they doe never misse
With solemne pomp to celebrate his feast from yeere to yeere.
    But if perchaunce that Amathus the rich in mettals, weere
    Demaunded if it would have bred the Propets it would sweare,   235
Yea even as gladly as the folke whose brewes sumtyme did beare
A payre of welked hornes: whereof they Cerastes named are.
Before theyr doore an Altar stood of Jove that takes the care
Of alyents and of travellers, which lothsome was to see,
For lewdnesse wrought theron. If one that had a straunger bee   240
Had lookt thereon, he would have thought there had on it beene killd
Sum sucking calves or lambes. The blood of straungers there was spilld.
Dame Venus sore offended at this wicked sacrifyse,
To leave her Cities and the land of Cyprus did devyse.
But then bethinking her, shee sayd: What hath my pleasant ground,   245

214 *syth:* since   236 *brewes:* brows
223 *orient:* radiant, dawn-red; *ingrayne:*   237 *welked:* twisted
    dyed in grain   239 *alyents:* aliens
230 *repreef:* shame

What have my Cities trespassed? what fault in them is found?
Nay rather let this wicked race by exyle punnisht beene,
Or death, or by sum other thing that is a meane betweene
Both death and exyle. What is that? save only for to chaunge
Theyr shape. In musing with herself what figure were most straunge, 250
Shee cast her eye uppon a horne. And therewithall shee thought
The same to bee a shape ryght meete uppon them to bee brought:
And so shee from theyr myghty limbes theyr native figure tooke,
And turnd them into boystous Bulles with grim and cruell looke.
Yit durst the filthy Propets stand in stiffe opinion that   255
Dame Venus was no Goddesse till shee beeing wroth thereat,
To make theyr bodies common first compelld them everychone
And after chaungd theyr former kynd. For when that shame was gone,
And that they wexed brazen faast, shee turned them to stone,
In which betweene their former shape was diffrence small or none.   260
      Whom forbycause Pygmalion saw to leade theyr lyfe in sin
      Offended with the vice whereof greate store is packt within
The nature of the womankynd, he led a single lyfe.
And long it was ere he could fynd in hart to take a wyfe.
Now in the whyle by wondrous Art an image he did grave   265
Of such proportion, shape, and grace as nature never gave
Nor can to any woman give. In this his worke he tooke
A certaine love. The looke of it was ryght a Maydens looke,
And such a one as that yee would beleeve had lyfe, and that
Would moved bee, if womanhod and reverence letted not: 270
So artificiall was the work. He woondreth at his Art
And of his counterfetted corse conceyveth love in hart.
He often toucht it, feeling if the woork that he had made
Were verie flesh or Ivorye still. Yit could he not perswade
Himself to think it Ivory, for he oftentymes it kist   275
And thought it kissed him ageine. He hild it by the fist,
And talked to it. He beleeved his fingars made a dint
Uppon her flesh, and feared lest sum blacke or broosed print
Should come by touching over hard. Sumtyme with pleasant boords
And wanton toyes he dalyingly dooth cast foorth amorous woords.   280
Sumtime (the giftes wherein yong Maydes are wonted to delyght)
He brought her owches, fyne round stones, and Lillyes fayre and
                                                                                whyght,

270 *letted:* prevented   280 *toyes:* caresses
271 *artificiall:* artistic, skillful   282 *owches:* buckles, brooches
279 *boords:* jests

And pretie singing birds, and flowres of thousand sorts and hew,
In gorgeous garments furthermore he did her also decke,   285
And peynted balles, and Amber from the tree distilled new.
And on her fingars put me rings, and cheynes about her necke.
Riche perles were hanging at her eares, and tablets at her brest.
All kynd of things became her well. And when she was undrest,
She seemed not lesse beawtifull. He layd her in a bed
The which with scarlet dyde in Tyre was richly overspred,   290
And terming her his bedfellow, he couched downe hir head
Uppon a pillow soft, as though shee could have felt the same.
     The feast of Venus hallowed through the Ile of Cyprus, came
     And Bullocks whyght with gilden hornes were slayne for sacrifyse,
And up to heaven of frankincence the smoky fume did ryse.   295
When as Pygmalion having doone his dutye that same day,
Before the altar standing, thus with fearefull hart did say:
If that you Goddes can all things give, then let my wife (I pray)
(He durst not say bee yoon same wench of Ivory, but) bee leeke
My wench of Ivory. Venus (who was nought at all to seeke   300
What such a wish as that did meene) then present at her feast,
For handsell of her freendly helpe did cause three tymes at least
The fyre to kindle and to spyre thryse upward in the ayre.
As soone as he came home, streyghtway Pygmalion did repayre
Unto the Image of his wench, and leaning on the bed,   305
Did kisse hir. In her body streyght a warmenesse seemd to spred.
He put his mouth againe to hers, and on her brest did lay
His hand. The Ivory wexed soft: and putting quyght away
All hardnesse, yeelded underneathe his fingars, as wee see
A peece of wax made soft ageinst the Sunne, or drawen to bee   310
In divers shapes by chaufing it betweene ones handes, and so
To serve to uses. He amazde stood wavering to and fro
Tweene joy, and feare to be beeguyld, ageine he burnt in love,
Ageine with feeling he began his wished hope to prove.
He felt it verrye flesh in deede. By laying on his thumb,   315
He felt her pulses beating. Then he stood no longer dumb
But thanked Venus with his hart, and at the length he layd
His mouth to hers who was as then become a perfect mayd.
Shee felt the kisse, and blusht therat: and lifting fearefully
Hir eyelidds up, hir Lover and the light at once did spye.   320
The mariage that her selfe had made the Goddesse blessed so,

299 *leeke:* like

That when the Moone with fulsum lyght nyne tymes her course had go,
This Ladye was delivered of a Sun that Paphus hyght,
Of whom the Iland takes that name. Of him was borne a knyght
Calld Cinyras who (had he had none issue) surely myght   325
Of all men underneathe the sun beene thought the happyest wyght.
    Of wicked and most cursed things to speake I now commence.
    Yee daughters and yee parents all go get yee farre from hence.
Or if yee mynded bee to heere my tale, beleeve mee nought
In this beehalfe: ne think that such a thing was ever wrought.   330
Or if yee will beeleeve the deede, beleeve the vengeance too
Which lyghted on the partye that the wicked act did doo.
But if that it be possible that any wyght so much
From nature should degenerate, as for to fall to such
A heynous cryme as this is, I am glad for Thracia, I   335
Am glad for this same world of ours, yea glad exceedingly
I am for this my native soyle, for that there is such space
Betweene it and the land that bred a chyld so voyd of grace.
I would the land Panchaya should of Amomie be rich,
And Cinnamom, and Costus sweete, and Incence also which   340
Dooth issue largely out of trees, and other flowers straunge,
As long as that it beareth Myrrhe: not woorth it was the chaunge,
Newe trees to have of such a pryce. The God of love denyes
His weapons to have hurted thee, O Myrrha, and he tryes
Himselfe ungiltie by thy fault. One of the Furies three   345
With poysonde Snakes and hellish brands hath rather blasted thee.
To hate ones father is a cryme as heynous as may bee,
But yit more wicked is this love of thine than any hate.
The youthfull Lordes of all the East and Peeres of cheef estate
Desyre to have thee to their wyfe, and earnest sute doo make.   350
Of all (excepting onely one) thy choyce, O Myrrha, take.
    Shee feeles her filthye love, and stryves ageinst it, and within
    Herself sayd: Whither roonnes my mynd? what thinke I to begin?
Yee Gods (I pray) and godlynesse, yee holy rites and awe
Of parents, from this heynous cryme my vicious mynd withdrawe,   355
And disappoynt my wickednesse. At leastwyse if it bee
A wickednesse that I intend. As farre as I can see,
This love infrindgeth not the bondes of godlynesse a whit.
For every other living wyght dame nature dooth permit

---

322 *fulsum:* full
339 *Amomie:* amomum, an aromatic plant
340 *Costus:* costum, an Oriental aromatic plant
356 *disappoynt:* frustrate

To match without offence of sin. The Heifer thinkes no shame   360
To beare her father on her backe: the horse bestrydes the same
Of whom he is the syre: the Gote dooth bucke the kid that hee
Himself begate: and birdes doo tread the selfsame birdes wee see
Of whom they hatched were before. In happye cace they are
That may doo so without offence. But mans malicious care   365
Hath made a brydle for it self, and spyghtfull lawes restreyne
The things that nature setteth free. Yit are their Realmes (men sayne)
In which the moother with the sonne, and daughter with the father
Doo match, wherethrough of godlynesse the bond augments the rather
With doubled love. Now wo is mee it had not beene my lot   370
In that same countrie to bee borne. And that this lucklesse plot
Should hinder mee. Why thinke I thus? Avaunt, unlawfull love.
I ought to love him, I confesse: but so as dooth behove
His daughter: were not Cinyras my father than, Iwis
I myght obtaine to lye with him. But now bycause he is   375
Myne owne, he cannot bee myne owne. The neerenesse of our kin
Dooth hurt me. Were I further off perchaunce I more myght win.
And if I wist that I therby this wickednesse myght shunne,
I would forsake my native soyle and farre from Cyprus runne.
This evill heate dooth hold mee backe, that beeing present still   380
I may but talke with Cinyras and looke on him my fill,
And touch, and kisse him, if no more may further graunted bee.
Why wicked wench, and canst thou hope for further? doost not see
How by thy fault thou doost confound the ryghts of name and kin?
And wilt thou make thy mother bee a Cucqueane by thy sin?   385
Wilt thou thy fathers leman bee? wilt thou bee both the moother
And suster of thy chyld? shall he bee both thy sonne and brother?
And standst thou not in feare at all of those same susters three
Whose heads with crawling snakes in stead of heare bematted bee?
Which pushing with theyr cruell bronds folks eyes and mouthes, doo
see   390
Theyr sinfull harts? but thou now whyle thy body yit is free,
Let never such a wickednesse once enter in thy mynd.
Defyle not myghtye natures hest by lust ageinst thy kynd.
What though thy will were fully bent? yit even the very thing
Is such as will not suffer thee the same to end to bring.   395
For why he beeing well disposde and godly, myndeth ay

372 *Avaunt:* away   393 *hest:* command
385 *Cucqueane:* female cuckold   396 *For why:* because
386 *leman:* sweetheart

So much his dewtye that from ryght and truth he will not stray.
Would Godlyke furie were in him as is in mee this day.
    This sayd, her father Cinyras (who dowted what to doo
    By reason of the worthy store of suters which did woo   400
His daughter,) bringing all theyr names did will her for to show
On which of them shee had herself most fancie to bestow.
At first shee hild her peace a whyle, and looking wistly on
Her fathers face, did boyle within: and scalding teares anon
Ran downe her visage. Cyniras, (who thought them to proceede   405
Of tender harted shamefastnesse) did say there was no neede
Of teares, and dryed her cheekes, and kist her. Myrrha tooke of it
Exceeding pleasure in her selfe: and when that he did wit
What husband shee did wish to have, shee sayd: One like to yow.
He undertanding not hir thought, did well her woordes allow,   410
And sayd: In this thy godly mynd continew. At the name
Of godlynesse, shee cast mee downe her looke for very shame.
For why her giltie hart did knowe shee well deserved blame.
    Hygh mydnight came, and sleepe bothe care and carkesses opprest.
    But Myrrha lying brode awake could neyther sleepe nor rest.   415
Shee fryes in Cupids flames, and woorkes continewally uppon
Her furious love. One while shee sinkes in deepe despayre. Anon
Shee fully myndes to give attempt, but shame doth hold her in.
Shee wishes and shee wotes not what to doo, nor how to gin.
And like as when a mightye tree with axes heawed rownd,   420
Now redy with a strype or twaine to lye uppon the grownd,
Uncerteine is which way to fall and tottreth every way:
Even so her mynd with dowtfull wound effeebled then did stray
Now heere now there uncerteinely, and tooke of bothe encreace.
No measure of her love was found, no rest, nor yit releace,   425
Save only death. Death likes her best. Shee ryseth, full in mynd
To hang herself. About a post her girdle she doth bynd,
And sayd: Farewell deere Cinyras, and understand the cause
Of this my death. And with that woord about her necke shee drawes
The nooze. Her trustye nurce that in another Chamber lay   430
By fortune heard the whispring sound of theis her woordes (folk say).
The aged woman rysing up unboltes the doore. And whan
Shee saw her in that plyght of death, shee shreeking out began
To smyght her self, and scratcht her brest, and quickly to her ran

---

403 *wistly:* intently, wistfully   419 *gin:* begin
408 *wit:* ask   421 *strype:* blow

And rent the girdle from her necke. Then weeping bitterly   435
And holding her betweene her armes, shee askt the question why
Shee went about to hang her self so unadvisedly.
The Lady hilld her peace as dumb, and looking on the ground
Unmovably, was sorye in her hart for beeing found
Before shee had dispatcht herself. Her nurce still at her lay,   440
And shewing her her emptie dugges and naked head all gray,
Besought her for the paynes shee tooke with her both night and day
In rocking and in feeding her, shee would vouchsafe to say
What ere it were that greeved her. The Ladye turnd away
Displeasde and fetcht a sygh. The nurce was fully bent in mynd   445
To bowlt the matter out: for which not onely shee did bynd
Her fayth, in secret things to keepe: but also sayd, put mee
In truth to fynd a remedye. I am not (thou shalt see)
Yit altogither dulld by age. If furiousenesse it bee,
I have bothe charmes and chaunted herbes to help. If any wyght   450
Bewitcheth thee, by witchcraft I will purge and set thee quyght.
Or if it bee the wrath of God, we shall with sacrifyse
Appease the wrath of God right well. What may I more surmyse?
No theeves have broken in uppon this house and spoyld the welth.
Thy mother and thy father bothe are living and in helth.   455
When Myrrha heard her father naamd, a greevous sygh she fet
Even from the bottom of her hart. Howbee't the nurce as yet
Misdeemd not any wickednesse. But nerethelesse shee gest
There was some love: and standing in one purpose made request
To breake her mynd unto her, and shee set her tenderly   460
Uppon her lappe. The Ladye wept and sobbed bitterly.
Then culling her in feeble armes, shee sayd: I well espye
Thou art in love. My diligence in this behalf I sweare
Shall servisable to thee bee. Thou shalt not neede to feare
That ere thy father shall it knowe. At that same woord shee lept   465
From nurces lappe like one that had beene past her witts, and stept
With fury to her bed. At which shee leaning downe hir face
Sayd: Hence I pray thee: force mee not to shewe my shamefull cace.
And when the nurce did urge her still, shee answered eyther: Get
Thee hence, or ceace to aske mee why myself I thus doo fret.   470
The thing that thou desyrste to knowe is wickednesse. The old
Poore nurce gan quake, and trembling both for age and feare did hold

440 *at her lay:* urged her   451 *quyght:* free
446 *bowlt:* sift   456 *fet:* fetched
450 *chaunted:* enchanted   460 *breake:* reveal

Her handes to her. And kneeling downe right humbly at her feete,
One whyle shee fayre intreated her with gentle woordes and sweete.
Another whyle (onlesse shee made her privie of her sorrow)   475
Shee threatned her, and put her in a feare shee would next morrow
Bewray her how shee went about to hang herself. But if
Shee told her, shee did plyght her fayth and help to her releef.
Shee lifted up her head, and then with teares fast gushing out
Beesloobered all her nurces brest: and going oft about   480
To speake, shee often stayd: and with her garments hid her face
For shame, and lastly sayd: O happye is my moothers cace
That such a husband hath. With that a greevous sygh shee gave,
And hilld her peace. Theis woordes of hers a trembling chilnesse drave
In nurcis limbes, which perst her bones: (for now shee understood   485
The cace) and all her horye heare up stiffly staring stood
And many things she talkt to put away her cursed love,
If that it had beene possible the madnesse to remove.
The Mayd herself to be full trew the councell dooth espye:
Yit if shee may not have her love shee fully myndes to dye.   490
Live still (quoth nurse) thou shalt obteine (shee durst not say thy
                                                              father,
But stayd at that). And forbycause that Myrrha should the rather
Beleeve her, shee confirmd her woordes by othe. The yeerely feast
Of gentle Ceres came, in which the wyves bothe moste and least
Appareld all in whyght are woont the firstlings of the feeld,   495
Fyne garlonds made of eares of corne, to Ceres for to yeeld.
And for the space of thryce three nyghts they counted it a sin
To have the use of any man, or once to towche his skin.
        Among theis women did the Queene freequent the secret rites.
        Now whyle that of his lawfull wyfe his bed was voyd a nightes,   500
The nurce was dooble diligent: and fynding Cinyras
Well washt with wyne, shee did surmyse there was a pretye lasse
In love with him. And hyghly shee her beawty setteth out.
And beeing asked of her yeeres, she sayd shee was about
The age of Myrrha. Well (quoth he) then bring her to my bed.   505
Returning home she sayd: bee glad my nurcechilde: we have sped.
Not all so wholly in her hart was wretched Myrrha glad,
But that her fore misgiving mynd did also make her sad.
Howbee't shee also did rejoyce as in a certaine kynd,

474 *whyle:* time
477 *Bewray:* reveal
486 *staring:* standing on end

502 *surmyse:* imply, pretend
506 *sped:* succeeded

Such discord of affections was within her combred mynd. ⁵¹⁰
   It was the tyme that all things rest. And now Bootes bryght,
   The driver of the Oxen seven, about the northpole pyght
Had sumwhat turnd his wayne asyde, when wicked Myrrha sped
About her buysnesse. Out of heaven the golden Phoebee fled.
With clowds more black than any pitch the starres did hyde their hed. ⁵¹⁵
The nyght beecommeth utter voyd of all her woonted lyght.
And first before all other hid their faces out of syght
Good Icar and Erigonee, his daughter, who for love
Most vertuous to her fatherward, was taken up above
And made a starre in heaven. Three tymes had Myrrha warning given ⁵²⁰
By stumbling, to retyre. Three tymes the deathfull Owle that eeven
With doolefull noyse prognosticates unhappie lucke. Yet came
Shee forward still: the darknesse of the nyght abated shame.
Her left hand held her nurce, her right the darke blynd way did grope.
Anon shee to the chamber came: anon the doore was ope: ⁵²⁵
Anon she entred in. With that her foltring hammes did quake:
Her colour dyde: her blood and hart did cleerly her forsake.
The neerer shee approched to her wickednesse, the more
She trembled: of her enterpryse it irked her full sore:
And fayne shee would shee might unknowen have turned back.
                              Nurce led ⁵³⁰
Her pawsing forward by the hand: and putting her to bed,
Heere, take this Damzell, Cinyras, shee is thine owne, shee sed.
And so shee layd them brest to brest. The wicked father takes
His bowelles into filthy bed, and there with wordes asslakes
The maydens feare, and cheeres her up. And lest this cryme of
                                  theyres ⁵³⁵
Myght want the ryghtfull termes, by chaunce as in respect of yeeres
He daughter did hir call, and shee him father. Beeing sped
With cursed seede in wicked womb, shee left her fathers bed,
Of which soone after shee became greate bagged with her shame.
Next night the lewdnesse doubled. And no end was of the same, ⁵⁴⁰
Untill at length that Cinyras desyrous for to knowe
His lover that so many nyghts uppon him did bestowe,
Did fetch a light: by which he sawe his owne most heynous cryme,
And eeke his daughter. Nathelesse, his sorrow at that time
Represt his speeche. Then hanging by he drew a Rapier bryght. ⁵⁴⁵
Away ran Myrrha, and by meanes of darknesse of the nyght

⁵¹² *pyght:* placed   ⁵³⁹ *greate bagged:* pregnant
⁵³⁴ *bowelles:* offspring; *asslakes:* assuages

Shee was delivered from the death: and straying in the broade
Datebearing feeldes of Arabye, shee through Panchaya yode,
And wandring full nyne moonethes at length shee rested beeing tyrde
In Saba land. And when the tyme was neere at hand expyrde,   550
And that uneath the burthen of her womb shee well could beare,
Not knowing what she might desyre, distrest betweene the feare
Of death, and tediousnesse of lyfe, this prayer shee did make:
O Goddes, if of repentant folk you any mercye take,
Sharpe vengeance I confesse I have deserved, and content   555
I am to take it paciently. How bee it to th'entent
That neyther with my lyfe the quick, nor with my death the dead
Anoyed bee, from both of them exempt mee this same sted,
And altring mee, deny to mee both lyfe and death. We see
To such as doo confesse theyr faults sum mercy shewd to bee.   560
The Goddes did graunt her this request, the last that she should make.
The ground did overgrow hir feete, and ancles as she spake.
And from her bursten toes went rootes, which wrything heere and there
Did fasten so the trunk within the ground shee could not steare.
Her bones did into timber turne, whereof the marie was   565
The pith, and into watrish sappe the blood of her did passe.
Her armes were turnd to greater boughes, her fingars into twig,
Her skin was hardned into bark. And now her belly big
The eatching tree had overgrowen, and overtane her brest,
And hasted for to win her neck, and hyde it with the rest.   570
Shee made no taryence nor delay, but met the comming tree,
And shroonk her face within the barke therof. Although that shee
Togither with her former shape her senses all did loose,
Yit weepeth shee, and from her tree warme droppes doo softly woose.
The which her teares are had in pryce and honour. And the Myrrhe   575
That issueth from her gummy bark dooth beare the name of her,
          And shall doo whyle the world dooth last. The misbegotten chyld
          Grew still within the tree, and from his mothers womb defyld
Sought meanes to bee delyvered. Her burthende womb did swell
Amid the tree, and stretcht her out. But woordes wherwith to tell   580
And utter foorth her greef did want. She had no use of speech
With which Lucina in her throwes shee might of help beseech.
Yit like a woman labring was the tree, and bowwing downe

548 *yode:* went
551 *uneath:* hardly, with difficulty
564 *steare:* stir

565 *marie:* marrow
569 *eatching:* growing
574 *woose:* ooze

Gave often sighes, and shed foorth teares as though shee there should
                                  drowne.
Lucina to this wofull tree came gently downe, and layd   585
Her hand theron, and speaking woordes of ease the midwife playd.
The tree did cranye, and the barke deviding made away,
And yeelded out the chyld alyve, which cryde and wayld streyght way.
The waternymphes uppon the soft sweete hearbes the chyld did lay,
And bathde him with his mothers teares. His face was such as spyght   590
Must needes have praysd. For such he was in all condicions right,
As are the naked Cupids that in tables picturde bee.
But to th'entent he may with them in every poynt agree,
Let eyther him bee furnisshed with wings and quiver light,
Or from the Cupids take theyr wings and bowes and arrowes quight.   595
    Away slippes fleeting tyme unspyde and mocks us to our face,
    And nothing may compare with yeares in swiftnesse of theyr pace.
That wretched imp whom wickedly his graundfather begate,
And whom his cursed suster bare, who hidden was alate
Within the tree, and lately borne, became immediatly   600
The beawtyfullyst babe on whom man ever set his eye.
Anon a stripling hee became, and by and by a man,
And every day more beawtifull than other he becam,
That in the end Dame Venus fell in love with him: wherby
He did revenge the outrage of his mothers villanye.   605
For as the armed Cupid kist Dame Venus, unbeware
An arrow sticking out did raze hir brest uppon the bare.
The Goddesse being wounded, thrust away her sonne. The wound
Appeered not to bee so deepe as afterward was found.
It did deceyve her at the first. The beawty of the lad   610
Nor unto Paphos where the sea beats round about the shore,
Inflaamd her. To Cythera Ile no mynd at all shee had.
Nor fisshy Gnyde, nor Amathus that hath of metalls store.
Yea even from heaven shee did absteyne. Shee lovd Adonis more
Than heaven. To him shee clinged ay, and bare him companye.   615
And in the shadowe woont shee was to rest continually,
And for to set her beawtye out most seemely to the eye
By trimly decking of her self. Through bushy grounds and groves,
And over Hills and Dales, and Lawnds and stony rocks shee roves,
Bare kneed with garment tucked up according to the woont   620

587 *cranye:* open in crannies   619 *Lawnds:* glades, pastures
592 *tables:* boards, pictures

Of Phebe, and shee cheerd the hounds with hallowing like a hunt,
Pursewing game of hurtlesse sort, as Hares made lowe before,
Or stagges with loftye heades, or bucks. But with the sturdy Boare
And ravening woolf, and Bearewhelpes armd with ugly pawes, and eeke
The cruell Lyons which delyght in blood, and slaughter seeke,   625
Shee meddled not. And of theis same shee warned also thee,
Adonis, for to shoonne them, if thou wooldst have warned bee.
Bee bold on cowards (Venus sayd) for whoso dooth advaunce
Himselfe against the bold, may hap to meete with sum mischaunce.
Wherfore I pray thee, my sweete boy, forbeare too bold to bee.   630
For feare thy rashnesse hurt thy self and woork the wo of me
Encounter not the kynd of beastes whom nature armed hath,
For dowt thou buy thy prayse too deere procuring thee sum scath.
Thy tender youth, thy beawty bryght, thy countnance fayre and brave
Although they had the force to win the hart of Venus, have   635
No powre ageinst the Lyons, nor ageinst the bristled swyne.
The eyes and harts of savage beasts doo nought to theis inclyne.
The cruell Boares beare thunder in theyr hooked tushes, and
Exceeding force and feercenesse is in Lyons to withstand.
And sure I hate them at my hart. To him demaunding why,   640
A monstrous chaunce (quoth Venus) I will tell thee by and by,
That hapned for a fault. But now unwoonted toyle hath made
Mee weerye: and beholde, in tyme this Poplar with his shade
Allureth, and the ground for cowch dooth serve to rest uppon.
I prey thee let us rest us here. They sate them downe anon.   645
And lying upward with her head uppon his lappe along,
Shee thus began, and in her tale shee bussed him among:
        Perchaunce thou hast or this tyme heard of one that overcame
        The swiftest men in footemanshippe. No fable was that fame.
She overcame them out of dowt. And hard it is to tell   650
Thee whither she did in footemanshippe or beawty more excell.
Uppon a season as she askt of Phebus, what he was
That should her husband bee, he sayd: For husband doo not passe,
O Atalanta, thou at all of husband hast no neede.
Shonne husbanding. But yit thou canst not shonne it, I thee reede.   655
Alyve thou shalt not be thy self. Shee being sore afrayd
Of this Apollos Oracle, did keepe herself a mayd,

633 *dowt:* fear; *scath:* harm   648 *or:* ere
638 *tushes:* tusks   653 *passe:* care
647 *bussed:* kissed   655 *reede:* tell

And lived in the shady woodes. When wooers to her came,
And were of her importunate, shee drave away the same
With boystous woordes, and with the sore condition of the game. 660
I am not to be had (quoth shee) onlesse yee able bee
In ronning for to vanquish mee. Yee must contend with mee
In footemanshippe. And who so winnes the wager, I agree
To bee his wife. But if that he bee found too slowe, then hee
Shall lose his head. This of your game the verrye law shall bee. 665
Shee was in deede unmercifull. But such is beawties powre,
That though the sayd condition were extreme and over sowre,
Yit many suters were so rash to undertake the same.
Hippomenes as a looker on of this uncurteous game,
Sate by, and sayd: Is any man so mad to seeke a wyfe 670
With such apparant perill and the hazard of his lyfe?
And utterly he did condemne the yongmens love. But when
He saw her face and bodye bare, (for why the Lady then
Did strippe her to her naked skin) the which was like to myne,
Or rather (if that thou wert made a woman) like to thyne: 675
He was amazde. And holding up his hands to heaven, he sayth:
Forgive mee you with whom I found such fault even now: in fayth
I did not know the wager that yee ran for. As hee prayseth
The beawty of her, in himselfe the fyre of love he rayseth.
And through an envy fearing lest shee should away be woonne, 680
He wisht that nere a one of them so swift as shee might roonne.
And wherfore (quoth hee) put not I myself in preace to trye
The fortune of this wager? God himself continually
Dooth help the bold and hardye sort. Now whyle Hippomenes
Debates theis things within himselfe and other like to these, 685
The Damzell ronnes as if her feete were wings. And though that shee
Did fly as swift as arrow from a Turkye bowe: yit hee
More woondred at her beawtye than at swiftnesse of her pace.
Her ronning greatly did augment her beawtye and her grace.
The wynd ay whisking from her feete the labells of her socks 690
Uppon her back as whyght as snowe did tosse her golden locks,
And eeke th'embroydred garters that were tyde beneathe her ham.
A rednesse mixt with whyght uppon her tender bodye cam,
As when a scarlet curtaine streynd ageinst a playstred wall
Dooth cast like shadowe, making it seeme ruddye therwithall. 695
Now whyle he straunger noted this, the race was fully ronne,

682 *preace:* crowd, mêlée, critical situation   690 *labells of her socks:* laces of her sandals

And Atalant (as shee that had the wager cleerely wonne)
Was crowned with a garlond brave. The vanquisht sighing sore,
Did lose theyr lyves according to agreement made before.
Howbeeit nought at all dismayd with theis mennes lucklesse cace   700
He stepped foorth, and looking full uppon the maydens face,
Sayd: Wherfore doost thou seeke renowne in vanquisshing of such
As were but dastards? Cope with mee. If fortune bee so much
My freend to give mee victorie, thou needest not hold scorne
To yeeld to such a noble man as I am. I am borne   705
The sonne of noble Megaree, Onchestyes sonne, and hee
Was sonne to Neptune. Thus am I great graundchyld by degree
In ryght descent, of him that rules the waters. Neyther doo
I out of kynd degenerate from vertue meete therto,
Or if my fortune bee so hard as vanquisht for to bee,   710
Thou shalt obteine a famous name by overcomming mee.
In saying thus, Atlanta cast a gentle looke on him:
And dowting whither shee rather had to lose the day or win,
    Sayd thus: What God, an enmy to the beawtyfull, is bent
        To bring this person to his end, and therefore hath him sent   715
To seeke a wyfe with hazard of his lyfe? If I should bee
Myselfe the judge in this behalfe, there is not sure in mee
That dooth deserve so deerely to bee earned. Neyther dooth
His beawty moove my hart at all. Yit is it such in sooth
As well might moove mee. But bycause as yit a chyld he is,   720
His person mooves mee not so much as dooth his age Iwis.
Beesydes that manhod is in him, and mynd unfrayd of death:
Beesydes that of the watrye race from Neptune as he seth
He is the fowrth: beesydes that he dooth love mee, and dooth make
So great accompt to win mee to his wyfe, that for my sake   725
He is contented for to dye, if fortune bee so sore
Ageinst him to denye him mee. Thou straunger hence therfore.
Away, I say, now whyle thou mayst, and shonne my bloody bed.
My mariage cruell is, and craves the losing of thy hed.
There is no wench but that would such a husband gladly catch.   730
And shee that wyse were myght desyre to meete with such a match.
But why now after heading of so many, doo I care
For thee? Looke thou to that. For sith so many men as are
Alreadye put to slawghter can not warne thee to beeware,
But that thou wilt bee weerye of thy lyfe, dye: doo not spare.   735

721 *Iwis:* certainly   732 *heading:* beheading
725 *accompt:* account

And shall he perrish then bycause he sought to live with mee?
And for his love unwoorthely with death rewarded bee?
All men of such a victory will speake too foule a shame.
But all the world can testifye that I am not to blame.
Would God thou wouldst desist. Or else bycause thou are so mad,   740
I would to God a little more thy feete of swiftnesse had.
Ah what a maydens countenance is in this chyldish face.
Ah, foolish boy Hippomenes, how wretched is thy cace.
I would thou never hadst mee seene. Thou woorthy art of lyfe.
And if so bee I happy were, and that to bee a wyfe   745
The cruell destnyes had not mee forbidden, sure thou art
The onely wyght with whom I would bee matcht with all my hart.
    This spoken: shee yit rawe and but new striken with the dart
    Of Cupid, beeing ignorant, did love and knew it nat.
Anon her father and the folk assembled, willed that   750
They should begin theyr woonted race. Then Neptunes issue prayd
With carefull hart and voyce to mee, and thus devoutly sayd:
O Venus, favour myne attempt, and send mee downe thyne ayd
To compasse my desyred love which thou hast on mee layd.
His prayer movd mee (I confesse,) and long I not delayd   755
Before I helpt him. Now there is a certaine feeld the which
The Cyprian folk call Damasene, most fertile and most rich
Of all the Cyprian feelds: the same was consecrate to mee
In auncient tyme, and of my Church the glebland woont to bee.
Amid this feeld, with golden leaves there growes a goodly tree   760
The crackling boughes whereof are all of yellow gold. I came
And gathered golden Apples three: and bearing thence the same
Within my hand, immediatly to Hippomen I gat
Invisible to all wyghts else save him and taught him what
To doo with them. The Trumpets blew: and girding forward, both   765
Set foorth, and on the hovering dust with nimble feete eche goth.
A man would think they able were uppon the Sea to go
And never wet theyr feete, and on the ayles of corne also
That still is growing in the feeld, and never downe them tread.
The man tooke courage at the showt and woordes of them that sed: 770
Now, now is tyme, Hippomenes, to ply it, hye apace:
Enforce thyself with all thy strength: lag not in any cace:

---

[748] *rawe:* inexperienced
[759] *glebland:* cultivated land, land assigned
    to a church
[763] *gat:* got, came

[765] *girding:* darting
[768] *ayles:* ails, the awn (beards) of corn
[771] *ply it:* exert yourself

Thou shalt obteine. It is a thing ryght dowtfull whither hee
At theis well willing woordes of theyrs rejoysed more, or shee.
O Lord, how often when shee might outstrippe him did shee stay,   775
And gazed long uppon his face, right loth to go her way.
A weerye breath proceeded from theyr parched lippes, and farre
They had to ronne. Then Neptunes imp her swiftnesse to disbarre,
Trolld downe at one side of the way an Apple of the three.
Amazde therat, and covetous of the goodly Apple, shee   780
Did step asyde and snatched up the rolling frute of gold.
With that Hippomenes coted her. The folke that did behold,
Made noyse with clapping of theyr hands. She recompenst her slothe
And losse of tyme with footemanshippe: and streight ageine outgothe
Hippomenes, leaving him behind. And beeing stayd agen   785
With taking up the second, shee him overtooke. And when
The race was almost at an end: He sayd: O Goddesse, thou
That art the author of this gift, assist mee freendly now,
And therwithall, of purpose that she might the longer bee
Askew at one side of the feelde. The Lady seemde to make
In comming, hee with all his might did bowle the last of three   790
A dowt in taking of it up. I forced her to take
It up, and to the Apple I did put a heavy weyght,
And made it of such massinesse shee could not lift it streight.
And lest that I in telling of my tale may longer bee,   795
Than they in ronning of their race, outstripped quight was shee.
And he that wan her, marying her enjoyd her for his fee.
    Thinkst thou I was not woorthy thanks, Adonis, thinkest thow
    I earned not that he to mee should frankincence allow?
But he forgetfull neyther thanks nor frankincence did give.   800
By meanes whereof to sooden wrath he justly did me drive.
For beeing greeved with the spyght, bycause I would not bee
Despysd of such as were to come, I thought it best for mee
To take such vengeance of them both as others might take heede
By them. And so ageinst them both in anger I proceede.   805
A temple of the mother of the Goddes that vowwed was
And buylded by Echion in a darksome grove, they passe.
There through my might Hippomenes was toucht and stirred so,
That needes he would to Venerie though out of season go.
Not farre from this same temple was with little light a den   810
With pommye vawlted naturally, long consecrate ere then

779 *Trolld:* rolled   811 *pommye:* pumice
782 *coted:* passed

For old religion, not unlike a cave: wher priests of yore
Bestowed had of Images of wooden Goddes good store.
Hippomenes entring herinto defyld the holy place,
With his unlawfull lust: from which the Idolls turnd theyr face.   815
And Cybell with the towred toppes disdeyning, dowted whither
Shee in the lake of Styx might drowne the wicked folk togither.
The pennance seemed over lyght. And therefore shee did cawse
Thinne yellow manes to growe uppon theyr necks: and hooked pawes
In stead of fingars to succeede. Theyr shoulders were the same   820
They were before: with woondrous force deepe brested they became.
Theyr looke beecame feerce, cruell, grim, and sowre: a tufted tayle
Stretcht out in length farre after them upon the ground dooth trayle.
In stead of speech they rore: in stead of bed they haunt the wood:
And dreadful unto others they for all theyr cruell moode   825
With tamed teeth chank Cybells bitts in shape of Lyons. Shonne
Theis beastes deere hart: and not from theis alonely see thou ronne,
But also from eche other beast that turnes not backe to flight
But offreth with his boystows brest to try the chaunce of fyght:
Lest that thyne overhardinesse bee hurtfull to us both.   830
    This warning given, with yoked swannes away through aire she
                                                                    goth.
But manhod by admonishment restreyned could not bee.
By chaunce his hounds in following of the tracke, a Boare did see,
And rowsed him. And as the swyne was comming from the wood,
Adonis hit him with a dart askew, and drew the blood.   835
The Boare streyght with his hooked groyne the hunting staffe out drew
Bestayned with his blood, and on Adonis did pursew.
Who trembling and retyring back, to place of refuge drew.
And hyding in his codds his tuskes as farre as he could thrust
He layd him all along for dead uppon the yellow dust.   840
Dame Venus in her chariot drawen with swannes was scarce arrived
At Cyprus, when shee knew afarre the sygh of him depryved
Of lyfe. Shee turnd her Cygnets backe and when shee from the skye
Beehilld him dead, and in his blood beweltred for to lye:
Shee leaped downe, and tare at once hir garments from her brist,   845
And rent her heare, and beate upon her stomack with her fist,
And blaming sore the destnyes, sayd: Yit shall they not obteine
Their will in all things. Of my greefe remembrance shall remayne
(Adonis) whyle the world doth last. From yeere to yeere shall growe

826 *chank:* champ   836 *groyne:* snout
829 *boystows:* boisterous, violent   839 *codds:* testicles

A thing that of my heavinesse and of thy death shall showe 850
The lively likenesse. In a flowre thy blood I will bestowe.
Hadst thou the powre, Persephonee, rank sented Mints to make
Of womens limbes? and may not I lyke powre upon mee take
Without disdeine and spyght, to turne Adonis to a flowre?
This sed, shee sprinckled Nectar on the blood, which through the
powre 855
Therof did swell like bubbles sheere that ryse in weather cleere
On water. And before that full an howre expyred weere,
Of all one colour with the blood a flowre she there did fynd
Even like the flowre of that same tree whose frute in tender rynde
Have pleasant graynes inclosde. Howbee't the use of them is short. 860
For why the leaves do hang so looce through lightnesse in such sort,
As that the windes that all things perce, with every little blast
Doo shake them off and shed them so as that they cannot last.

FINIS DECIMI LIBRI.

◙◙◙

THE. XI. BOOKE OF

OVIDS METAMORPHOSIS.

[Orpheus and the Thracian Women. Midas. Peleus and Thetis. Daedalion. Ceyx and Alcyone.]

Now whyle the Thracian Poet with this song delyghts the mynds
Of savage beastes, and drawes both stones and trees ageynst their
                                               kynds,
Behold the wyves of Ciconie with red deer skinnes about
Their furious brists as in the feeld they gadded on a rout,
Espyde him from a hillocks toppe still singing to his harp.   5
Of whom one shooke her head at him, and thus began to carp:
Behold (sayes shee) behold yoon same is he that doth disdeine
Us women. And with that same woord shee sent her lawnce amayne
At Orphyes singing mouth. The Lawnce armd round about with leaves,
Did hit him, and without a wound a marke behynd it leaves.   10
Another threw a stone at him, which vanquisht with his sweete
And most melodius harmonye, fell humbly at his feete
As sorye for the furious act it purposed. But rash
And heady ryot out of frame all reason now did dash,
And frantik outrage reigned. Yit had the sweetenesse of his song   15
Appeasd all weapons, saving that the noyse now growing strong
With blowing shalmes, and beating drummes, and bedlem howling out,
And clapping hands on every syde by Bacchus drunken rout,
Did drowne the sownd of Orphyes harp. Then first of all stones were
Made ruddy with the prophets blood, and could not give him eare.   20
And first the flocke of Bacchus froes by violence brake the ring

2 *kynds:* natures
4 *rout:* riotous excursion
6 *carp:* complain, attack verbally
8 *amayne:* with full force

14 *frame:* order, control
17 *shalmes:* shawms, oboe-like instruments
21 *froes:* women

Of Serpents, birds, and savage beastes that for to heere him sing
Sate gazing round about him there. And then with bluddy hands
They ran uppon the prophet who among them singing stands.
They flockt about him like as when a sort of birds have found   25
An Owle a daytymes in a tod: and hem him in full round,
As when a Stag by hungrye hownds is in a morning found,
The which forestall him round about and pull him to the ground.
Even so the prophet they assayle, and throwe their Thyrses greene
At him, which for another use than that invented beene.   30
Sum cast mee clods, sum boughes of trees, and sum threw stones. And
                                                                 lest
That weapons wherwithall to wreake theyr woodnesse which increast
Should want, it chaunst that Oxen by were tilling of the ground
And labring men with brawned armes not farre fro thence were found
A digging of the hardned earth, and earning of theyr food,   35
With sweating browes. They seeing this same rout, no longer stood,
But ran away and left theyr tooles behynd them. Every where
Through all the feeld theyr mattocks, rakes, and shovells scattred were.
Which when the cruell feends had caught, and had asunder rent
The horned Oxen, backe ageine to Orphy ward they went,   40
And (wicked wights) they murthred him, who never till that howre
Did utter woordes in vaine, nor sing without effectuall powre.
And through that mouth of his (oh lord) which even the stones had
                                                                 heard,
And unto which the witlesse beastes had often given regard,
His ghost then breathing into aire, departed. Even the fowles   45
Were sad for Orphye, and the beast with sorye syghing howles:
The rugged stones did moorne for him, the woods which many a tyme
Had followed him to heere him sing, bewayled this same cryme.
Yea even the trees lamenting him did cast theyr leavy heare.
The rivers also with theyr teares (men say) encreased were.   50
Yea and the Nymphes of brookes and woods uppon theyr streames
                                                              did sayle
With scattred heare about theyr eares, in boats with sable sayle.
His members lay in sundrie steds. His head and harp both cam
To Hebrus, and (a woondrous thing) as downe the streame they swam,
His Harp did yeeld a moorning sound: his livelesse toong did make   55

26 *tod:* clump, cluster (of ivy, etc.)   32 *wreake:* give vent to; *woodnesse:* mad-
29 *Thyrses:* thyrsi, decorated staffs associ-   ness, fury
    ated with Dionysius. Cf IV, 8.   53 *steds:* places

A certeine lamentable noyse as though it still yit spake,
And bothe the banks in moorning wyse made answer to the same.
At length adowne theyr country streame to open sea they came,
And lyghted on Methymnye shore in Lesbos land. And there
No sooner on the forreine coast now cast aland they were,
But that a cruell naturde Snake did streyght uppon them fly,
And licking on his ruffled heare the which was dropping drye,
Did gape to tyre uppon those lippes that had beene woont to sing
Most heavenly hymnes. But Phebus streyght preventing that same
                                                    thing,
Dispoynts the Serpent of his bit, and turnes him into stone
With gaping chappes. Already was the Ghost of Orphye gone
To Plutos realme, and there he all the places eft beehild
The which he heretofore had seene. And as he sought the feeld
Of fayre Elysion (where the soules of godly folk doo woonne,)
He found his wyfe Eurydicee, to whom he streyght did roonne,
And hilld her in imbracing armes. There now he one while walks
Togither with hir cheeke by cheeke: another while he stalks
Before her, and another whyle he followeth her. And now
Without all kinde of forfeyture he saufly myght avow
His looking backward at his wyfe. But Bacchus greeved at
The murther of the Chapleine of his Orgies, suffred not
The mischeef unrevengd to bee. For by and by he bound
The Thracian women by the feete with writhen roote in ground,
As many as consenting to this wicked act were found.
And looke how much that eche of them the prophet did pursew,
So much he sharpening of their toes, within the ground them drew.
And as the bird that fynds her legs besnarled in the net
The which the fowlers suttletye hathe clocely for her set,
And feeles shee cannot get away, stands flickering with her wings,
And with her fearefull leaping up drawes clocer still the strings:
So eche of theis when in the ground they fastned were, assayd
Aflayghted for to fly away. But every one was stayd
With winding roote which hilld her downe. Her frisking could not
                                                    boote.
And whyle she lookte what was become of Toe, of nayle, and foote,
Shee sawe her leggs growe round in one, and turning into woode.

60

65

70

75

80

85

90

---

63 *tyre:* feed on, tear   71 *while:* time
65 *Dispoynts:* disappoints   78 *writhen:* twisted
67 *eft:* again   87 *Aflayghted:* frightened
69 *woonne:* dwell   88 *boote:* help

And as her thyghes with violent hand shee sadly striking stoode,
Shee felt them tree: her brest was tree: her shoulders eeke were tree.
Her armes long boughes yee myght have thought, and not deceyved bee.
    But Bacchus was not so content: he quyght forsooke their land:
    And with a better companye removed out of hand   95
Unto the Vyneyarde of his owne mount Tmolus, and the river
Pactolus though as yit no streames of gold it did deliver,
Ne spyghted was for precious sands. His olde accustomd rout
Of woodwards and of franticke froes envyrond him about.
But old Silenus was away. The Phrygian ploughmen found   100
Him reeling bothe for droonkennesse and age, and brought him bound
With garlands unto Midas, king of Phrygia, unto whom
The Thracian Orphye and the preest Eumolphus comming from
The towne of Athens erst had taught the Orgies. When he knew
His fellowe and companion of the selfesame badge and crew,   105
Uppon the comming of this guest, he kept a feast the space
Of twyce fyve dayes and twyce fyve nyghts togither in that place.
And now th'eleventh tyme Lucifer had mustred in the sky
The heavenly host, when Midas commes to Lydia jocundly
And yeeldes the old Silenus to his fosterchyld. He, glad   110
That he his fosterfather had eftsoones recovered, bad
King Midas ask him what he would. Right glad of that was hee,
But not a whit at latter end the better should he bee.
He minding to misuse his giftes, sayd: Graunt that all and some
The which my body towcheth bare may yellow gold become.   115
God Bacchus graunting his request, his hurtfull gift performd,
And that he had not better wisht he in his stomacke stormd.
    Rejoycing in his harme away full merye goes the king:
    And for to try his promis true he towcheth every thing.
Scarce giving credit to himself, he pulled yoong greene twiggs   120
From off an Holmetree: by and by all golden were the spriggs.
He tooke a flintstone from the ground, the stone likewyse became
Pure gold. He towched next a clod of earth, and streight the same
By force of towching did become a wedge of yellow gold.
He gathered eares of rypened corne: immediatly beholde   125
The corne was gold. An Apple then he pulled from a tree:
Yee would have thought the Hesperids had given it him. If hee
On Pillars high his fingars layd, they glistred like the sonne.
The water where he washt his hands did from his hands so ronne,

As Danae might have beene therwith beguyld. He scarce could hold ¹³⁰
His passing joyes within his hart, for making all things gold.
Whyle he thus joyd, his officers did spred the boord anon,
And set downe sundry sorts of meate and mancheate theruppon.
Then whither his hand did towch the bread, the bread was massy gold:
Or whither he chawde with hungry teeth his meate, yee might behold ¹³⁵
The peece of meate betweene his jawes a plat of gold to bee.
In drinking wine and water mixt, yee myght discerne and see
The liquid gold ronne downe his throte. Amazed at the straunge
Mischaunce, and being both a wretch and rich, he wisht to chaunge
His riches for his former state, and now he did abhorre ¹⁴⁰
The thing which even but late before he cheefly longed for.
No meate his hunger slakes: his throte is shrunken up with thurst:
And justly dooth his hatefull gold torment him as accurst.
Then lifting up his sory armes and handes to heaven, he cryde:
O father Bacchus, pardon mee. My sinne I will not hyde. ¹⁴⁵
Have mercy, I beseech thee, and vouchsauf to rid mee quyght
From this same harme that seemes so good and glorious unto syght.
The gentle Bacchus streight uppon confession of his cryme
Restored Midas to the state hee had in former tyme.
And having made performance of his promis, hee beereft him ¹⁵⁰
The gift that he had graunted him. And lest he should have left him
Beedawbed with the dregges of that same gold which wickedly
Hee wished had, he willed him to get him by and by
To that great ryver which dooth ronne by Sardis towne, and there
Along the chanell up the streame his open armes to beare ¹⁵⁵
Untill he commeth to the spring: and then his head to put
Full underneathe the foming spowt where greatest was the gut,
And so in washing of his limbes to wash away his cryme.
The king (as was commaunded him) ageinst the streame did clyme.
And streyght the powre of making gold departing quyght from him, ¹⁶⁰
Infects the ryver, making it with golden streame to swim.
The force whereof the bankes about so soked in theyr veynes,
That even as yit the yellow gold uppon the cloddes remaynes.
    Then Midas, hating riches, haunts the pasturegrounds and groves,
    And up and down with Pan among the Lawnds and mountaines
                                                    roves. ¹⁶⁵
But still a head more fat than wyse, and doltish wit he hath,

¹³¹ *passing:* surpassing   ¹⁵⁷ *gut:* channel
¹³³ *mancheate:* fine bread   ¹⁶⁵ *Lawnds:* glades, pastures
¹³⁶ *plat:* flat piece

The which as erst, yit once againe must woork theyr mayster scath.
The mountayne Tmole from loftye toppe to seaward looketh downe,
And spreading farre his boorely sydes, extendeth to the towne
Of Sardis with the t'one syde and to Hypep with the tother.   170
There Pan among the fayrye elves that dawnced round togither
In setting of his conning out for singing and for play
Uppon his pype of reedes and wax, presuming for to say
Apollos musick was not like to his, did take in hand
A farre unequall match, wherof the Tmole for judge should stand.   175
The auncient judge sitts downe uppon his hill, and ridds his eares
From trees, and onely on his head an Oken garlond weares,
Wherof the Acornes dangled downe about his hollow brow.
And looking on the God of neate he sayd: Yee neede not now
To tarry longer for your judge. Then Pan blew lowd and strong   180
His country pype of reedes, and with his rude and homely song
Delighted Midas eares, for he by chaunce was in the throng.
When Pan had doone, the sacred Tmole to Phebus turnd his looke,
And with the turning of his head his busshye heare he shooke.
Then Phebus with a crowne of Bay upon his golden heare   185
Did sweepe the ground with scarlet robe. In left hand he did beare
His viol made of precious stones and Ivorye intermixt.
And in his right hand for to strike, his bowe was redy fixt.
He was the verrye paterne of a good Musician ryght
Anon he gan with conning hand the tuned strings to smyght.   190
The sweetenesse of the which did so the judge of them delyght,
That Pan was willed for to put his Reedepype in his cace,
And not to fiddle nor to sing where viols were in place.
     The judgement of the holy hill was lyked well of all,
     Save Midas, who found fault therwith and wrongfull did it call. 195
Apollo could not suffer well his foolish eares to keepe
Theyr humaine shape, but drew them wyde, and made them long
                                                    and deepe.
And filld them full of whytish heares, and made them downe to sag,
And through too much unstablenesse continually to wag.
His body keeping in the rest his manly figure still,   200
Was ponnisht in the part that did offend for want of skill.
And so a slowe paaste Asses eares his heade did after beare.
This shame endevereth he to hyde. And therefore he did weare

167 *scath:* harm   179 *neate:* cattle
169 *boorely:* burly, sturdy, stately 202 *paaste:* paced

A purple nyghtcappe ever since. But yit his Barber who
Was woont to notte him spyed it: and beeing eager to   205
Disclose it, when he neyther durst to utter it, nor could
It keepe in secret still, he went and digged up the mowld,
And whispring softly in the pit, declaard what eares hee spyde
His mayster have, and turning downe the clowre ageine, did hyde
His blabbed woordes within the ground, and closing up the pit   210
Departed thence and never made mo woordes at all of it.
Soone after, there began a tuft of quivering reedes to growe
Which beeing rype bewrayd theyr seede and him that did them sowe.
For when the gentle sowtherne wynd did lyghtly on them blowe,
They uttred foorth the woordes that had beene buried in the ground   215
And so reprovde the Asses eares of Midas with theyr sound.
        Apollo after this revenge from Tmolus tooke his flyght:
        And sweeping through the ayre, did on the selfsame syde alyght
Of Hellespontus, in the Realme of king Laomedon.
There stoode uppon the right syde of Sigaeum, and uppon   220
The left of Rhetye cliffe that tyme, an Altar buylt of old
To Jove that heereth all mennes woordes. Heere Phebus did behold
The foresayd king Laomedon beginning for to lay
Foundation of the walles of Troy: which woork from day to day
Went hard and slowly forward, and requyrd no little charge,   225
Then he togither with the God that rules the surges large,
Did put themselves in shape of men, and bargaynd with the king
Of Phrygia for a summe of gold his woork to end to bring.
Now when the woork was done, the king theyr wages them denayd,
And falsly faaste them downe with othes it was not as they sayd.   230
Thou shalt not mock us unrevendgd (quoth Neptune). And anon
He caused all the surges of the sea to rush uppon
The shore of covetous Troy, and made the countrye like the deepe.
The goodes of all the husbandmen away he quight did sweepe,
And overwhelmd theyr feeldes with waves. And thinking this too
                                                        small   235
A pennance for the falsehod, he demaunded therwithall
His daughter for a monster of the Sea. Whom beeing bound
Untoo a rocke, stout Hercules delivering saufe and sound,
Requyrd his steeds which were the hyre for which he did compound.
And when that of so great desert the king denyde the hyre.   240

205 *notte*: not, cut short   229 *denayd*: denied
209 *clowre*: sward, grassy ground   230 *faaste*: faced
213 *bewrayd*: revealed

The twyce forsworne false towne of Troy he sacked in his ire.
And Telamon in honour of his service did enjoy.
The Lady Hesion, daughter of the covetous king of Troy.
For Peleus had already got a Goddesse to his wife,
And lived unto both theyr joyes a right renowmed lyfe.   245
And sure he was not prowder of his graundsyre, than of thee
That wert become his fathrinlaw. For many mo than hee
Have had the hap of mighty Jove the nephewes for to bee.
But never was it heeretofore the chaunce of any one
To have a Goddesse to his wyfe, save only his alone.   250
For unto watry Thetis thus old Protew did foretell:
Go marry: thou shalt beare a sonne whose dooings shall excell
His fathers farre in feates of armes, and greater he shall bee
In honour, high renowme, and fame, than ever erst was hee.
This caused Jove the watry bed of Thetis to forbeare   255
Although his hart were more than warme with love of her, for feare
The world sum other greater thing than Jove himself should breede,
And willd the sonne of Aeacus this Peleus to succeede
In that which he himself would faine have done, and for to take
The Lady of the sea in armes a mother her to make.   260
        There is a bay of Thessaly that bendeth lyke a boawe.
        The sydes shoote foorth, where if the sea of any depth did flowe
It were a haven. Scarcely dooth the water hyde the sand.
It hath a shore so firme, that if a man theron doo stand,
No print of foote remaynes behynd: it hindreth not ones pace,   265
Ne covered is with hovering reeke. Adjoyning to this place,
There is a grove of Myrtletrees with frute of dowle colour,
And in the midds thereof a Cave. I can not tell you whither
That nature or the art of man were maker of the same.
It seemed rather made by arte. Oft Thetis hither came   270
Starke naked, ryding bravely on a brydled Dolphins backe.
There Peleus as shee lay asleepe uppon her often bracke.
And forbycause that at her handes entreatance nothing winnes,
He folding her about the necke with both his armes, beginnes
To offer force. And surely if shee had not falne to wyles   275
And shifted oftentymes her shape, he had obteind erewhyles.
But shee became sumtymes a bird: he hilld her like a bird.
Anon shee was a massye log: but Peleus never stird
A whit for that. Then thirdly shee of speckled Tyger tooke

266 *reeke:* wrack, seaweed   272 *bracke:* burst
267 *dowle:* double   277 *hilld:* held

The ugly shape: for feare of whose most feerce and cruell looke,   280
His armes he from her body twicht. And at his going thence,
In honour of the watry Goddes he burned frankincence,
And powred wyne uppon the sea, with fat of neate and sheepe:
Untill the prophet that dooth dwell within Carpathian deepe,
Sayd thus: Thou sonne of Aeacus, thy wish thou sure shalt have   285
Alonely when shee lyes asleepe within her pleasant Cave,
Cast grinnes to trappe her unbewares: hold fast with snarling knot:
And though shee fayne a hundreth shapes, deceyve thee let her not.
But sticke unto't what ere it bee, untill the tyme that shee
Returneth to the native shape shee erst was woont to bee.   290
When Protew thus had sed, within the sea he duckt his head,
And suffred on his latter woordes the water for to spred.
The lyghtsum Titan downeward drew, and with declyning chayre
Approched to the westerne sea, when Neryes daughter fayre
Returning from the sea, resorts to her accustomd cowch.   295
And Peleus scarcely had begon hir naked limbes to towch,
But that shee chaungd from shape to shape, untill at length shee found
Herself surprysd. Then stretching out her armes with sighes profound,
She sayd: Thou overcommest mee, and not without the ayd
Of God. And then she, Thetis like, appeerd in shape of mayd.   300
The noble prince imbracing her obteynd her at his will,
To both theyr joyes, and with the great Achylles did her fill.
      A happye wyght was Peleus in his wyfe: a happy wyght
      Was Peleus also in his sonne. And if yee him acquight
Of murthring Phocus, happy him in all things count yee myght.   305
But giltye of his brothers blood, and bannisht for the same
From bothe his fathers house and Realme, to Trachin sad he came.
The sonne of lyghtsum Lucifer, king Ceyx (who in face
Exprest the lively beawtye of his fathers heavenly grace,)
Without all violent rigor and sharpe executions reignd   310
In Trachin. He right sad that tyme unlike himself, remaynd
Yit moorning for his brothers chaunce transformed late before.
When Peleus thither came, with care and travayle tyred sore,
He left his cattell and his sheepe (whereof he brought great store)
Behynd him in a shady vale not farre from Trachin towne,   315
And with a little companye himself went thither downe.
Assoone as leave to come to Court was graunted him, he bare
A braunche of Olyf in his hand, and humbly did declare
His name and lynage. Onely of his crime no woord hee spake,

287 *grinnes:* snares, nooses   293 *lyghtsum:* bright; *chayre:* chariot

But of his flyght another cause pretensedly did make: 320
Desyring leave within his towne or countrye to abyde.
The king of Trachin gently thus to him ageine replyde:
Our bownty to the meanest sort (O Peleus) dooth extend:
Wee are not woont the desolate our countrye to forfend.
And though I bee of nature most inclyned good to doo: 325
Thyne owne renowme, thy graundsyre Jove are forcements thereunto.
Misspend no longer tyme in sute. I gladly doo agree
To graunt thee what thou wilt desyre. Theis things that thou doost see
I would thou should account them as thyne owne, such as they bee
I would they better were. With that he weeped. Peleus and   330
His freends desyred of his greef the cause to understand.
          He answerd thus: Perchaunce yee think this bird that lives by pray
          And putts all other birds in feare had wings and fethers ay.
He was a man. And as he was right feerce in feats of armes,
And stout and readye bothe to wreake and also offer harmes: 335
So was he of a constant mynd. Daedalion men him hyght.
Our father was that noble starre that brings the morning bryght,
And in the welkin last of all gives place to Phebus lyght.
My study was to maynteine peace, in peace was my delyght,
And for to keepe mee true to her to whom my fayth is plyght.   340
My brother had felicite in warre and bloody fyght.
His prowesse and his force which now dooth chase in cruell flyght
The Dooves of Thisbye since his shape was altred thus anew,
Ryght puyssant Princes and theyr Realmes did heeretofore subdew.
He had a chyld calld Chyone, whom nature did endew   345
With beawtye so, that when to age of fowreteene yeeres shee grew,
A thousand Princes liking her did for hir favour sew.
By fortune as bryght Phebus and the sonne of Lady May
Came t'one from Delphos, toother from mount Cyllen, by the way
They saw her bothe at once, and bothe at once were tane in love.   350
Apollo till the tyme of nyght differd his sute to move.
But Hermes could not beare delay. He stroked on the face
The mayden with his charmed rod which hath the powre to chace
And bring in sleepe: the touch whereof did cast her in so dead
A sleepe, that Hermes by and by his purpose of her sped.   355
As soone as nyght with twinckling starres the welkin had beesprent,
Apollo in an old wyves shape to Chyon clocely went,

324 *forfend:* forbid   336 *hyght:* called
335 *wreake:* avenge   356 *beesprent:* sprinkled, scattered

And tooke the pleasure which the sonne of Maya had forehent.
Now when shee full her tyme had gone, shee bare by Mercurye
A sonne that hyght Awtolychus, who provde a wyly pye, 360
And such a fellow as in theft and filching had no peere.
He was his fathers owne sonne right: he could mennes eyes so bleere,
As for to make the black things whyght, and whyght things black
appeere.

And by Apollo (for shee bare a payre) was borne his brother
Philammon, who in musick arte excelled farre all other, 365
As well in singing as in play. But what avayled it
To beare such twinnes, and of two Goddes in favour to have sit?
And that shee to her father had a stowt and valeant knight,
Or that her graundsyre was the sonne of Jove that God of might?
Dooth glorie hurt to any folk? It surely hurted her. 370
For standing in her owne conceyt shee did herself prefer
Before Diana, and dispraysd her face, who there with all
Inflaamd with wrath, sayd: Well, with deedes we better please her shall.
Immediatly shee bent her bowe, and let an arrow go,
Which strake her through the toong, whose spight deserved
wounding so. 375
Her toong wext dumb, her speech gan fayle that erst was over ryfe,
And as shee stryved for to speake, away went blood and lyfe.
How wretched was I then, O God? how strake it to my hart?
What woordes of comfort did I speake to ease my brothers smart?
To which he gave his eare as much as dooth the stony rocke 380
To hideous roring of the waves that doo against it knocke.
There was no measure nor none ende in making of his mone,
Nor in bewayling comfortlesse his daughter that was gone.
But when he sawe her bodye burne, fowre tymes with all his myght
He russhed foorth to thrust himself amid the fyre in spyght. 385
Fowre tymes hee beeing thence repulst, did put himself to flyght.
And ran mee wheras was no way, as dooth a Bullocke when
A hornet stings him in the necke. Mee thought hee was as then
More wyghter farre than any man. Yee would have thought his feete
Had had sum wings. So fled he quyght from all, and being fleete 390
Through eagernesse to dye, he gat to mount Parnasos knappe
And there Apollo pitying him and rewing his missehappe,

358 *forehent:* taken beforehand   389 *wyghter:* swifter
360 *pye:* magpie, thief   391 *knappe:* summit
362 *eyes . . . bleere:* hoodwink

When as Daedalion from the cliffe himself had headlong floong,
Transformd him to a bird, and on the soodaine as hee hung
Did give him wings, and bowwing beake, and hooked talants keene,   395
And eeke a courage full as feerce as ever it had beene.
And furthermore a greater strength he lent him therwithall,
Than one would thinke conveyd myght bee within a roome so small.
And now in shape of Gossehawke hee to none indifferent is,
But wreakes his teene on all birds. And bycause him selfe ere this   400
Did feele the force of sorrowes sting within his wounded hart,
Hee maketh others oftentymes to sorrow and to smart.
      As Caeyx of his brothers chaunce this wondrous story seth,
      Commes ronning thither all in haste and almost out of breth
Anaetor the Phocayan who was Pelyes herdman. Hee   405
Sayd: Pelye Pelye, I doo bring sad tydings unto thee.
Declare it man (quoth Peleus) what ever that it bee.
King Ceyx at his fearefull woordes did stand in dowtfull stowne.
This noonetyde (quoth the herdman) Iche did drive your cattell downe
To zea, and zum a them did zit uppon the yellow zand   410
And looked on the large mayne poole of water neere at hand.
Zum roayled zoftly up and downe, and zum a them did zwim
And bare their jolly horned heades aboove the water trim.
A Church stondes neere the zea not deckt with gold nor marble stone
But made of wood, and hid with trees that dreeping hang theron.   415
A visherman that zat and dryde hiz netts uppo the zhore
Did tell'z that Nereus and his Nymphes did haunt the place of yore,
And how that thay beene Goddes a zea. There butts a plot vorgrowne
With zallow trees uppon the zame, the which is overblowne
With tydes, and is a marsh. From thence a woolf, an orped wyght,   420
With hideous noyse of rustling made the groundes neere hand afryght.
Anon he commes mee buskling out bezmeared all his chappes
With blood daubaken and with vome as veerce as thunder clappes.
Hiz eyen did glaster red as vyre, and though he raged zore
Vor vamin and vor madnesse bothe, yit raged he much more   425
In madnesse. Vor hee cared not his hunger vor to zlake,
Or i'the death of oxen twoo or three an end to make.

---

395 *bowwing:* curving
400 *wreakes:* vents; *teene:* grief, rage
408 *stowne:* stupefaction
409 *Iche:* I
410 *zea, zum, zit:* sea, some, sit. In this
passage of rustic dialect, *s*'s change to
z's, *f*'s to *v*'s (vorgrowne, vrom). Cf.
II, 869 ff.

412 *roayled:* wandered
415 *dreeping:* drooping
420 *orped:* fierce
422 *buskling:* prowling
423 *daubaken:* smeared, caked
424 *glaster:* glitter

But wounded all the herd and made a havocke of them all,
And zum of us too, in devence did happen vor to vall,
In daunger of his deadly chappes, and lost our lyves. The zhore   430
And zea is staynd with blood, and all the ven is on a rore.
Delay breedes losse. The cace denyes now dowting vor to stond,
Whyle owght remaynes let all of us take weapon in our hond.
Let's arme our zelves, and let uz altogither on him vall.
    The herdman hilld his peace. The losse movde Peleus not at all.   435
    But calling his offence to mynde, he thought that Neryes daughter,
The chyldlesse Ladye Psamathe, determynd with that slaughter
To keepe an Obit to her sonne whom hee before had killd.
Immediatly uppon this newes the king of Trachin willd
His men to arme them, and to take their weapons in theyr hand,   440
And he addrest himself to bee the leader of the band.
His wyfe, Alcyone, by the noyse admonisht of the same,
In dressing of her head, before shee had it brought in frame,
Cast downe her heare, and ronning foorth caught Ceyx fast about
The necke, desyring him with teares to send his folk without   445
Himself, and in the lyfe of him to save the lyves of twayne.
O Princesse, cease your godly feare (quoth Peleus then agayne).
Your offer dooth deserve great thanks. I mynd not warre to make
Ageinst straunge monsters. I as now another way must take.
The seagods must bee pacifyde. There was a Castle hye,   450
And in the same a lofty towre whose toppe dooth face the skye,
A joyfull mark for maryners to guyde theyr vessells by.
To this same Turret up they went, and there with syghes behilld
The Oxen lying every where stark dead uppon the feelde
And eeke the cruell stroygood with his bluddy mouth and heare.   455
Then Peleus stretching foorth his handes to Seaward, prayd in feare
To watrish Psamath that she would her sore displeasure stay,
And help him. She no whit relents to that that he did pray.
But Thetis for hir husband made such earnest sute, that shee
Obteynd his pardon. For anon the woolfe (who would not bee   460
Revoked from the slaughter for the sweetenesse of the blood)
Persisted sharpe and eager still, untill that as he stood
Fast byghting on a Bullocks necke, shee turnd him intoo stone
As well in substance as in hew, the name of woolf alone
Reserved. For although in shape hee seemed still yit one,   465

---

438 *Obit:* funeral rites, memorial service   455 *stroygood:* destructive or wasteful crea-
                                                                    ture

The verry colour of the stone beewrayd him to bee none,
And that he was not to bee feard. How be it froward fate
Permitts not Peleus in that land to have a setled state.
He wandreth like an outlaw to the Magnets. There at last
Acastus the Thessalien purgd him of his murther past.   470
    In this meane tyme the Trachine king sore vexed in his thought
    With signes that both before and since his brothers death were
        wrought,
For counsell at the sacret Spelles (which are but toyes to foode
Fond fancyes, and not counsellers in perill to doo goode)
Did make him reedy to the God of Claros for to go.   475
For heathenish Phorbas and the folk of Phlegia had as tho
The way to Delphos stopt, that none could travell to or fro.
But ere he on his journey went, he made his faythfull make
Alcyone preevye to the thing. Immediatly theyr strake
A chilnesse to her verry bones, and pale was all her face   480
Like box and downe her heavy cheekes the teares did gush apace.
Three times about to speake, three times shee washt her face with teares,
And stinting oft with sobbes, shee thus complayned in his eares:
    What fault of myne, O husband deere, hath turnd thy hart fro
        mee?
    Where is that care of mee that erst was woont to bee in thee?   485
And canst thou having left thy deere Alcyone merrye bee?
Doo journeyes long delyght thee now? dooth now myne absence please
Thee better then my presence dooth? Think I that thou at ease
Shalt go by land? Shall I have cause but onely for to moorne?
And not to bee afrayd? And shall my care of thy returne   490
Bee voyd of feare? No no. The sea mee sore afrayd dooth make.
To think uppon the sea dooth cause my flesh for feare to quake.
I sawe the broken ribbes of shippes alate uppon the shore.
And oft on Tumbes I reade theyr names whose bodyes long before
The sea had swallowed. Let not fond vayne hope seduce thy mynd,   495
That Aeolus is thy fathrinlaw who holdes the boystous wynd
In prison, and can calme the seas at pleasure. When the wynds
Are once let looce uppon the sea, no order then them bynds.
Then neyther land hathe priviledge, nor sea exemption fynds.
Yea even the clowdes of heaven they vex, and with theyr meeting
        stout   500

---

467 *froward:* adverse, perverse   481 *box:* boxwood
473 *foode:* fode, encourage, beguile   496 *boystous:* boisterous, violent
478 *make:* mate

Enforce the fyre with hideous noyse to brust in flashes out.
The more that I doo know them, (for ryght well I know theyr powre,
And saw them oft a little wench within my fathers bowre)
So much the more I think them to bee feard. But if thy will
By no intreatance may bee turnd at home to tarry still, 505
But that thou needes wilt go: then mee, deere husband, with thee take.
So shall the sea us equally togither tosse and shake.
So woorser than I feele I shall bee certeine not to feare.
So shall we whatsoever happes togither joyntly beare.
So shall wee on the broad mayne sea togither joyntly sayle. 510
  Theis woordes and teares wherewith the imp of Aeolus did assayle
  Her husbond borne of heavenly race, did make his hart relent.
(For he lovd her no lesse than shee lovd him.) But fully bent
He seemed, neyther for to leave the journey which he ment
To take by sea, nor yit to give Alcyone leave as tho 515
Companion of his perlous course by water for to go.
He many woordes of comfort spake her feare away to chace.
But nought hee could perswade therein to make her like the cace.
This last asswagement of her greef he added in the end,
Which was the onely thing that made her loving hart to bend: 520
All taryance will assuredly seeme over long to mee.
And by my fathers blasing beames I make my vow to thee
That at the furthest ere the tyme (if God therto agree)
The moone doo fill her circle twyce, ageine I will heere bee.
When in sum hope of his returne this promis had her set, 525
He willd a shippe immediatly from harbrough to bee fet,
And throughly rigged for to bee, that neyther maast, nor sayle,
Nor tackling, no nor other thing should apperteyning fayle.
Which when Alcyone did behold, as one whoose hart misgave
The happes at hand, shee quaakt ageine, and teares out gusshing
                                                             drave. 530
And streyning Ceyx in her armes with pale and piteous looke,
Poore wretched soule, her last farewell at length shee sadly tooke,
And swounded flat uppon the ground. Anon the watermen
(As Ceyx sought delayes and was in dowt to turne agen)
Set hand to Ores, of which there were two rowes on eyther syde, 535
And all at once with equall stroke the swelling sea devyde.
Shee lifting up her watrye eyes behilld her husband stand
Uppon the hatches making signes by beckening with his hand:

501 *brust:* burst
511 *imp:* offspring
526 *harbrough:* harbor; *fet:* fetched
533 *swounded:* swooned; *watermen:* sailors

And shee made signes to him ageine. And after that the land
Was farre removed from the shippe, and that the sight began   540
To bee unable to discerne the face of any man,
As long as ere shee could shee lookt uppon the rowing keele.
And when shee could no longer tyme for distance ken it weele,
Shee looked still uppon the sayles that flasked with the wynd
Uppon the maast. And when shee could the sayles no longer fynd,   545
She gate her to her empty bed with sad and sorye hart,
And layd her downe. The chamber did renew afresh her smart,
And of her bed did bring to mynd the deere departed part.
          From harbrough now they quyght were gone: and now a
                                                  plasant gale
          Did blowe. The mayster made his men theyr Ores asyde to hale,   550
And hoysed up the toppesayle on the hyghest of the maast,
And clapt on all his other sayles bycause no wind should waast.
Scarce full t'one half, (or sure not much above) the shippe had ronne
Uppon the sea and every way the land did farre them shonne,
When toward night the wallowing waves began to waxen whyght,   555
And eeke the heady easterne wynd did blow with greater myght,
Anon the Mayster cryed: Strike the toppesayle, let the mayne
Sheate flye and fardle it to the yard. Thus spake he, but in vayne,
For why so hideous was the storme uppon the soodeine brayd,
That not a man was able there to heere what other sayd.   560
And lowd the sea with meeting waves extreemely raging rores.
Yit fell they to it of them selves. Sum haalde asyde the Ores:
Sum fensed in the Gallyes sydes, sum downe the sayleclothes rend:
Sum pump the water out, and sea to sea ageine doo send.
Another hales the sayleyards downe. And whyle they did eche thing   565
Disorderly, the storme increast, and from eche quarter fling
The wyndes with deadly foode, and bownce the raging waves togither.
The Pilot being sore dismayd sayth playne, he knowes not whither
To wend himself, nor what to doo or bid, nor in what state
Things stood. So huge the mischeef was, and did so overmate   570
All arte. For why of ratling ropes, of crying men and boyes,
Of flusshing waves and thundring ayre, confused was the noyse.
The surges mounting up aloft did seeme to mate the skye,

543 *ken:* see
544 *flasked:* flapped, fluttered
551 *hoysed:* raised
556 *heady:* headstrong, violent
558 *fardle:* furl

559 *For why:* because; *brayd:* assault, onset
567 *foode:* feud
570 *overmate:* overcome
573 *mate:* equal, vie with

And with theyr sprinckling for to wet the clowdes that hang on hye.
One whyle the sea, when from the brink it raysd the yellow sand,   575
Was like in colour to the same. Another whyle did stand
A colour on it blacker than the Lake of Styx. Anon
It lyeth playne and loometh whyght with seething froth thereon.
And with the sea the Trachin shippe ay alteration tooke.
One whyle as from a mountaynes toppe it seemed downe to looke   580
To vallyes and the depth of hell. Another whyle beset
With swelling surges round about which neere above it met,
It looked from the bottom of the whoorlepoole up aloft
As if it were from hell to heaven. A hideous flusshing oft
The waves did make in beating full against the Gallyes syde.   585
The Gallye being striken gave as great a sownd that tyde
As did sumtyme the Battellramb of steele, or now the Gonne
In making battrye to a towre. And as feerce Lyons ronne
Full brist with all theyr force ageinst the armed men that stand
In order bent to keepe them off with weapons in theyr hand,   590
Even so as often as the waves by force of wynd did rave,
So oft uppon the netting of the shippe they maynely drave,
And mounted farre above the same. Anon off fell the hoopes:
And having washt the pitch away, the sea made open loopes
To let the deadly water in. Behold the clowdes did melt,   595
And showers large came pooring downe. The seamen that them felt
Myght thinke that all the heaven had falne uppon them that same tyme,
And that the swelling sea likewyse above the heaven would clyme.
The sayles were throughly wet with showers, and with the heavenly
                                                            raine
Was mixt the waters of the sea. No lyghts at all remayne   600
Of sunne, or moone, or starres in heaven. The darknesse of the nyght
Augmented with the dreadfull storme, takes dowble powre and myght.
Howbee't the flasshing lyghtnings oft doo put the same to flyght,
And with theyr glauncing now and then do give a soodeine lyght.
The lightnings setts the waves on fyre. Above the netting skippe   605
The waves, and with a violent force doo lyght within the shippe.
And as a souldyer stowter than the rest of all his band
That oft assayles a citie walles defended well by hand,
At length atteines his hope, and for to purchace prayse withall
Alone among a thousand men getts up uppon the wall: 610
So when the loftye waves had long the Gallyes sydes assayd,

At length the tenth wave rysing up with huger force and brayd,
Did never cease assaulting of the weery shippe, till that
Uppon the hatches lyke a fo victoriously it gat.
A part thereof did still as yit assault the shippe without,   615
And part had gotten in. The men all trembling ran about,
As in a Citie commes to passe, when of the enmyes sum
Dig downe the walles without, and sum already in are come.
All arte and conning was to seeke. Theyr harts and stomacks fayle:
And looke, how many surges came theyr vessell to assayle,   620
So many deathes did seeme to charge and breake uppon them all.
One weepes: another stands amazde: the third them blist dooth call
Whom buryall dooth remayne. To God another makes his vow,
And holding up his handes to heaven the which hee sees not now,
Dooth pray in vayne for help. The thought of this man is uppon   625
His brother and his parents whom he cleerely hath forgone.
Another calles his house and wyfe and children unto mynd,
And every man in generall the things he left behynd.
Alcyone moveth Ceyx hart. In Ceyx mouth is none
But onely one Alcyone. And though shee were alone   630
The wyght that he desyred most, yit was he verry glad
Shee was not there. To Trachin ward to looke desyre he had,
And homeward fayne he would have turnd his eyes which never more
Should see the land. But then he knew not which way was the shore,
Nor where he was. The raging sea did rowle about so fast: 635
And all the heaven with clowds as black as pitch was over cast,
That never nyght was halfe so dark. There came a flaw at last,
That with his violence brake the maste, and strake the sterne away.
A billowe proudly pranking up as vaunting of his pray
By conquest gotten, walloweth hole and breaketh not asunder,   640
Beholding with a lofty looke the waters woorking under.
And looke, as if a man should from the places where they growe
Rend downe the mountaynes, Athe and Pind, and whole them
                                                         overthrowe
Into the open sea: so soft the Billowe tumbling downe,
With weyght and violent stroke did sink and in the bottom drowne   645
The Gallye. And the moste of them that were within the same
Went downe therwith and never up to open aier came,
But dyed strangled in the gulf. Another sort againe

612 *brayd*: assault, sudden movement   626 *forgone*: gone from, left
622 *blist*: blest   639 *pranking*: swanking, swaggering
623 *remayne*: await

Caught peeces of the broken shippe. The king himself was fayne
A shiver of the sunken shippe in that same hand to hold, 650
In which hee erst a royall mace had hilld of yellow gold.
His father and his fathrinlawe he calles uppon (alas
In vayne.) But cheefly in his mouth his wife Alcyone was.
In hart was shee: in toong was shee: he wisshed that his corse
To land where shee myght take it up the surges myght enforce: 655
And that by her most loving handes he might be layd in grave.
In swimming still (as often as the surges leave him gave
To ope his lippes) he harped still upon Alcyones name,
And when he drowned in the waves he muttred still the same.
Behold, even full uppon the wave a flake of water blacke 660
Did breake, and underneathe the sea the head of Ceyx stracke.
That nyght the lyghtsum Lucifer for sorrowe was so dim,
As scarcely could a man discerne or thinke it to bee him.
And forasmuch as out of heaven he might not steppe asyde,
With thick and darksum clowds that nyght his countnance he did
                                                                hyde. 665
    Alcyone of so great mischaunce not knowing aught as yit,
    Did keepe a reckening of the nyghts that in the whyle did flit,
And hasted garments both for him and for herself likewyse,
To weare at his homecomming which shee vaynely did surmyse.
To all the Goddes devoutly shee did offer frankincence: 670
But most above them all the Church of Juno shee did sence.
And for her husband (who as then was none) shee kneeld before
The Altar, wisshing health and soone arrivall at the shore,
And that none other woman myght before her be preferd.
Of all her prayers this one peece effectually was heard. 675
For Juno could not fynd in hart intreated for to bee
For him that was already dead. But to th'entent that shee
From dame Alcyones deadly hands might keepe her Altars free,
Shee sayd: Most faythfull messenger of my commaundments, O
Thou Raynebowe, to the sluggish house of Slomber swiftly go. 680
And bid him send a Dreame in shape of Ceyx to his wyfe
Alcyone, for to shew her playne the losing of his lyfe.
Dame Iris takes her pall wherein a thousand colours were
And bowwing lyke a stringed bow upon the clowdy sphere,
Immediatly descended to the drowzye house of Sleepe 685

---

649 *fayne:* glad   671 *sence:* cense, offer incense to
655 *enforce:* compel   683 *pall:* mantle

Whose Court the clowdes continually doo clocely overdreepe.
    Among the darke Cimmerians is a hollow mountaine found
    And in the hill a Cave that farre dooth ronne within the ground,
The Chamber and the dwelling place where slouthfull sleepe dooth
                                                                cowch.
The lyght of Phebus golden beames this place can never towch.   690
A foggye mist with dimnesse mixt streames upwarde from the ground,
And glimmering twylyght evermore within the same is found.
No watchfull bird with barbed bill, and combed crowne dooth call
The morning foorth with crowing out. There is no noyse at all
Of waking dogge, nor gagling goose more waker than the hound   695
To hinder sleepe. Of beast ne wyld ne tame there is no sound.
No bowghes are stird with blastes of wynd, no noyse of tatling toong
Of man or woman ever yit within that bower roong.
Dumb quiet dwelleth there. Yit from the Roches foote dooth go
The ryver of forgetfulnesse, which ronneth trickling so   700
Uppon the little pebble stones which in the channell lye,
That unto sleepe a great deale more it dooth provoke thereby.
Before the entry of the Cave, there growes of Poppye store,
With seeded heades, and other weedes innumerable more,
Out of the milkye jewce of which the night dooth gather sleepes,   705
And over all the shadowed earth with dankish deawe them dreepes.
Bycause the craking hindges of the doore no noyse should make,
There is no doore in all the house, nor porter at the gate.
Amid the Cave, of Ebonye a bedsted standeth hye,
And on the same a bed of downe with keeverings blacke dooth lye: 710
In which the drowzye God of sleepe his lither limbes dooth rest.
About him, forging sundrye shapes as many dreames lye prest
As eares of corne doo stand in feeldes in harvest tyme, or leaves
Doo grow on trees, or sea to shore of sandye cinder heaves.
As soone as Iris came within this house, and with her hand   715
Had put asyde the dazeling dreames that in her way did stand,
The brightnesse of her robe through all the sacred house did shine.
The God of sleepe scarce able for to rayse his heavy eyen,
A three or fowre tymes at the least did fall ageine to rest,
And with his nodding head did knocke his chinne ageinst his brest.   720
At length he shaking of himselfe, uppon his elbowe leande.
And though he knew for what shee came: he askt her what shee meand.

686 *overdreepe:* droop over   710 *keeverings:* coverings
706 *dreepes:* drips   711 *lither:* sluggish, lazy

O sleepe (quoth shee,) the rest of things, O gentlest of the Goddes,
Sweete sleepe, the peace of mynd, with whom crookt care is aye at
                                                              oddes:
Which cherrishest mennes weery limbes appalld with toyling sore, 725
And makest them as fresh to woork and lustye as beefore,
Commaund a dreame that in theyr kyndes can every thing expresse,
To Trachine, Hercles towne, himself this instant to addresse.
And let him lively counterfet to Queene Alcyonea
The image of her husband who is drowned in the sea   730
By shipwrecke. Juno willeth so. Her message beeing told,
Dame Iris went her way. Shee could her eyes no longer hold
From sleepe. But when shee felt it come shee fled that instant tyme,
And by the boawe that brought her downe to heaven ageine did clyme.
      Among a thousand sonnes and mo that father slomber had   735
      He calld up Morph, the feyner of mannes shape, a craftye lad.
None other could so conningly expresse mans verrye face,
His gesture and his sound of voyce, and manner of his pace,
Togither with his woonted weede, and woonted phrase of talk.
But this same Morphye onely in the shape of man dooth walk.   740
There is another who the shapes of beast or bird dooth take,
Or else appeereth unto men in likenesse of a snake.
The Goddes doo call him Icilos, and mortall folke him name
Phobetor. There is also yit a third who from theis same
Woorkes diversly, and Phantasos he highteth. Into streames   745
This turnes himself, and into stones, and earth, and timber beames,
And into every other thing that wanteth life. Theis three,
Great kings and Capteines in the night are woonted for to see.
The meaner and inferiour sort of others haunted bee.
Sir Slomber overpast the rest, and of the brothers all   750
To doo dame Iris message he did only Morphye call.
Which doone he waxing luskish, streyght layd downe his drowzy head
And softly shroonk his layzye limbes within his sluggish bed.
      Away flew Morphye through the aire: no flickring made his wings:
      And came anon to Trachine. There his fethers off he flings, 755
And in the shape of Ceyx standes before Alcyones bed,
Pale, wan, stark naakt, and like a man that was but lately deade.
His berde seemd wet, and of his head the heare was dropping drye,
And leaning on her bed, with teares he seemed thus to cry:
Most wretched woman, knowest thou thy loving Ceyx now   760

752 *luskish:* lazy, sluggish

Or is my face by death disformd? behold mee well, and thow
Shalt know mee. For thy husband, thou thy husbandes Ghost shalt see.
No good thy prayers and thy vowes have done at all to mee.
For I am dead. In vayne of my returne no reckning make.
The clowdy sowth amid the sea our shippe did tardy take,   765
And tossing it with violent blastes asunder did it shake.
And floodes have filld my mouth which calld in vayne uppon thy name.
No persone whom thou mayst misdeeme brings tydings of the same.
Thou hearest not thereof by false report of flying fame.
But I myself: I presently my shipwrecke to thee showe.   770
Aryse therefore and wofull teares uppon thy spouse bestowe.
Put moorning rayment on, and let mee not to Limbo go
Unmoorned for. In shewing of this shipwrecke Morphye so
Did feyne the voyce of Ceyx, that shee could none other deeme,
But that it should bee his in deede. Moreover he did seeme   775
To weepe in earnest: and his handes the verry gesture had
Of Ceyx. Queene Alcyone did grone, and beeing sad
Did stirre her armes, and thrust them foorth his body to embrace.
In stead whereof shee caught but ayre. The teares ran downe her face.
Shee cryed, Tarry: whither flyste? togither let us go.   780
And all this whyle she was asleepe. Both with her crying so,
And flayghted with the image of her husbands gastly spryght,
She started up: and sought about if fynd him there shee myght.
(For why her Groomes awaking with the shreeke had brought a light.)
And when shee no where could him fynd, shee gan her face to
                                                         smyght,   785
And tare her nyghtclothes from her brest, and strake it feercely, and
Not passing to unty her heare shee rent it with her hand.
And when her nurce of this her greef desyrde to understand
The cause: Alcyone is undoone, undoone and cast away
With Ceyx her deare spouse (shee sayd). Leave comforting I pray.   790
By shipwrecke he is perrisht: I have seene him: and I knew
His handes. When in departing I to hold him did pursew
I caught a Ghost: but such a Ghost as well discerne I myght
To bee my husbands. Nathelesse he had not to my syght
His woonted countenance, neyther did his visage shyne so bryght,   795
As heeretofore it had beene woont. I saw him, wretched wyght,
Starke naked, pale, and with his heare still wet: even verry heere

768 *misdeeme*: mistake, be mistaken in   787 *passing*: caring
782 *flayghted*: frightened

I saw him stand. With that shee lookes if any print appeere
Of footing where as he did stand uppon the floore behynd.
This this is it that I did feare in farre forecasting mynd,   800
When flying mee I thee desyrde thou shouldst not trust the wynd.
But syth thou wentest to thy death, I would that I had gone
With thee. Ah meete, it meete had beene thou shouldst not go alone
Without mee. So it should have come to passe that neyther I
Had overlived thee, nor yit beene forced twice to dye.   805
Already, absent in the waves now tossed have I bee.
Already have I perrished. And yit the sea hath thee
Without mee. But the cruelnesse were greater farre of mee
Than of the sea, if after thy decease I still would strive
In sorrow and in anguish still to pyne away alive.   810
But neyther will I strive in care to lengthen still my lyfe,
Nor (wretched wyght) abandon thee: but like a faythfull wyfe
At leastwyse now will come as thy companion. And the herse
Shall joyne us, though not in the selfsame coffin: yit in verse.
Although in tumb the bones of us togither may not couch,   815
Yit in a graven Epitaph my name thy name shall touch.
Her sorrow would not suffer her to utter any more.
Shee sobd and syghde at every woord, untill her hart was sore.
    The morning came, and out shee went ryght pensif to the shore
    To that same place in which shee tooke her leave of him before.   820
Whyle there shee musing stood, and sayd: He kissed mee even heere,
Heere weyed hee his Anchors up, heere loosd he from the peere.
And whyle shee calld to mynd the things there marked with her eyes:
In looking on the open sea, a great way off shee spyes
A certaine thing much like a corse come hovering on the wave.   825
At first shee dowted what it was. As tyde it neerer drave,
Although it were a good way off, yit did it plainely showe
To bee a corce. And though that whose it was shee did not knowe,
Yit forbycause it seemd a wrecke, her hart therat did ryse:
And as it had sum straunger beene, with water in her eyes   830
She sayd: Alas poore wretch who ere thou art, alas for her
That is thy wyfe, if any bee. And as the waves did stirre,
The body floted neerer land: the which the more that shee
Behilld, the lesse began in her of stayed wit to bee.
Anon it did arrive on shore. Then plainely shee did see   835
And know it, that it was her feere. Shee shreeked, It is hee.

---

803 *meete:* fitting, proper   836 *feere:* mate
829 *wrecke:* one shipwrecked

And therewithall her face, her heare, and garments shee did teare,
And unto Ceyx stretching out her trembling handes with feare,
Sayd: cumst thou home in such a plyght to mee, O husband deere?
Returnst in such a wretched plyght? There was a certeine peere   840
That buylded was by hand, of waves the first assaults to breake,
And at the havons mouth to cause the tyde to enter weake.
Shee lept thereon. (A wonder sure it was shee could doo so)
Shee flew, and with her newgrowen winges did beate the ayre as tho.
And on the waves a wretched bird shee whisked to and fro.   845
And with her crocking neb then growen to slender bill and round,
Like one that wayld and moorned still shee made a moaning sound.
Howbee't as soone as she did touch his dumb and bloodlesse flesh,
And had embraast his loved limbes with winges made new and fresh,
And with her hardened neb had kist him coldly, though in vayne,   850
Folk dowt if Ceyx feeling it to rayse his head did strayne,
Or whither that the waves did lift it up. But surely hee
It felt: and through compassion of the Goddes both hee and shee
Were turnd to birdes. The love of them eeke subject to their fate,
Continued after: neyther did the faythfull bond abate   855
Of wedlocke in them beeing birdes: but standes in stedfast state.
They treade, and lay, and bring foorth yoong and now the Alcyon sitts
In wintertime uppon her nest, which on the water flitts
A sevennyght. During all which tyme the sea is calme and still,
And every man may to and fro sayle saufly at his will,   860
For Aeolus for his offsprings sake the windes at home dooth keepe,
And will not let them go abroade for troubling of the deepe.
        An auncient father seeing them about the brode sea fly,
        Did prayse theyr love for lasting to the end so stedfastly.
His neyghbour or the selfsame man made answer (such is chaunce):   865
Even this fowle also whom thou seest uppon the surges glaunce
With spindle shanks, (he poynted to the wydegoawld Cormorant)
Before that he became a bird, of royall race might vaunt.
And if thou covet lineally his pedigree to seeke,
His Auncetors were Ilus, and Assaracus, and eeke   870
Fayre Ganymed who Jupiter did ravish as his joy,
Laomedon and Priamus the last that reygnd in Troy.
Stout Hectors brother was this man. And had he not in pryme
Of lusty youth beene tane away, his deedes perchaunce in tyme

846 *crocking:* croaking; *neb:* bill   867 *wydegoawld:* wide-jowled, wide-
                                               cropped

Had purchaast him as great a name as Hector, though that hee   875
Of Dymants daughter Hecuba had fortune borne to bee.
For Aesacus reported is begotten to have beene
By scape, in shady Ida on a mayden fayre and sheene
Whose name was Alyxothoe, a poore mans daughter that
With spade and mattocke for himselfe and his a living gat.   880
This Aesacus the Citie hates, and gorgious Court dooth shonne,
And in the unambicious feeldes and woods alone dooth wonne.
He seeldoom haunts the towne of Troy, yit having not a rude
And blockish wit, nor such a hart as could not be subdewd
By love, he spyde Eperie (whom oft he had pursewd   885
Through all the woodes) then sitting on her father Cebrius brim
A drying of her heare ageinst the sonne, which hanged trim
Uppon her back. As soone as that the Nymph was ware of him,
She fled as when the grisild woolf dooth scare the fearefull hynd
Or when the Fawcon farre from brookes a Mallard happes to fynd.   890
The Trojane knyght ronnes after her, and beeing swift through love,
Purseweth her whom feare dooth force apace her feete to move.
Behold an Adder lurking in the grasse there as shee fled,
Did byght her foote with hooked tooth, and in her bodye spred
His venim. Shee did cease her flyght and soodein fell downe dead.   895
Her lover being past his witts her carkesse did embrace,
And cryde: Alas it irketh mee, it irkes mee of this chace.
But this I feard not. Neyther was the gaine of that I willd
Woorth halfe so much. Now two of us thee (wretched soule) have killd.
The wound was given thee by the snake, the cause was given by mee.   900
The wickedder of both am I: who for to comfort thee
Will make thee satisfaction with my death. With that at last
Downe from a rocke (the which the waves had undermynde) he cast
Himself into the sea. Howbee't dame Tethys pitying him,
Receyvd him softly, and as he uppon the waves did swim,   905
Shee covered him with fethers. And though fayne he would have dyde,
Shee would not let him. Wroth was he that death was him denyde,
And that his soule compelld should bee ageinst his will to byde
Within his wretched body still, from which it would depart,
And that he was constreynd to live perforce ageinst his hart.   910
And as he on his shoulders now had newly taken wings,

---

878 *scape:* transgression; here, Ovid's *fur-*   882 *wonne:* live
    tim, in secrecy   886 *brim:* brink, bank

He mounted up, and downe uppon the sea his boddye dings.
His fethers would not let him sinke. In rage he dyveth downe,
And despratly he strives himself continually to drowne.
His love did make him leane, long leggs: long neck dooth still
remayne.   915
His head is from his shoulders farre: of Sea he is most fayne.
And for he underneath the waves delyghteth for to drive
A name according thereunto the Latins doo him give.

FINIS UNDECIMI LIBRI.

912 *dings:* dashes

THE. XII. BOOKE OF

OVIDS METAMORPHOSIS.

[The Trojan War. Cygnet, Caenis-Caeneus. The Centaurs and the Lapithae. The Death of Achilles.]

King Priam beeing ignorant that Aesacus his sonne
Did live in shape of bird, did moorne: and at a tumb wheron
His name was written, Hector and his brother solemly
Did keepe an Obit. Paris was not at this obsequye.
Within a whyle with ravisht wyfe he brought a lasting warre   5
Home unto Troy. There followed him a thowsand shippes not farre
Conspyrd togither, with the ayde that all the Greekes could fynd:
And vengeance had beene tane foorthwith but that the cruell wynd
Did make the seas unsaylable, so that theyr shippes were fayne
At rode at fisshye Awlys in Baeotia to remayne.   10
Heere as the Greekes according to theyr woont made sacrifyse
To Jove, and on the Altar old the flame aloft did ryse,
They spyde a speckled Snake creepe up uppon a planetree bye
Uppon the toppe whereof there was among the braunches hye
A nest, and in the nest eyght birdes, all which and eeke theyr dam 15
That flickering flew about her losse, the hungry snake did cram
Within his mawe. The standers by were all amazde therat.
But Calchas, Thestors sonne, who knew what meening was in that,
Sayd: We shall win. Rejoyce, yee Greekes, by us shall perish Troy,
But long the tyme will bee before wee may our will enjoy.   20
And then he told them how the birds nyne yeeres did signifie
Which they before the towne of Troy not taking it should lye.
The Serpent as he wound about the boughes and braunches greene,

---

⁴ *Obit:* funeral rites   ⁹ *fayne:* obliged
⁷ *Conspyrd:* cooperating   ¹⁰ *rode:* roadstead

Became a stone, and still in stone his snakish shape is seene.
The seas continewed verry rough and suffred not theyr hoste   25
Imbarked for to passe from thence to take the further coast.
Sum thought that Neptune favored Troy bycause himself did buyld
The walles therof. But Calchas (who both knew, and never hilld
His peace in tyme) declared that the Goddesse Phebe must
Appeased bee with virgins blood for wrath conceyved just.   30
As soone as pitie yeelded had to cace of publicke weale,
And reason got the upper hand of fathers loving zeale,
So that the Ladye Iphigen before the altar stood
Among the weeping ministers, to give her maydens blood:
The Goddesse taking pitie, cast a mist before theyr eyes,   35
And as they prayd and stird about to make the sacrifyse,
Conveyes her quight away, and with a Hynd her roome supplyes.
Thus with a slaughter meete for her Diana beeing pleasd,
The raging surges with her wrath togither were appeasd,
The thousand shippes had wynd at poope. And when they had abode   40
Much trouble, at the length all safe they gat the Phrygian rode.
        Amid the world tweene heaven, and earth, and sea, there is a place,
        Set from the bounds of eche of them indifferently in space,
From whence is seene what ever thing is practisd any where,
Although the Realme bee nere so farre, and roundly to the eare   45
Commes whatsoever spoken is. Fame hath his dwelling there.
Who in the toppe of all the house is lodged in a towre.
A thousand entryes, glades, and holes are framed in this bowre.
There are no doores to shet. The doores stand open nyght and day.
The house is all of sounding brasse, and roreth every way,   50
Reporting dowble every woord it heareth people say.
There is no rest within, there is no silence any where.
Yit is there not a yelling out: but humming, as it were
The sound of surges beeing heard farre off, or like the sound
That at the end of thunderclappes long after dooth redound,   55
When Jove dooth make the clowdes to crack. Within the courts is preace
Of common people, which to come and go doo never ceace.
And millions both of trothes and lyes ronne gadding every where,
And woordes confusely flye in heapes. Of which, sum fill the eare
That heard not of them erst, and sum Colcaryers part doo play   60
To spread abrode the things they heard. And ever by the way
The thing that was invented growes much greater than before,

60 *Colcaryers:* coal carriers, hirelings, those who do the "dirty work"

And every one that getts it by the end addes sumwhat more.
Lyght credit dwelleth there. There dwells rash error: there dooth dwell
Vayne joy: there dwelleth hartlesse feare, and Bruit that loves to tell   65
Uncertayne newes uppon report, whereof he dooth not knowe
The author, and Sedition who fresh rumors loves to sowe.
This Fame beholdeth what is doone in heaven, on sea, and land,
And what is wrought in all the world he layes to understand.
    He gave the Trojans warning that the Greekes with valeant men 70
    And shippes approched, that unwares they could not take them
                                      then.
For Hector and the Trojan folk well armed were at hand
To keepe the coast and bid them bace before they came aland.
Protesilay by fatall doome was first that dyde in feeld
Of Hectors speare: and after him great numbers mo were killd   75
Of valeant men. That battell did the Greeks full deerly cost.
And Hector with his Phrygian folk of blood no little lost,
In trying what the Greekes could doo. The shore was red with blood.
And now king Cygnet, Neptunes sonne, had killed where he stood
A thousand Greekes. And now the stout Achilles causd to stay   80
His Charyot: and his lawnce did slea whole bandes of men that day.
And seeking Cygnet through the feeld or Hector, he did stray.
At last with Cygnet he did meete. For Hector had delay
Untill the tenth yeare afterward. Then hasting foorth his horses
With flaxen manes, ageinst his fo his Chariot he enforces.   85
And brandishing his shaking dart, he sayd: O noble wyght,
A comfort let it bee to thee that such a valeant knyght
As is Achilles killeth thee. In saying so he threw
A myghty dart, which though it hit the mark at which it flew,
Yit perst it not the skinne at all. Now when this blunted blowe   90
Had hit on Cygnets brest, and did no print of hitting showe,
Thou, Goddesse sonne (quoth Cygnet), for by fame we doo thee
                                   knowe.
Why woondrest at mee for to see I can not wounded bee?
(Achilles woondred much thereat.) This helmet which yee see
Bedect with horses yellow manes, this sheeld that I doo beare,   95
Defend mee not. For ornaments alonly I them weare.
For this same cause armes Mars himself likewyse. I will disarme
Myself, and yit unrazed will I passe without all harme.

65 *hartlesse:* spiritless   73 *bid them bace:* challenge them
69 *layes:* applies himself, seeks   98 *unrazed:* ungrazed, unwounded

It is to sum effect, not borne to bee of Neryes race,
So that a man be borne of him that with threeforked mace   100
Rules Nereus and his daughters too, and all the sea besyde.
This sayd, he at Achilles sent a dart that should abyde
Uppon his sheeld. It perced through the steele and through nyne fold
Of Oxen hydes, and stayd uppon the tenth. Achilles bold
Did wrest it out, and forcybly did throwe the same agayne.   105
His bodye beeing hit ageine, unwounded did remayne,
And cleere from any print of wound. The third went eeke in vayne.
And yit did Cygnet to the same give full his naked brist.
Achilles chafed like a Bull that in the open list
With dreadfull hornes dooth push ageinst the scarlet clothes that
                                                                there   110
Are hanged up to make him feerce, and when he would them teare
Dooth fynd his wounds deluded. Then Achilles lookt uppon
His Javelings socket, if the head thereof were looce or gone.
The head stacke fast. My hand byleeke is weakened then (quoth hee),
And all the force it had before is spent on one I see.   115
For sure I am it was of strength, both when I first downe threw
Lyrnessus walles, and when I did Ile Tenedos subdew,
And eeke Aetions Thebe with her proper blood embrew.
And when so many of the folke of Tewthranie I slew,
That with theyr blood Caycus streame became of purple hew.   120
And when the noble Telephus did of my Dart of steele
The dowble force, of wounding and of healing also feele.
Yea even the heapes of men slayne heere by mee, that on this strond
Are lying still to looke uppon, doo give to understond
That this same hand of myne both had and still hath strength. This
                                                                sed,   125
(As though he had distrusted all his dooings ere that sted,)
He threw a Dart ageinst a man of Lycia land that hyght
Menetes, through whose Curets and his brest he strake him quyght.
And when he saw with dying limbes him sprawling on the ground,
He stepped to him streyght, and pulld the Javeling from the wound,   130
And sayd alowd: This is the hand, this is the selfsame dart
With which my hand did strike even now Menetes to the hart.
Ageinst my tother Copemate will I use the same: I pray
To God it may have like successe. This sed, without delay

---

102 *abyde:* remain   128 *Curets:* cuirass
114 *byleeke:* probably   133 *Copemate:* adversary
126 *sted:* time

He sent it toward Cygnet, and the weapon did not stray,   135
Nor was not shunned. Insomuch it lighted full uppon
His shoulder: and it gave a rappe as if uppon sum ston
It lyghted had, rebownding backe. Howbeeit where it hit,
Achilles sawe it bloodye, and was vaynly glad of it.
For why there was no wound. It was Menetes blood. Then lept   140
He hastly from his Charyot downe, and like a madman stept
To carelesse Cygnet with his swoord. He sawe his swoord did pare
His Target and his morion bothe. But when it toucht the bare,
His bodye was so hard, it did the edge thereof abate.
He could no lengar suffer him to tryumph in that rate,   145
But with the pommell of his swoord did thump him on the pate,
And bobd him well about the brewes a doozen tymes and more,
And preacing on him as he still gave backe amaazd him sore,
And troubled him with buffetting, not respecting a whit.
Then Cygnet gan to bee afrayd, and mistes beegan to flit   150
Before his eyes, and dimd his syght. And as he still did yeeld,
In giving back, by chaunce he met a stone amid the feeld,
Ageinst the which Achilles thrust him back with all his myght,
And throwing him ageinst the ground, did cast him bolt upryght.
Then bearing bostowsely with both his knees ageinst his chest,   155
And leaning with his elbowes and his target on his brest,
He shet his headpeece cloce and just, and underneathe his chin
So hard it straynd, that way for breath was neyther out nor in,
And closed up the vent of lyfe. And having gotten so
The upper hand, he went about to spoyle his vanquisht fo.   160
But nought he in his armour found. For Neptune had as tho
Transformd him to the fowle whose name he bare but late ago.
This labour, this encounter brought the rest of many dayes,
And eyther partye in theyr strength a whyle from battell stayes.
    Now whyle the Phrygians watch and ward uppon the walles of
                                                        Troy,   165
    And Greekes likewyse within theyr trench, there came a day of
                                                        joy,
In which Achilles for his luck in Cygnets overthrow,
A Cow in way of sacrifyse on Pallas did bestowe,
Whose inwards when he had uppon the burning altar cast

139 *vaynly:* in vain   149 *respetting:* giving respite
140 *For why:* because   154 *bolt upryght:* on his back
143 *Target:* round shield; *morion:* helmet   155 *bostowsely:* violently
147 *bobd:* struck; *brewes:* brows

And that the acceptable fume had through the ayer past   170
To Godward, and the holy rytes had had theyr dewes, the rest
Was set on boords for men to eate in disshes fynely drest.
The princes sitting downe, did feede uppon the rosted flesh,
And both theyr thirst and present cares with wyne they did refresh.
Not Harpes, nor songs, nor hollowe flutes to heere did them delyght.   175
They talked till they nye had spent the greatest part of nyght.
And all theyr communication was of feates of armes in fyght
That had beene doone by them or by theyr foes. And every wyght
Delyghts to uppen oftentymes by turne as came about
The perills and the narrow brunts himself had shifted out.   180
For what thing should bee talkt beefore Achilles rather? Or
What kynd of things than such as theis could seeme more meeter for
Achilles to bee talking of? But in theyr talk most breeme
Was then Achilles victory of Cygnet. It did seeme
A woonder that the flesh of him should bee so hard and tough   185
As that no weapon myght have powre to raze or perce it through,
But that it did abate the edge of steele: it was a thing
That both Achilles and the Greekes in woondrous maze did bring.
Then Nestor sayd: This Cygnet is the person now alone
Of your tyme that defyed steele, and could bee perst of none.   190
But I have seene now long ago one Cene of Perrhebye,
I sawe one Cene of Perrhebye a thousand woundes defye
With unatteynted bodye. In mount Othris he did dwell:
And was renowmed for his deedes: (and which in him ryght well
A greater woonder did appeere) he was a woman borne.   195
This uncouth made them all much more amazed than beforne,
And every man desyred him to tell it. And among
The rest, Achilles sayd: Declare, I pray thee (for wee long
To heare it every one of us), O eloquent old man,
The wisedome of our age: what was that Cene and how he wan   200
Another than his native shape, and in what rode, or in
What fyght or skirmish, tweene you first acquaintance did beegin,
And who in fyne did vanquish him if any vanquisht him.
     Then Nestor: Though the length of tyme have made my senses
                                                                            dim,
     And dyvers things erst seene in youth now out of mynd be gone: 205

179 *uppen:* mention   193 *unatteynted:* untouched
180 *shifted out:* handled successfully 196 *uncouth:* news, wonder
183 *breeme:* celebrated   203 *in fyne:* finally
188 *maze:* amazement

Yit beare I still mo things in mynd: and of them all is none
Among so many both of peace and warre, that yit dooth take
More stedfast roote in memorye. And if that tyme may make
A man great store of things through long continuance for to see,
Two hundred yeeres already of my lyfe full passed bee, 210
And now I go uppon the third. This foresayd Ceny was
The daughter of one Elatey. In beawty shee did passe
The maydens all of Thessaly. From all the Cities bye
And from thy Cities also, O Achilles, came (for why
Shee was thy countrywoman) store of wooers who in vayne 215
In hope to win her love did take great travail, suit and payne.
Thy father also had perchaunce attempted heere to matcht
But that thy moothers maryage was alreadye then dispatcht,
Or shee at least affyanced. But Ceny matcht with none,
Howbeeit as shee on the shore was walking all alone, 220
The God of sea did ravish her. (So fame dooth make report.)
And Neptune for the great delight he had in Venus sport,
Sayd: Ceny, aske mee what thou wilt, and I will give it thee.
(This also bruited is by fame.) The wrong heere doone to mee
(Quoth Ceny) makes mee wish great things. And therfore to
             th'entent 225
I may no more constreyned bee to such a thing, consent
I may no more a woman bee. And if thou graunt thereto,
It is even all that I desyre, or wish thee for to doo.
In bacer tune theis latter woordes were uttred, and her voyce
Did seeme a mannes voyce as it was in deede. For to her choyce 230
The God of sea had given consent. He graunted him besyde
That free from wounding and from hurt he should from thence abyde,
And that he should not dye of steele. Right glad of this same graunt
Away went Ceny, and the feeldes of Thessaly did haunt,
And in the feates of Chevalrye from that tyme spent his lyfe. 235
  The over bold Ixions sonne had taken to his wyfe
  Hippodame. And kevering boordes in bowres of boughes of trees
His Clowdbred brothers one by one he placed in degrees.
There were the Lordes of Thessaly. I also was among
The rest: a cheerefull noyse of feast through all the Pallace roong. 240
Sum made the altars smoke, and sum the brydale carrolls soong.
Anon commes in the mayden bryde, a goodly wench of face,
With wyves and maydens following her with comly gate and grace.

²³⁷ *kevering:* covering

Wee sayd that sir Pirithous was happy in his wyfe:
Which handsell had deceyved us wellneere through soodeine stryfe.   245
For of the cruell Centawres thou most cruell Ewryt, tho
Like as thy stomacke was with wyne farre over charged: so
As soone as thou behilldst the bryde, thy hart began to frayne,
And doubled with thy droonkennesse thy raging lust did reigne.
The feast was troubled by and by with tables overthrowen.   250
The bryde was hayled by the head, so farre was furye growen.
Feerce Ewryt caught Hippodame, and every of the rest
Caught such as commed next to hand, or such as likte him best.
It was the lively image of a Citie tane by foes.
The house did ring of womens shreekes. We all up quickly rose.   255
And first sayd Theseus thus: What aylst? art mad, O Ewrytus?
That darest (seeing mee alive) misuse Pirithous?
Not knowing that in one thou doost abuse us both? And least
He myght have seemd to speake in vayne, he thrust way such as preast
About the bryde, and tooke her from them freating sore thereat.   260
No answere made him Ewrytus: (for such a deede as that
Defended could not bee with woordes) but with his sawcye fist
He flew at gentle Theseus face, and bobd him on the brist.
By chaunce hard by, an auncient cuppe of image woork did stand,
Which being huge, himself more huge sir Theseus tooke in hand,   265
And threw't at Ewryts head. He spewd as well at mouth as wound
Mixt cloddes of blood, and brayne and wyne, and on the soyled ground
Lay sprawling bolt upryght. The death of him did set the rest,
His dowblelimbed brothers, so on fyre, that all the quest
With one voyce cryed out, Kill, kill. The wyne had given them hart.   270
Theyr first encounter was with cuppes and cannes throwen overthwart,
And brittle tankerds, and with boawles, pannes, dishes, potts, and
                                                              trayes,
Things serving late for meate and drinke, and then for bluddy frayes.
First Amycus, Ophions sonne, without remorse began
To reeve and rob the brydehouse of his furniture. He ran   275
And pulled downe a Lampbeame full of lyghtes, and lifting it
Aloft like one that with an Ax dooth fetch his blowe to slit
An Oxis necke in sacrifyse, he on the forehead hit
A Lapith named Celadon, and crusshed so his bones

245 *handsell:* omen
248 *frayne:* (?) this word translates Ovid's
    ardet (burn, glow, flame)
258 *least:* lest
269 *quest:* pack

271 *cannes:* metal drinking cups; *overthwart:*
    across, against each other
275 *reeve:* plunder, strip
276 *Lampbeame:* chandelier, candelabrum

That none could know him by the face: both eyes flew out at ones. [280]
His nose was beaten backe and to his pallat battred flat.
One Pelates, a Macedone, exceeding wroth therat,
Pulld out a maple tressles foote, and napt him in the necks,
That bobbing with his chin ageinst his brest to ground he becks.
And as he spitted out his teeth with blackish blood, he lent [285]
Another blowe to Amycus, which streyght to hell him sent.
Gryne standing by and lowring with a fell grim visage at
The smoking Altars, sayd: Why use we not theis same? with that
He caught a myghty altar up with burning fyre thereon,
And it among the thickest of the Lapithes threw anon. [290]
And twoo he over whelmd therewith calld Brote and Orion.
This Orions moother, Mycale, is knowne of certeintye
The Moone resisting to have drawne by witchcraft from the skye.
Full dearely shalt thou by it (quoth Exadius) may I get
A weapon: and with that in stead of weapon, he did set [295]
His hand uppon a vowd harts horne that on a Pynetree hye
Was nayld, and with two tynes therof he strake out eyther eye
Of Gryne: whereof sum stacke uppon the horne, and sum did flye
Uppon his beard, and there with blood like jelly mixt did lye.
A flaming fyrebrand from amids an Altar Rhaetus snatcht, [300]
With which uppon the leftsyde of his head Charaxus latcht
A blow that crackt his skull. The blaze among his yellow heare
Ran sindging up, as if dry corne with lightning blasted were.
And in his wound the seared blood did make a greevous sound,
As when a peece of steele red hot tane up with tongs is drownd [305]
In water by the smith, it spirts and hisseth in the trowgh.
Charaxus from his curled heare did shake the fyre, and thowgh
He wounded were, yit caught he up uppon his shoulders twayne
A stone, the Jawme of eyther doore that well would loade a wayne.
The masse theof was such as that it would not let him hit [310]
His fo. It lighted short: and with the falling downe of it
A mate of his that Comet hyght, it all in peeces smit.
Then Rhaete restreyning not his joy, sayd thus: I would the rowt
Of all thy mates myght in the selfsame maner prove them stowt.
And with his halfeburnt brond the wound he searched new agayne, [315]
Not ceasing for to lay on loade uppon his pate amayne,
Untill his head was crusht, and of his scalp the bones did swim

283 *napt:* knocked
284 *becks:* bows
294 *by:* pay for

301 *latcht:* received
309 *Jawme:* jamb; *wayne:* wagon
313 *rowt:* crowd, mob

Among his braynes. In jolly ruffe he passed streyght from him
To Coryt, and Euagrus, and to Dryant on a rowe.
Of whom when Coryt (on whose cheekes yoong mossy downe gan
grow)   320
Was slayne, What prayse or honour (quoth Euagrus) hast thou got
By killing of a boy? mo woordes him Rhetus suffred not
To speake, but in his open mouth did thrust his burning brand,
And downe his throteboll to his chest. Then whisking in his hand
His fyrebrand round about his head he feercely did assayle   325
The valyant Dryant. But with him he could not so prevayle.
For as he triumpht in his lucke, proceeding for to make
Continuall slaughter of his foes, sir Dryant with a stake
(Whose poynt was hardned in the fyre) did cast at him a foyne
And thrust him through the place in which the neck and shoulders
joyne.   330
He groand and from his cannell bone could scarcely pull the stake.
And beeing foyled with his blood to flyght he did him take.
Arnaeus also ran away, and Lycidas likewyse.
And Medon (whose ryght shoulderplate was also wounded) flyes.
So did Pisenor, so did Cawne, and so did Mermeros   335
Who late outronning every man, now wounded slower goes:
And so did Phole, and Menelas, and Abas who was woont
To make a spoyle among wylde Boares as oft as he did hunt:
And eeke the wyzarde Astylos who counselled his mates
To leave that fray: but he to them in vayne of leaving prates.   340
He eeke to Nessus (who for feare of wounding seemed shye)
Sayd: Fly not, thou shalt scape this fray of Hercles bowe to dye.
But Lycid and Ewrinomos, and Imbreus, and Are
Escapte not death. Sir Dryants hand did all alike them spare.
Cayneius also (though that he in flying were not slacke,)   345
Yit was he wounded on the face: for as he looked backe,
A weapons poynt did hit him full midway betweene the eyes,
Wheras the noze and forehead meete. For all this deane, yit lyes
Aphipnas snorting fast asleepe not mynding for to wake,
Wrapt in a cloke of Bearskinnes which in Ossa mount were take.   350
And in his lither hand he hilld a potte of wyne. Whom when
That Phorbas saw (although in vayne) not medling with them, then

---

318 *jolly:* exhilarated, brave, arrogant; *ruffe:*
    elation, excitement, fury
324 *throteball:* Adam's-apple
329 *foyne:* thrust

331 *cannell bone:* collarbone
332 *foyled:* stained
348 *deane:* din
351 *lither:* sluggish, lazy

He set his fingars to the thong: and saying: Thou shalt drink
Thy wyne with water taken from the Stygian fountaynes brink,
He threw his dart at him. The dart (as he that tyme by chaunce   355
Lay bolt upright uppon his backe) did through his throteboll glaunce.
He dyde and felt no payne at all. The blacke swart blood gusht out,
And on the bed and in the potte fell flushing lyke a spout.
I saw Petreius go about to pull out of the ground
An Oken tree. But as he had his armes about it round,   360
And shaakt it too and fro to make it looce, Pirithous cast
A Dart which nayled to the tree his wrything stomacke fast.
Through prowesse of Pirithous (men say) was Lycus slayne.
Through prowesse of Pirithous dyde Crome. But they both twayne
Lesse honour to theyr conquerour were, than Dyctis was, or than   365
Was Helops. Helops with a dart was striken, which through ran
His head, and entring at the ryght eare to the left eare went.
And Dyctis from a slipprye knappe downe slyding, as he ment
To shonne Perithous preacing on, fell headlong downe, and with
His hugenesse brake the greatest Ash that was in all the frith,   370
And goard his gutts uppon the stump. To wreake his death comes Phare:
And from the mount a mighty rocke with bothe his handes he tare:
Which as he was about to throwe, Duke Theseus did prevent,
And with an Oken plant uppon his mighty elbowe lent
Him such a blowe, as that he brake the bones, and past no further.   375
For leysure would not serve him then his maymed corce to murther.
He lept on hygh Bianors backe, who none was woont to beare
Besydes himself. Ageinst his sydes his knees fast nipping were,
And with his left hand taking hold uppon his foretoppe heare
He cuft him with his knubbed plant about the frowning face,   380
And made his wattled browes to breake. And with his Oken mace
He overthrew Nedimnus: and Lycespes with his dart,
And Hippasus whose beard did hyde his brest the greater part:
And Riphey tallar than the trees, and Therey who was woont
Among the hilles of Thessaly for cruell Beares to hunt,   385
And beare them angry home alyve. It did Demoleon spyght
That Theseus had so good successe and fortune in his fyght.
An old long Pynetree rooted fast he strave with all his myght
To pluck up whole bothe trunk and roote, which when he could not
                                                              bring

368 *knappe:* summit   386 *spyght:* fill with spite
370 *frith:* wood

To passe, he brake it off, and at his emnye did it fling.   390
But Theseus by admonishment of heavenly Pallas (so
He would have folke beleve it were) start backe a great way fro
The weapon as it came. Yit fell it not without some harme.
It cut from Crantors left syde bulke, his shoulder, brest, and arme.
This Crantor was thy fathers Squyre (Achilles) and was given   395
Him by Amyntor ruler of the Dolops, who was driven
By battell for to give him as an hostage for the peace
To bee observed faythfully. When Peleus in the preace
A great way off behilld him thus falne dead of this same wound,
O Crantor, deerest man to mee of all above the ground,   400
Hold heere an obitgift hee sayd: and both with force of hart
And hand, at stout Demoleons head he threw an asshen dart,
Which brake the watling of his ribbes, and sticking in the bone,
Did shake. He pulled out the steale with much adoo alone.
The head therof stacke still behynd among his lungs and lyghts.   405
Enforst to courage with his payne, he ryseth streight uprights,
And pawing at his emny with his horsish feete, he smyghts
Uppon him. Peleus bare his strokes uppon his burganet,
And fenst his shoulders with his sheeld, and evermore did set
His weapon upward with the poynt, which by his shoulders perst   410
Through both his brestes at one full blowe. Howbee't your father erst
Had killed Hyle and Phlegrye, and Hiphinous aloof
And Danes who boldly durst at hand his manhod put in proof.
To theis was added Dorylas, who ware uppon his head
A cap of woolves skinne. And the hornes of Oxen dyed red   415
With blood were then his weapon. I (for then my courage gave
Mee strength) sayd: See how much thy hornes lesse force than Iron
                                        have.
And therewithall with manly might a dart at him I drave.
Which when he could not shonne, he clapt his right hand flat uppon
His forehead where the wound should bee. For why his hand anon   420
Was nayled to his forehead fast. Hee roared out amayne.
And as he stood amazed and began to faynt for payne,
Your father Peleus (for he stood hard by him) strake him under
The middle belly with his swoord, and ript his womb asunder.

390 *emnye:* enemy   412 *aloof:* from a distance
401 *obitgift:* funeral offering   413 *at hand:* in hand-to-hand fighting
403 *watling:* woven framework   421 *amayne:* mightily
408 *burganet:* helmet   424 *womb:* abdomen

Out girdes mee Dorill streyght, and trayles his guttes uppon the
ground   ⁴²⁵
And trampling underneath his feete did breake them, and they wound
About his leggs so snarling, that he could no further go,
But fell downe dead with empty womb. Nought booted Cyllar tho
His beawtye in that frentick fray, (at leastwyse if wee graunt
That any myght in that straunge shape, of natures beawtye vaunt.)   ⁴³⁰
His beard began but then to bud: his beard was like the gold:
So also were his yellowe lokes, which goodly to behold
Midway beneath his shoulders hung. There rested in his face
A sharpe and lively cheerfulnesse with sweete and pleasant grace.
His necke, brest, shoulders, armes, and hands, as farre as he was man,   ⁴³⁵
Were such as never carvers woork yit stayne them could or can.
His neather part likewyse (which was a horse) was every whit
Full equall with his upper part, or little woorse than it.
For had yee given him horses necke, and head, he was a beast
For Castor to have ridden on. So bourly was his brest: ⁴⁴⁰
So handsome was his backe to beare a saddle: and his heare
Was blacke as jeate, but that his tayle and feete milk whyghtish were.
Full many Females of his race did wish him to theyr make.
But only dame Hylonome for lover he did take.
Of all the halfbrutes in the woodes there did not any dwell   ⁴⁴⁵
More comly than Hylonome. She usde herself so well
In dalyance, and in loving, and in uttring of her love,
That shee alone hilld Cyllarus. As much as did behove
In suchye limbes, shee trimmed them as most the eye might move.
With combing, smoothe shee made her heare: shee wallowed her full
oft   ⁴⁵⁰
In Roses and in Rosemarye, or Violets sweete and soft:
Sumtyme shee caryed Lillyes whyght: and twyce a day shee washt
Her visage in the spring that from the toppe of Pagase past:
And in the streame shee twyce a day did bath her limbes: and on
Her left syde or her shoulders came the comlyest things, and none   ⁴⁵⁵
But fynest skinnes of choycest beasts. Alike eche loved other:
Togither they among the hilles roamd up and downe: togither
They went to covert: and that tyme togither they did enter
The Lapithes house, and there the fray togither did adventer.
A dart on Cyllars left syde came, (I know not who it sent)   ⁴⁶⁰

---

⁴²⁵ *girdes:* springs   ⁴⁴³ *make:* mate
⁴⁴⁰ *bourly:* burly   ⁴⁴⁹ *suchye:* such

Which sumwhat underneathe his necke his brest asunder splent.
As lyghtly as his hart was raazd, no sooner was the dart
Pluckt out, but all his bodye wext stark cold and dyed swart.
Immediatly Hylonome his dying limbes up stayd,
And put her hand uppon the wound to stoppe the blood, and layd   465
Her mouth to his, and labored sore to stay his passing spryght.
But when shee sawe him throughly dead, then speaking woordes which
                                                                might
Not to my hearing come for noyse, shee stikt herself uppon
The weapon that had gored him, and dyde with him anon
Embracing him beetweene her armes. There also stood before   470
Myne eyes the grim Pheocomes both man and horse who wore
A Lyons skinne uppon his backe fast knit with knotts afore.
He snatching up a timber log (which scarcely two good teeme
Of Oxen could have stird) did throwe the same with force extreeme
At Phonolenyes sonne. The logge him all in fitters strake,   475
And of his head the braynepan in a thousand peeces brake,
That at his mouth, his eares, and eyes, and at his nosethrills too,
His crusshed brayne came roping out as creame is woont to doo
From sives or riddles made of wood, or as a Cullace out
From streyner or from Colender. But as he went about   480
To strippe him from his harnesse as he lay uppon the ground,
(Your father knoweth this full well) my sword his gutts did wound,
Teleboas and Cthonius bothe, were also slaine by mee.
Sir Cthonius for his weapon had a forked bough of tree.
The tother had a dart. His dart did wound mee. You may see   485
The scarre therof remayning yit. Then was the tyme that I
Should sent have beene to conquer Troy. Then was the tyme that I
Myght through my force and prowesse, if not vanquish Hector stout,
Yit at the least have hilld him wag, I put you out of Dout.
But then was Hector no body: or but a babe. And now   490
Am I forspent and worne with yeeres. What should I tell you how
Piretus dyde by Periphas? Or wherefore should I make
Long processe for to tell you of sir Ampycus that strake
The fowrefoote Oecle on the face with dart of Cornell tree,
The which had neyther head nor poynt? Or how that Macaree   495
Of Mountaine Pelithronye with a leaver lent a blowe
To Erigdupus on the brest which did him overthrowe?

461 *splent:* split   479 *riddles:* coarse sieves; *Cullace:* broth
475 *fitters:* pieces   489 *hilld . . . wag:* kept at bay

Full well I doo remember that Cymelius threw a dart
Which lyghted full in Nesseyes flank about his privie part.
And think not you that Mops, the sonne of Ampycus, could doo   500
No good but onely prophesye. This stout Odites whoo
Had bothe the shapes of man and horse, by Mopsis dart was slayne,
And labouring for to speake his last he did but strive in vayne.
For Mopsis dart togither nayld his toong and neather chappe,
And percing through his throte did make a wyde and deadly gappe.   505
Fyve men had Cene already slayne: theyr wounds I cannot say:
The names and nomber of them all ryght well I beare away.
The names of them were Stiphelus, and Brome, and Helimus,
Pyracmon with his forest bill, and stout Antimachus.
Out steppes the biggest Centawre there, huge Latreus, armed in   510
Alesus of Aemathias spoyle slayne late before by him.
His yeeres were mid tweene youth and age, his courage still was yoong,
And on his abrun head hore heares peerd heere and there amoong.
His furniture was then a swoord, a target and a lawnce
Aemathian like. To bothe the parts he did his face advaunce,   515
And brandishing his weapon brave, in circlewyse did prawnce
About, and stoutly spake theis woordes: And must I beare with yow,
Dame Cenye? for none other than a moother (I avow)
No better than a moother will I count thee whyle I live.
Remembrest not what shape by birth dame nature did thee give?   520
Forgettst thou how thou purchasedst this counterfetted shape
Of man? Consyderest what thou art by birth? and how for rape
Thou art become the thing thou art? Go take thy distaffe, and
Thy spindle, and in spinning yarne go exercyse thy hand.
Let men alone with feates of armes. As Latreus made this stout   525
And scornefull taunting in a ring still turning him about,
This Cenye with a dart did hit him full uppon the syde
Where as the horse and man were joyned togither in a hyde.
The strype made Latreus mad: and with his lawnce in rage he stracke
Uppon sir Cenyes naked ribbes. The lawnce rebounded backe   530
Like haylestones from a tyled house, or as a man should pat
Small stones uppon a dromslets head. He came more neere with that,
And in his brawned syde did stryve to thrust his swoord. There was
No way for swoord to enter in. Yit shalt thou not so passe

507 *beare away:* remember
509 *bill:* weapon with hook-shaped blade on
    wooden shaft
513 *abrun:* auburn

514 *furniture:* equipment
518 *moother:* mauther, young girl
529 *strype:* blow
532 *dromslet:* drum

My handes (sayd he.) Well sith the poynt is blunted thou shalt dye 535
Uppon the edge: and with that woord he fetcht his blow awrye,
And sydling with a sweeping stroke along his belly smit.
The strype did give a clinke as if it had on marble hit.
And therewithall the swoord did breake, and on his necke did lyght.
When Ceny had sufficiently given Latreus leave to smyght   540
His flesh which was unmaymeable, Well now (quoth he) lets see,
If my swoord able bee or no to byght the flesh of thee.
In saying so, his dreadfull swoord as farre as it would go
He underneathe his shoulder thrust, and wrinching to and fro
Among his gutts, made wound in wound. Behold with hydeous crye 545
The dowblemembred Centawres sore abasht uppon him flye,
And throwe theyr weapons all at him. Theyr weapons downe did fall
As if they had rebated beene, and Cenye for them all
Abydes unstriken through. Yea none was able blood to drawe.
The straungenesse of the cace made all amazed that it sawe.   550
Fy, fy for shame (quoth Monychus) that such a rable can
Not overcome one wyght alone, who scarcely is a man.
Although (to say the very truthe) he is the man, and wee
Through fayntnesse that that he was borne by nature for to bee.
What profits theis huge limbes of ours? what helpes our dowble force? 555
Or what avayles our dowble shape of man as well as horse
By puissant nature joynd in one? I can not thinke that wee
Of sovereigne Goddesse Juno were begot, or that wee bee
Ixions sonnes, who was so stout of courage and so hault,
As that he durst on Junos love attempt to give assault.   560
The emny that dooth vanquish us is scarcely half a man
Whelme blocks, and stones, and mountaynes whole uppon his hard
                                        brayne pan:
And presse yee out his lively ghoste with trees. Let timber choke
His chappes, let weyght enforce his death in stead of wounding stroke.
This sayd: by chaunce he gets a tree blowne downe by blustring blasts 565
Of Southerne wynds, and on his fo with all his myght it casts,
And gave example to the rest to doo the like. Within
A whyle the shadowes which did hyde mount Pelion waxed thin:
And not a tree was left uppon mount Othris ere they went.
Sir Cenye underneathe this greate huge pyle of timber pent,   570
Did chauf and on his shoulders hard the heavy logges did beare.
But when above his face and head the trees up stacked were,

548 *rebated:* blunted   564 *chappes:* jaws
559 *hault:* proud, high-minded, high-born   571 *chauf:* chafe, rage

So that he had no venting place to drawe his breth: One whyle
He faynted: and another whyle he heaved at the pyle,
To tumble downe the loggs that lay so heavy on his backe,   575
And for to winne the open ayre ageine above the stacke:
As if the mountayne Ida (lo) which yoonder we doo see
So hygh, by earthquake at a tyme should chaunce to shaken bee.
Men dowt what did become of him. Sum hold opinion that
The burthen of the woodes had driven his soule to Limbo flat.   580
But Mopsus sayd it was not so. For he did see a browne
Bird flying from amid the stacke and towring up and downe.
It was the first tyme and the last that ever I behild
That fowle. When Mopsus softly saw him soring in the feeld,
He looked wistly after him, and cryed out on hye: 585
Hayle peerlesse perle of Lapith race, hayle Ceny, late ago
A valeant knyght, and now a bird of whom there is no mo.
The author caused men beleeve the matter to bee so.
Our sorrow set us in a rage. It was too us a greef
That by so many foes one knyght was killd without releef.   590
Then ceast wee not to wreake our teene till most was slaine in fyght,
And that the rest discomfited were fled away by nyght.
       As Nestor all the processe of this battell did reherce
       Betweene the valeant Lapithes and misshapen Centawres ferce,
Tlepolemus displeased sore that Hercules was past   595
With silence, could not hold his peace, but out theis woordes did cast:
My Lord, I muse you should forget my fathers prayse so quyght.
For often unto mee himself was woonted to recite,
How that the clowdbred folk by him were cheefly put to flyght.
       Ryght sadly Nestor answerd thus: Why should you mee
                                                     constreyne   600
       To call to mynd forgotten greefs? and for to reere ageine
The sorrowes now outworne by tyme? or force mee to declare
The hatred and displeasure which I to your father bare?
In sooth his dooings greater were than myght bee well beleeved.
He fild the world with high renowme which nobly he atcheeved.   605
Which thing I would I could denye. For neyther set wee out
Deiphobus, Polydamas, nor Hector that most stout
And valeant knyght, the strength of Troy. For whoo will prayse his fo?

---

573 *whyle:* time
580 *flat:* (1) absolutely, directly, quite;
    (2) swamp, field
585 *wistly:* intently, wistfully
588 *author:* authority
591 *wreake:* vent, express; *teene:* grief
595 *past:* passed over
601 *reere:* raise, rouse

Your father overthrew the walles of Messen long ago,
And razed Pyle, and Ely townes unwoorthye serving so.   610
And feerce ageinst my fathers house hee usde bothe swoord and fyre.
And (not to speake of others whom he killed in his ire)
Twyce six wee were the sonnes of Nele all lusty gentlemen.
Twyce six of us (excepting mee) by him were murthred then.
The death of all the rest myght seeme a matter not so straunge: 615
But straunge was Periclymens death whoo had the powre to chaunge
And leave and take what shape he list (by Neptune to him given,
The founder of the house of Nele). For when he had beene driven
To try all shapes, and none could help: he last of all became
The fowle that in his hooked feete dooth beare the flasshing flame   620
Sent downe from heaven by Jupiter. He practising those birds,
With flapping wings, and bowwing beake, and hooked talants girds
At Hercle, and beescratcht his face. Too certeine (I may say)
Thy father amde his shaft at him. For as he towring lay
Among the clowdes, he hit him underneath the wing. The stroke   625
Was small: howbee't bycause therwith the sinewes being broke,
He wanted strength to maynteine flyght, he fell me to the ground,
Through weakenesse of his wing. The shaft that sticked in the wound,
By reason of the burthen of his bodye perst his syde,
And at the leftsyde of his necke all bloodye foorth did glyde.   630
Now tell mee, O thou beawtyfull Lord Amirall of the fleete
Of Rhodes, if mee to speake the prayse of Hercle it bee meete.
But lest that of my brothers deathes men think I doo desyre
A further vendge than silence of the prowesse of thy syre,
I love thee even with all my hart, and take thee for my freend.   635
When Nestor of his pleasant tales had made this freendly end,
They called for a boll of wyne, and from the table went,
And all the resdew of the nyght in sleeping soundly spent.
      But Neptune like a father tooke the matter sore to hart
      That Cygnet to a Swan he was constreyned to convert.   640
And hating feerce Achilles, he did wreake his cruell teene
Uppon him more uncourteously than had beseeming beene.
For when the warres well neere full twyce fyve yeeres had lasted, hee
Unshorne Apollo thus bespake: O nevew, unto mee
Most deere of all my brothers impes, who helpedst mee to lay   645
Foundation of the walles of Troy for which we had no pay,

---

621 *practising:* (?) putting into practice,   634 *vendge:* vengeance
     exercising himself as?   645 *impes:* offspring
622 *bowwing:* curving; *girds:* darts

And canst thou syghes forbeare to see the Asian Empyre fall?
And dooth it not lament thy hart when thou to mynd doost call
So many thousand people slayne in keeping Ilion wall?
Or (too th'entent particlerly I doo not speake of all)   650
Remembrest thou not Hectors Ghost whoo harryed was about
His towne of Troy? where nerethelesse Achilles that same stout
And farre in fyght more butcherly, whoo stryves with all his myght
To stroy the woorke of mee and thee, lives still in healthfull plyght?
If ever hee doo come within my daunger he shall feele   655
What force is in my tryple mace. But sith with swoord of steele
I may not meete him as my fo, I pray thee unbeeware
Go kill him with a sodeine shaft and rid mee of my care.
Apollo did consent: as well his uncle for to please,
As also for a pryvate grudge himself had for to ease.   660
And in a clowd he downe among the host of Troy did slyde,
Where Paris dribbling out his shaftes among the Greekes hee spyde:
And telling him what God he was, sayd: Wherfore doost thou waast
Thyne arrowes on the simple sort? If any care thou haste
Of those that are thy freendes, go turne ageinst Achilles head,   665
And like a man revendge on him thy brothers that are dead.
In saying this, he brought him where Achilles with his brond
Was beating downe the Trojane folk, and leveld so his hond
As that Achilles tumbled downe starke dead uppon the lond.
    This was the onely thing wherof the old king Priam myght   670
    Take comfort after Hectors death. That stout and valeant knyght
Achilles whoo had overthrowen so many men in fyght,
Was by that coward carpet knyght beereeved of his lyfe,
Whoo like a caytif stale away the Spartane princes wyfe.
But if of weapon womanish he had foreknowen it had   675
His destnye beene to lose his lyfe, he would have beene more glad
That Queene Penthesileas bill had slaine him out of hand.
Now was the feare of Phrygian folk, the onely glory, and
Defence of Greekes, that peerelesse prince in armes, Achilles turnd
To asshes. That same God that had him armd, him also burnd.   680
Now is he dust: and of that great Achilles bydeth still
A thing of nought, that scarcely can a little coffin fill.
Howbee't his woorthy fame dooth lyve, and spreadeth over all
The world, a measure meete for such a persone to beefall.

647 *syghes:* sighs   655 *daunger:* power, dominion
651 *harryed:* dragged   657 *unbeeware:* unaware
652 *stout:* stalwart   673 *carpet knyght:* stay-at-home knight

This matcheth thee, Achilles, full. And this can never dye.   685
His target also (too th'entent that men myght playnly spye
What wyghts it was) did move debate, and for his armour burst
Out deadly foode. Not Diomed, nor Ajax Oylye durst
Make clayme or chalendge to the same, nor Atreus yoonger sonne,
Nor yit his elder, though in armes much honour they had wonne.   690
Alone the sonnes of Telamon and Laert did assay
Which of them two of that great pryse should beare the bell away.
But Agamemnon from himself the burthen putts, and cleeres
His handes of envye, causing all the Capteines and the Peeres
Of Greece to meete amid the camp togither in a place,   695
To whom he put the heering and the judgement of the cace.

FINIS DUODECIMI LIBRI.

688 *foode:* feud   692 *beare the bell away:* win

꠲꠲꠲

THE. XIII. BOOKE OF

OVIDS METAMORPHOSIS.

[*The Contention of Ajax and Ulysses. The Fall of Troy. Polyxena,
Polydorus, and Hecuba. Memnon. Aeneas. Acis, Galatea, and Polyphe-
mus. Glaucus and Scylla.*]

The Lordes and Capteynes being set toogither with the King,
And all the souldiers standing round about them in a ring,
The owner of the sevenfold sheeld, to theis did Ajax ryse.
And (as he could not brydle wrath) he cast his frowning eyes
Uppon the shore and on the fleete that there at Anchor lyes   5
And throwing up his handes: O God and must wee plead (quoth hee)
Our case before our shippes? and must Ulysses stand with mee?
But like a wretch he ran his way when Hector came with fyre,
Which I defending from theis shippes did force him to retyre.
It easyer is therefore with woordes in print to maynteine stryfe,   10
Than for to fyght it out with fists. But neyther I am ryfe
In woordes, nor hee in deedes. For looke how farre I him excell
In battell and in feates of armes: so farre beares hee the bell
From mee in talking. Neyther think I requisite to tell
My actes among you. You your selves have seene them verry well.   15
But let Ulysses tell you his doone all in hudther mudther,
And wherunto the only nyght is privy and none other.
The pryse is great (I doo confesse) for which wee stryve. But yit
It is dishonour unto mee, for that in clayming it
So bace a persone standeth in contention for the same.   20
To think it myne already, ought to counted bee no shame

11 *ryfe:* abundant, rich
13 *beares . . . the bell:* wins over

16 *hudther   mudther:* hugger-mugger, se-
crecy
17 *the only nyght:* the night alone

319

Nor pryde in mee: although the thing of ryght great valew bee
Of which Ulysses standes in hope. For now alreadye hee
Hath wonne the honour of this pryse, in that when he shall sit
Besydes the cuishon, he may brag he strave with mee for it.   25
And though I wanted valiantnesse, yit should nobilitee
Make with mee. I of Telamon am knowne the sonne to bee
Who under valeant Hercules the walles of Troy did scale,
And in the shippe of Pagasa to Colchos land did sayle.
His father was that Aeacus whoo executeth ryght   30
Among the ghostes where Sisyphus heaves up with all his myght
The massye stone ay tumbling downe. The hyghest Jove of all
Acknowledgeth this Aeacus, and dooth his sonne him call.
Thus am I Ajax third from Jove. Yit let this Pedegree,
O Achyves, in this case of myne avaylable not bee,   35
Onlesse I proove it fully with Achylles to agree.
He was my brother, and I clayme that was my brothers. Why
Shouldst thou that art of Sisyphs blood, and for to filch and lye
Expressest him in every poynt, by foorged pedegree
Aly thee to the Aeacyds, as though we did not see   40
Thee to the house of Aeacus a straunger for to bee?
And is it reason that you should this armour mee denye
Bycause I former was in armes, and needed not a spye
To fetch mee foorth? Or think you him more woorthye it to have,
That came to warrefare hindermost, and feynd himself to rave,   45
Bycause he would have shund the warre? untill a suttler head
And more unprofitable for himself, sir Palamed,
Escryde the crafty fetches of his fearefull hart, and drew
Him foorth a warfare which he sought so cowardly to eschew?
Must he now needes enjoy the best and richest armour, whoo   50
Would none at all have worne onlesse he forced were thertoo?
And I with shame bee put besyde my cousin germanes gifts
Bycause to shun the formest brunt of warres I sought no shifts?
Would God this mischeef mayster had in verrye deede beene mad,
Or else beleeved so to bee: and that wee never had   55
Brought such a panion unto Troy. Then should not Paeans sonne
In Lemnos like an outlawe to the shame of all us wonne.
Who lurking now (as men report) in woodes and caves, dooth move
The verry flints with syghes and grones, and prayers to God above

37 *that*: that which
43 *former*: earlier
48 *Escryde*: descried; *fetches*: tricks
52 *put besyde*: deprived of

53 *formest*: foremost; *shifts*: evasions, tricks
56 *panion*: companion
57 *wonne*: live

To send Ulysses his desert. Which prayer (if there bee   60
A God) must one day take effect. And now beehold how hee
By othe a Souldier of our Camp, yea and as well as wee
A Capteine too, alas, (who was by Hercules assignde
To have the keeping of his shafts,) with payne and hungar pynde,
Is clad and fed with fowles, and dribs his arrowes up and downe   65
At birds, which were by destinye preparde to stroy Troy towne.
Yit liveth hee bycause hee is not still in companie
With sly Ulysses. Palamed that wretched knyght perdie,
Would eeke he had abandond beene. For then should still the same
Have beene alyve: or at the least have dyde without our shame.   70
But this companion bearing (ah) too well in wicked mynd
His madnesse which sir Palamed by wisdome out did fynd,
Appeached him of treason that he practysde to betray
The Greekish hoste. And for to vouch the fact, he shewd streyght way
A masse of goold that he himself had hidden in his tent,   75
And forged Letters which he feynd from Priam to bee sent.
Thus eyther by his murthring men or else by banishment
Abateth hee the Greekish strength. This is Ulysses fyght.
This is the feare he puttes men in. But though he had more might
Than Nestor hath, in eloquence he shal not compasse mee   80
To think his leawd abandoning of Nestor for to bee
No fault: who beeing cast behynd by wounding of his horse,
And slowe with age, with calling on Ulysses waxing hoarce,
Was nerethelesse betrayd by him. Sir Diomed knowes this cryme
Is unsurmysde. For he himselfe did at that present tyme   85
Rebuke him oftentymes by name, and feercely him upbrayd
With flying from his fellowe so who stood in neede of ayd.
With ryghtfull eyes dooth God behold the deedes of mortall men.
Lo, he that helped not his freend wants help himself agen.
And as he did forsake his freend in tyme of neede: so hee   90
Did in the selfsame perrill fall forsaken for to bee.
He made a rod to beat himself. He calld and cryed out
Uppon his fellowes. Streight I came: and there I saw the lout
Bothe quake and shake for feare of death, and looke as pale as clout.
I set my sheeld betweene him and his foes, and him bestrid: 95
And savde the dastards lyfe. Small prayse redoundes of that I did.
But if thou wilt contend with mee, lets to the selfesame place

---

65 *dribs:* shoots short or wide
66 *stroy:* destroy
73 *Appeached:* impeached, accused

85 *unsurmysde:* not merely imagined, actual
94 *clout:* cloth

Agein: bee wounded as thou wart: and in the foresayd case
Of feare, beset about with foes: cowch underneath my sheeld:
And then contend thou with mee there amid the open feeld.   100
Howbee't, I had no sooner rid this champion of his foes,
But where for woundes he scarce before could totter on his toes,
He ran away apace, as though he nought at all did ayle.
Anon commes Hector to the feeld and bringeth at his tayle
The Goddes. Not only thy hart there (Ulysses) did thee fayle,   105
But even the stowtest courages and stomacks gan to quayle.
So great a terrour brought he in. Yit in the midds of all
His bloody ruffe, I coapt with him, and with a foyling fall
Did overthrowe him to the ground. Another tyme, when hee
Did make a chalendge, you my Lordes by lot did choose out mee,   110
And I did match him hand to hand. Your wisshes were not vayne.
For if you aske mee what successe our combate did obteine,
I came away unvanquished. Behold the men of Troy
Brought fyre and swoord, and all the feendes our navye to destroy.
And where was slye Ulysses then with all his talk so smooth?   115
This brest of myne was fayne to fence your thousand shippes forsooth,
The hope of your returning home. For saving that same day
So many shippes, this armour give. But (if that I shall say
The truth) the greater honour now this armour beares away.
And our renownes togither link. For (as of reason ought)   120
An Ajax for this armour, not an armour now is sought
For Ajax. Let Dulychius match with theis, the horses whyght
Of Rhesus, dastard Dolon, and the coward carpetknyght
King Priams Helen, and the stelth of Palladye by nyght.
Of all theis things was nothing doone by day nor nothing wrought   125
Without the helpe of Diomed. And therefore if yee thought
To give them to so small deserts, devyde the same, and let
Sir Diomed have the greater part. But what should Ithacus get
And if he had them, who dooth all his matters in the dark,
Who never weareth armour, who shootes ay at his owne mark   130
To trappe his fo by stelth unwares? The very headpeece may
With brightnesse of the glistring gold his privie feates bewray
And shew him lurking. Neyther well of force Dulychius were
The weyght of great Achilles helme uppon his pate to weare.
It cannot but a burthen bee (and that ryght great) to beare   135
(With those same shrimpish armes of his) Achilles myghty speare.

108 *ruffe:* excitement, fury; *foyling:* over-   123 *carpetknyght:* stay-at-home knight
throwing

Agen his target graven with the whole huge world theron
Agrees not with a fearefull hand, and cheefly such a one
As taketh filching even by kynd. Thou Lozell, thou doost seeke
A gift that will but weaken thee, which if the folk of Greeke   140
Shall give thee through theyr oversyght, it will be unto thee
Occasion, of thyne emnyes spoyld not feared for to bee,
And flyght (wherein thou, coward, thou all others mayst outbrag)
Will hindred bee when after thee such masses thou shalt drag.
Moreover this thy sheeld that feeles so seeld the force of fyght   145
Is sound. But myne is gasht and hakt and stricken thurrough quyght
A thousand tymes, with bearing blowes. And therfore myne must walk
And put another in his stead. But what needes all this talk?
Lets now bee seene another whyle what eche of us can doo.
The thickest of our armed foes this armour throwe into,   150
And bid us fetch the same fro thence. And which of us dooth fetch
The same away, reward yee him therewith. Thus farre did stretch
The woordes of Ajax. At the ende whereof there did ensew
A muttring of the souldiers, till Laertis sonne the prew
Stood up, and raysed soberly his eyliddes from the ground   155.
(On which he had a little whyle them pitched in a stound)
And looking on the noblemen who longd his woordes to heere
He thus began with comly grace and sober pleasant cheere:
    My Lordes, if my desyre and yours myght erst have taken place,
    It should not at this present tyme have beene a dowtfull cace,   160
What person hath most ryght to this great pryse for which wee stryve.
Achilles should his armour have, and wee still him alyve.
Whom sith that cruell destinie to both of us denyes,
(With that same woord as though he wept, he wypte his watry eyes)
What wyght of reason rather ought to bee Achilles heyre,   165
Than he through whom to this your camp Achilles did repayre?
Alonly let it not avayle sir Ajax heere, that hee
Is such a dolt and grossehead, as he shewes himself to bee
Ne let my wit (which ay hath done you good, O Greekes) hurt mee.
But suffer this mine eloquence (such as it is) which now   170
Dooth for his mayster speake, and oft ere this hath spoke for yow,
Bee undisdeynd. Let none refuse his owne good gifts he brings.
For as for stocke and auncetors, and other such like things
Wherof our selves no fownders are, I scarcely dare them graunt

---

139 *kynd:* nature; *Lozell:* scoundrel, good-   147 *walk:* go, be got rid of
    for-nothing   154 *prew:* valiant
145 *seeld:* seldom   156 *a stound:* wonder, absorption

To bee our owne. But forasmuch as Ajax makes his vaunt   175
To bee the fowrth from Jove: even Jove the founder is also
Of my house: and than fowre descents I am from him no mo.
Laertes is my father, and Arcesius his, and hee
Begotten was of Jupiter. And in this pedegree
Is neyther any damned soule, nor outlaw as yee see.   180
Moreover by my moothers syde I come of Mercuree,
Another honor to my house. Thus both by fathers syde
And moothers (as you may perceyve) I am to Goddes alyde.
But neyther for bycause I am a better gentleman
Then Ajax by the moothers syde, nor that my father can   185
Avouch himself ungiltye of his brothers blood, doo I
This armour clayme. Wey you the case by merits uprightly,
Provyded no prerogatyve of birthryght Ajax beare,
For that his father Telamon, and Peleus brothers were.
Let only prowesse in this pryse the honour beare away.   190
Or if the case on kinrid or on birthryght seeme to stay,
His father Peleus is alive, and Pyrrhus eeke his sonne.
What tytle then can Ajax make? This geere of ryght should woone
To Phthya, or to Scyros Ile. And Tewcer is as well
Achilles uncle as is hee. Yit dooth not Tewcer mell.   195
And if he did, should hee obteyne? Well, sith the cace dooth rest
On tryall which of us can prove his dooings to bee best,
I needes must say my deedes are mo than well I can expresse:
Yit will I shew them orderly as neere as I can gesse.
Foreknowing that her sonne should dye, the Lady Thetis hid   200
Achilles in a maydes attyre. By which fyne slyght shee did
All men deceyve, and Ajax too. This armour in a packe
With other womens tryflyng toyes I caryed on my backe,
A bayte to treyne a manly hart. Apparelld like a mayd
Achilles tooke the speare and sheeld in hand, and with them playd.   205
Then sayd I: O thou Goddesse sonne, why shouldst thou bee afrayd
To raze great Troy, whoose overthrowe for thee is onely stayd?
And laying hand uppon him I did send him (as you see)
To valeant dooings meete for such a valeant man as hee.
And therfore all the deedes of him are my deedes. I did wound   210
King Teleph with his speare, and when he lay uppon the ground,
I was intreated with the speare to heale him safe and sound.
That Thebe lyeth overthrowne, is my deede. You must think

---

193 *woone/To:* remain at, go to stay at   204 *treyne:* draw, entice
195 *mell:* meddle

I made the folk of Tenedos and Lesbos for to shrink.
Both Chryse and Cillas, Phebus townes, and Scyros I did take. 215
And my ryght hand Lyrnessus walles to ground did levell make.
I gave you him that should confound (besydes a number mo)
The valeant Hector. Hector, that our most renowmed fo,
Is slayne by mee. This armour heere I sue agein to have
This armour by the which I found Achilles. I it gave 220
Achilles whyle he was alive: and now that he is gone
I clayme it as myne owne agein. What tyme the greefe of one
Had perst the harts of all the Greekes, and that our thousand sayle
At Awlis by Ewboya stayd, bycause the wyndes did fayle,
Continewing eyther none at all or cleene ageinst us long, 225
And that our Agamemnon was by destnyes overstrong
Commaunded for to sacrifyse his giltlesse daughter to
Diana, which her father then refusing for to doo
Was angry with the Godds themselves, and though he were a king
Continued also fatherlyke: by reason, I did bring 230
His gentle nature to relent for publike profits sake.
I must confesse (whereat his grace shall no displeasure take)
Before a parciall judge I undertooke a ryght hard cace.
Howbeeit for his brothers sake, and for the royall mace
Committed, and his peoples weale, at length he was content 235
To purchace prayse wyth blood. Then was I to the moother sent,
Who not perswaded was to bee, but compast with sum guyle.
Had Ajax on this errand gone, our shippes had all this whyle
Lyne still there yit for want of wynd. Moreover I was sent
To Ilion as ambassadour. I boldly thither went, 240
And entred and behilld the Court, wherin there was as then
Great store of princes, Dukes, Lords, knyghts, and other valeant men.
And yit I boldly nerethelesse my message did at large
The which the whole estate of Greece had given mee erst in charge.
I made complaint of Paris, and accusde him to his head. 245
Demaunding restitution of Queene Helen that same sted
And of the bootye with her tane. Both Priamus the king
And eeke Antenor his alye the woordes of mee did sting.
And Paris and his brothers, and the resdew of his trayne
That under him had made the spoyle, could hard and scarce refrayne 250
There wicked hands. You, Menelay, doo know I doo not feyne.
And that day was the first in which wee joyntly gan susteyne

222 *What tyme:* when   246 *sted:* time
237 *compast:* taken in, won over

A tast of perrills, store whereof did then behind remayne.
It would bee overlong to tell eche profitable thing
That during this long lasting warre I well to passe did bring,   255
By force as well as pollycie. For after that the furst
Encounter once was overpast, our emnyes never durst
Give battell in the open feeld, but hild themselves within
Theyr walles and bulwarks till the tyme the tenth yeere did begin,
Now what didst thou of all that whyle, that canst doo nought but
                                                          streeke?   260
Or to what purpose servedst thou? For if thou my deedes seeke,
I practysd sundry pollycies to trappe our foes unware:
I fortifyde our Camp with trench which heretofore lay bare:
I hartned our companions with a quiet mynd to beare
The longnesse of the weery warre: I taught us how wee were   265
Bothe to bee fed and furnished: and to and fro I went
To places where the Counsell thought most meete I should bee sent.
Behold the king deceyved in his dreame by false pretence
Of Joves commaundement, bade us rayse our seedge and get us hence.
The author of his dooing so may well bee his defence.   270
Now Ajax should have letted this, and calld them backe ageine
To sacke the towne of Troy. He should have fought with myght and
                                                          maine.
Why did he not restreyne them when they ready were to go?
Why tooke he not his swoord in hand? why gave he not as tho
Sum counsell for the fleeting folk to follow at the brunt?   275
In fayth it had a tryfle beene to him that ay is woont
Such vaunting in his mouth to have. But he himself did fly
As well as others. I did see, and was ashamed, I,
To see thee when thou fledst, and didst prepare so cowardly
To sayle away. And thereuppon I thus aloud did cry: 280
What meene yee, sirs? what madnesse dooth you move to go to shippe
And suffer Troy as good as tane, thus out of hand to slippe?
What else this tenth yeere beare yee home than shame? with such
                                                          like woord
And other, (which the eloquence of sorrowe did avoord,)
I brought them from theyr flying shippes. Then Agamemnon calld   285
Toogither all the capteines who with feare were yit appalld.

256 *pollycie:* craftiness   274 *as tho:* then
260 *streeke:* strike   275 *brunt:* attack, critical moment
271 *letted:* prevented   284 *avoord:* afford

But Ajax durst not then once creake. Yit durst Thersites bee
So bold as rayle uppon the kings, and he was payd by mee
For playing so the sawcye Jacke. Then stood I on my toes
And to my fearefull countrymen gave hart ageinst theyr foes.   290
And shed new courage in theyr mynds through talk that fro mee goes.
From that tyme foorth what ever thing hath valeantly atcheeved
By this good fellow beene, is myne, whoo him from flyght repreeved.
And now to touche thee: which of all the Greekes commendeth thee?
Or seeketh thee? But Diomed communicates with mee   295
His dooings, and alloweth mee, and thinkes him well apayd
To have Ulysses ever as companion at the brayd.
And sumwhat woorth you will it graunt (I trow) alone for mee
Out of so many thousand Greekes by Diomed pikt to bee.
No lot compelled mee to go, and yit I setting lyght   300
As well the perrill of my foes as daunger of the nyght,
Killd Dolon who about the selfsame feate that nyght did stray,
That wee went out for. But I first compelld him to bewray
All things concerning faythlesse Troy, and what it went about.
When all was learnd, and nothing left behynd to harken out,   305
I myght have then come home with prayse. I was not so content.
Proceeding further to the Camp of Rhesus streyght I went,
And killed bothe himself and all his men about his tent.
And taking bothe his chariot and his horses which were whyght,
Returned home in tryumph like a conquerour from fyght.   310
Denye you mee the armour of the man whoose steedes the fo
Requyred for his playing of the spye a nyght, and so
May Ajax bee more kynd to mee than you are. What should I
Declare unto you how my sword did waste ryght valeantly
Sarpedons hoste of Lycia? I by force did overthrowe   315
Alastor, Crome, and Ceranos, and Haly on a rowe.
Alcander, and Noemon too, and Prytanis besyde,
And Thoon and Theridamas, and Charops also dyde
By mee, and so did Ewnomos enforst by cruell fate.
And many mo in syght of Troy I slew of bacer state.   320
There also are (O countrymen) about mee woundings, which
The place of them make beawtyfull. See heere (his hand did twich
His shirt asyde) and credit not vayne woordes. Lo heere the brist
That alwayes to bee one in your affayres hath never mist.

287 *creake:* squeak, open his mouth
296 *apayd:* satisfied
297 *brayd:* onset, attack
303 *bewray:* reveal

305 *harken out:* learn by hearing, search
out
313 *What:* why

And yit of all this whyle no droppe of blood hath Ajax spent   325
Uppon his fellowes. Woundlesse is his body and unrent.
But what skills that, as long as he is able for to vaunt
He fought against bothe Troy and Jove to save our fleete? I graunt
He did so. For I am not of such nature as of spyght
Well dooings to deface: so that he chalendge not the ryght   330
Of all men to himself alone, and that he yeeld to mee
Sum share, whoo of the honour looke a partener for to bee.
Patroclus also having on Achilles armour, sent
The Trojans and theyr leader hence, to burne our navye bent.
And yit thinks hee that none durst meete with Hector saving hee,   335
Forgetting bothe the king, and eeke his brother, yea and mee.
Where hee himself was but the nyneth, appoynted by the king,
And by the fortune of his lot preferd to doo the thing.
But now for all your valeantnesse, what Issue had I pray
Your combate? Shall I tell? Forsoothe, that Hector went his way   340
And had no harme. Now wo is mee how greeveth it my hart
To think uppon that season when the bulwark of our part
Achilles dyde. When neyther teares, nor greef, nor feare could make
Mee for to stay, but that uppon theis shoulders I did take,
I say uppon theis shoulders I Achilles body tooke,   345
And this same armour claspt theron, which now to weare I looke.
Sufficient strength I have to beare as great a weyght as this,
And eeke a hart wherein regard of honour rooted is.
Think you that Thetis for her sonne so instantly besought
Sir Vulcane this same heavenly gift to give her, which is wrought   350
With such exceeding cunning, to th'entent a souldier that
Hath neyther wit nor knowledge should it weare? He knowes not what
The things ingraven on the sheeld doo meene. Of Ocean se,
Of land, of heaven, and of the starres no skill at all hath he.
The Beare that never dyves in sea he dooth not understand,   355
The Pleyads, nor the Hyads, nor the cities that doo stand
Uppon the earth, nor yit the swoord that Orion holdes in hand.
He seekes to have an armour of the which he hath no skill.
And yit in fynding fault with mee bycause I had no will
To follow this same paynfull warre and sought to shonne the same,   360
And made it sumwhat longer tyme before I thither came,
He sees not how hee speakes reproch to stout Achilles name.
For if to have dissembled in this case, yee count a cryme,
Wee both offenders bee. Or if protracting of the tyme

327 _skills:_ matters   358 _skill:_ understanding

Yee count blame woorthye, yit was I the tymelyer of us twayne. 365
Achilles loving moother him, my wyfe did mee deteyne.
The former tyme was given to them, the rest was given to yow.
And therefore doo I little passe although I could not now
Defend my fault, sith such a man of prowesse, birth and fame
As was Achilles, was with mee offender in the same. 370
But yit was he espyed by Ulysses wit, but nat
Ulysses by sir Ajax wit. And lest yee woonder at
The rayling of this foolish dolt at mee, hee dooth object
Reproche to you. For if that I offended to detect
Sir Palamed of forged fault, could you without your shame 375
Arreyne him, and condemne him eeke to suffer for the same?
But neyther could sir Palamed excuse him of the cryme
So heynous and so manifest: and you your selves that tyme
Not onely his indytement heard, but also did behold
His deed avowched to his face by bringing in the gold. 380
And as for Philoctetes, that he is in Lemnos, I
Deserve not to bee toucht therwith. Defend your cryme: for why
You all consented therunto. Yit doo I not denye,
But that I gave the counsell to convey him out of way
From toyle of warre and travell that by rest he myght assay 385
To ease the greatnesse of his peynes. He did thereto obey
And by so dooing is alyve. Not only faythfull was
This counsell that I gave the man, but also happye, as
The good successe hath shewed since. Whom sith the destnyes doo
Requyre in overthrowing Troy, appoynt not mee thertoo: 390
But let sir Ajax rather go. For he with eloquence
Or by some suttle pollycie, shall bring the man fro thence
And pacyfie him raging through disease, and wrathfull ire.
Nay, first the river Simois shall to his spring retyre,
And mountaine Ida shall theron have stonding never a tree, 395
Yea and the faythlesse towne of Troy by Greekes shall reskewd bee,
Before that Ajax blockish wit shall aught at all avayle,
When my attempts and practyses in your affayres doo fayle.
For though thou, Philoctetes, with the king offended bee,
And with thy fellowes everychone, and most of all with mee, 400
Although thou cursse and ban mee to the hellish pit for ay,
And wisshest in thy payne that I by chaunce myght crosse thy way,
Of purpose for to draw my blood: yit will I give assay

400 *everychone:* everyone   401 *ban:* damn

To fetch thee hither once ageine. And (if that fortune say
Amen,) I will as well have thee and eeke thyne arrowes, as   405
I have the Trojane prophet whoo by mee surprysed was,
Or as I did the Oracles and Trojane fates disclose,
Or as I from her chappell through the thickest of her foes
The Phrygian Pallads image fetcht: and yit dooth Ajax still
Compare himself with mee. Yee knowe it was the destinyes will   410
That Troy should never taken bee by any force, untill
This Image first were got. And where was then our valeant knight
Sir Ajax? Where the stately woordes of such a hardy wyght?
Why feareth hee? Why dares Ulysses ventring through the watch
Commit his persone to the nyght his buysnesse to dispatch?   415
And through the pykes not only for to passe the garded wall
But also for to enter to the strongest towre of all
And for to take the Idoll from her Chappell and her shryne
And beare her thence amid his foes? For had this deede of myne
Beene left undoone, in vayne his sheeld of Oxen hydes seven fold   420
Should yit the Sonne of Telamon have in his left hand hold.
That nyght subdewed I Troy towne. That nyght did I it win,
And opened it for you likewyse with ease to enter in.
Cease to upbrayd mee by theis lookes and mumbling woordes of thyne
With Diomed: his prayse is in this fact as well as myne.   425
And thou thy selfe when for our shippes thou diddest in reskew stand,
Wart not alone: the multitude were helping thee at hand.
I had but only one with mee. Whoo (if he had not thought
A wyseman better than a strong, and that preferment ought
Not alway followe force of hand) would now himself have sought   430
This Armour. So would toother Ajax better stayed doo,
And feerce Ewrypyle, and the sonne of hault Andremon too.
No lesse myght eeke Idominey, and eeke Meriones,
His countryman, and Menelay. For every one of these
Are valeant men of hand, and not inferior unto thee   435
In martiall feates. And yit they are contented rulde to bee
By myne advyce. Thou hast a hand that serveth well in fyght.
Thou hast a wit that stands in neede of my direction ryght.
Thy force is witlesse. I have care of that that may ensew.
Thou well canst fyght: the king dooth choose the tymes for fyghting
                                                                dew   440
By myne advyce. Thou only with thy body canst avayle.

421 *hold:* held   432 *hault:* lofty, proud
431 *better stayed:* more controlled

But I with bodye and with mynd to profite doo not fayle,
And looke how much the mayster dooth excell the gally slave,
Or looke how much preheminence the Capteine ought to have
Above his souldyer: even so much excell I also thee.   445
A wit farre passing strength of hand inclosed is in mee.
In wit rests cheefly all my force. My Lordes, I pray bestowe
This gift on him who ay hath beene your watchman as yee knowe.
And for my tenne yeeres cark and care endured for your sake
Full recompence for my deserts with this same honour make.   450
Our labour draweth to an end, all lets are now by mee
Dispatched. And by bringing Troy in cace to taken bee
I have already taken it. Now by the hope that yee
Conceyve, within a whyle of Troy the ruine for to see,
And by the Goddes of whom alate our emnyes I bereft,   455
And as by wisedome to bee doone yit any thing is left,
If any bold aventrous deede, or any perlous thing,
That asketh hazard both of lyfe and limb to passe to bring,
Or if yee think of Trojane fates there yit dooth ought remayne,
Remember mee. Or if from mee this armour you restrayne,   460
Bestowe it on this same. With that he shewed with his hand
Minervas fatall image, which hard by in syght did stand.
    The Lords were moved with his woordes, and then appeared playne
    The force that is in eloquence. The lerned man did gayne
The armour of the valeant. He that did so oft susteine   465
Alone both fyre, and swoord, and Jove, and Hector could not byde
One brunt of wrath. And whom no force could vanquish ere that tyde,
Now only anguish overcommes. He drawes his swoord and sayes:
Well: this is myne yit. Unto this no clayme Ulysses layes.
This must I use ageinst myself: this blade that heretofore   470
Hath bathed beene in Trojane blood, must now his mayster gore
That none may Ajax overcome save Ajax. With that woord
Into his brest (not wounded erst) he thrust his deathfull swoord.
His hand to pull it out ageine unable was. The blood
Did spout it out. Anon the ground bestayned where he stood,   475
Did breede the pretye purple flowre uppon a clowre of greene,
Which of the wound of Hyacinth had erst engendred beene.
The selfsame letters eeke that for the chyld were written than,
Were now againe amid the flowre new written for the man.

449 *cark*: anxiety, toil   460 *restrayne*: hold back
451 *lets*: obstacles   476 *clowre*: sward, grassy surface
452 *cace*: condition

The former tyme complaynt, the last a name did represent.   480
Ulysses, having wonne the pryse, within a whyle was sent
To Thoants and Hysiphiles realme, the land defamde of old
For murthering all the men therin by women over bold.
At length attayning land and lucke according to his mynd,
To carry Hercles arrowes backe he set his sayles to wynd.   485
Which when he with the lord of them among the Greekes had brought,
And of the cruell warre at length the utmost feate had wrought,
At once both Troy and Priam fell. And Priams wretched wife
Lost (after all) her womans shape, and barked all her lyfe
In forreine countrye. In the place that bringeth to a streight   490
The long spred sea of Hellespont, did Ilion burne in height.
The kindled fyre with blazing flame continewed unalayd,
And Priam with his aged blood Joves Altar had berayd.
And Phebus preestesse casting up her handes to heaven on hye,
Was dragd and haled by the heare. The Grayes most spyghtfully   495
(As eche of them had prisoners tane in meede of victorye)
Did drawe the Trojane wyves away, who lingring whyle they mought
Among the burning temples of theyr Goddes, did hang about
Theyr sacred shrynes and images. Astyanax downe was cast
From that same turret from the which his moother in tyme past   500
Had shewed him his father stand oft fyghting to defend
Himself and that same famous realme of Troy that did descend
From many noble auncetors. And now the northerne wynd
With prosperous blasts, to get them thence did put the Greekes in mynd.
The shipmen went aboord, and hoyst up sayles, and made fro thence.   505
Adeew deere Troy (the women cryde), wee haled are from hence.
And therwithall they kist the ground, and left yit smoking still
Theyr native houses. Last of all tooke shippe ageinst her will
Queene Hecub: who (a piteous cace to see) was found amid
The tumbes in which her sonnes were layd. And there as Hecub did   510
Embrace theyr chists and kisse theyr bones, Ulysses voyd of care
Did pull her thence. Yit raught shee up, and in her boosom bare
Away a crum of Hectors dust, and left on Hectors grave
Her hory heares and teares, which for poore offrings shee him gave.
    Ageinst the place where Ilion was, there is another land   515
    Manured by the Biston men. In this same Realme did stand
King Polemnestors palace riche, to whom king Priam sent
His little infant Polydore to foster, to th'entent

493 *berayd:* stained   512 *raught:* reached, seized
495 *Grayes:* Graii, Greeks   516 *Manured:* held, cultivated

He might bee out of daunger from the warres: wherin he ment
Ryght wysely, had he not with him great riches sent, a bayt   520
To stirre a wicked covetous mynd to treason and deceyt.
For when the state of Troy decayd, the wicked king of Thrace
Did cut his nurcechylds weazant, and (as though the sinfull cace
Toogither with the body could have quyght beene put away)
He threw him also in the sea. It happened by the way,   525
That Agamemnon was compeld with all his fleete to stay
Uppon the coast of Thrace, untill the sea were wexen calme,
And till the hideous stormes did cease, and furious wynds were falne.
Heere rysing gastly from the ground which farre about him brake,
Achilles with a threatning looke did like resemblance make   530
As when at Agamemnon he his wrongfull swoord did shake,
And sayd: Unmyndfull part yee hence of mee, O Greekes, and must
My merits thanklesse thus with mee be buryed in the dust?
Nay, doo not so. But to th'entent my death dew honour have,
Let Polyxene in sacrifyse bee slayne uppon my grave.   535
Thus much he sayd: and shortly his companions dooing as
By vision of his cruell ghost commaundment given them was,
Did fetch her from her mothers lappe, whom at that tyme, well neere,
In that most great adversitie alonly shee did cheere.
The haultye and unhappye mayd, and rather to bee thought   540
A man than woman, to the tumb with cruell hands was brought,
To make a cursed sacrifyse. Whoo mynding constantly
Her honour, when shee standing at the Altar prest to dye,
Perceyvd the savage ceremonies in making ready, and
The cruell Neoptolemus with naked swoord in hand   545
Stand staring with ungentle eyes uppon her gentle face,
        She sayd: Now use thou when thou wilt my gentle blood. The cace
        Requyres no more delay. Bestow thy weapon in my chest,
Or in my throte: (in saying so shee proferred bare her brest,
And eeke her throte). Assure your selves it never shalbee seene,   550
That any wyght shall (by my will) have slave of Polyxeene.
Howbee't with such a sacrifyse no God yee can delyght.
I would desyre no more but that my wretched moother myght
Bee ignorant of this my death. My moother hindreth mee,
And makes the pleasure of my death much lesser for to bee.   555
Howbeeit not the death of mee should justly greeve her hart:
But her owne lyfe. Now to th'entent I freely may depart
To Limbo, stand yee men aloof: and sith I aske but ryght

523 *weazant:* windpipe

Forebeare to touch mee. So my blood unsteyned in his syght
Shall farre more acceptable been what ever wyght he bee   560
Whom you prepare to pacifye by sacrifysing mee.
Yit (if that these last woordes of myne may purchace any grace),
I, daughter of king Priam erst, and now in prisoners cace,
Beeseeche you all unraunsomed to render to my moother
My bodye: and for buriall of the same to take none other   565
Reward than teares: for whyle shee could shee did redeeme with gold.
This sayd: the teares that shee forbare the people could not hold.
And even the verry preest himself full sore ageinst his will
And weeping, thrust her through the brest which she hild stoutly still.
Shee sinking softly to the ground with faynting legges, did beare   570
Even to the verry latter gasp a countnance voyd of feare.
And when shee fell, shee had a care such parts of her to hyde,
As womanhod and chastitie forbiddeth to be spyde.
     The Trojane women tooke her up, and moorning reckened
     King Priams children, and what blood that house alone had
                                                        shed.   575
They syghde for fayer Polyxeene: they syghed eeke for thee
Who late wart Priams wyfe, whoo late wart counted for to bee
The flowre of Asia in his flowre, and Queene of moothers all:
But now the bootye of the fo as evill lot did fall,
And such a bootye as the sly Ulysses did not passe   580
Uppon her, saving that erewhyle shee Hectors moother was.
So hardly for his moother could a mayster Hector fynd.
Embracing in her aged armes the bodye of the mynd
That was so stout, shee powrd theron with sobbing syghes unsoft
The teares that for her husband and her children had so oft   585
And for her countrye sheaded beene. Shee weeped in her wound
And kist her pretye mouth, and made her brist with shrekes to sound,
According to her woonted guyse, and in the jellyed blood
Beerayed all her grisild heare, and in a sorrowfull mood
Sayd theis and many other woordes with brest bescratcht and rent: 590
     O daughter myne, the last for whom thy moother may lament,
     (For what remaynes?) O daughter, thou art dead and gone. I see
Thy wound which at the verry hart strikes mee as well as thee.
And lest that any one of myne unwounded should depart,
Thou also gotten hast a wound. Howbee't bycause thou wart   595
A woman, I beleeved thee from weapon to bee free.

---

580 *passe/Uppon:* care for   589 *Beerayed:* stained

But notwithstanding that thou art a woman, I doo see
Thee slayne by swoord. Even he that kild thy brothers killeth thee,
Achilles, the decay of Troy and maker bare of mee.
What tyme that he of Paris shaft by Phebus meanes was slayne,   600
I sayd of feerce Achilles now no feare dooth more remayne.
But then, even then he most of all was feared for to bee.
The asshes of him rageth still ageinst our race I see.
Wee feele an emny of him dead and buryed in his grave.
To feede Achilles furie, I a frutefull issue gave.   605
Great Troy lyes under foote, and with a ryght great greevous fall
The mischeeves of the common weale are fully ended all.
But though to others Troy be gone, yit standes it still to mee:
My sorrowes ronne as fresh a race as ever and as free.
I late ago a sovereine state, advaunced with such store   610
Of daughters, sonnes, and sonneinlawes, and husband over more
And daughtrinlawes, am caryed like an outlawe bare and poore,
By force and violence haled from my childrens tumbes, to bee
Presented to Penelope a gift, who shewing mee
In spinning my appoynted taske, shall say: This same is shee   615
That was sumtyme king Priams wyfe, this was the famous moother
Of Hector. And now after losse of such a sort of other,
Thou (whoo alonly in my greefe my comfort didst remayne,)
To pacifye our emnyes wrath uppon his tumb art slayne.
Thus bare I deathgyfts for my foes. To what intent am I   620
Most wretched wyght remayning still? Why doo I linger? Why
Dooth hurtfull age preserve mee still alive? To what intent,
Yee cruell Goddes, reserve yee mee that hath already spent
Too manye yeeres, onlesse it bee new buryalls for to see?
And whoo would think that Priamus myght happy counted bee   625
Sith Troy is razed? Happy man is hee in being dead.
His lyfe and kingdoome he forwent toogither: and this stead
He sees not thee, his daughter, slaine. But peradventure thou
Shall like the daughter of a king have sumptuous buryall now,
And with thy noble auncetors thy bodye layd shall bee.   630
Our linage hath not so good lucke. The most that shall to thee
Bee yeelded are thy moothers teares, and in this forreine land
To hyde thy murthered corce withall a little heape of sand.
For all is lost. Nay yit remaynes (for whome I well can fynd

---

610 *sovereine state:* person of highest rank   627 *forwent:* went from, gave up; *stead:*
611 *over more:* moreover   time

In hart to live a little whyle) an imp unto my mynd   635
Most deere, now only left alone, sumtyme of many mo
The yoongest, little Polydore, delivered late ago
To Polemnestor, king of Thrace, whoo dwelles within theis bounds.
But wherefore doo I stay so long in wasshing of her wounds,
And face berayd with gory blood? In saying thus, shee went   640
To seaward with an aged pace and hory heare beerent.
And (wretched woman) as shee calld for pitchers for to drawe
Up water, shee of Polydore on shore the carkesse sawe,
And eeke the myghty wounds at which the Tyrants swoord went
                                                                                          thurrow.
The Trojane Ladyes shreeked out. But shee was dumb for sorrow. 645
The anguish of her hart forclosde as well her speech as eeke
Her teares devowring them within. Shee stood astonyed leeke
As if shee had beene stone. One whyle the ground shee staard uppon.
Another whyle a gastly looke shee kest to heaven. Anon
Shee looked on the face of him that lay before her killd.   650
Sumtymes his woundes, (his woundes I say) shee specially behilld.
And therwithall shee armd her selfe and furnisht her with ire:
Wherethrough as soone as that her hart was fully set on fyre,
As though shee still had beene a Queene, to vengeance shee her bent
Enforcing all her witts to fynd some kynd of ponnishment.   655
And as a Lyon robbed of her whelpes becommeth wood,
And taking on the footing of her emnye where hee stood,
Purseweth him though out of syght: even so Queene Hecubee
(Now having meynt her teares with wrath) forgetting quyght that shee
Was old, but not her princely hart, to Polemnestor went   660
The cursed murtherer, and desyrde his presence to th'entent
To shew to him a masse of gold (so made shee her pretence)
Which for her lyttle Polydore was hid not farre from thence.
The Thracian king beleeving her, as eager of the pray,
Went with her to a secret place. And as they there did stay,   665
With flattring and deceytfull toong he thus to her did say:
Make speede I prey thee, Hecuba, and give thy sonne this gold.
I sweare by God it shall bee his, as well that I doo hold
Already, as that thou shalt give. Uppon him speaking so,
And swearing and forswearing too, shee looked sternely tho,   670
And beeing sore inflaamd with wrath, caught hold uppon him, and

635 *imp*: child   647 *leeke*: like
641 *beerent*: torn   656 *wood*: enraged, furious
646 *forclosde*: barred   659 *meynt*: mixed

Streyght calling out for succor to the wyves of Troy at hand
Did in the traytors face bestowe her nayles, and scratched out
His eyes, her anger gave her hart and made her strong and stout.
Shee thrust her fingars in as farre as could bee, and did bore 675
Not now his eyes (for why his eyes were pulled out before)
But bothe the places of the eyes berayd with wicked blood.
  The Thracians at theyr Tyrannes harme for anger wexing wood,
  Began to scare the Trojane wyves with darts and stones. Anon
Queene Hecub ronning at a stone, with gnarring seazd theron, 680
And wirryed it beetweene her teeth. And as shee opte her chappe
To speake, in stead of speeche shee barkt. The place of this missehappe
Remayneth still, and of the thing there done beares yit the name.
Long myndfull of her former illes, shee sadly for the same
Went howling in the feeldes of Thrace. Her fortune moved not 685
Her Trojans only, but the Greekes her foes to ruthe: her lot
Did move even all the Goddes to ruthe: and so effectually,
That Hecub to deserve such end even Juno did denye.
  Although the Morning of the selfsame warres had favorer beene:
  Shee had no leysure to lament the fortune of the Queene, 690
Nor on the slaughters and the fall of Ilion for to think.
A household care more neerer home did in her stomacke sink,
For Memnon her beloved sonne, whom dying shee behild
Uppon the feerce Achilles speare amid the Phrygian feeld.
She saw it, and her ruddy hew with which shee woonted was 695
To dye the breaking of the day, did into palenesse passe:
And all the skye was hid with clowdes. But when his corce was gone
To burningward, shee could not fynd in hart to looke theron:
But with her heare about her eares shee kneeled downe before
The myghtye Jove, and thus gan speake unto him weeping sore: 700
  Of al that have theyr dwelling place uppon the golden skye
  The lowest (for through all the world the feawest shrynes have I)
But yit a Goddesse, I doo come, not that thou shouldst decree
That Altars, shrynes, and holydayes bee made to honour mee.
Yit if thou marke how much that I a woman doo for thee, 705
In keeping nyght within her boundes, by bringing in the light,
Thou well mayst thinke mee worthy sum reward to clayme of ryght.
But neyther now is that the thing the Morning cares to have,
Ne yit her state is such as now dew honour for to crave.
Bereft of my deere Memnon who in fyghting valeantly 710

680 *gnarring:* growling, snarling

To help his uncle, (so it was your will, O Goddes) did dye
Of stout Achilles sturdye speare even in his flowring pryme,
I sue to thee, O king of Goddes, to doo him at this tyme
Sum honour as a comfort of his death, and ease this hart
Of myne which greatly greeved is with wound of percing smart.   715
    No sooner Jove had graunted dame Aurora her desyre
    But that the flame of Memnons corce that burned in the fyre
Did fall: and flaky rolles of smoke did dark the day, as when
A foggy mist steames upward from a River or a fen,
And suffreth not the Sonne to shyne within it. Blacke as cole   720
The cinder rose: and into one round lump assembling whole
Grew grosse, and tooke bothe shape and hew. The fyre did lyfe it send,
The lyghtnesse of the substance self did wings unto it lend.
And at the first it flittred like a bird: and by and by
It flew a fethered bird in deede. And with that one gan fly   725
Innumerable mo of selfsame brood: whoo once or twyce
Did sore about the fyre, and made a piteous shreeking thryce.
The fowrth tyme in theyr flying round, themselves they all withdrew
In battells twayne, and feercely foorth of eyther syde one flew
To fyght a combate. With theyr billes and hooked talants keene   730
And with theyr wings couragiously they wreakt theyr wrathfull teene.
And myndfull of the valeant man of whom they issued beene,
They never ceased jobbing eche uppon the others brest,
Untill they falling both downe dead with fyghting overprest,
Had offred up theyr bodyes as a woorthy sacrifyse   735
Unto theyr cousin Memnon who to Asshes burned lyes.
Theis soodeine birds were named of the founder of theyr stocke:
For men doo call them Memnons birds. And every yeere a flocke
Repayre to Memnons tumb, where twoo doo in the foresayd wyse
In manner of a yeeremynd slea themselves in sacrifyse.   740
Thus where as others did lament that Dymants daughter barkt,
Auroras owne greef busyed her, that smally shee it markt
Which thing shee to this present tyme with piteous teares dooth shewe:
For through the universall world shee sheadeth moysting deawe.
    Yit suffred not the destinyes all hope to perrish quyght   745
    Togither with the towne of Troy. That good and godly knyght
The sonne of Venus bare away by nyght uppon his backe
His aged father and his Goddes, an honorable packe.

731 *wreakt:* vented, expressed; *teene:* rage,   740 *yeeremynd:* commemoration of a death
grief   on its anniversary
733 *jobbing:* pecking, jabbing

Of all the riches of the towne that only pray he chose,
So godly was his mynd: and like a bannisht man he goes   750
By water with his owne yoong sonne Ascanius from the Ile
Antandros, and he shonnes the shore of Thracia which ere whyle
The wicked Tyrants treason did with Polydores blood defyle.
And having wynd and tyde at will, he saufly wyth his trayne
Arryved at Apollos towne where Anius then did reigne.   755
Whoo being both Apollos preest and of that place the king,
Did enterteyne him in his house and unto church him bring,
And shewd him bothe the Citie and the temples knowen of old,
And eeke the sacred trees by which Latona once tooke hold
When shee of chyldbirth travailed. As soone as sacrifyse   760
Was doone with Oxens inwards burnt according to the guyse,
And casting incence in the fyre, and sheading wyne thereon,
They joyfull to the court returnd, and there they took anon
Repaste of meate and drink. Then sayd the good Anchyses this:
O Phebus, sovereine preest, onlesse I take my markes amisse,   765
(As I remember) when I first of all this towne did see,
Fowre daughters and a sonne of thyne thou haddest heere with thee.
    King Anius shooke his head wheron he ware a myter whyght,
    And answerd thus: O noble prince, in fayth thou gessest ryght.
Of children fyve a father then, thou diddest mee behold,   770
Whoo now (with such unconstancie are mortall matters rolld)
Am in a manner chyldlesse quyght. For what avayles my sonne
Who in the Ile of Anderland a great way hence dooth wonne?
Which country takes his name of him, and in the selfsayd place,
In stead of father, like a king he holdes the royall mace.   775
Apollo gave his lot to him: and Bacchus for to showe
His love, a greater gift uppon his susters did bestowe
Then could bee wisht or credited. For whatsoever they
Did towche, was turned into corne, and wyne, and oyle streyghtway.
And so theyr was riche use in them. As soone as that the fame 780
Hereof to Agamemnons eares, the scourge of Trojans, came,
Lest you myght tast your stormes alone and wee not feele the same
In part, an hoste he hither sent, and whither I would or no
Did take them from mee, forcing them among the Greekes to go
To feede the Greekish army with theyr heavenly gift. But they 785
Escapde whither they could by flyght. A couple tooke theyr way
To Ile Ewboya: tother two to Anderland did fly,

761 *guyse:* usual manner   774 *selfsayd:* selfsame
773 *wonne:* dwell

Theyr brothers Realme. An host of men pursewd them by and by,
And threatened warre onlesse they were deliverde. Force of feare
Subdewing nature, did constreyne the brother (men must beare   790
With fearfulnesse) to render up his susters to theyr fo.
For neyther was Aenaeas there, nor valeant Hector (who
Did make your warre last ten yeeres long) the countrye to defend.
Now when they should like prisoners have beene fettred, in the end
They casting up theyr handes (which yit were free) to heaven, did
                                                              cry   795
To Bacchus for to succour them, who helpt them by and by,
At leastwyse if it may bee termd a help, in woondrous wyse
To alter folke. For never could I lerne ne can surmyse
The manner how they lost theyr shape. The thing it selfe is knowen.
With fethered wings as whyght as snow they quyght away are flowen   800
Transformed into doovehouse dooves, thy wyfe dame Venus burdes.
     When that the time of meate was spent with theis and such like
                                                              woordes,
     The table was removed streyght, and then they went to sleepe.
Next morrow rysing up as soone as day began to peepe,
They went to Phebus Oracle, which willed them to go   805
Unto theyr moother countrey and the coastes theyr stocke came fro.
King Anius bare them companie. And when away they shoold,
He gave them gifts. Anchises had a scepter all of goold.
Ascanius had a quiver and a Cloke right brave and trim.
Aenaeas had a standing Cup presented unto him.   810
The Thebane Therses whoo had been king Anius guest erewhyle
Did send it out of Thessaly: but Alcon one of Myle
Did make the cuppe. And hee theron a story portrayd out.
It was a Citie with seven gates in circuit round about,
Which men myght easly all discerne. The gates did represent   815
The Cities name, and showed playne what towne thereby was ment.
Without the towne were funeralls a dooing for the dead,
With herces, tapers, fyres, and tumbes. The wyves with ruffled head
And stomacks bare pretended greef. The nymphes seemd teares to
                                                              shead,
And wayle the drying of theyr welles. The leavelesse trees did seare. 820
And licking on the parched stones Goats romed heere and there.
Behold amid this Thebane towne was lyvely portrayd out

796 *by and by:* immediately   820 *seare:* wither
819 *pretended:* signified

Echions daughters twayne, of which the one with courage stout
Did profer bothe her naked throte and stomacke to the knyfe:
And tother with a manly hart did also spend her lyfe, 825
For saufgard of her countryfolk: and how that theruppon
They both were caryed solemly on herces, and anon
Were burned in the cheefest place of all the Thebane towne.
Then (least theyr linage should decay whoo dyde with such renowne,)
Out of the Asshes of the maydes there issued twoo yong men, 830
And they unto theyr moothers dust did obsequies agen.
Thus much was graved curiously in auncient precious brasse,
And on the brim a trayle of flowres of bearbrich gilded was.
The Trojans also gave to him as costly giftes agen.
Bycause he was Apollos preest they gave to him as then 835
A Chist to keepe in frankincence. They gave him furthermore
A Crowne of gold wherin were set of precious stones great store.
Then calling to remembrance that the Trojans issued were
Of Tewcers blood, they sayld to Crete. But long they could not
there
Abyde th'infection of the aire: and so they did forsake 840
The hundred Cities, and with speede to Itayleward did make.
The winter wexed hard and rough, and tost them verry sore.
And when theyr shippes arrived were uppon the perlous shore
Among the Strophad Iles, the bird Aello did them feare.
The costes of Dulich, Ithaca, and Same they passed were, 845
And eeke the Court of Neritus where wyse Ulysses reignd,
And came to Ambrace for the which the Gods strong stryfe maynteind.
There sawe they turned into stone the judge whoose image yit
At Actium in Appollos Church in signe therof dooth sit.
They vewed also Dodon grove where Okes spake: and the coast 850
Of Chaon where the sonnes of king Molossus scapt a most
Ungracious fyre by taking wings. From thence they coasted by
The countrye of the Pheaks fraught with frute abundantly.
Then tooke they land in Epyre, and to Buthrotos they went
Wheras the Trojane prophet dwelt, whoose reigne did represent 855
An image of theyr auncient Troy. There being certifyde
Of things to come by Helen (whoo whyle there they did abyde
Informed them ryght faythfully of all that should betyde)
They passed into Sicilie. With corners three this land
Shootes out into the Sea: of which Pachinnus front dooth stand 860

833 *bearbrich:* bear's-breech, acanthus   844 *feare:* frighten

Ageinst the southcoast: Lilibye dooth face the gentle west,
And Pelore unto Charlsis wayne dooth northward beare his brest.
The Trojanes under Pelore gat with ores and prosprous tydes
And in the even by Zanclye shore theyr fleete at anchor rydes.
Uppon the left syde restlessely Charybdis ay dooth beate them,   865
And swalloweth shippes and spewes them up as fast as it dooth eate
them.
And Scylla beateth on theyr ryght: which from the navell downe
Is patched up with cruell curres: and upward to the crowne
Dooth keepe the countnance of a mayd, and (if that all bee trew
That Poets fayne) shee was sumtyme a mayd ryght fayre of hew.   870
To her made many wooers sute: all which shee did eschew.
And going to the salt Sea nymphes (to whom shee was ryght deere)
She vaunted, to how many men shee gave the slippe that yeere.
To whom the Lady Galate in kembing of her heare
Sayd thus with syghes: But they that sought to thee (O Lady) were   875
None other than of humane kynd, to whom without all feare
Of harme, thou myghtest (as thou doost) give nay. But as for mee
Although that I of Nereus and gray Doris daughter bee,
And of my susters have with mee continually a gard,
I could not scape the Cyclops love, but to my greef full hard.   880
(With that her teares did stoppe her speeche.) As soone as that the mayd
Had dryde them with her marble thomb, and moande the nymph,
she sayd:
Deere Goddesse, tell mee all your greef, and hyde it not from mee:
For trust mee, I will unto you bothe true and secret bee.
Then unto Cratyes daughter thus the nymph her playnt did frame: 885
    Of Fawne and nymph Simethis borne was Acis, whoo became
    A joy to bothe his parents, but to mee the greater joy.
For being but a sixteene yeeres of age, this fayre sweete boy
Did take mee to his love, what tyme about his chyldish chin
The tender heare like mossy downe to sprowt did first begin.   890
I loved him beyond all Goddes forbod, and likewyse mee
The Giant Cyclops. Neyther (if demaunded it should bee)
I well were able for to tell you whither that the love
Of Acis, or the Cyclops hate did more my stomacke move.
There was no oddes betweene them. Oh deere Goddesse Venus, what 895
A powre haste thou? Behold how even this owgly Giant that

862 *wayne:* wagon, chariot   891 *forbod:* forbidding, prohibition
868 *patched up:* put together like patchwork

No sparke of meekenesse in him hath, whoo is a terrour to
The verrye woodes, whom never guest nor straunger came unto
Without displeasure, whoo the heavens and all the Goddes despyseth,
Dooth feele what thing is love. The love of mee him so surpryseth, 900
That Polypheme regarding not his sheepe and hollowe Cave,
And having care to please dooth go about to make him brave.
His sturre stiffe heare he kembeth nowe with strong and sturdy rakes,
And with a sythe dooth marcussotte his bristled berd: and takes
Delyght to looke uppon himself in waters, and to frame 905
His countnance. Of his murtherous hart the wyldnesse wexeth tame.
His unastaunched thyrst of blood is quenched: shippes may passe
And repasse saufly. In the whyle that he in love thus was,
One Telemus, Ewrymeds sonne, a man of passing skill
In birdflyght, taking land that tyme in Sicill, went untill 910
The orped Gyant Polypheme, and sayd: This one round eye
That now amid thy forehead stands shall one day ere thou dye
By sly Ulysses blinded bee. The Gyant laught therat,
And sayd: O foolish soothsayre, thou deceyved art in that.
For why another (even a wench) already hathe it blynded. 915
Thus skorning him that told him truthe bycause he was hygh mynded,
He eyther made the ground to shake in walking on the shore,
Or rowzd him in his shadye Cave. With wedged poynt before
There shoots a hill into the Sea: whereof the sea dooth beate
On eyther syde. The one eyd feend came up and made his seate 920
Theron, and after came his sheepe undriven. As soone as hee
Had at his foote layd downe his staffe which was a whole Pyne tree
Well able for to bee a maast to any shippe, he takes
His pype compact of fyvescore reedes, and therwithall he makes
So loud a noyse that all the hilles and waters therabout 925
Myght easly heere the shirlnesse of the shepeherds whistling out.
I lying underneathe the rocke, and leaning in the lappe
Of Acis markt theis woordes of his which farre I heard by happe:
   More whyght thou art then Primrose leaf, my Lady Galatee.
   More fresh than meade, more tall and streyght than lofty
                                                  Aldertree. 930
More bright than glasse, more wanton than the tender kid forsooth.
Than Cockleshelles continually with water worne, more smoothe.

903 *sturre:* harsh
904 *marcussotte:* to cut beard à la mar-
   quisotte (in the Turkish fashion, leaving
   mustachios)
910 *untill:* unto

911 *orped:* fierce
915 *For why:* because
916 *hygh mynded:* arrogant
918 *rowzd him:* rested

More cheerefull than the winters Sun, or Sommers shadowe cold,
More seemely and more comly than the Planetree to behold,
Of valew more than Apples bee although they were of gold.   935
More cleere than frozen yce, more sweete than Grape through rype
                                                            ywis,
More soft than butter newly made, or downe of Cygnet is.
And much more fayre and beawtyfull than gardein to myne eye,
But that thou from my companye continually doost flye.
And thou the selfsame Galate art more tettish for to frame   940
Than Oxen of the wildernesse whom never wyght did tame.
More fleeting than the waves, more hard than warryed Oke to twyne,
More tough than willow twiggs, more lyth than is the wyld whyght
                                                            vyne.
More than this rocke unmovable, more violent than a streame.
More prowd than Peacocke praysd, more feerce than fyre and more
                                                    extreeme.   945
More rough than Breers, more cruell than the new delivered Beare,
More mercilesse than troden snake, than sea more deafe of eare.
And which (and if it lay in mee I cheefly would restrayne)
Not only swifter paced than the stag in chace on playne,
But also swifter than the wynd and flyghtfull ayre. But if   950
Thou knew me well, it would thee irke to flye and bee a greef
To tarrye from mee. Yea thou wouldst endeavour all thy powre
To keepe mee wholly to thy self. The Quarry is my bowre
Heawen out of whole mayne stone. No Sun in sommer there can swelt.
No nipping cold in wintertyme within the same is felt.   955
Gay Apples weying downe the boughes have I, and Grapes like gold,
And purple Grapes on spreaded Vynes as many as can hold.
Bothe which I doo reserve for thee. Thyself shalt with thy hand
The soft sweete strawbryes gather, which in wooddy shadowe stand.
The Cornell berryes also from the tree thy self shall pull: 960
And pleasant plommes, sum yellow lyke new wax, sum blew, sum full
Of ruddy jewce. Of Chestnutts eeke (if my wyfe thou wilt bee)
Thou shalt have store: and frutes all sortes: all trees shall serve for thee.
This Cattell heere is all myne owne. And many mo besyde
Doo eyther in the bottoms feede, or in the woodes them hyde,   965
And many standing at theyr stalles doo in my Cave abyde.

936 *ywis:* certainly
937 *Cygnet:* young swan
940 *tettish:* peevish, irritable; *frame:* man-
age, train

942 *warryed:* knotty; *twyne:* cleave
943 *lyth:* lithe
950 *flyghtfull:* flying, fleeting
954 *mayne:* solid; *swelt:* swelter

The number of them (if a man should ask) I cannot showe.
Tush, beggars of theyr Cattell use the number for to knowe.
And for the goodnesse of the same, no whit beleeve thou mee.
But come thyself (and if thou wilt) the truth therof to see.   970
See how theyr udders full doo make them straddle. Lesser ware
Shet up at home in cloce warme peends, are Lambes. There also are
In other pinfolds Kidds of selfsame yeaning tyme. Thus have
I alwayes mylke as whyte as snow. Wherof I sum doo save
To drink, and of the rest is made good cheese. And furthermore   975
Not only stale and common gifts and pleasures wherof store
Is to bee had at eche mannes hand, (as Leverets, Kidds, and Does,
A payre of pigeons, or a nest of birds new found, or Roes,)
Shall unto thee presented bee. I found this tother day
A payre of Bearewhelpes, eche so lyke the other as they lay   980
Uppon a hill, that scarce yee eche discerne from other may.
And when that I did fynd them I did take them up, and say
Theis will I for my Lady keepe for her therwith to play.
Now put thou up thy fayre bryght head, good Galat, I thee pray,
Above the greenish waves: now come my Galat, come away.   985
And of my present take no scorne. I know my selfe to bee
A jollye fellow. For even now I did behold and see
Myne image in the water sheere, and sure mee thought I tooke
Delyght to see my goodly shape, and favor in the brooke.
Behold how big I am: not Jove in heaven (for so you men   990
Report one Jove to reigne, of whom I passe not for to ken)
Is huger than this doughty corce of myne. A bush of heare
Dooth overdreepe my visage grim, and shadowes as it were
A grove uppon my shoulders twayne. And think it not to bee
A shame for that with bristled heare my body rough yee see.   995
A fowle ilfavored syght it is to see a leavelesse tree.
A lothely thing it is, a horse without a mane to keepe.
As fethers doo become the birdes, and wooll becommeth sheepe,
Even so a beard and bristled skin becommeth also men.
I have but one eye, which dooth stand amid my frunt. What then?   1000
This one round eye of myne is lyke a myghty target. Why?
Vewes not the Sun all things from heaven? Yit but one only eye
Hath hee. Moreover in your Seas my father beares the sway.
Him will I make thy fathrinlaw. Have mercy I thee pray,

972 *peends:* pens   989 *favor:* face, features
973 *yeaning:* birth   991 *passe:* care; *ken:* know
977 *Leverets:* young hares   993 *overdreepe:* droop over

And harken to myne humble sute. For only unto thee   1005
Yeeld I. Even I of whom bothe heaven and Jove despysed bee
And eeke the percing thunderbolt, doo stand in awe and feare
Of thee, O Nerye. Thyne ill will is greevouser to beare
Than is the deadly Thunderclappe. Yit could I better fynd
In hart to suffer this contempt of thyne with pacient mynd   1010
If thou didst shonne all other folk as well as mee. But why
Rejecting Cyclops doost thou love dwarf Acis? Why say I
Preferst thou Acis unto mee? Well, let him liked bee
Both of himself, and also (which I would be lothe) of thee.
And if I catch him he shall feele that in my body is   1015
The force that should bee. I shall paunch him quicke. Those limbes of
                                                                   his
I will in peeces teare, and strew them in the feeldes, and in
Thy waters, if he doo thee haunt. For I doo swelt within.
And being chaafte the flame dooth burne more feerce to my unrest.
Mee thinks mount Aetna with his force is closed in my brest.   1020
And yit it nothing moveth thee. As soone as he had talkt
     Thus much in vayne, (I sawe well all) he rose: and fuming stalkt
     Among his woodes and woonted Lawndes, as dooth a Bulchin,
                                                                   when
The Cow is from him tane. He could him no where rest as then.
Anon the feend espyed mee and Acis where wee lay,   1025
Before wee wist or feared it: and crying out gan say:
I see yee. And confounded myght I bee with endlesse shame,
But if I make this day the last agreement of your game.
Theis woordes were spoke with such a reere as verry well became
An angry Giant. Aetna shooke with lowdnesse of the same.   1030
I scaard therwith dopt underneathe the water, and the knyght
Simethus turning streyght his backe, did give himself to flyght,
And cryed: Help mee Galate, help parents I you pray,
And in your kingdome mee receyve whoo perrish must streyghtway.
The roundeyd devill made pursewt: and rending up a fleece   1035
Of Aetna Rocke, threw after him: of which a little peece
Did Acis overtake. And yit as little as it was,
It overwhelmed Acis whole. I wretched wyght (alas)
Did that which destnyes would permit. Foorthwith I brought to passe
That Acis should receyve the force his father had before.   1040

1016 *paunch:* stab in paunch, eviscerate   1029 *reere:* roar, shout
1023 *Lawndes:* glades, pastures; *Bulchin:*   1031 *dopt:* ducked, dipped
    bull calf   1035 *fleece:* fleech, flitch, slice

His scarlet blood did issue from the lump, and more and more
Within a whyle the rednesse gan to vannish: and the hew
Resembled at the first a brooke with rayne distroubled new,
Which wexeth cleere by length of tyme. Anon the lump did clyve,
And from the hollow cliffe therof hygh reedes sprang up alyve.   1045
And at the hollow issue of the stone the bubling water
Came trickling out. And by and by (which is a woondrous matter)
The stripling with a wreath of reede about his horned head
Avaunst his body to the waste. Whoo (save he was that stead
Much biggar than he erst had beene, and altogither gray)   1050
Was Acis still. And being turnd to water, at this day
In shape of river still he beares his former name away.
       The Lady Galat ceast her talk and streyght the companye brake.
       And Neryes daughters parting thence, swam in the gentle lake.
Dame Scylla home ageine returnd. (Shee durst not her betake   1055
To open sea) and eyther roamd uppon the sandy shore
Stark naakt, or when for weerinesse shee could not walk no more,
Shee then withdrew her out of syght and gate her to a poole,
And in the water of the same, her heated limbes did coole.
Behold the fortune. Glaucus (whoo then being late before   1060
Transformed in Ewboya Ile uppon Anthedon shore,
Was new becomme a dweller in the sea) as he did swim
Along the coast was tane in love at syght of Scylla trim,
And spake such woordes as he did think myght make her tarry still.
Yit fled shee still, and swift for feare shee gate her to a hill   1065
That butted on the Sea. Ryght steepe and upward sharp did shoote
A loftye toppe with trees, beneathe was hollowe at the foote.
Heere Scylla stayd and being sauf by strongnesse of the place,
(Not knowing if he monster were, or God, that did her chace,)
Shee looked backe. And woondring at his colour and his heare   1070
With which his shoulders and his backe all wholly covered were,
Shee saw his neather parts were like a fish with tayle wrythde round
Who leaning to the neerest Rocke, sayd thus with lowd cleere sound:
       Fayre mayd, I neyther monster am nor cruell savage beast:
       But of the sea a God, whoose powre and favour is not least.   1075
For neyther Protew in the sea nor Triton have more myght
Nor yit the sonne of Athamas that now Palaemon hyght.

1041 *lump:* mound   1066 *butted:* abutted, jutted
1043 *distroubled:* greatly disturbed 1068 *sauf:* safe
1045 *cliffe:* cleft   1072 *wrythde:* twisted
1049 *Avaunst:* raised

Yit once I was a mortall man. But you must know that I
Was given to seawoorkes, and in them mee only did apply.
For sumtyme I did draw the drag in which the fishes were,   1080
And sumtyme sitting on the cliffes I angled heere and there.
There butteth on a fayre greene mede a bank wherof t'one half
Is cloasd with sea, the rest is clad with herbes which never calf,
Nor horned Ox, nor seely sheepe, nor shakheard Goate did feede.
The busye Bee did never there of flowres sweet smelling speede.   1085
No gladsum garlonds ever there were gathered for the head.
No hand those flowers ever yit with hooked sythe did shred.
I was the first that ever set my foote uppon that plot.
Now as I dryde my dropping netts, and layd abrode my lotte,
To tell how many fishes had bychaunce to net beene sent,   1090
Or through theyr owne too lyght beeleefe on bayted hooke beene hent:
(The matter seemeth like a lye, but what avayles to lye?)
As soone as that my pray had towcht the grasse, it by and by
Began to move, and flask theyr finnes, and swim uppon the drye,
As in the Sea. And as I pawsd and woondred at the syght,   1095
My draught of fishes everychone to seaward tooke theyr flyght,
And leaping from the shore, forsooke theyr newfound mayster quyght.
I was amazed at the thing: and standing long in dowt,
I sought the cause if any God had brought this same abowt,
Or else sum jewce of herb. And as I so did musing stand,   1100
What herb (quoth I) hath such a powre? And gathering with my hand
The grasse, I bote it with my toothe. My throte had scarcely yit
Well swallowed downe the uncouth jewce, when like an agew fit
I felt myne inwards soodeinly to shake, and with the same,
A love of other nature in my brest with violence came.   1105
And long I could it not resist, but sayd: Deere land, adeew,
For never shall I haunt thee more. And with that woord I threw
My bodye in the sea. The Goddes thereof receyving mee,
Vouchsaved in theyr order mee installed for to bee,
Desyring old Oceanus and Thetis for theyr sake,   1110
The rest of my mortalitie away from mee to take.
They hallowed mee, and having sayd nyne tymes the holy ryme
That purgeth all prophanednesse, they charged mee that tyme
To put my brestbulk underneathe a hundred streames. Anon

1084 *seely:* simple, harmless; *shakheard:*   1094 *flask:* flap, flutter
     shag-haired   1103 *uncouth:* unfamiliar, strange
1085 *speede:* succeed   1114 *brestbulk:* chest, breast
1091 *hent:* taken

The brookes from sundry coastes and all the Seas did ryde uppon [1115]
My head. From whence as soone as I returned, by and by
I felt my self farre otherwyse through all my limbes, than I
Had beene before. And in my mynd I was another man.
Thus farre of all that mee befell make just report I can.
Thus farre I beare in mynd. The rest my mynd perceyved not. [1120]
Then first of all this hory greene gray grisild beard I got,
And this same bush of heare which all along the seas I sweepe,
And theis same myghty shoulders, and theis grayish armes, and feete
Confounded into finned fish. But what avayleth mee
This goodly shape, and of the Goddes of sea to loved bee? [1125]
Or for to be a God my self, if they delyght not thee?
　　As he was speaking this, and still about to utter more,
　　Dame Scylla him forsooke: wherat he wexing angry sore,
And beeing quickened with repulse, in rage he tooke his way
To Circes, Titans daughters, Court which full of monsters lay. [1130]

FINIS LIBRI DECIMI TERTII.

囸囸囸
THE. XIIII. BOOKE OF

OVIDS METAMORPHOSIS.

[*Glaucus and Scylla. The Cumaean Sibyl. Achaemenides and Poly-
phemus. Circe. Canens and Picus. Aeneas in Italy. Vertumnus and
Pomona. Iphis and Anaxarete. The Beginnings of Rome.*]

Now had th'Ewboyan fisherman (whoo lately was becomme
A God of sea to dwell in sea for ay,) alreadye swomme
Past Aetna which uppon the face of Giant Typho lyes,
Toogither with the pasture of the Cyclops which defyes
Both Plough and harrowe, and by teemes of Oxen sets no store: 5
And Zancle, and crackt Rhegion which stands a tother shore:
And eeke the rough and shipwrecke sea which being hemmed in
With two mayne landes on eyther syde, is as a bound betwin
The frutefull Realmes of Italy and Sicill. From that place
He cutting through the Tyrrhene sea with both his armes apace,   10
Arryved at the grassye hilles and at the Palace hye
Of Circe, Phoebus imp, which full of sundry beastes did lye.
When Glaucus in her presence came, and had her greeted, and
Receyved freendly welcomming and greeting at her hand,
He sayd: O Goddesse, pitie mee a God, I thee desyre.   15
Thou only (if at least thou think mee woorthy so great hyre)
Canst ease this love of myne. No wyght dooth better know than I
The powre of herbes, whoo late ago transformed was therby.
And now to open unto thee of this my greef the ground,
Uppon th'Italyan shore ageinst Messene walls I found   20
Fayre Scylla. Shame it is to tell how scornfull shee did take
The gentle woordes and promises and sute that I did make.
But if that any powre at all consist in charmes, then let

12 *imp:* child

350

That sacret mouth of thyne cast charmes: or if more force bee set
In herbes to compasse things withall, then use the herbes that have 25
Most strength in woorking. Neyther think, I hither come to crave
A medcine for to heale myself and cure my wounded hart:
I force no end. I would have her bee partener of my smart.
   But Circe (for no natures are more lyghtly set on fyre
   Than such as shee is) (whither that the cause of this desyre 30
Were only in herself, or that Dame Venus bearing ay
In mynd her fathers deede in once disclosing of her play,
Did stirre her heereunto) sayd thus: It were a better way
For thee to fancye such a one whoose will and whole desyre
Is bent to thine, and whoo is sindgd with selfsame kynd of fyre. 35
Thou woorthye art of sute to thee. And (credit mee) thou shouldst
Bee woode in deede, if any hope of speeding give thou wouldst.
And therefore dowt not. Only of thy beawtye lyking have.
Lo, I whoo am a Goddesse and the imp of Phoebus brave,
Whoo can so much by charmes, whoo can so much by herbes, doo vow 40
My self to thee. If I disdeine, disdeine mee also thow.
And if I yeeld, yeeld thou likewyse: and in one only deede
Avenge thy self of twayne. To her intreating thus to speede,
First trees shall grow (quoth Glaucus) in the sea, and reeke shall thryve
In toppes of hilles, ere I (as long as Scylla is alyve) 45
Doo chaunge my love. The Goddesse wext ryght wroth: and sith she
                                    could
Not hurt his persone beeing falne in love with him, ne would:
Shee spyghted her that was preferd before her. And uppon
Displeasure tane of this repulse, shee went her way anon.
And wicked weedes of grisly jewce toogither shee did bray, 50
And in the braying, witching charmes shee over them did say.
And putting on a russet cloke, shee passed through the rowt
Of savage beastes that in her court came fawning round abowt,
And going unto Rhegion cliffe which standes ageinst the shore
Of Zancle, entred by and by the waters that doo rore 55
With violent tydes, uppon the which shee stood as on firme land,
And ran and never wet her feete a whit. There was at hand
A little plash that bowwed like a bowe that standeth bent,
Where Scylla woonted was to rest herself, and thither went
From rage of sea and ayre, what tyme the sonne amid the skye 60

37 *woode:* wooed; *speeding:* succeeding
44 *reeke:* wrack, seaweed
48 *spyghted:* felt anger, spite toward
50 *bray:* grind up
55 *by and by:* immediately
58 *plash:* pool

Is hotest making shadowes short by mounting up on hye.
This plash did Circe then infect ageinst that Scylla came,
And with her poysons which had powre most monstrous shapes to frame
Defyled it. Shee sprincled there the jewce of venymd weedes,
And thryce nyne tymes with witching mouth shee softly mumbling,
　　　　　　　　　　　　　　　　　　　　　　　　　reedes　65
A charme ryght darke of uncouth woordes. No sooner Scylla came
Within this plash, and to the waast had waded in the same,
But that shee sawe her hinderloynes with barking buggs atteint.
And at the first, not thinking with her body they were meynt
As parts therof, shee started back, and rated them. And sore　70
Shee was afrayd the eager curres should byght her. But the more
Shee shonned them, the surer still shee was to have them there.
In seeking where her loynes, and thyghes, and feet and ancles were,
Chappes like the chappes of Cerberus in stead of them shee found.
Nought else was there than cruell curres from belly downe to ground.　75
So underneathe misshaped loynes and womb remayning sound,
Her mannish mastyes backes were ay within the water drownd.
　　　Her lover Glaucus wept therat, and Circes bed refusde
That had so passing cruelly her herbes on Scylla usde.
But Scylla in that place abode. And for the hate shee bore　80
To Circeward, (assoone as meete occasion servde therfore)
Shee spoyld Ulysses of his mates. And shortly after, shee
Had also drownd the Trojane fleete, but that (as yit wee see)
Shee was transformd to rock of stone, which shipmen warely shonne.
When from this Rocke the Trojane fleete by force of Ores had wonne,　85
And from Charybdis greedye gulf, and were in manner readye
To have arryvde in Italy, the wynd did ryse so heady,
And that it drave them backe uppon the coast of Affricke. There
The Tyrian Queene (whoo afterward unpaciently should beare
The going of this Trojane prince away) did enterteine　90
Aenaeas in her house, and was ryght glad of him and fayne.
Uppon a Pyle made underneathe pretence of sacrifyse
Shee goard herself upon a swoord, and in most wofull wyse
As shee herself had beene beguyld: so shee beguyled all.
Eftsoone Aenaeas flying from the newly reered wall　95
Of Carthage in that sandy land, retyred backe agen

---

65 *reedes:* says　　　　　　　　　　87 *heady:* headstrong, violent
66 *uncouth:* strange　　　　　　　　91 *fayne:* glad
68 *buggs:* bugbears, monsters　　　92 *Pyle:* pyre
69 *meynt:* mixed　　　　　　　　　　95 *Eftsoone:* soon after
77 *mastyes:* mastiffs

To Sicill, where his faythfull freend Acestes reignd. And when
He there had doone his sacrifyse, and kept an Obit at
His fathers tumb, he out of hand did mend his Gallyes that
Dame Iris, Junos messenger, had burned up almost. 100
And sayling thence he kept his course aloof along the coast
Of Aeolye and of Vulcanes Iles the which of brimston smoke.
And passing by the Meremayds rocks, (His Pilot by a stroke
Of tempest being drownd in sea) he sayld by Prochite, and
Inarime, and (which uppon a barreine hill dooth stand) 105
The land of Ape Ile, which dooth take that name of people slye
There dwelling. For the Syre of Goddes abhorring utterly
The leawdnesse of the Cercops, and theyr wilfull perjurye,
And eeke theyr guylefull dealing did transforme them everychone
Into an evillfavored kynd of beast: that beeing none 110
They myght yit still resemble men. He knit in lesser space
Theyr members, and he beate mee flat theyr noses to theyr face,
The which he filled furrowlike with wrinckles every where.
He clad theyr bodyes over all with fallow coulourd heare,
And put them into this same Ile to dwell forever there. 115
But first he did bereeve them of the use of speeche and toong,
Which they to cursed perjurye did use bothe old and yoong.
To chatter hoarcely, and to shreeke, to jabber, and to squeake,
He hath them left, and for to moppe and mowe, but not to speake.
 Aenaeas having past this Ile, and on his ryght hand left 120
 The towne of Naples, and the tumb of Mysen on his left,
Toogither with the fenny grounds: at Cumye landed, and
Went unto longlyvde Sybills house, with whom he went in hand
That he to see his fathers ghoste myght go by Averne deepe.
Shee long uppon the earth in stownd her eyes did fixed keepe, 125
And at the length as soone as that the spryght of prophesye
Was entred her, shee raysing them did thus ageine reply:
O most renowmed wyght, of whom the godlynesse by fyre
And valeantnesse is tryde by swoord, great things thou doost requyre.
But feare not, Trojane: for thou shalt bee lord of thy desyre. 130
To see the reverend image of thy deerebeeloved syre,
Among the fayre Elysian feeldes where godly folke abyde,
And all the lowest kingdoomes of the world I will thee guyde.

---

98 *Obit:* funeral rites
119 *moppe and mowe:* make grimaces
123 *went in hand [with]:* dealt with, talked
 with, endeavored to persuade

125 *stownd:* wonder, absorption
129 *requyre:* ask, request

No way to vertue is restreynd. This spoken, shee did showe
A golden bowgh that in the wood of Proserpine did growe,   135
And willed him to pull it from the tree. He did obey:
And sawe the powre of dreadfull hell, and where his graundsyres lay
And eeke the aged Ghost of stowt Anchises. Furthermore
He lernd the customes of the land arryvd at late before,
And what adventures should by warre betyde him in that place.   140
From thence retyring up ageine a slow and weery pace,
He did asswage the tediousnesse by talking with his guyde.
For as he in the twylyght dim this dreadfull way did ryde,
He sayed: Whither present thou thyself a Goddesse bee,
Or such a one as God dooth love most dearly, I will thee   145
For ever as a Goddesse take, and will acknowledge mee
Thy servant, for saufguyding mee the place of death to see,
And for thou from the place of death hast brought me sauf and free.
For which desert, what tyme I shall atteyne to open ayre,
I will a temple to thee buyld ryght sumptuous, large, and fayre,   150
And honour thee with frankincence. The prophetisse did cast
Her eye uppon Aenaeas backe, and syghing sayd at last:
I am no Goddesse. Neyther think thou canst with conscience ryght,
With holy incence honour give to any mortall wyght.
But to th'entent through ignorance thou erre not, I had beene   155
Eternall and of worldly lyfe I should none end have seene,
If that I would my maydenhod on Phebus have bestowde.
Howbeeit whyle he stood in hope to have the same, and trowde
To overcome mee with his gifts: Thou mayd of Cumes (quoth he)
Choose what thou wilt, and of thy wish the owner thou shalt bee.   160
I taking full my hand of dust, and shewing it him there,
Desyred like a foole to live as many yeeres as were
Small graynes of cinder in that heape. I quight forgot to crave
Immediately, the race of all those yeeres in youth to have.
Yit did he graunt mee also that, uppon condicion I   165
Would let him have my maydenhod, which thing I did denye.
And so rejecting Phebus gift a single lyfe I led.
But now the blessefull tyme of youth is altogither fled,
And irksome age with trembling pace is stolne uppon my head,
Which long I must endure. For now already as you see   170
Seven hundred yeares are come and gone and that the number bee
Full matched of the granes of dust, three hundred harvestes mo,

148 *sauf:* safe   164 *race:* course
158 *trowde:* thought

I must three hundred vintages see more before I go.
The day will come that length of tyme shall make my body small,
And little of my withered limbes shall leave or naught at all.   175
And none shall think that ever God was tane in love with mee.
Even out of Phebus knowledge then perchaunce I growen shall bee,
Or at the least that ever he mee lovde he shall denye,
So sore I shall be altered. And then shall no mannes eye
Discerne mee. Only by my voyce I shall bee knowen. For why   180
The fates shall leave mee still my voyce for folke to know mee by.
    As Sybill in the vaulted way such talk as this did frame,
    The Trojane knyght Aeneaes up at Cumes fro Limbo came.
And having doone the sacrifyse accustomd for the same,
He tooke his journey to the coast which had not yit the name   185
Receyved of his nurce. In this same place he found a mate
Of wyse Ulysses, Macare of Neritus, whoo late
Before, had after all his long and tediouse toyles, there stayd.
He spying Achemenides (whom late ago afrayd
They had among mount Aetnas Cliffs abandond when they fled   190
From Polypheme): and woondring for to see he was not dead,
Sayd thus: O Achemenides, what chaunce, or rather what
Good God hathe savde the lyfe of thee? What is the reason that
A barbrous shippe beares thee a Greeke? Or whither saylest thou?
    To him thus, Achemenides, his owne man freely now   195
    And not forgrowen as one forlorne, nor clad in bristled hyde,
Made answer: Yit ageine I would I should in perrill byde
Of Polypheme, and that I myght those chappes of his behold
Beesmeared with the blood of men, but if that I doo hold
This shippe more deere than all the Realme of wyse Ulysses, or   200
If lesser of Aenaeas I doo make account than for
My father, neyther (though I did as much as doone myght bee,)
I could ynough bee thankfull for his goodnesse towards mee.
That I still speake and breathe, that I the Sun and heaven doo see,
Is his gift. Can I thanklesse then or myndlesse of him bee,   205
That downe the round eyed gyants throte this soule of myne went not?
And that from hencefoorth when to dye it ever be my lot
I may be layd in grave, or sure not in the Gyants mawe?
What hart had I that tyme (at least if feare did not withdrawe
Both hart and sence) when left behynd, you taking shippe I sawe?   210
I would have called after you but that I was afrayd

180 *For why:* because   196 *forgrowen:* grown shaggy

By making outcrye to my fo myself to have beewrayd.
For even the noyse that you did make did put Ulysses shippe
In daunger. I did see him from a cragged mountaine strippe
A myghty rocke, and into sea it throwe midway and more.   215
Ageine I sawe his giants pawe throwe huge big stones great store
As if it were a sling. And sore I feared lest your shippe
Should drowned by the water bee that from the stones did skippe,
Or by the stones themselves, as if my self had beene therin.
But when that flyght had saved you from death, he did begin   220
On Aetna syghing up and downe to walke: and with his pawes
Went groping of the trees among the woodes. And forbycause
He could not see, he knockt his shinnes ageinst the rocks eche where.
And stretching out his grisly armes (which all beegrymed were
With baken blood) to seaward, he the Greekish nation band,   225
And sayd: O if that sum good chaunce myght bring unto my hand
Ulysses or sum mate of his, on whom to wreake myne ire,
Uppon whose bowells with my teeth I like a Hawke myght tyre:
Whose living members myght with theis my talants teared beene:
Whoose blood myght bubble down my throte: whose flesh myght pant
                                                        between   230
My jawes: how lyght or none at all this losing of myne eye
Would seeme. Theis woordes and many mo the cruell feend did cry.
A shuddring horror perced mee to see his smudged face,
And cruell handes, and in his frunt the fowle round eyelesse place,
And monstrous members, and his beard beslowbered with the blood   235
Of man. Before myne eyes then death the smallest sorrow stood.
I loked every minute to bee seased in his pawe.
I looked ever when he should have cramd mee in his mawe.
And in my mynd I of that tyme mee thought the image sawe
When having dingd a doozen of our fellowes to the ground   240
And lying lyke a Lyon feerce or hunger sterved hownd
Uppon them, very eagerly he downe his greedy gut
Theyr bowwels and theyr limbes yit more than half alive did put,
And with theyr flesh toogither crasht the bones and maree whyght.
I trembling like an aspen leaf stood sad and bloodlesse quyght.   245
And in beholding how he fed and belked up againe
His bloody vittells at his mouth, and uttred out amayne

212 *beewrayd:* revealed   240 *dingd:* dashed
225 *baken:* caked; *band:* cursed   244 *maree:* marrow
227 *wreake:* vent   246 *belked:* belched
228 *tyre:* prey, tear at   247 *uttred:* ejected; *amayne:* violently

The clottred gobbets mixt with wyne, I thus surmysde: Like lot
Hangs over my head now, and I must also go to pot.
And hyding mee for many dayes, and quaking horribly   250
At every noyse, and dreading death, and wisshing for to dye,
Appeasing hunger with the leaves of trees, and herbes and mast,
Alone, and poore, and footelesse, and to death and pennance cast,
A long tyme after I espyde this shippe afarre at last,
And ronning downeward to the sea by signes did succour seeke.   255
Where fynding grace, this Trojane shippe receyved mee, a Greeke.
But now I prey thee, gentle freend, declare thou unto mee
Thy Capteines and thy fellowes lucke that tooke the sea with thee.
    He told him how that Aeolus, the sonne of Hippot, he
    That keepes the wyndes in pryson cloce did reigne in Tuskane
                                                        sea.   260
And how Ulysses having at his hand a noble gift,
The wynd enclosde in leather bagges, did sayle with prosperous drift
Nyne dayes toogither: insomuch they came within the syght
Of home: but on the tenth day when the morning gan give lyght,
His fellowes being somewhat toucht with covetousenesse and spyght,   265
Supposing that it had beene gold, did let the wyndes out quyght.
The which returning whence they came, did drive them backe amayne
That in the Realme of Aeolus they went aland agayne.
From thence (quoth he) we came unto the auncient Lamyes towne
Of which the feerce Antiphates that season ware the crowne.   270
A cowple of my mates and I were sent unto him: and
A mate of myne and I could scarce by flyght escape his hand.
The third of us did with his blood embrew the wicked face
Of leawd Antiphate, whoo with swoord us flying thence did chace,
And following after with a rowt threw stones and loggs which
                                                        drownd   275
Both men and shippes. Howbeeit one by chaunce escaped sound,
Which bare Ulysses and my self. So having lost most part
Of all our deare companions, we with sad and sory hart
And much complayning, did arryve at yoonder coast which yow
May ken farre hence. A great way hence (I say) wee see it now   280
But trust mee truly over neere I saw it once. And thow
Aenaeas, Goddesse Venus sonne, the justest knight of all
The Trojane race (for sith the warre is doone, I can not call

252 *mast:* acorns and fruit of other forest   275 *rowt:* crowd, rabble
    trees   280 *ken:* see
253 *footelesse:* with not a leg to stand on

Thee fo) I warne thee get thee farre from Circes dwelling place.
For when our shippes arryved there, remembring eft the cace   285
Of cruell king Antiphates, and of that hellish wyght
The round eyed gyant Polypheme, wee had so small delyght
To visit uncowth places, that wee sayd wee would not go.
Then cast we lotts. The lot fell out uppon myself as tho,
And Polyte, and Eurylocus, and on Elpenor who   290
Delyghted too too much in wyne, and eyghteene other mo.
All wee did go to Circes houses. As soone as wee came thither,
And in the portall of the Hall had set our feete toogither,
A thousand Lyons, wolves and beares did put us in a feare
By meeting us. But none of them was to bee feared there.   295
For none of them could doo us harme: but with a gentle looke
And following us with fawning feete theyr wanton tayles they shooke.
Anon did Damzells welcome us and led us through the hall
(The which was made of marble stone, floore, arches, roof, and wall)
To Circe. Shee sate underneathe a traverse in a chayre   300
Aloft ryght rich and stately, in a chamber large and fayre.
Shee ware a goodly longtreynd gowne: and all her rest attyre
Was every whit of goldsmithes woork. There sate mee also by her
The Sea nymphes and her Ladyes whoose fyne fingers never knew
What toozing wooll did meene, nor threede from whorled spindle
          drew.   305
They sorted herbes, and picking out the flowers that were mixt,
Did put them into mawnds, and with indifferent space betwixt
Did lay the leaves and stalks on heapes according to theyr hew,
And shee herself the woork of them did oversee and vew.
The vertue and the use of them ryght perfectly shee knew,   310
And in what leaf it lay, and which in mixture would agree.
And so perusing every herb by good advysement, shee
Did wey them out. Assoone as shee us entring in did see,
And greeting had bothe given and tane, shee looked cheerefully,
And graunting all that we desyrde, commaunded by and by   315
A certeine potion to bee made of barly parched drye
And wyne and hony mixt with cheese. And with the same shee slye
Had meynt the jewce of certeine herbes which unespyde did lye
By reason of the sweetenesse of the drink. Wee tooke the cup
Delivered by her wicked hand, and quaft it cleerely up   320

285 *eft*: after, again
288 *uncowth*: unknown, unfamiliar
289 *as tho*: then
297 *wanton*: frolicsome

300 *traverse*: curtain, lattice, etc.
305 *toozing*: teasing, combing; *whorled*: whirling
307 *mawnds*: woven baskets

With thirstye throtes. Which doone, and that the cursed witch had smit
Our highest heare tippes with her wand, (it is a shame, but yit
I will declare the truth) I wext all rough with bristled heare,
And could not make complaint with woordes. In stead of speech I there
Did make a rawghtish grunting, and with groveling face gan beare   325
My visage downeward to the ground. I felt a hooked groyne
To wexen hard uppon my mouth, and brawned neck to joyne
My head and shoulders. And the handes with which I late ago
Had taken up the charmed cup, were turnd to feete as tho.
Such force there is in Sorcerie. In fyne wyth other mo   330
That tasted of the selfsame sawce, they shet mee in a Stye.
From this missehappe Eurilochus alonly scapte. For why
He only would not taste the cup, which had he not fled fro,
He should have beene a bristled beast as well as we. And so
Should none have borne Ulysses woorde of our mischaunce, nor hee   335
Have come to Circe to revenge our harmes and set us free.
The peaceprocurer Mercurie had given to him a whyght
Fayre flowre whoose roote is black, and of the Goddes it Moly hyght
Assurde by this and heavenly hestes, he entred Circes bowre.
And beeing bidden for to drink the cup of baleful powre,   340
As Circe was about to stroke her wand uppon his heare,
He thrust her backe, and put her with his naked swoord in feare.
Then fell they to agreement streyght, and fayth in hand was plyght.
And beeing made her bedfellowe, he claymed as in ryght
Of dowrye, for to have his men ageine in perfect plyght.   345
Shee sprincled us with better jewce of uncowth herbes, and strake
The awk end of her charmed rod uppon our heades, and spake
Woordes to the former contrarie. The more shee charmd, the more
Arose wee upward from the ground on which wee daarde before.
Our bristles fell away, the clift our cloven clees forsooke.   350
Our shoulders did returne agein: and next our elbowes tooke
Our armes and handes theyr former place. Then weeping wee enbrace
Our Lord, and hing about his necke whoo also wept apace.
And not a woord wee rather spake than such as myght appeere
From harts most thankfull to proceede. Wee taryed theyr a yeere.   355
 I in that whyle sawe many things, and many things did heere.
 I marked also this one thing with store of other geere

325 *rawghtish:* harsh   345 *plyght:* condition
326 *groyne:* snout   347 *awk:* wrong, reversed
338 *hyght:* is called   349 *daarde:* crouched
339 *hestes:* commands   350 *clees:* claws

Which one of Circes fowre cheef maydes (whoose office was alway
Uppon such hallowes to attend) did secretly bewray
To mee. For in the whyle my Lord with Circe kept alone,   360
This mayd a yoongmannes image sheawd of fayre whyght marble stone
Within a Chauncell. On the head therof were garlonds store
And eeke a woodspecke. And as I demaunded her wherfore
And whoo it was they honord so in holy Church, and why
He bare that bird uppon his head: shee answeering by and by   365
Sayd: Lerne hereby, sir Macare, to understand the powre
My lady hathe, and marke thou well what I shall say this howre.
    There reignd erewhyle in Italy one Picus, Saturnes sonne,
    Whoo loved warlike horse and had delyght to see them ronne.
He was of feature as yee see. And by this image heere   370
The verry beawtye of the man dooth lyvelely appeere.
His courage matcht his personage. And scarcely had he well
Seene twentye yeeres. His countnance did allure the nymphes that
                              dwell
Among the Latian hilles. The nymphes of fountaines and of brookes,
As those that haunted Albula were ravisht with his lookes   375
And so were they that Numicke beares, and Anio too, and Alme
That ronneth short, and heady Nar, and Farfar coole and calme.
And all the nymphes that usde to haunt Dianas shadye poole,
Or any lakes or meeres neere hand, or other waters coole.
But he disdeyning all the rest did set his love uppon   380
A lady whom Venilia bare (so fame reporteth) on
The stately mountayne Palatine by Janus that dooth beare
The dowble face. Assoone as that her yeeres for maryage were
Thought able, shee preferring him before all other men,
Was wedded to this Picus whoo was king of Lawrents then.   385
Shee was in beawtye excellent, but yit in singing, much
More excellent: and theruppon they naamd her Singer. Such
The sweetenesse of her musicke was, that shee therwith delyghts
The savage beastes, and caused birdes to cease theyr wandring flyghts,
And moved stones and trees, and made the ronning streames to stay.   390
Now whyle that shee in womans tune recordes her pleasant lay
At home, her husband rode abrode uppon a lustye horse
To hunt the Boare, and bare in hand twoo hunting staves of force.
His cloke was crymzen butned with a golden button fast.
Into the selfsame forest eeke was Phebus daughter past   395

359 *hallowes*: shrines   363 *woodspecke*: woodpecker

From those same feeldes that of herself the name of Circe beare,
To gather uncowth herbes among the fruteful hillocks there.
As soone as lurking in the shrubbes shee did the king espye,
Shee was astrawght. Downe fell her herbes to ground. And by and by
Through all her bones the flame of love the maree gan to frye.   400
And when shee from this forced heate had cald her witts agen,
Shee purposde to bewray her mynd. But unto him as then
Shee could not come for swiftnesse of his horse and for his men
That garded him on every syde. Yit shalt thou not (quoth shee)
So shift thee fro my handes although the wynd should carrye thee,   405
If I doo knowe myself, if all the strength of herbes fayle not,
Or if I have not quyght and cleene my charmes and spelles forgotte.
In saying theis same wordes, shee made the likenesse of a Boare
Without a body, causing it to swiftly passe before
King Picus eyes, and for to seeme to get him to the woode,   410
Where for the thickenesse of the trees a horse myght do no good.
Immediatly the king unwares a hote pursute did make
Uppon the shadowe of his pray, and quikly did forsake
His foming horses sweating backe: and following vayne wan hope,
Did runne afoote among the woodes, and through the bushes crope.   415
Then Circe fell a mumbling spelles, and praying like a witch
Did honour straunge and uncowth Goddes with uncowth charmes, by
                                                                which
Shee usde to make the moone looke dark, and wrappe her fathers head
In watry clowdes. And then likewyse the heaven was overspred
With darknesse, and a foggye mist steamd upward from the ground.   420
And nere a man about the king to gard him could bee found,
But every man in blynd bywayes ran scattring in the chace,
Through her inchauntments. At the length shee getting tyme and place,
Sayd: By those lyghtsum eyes of thyne which late have ravisht myne,
And by that goodly personage and lovely face of thyne,   425
The which compelleth mee that am a Goddesse to enclyne
To make this humble sute to thee that art a mortall wyght,
Asswage my flame, and make this sonne (whoo by his heavenly syght
Foresees all things) thy fathrinlawe: and hardly hold not scorne
Of Circe whoo by long discent of Titans stocke am borne.   430
Thus much sayd Circe. He ryght feerce rejecting her request,
And her, sayd: Whooso ere thou art, go set thy hart at rest.
I am not thyne, nor will not bee. Another holdes my hart:

399 *astrawght:* distraught, distracted   429 *hardly:* obdurately
415 *crope:* crept

And long God graunt shee may it hold, that I may never start
To leawdnesse of a forreigne lust from bond of lawfull bed,   435
As long as Janus daughter, my sweete Singer, is not dead.
Dame Circe having oft renewd her sute in vayne beefore,
Sayd: Dearely shalt thou bye thy scorne. For never shalt thou more
Returne to Singer. Thou shalt lerne by proof what one can doo
That is provoked, and in love, yea and a woman too.   440
But Circe is bothe stird to wrath, and also tane in love,
Yea and a woman. Twyce her face to westward she did move,
And twyce to Eastward. Thryce shee layd her rod uppon his head.
And therwithall three charmes shee cast. Away king Picus fled.
And woondring that he fled more swift than earst he had beene
                                                    woont,   445
He saw the fethers on his skin, and at the sodein brunt
Became a bird that haunts the wooddes. Wherat he taking spyght,
With angrye bill did job uppon hard Okes with all his myght,
And in his moode made hollowe holes uppon theyr boughes. The hew
Of Crimzen which was in his cloke, uppon his fethers grew.   450
The gold that was a clasp and did his cloke toogither hold,
Is fethers, and about his necke goes circlewyse like gold.
His servants luring in that whyle oft over all the ground
In vayne, and fynding no where of theyr kyng no inkling, found
Dame Circe. (For by that tyme shee had made the ayer sheere,   455
And suffred both the sonne and wyndes the mistye steames to cleere)
And charging her with matter trew, demaunded for theyr kyng,
And offring force, began theyr darts and Javelings for to fling.
Shee sprincling noysom venim streyght and jewce of poysoning myght,
Did call togither Eribus and Chaos, and the nyght,   460
And all the feendes of darknesse, and with howling out along
Made prayers unto Hecate. Scarce ended was her song,
But that (a woondrous thing to tell) the woodes lept from theyr place.
The ground did grone: the trees neere hand lookt pale in all the chace:
The grasse besprent with droppes of blood lookt red: the stones did
                                                    seem   465
To roare and bellow horce: and doggs to howle and raze extreeme:
And all the ground to crawle with snakes blacke scaalde: and gastly
                                                    spryghts
Fly whisking up and downe. The folke were flayghted at theis syghts.

438 *bye:* aby, pay for   455 *sheere:* clear
448 *job:* jab, peck   466 *raze:* rase, rage, growl, bark
453 *luring:* calling   468 *flayghted:* frightened

And as they woondring stood amaazd, shee strokte her witching wand
Uppon theyr faces. At the touche wherof, there out of hand   470
Came woondrous shapes of savage beastes uppon them all. Not one
Reteyned still his native shape. The setting sonne was gone
Beyond the utmost coast of Spaine, and Singer longd in vayne
To see her husband. Bothe her folke and people ran agayne
Through all the woodes. And ever as they went, they sent theyr eyes   475
Before them for to fynd him out, but no man him espyes.
Then Singer thought it not ynough to weepe and teare her heare,
And beat herself (all which shee did). Shee gate abrode, and there
Raundgd over all the broade wyld feelds like one besyds her witts.
Six nyghts and full as many dayes (as fortune led by fitts)   480
She strayd mee over hilles and dales, and never tasted rest,
Nor meate, nor drink of all the whyle. The seventh day, sore opprest
And tyred bothe with travell and with sorrowe, downe shee sate
Uppon cold Tybers bank, and there with teares in moorning rate
Shee warbling on her greef in tune not shirle nor over hye,   485
Did make her moane, as dooth the swan: whoo ready for to dye
Dooth sing his buriall song before. Her maree molt at last
With moorning, and shee pynde away: and finally shee past
To lither ayre. But yit her fame remayned in the place.
For why the auncient husbandmen according to the cace,   490
Did name it Singer of the nymph that dyed in the same.
Of such as these are, many things that yeere by fortune came
Bothe to my heering and my sight. Wee wexing resty then
And sluggs by discontinuance, were commaunded yit agen
To go aboord and hoyse up sayles. And Circe told us all   495
That long and dowtfull passage and rowgh seas should us befall.
I promis thee those woordes of hers mee throughly made afrayd:
And therfore hither I mee gate, and heere I have mee stayd.
     This was the end of Macars tale. And ere long tyme was gone,
     Aenaeas Nurce was buryed in a tumb of marble stone,   500
And this short verse was set theron: *In this same verry place*
My Nurcechyld whom the world dooth know to bee a chyld of grace
Delivering mee, Caieta, quicke from burning by the Grayes,
Hathe burnt mee dead with such a fyre as justly winnes him prayse.
Theyr Cables from the grassye strond were loosde, and by and by   505
From Circes slaunderous house and from her treasons farre they fly.

---

484 *rate:* manner
487 *molt:* melted
489 *lither:* yielding

493 *resty:* sluggish, lazy
495 *hoyse:* hoist
503 *quicke:* alive; *Grayes:* Graii, Greeks

And making to the thickgrowen groves where through the yellow dust
The shady Tyber into sea his gusshing streame dooth thrust,
Aenaeas got the Realme of king Latinus, Fawnus sonne,
And eeke his daughter, whom in feyght by force of armes he wonne. 510
He enterprysed warre ageinst a Nation feerce and strong.
And Turne was wrothe for holding of his wyfe away by wrong.
Ageinst the Shyre of Latium met all Tyrrhene, and long
With busye care hawlt victorie by force of armes was sought.
Eche partie to augment theyr force by forreine succour wrought.   515
And many sent the Rutills help, and many came to ayd
The Trojanes: neyther was the good Aenaeas ill apayd
Of going to Evanders towne. But Venulus in vayne
To outcast Diomeds citie went his succour to obteine.
        This Diomed under Dawnus, king of Calabrye, did found   520
        A myghtye towne, and with his wyfe in dowrye hild the ground.
Now when from Turnus, Venulus his message had declaard,
Desyring help: th'Aetolian knyght sayd none could well bee spaard.
And in excuce, he told him how he neyther durst be bold
To prest his fathers folk to warre of whom he had no hold,   525
Nor any of his countrymen had left as then alyve
To arme. And lest yee think (quoth hee) I doo a shift contryve,
Although by uppening of the thing my bitter greef revyve
I will abyde to make a new rehersall. After that
The Greekes had burned Troy and on the ground had layd it flat,   530
And that the Prince of Narix by his ravishing the mayd
In Pallas temple, on us all the pennance had displayd
Which he himself deservd alone: then scattred heere and there
And harryed over all the seas, wee Greekes were fayne to beare
Nyght, thunder, tempest, wrath of heaven and sea, and last of all   535
Sore shipwrecke at mount Capharey to mend our harmes withall.
And lest that mee to make too long a processe yee myght deeme
In setting forth our heavy happes, the Greekes myght that tyme seeme
Ryght rewfull even to Priamus. Howbee't Minerva, shee
That weareth armour, tooke mee from the waves and saved mee.   540
But from my fathers Realme ageine by violence I was driven.
For Venus bearing still in mynd the wound I had her given
Long tyme before, did woork revendge. By meanes wherof such toyle
Did tosse mee on the sea, and on the land I found such broyle

514 *hawlt:* lofty
517 *apayd:* satisfied
525 *prest:* press, levy

527 *shift:* trick
528 *uppening:* mentioning
544 *broyle:* turmoil

By warres, that in my hart I thought them blist of God whom erst   ⁵⁴⁵
The violence of the raging sea and hideous wynds had perst,
And whom the wrathfull Capharey by shipwrecke did confound:
Oft wisshing also I had there among the rest beene drownd.
My company now having felt the woorst that sea or warre
Could woorke, did faynt, and wisht an end of straying out so farre.   ⁵⁵⁰
But Agmon hot of nature and too feerce through slaughters made
Sayd: What remayneth, sirs, through which our pacience cannot wade?
What further spyght hath Venus yit to woork ageinst us more?
When woorse misfortunes may be feard than have beene felt before,
Then prayer may advauntadge men, and vowwing may then boote.   ⁵⁵⁵
But when the woorst is past of things, then feare is under foote.
And when that bale is hyghest growne, then boote must next ensew.
Although shee heere mee, and doo hate us all (which thing is trew)
That serve heere under Diomed: Yit set wee lyght her hate.
And deerely it should stand us on to purchase hygh estate.   ⁵⁶⁰
With such stowt woordes did Agmon stirre dame Venus unto ire
And raysd ageine her settled grudge. Not many had desyre
To heere him talk thus out of square. The moste of us that are
His freendes rebukte him for his woordes. And as he did prepare
To answere, bothe his voyce and throte by which his voyce should go, ⁵⁶⁵
Were small: his heare to feathers turnd: his necke was clad as tho
With feathers: so was brist and backe. The greater fethers stacke
Uppon his armes: and into wings his elbowes bowwed backe.
The greatest portion of his feete was turned into toes.
A hardened bill of horne did growe uppon his mouth and noze,   ⁵⁷⁰
And sharpened at the neather end. His fellowes, Lycus, Ide,
Rethenor, Nyct, and Abas all stood woondring by his syde.
And as they woondred, they receyvd the selfsame shape and hew.
And finally the greater part of all my band up flew,
And clapping with theyr newmade wings, about the ores did gird.   ⁵⁷⁵
And if yee doo demaund the shape of this same dowtfull bird,
Even as they bee not verry Swannnes: so drawe they verry neere
The shape of Cygnets whyght. With much adoo I settled heere,
And with a little remnant of my people doo obteyne
The dry grownds of my fathrinlaw, king Dawnus, whoo did reigne   ⁵⁸⁰

⁵⁴⁶ *perst:* perished, destroyed (?). Ovid's
    word is *mersit* (sunk, overwhelmed).
⁵⁵⁵ *boote:* help
⁵⁵⁷ *bale:* suffering, misery
⁵⁵⁹ *set . . . lyght:* despise
⁵⁶⁰ *it should stand us on:* it is incumbent

on us, we ought; *purchase:* acquire,
    gain
⁵⁶³ *out of square:* improperly
⁵⁶⁶ *as tho:* then
⁵⁶⁷ *stacke:* stuck
⁵⁷⁵ *gird:* dart

In Calabry. Thus much the sonne of Oenye sayd. Anon
  Sir Venulus returning from the king of Calydon,
  Forsooke the coast of Puteoll and the feeldes of Messapie,
In which hee saw a darksome denne forgrowne with busshes hye,
And watred with a little spring. The halfegoate Pan that howre   585
Possessed it: but heertofore it was the fayryes bowre.
A shepeherd of Appulia from that countrye scaard them furst.
But afterward recovering hart and hardynesse they durst
Despyse him when he chaced them, and with theyr nimble feete
Continewed on theyr dawncing still in tyme and measure meete.   590
The shepeherd fownd mee fault with them: and with his lowtlike leapes
Did counterfette theyr minyon dawnce, and rapped out by heapes
A rabble of unsavery taunts even like a country cloyne,
To which, most leawd and filthy termes of purpose he did joyne.
And after he had once begon, he could not hold his toong,   595
Untill that in the timber of a tree his throte was cloong.
For now he is a tree, and by his jewce discerne yee may
His manners. For the Olyf wyld dooth sensibly bewray
By berryes full of bitternesse his rayling toong. For ay
The harshnesse of his bitter woordes the berryes beare away.   600
  Now when the kings Ambassadour returned home without
  The succour of th'Aetolian prince, the Rutills being stout
Made luckelesse warre without theyr help: and much on eyther syde
Was shed of blood. Behold king Turne made burning bronds to glyde
Uppon theyr shippes, and they that had escaped water, stoode   605
In feare of fyre. The flame had sindgd the pitch, the wax, and wood,
And other things that nourish fyre, and ronning up the maste
Caught hold uppon the sayles, and all the takling gan to waste,
The Rowers seates did also smoke: when calling to her mynd
That theis same shippes were pynetrees erst and shaken with the
                                                              wynd   610
On Ida mount, the moother of the Goddes, dame Cybel, filld
The ayre with sound of belles, and noyse of shalmes. And as shee hilld
The reynes that rulde the Lyons tame which drew her charyot, shee
Sayd thus: O Turnus, all in vayne theis wicked hands of thee
Doo cast this fyre. For by myself dispoynted it shall bee.   615
I wilnot let the wasting fyre consume theis shippes which are
A parcell of my forest Ide of which I am most chare.

592 *minyon*: pretty   612 *shalmes*: shawms, oboe-like instruments
593 *cloyne*: clown, boor   615 *dispoynted*: thwarted
596 *cloong*: caught   617 *chare*: careful

It thundred as the Goddesse spake, and with the thunder came
A storme of rayne and skipping hayle, and soodeyne with the same
The sonnes of Astrey meeting feerce and feyghting verry sore,   620
Did trouble bothe the sea and ayre and set them on a rore.
Dame Cybel using one of them to serve her turne that tyde,
Did breake the Cables at the which the Trojane shippes did ryde,
And bare them prone, and underneathe the water did them dryve.
The Timber of them softning turnd to bodyes streyght alyve.   625
The stemmes were turnd to heades, the ores to swimming feete and toes,
The sydes to ribbes, the keele that through the middle gally goes
Became the ridgebone of the backe, the sayles and tackling, heare:
And into armes on eyther syde the sayleyards turned were.
Theyr hew is duskye as before, and now in shape of mayd   630
They play among the waves of which even now they were afrayd.
And beeing Sea nymphes, wheras they were bred in mountaynes hard,
They haunt for ay the water soft, and never afterward
Had mynd to see theyr natyve soyle. But yit forgetting not
How many perills they had felt on sea by lucklesse lot,   635
They often put theyr helping hand to shippes distrest by wynd,
Onlesse that any caryed Greekes. For bearing still in mynd
The burning of the towne of Troy, they hate the Greekes by kynd.
And therfore of Ulysses shippes ryght glad they were to see
The shivers, and as glad they were as any glad myght bee,   640
To see Alcinous shippes wex hard and turned into stone.
      Theis shippes thus having gotten lyfe and beeing turnd each one
      To nymphes, a body would have thought the miracle so greate
Should into Turnus wicked hart sum godly feare have beate,
And made him cease his wilfull warre. But he did still persist.   645
And eyther partye had theyr Goddes theyr quarrell to assist,
And courage also: which as good as Goddes myght well be thought.
In fyne they neyther for the Realme nor for the scepter sought,
Nor for the Lady Lavine: but for conquest. And for shame
To seeme to shrinke in leaving warre, they still prolongd the same.   650
At length dame Venus sawe her sonne obteyne the upper hand.
King Turnus fell, and eeke the towne of Ardea which did stand
Ryght strong in hygh estate as long as Turnus lived. But
Assoone as that Aenaeas swoord to death had Turnus put,
The towne was set on fyre: and from amid the embers flew   655
A fowle which till that present tyme no persone ever knew,
And beete the ashes feercely up with flapping of his wing.

638 *by kynd*: (1) naturally, (2) as a race   640 *shivers*: pieces, wreckage

The leanenesse, palenesse, dolefull sound, and every other thing
That may expresse a Citie sakt, yea and the Cities name
Remayned still unto the bird. And now the verrye same   660
With Hernesewes fethers dooth bewayle the towne wherof it came.
    And now Aenaeas prowesse had compelled all the Goddes
    And Juno also (whoo with him was most of all at oddes)
To cease theyr old displeasure quyght. And now he having layd
Good ground wheron the growing welth of July myght be stayd,   665
Was rype for heaven. And Venus had great sute already made
To all the Goddes, and cleeping Jove did thus with him perswade:
Deere father, whoo hast never beene uncurtuous unto mee,
Now shewe the greatest courtesie (I pray thee) that may bee.
And on my sonne Aenaeas (whoo a graundchyld unto thee   670
Hath got of my blood) if thou wilt vouchsafe him awght at all)
Vouchsafe sum Godhead to bestowe, although it bee but small.
It is ynough that once he hathe alreadye seene the Realme
Of Pluto utter pleasurelesse, and passed Styxis streame.
The Goddes assented: neyther did Queene Juno then appeere   675
In countnance straunge, but did consent with glad and merry cheere.
Then Jove: Aenaeas woorthy is a saynct in heaven to bee.
Thy wish for whom thou doost it wish I graunt thee frank and free.
This graunt of his made Venus glad. Shee thankt him for the same.
And glyding through the aire uppon her yoked doves, shee came   680
To Lawrent shore, where clad with reede the river Numicke deepe
To seaward (which is neere at hand) with stealing pace dooth creepe.
Shee bade this river wash away what ever mortall were
In good Aenaeas bodye, and them under sea to beare.
The horned brooke fulfilld her hest, and with his water sheere   685
Did purge and clenze Aenaeas from his mortall body cleere.
The better porcion of him did remayne unto him sownd.
His moother having hallowed him did noynt his bodye rownd
With heavenly odours, and did touch his mouth with Ambrosie
The which was mixt with Nectar sweete, and made him by and by   690
A God to whom the Romanes give the name of Indiges,
Endevering with theyr temples and theyr altars him to please.
    Ascanius with the dowble name from thence began to reigne,
    In whom the rule of Alba and of Latium did remayne.
Next him succeeded Silvius, whoose sonne Latinus hild   695

661 *Hernesewes:* heronshaw, young heron,   667 *cleeping:* embracing
    heron   676 *cheere:* expression
665 *stayd:* based, supported

The auncient name and scepter which his graundsyre erst did weeld.
The famous Epit after this Latinus did succeede.
Then Capys and king Capetus. But Capys was indeede
The formest of the two. From this the scepter of the Realme
Descended unto Tyberine, whoo drowning in the streame   700
Of Tyber left that name thereto. This Tyberine begat
Feerce Remulus and Acrota. By chaunce it hapned that
The elder brother Remulus for counterfetting oft
The thunder, with a thunderbolt was killed from aloft.
From Acrota whoose stayednesse did passe his brothers skill,   705
The crowne did come to Aventine, whoo in the selfsame hill
In which he reygned buryed lyes, and left therto his name.
The rule of nation Palatine at length to Proca came.
    In this Kings reigne Pomona livd. There was not to bee found
    Among the woodnymphes any one in all the Latian ground   710
That was so conning for to keepe an Ortyard as was shee,
Nor none so paynefull to preserve the frute of every tree.
And theruppon shee had her name. Shee past not for the woodes
Nor rivers, but the villages and boughes that bare bothe buddes
And plentuous frute. In sted of dart a shredding hooke shee bare, 715
With which the overlusty boughes shee eft away did pare
That spreaded out too farre, and eft did make therwith a rift
To greffe another imp uppon the stocke within the clift.
And lest her trees should die through drought, with water of the springs
Shee moysteth of theyr sucking roots the little crumpled strings.   720
This was her love and whole delyght. And as for Venus deedes,
Shee had no mynd at all of them. And forbycause shee dreedes
Enforcement by the countrye folke, shee walld her yards about,
Not suffring any man at all to enter in or out.
What have not those same nimble laddes so apt to frisk and daunce   725
The Satyrs doone? Or what the Pannes that wantonly doo praunce
With horned forheads? And the old Silenus whoo is ay
More youthfull than his yeeres? And eeke the feend that scares away
The theeves and robbers with his hooke, or with his privy part
To winne her love? But yit than theis a farre more constant hart   730
Had sly Vertumnus, though he sped no better than the rest.
O Lord, how often being in a moawers garment drest,
Bare he in bundells sheaves of corne? And when he so was dyght,

699 *formest:* foremost   716 *eft:* again
705 *stayednesse:* restraint, seriousness   718 *greffe:* graft; *imp:* scion
713 *past:* cared   723 *Enforcement:* force, violence
715 *shredding:* pruning   733 *dyght:* dressed

He was the verry patterne of a harvest moawer ryght.
Oft bynding newmade hay about his temples he myght seeme   735
A haymaker. Oft tymes in hand made hard with woork extreeme
He bare a goade, that men would sweere he had but newly then
Unyoakt his weerye Oxen. Had he tane in hand agen
A shredding hooke, yee would have thought hee had a gardener beene,
Or proyner of sum vynes. Or had you him with ladder seene   740
Uppon his necke, a gatherer of frute yee would him deeme.
With swoord a souldier, with his rod an Angler he did seeme.
And finally in many shapes he sought to fynd accesse
To joy the beawty but by syght, that did his hart oppresse.
Moreover, putting on his head a womans wimple gay,   745
And staying by a staffe, graye heares he foorth to syght did lay
Uppon his forehead, and did feyne a beldame for to bee,
By meanes wherof he came within her goodly ortyards free.
And woondring at the frute, sayd: Much more skill hast thou I see
Than all the Nymphes of Albula. Hayle, Lady myne, the flowre   750
Unspotted of pure maydenhod in all the world this howre.
And with that woord he kissed her a little: but his kisse
Was such as trew old women would have never given ywis.
Then sitting downe uppon a bank, he looked upward at
The braunches bent with harvests weyght. Ageinst him where he sat   755
A goodly Elme with glistring grapes did growe: which after hee
Had praysed, and the vyne likewyse that ran uppon the tree:
    But if (quoth hee) this Elme without the vyne did single stand,
    It should have nothing (saving leaves) to bee desyred: and
Ageine if that the vyne which ronnes uppon the Elme had nat   760
The tree to leane unto, it should uppon the ground ly flat.
Yit art not thou admonisht by example of this tree
To take a husband, neyther doost thou passe to maryed bee.
But would to God thou wouldest. Sure Queene Helen never had
Mo suters, nor the Lady that did cause the battell mad   765
Betweene the halfbrute Centawres and the Lapythes, nor the wyfe
Of bold Ulysses whoo was eeke ay fearefull of his lyfe,
Than thou shouldst have. For thousands now (even now most cheefly
                                                        when
Thou seemest suters to abhorre) desyre thee, both of men,
And Goddes and halfgoddes, yea and all the fayryes that doo dwell   770
In Albane hilles. But if thou wilt bee wyse, and myndest well

740 *proyner:* pruner   747 *beldame:* old lady
746 *staying by:* leaning on   753 *ywis:* certainly

To match thy self, and wilt give eare to this old woman heere,
(To whom thou more than to them all art (trust mee) leef and deere,
And more than thou thyself beleevst) the common matches flee,
And choose Vertumnus to thy make. And take thou mee to bee   775
His pledge. For more he to himself not knowen is, than to mee.
He roves not like a ronneagate through all the world abrode,
This countrye heerabout (the which is large) is his abode.
He dooth not (like a number of theis common wooers) cast
His love to every one he sees. Thou art the first and last   780
That ever he set mynd uppon. Alonly unto thee
Hee vowes himself as long as lyfe dooth last. Moreover hee
Is youthfull, and with beawtye sheene endewd by natures gift,
And aptly into any shape his persone he can shift.
Thou canst not bid him bee the thing, (though al things thou shouldst
                                              name)   785
But that he fitly and with ease will streyght becomme the same.
Besydes all this, in all one thing bothe twayne of you delyght,
And of the frutes that you love best the firstlings are his ryght:
And gladly he receyves thy gifts. But neyther covets hee
Thy Apples, Plommes, nor other frutes new gathered from the tree,   790
Nor yit the herbes of pleasant sent that in thy gardynes bee:
Nor any other kynd of thing in all the world, but thee.
Have mercy on his fervent love, and think himself to crave
Heere present by the mouth of mee, the thing that he would have.
And feare the God that may revenge: as Venus whoo dooth hate   795
Hard harted folkes, and Rhamnuse whoo dooth eyther soone or late
Expresse her wrath with myndfull wreake. And to th'entent thou may
The more beware, of many things which tyme by long delay
Hathe taught mee, I will shewe thee one which over all the land
Of Cyprus blazed is abrode, which being ryghtly skand   800
May easly bow thy hardned hart and make it for to yild.
      One Iphis borne of lowe degree by fortune had behild
      The Ladye Anaxarete descended of the race
Of Tewcer, and in vewwing her the fyre of love apace
Did spred it self through all his bones. With which he stryving long,   805
When reason could not conquer rage bycause it was too strong,
Came humbly to the Ladyes house: and one whyle laying ope

773 *leef:* beloved   783 *sheene:* bright
775 *make:* mate   797 *wreake:* vengeance
777 *ronneagate:* renegade, runaway, vag-
    abond

His wretched love before her nurce, besought her by the hope
Of Lady Anaxarete her nurcechylds good successe,
Shee would not bee ageinst him in that cace of his distresse.   810
Another whyle entreating fayre sum freend of hers, he prayd
Him earnestly with carefull voyce, of furthrance and of ayd.
Oftymes he did preferre his sute by gentle letters sent.
Oft garlonds moysted with the deawe of teares that from him went
He hanged on her postes. Oft tymes his tender sydes he layd   815
Ageinst the threshold hard, and oft in sadnesse did upbrayd
The locke with much ungentlenesse. The Lady crueller
Than are the rysing narrowe seas, or falling Kiddes, and farre
More hard than steele of Noricum, and than the stonny rocke
That in the quarrye hath his roote, did him despyse and mocke.   820
Besyde her dooings mercylesse, of statelynesse and spyght
Shee adding prowd and skornefull woordes, defrauds the wretched
wyght
Of verry hope. But Iphis now unable any more
To beare the torment of his greef, still standing there before
Her gate, spake theis his latest woordes: Well, Anaxarete,   825
Thou hast the upper hand. Hencefoorth thou shalt not neede to bee
Agreeved any more with mee. Go tryumph hardely:
Go vaunt thy self with joy: go sing the song of victorye:
Go put a crowne of glittring bay uppon thy cruell head.
For why thou hast the upper hand, and I am gladly dead.   830
Well, steely harted, well: rejoyce. Compeld yit shalt thou bee
Of sumwhat in mee for to have a lyking. Thou shalt see
A poynt wherein thou mayst mee deeme most thankfull unto thee,
And in the end thou shalt confesse the great desert of mee.
But yit remember that as long as lyfe in mee dooth last,   835
The care of thee shall never from this hart of myne be cast.
For bothe the lyfe that I doo live in hope of thee, and tother
Which nature giveth, shall have end and passe away toogither.
The tydings neyther of my death shall come to thee by fame.
Myself (I doo assure thee) will bee bringer of the same.   840
Myself (I say) will present bee that those same cruell eyen
Of thyne may feede themselves uppon this livelesse corce of myne.
But yit, O Goddes, (if you behold mennes deedes) remember mee.
(My toong will serve to pray no more) and cause that I may bee
Longtyme heerafter spoken of: and length the lyfe by fame   845

821 *statelynesse:* aloofness, arrogance   842 *corce:* corpse
827 *hardely:* boldly   845 *length:* lengthen

The which yee have abridgd in yeeres. In saying of this same
He lifted up his watrye eyes and armes that wexed wan
To those same stulpes which oft he had with garlondes deckt ere than,
And fastning on the topps therof a halter thus did say:
Thou cruell and ungodly wyght, theis are the wreathes that may   850
Most pleasure thee. And with that woord he thrusting in his head,
Even then did turne him towards her as good as being dead,
And wretchedly did totter on the poste with strangled throte.
The wicket which his feerefull feete in sprawling maynely smote,
Did make a noyse: and flying ope bewrayd his dooing playne.   855
The servants shreekt, and lifting up his bodye, but in vayne,
Conveyd him to his moothers house, his father erst was slayne.
His moother layd him in her lappe, and cleeping in her armes
Her sonnes cold bodye, after that shee had bewayld her harmes
With woordes and dooings mootherlyke, the corce with moorning
                                                          cheere   860
To buryall sadly through the towne was borne uppon a beere.
The house of Anaxarete by chaunce was neere the way
By which this piteous pomp did passe. And of the doolefull lay
The sound came to the eares of her, whom God alreadye gan
To strike. Yit let us see (quoth shee) the buryall of this man.   865
And up the hygh wyde windowde house in saying so, shee ran.
Scarce had shee well on Iphis lookt that on the beere did lye,
But that her eyes wext stark: and from her limbes the blood gan flye.
In stead therof came palenesse in. And as shee backeward was
In mynd to go, her feete stacke fast and could not stirre. And as   870
Shee would have cast her countnance backe, shee could not doo it. And
The stonny hardnesse which alate did in her stomacke stand,
Within a whyle did overgrow her whole from sole to crowne.
And lest you think this geere surmysde, even yit in Salamin towne
Of Lady Anaxarete the image standeth playne.   875
The temple also in the which the image dooth remayne,
Is unto Venus consecrate by name of Looker Out.
And therfore weying well theis things, I prey thee looke about
Good Lady, and away with pryde: and be content to frame
Thy self to him that loveth thee and cannot quench his flame.   880
So neyther may the Lentons cold thy budding frutetrees kill

---

848 *stulpes:* posts, pillars
863 *pomp:* funeral procession
868 *stark:* stiff
874 *geere surmysde:* matter imagined

879 *frame:* adapt, fit
881 *Lentons:* springs, spring's, springs' (the season)

Nor yit the sharp and boystous wyndes thy flowring Gardynes spill.
The God that can uppon him take what kynd of shape he list
Now having sayd thus much in vayne, omitted to persist
In beldames shape, and shewde himself a lusty gentleman,   885
Appeering to her cheerefully, even like as Phebus whan
Hee having overcomme the clowdes that did withstand his myght,
Dooth blaze his brightsum beames agein with fuller heate and lyght.
He offred force, but now no force was needfull in the cace.
For why shee beeing caught in love with beawty of his face,   890
Was wounded then as well as hee, and gan to yeeld apace.
    Next Proca, reignd Amulius in Awsonye by wrong,
    Till Numitor, the ryghtfull heyre, deposed verry long,
Was by his daughters sonnes restorde. And on the feastfull day
Of Pale, foundation of the walles of Rome they gan to lay.   895
Soone after Tacye, and the Lordes of Sabine stird debate:
And Tarpey for her traytrous deede in opening of the gate
Of Tarpey towre was prest to death according to desert
With armour heapt uppon her head. Then feerce and stowt of hart
The Sabines like to toonglesse woolves without all noyse of talke   900
Assayld the Romanes in theyr sleepe, and to the gates gan stalke
Which Ilias sonne had closed fast with lockes and barres. But yit
Dame Juno had set open one, and as shee opened it
Had made no noyse of craking with the hindges, so that none
Perceyvd the opening of the gate but Venus all alone.   905
And shee had shet it up, but that it is not lawfull to
One God to undoo any thing another God hath doo.
The water nymphes of Awsonie hild all the groundes about
The Church of Janus where was store of springs fresh flowing out.
Dame Venus prayd theis nymphes of help. And they considering that 910
The Goddesse did request no more but ryght, denyde it nat.
They opened all theyr fountayne veynes and made them flowe apace.
Howbee't the passage was not yit to Janus open face
Forclosed: neyther had as yit the water stopt the way.
They put rank brimstone underneathe the flowing spring that day,   915
And eeke with smokye rozen set theyr veynes on fyre for ay.
Through force of theis and other things, the vapour perced lowe
Even downe unto the verry rootes on which the springs did growe.
So that the waters which alate in coldnesse myght compare
Even with the frozen Alpes, now hot as burning furnace are.   920

882 *spill:* destroy, kill   904 *craking:* creaking

The two gate posts with sprinkling of the fyry water smoakt.
Wherby the gate beehyghted to the Sabines quyght was choakt
With rysing of this fountaine straunge, untill that Marsis knyght
Had armed him. Then Romulus did boldly offer fyght.
The Romane ground with Sabines and with Romanes bothe were
          spred.   925
And with the blood of fathrinlawes which wicked swoord had shed
Flowde mixt the blood of sonneinlawes. Howbee't it seemed best
To bothe the partyes at the length from battell for to rest,
And not to fyght to uttrance: and that Tacye should becoome
Copartner with king Romulus of sovereintye in Rome.   930
Within a whyle king Tacye dyde: and bothe the Sabines and
The Romanes under Romulus in equall ryght did stand.
The God of battell putting off his glittring helmet then,
With such like woordes as theis bespake the syre of Goddes and men:
    The tyme, O father (in as much as now the Romane state   935
    Is wexen strong uppon the good foundation layd alate,
Depending on the stay of one) is comme for thee to make
Thy promis good which thou of mee and of thy graundchyld spake:
Which was to take him from the earth and in the heaven him stay.
Thou once (I markt thy gracious woordes and bare them well away)   940
Before a great assembly of the Goddes didst to mee say
There shalbee one whom thou shalt rayse above the starry skye.
Now let thy saying take effect. Jove graunting by and by
The ayre was hid with darksom clowdes, and thunder foorth did fly,
And lyghtning made the world agast. Which Mars perceyving to   945
Bee luckye tokens for himself his enterpryse to do,
Did take his rist uppon his speare and boldly lept into
His bloodye charyot. And he lent his horses with his whippe
A yirking lash, and through the ayre full smoothely downe did slippe.
And staying on the woody toppe of mountayne Palatine,   950
He tooke away king Romulus whoo there did then defyne
The pryvate caces of his folk unseemly for a king.
And as a leaden pellet broade enforced from a sling
Is woont to dye amid the skye: even so his mortall flesh
Sank from him downe the suttle ayre. In sted wherof a fresh   955
And goodly shape more stately and more meete for sacred shryne
Succeeded, like our Quirin that in stately robe dooth shyne.

922 *beehyghted:* promised   940 *bare . . . away:* remembered
929 *to uttrance:* to the bitter end   949 *yirking:* cracking
939 *stay:* set firmly, fix   951 *defyne:* settle

Hersilia for her feere as lost, of moorning made none end,
Untill Queene Juno did commaund dame Iris to discend
Uppon the Raynebowe downe, and thus her message for to doo: 960
O of the Latian country and the Sabine nacion too
Thou peerlesse perle of womanhod, most woorthy for to bee
The wyfe of such a noble prince as heertofore was hee,
And still to bee the wyfe of him canonized by name,
Of Quirin: cease thy teares. And if thou have desyre the same   965
Thy holy husband for to see, ensew mee to the queache
That groweth greene on Quirins hill, whoose shadowes overreache
The temple of the Romane king. Dame Iris did obey.
And slyding by her paynted bowe, in former woordes did say
Her errand to Hersilia. Shee scarce lifting up her eyes   970
With sober countnance answerd: O thou Goddesse (for surmyse
I cannot whoo thou art, but yit I well may understand
Thou art a Goddesse) leede mee, O deere Goddesse, leede mee, and
My husband to mee shewe. Whom if the fatall susters three
Will of theyr gracious goodnesse graunt mee leave but once to see,   975
I shall account mee into heaven receyved for to bee.
Immediatly with Thawmants imp to Quirins hill shee went.
There glyding from the sky a starre streyght downe to ground was sent,
The sparkes of whoose bryght blazing beames did burne Hersilias heare.
And with the starre the ayre did up her heare to heavenward beare.   980
The buylder of the towne of Rome receyving streyght the same
Betweene his old acquaynted handes, did alter both her name
And eeke her bodye, calling her dame Ora. And by this
Shee joyntly with her husband for a Goddesse woorshipt is.

FINIS LIBRI DECIMI QUARTI.

958 *feere:* mate   966 *ensew:* follow; *queache:* thicket

THE. XV. BOOKE OF

OVIDS METAMORPHOSIS.

[*Numa. Pythagoras. Hippolytus. Cipus. Aesculapius. Julius Caesar.*]

A Persone in the whyle was sought sufficient to susteine
The burthen of so great a charge, and woorthy for to reigne
In stead of such a mighty prince. The noble Nume by fame
(Whoo harped then uppon the truthe before to passe it came)
Appoynted to the Empyre was. This Numa thought it not   5
Inough that he the knowledge of the Sabine rites had got.
The deepenesse of the noble wit to greater things was bent,
To serch of things the natures out. The care of this intent
Did cause that he from Curie and his native Countrye went
With peynfull travell, to the towne where Hercules did hoste.   10
And asking who it was of Greece that in th'Italian coast
Had buylt that towne, an aged man well seene in storyes old,
To satisfye his mynd therin the processe thus him told:
    As Hercules enriched with the Spannish kyne did hold
    His voyage from the Ocean sea, men say with lucky cut   15
He came aland on Lacine coast. And whyle he there did put
His beace to grazing, he himself in Crotons house did rest,
The greatest man in all those parts and unto straungers best:
And that he there refresht him of his tedious travell, and
That when he should depart, he sayd: Where now thy house dooth
                                                  stand,   20
Shall in thy childers childrens tyme a Citie buylded bee.
Which woordes of his have proved trew as playnly now wee see.

---

10 *did hoste:* was a guest   17 *beace:* beasts, cattle
12 *well seene:* well versed   21 *childers:* children's
15 *cut:* course, crossing

For why there was one Myscelus, a Greeke, Alemons sonne,
A persone more in favour of the Goddes than any one
In those dayes was. The God that beares the boystous club did stay   25
Uppon him being fast asleepe, and sayd: Go seeke streyght way
The stonny streame of Aeserie. Thy native soyle for ay
Forsake. And sore he threatned him onlesse he did obey.
The God and sleepe departed both togither. Up did ryse
Alemons sonne, and in himself did secretly devyse   30
Uppon this vision. Long his mynd strove dowtfull to and fro.
The God bad go. His country lawes did say he should not go,
And death was made the penaltie for him that would doo so.
Cleere Titan in the Ocean sea had hid his lyghtsomme head,
And duskye nyght had put up hers most thick with starres bespred.   35
The selfsame God by Myscelus did seeme to stand eftsoone,
Commaunding him the selfsame thing that he before had doone,
And threatning mo and greater plages onlesse he did obey.
Then being stricken sore in feare he went about streyghtway
His household from his natyve land to forreine to convey.   40
A rumor heereuppon did ryse through all the towne of Arge
And disobedience of the lawe was layed to his charge.
Assoone as that the cace had first beene pleaded and the deede
Apparantly perceyved, so that witnesse did not neede,
Arreyned and forlorne to heaven he cast his handes and eyes,   45
And sayd: O God whoose labours twelve have purchaste thee the skyes,
Assist mee, I thee pray. For thou art author of my cryme.
When judgement should bee given it was the guyse in auncient tyme
With whyght stones to acquit the cleere, and eeke with blacke to cast
The giltye. That tyme also so the heavy sentence past.   50
The stones were cast unmercifull all blacke into the pot.
But when the stones were powred out to number, there was not
A blacke among them. All were whyght. And so through Hercles powre
A gentle judgement did proceede, and he was quit that howre.
Then gave he thankes to Hercules, and having prosprous blast,   55
Cut over the Ionian sea, and so by Tarent past
Which Spartanes buylt, and Cybaris, and Neaeth Salentine,
And Thurine bay, and Emese, and eeke the pastures fyne
Of Calabrye. And having scarce well sought the coastes that lye

25 *boystous:* violent; *stay/Uppon:* lean over   48 *guyse:* custom
30 *devyse:* think, consider   49 *cleere:* innocent
36 *eftsoone:* again   54 *quit:* acquitted
38 *plages:* evils, calamities

Uppon the sea, he found the mouth of fatall Aeserye.　　60
Not farre from thence, he also found the tumb in which the ground
Did kiver Crotons holy bones, and in that place did found
The Citie that was willed him, and gave thereto the name
Of him that there lay buryed. Such originall as this same
This Citie in th'Italian coast is sayd to have by fame.　　65
　　Heere dwelt a man of Samos Ile, who for the hate he had
To Lordlynesse and Tyranny, though unconstreynd was glad
To make himself a bannisht man. And though this persone weere
Farre distant from the Goddes by site of heaven: yit came he neere
To them in mynd. And he by syght of soule and reason cleere　　70
Behild the things which nature dooth to fleshly eyes denye.
And when with care most vigilant he had assuredly
Imprinted all things in his hart, he set them openly
Abroade for other folk to lerne. He taught his silent sort
(Which woondred at the heavenly woordes theyr mayster did report)　　75
The first foundation of the world: the cause of every thing:
What nature was: and what was God: whence snow and lyghtning
　　　　　　　　　　　　　　　　　　　　　　　　　　spring:
And whither Jove or else the wynds in breaking clowdes doo thunder:
What shakes the earth: what law the starres doo keepe theyr courses
　　　　　　　　　　　　　　　　　　　　　　　　　　under:
And what soever other thing is hid from common sence.　　80
He also is the first that did injoyne an abstinence
To feede of any lyving thing. He also first of all
Spake thus: although ryght lernedly, yit to effect but small:
　　Yee mortall men, forbeare to frank your flesh with wicked foode.
　　Yee have both corne and frutes of trees and grapes and herbes right
　　　　　　　　　　　　　　　　　　　　　　　　　　good.　　85
And though that sum bee harsh and hard: yit fyre may make them well
Both soft and sweete. Yee may have milk, and honny which dooth smell
Of flowres of tyme. The lavish earth dooth yeeld you plentiously
Most gentle foode, and riches to content bothe mynd and eye.
There needes no slaughter nor no blood to get your living by.　　90
The beastes do breake theyr fast with flesh: and yit not all beastes
　　　　　　　　　　　　　　　　　　　　　　　　　　neyther.
For horses, sheepe, and Rotherbeastes to live by grasse had lever.
The nature of the beast that dooth delyght in bloody foode,

62 kiver: cover　　　　　　　　88 tyme: thyme
64 originall: origin　　　　　　　92 Rotherbeastes: animals of the ox kind;
84 frank: cram　　　　　　　　　　lever: rather

Is cruell and unmercifull. As Lyons feerce of moode,
Armenian Tigers, Beares, and Woolves. Oh, what a wickednesse   95
It is to cram the mawe with mawe, and frank up flesh with flesh,
And for one living thing to live by killing of another:
As whoo should say, that of so great abundance which our moother
The earth dooth yeeld most bountuously, none other myght delyght
Thy cruell teethe to chawe uppon, than grisly woundes that myght   100
Expresse the Cyclops guyse? or else as if thou could not stawnche
The hunger of thy greedye gut and evill mannerd pawnche,
Onlesse thou stroyd sum other wyght. But that same auncient age
Which wee have naamd the golden world, cleene voyd of all such rage,
Livd blessedly by frute of trees and herbes that grow on ground,   105
And stayned not their mouthes with blood. Then birds might safe and
                                                            sound
Fly where they listed in the ayre. The hare unscaard of hound
Went pricking over all the feeldes. No angling hooke with bayt
Did hang the seely fish that bote mistrusting no deceyt.
All things were voyd of guylefulnesse: no treason was in trust: 110
But all was freendshippe, love and peace. But after that the lust
Of one (what God so ere he was) disdeyning former fare,
To cram that cruell croppe of his with fleshmeate did not spare,
He made a way for wickednesse. And first of all the knyfe
Was staynd with blood of savage beastes in ridding them of lyfe.   115
And that had nothing beene amisse, if there had beene the stay.
For why wee graunt, without the breach of godlynesse wee may
By death confound the things that seeke to take our lyves away.
But as to kill them reason was: even so agein theyr was
No reason why to eate theyr flesh. This leawdnesse thence did passe   120
On further still. Wheras there was no sacrifyse beforne,
The Swyne (bycause with hoked groyne he rooted up the corne,
And did deceyve the tillmen of theyr hope next yeere thereby)
Was deemed woorthy by desert in sacrifyse to dye.
The Goate for byghting vynes was slayne at Bacchus altar whoo   125
Wreakes such misdeedes. Theyr owne offence was hurtful to theis two.
But what have you poore sheepe misdoone, a cattell meeke and meeld,
Created for to maynteine man, whoose fulsomme duggs doo yeeld
Sweete Nectar, whoo dooth clothe us with your wooll in soft aray?

103 *stroyd:* destroyed
108 *pricking:* running, leaving tracks
109 *seely:* simple, harmless; *bote:* bit
120 *leawdness:* wickedness

122 *groyne:* snout
123 *tillmen:* farmers
128 *fulsomme:* abundant, full

Whoose lyfe dooth more us benefite than dooth your death farreway? [130]
What trespasse have the Oxen doone, a beast without all guyle
Or craft, unhurtfull, simple, borne to labour every whyle?
In fayth he is unmyndfull and unwoorthy of increace
Of corne, that in his hart can fynd his tilman to releace
From plowgh, to cut his throte: that in his hart can fynde (I say) [135]
Those neckes with hatchets off to strike, whoose skinne is worne away
With labring ay for him: whoo turnd so oft his land most tough,
Whoo brought so many harvestes home. Yit is it not ynough
That such a great outrageousenesse committed is. They father
Theyr wickednesse uppon the Goddes. And falsly they doo gather [140]
That in the death of peynfull Ox the Hyghest dooth delyght.
A sacrifyse unblemished and fayrest unto syght,
(For beawtye woorketh them theyr bane) adornd with garlonds, and
With glittring gold, is cyted at the altar for to stand.
There heeres he woordes (he wotes not what) the which the preest
dooth pray, [145]
And on his forehead suffereth him betweene his hornes to lay
The eares of corne that he himself hath wrought for in the clay,
And stayneth with his blood the knyfe that he himself perchaunce
Hathe in the water sheere ere then behild by soodein glaunce.
Immediatly they haling out his hartstrings still alive, [150]
And poring on them, seeke therein Goddes secrets to retryve.
Whence commes so greedy appetyte in men, of wicked meate?
And dare yee, O yee mortall men, adventure thus to eate?
Nay doo not (I beseeche yee) so. But give good eare and heede
To that that I shall warne you of, and trust it as your creede, [155]
That whensoever you doo eate your Oxen, you devowre
Your husbandmen. And forasmuch as God this instant howre
Dooth move my toong to speake, I will obey his heavenly powre.
My God Apollos temple I will set you open, and
Disclose the woondrous heavens themselves, and make you
understand [160]
The Oracles and secrets of the Godly majestye.
Greate things, and such as wit of man could never yit espye,
And such as have beene hidden long, I purpose to descrye.
I mynd to leave the earth, and up among the starres to stye.
I mynd to leave this grosser place, and in the clowdes to flye, [165]
And on stowt Atlas shoulders strong to rest my self on hye,

130 *farreway:* by far
144 *cyted:* summoned, brought
149 *sheere:* clear
164 *stye:* climb, soar

And looking downe from heaven on men that wander heere and there
In dreadfull feare of death as though they voyd of reason were,
To give them exhortation thus: and playnely to unwynd
The whole discourse of destinie as nature hath assignd.   170
O men amaazd with dread of death, why feare yee Limbo Styx,
And other names of vanitie, which are but Poets tricks?
And perrills of another world, all false surmysed geere?
For whether fyre or length of tyme consume the bodyes heere,
Yee well may thinke that further harmes they cannot suffer more.   175
For soules are free from death. Howbee't, they leaving evermore
Theyr former dwellings, are receyvd and live ageine in new.
For I myself (ryght well in mynd I beare it to be trew)
Was in the tyme of Trojan warre Euphorbus, Panthewes sonne,
Quyght through whoose hart the deathfull speare of Menelay did
                                                             ronne.   180
I late ago in Junos Church at Argos did behold
And knew the target which I in my left hand there did hold.
Al things doo chaunge. But nothing sure dooth perrish. This same
                                                             spright
Dooth fleete, and fisking heere and there dooth swiftly take his flyght
From one place to another place, and entreth every wyght,   185
Removing out of man to beast, and out of beast to man.
But yit it never perrisheth nor never perrish can.
And even as supple wax with ease receyveth fygures straunge,
And keepes not ay one shape, ne bydes assured ay from chaunge,
And yit continueth alwayes wax in substaunce: so I say   190
The soule is ay the selfsame thing it was and yit astray
It fleeteth into sundry shapes. Therfore lest Godlynesse
Bee vanquisht by outragious lust of belly beastlynesse,
Forbeare (I speake by prophesie) your kinsfolkes ghostes to chace
By slaughter: neyther nourish blood with blood in any cace.   195
And sith on open sea the wynds doo blow my sayles apace,
In all the world there is not that that standeth at a stay.
Things eb and flow: and every shape is made to passe away.
The tyme itself continually is fleeting like a brooke.
For neyther brooke nor lyghtsomme tyme can tarrye still. But looke   200
As every wave dryves other foorth, and that that commes behynd
Bothe thrusteth and is thrust itself: even so the tymes by kynd

---

173 *geere:* matter   194 *chace:* persecute, harass
183 *spright:* spirit   202 *kynd:* nature
184 *fisking:* frisking, whisking

Doo fly and follow bothe at once, and evermore renew.
For that that was before is left, and streyght there dooth ensew
Anoother that was never erst. Eche twincling of an eye   205
Dooth chaunge. Wee see that after day commes nyght and darks the sky,
And after nyght the lyghtsum Sunne succeedeth orderly.
Like colour is not in the heaven when all things weery lye
At midnyght sound asleepe, as when the daystarre cleere and bryght
Commes foorth uppon his milkwhyght steede. Ageine in other plyght 210
The Morning, Pallants daughter fayre, the messenger of lyght
Delivereth into Phebus handes the world of cleerer hew.
The circle also of the sonne what tyme it ryseth new
And when it setteth, looketh red, but when it mounts most hye,
Then lookes it whyght, bycause that there the nature of the skye   215
Is better, and from filthye drosse of earth dooth further flye.
The image also of the Moone that shyneth ay by nyght,
Is never of one quantitie. For that that giveth lyght
Today, is lesser than the next that followeth, till the full.
And then contrarywyse eche day her lyght away dooth pull.   220
What? Seest thou not how that the yeere as representing playne
The age of man, departes itself in quarters fowre? First bayne
And tender in the spring it is, even like a sucking babe.
Then greene, and voyd of strength, and lush, and foggye, is the blade,
And cheeres the husbandman with hope. Then all things florish gay. 225
The earth with flowres of sundry hew then seemeth for to play,
And vertue small or none to herbes there dooth as yit belong.
The yeere from springtyde passing foorth to sommer, wexeth strong,
Becommeth lyke a lusty youth. For in our lyfe through out
There is no tyme more plentifull, more lusty, hote and stout.   230
Then followeth Harvest when the heate of youth growes sumwhat cold,
Rype, meeld, disposed meane betwixt a yoongman and an old,
And sumwhat sprent with grayish heare. Then ugly winter last
Like age steales on with trembling steppes, all bald, or overcast
With shirle thinne heare as whyght as snowe. Our bodies also ay   235
Doo alter still from tyme to tyme, and never stand at stay.
Wee shall not bee the same wee were today or yisterday.
The day hath beene wee were but seede and only hope of men,
And in our moothers womb wee had our dwelling place as then:
Dame Nature put to conning hand and suffred not that wee   240
Within our moothers streyned womb should ay distressed bee,

210 *plyght:* condition, state   233 *sprent:* besprinkled, strewed
222 *departes:* divides; *bayne:* limber   235 *shirle:* rough

But brought us out to aire, and from our prison set us free.
The chyld newborne lyes voyd of strength. Within a season tho
He wexing fowerfooted lernes like savage beastes to go.
Then sumwhat foltring, and as yit not firme of foote, he standes   245
By getting sumwhat for to helpe his sinewes in his handes.
From that tyme growing strong and swift, he passeth foorth the space
Of youth: and also wearing out his middle age apace,
Through drooping ages steepye path he ronneth out his race.
This age dooth undermyne the strength of former yeares, and throwes   250
It downe. Which thing old Milo by example playnely showes.
For when he sawe those armes of his (which heeretofore had beene
As strong as ever Hercules in woorking deadly teene
Of biggest beastes) hang flapping downe, and nought but empty skin,
He wept. And Helen when shee saw her aged wrincles in   255
A glasse wept also: musing in herself what men had seene,
That by two noble princes sonnes shee twyce had ravisht beene.
Thou tyme the eater up of things, and age of spyghtfull teene,
Destroy all things. And when that long continuance hath them bit,
You leysurely by lingring death consume them every whit.   260
And theis that wee call Elements doo never stand at stay.
The enterchaunging course of them I will before yee lay.
Give heede therto. This endlesse world conteynes therin I say
Fowre substances of which all things are gendred. Of theis fower
The Earth and Water for theyr masse and weyght are sunken lower.   265
The other cowple Aire and Fyre, the purer of the twayne,
Mount up, and nought can keepe them downe. And though there doo
                                                               remayne
A space betweene eche one of them: yit every thing is made
Of themsame fowre, and into them at length ageine doo fade.
The earth resolving leysurely dooth melt to water sheere.   270
The water fyned turnes to aire. The aire eeke purged cleere
From grossenesse, spyreth up aloft, and there becommeth fyre.
From thence in order contrary they backe ageine retyre.
Fyre thickening passeth into Aire, and Ayer wexing grosse,
Returnes to water: Water eeke congealing into drosse,   275
Becommeth earth. No kind of thing keepes ay his shape and hew.
For nature loving ever chaunge repayres one shape anew
Uppon another. Neyther dooth there perrish aught (trust mee)
In all the world, but altring takes new shape. For that which wee

---

253 *teene*: harm, grief   269 *themsame*: those same
264 *gendred*: engendered   271 *fyned*: refined, purified

Doo terme by name of being borne, is for to gin to bee   280
Another thing than that it was: and likewise for to dye,
To cease to bee the thing it was. And though that varyably
Things passe perchaunce from place to place: yit all from whence they
                                                              came
Returning, do unperrisshed continew still the same.
But as for in one shape, bee sure that nothing long can last.   285
Even so the ages of the world from gold to Iron past.
Even so have places oftentymes exchaunged theyr estate.
For I have seene it sea which was substanciall ground alate,
Ageine where sea was, I have seene the same become dry lond,
And shelles and scales of Seafish farre have lyen from any strond,   290
And in the toppes of mountaynes hygh old Anchors have beene found.
Deepe valleyes have by watershotte beene made of levell ground,
And hilles by force of gulling oft have into sea beene worne.
Hard gravell ground is sumtyme seene where marris was beforne,
And that that erst did suffer drowght, becommeth standing lakes.   295
Heere nature sendeth new springs out, and there the old in takes.
Full many rivers in the world through earthquakes heretofore
Have eyther chaundgd theyr former course, or dryde and ronne no more.
Soo Lycus beeing swallowed up by gaping of the ground,
A greatway off fro thence is in another channell found.   300
Even so the river Erasine among the feeldes of Arge
Sinkes one whyle, and another whyle ronnes greate ageine at large.
Caycus also of the land of Mysia (as men say)
Misliking of his former head, ronnes now another way.
In Sicill also Amasene ronnes sumtyme full and hye,   305
And sumtyme stopping up his spring, he makes his chanell drye.
Men drank the waters of the brooke Anigrus heretofore,
Which now is such that men abhorre to towche them any more.
Which commes to passe, (onlesse wee will discredit Poets quyght)
Bycause the Centaures vanquisshed by Hercules in fyght   310
Did wash theyr woundes in that same brooke. But dooth not Hypanis
That springeth in the Scythian hilles, which at his fountaine is
Ryght pleasant, afterward becomme of brackish bitter taste?
Antissa, and Phenycian Tyre, and Pharos in tyme past
Were compast all about with waves: but none of all theis three   315
Is now an Ile. Ageine the towne of Lewcas once was free
From sea, and in the auncient tyme was joyned to the land.

292 *watershotte:* overflow of water   294 *marris:* marsh
293 *gulling:* channeling, gullying

But now environd round about with water it dooth stand.
Men say that Sicill also hath beene joynd to Italy
Untill the sea consumde the bounds beetweene, and did supply   320
The roome with water. If yee go to seeke for Helicee
And Burye which were Cities of Achaia, you shall see
Them hidden under water, and the shipmen yit doo showe
The walles and steeples of the townes drownd under as they rowe.
Not farre from Pitthey Troyzen is a certeine high ground found   325
All voyd of trees, which heeretofore was playne and levell ground,
But now a mountayne. For the wyndes (a woondrous thing to say)
Inclosed in the hollow caves of ground, and seeking way
To passe therefro, in struggling long to get the open skye
In vayne, (bycause in all the cave there was no vent wherby   330
To issue out,) did stretch the ground and make it swell on hye,
As dooth a bladder that is blowen by mouth, or as the skinne
Of horned Goate in bottlewyse when wynd is gotten in.
The swelling of the foresayd place remaynes at this day still,
And by continuance waxing hard is growen a pretye hill.   335
Of many things that come to mynd by heersay, and by skill
Of good experience, I a fewe will utter to you mo.
What? Dooth not water in his shapes chaunge straungely to and fro?
The well of horned Hammon is at noonetyde passing cold.
At morne and even it wexeth warme. At midnyght none can hold   340
His hand therin for passing heate. The well of Athamane,
Is sayd to kindle woode what tyme the moone is in the wane.
The Cicons have a certeine streame which beeing droonk dooth bring
Mennes bowwelles into Marble hard: and whatsoever thing
Is towcht therwith, it turnes to stone. And by your bounds behold   345
The rivers Crathe and Sybaris make yellow heare like gold
And Amber. There are also springs (which thing is farre more straunge)
Which not the bodye only, but the mynd doo also chaunge.
Whoo hath not heard of Salmacis, that fowle and filthye sink?
Or of the lake of Aethyop, which if a man doo drink,   350
He eyther ronneth mad, or else with woondrous drowzinesse
Forgoeth quyght his memorie? Whoo ever dooth represse
His thirst with drawght of Clitor well, hates wyne, and dooth delyght
In only water: eyther for bycause there is a myght
Contrary unto warming wyne by nature in the well,   355
Or else bycause (for so the folk of Arcadye doo tell)
Melampus, Amythaons sonne (when he delivered had

352 *Forgoeth:* goes from, loses

King Praetus daughters by his charmes and herbes from being mad),
Cast into that same water all the baggage wherewithall
He purdgd the madnesse of theyr mynds. And so it did befall,   360
That lothsomnesse of wyne did in those waters ay remayne.
Ageine in Lyncest contrarie effect to this dooth reigne.
For whoo so drinkes too much therof, he reeleth heere and there
As if by quaffing wyne no whyt alayd he droonken were.
There is a Lake in Arcadye which Pheney men did name   365
In auncient tyme, whoose dowtfulnesse deserveth justly blame.
A nyght tymes take thou heede of it, for if thou taste the same
A nyghttymes, it will hurt. But if thou drink it in the day
It hurteth not. Thus lakes and streames (as well perceyve yee may)
Have divers powres and diversly. Even so the tyme hathe beene   370
That Delos which stands stedfast now, on waves was floting seene.
And Galyes have beene sore afrayd of frusshing by the Iles
Symplegads which togither dasht uppon the sea erewhyles,
But now doo stand unmovable ageinst bothe wynde and tyde.
Mount Aetna with his burning Oovens of brimstone shall not byde   375
Ay fyrye: neyther was it so for ever erst. For whither
The earth a living creature bee, and that to breathe out hither
And thither flame, great store of vents it have in sundry places,
And that it have the powre to shift those vents in divers caces,
Now damming theis, now opening those, in moving to and fro: 380
Or that the whisking wynds restreynd within the earth bylowe,
Doo beate the stones ageinst the stones, and other kynd of stuffe
Of fyrye nature, which doo fall on fyre with every puffe:
Assoone as those same wynds doo cease, the caves shall streight bee
                                                             cold.
Or if it bee a Rozen mowld that soone of fyre takes hold,   385
Or brimstone mixt with clayish soyle on fyre dooth lyghtly fall:
Undowtedly assoone as that same soyle consumed shall
No longer yeeld the fatty foode to feede the fyre withall,
And ravening nature shall forgo her woonted nourishment,
Then being able to abyde no longer famishment,   390
For want of sustenance it shall cease his burning. I doo fynd
By fame, that under Charlsis wayne in Pallene are a kynd
Of people which by dyving thryce three tymes in Triton lake
Becomme all fethred, and the shape of birdes uppon them take.
The Scythian witches also are reported for to doo   395
The selfsame thing (but hardly I give credit therunto)

364 *alayd:* diluted   372 *frusshing:* crushing, squashing

By smearing poyson over all theyr bodyes. But (and if
A man to matters tryde by proof may saufly give beleef,)
Wee see how flesh by lying still a whyle and ketching heate
Dooth turne to little living beastes. And yit a further feate,   400
Go kill an Ox and burye him, (the thing by proof man sees)
And of his rotten flesh will breede the flowergathering Bees,
Which as theyr father did before, love feeldes exceedingly,
And unto woork in hope of gayne theyr busye limbes apply.
The Hornet is engendred of a lustye buryed Steede.   405
Go pull away the cleas from Crabbes that in the sea doo breede,
And burye all the rest in mowld, and of the same will spring
A Scorpion which with writhen tayle will threaten for to sting.
The Caterpillers of the feelde the which are woont to weave
Hore filmes uppon the leaves of trees, theyr former nature leave,   410
(Which thing is knowen to husbandmen) and turne to Butterflyes.
The mud hath in it certeine seede wherof greene frosshes ryse.
And first it brings them footelesse foorth. Then after, it dooth frame
Legges apt to swim: and furthermore of purpose that the same
May serve them for to leape afarre, theyr hinder part is mych   415
More longer than theyr forepart is. The Bearwhelp also which
The Beare hath newly littred, is no whelp immediatly.
But like an evill favored lump of flesh alyve dooth lye.
The dam by licking shapeth out his members orderly
Of such a syse, as such a peece is able to conceyve.   420
Or marke yee not the Bees of whom our hony wee receyve,
How that theyr yoong ones which doo lye within the sixsquare wax
Are limblesse bodyes at the first, and after as they wex
In processe take bothe feete and wings? What man would think it trew
That Ladye Venus simple birdes, the Dooves of silver hew,   425
Or Junos bird that in his tayle beares starres, or Joves stowt knyght
The Earne, and every other fowle of whatsoever flyght,
Could all bee hatched out of egges, onlesse he did it knowe?
Sum folk doo hold opinion when the backebone which dooth growe
In man, is rotten in the grave, the pith becommes a snake.   430
Howbee't of other things all theis theyr first beginning take.
One bird there is that dooth renew itself and as it were
Beget it self continually. The Syrians name it there
A Phoenix. Neyther corne nor herbes this Phoenix liveth by,

398 *saufly:* safely   410 *Hore:* gray
406 *cleas:* claws   412 *frosshes:* frogs
408 *writhen:* twisted   427 *Earne:* erne, eagle

But by the jewce of frankincence and gum of Amomye.   435
And when that of his lyfe well full fyve hundred yeeres are past,
Uppon a Holmetree or uppon a Date tree at the last
He makes him with his talants and his hardened bill a nest.
Which when that he with Casia sweete and Nardus soft hathe drest,
And strowed it with Cynnamom and Myrrha of the best,   440
He rucketh downe uppon the same, and in the spyces dyes.
Soone after, of the fathers corce men say there dooth aryse
Another little Phoenix which as many yeeres must live
As did his father. He (assoone as age dooth strength him give
To beare the burthen) from the tree the weyghty nest dooth lift,   445
And godlyly his cradle thence and fathers herce dooth shift.
And flying through the suttle aire he gettes to Phebus towne,
And there before the temple doore dooth lay his burthen downe.
But if that any noveltye woorth woondring bee in theis,
Much rather may we woonder at the Hyen if we please.   450
To see how interchaungeably it one whyle dooth remayne
A female, and another whyle becommeth male againe.
The creature also which dooth live by only aire and wynd,
All colours that it leaneth to dooth counterfet by kynd.
The Grapegod Bacchus, when he had subdewd the land of Inde,   455
Did fynd a spotted beast cald Lynx, whoose urine (by report)
By towching of the open aire congealeth in such sort,
As that it dooth becomme a stone. So Corall (which as long
As water hydes it is a shrub and soft) becommeth strong
And hard assoone as it dooth towch the ayre. The day would end,   460
And Phebus panting steedes should in the Ocean deepe descend,
Before all alterations I in woordes could comprehend.
So see wee all things chaungeable. One nation gathereth strength:
Another wexeth weake: and bothe doo make exchaunge at length.
So Troy which once was great and strong as well in welth as men,   465
And able tenne yeeres space to spare such store of blood as then,
Now beeing bace hath nothing left of all her welth to showe,
Save ruines of the auncient woorkes which grasse dooth overgrowe,
And tumbes wherin theyr auncetours lye buryed on a rowe.
Once Sparta was a famous towne: Great Mycene florisht trim: 470
Bothe Athens and Amphions towres in honor once did swim.
A pelting plot is Sparta now: great Mycene lyes on ground.

435 *Amomye:* amomum   454 *by kynd:* naturally
437 *Holmetree:* holm-oak   472 *pelting:* paltry, insignificant
441 *rucketh:* crouches

Of Theab the towne of Oedipus what have we more than sound?
Of Athens, king Pandions towne, what resteth more than name?
Now also of the race of Troy is rysing (so sayth fame)   475
The Citie Rome, which at the bank of Tyber that dooth ronne
Downe from the hill of Appennyne) already hath begonne
With great advysement for to lay foundation of her state.
This towne then chaungeth by increase the forme it had alate,
And of the universall world in tyme to comme shall hold   480
The sovereintye, so prophesies and lotts (men say) have told.
And as (I doo remember mee) what tyme that Troy decayd,
The prophet Helen, Priams sonne, theis woordes ensewing sayd
Before Aenaeas dowting of his lyfe in weeping plyght:
O Goddesse sonne, beleeve mee (if thou think I have foresyght   485
Of things to comme) Troy shalnot quyght decay whyle thou doost live.
Bothe fyre and swoord shall unto thee thy passage freely give.
Thou must from hence: and Troy with thee convey away in haste,
Untill that bothe thyself and Troy in forreine land bee plaast
More freendly than thy native soyle. Moreover I foresee,   490
A Citie by the offspring of the Trojans buylt shall bee,
So great as never in the world the lyke was seene before
Nor is this present, neyther shall be seene for evermore.
A number of most noble peeres for manye yeeres afore
Shall make it strong and puyssant: but hee that shall it make   495
The sovereine Ladye of the world, by ryght descent shall take
His first beginning from thy sonne the little Jule. And when
The earth hathe had her tyme of him, the sky and welkin then
Shall have him up for evermore, and heaven shall bee his end.
Thus farre (I well remember mee) did Helens woordes extend   500
To good Aenaeas. And it is a pleasure unto mee
The Citie of my countrymen increasing thus to see:
And that the Grecians victorie becommes the Trojans weale.
But lest forgetting quyght themselves our horses happe to steale
Beyond the mark: the heaven and all that under heaven is found,   505
Dooth alter shape. So dooth the ground and all that is in ground.
And wee that of the world are part (considring how wee bee
Not only flesh, but also sowles, which may with passage free
Remove them into every kynd of beast both tame and wyld)
Let live in saufty honestly with slaughter undefyld,   510
The bodyes which perchaunce may have the spirits of our brothers,
Our sisters, or our parents, or the spirits of sum others

503 *weale:* welfare, prosperity

Alyed to us eyther by sum freendshippe or sum kin,
Or at the least the soules of men abyding them within.
And let us not Thyesteslyke thus furnish up our boordes 515
With bloodye bowells. Oh how leawd example he afoordes.
How wickedly prepareth he himself to murther man
That with a cruell knyfe dooth cut the throte of Calf, and can
Unmovably give heering to the lowing of the dam
Or sticke the kid that wayleth lyke the little babe, or eate 520
The fowle that he himself before had often fed with meate.
What wants of utter wickednesse in woorking such a feate?
What may he after passe to doo? well eyther let your steeres
Weare out themselves with woork, or else impute theyr death to yeeres.
Ageinst the wynd and weather cold let Wethers yeeld yee cotes, 525
And udders full of batling milk receyve yee of the Goates.
Away with sprindges, snares, and grinnes, away with Risp and net.
Away with guylefull feates: for fowles no lymetwiggs see yee set.
No feared fethers pitche yee up to keepe the Red deere in,
Ne with deceytfull bayted hooke seeke fishes for to win. 530
If awght doo harme, destroy it, but destroy't and doo no more.
Forbeare the flesh: and feede your mouthes with fitter foode therfore.
    Men say that Numa furnisshed with such philosophye
    As this and like, returned to his native soyle, and by
Entreatance was content of Rome to take the sovereintye. 535
Ryght happy in his wyfe which was a nymph, ryght happy in
His guydes which were the Muses nyne, this Numa did begin
To teach Religion, by the meanes whereof hee shortly drew
That people unto peace whoo erst of nought but battell knew.
And when through age he ended had his reigne and eeke his lyfe, 540
Through Latium he was moorned for of man and chyld and wyfe
As well of hygh as low degree. His wyfe forsaking quyght
The Citie, in vale Aricine did hyde her out of syght,
Among the thickest groves, and there with syghes and playnts did let
The sacrifyse of Diane whom Orestes erst had fet 545
From Taurica in Chersonese, and in that place had set.
How oft ah did the woodnymphes and the waternymphes perswade
Egeria for to cease her mone. What meanes of comfort made
They. Ah how often Theseus sonne her weeping thus bespake.

[523] *passe:* go on, proceed
[526] *batling:* rich
[527] *sprindges:* snares, nooses; *grinnes:* snares, nooses; *Risp:* branch, twig (here, limetwig)
[528] *lymetwiggs:* twigs smeared with a sticky substance to catch birds
[544] *let:* hinder, be an obstacle to

O Nymph, thy moorning moderate: thy sorrow sumwhat slake: ⁵⁵⁰
Not only thou hast cause to heart thy fortune for to take.
Behold like happes of other folkes, and this mischaunce of thyne
Shall greeve thee lesse. Would God examples (so they were not myne)
Myght comfort thee. But myne perchaunce may comfort thee. If thou
In talk by hap hast heard of one Hippolytus ere now,   ⁵⁵⁵
That through his fathers lyght beleefe, and stepdames craft was slayne,
It will a woonder seeme to thee, and I shall have much payne
To make thee to beleeve the thing. But I am very hee.
The daughter of Pasyphae in vayne oft tempting mee
My fathers chamber to defyle, surmysde mee to have sought   ⁵⁶⁰
The thing that shee with al her hart would fayne I should have wrought.
And whither it were for feare I should her wickednesse bewray,
Or else for spyght bycause I had so often sayd her nay,
Shee chardgd mee with hir owne offence. My father by and by
Condemning mee, did banish mee his Realme without cause whye.   ⁵⁶⁵
And at my going like a fo did ban me bitterly.
To Pitthey Troyzen outlawelike my chariot streight tooke I.
My way lay hard uppon the shore of Corinth. Soodeinly
The sea did ryse, and like a mount the wave did swell on hye,
And seemed huger for to growe in drawing ever nye,   ⁵⁷⁰
And roring clyved in the toppe. Up starts immediatly
A horned bullocke from amid the broken wave, and by
The brest did rayse him in the ayre, and at his nostrills and
His platter mouth did puffe out part of sea uppon the land.
My servants harts were sore afrayd. But my hart musing ay   ⁵⁷⁵
Uppon my wrongfull banishment, did nought at all dismay.
My horses setting up theyr eares and snorting wexed shye,
And beeing greatly flayghted with the monster in theyr eye,
Turnd downe to sea: and on the rockes my wagon drew. In vayne
I stryving for to hold them backe, layd hand uppon the reyne   ⁵⁸⁰
All whyght with fome, and haling backe lay almost bolt upryght.
And sure the feercenesse of the steedes had yeelded to my might,
But that the wheele that ronneth ay about the Extree round,
Did breake by dashing on a stub, and overthrew to ground.
Then from the Charyot I was snatcht the brydles beeing cast   ⁵⁸⁵
About my limbes. Yee myght have seene my sinewes sticking fast
Uppon the stub: my gutts drawen out alyve: my members, part

⁵⁶⁰ *surmysde:* charged falsely, pretended   ⁵⁷⁸ *flayghted:* frightened
⁵⁶² *bewray:* reveal   ⁵⁸¹ *bolt upryght:* on one's back
⁵⁶⁶ *ban:* curse   ⁵⁸³ *Extree:* axle-tree
⁵⁷¹ *clyved:* divided, split   ⁵⁸⁴ *stub:* stump

Still left uppon the stump, and part foorth harryed with the cart:
The crasshing of my broken bones: and with what passing peyne
I breathed out my weery ghoste. There did not whole remayne   590
One peece of all my corce by which yee myght discerne as tho
What lump or part it was. For all was wound from toppe to toe.
Now canst thou, nymph, or darest thou compare thy harmes with myne?
Moreover I the lightlesse Realme behild with theis same eyne,
And bathde my tattred bodye in the river Phlegeton,   595
And had not bright Apollos sonne his cunning shewde uppon
My bodye by his surgery, my lyfe had quyght bee gone.
Which after I by force of herbes and leechecraft had ageine
Receyvd by Aesculapius meanes, though Pluto did disdeine,
Then Cynthia (lest this gift of hers myght woorke mee greater
                                                   spyght)   600
Thicke clowds did round about mee cast. And to th'entent I myght
Bee saufe myself, and harmelessely appeere to others syght:
Shee made mee old. And for my face, shee left it in such plyght,
That none can knowe mee by my looke. And long shee dowted whither
To give mee Dele or Crete. At length refusing bothe togither,   605
Shee plaast mee heere. And therwithall shee bade me give up quyght
The name that of my horses in remembrance put mee myght.
For whereas erst Hippolytus hath beene thy name (quoth shee)
I will that Virbie afterward thy name for ever bee.
From that tyme foorth within this wood I keepe my residence,   610
As of the meaner Goddes, a God of small magnificence,
And heere I hyde mee underneathe my sovereine Ladyes wing
Obeying humbly to her hest in every kynd of thing.
      But yit the harmes of other folk could nothing help nor boote
      Aegerias sorrowes to asswage. Downe at a mountaines foote   615
Shee lying melted into teares, till Phebus sister sheene
For pitie of her greate distresse in which shee had her seene,
Did turne her to a fountaine cleere, and melted quyght away
Her members into water thinne that never should decay.
The straungenesse of the thing did make the nymphes astonyed: and 620
The Ladye of Amázons sonne amaazd therat did stand,
As when the Tyrrhene Tilman sawe in earing of his land
The fatall clod first stirre alone without the help of hand,

588 *harryed:* dragged
591 *as tho:* then
598 *leechecraft:* medical science
600 *spyght:* ill will
613 *hest:* command
616 *sheene:* bright
620 *astonyed:* astonished
622 *earing:* plowing

And by and by forgoing quyght the earthly shape of clod,
To take the seemely shape of man, and shortly like a God   625
To tell of things as then to comme. The Tyrrhenes did him call
By name of Tages. He did teach the Tuskanes first of all
To gesse by searching bulks of beastes what after should befall.
Or like as did king Romulus when soodeinly he found
His lawnce on mountayne Palatine fast rooted in the ground,   630
And bearing leaves, no longer now a weapon but a tree,
Which shadowed such as woondringly came thither for to see.
Or else as Cippus when he in the ronning brooke had seene
His hornes. For why he saw them, and supposing there had beene
No credit to bee given unto the glauncing image, hee   635
Put oft his fingers to his head, and felt it so to bee.
And blaming now no more his eyes, in comming from the chase
With conquest of his foes, he stayd. And lifting up his face
And with his face, his hornes to heaven, he sayd: What ever thing
Is by this woonder meant, O Goddes, if joyfull newes it bring   640
I pray yee let it joyfull to my folk and countrye bee:
But if it threaten evill, let the evill light on mee.
In saying so, an altar greene of clowwers he did frame,
And offred fuming frankincence in fyre uppon the same,
And powred boawles of wyne theron, and searched therwithall   645
The quivering inwards of a sheepe to know what should befall.
A Tyrrhene wizard having sought the bowelles, saw therin
Great chaunges and attempts of things then readye to begin,
Which were not playnly manifest. But when that he at last
His eyes from inwards of the beast on Cippus hornes had cast,   650
Hayle king (he sayd). For untoo thee, O Cippus, unto thee,
And to thy hornes shall this same place and Rome obedyent bee.
Abridge delay: and make thou haste to enter at the gates
Which tarrye open for thee. So commaund the soothfast fates.
Thou shalt bee king assoone as thou hast entred once the towne,   655
And thou and thyne for evermore shalt weare the royall crowne.
With that he stepping back his foote, did turne his frowning face
From Romeward, saying: Farre, O farre, the Goddes such handsel
                                                                    chace.
More ryght it were I all my lyfe a bannisht man should bee,

---

628 *bulks:* bodies   654 *soothfast:* truthful
634 *For why:* because   658 *handsel:* omen
643 *clowwers:* pieces of turf, grassy sod

Than that the holy Capitoll mee reigning there should see. 660
Thus much he sayd: and by and by toogither he did call
The people and the Senators. But yit he first of all
Did hyde his hornes with Lawrell leaves: and then without the wall
He standing on a mount the which his men had made of soddes,
And having after auncient guyse made prayer to the Goddes 665
Sayd: Heere is one that shall (onlesse yee bannish him your towne
Immediatly) bee king of Rome and weare a royall crowne.
What man it is, I will by signe, but not by name bewray.
He hath uppon his brow two hornes. The wizard heere dooth say,
That if he enter Rome, you shall lyke servants him obey. 670
He myght have entred at your gates which open for him lay,
But I did stay him thence. And yit there is not unto mee
A neerer freend in all the world. Howbee't forbid him yee
O Romanes, that he comme not once within your walles. Or if
He have deserved, bynd him fast in fetters like a theef. 675
Or in this fatall Tyrants death, of feare dispatch your mynd.
Such noyse as Pynetrees make what tyme the heady easterne wynde
Dooth whiz amongst them, or as from the sea dooth farre rebound:
Even such among the folk of Rome that present was the sound.
Howbee't in that confused roare of fearefull folk, did fall 680
Out one voyce asking, Whoo is hee? And staring therewithall
Uppon theyr foreheads, they did seeke the foresayd hornes. Agen
(Quoth Cippus) Lo, yee have the man for whom yee seeke. And then
He pulld (ageinst his peoples will) his garlond from his head,
And shewed them the two fayre hornes that on his browes were spred. 685
At that the people dassheth downe theyr lookes and syghing is
Ryght sorye (whoo would think it trew?) to see that head of his,
Most famous for his good deserts. Yit did they not forget
The honour of his personage, but willingly did set
The Lawrell garlond on his head ageine. And by and by 690
The Senate sayd: Well Cippus, sith untill the tyme thou dye
Thou mayst not come within theis walles, wee give thee as much ground
In honour of thee, as a teeme of steeres can plough thee round,
Betweene the dawning of the day, and shetting in of nyght.
Moreover on the brazen gate at which this Cippus myght 695
Have entred Rome, a payre of hornes were gravde to represent
His woondrous shape, as of his deede an endlesse monument.

677 *heady:* headstrong, violent   679 *present:* time

396 OVID'S METAMORPHOSES

Yee Muses whoo to Poets are the present springs of grace,
Now shewe (for you knowe, neyther are you dulld by tyme or
space)
How Aesculapius in the Ile that is in Tyber deepe   700
Among the sacred sayncts of Rome had fortune for to creepe.
A cruell plage did heertofore infect the Latian aire,
And peoples bodyes pyning pale the murreine did appayre.
When tyred with the buriall of theyr freends, they did perceyve
Themselves no helpe at mannes hand nor by Phisicke to receyve.   705
Then seeking help from heaven, they sent to Delphos (which dooth
stand
Amid the world) for counsell to bee had at Phebus hand.
Beseeching him with helthfull ayd to succour theyr distresse,
And of the myghtye Citie Rome the mischeef to redresse.
The quivers which Apollo bryght himself was woont to beare,   710
The Baytrees, and the place itself togither shaken were.
And by and by the table from the furthest part of all
The Chauncell spake theis woords, which did theyr harts with feare
appal:
The thing yee Romanes seeke for heere, yee should have sought more ny
Your countrye. Yea and neerer home go seeke it now. Not I,   715
Apollo, but Apollos sonne is hee that must redresse
Your sorrowes. Take your journey with good handsell of successe,
And fetch my sonne among you. When Apollos hest was told
Among the prudent Senators, they sercht what towne did hold
His sonne, and unto Epidawre a Gallye for him sent.   720
Assoone as that th'Ambassadours arryved there they went
Unto the counsell and the Lordes of Greekland: whom they pray
To have the God the present plages of Romanes for to stay,
And for themselves the Oracle of Phebus foorth they lay.
The Counsell were of sundry mynds and could not well agree.   725
Sum thought that succour in such neede denyed should not bee.
And divers did perswade to keepe theyr helpe, and not to send
Theyr Goddes away sith they themselves myght neede them in the end.
Whyle dowtfully they off and on debate this curious cace,
The evening twylyght utterly the day away did chace,   730
And on the world the shadowe of the earth had darknesse brought.
That nyght the Lord Ambassadour as sleepe uppon him wrought,

702 *plage:* plague   707 *Amid:* in the middle of
703 *murreine:* pestilence; *appayre:* impair,   718 *hest:* bidding
injure

Did dreame he saw before him stand the God whose help he sought,
In shape as in his chappell he was woonted for to stand,
With ryght hand stroking downe his berd, and staffe in tother hand, 735
And meekely saying: Feare not, I will comme and leave my shryne.
This serpent which dooth wreath with knottes about this staffe of mine
Mark well, and take good heede therof: that when thou shalt it see,
Thou mayst it knowe. For into it transformed will I bee.
But bigger I will bee, for I will seeme of such a syse, 740
As may celestiall bodyes well to turne into suffise.
Streyght with the voyce, the God, and with the voyce and God, away
Went sleepe: and after sleepe was gone ensewed cheerfull day.
Next morning having cleerely put the fyrye starres to flyght,
The Lordes not knowing what to doo, assembled all foorthryght 745
Within the sumptuous temple of the God that was requyrde,
And of his mynd by heavenly signe sum knowledge they desyrde.
They scarce had doone theyr prayers, when the God in shape of snake
With loftye crest of gold, began a hissing for to make,
Which was a warning given. And with his presence he did shake 750
The Altar, shryne, doores, marble floore, and roofe all layd with gold,
And vauncing up his brest he stayd ryght stately to behold
Amid the Church, and round about his fyrye eyes he rold.
The syght did fray the people. But the wyvelesse preest (whoose heare
Was trussed in a fayre whyght Call) did know the God was there. 755
And sayd: Behold, tiz God, tiz God. As many as bee heere
Pray both with mouth and mynd. O thou our glorious God, appeere
To our beehoofe, and helpe thy folke that keepe thy hallowes ryght.
The people present woorshipped his Godhead there in syght,
Repeating dowble that the preest did say. The Romaynes eeke 760
Devoutly did with Godly voyce and hart his favour seeke.
The God by nodding did consent, and gave assured signe
By shaking of his golden crest that on his head did shyne,
And hissed twyce with spirting toong. Then trayld he downe the fyne
And glistring greeces of his church. And turning backe his eyen, 765
He looked to his altarward and to his former shryne
And temple, as to take his leave and bid them all fare well.
From thence ryght huge uppon the ground (which sweete of flowres
                                                                did smell

---

745 *foorthryght:* directly
746 *requyrde:* sought out, petitioned
752 *vauncing:* raising
754 *fray:* frighten

755 *Call:* caul, chaplet
758 *beehoofe:* benefit; *hallowes:* rites, shrines
765 *greeces:* steps

That people strewed in his way), he passed stately downe,
And bending into bowghts went through the hart of all the towne,   770
Untill that hee the bowwing wharf besyde the haven tooke.
Where staying, when he had (as seemd) dismist with gentle looke
His trayne of Chapleynes and the folke that wayted on him thither,
Hee layd him in the Romane shippe to sayle away toogither.
The shippe did feele the burthen of his Godhed to the full,   775
And for the heavye weyght of him did after passe more dull.
The Romanes being glad of him, and having killd a steere
Uppon the shore, untyde theyr ropes and cables from the peere.
    The lyghtsum wynd did dryve the shippe. The God avauncing
                                                              hye,
    And leaning with his necke uppon the Gallyes syde, did lye   780
And looke uppon the greenish waves, and cutting easly through
Th'Ionian sea with little gales of westerne wynd not rough,
The sixt day morning came uppon the coast of Italy.
And passing foorth by Junos Church that mustreth to the eye
Uppon the head of Lacine he was caryed also by   785
The rocke of Scylley. Then he left the land of Calabrye
And rowing softly by the rocke Zephyrion, he did draw
To Celen cliffs the which uppon the ryght syde have a flawe.
By Romeche and by Cawlon, and by Narice thence he past,
And from the streyghtes of Sicily gate quyght and cleere at last.   790
Then ran he by th'Aeolian Iles and by the metall myne
Of Tempsa, and by Lewcosye, and temprate Pest where fyne
And pleasant Roses florish ay. From thence by Capreas
And Atheney the headlond of Minerva he did passe
To Surrent, where with gentle vynes the hilles bee overclad,   795
And by the towne of Hercules and Stabye ill bestad
And Naples borne to Idlenesse, and Cumes where Sybell had
Hir temples, and the scalding bathes, and Linterne where growes store
Of masticke trees, and Vulturne which beares sand apace from shore,
And Sinuesse where as Adders are as whyght as any snowe,   800
And Minturne of infected ayre bycause it stands so lowe,
And Caiete where Aeneas did his nurce in tumbe bestowe,
And Formy where Antiphates the Lestrigon did keepe,

---

770 *bowghts:* loops
771 *bowwing:* curving
779 *avauncing:* rising
784 *mustreth:* shows up, makes a good appearance

788 *flawe:* crack, breach
790 *gate quyght:* got free
796 *bestad:* (1) situated, (2) in trouble

And Trache envyrond with a fen, and Circes mountayne steepe:
To Ancon with the boystous shore. Assoone as that the shippe   805
Arryved heere, (for now the sea was rough,) the God let slippe
His circles, and in bending bowghts and wallowing waves did glyde
Into his fathers temple which was buylded there besyde
Uppon the shore, and when the sea was calme and pacifyde,
The foresayd God of Epidawre, his fathers Church forsooke,   810
(The lodging of his neerest freend which for a tyme hee tooke,)
And with his crackling scales did in the sand a furrowe cut,
And taking hold uppon the sterne did in the Galy put
His head, and rested till he came past Camp and Lavine sands,
And entred Tybers mouth at which the Citie Ostia stands.   815
The folke of Rome came hither all by heapes bothe men and wyves
And eeke the Nunnes that keepe the fyre of Vesta as theyr lyves,
To meete the God, and welcomd him with joyfull noyse. And as
The Gally rowed up the streame, greate store of incence was
On altars burnt on bothe the banks, so that on eyther syde   820
The fuming of the frankincence the very aire did hyde,
And also slaine in sacrifyse full many cattell dyde.
Anon he came to Rome, the head of all the world: and there
The serpent lifting up himself, began his head to beare
Ryght up along the maast, uppon the toppe whereof on hye   825
He looked round about, a meete abyding place to spye.
The Tyber dooth devyde itself in twaine, and dooth embrace
A little pretye Iland (so the people terme the place)
From eyther syde whereof the bankes are distant equall space.
Apollos Snake descending from the maast conveyd him thither,   830
And taking eft his heavenly shape, as one repayring hither
To bring our Citie healthfulnesse, did end our sorrowes quyght.
　　Although to bee a God with us admitted were this wyght,
Yit was he borne a forreiner. But Caesar hathe obteynd
His Godhead in his native soyle and Citie where he reignd.   835
Whom peerelesse both in peace and warre, not more his warres up knit
With triumph, nor his great exployts atcheeved by his wit,
Nor yit the great renowme that he obteynd so speedely,
Have turned to a blazing starre, than did his progenie.
For of the actes of Caesar, none is greater than that hee   840
Left such a sonne behynd him as Augustus is, to bee
His heyre. For are they things more hard: to overcomme thy Realme

831 *eft:* again

Of Britaine standing in the sea, or up the sevenfold streame
Of Nyle that beareth Paperreede victorious shippes to rowe,
Or to rebelliouse Numidye to give an overthrowe,   845
Or Juba, king of Moores, and Pons (which proudely did it beare
Uppon the name of Mythridate) to force by swoord and speare
To yeeld them subjects unto Rome, or by his just desert
To merit many triumphes, and of sum to have his part,
Than such an heyre to leave beehynd, in whom the Goddes doo
                                                        showe   850
Exceeding favour unto men for that they doo bestowe
So great a prince uppon the world? Now to th'entent that hee
Should not bee borne of mortall seede, the other was too bee
Canonyzde for a God. Which thing when golden Venus see,
(Shee also sawe how dreadfull death was for the bisshop then   855
Prepaard, and how conspiracye was wrought by wicked men)
Shee looked pale. And as the Goddes came any in her way,
Shee sayd unto them one by one: Behold and see, I pray,
With how exceeding eagernesse they seeke mee to betray,
And with what woondrous craft they stryve to take my lyfe away,   860
I meene the thing that only now remayneth unto mee
Of Jule the Trojans race. Must I then only ever bee
Thus vext with undeserved cares? How seemeth now the payne
Of Diomeds speare of Calydon to wound my hand ageyne?
How seemes it mee that Troy ageine is lost through ill defence?   865
How seemes my sonne Aenaeas like a bannisht man, from thence
To wander farre ageine, and on the sea to tossed bee,
And warre with Turnus for to make? or rather (truth to say)
With Juno? What meene I about harmes passed many a day
Ageinst myne ofspring, thus to stand? This present feare and wo   870
Permit mee not to think on things now past so long ago.
Yee see how wicked swoordes ageinst my head are whetted. I
Beseeche yee keepe them from my throte, and set the traytors by
Theyr purpose. Neyther suffer you dame Vestas fyre to dye
By murthering of her bisshop. Thus went Venus wofully   875
Complayning over all the heaven, and moovde the Goddes therby.
And for they could not breake the strong decrees of destinye,
They shewed signes most manifest of sorrowe to ensew.
For battells feyghting in the clowdes with crasshing armour flew.

873 *set . . . by:* thwart, frustrate of

And dreadfull trumpets sownded in the aire, and hornes eeke blew,   880
As warning men before hand of the mischeef that did brew.
And Phebus also looking dim did cast a drowzy lyght
Uppon the earth, which seemd lykewyse to bee in sorrye plyght.
From underneathe amid the starres brands oft seemd burning bryght.
It often rayned droppes of blood. The morning starre lookt blew,   885
And was bespotted heere and there with specks of rusty hew.
The moone had also spottes of blood. The Screeche owle sent from hell
Did with her tune unfortunate in every corner yell.
Salt teares from Ivory images in sundry places fell.
And in the Chappells of the Goddes was singing heard, and woordes   890
Of threatning. Not a sacrifyse one signe of good afoordes.
But greate turmoyle to bee at hand theyr hartstrings doo declare.
And when the beast is ripped up the inwards headlesse are.
About the Court, and every house, and Churches in the nyghts
The doggs did howle, and every where appeered gastly spryghts.   895
And with an earthquake shaken was the towne. Yit could not all
Theis warnings of the Goddes dispoynt the treason that should fall,
Nor overcomme the destinies. The naked swoordes were brought
Into the temple. For no place in all the towne was thought
So meete to woork the mischeef in, or for them to commit   900
The heynous murder, as the Court in which they usde to sit
In counsell. Venus then with both her hands her stomacke smit,
And was about to hyde him with the clowd in which shee hid
Aenaeas, when shee from the swoord of Diomed did him rid,
Or Paris, when from Menelay shee did him saufe convey.   905
But Jove her father staying her did thus unto hir say:
Why, daughter myne, wilt thou alone bee stryving to prevent
Unvanquishable destinie? In fayth and if thou went
Thy self into the house in which the fatall susters three
Doo dwell, thou shouldest there of brasse and steele substantiall see   910
The registers of things so strong and massye made to bee,
That sauf and everlasting, they doo neyther stand in feare
Of thunder, nor of lyghtning, nor of any ruine there.
The destnyes of thyne offspring thou shalt there fynd graven deepe
In Adamant. I red them: and in mynd I doo them keepe.   915
And forbycause thou shalt not bee quyght ignorant of all,
I will declare what things I markt herafter to befall.

893 *headlesse:* with tip or lobe cut off   897 *dispoynt:* frustrate

The man for whom thou makest sute, hath lived full his tyme
And having ronne his race on earth must now to heaven up clyme.
Where thou shalt make a God of him ay honord for to bee   920
With temples and with Altars on the earth. Moreover hee
That is his heyre and beares his name, shall all alone susteyne
The burthen layd uppon his backe, and shall our help obteyne
His fathers murther to revenge. The towne of Mutinye
Beseedged by his powre, shall yeeld. The feelds of Pharsaly   925
Shall feele him, and Philippos in the Realme of Macedonne
Shall once ageine bee staynd with blood. The greate Pompeius sonne
Shall vanquisht be by him uppon the sea of Sicilye.
The Romane Capteynes wyfe, the Queene of Aegypt, through her hye
Presumption trusting to her match too much, shall threate in vayne   930
To make her Canop over our hygh Capitoll to reigne.
What should I tell thee of the wyld and barbrous nacions that
At bothe the Oceans dwelling bee? The universall plat
Of all the earth inhabited, shall all be his. The sea
Shall unto him obedient bee likewyse. And when that he   935
Hathe stablisht peace in all the world, then shall he set his mynd
To civill matters, upryght lawes by justice for to fynd,
And by example of himself all others he shall bynd.
Then having care of tyme to comme, and of posteritye,
A holy wyfe shall beare to him a sonne that may supply   940
His carefull charge and beare his name. And lastly in the end
He shall to heaven among the starres, his auncetors, ascend,
But not before his lyfe by length to drooping age doo tend.
And therfore from the murthred corce of Julius Caesar take
His sowle with speede, and of the same a burning cresset make,   945
That from our heavenly pallace he may evermore looke downe
Uppon our royall Capitoll and Court within Rome towne.
    He scarcely ended had theis woordes, but Venus out of hand
    Amid the Senate house of Rome invisible did stand,
And from her Caesars bodye tooke his new expulsed spryght   950
The which shee not permitting to resolve to ayer quyght,
Did place it in the skye among the starres that glister bryght
And as shee bare it, shee did feele it gather heavenly myght,
And for to wexen fyrye. Shee no sooner let it flye,

931 *Canop:* a city in Egypt   948 *out of hand:* immediately
933 *plat:* plot, place   951 *resolve:* dissolve

But that a goodly shyning starre it up aloft did stye 955
And drew a greate way after it bryght beames like burning heare.
Whoo looking on his sonnes good deedes confessed that they were
Farre greater than his owne, and glad he was to see that hee
Excelled him. Although his sonne in no wyse would agree
To have his deedes preferd before his fathers: yit dooth fame, 960
(Whoo ay is free, and bound to no commaund) withstand the same
And stryving in that one behalf ageinst his hest and will,
Proceedeth to preferre his deedes before his fathers still.
Even so to Agamemnons great renowne gives Atreus place,
Even so Achilles deedes, the deedes of Peleus doo abace. 965
Even so beyond Aegaeus, farre dooth Theseyes prowesse go.
And (that I may examples use full matching theis) even so
Is Saturne lesse in fame than Jove. Jove rules the heavenly spheres,
And all the tryple shaped world. And our Augustus beares
Dominion over all the earth. They bothe are fathers: they 970
Are rulers both. Yee Goddes to whom both fyre and swoord gave way,
What tyme yee with Aenaeas came from Troy: yee Goddes that were
Of mortall men canonyzed: thou Quirin whoo didst reere
The walles of Rome: and Mars who wart the valeant Quirins syre
And Vesta of the household Goddes of Caesar with thy fyre 975
Most holy: and thou Phebus whoo with Vesta also art
Of household: and thou Jupiter whoo in the hyghest part
Of mountayne Tarpey hast thy Church: and all yee Goddes that may
With conscience sauf by Poets bee appealed to: I pray
Let that same day bee slowe to comme and after I am dead, 980
In which Augustus (whoo as now of all the world is head)
Quyght giving up the care therof ascend to heaven for ay,
There (absent hence) to favour such as unto him shall pray.
Now have I brought a woork to end which neither Joves feerce
wrath,
Nor swoord, nor fyre, nor freating age with all the force it hath 985
Are able to abolish quyght. Let comme that fatall howre
Which (saving of this brittle flesh) hath over mee no powre,
And at his pleasure make an end of myne uncerteyne tyme.
Yit shall the better part of mee assured bee to clyme
Aloft above the starry skye. And all the world shall never 990
Be able for to quench my name. For looke how farre so ever

⁹⁷³ *reere:* raise ⁹⁸⁵ *freating:* fretting, gnawing

The Romane Empyre by the ryght of conquest shall extend,
So farre shall all folke reade this woork. And tyme without all end
(If Poets as by prophesie about the truth may ame)
My lyfe shall everlastingly bee lengthened still by fame.   995

FINIS LIBRI DECIMI QUINTI.

Laus & honor soli Deo.

IMPRINTED AT LON-
don by Willyam Seres dwelling at the west
end of Paules church, at the
signe of the Hedgehogge.

[THE EPISTLE]

To the ryght Honorable
and his singu-
lar good Lord, Robert Erle of Leycester,
BARON OF DENBYGH, KNYGHT OF THE

most noble order of the Garter, &c. Arthur Gol-
ding Gent. wisheth continuance of health,
with prosperous estate and felicitie.

At length my chariot wheele about the mark hath found the way,
And at their weery races end, my breathlesse horses stay.
The woork is brought to end by which the author did account
(And rightly) with externall fame above the starres to mount.
For whatsoever hath bene writ of auncient tyme in greeke   5
By sundry men dispersedly, and in the latin eeke,
Of this same dark Philosophie of turned shapes, the same
Hath Ovid into one whole masse in this booke brought in frame.
Fowre kynd of things in this his worke the Poet dooth conteyne.
That nothing under heaven dooth ay in stedfast state remayne.   10
And next that nothing perisheth: but that eche substance takes
Another shape than that it had. Of theis twoo points he makes
The proof by shewing through his woorke the wonderfull exchaunge
Of Goddes, men, beasts, and elements, to sundry shapes right straunge,
Beginning with creation of the world, and man of slyme,   15
And so proceeding with the turnes that happened till his tyme.
Then sheweth he the soule of man from dying to be free,
By samples of the noblemen, who for their vertues bee
Accounted and canonized for Goddes by heathen men,
And by the peynes of Lymbo lake, and blysfull state agen   20
Of spirits in th'Elysian feelds. And though that of theis three
He make discourse dispersedly: yit specially they bee
Discussed in the latter booke in that oration where
He bringeth in Pythagoras disswading men from feare

⁶ *eeke:* also   ¹⁸ *samples:* examples

405

Of death, and preaching abstinence from flesh of living things.   25
But as for that opinion which Pythagoras there brings
Of soules removing out of beasts to men, and out of men
To birdes and beasts both wyld and tame, both to and fro agen:
It is not to be understand of that same soule whereby
Wee are endewd with reason and discretion from on hie: 30
But of that soule or lyfe the which brute beasts as well as wee
Enjoy. Three sortes of lyfe or soule (for so they termed bee)
Are found in things. The first gives powre to thryve, encrease and grow,
And this in senselesse herbes and trees and shrubs itself dooth show.
The second giveth powre to move and use of senses fyve,   35
And this remaynes in brutish beasts, and keepeth them alyve.
Both theis are mortall, as the which receyved of the aire
By force of Phebus, after death doo thither eft repayre.
The third gives understanding, wit, and reason: and the same
Is it alonly which with us of soule dooth beare the name.   40
And as the second dooth conteine the first: even so the third
Conteyneth both the other twaine. And neyther beast, nor bird,
Nor fish, nor herb, nor tree, nor shrub, nor any earthly wyght
(Save only man) can of the same partake the heavenly myght.
I graunt that when our breath dooth from our bodies go away,   45
It dooth eftsoones returne to ayre: and of that ayre there may
Both bird and beast participate, and wee of theirs likewyse.
For whyle wee live, (the thing itself appeereth to our eyes)
Bothe they and wee draw all one breath. But for to deeme or say
Our noble soule (which is divine and permanent for ay)   50
Is common to us with the beasts, I think it nothing lesse
Than for to bee a poynt of him that wisdome dooth professe.
Of this I am ryght well assurde, there is no Christen wyght
That can by fondnesse be so farre seduced from the ryght.
And finally hee dooth proceede in shewing that not all   55
That beare the name of men (how strong, feerce, stout, bold, hardy, tall,
How wyse, fayre, rych, or hyghly borne, how much renownd by fame,
So ere they bee, although on earth of Goddes they beare the name)
Are for to be accounted men: but such as under awe
Of reasons rule continually doo live in vertues law: 60
And that the rest doo differ nought from beasts, but rather bee
Much woorse than beasts, bicause they doo abace theyr owne degree.

---

30 *endewd:* endowed   46 *eftsoones:* soon after
38 *eft:* again   52 *poynt:* smallest part
43 *wyght:* creature   54 *fondnesse:* foolishness

To naturall philosophye the formest three perteyne,
The fowrth to morall: and in all are pitthye, apt and playne
Instructions which import the prayse of vertues and the shame 65
Of vices, with the due rewardes of eyther of the same.

Book I

As for example, in the tale of Daphnee turnd to Bay,
A myrror of virginitie appeere unto us may,
Which yeelding neyther unto feare, nor force, nor flatterye,
Doth purchace everlasting fame and immortalitye. 70

Book II

In Phaetons fable unto syght the Poet dooth expresse
The natures of ambition blynd, and youthfull wilfulnesse.
The end whereof is miserie, and bringeth at the last
Repentance when it is too late that all redresse is past.
And how the weaknesse and the want of wit in magistrate 75
Confoundeth both his common weale and eeke his owne estate.
This fable also dooth advyse all parents and all such
As bring up youth, to take good heede of cockering them too much.
It further dooth commende the meane: and willeth to beware
Of rash and hasty promises which most pernicious are, 80
And not to bee performed: and in fine it playnly showes
What sorrow to the parents and to all the kinred growes
By disobedience of the chyld: and in the chyld is ment
The disobedient subject that ageinst his prince is bent.
The transformations of the Crow and Raven doo declare 85
That Clawbacks and Colcariers ought wysely to beware
Of whom, to whom, and what they speake. For sore against his will
Can any freendly hart abyde to heare reported ill
The partie whom he favoureth. This tale dooth eeke bewray
The rage of wrath and jelozie to have no kynd of stay: 90
And that lyght credit to reportes in no wyse should be given,
For feare that men too late to just repentance should bee driven.
The fable of Ocyroee by all such folk is told
As are in serching things to come too curious and too bold.

63 *formest:* foremost, first
70 *purchace:* earn, win
78 *cockering:* pampering
86 *Clawbacks:* flatterers, toadies; *Colcariers:* coal carriers, hirelings, those who do the "dirty work"
89 *bewray:* reveal
90 *stay:* restraint, control

A very good example is describde in Battus tale 95
For covetous people which for gayne doo set theyr toongs to sale.

Book III

All such as doo in flattring freaks, and hawks, and hownds delyght,
And dyce, and cards, and for to spend the tyme both day and nyght
In foule excesse of chamberworke, or too much meate and drink:
Uppon the piteous storie of Acteon ought to think. 100
For theis and theyr adherents usde, excessive are in deede
The dogs that dayly doo devour theyr followers on with speede.
Tyresias willes inferior folk in any wyse to shun
To judge betweene their betters least in perill they doo run.
Narcissus is of scornfulnesse and pryde a myrror cleere, 105
Where beawties fading vanitie most playnly may appeere.
And Echo in the selfsame tale dooth kyndly represent
The lewd behaviour of a bawd, and his due punishment.

Book IV

The piteous tale of Pyramus and Thisbee doth conteine
The headie force of frentick love whose end is wo and payne. 110
The snares of Mars and Venus shew that tyme will bring to lyght
The secret sinnes that folk commit in corners or by nyght.
Hermaphrodite and Salmacis declare that idlenesse
Is cheefest nurce and cherisher of all volupteousnesse,
And that voluptuous lyfe breedes sin: which linking all toogither 115
Make men to bee effeminate, unweeldy, weake and lither.

Book V

Rich Piers daughters turnd to Pies doo openly declare
That none so bold to vaunt themselves as blindest bayardes are.
The Muses playnly doo declare ageine a tother syde,
That whereas cheefest wisdom is, most meeldnesse dooth abyde. 120

Book VI

Arachnee may example bee that folk should not contend
Ageinst their betters, nor persist in error to the end.
So dooth the tale of Niobee and of her children: and

97 *freaks:* capers, vagaries
99 *chamberworke:* lechery
101 *usde:* customary
107 *kyndly:* naturally

110 *headie:* rash, violent
116 *unweeldy:* feeble, clumsy; *lither:* lazy,
spiritless
118 *bayardes:* vain ignoramuses

The transformation of the Carles that dwelt in Lycie land,
Toogither with the flaying off of piper Marsies skin.   125
The first doo also show that long it is ere God begin
To pay us for our faults, and that he warnes us oft before
To leave our folly: but at length his vengeance striketh sore.
And therfore that no wyght should strive with God in word nor thought
Nor deede. But pryde and fond desyre of prayse have ever wrought   130
Confusion to the parties which accompt of them do make.
For some of such a nature bee that if they once doo take
Opinion (be it ryght or wrong) they rather will agree
To dye, than seeme to take a foyle: so obstinate they bee.
The tale of Tereus, Philomele, and Prognee dooth conteyne   135
That folke are blynd in thyngs that to their proper weale perteyne.
And that the man in whom the fyre of furious lust dooth reigne
Dooth run to mischeefe like a horse that getteth loose the reyne.
It also shewes the cruell wreake of women in their wrath
And that no hainous mischiefe long delay of vengeance hath.   14c
And lastly that distresse doth drive a man to looke about
And seeke all corners of his wits, what way to wind him out.

Book VII

The good successe of Jason in the land of Colchos, and
The dooings of Medea since, doo give to understand
That nothing is so hard but peyne and travail doo it win,   145
For fortune ever favoreth such as boldly doo begin:
That women both in helping and in hurting have no match
When they to eyther bend their wits: and how that for to catch
An honest meener under fayre pretence of frendship, is
An easie matter. Also there is warning given of this,   150
That men should never hastely give eare to fugitives,
Nor into handes of sorcerers commit their state or lyves.
It shewes in fine of stepmoothers the deadly hate in part,
And vengeaunce most unnaturall that was in moothers hart.
The deedes of Theseus are a spurre to prowesse, and a glasse   155
How princes sonnes and noblemen their youthfull yeeres should passe.
King Minos shewes that kings in hand no wrongfull wars should take,
And what provision for the same they should before hand make.
King Aeacus gives also there example how that kings

124 *Carles:* churls   136 *weale:* welfare
131 *accompt:* account   139 *wreake:* revenge
134 *foyle:* repulse, setback 142 *wind him out:* extricate himself

Should keepe their promise and their leages above all other things.   160
His grave description of the plage and end thereof, expresse
The wrath of God on man for sin: and how that nerethelesse
He dooth us spare and multiply ageine for goodmens sakes.
The whole discourse of Cephalus and Procris mention makes
That maried folke should warely shunne the vyce of jealozie   165
And of suspicion should avoyd all causes utterly,
Reproving by the way all such as causelesse doo misdeeme
The chaste and giltlesse for the deedes of those that faultie seeme.

Book VIII

The storie of the daughter of king Nisus setteth out
What wicked lust drives folk unto to bring their wills about.   170
And of a rightuous judge is given example in the same,
Who for no meede nor frendship will consent to any blame.
Wee may perceyve in Dedalus how every man by kynd
Desyres to bee at libertie, and with an earnest mynd
Dooth seeke to see his native soyle, and how that streight distresse   175
Dooth make men wyse, and sharpes their wits to fynd their own redresse.
Wee also lerne by Icarus how good it is to bee
In meane estate and not to clymb too hygh, but to agree
To wholsome counsell: for the hyre of disobedience is
Repentance when it is too late forthinking things amisse.   180
And Partrich telles that excellence in any thing procures
Men envie, even among those frendes whom nature most assures.
Philemon and his feere are rules of godly pacient lyfe,
Of sparing thrift, and mutuall love betweene the man and wyfe,
Of due obedience, of the feare of God, and of reward   185
For good or evill usage shewd to wandring straungers ward.
In Erisicthon dooth appeere a lyvely image both
Of wickednesse and crueltie which any wyght may lothe,
And of the hyre that longs thereto. He sheweth also playne
That whereas prodigalitie and gluttony dooth reigne,   190
A world of riches and of goods are ever with the least
To satisfye the appetite and eye of such a beast.

---

160 *leages:* covenants, agreements
161 *plage:* plague
167 *misdeeme:* mistake
172 *meede:* wages, reward, bribery
173 *by kynd:* naturally
179 *hyre:* wages, payment

180 *forthinking:* repenting, regretting
183 *feere:* mate
186 *to . . . ward:* toward
188 *wyght:* man, creature
189 *hyre:* payment

Book IX

In Hercules and Acheloyes encounters is set out
The nature and behaviour of two wooers that be stout.
Wherein the Poet covertly taunts such as beeing bace   195
Doo seeke by forged pedegrees to seeme of noble race.
Who when they doo perceyve no truth uppon their syde to stand,
In stead of reason and of ryght use force and myght of hand.
This fable also signifies that valiantnesse of hart
Consisteth not in woords, but deedes: and that all slyght and Art   200
Give place to prowesse. Furthermore in Nessus wee may see
What breach of promise commeth to, and how that such as bee
Unable for to wreake theyr harmes by force, doo oft devyse
To wreake themselves by policie in farre more cruell wise.
And Deyanira dooth declare the force of jealozie   205
Deceyved through too lyght beleef and fond simplicitie.
The processe following peinteth out true manlynesse of hart
Which yeeldeth neyther unto death, to sorrow, greef, nor smart.
And finally it shewes that such as live in true renowne
Of vertue heere, have after death an everlasting crowne   210
Of glorie. Cawne and Byblis are examples contrarie:
The Mayd of most outrageous lust, the man of chastitie.

Book X

The tenth booke cheefly dooth containe one kynd of argument
Reproving most prodigious lusts of such as have bene bent
To incest most unnaturall. And in the latter end   215
It showeth in Hippomenes how greatly folk offend
That are ingrate for benefits which God or man bestow
Uppon them in the time of neede. Moreover it dooth show
That beawty (will they nill they) aye dooth men in daunger throw:
And that it is a foolyshnesse to stryve ageinst the thing   220
Which God before determineth to passe in tyme to bring.
And last of all Adonis death dooth shew that manhod strives
Against forewarning though men see the perill of theyr lyves.

Book XI

The death of Orphey sheweth Gods just vengeance on the vyle
And wicked sort which horribly with incest them defyle.   225

203 *wreake:* avenge   206 *simplicitie:* ignorance
204 *policie:* trickery

In Midas of a covetous wretch the image wee may see
Whose riches justly to himself a hellish torment bee,
And of a foole whom neyther proof nor warning can amend,
Untill he feele the shame and smart that folly doth him send.
His Barbour represents all blabs which seeme with chyld to bee   230
Untill that they have blaazd abrode the things they heare or see.
In Ceyx and Alcyone appeeres most constant love,
Such as betweene the man and wyfe to bee it dooth behove.
This Ceyx also is a lyght of princely courtesie
And bountie toward such whom neede compelleth for too flie.   235
His viage also dooth declare how vainly men are led
To utter perill through fond toyes and fansies in their head.
For Idols, doubtfull oracles and soothsayres prophecies
Doo nothing else but make fooles fayne and blynd their bleared eyes.
Dedalions daughter warnes to use the toong with modestee   240
And not to vaunt with such as are their betters in degree.

Book XII

The seege of Troy, the death of men, the razing of the citie,
And slaughter of king Priams stock without remors of pitie,
Which in the xii. and xiii. bookes bee written, doo declare
How heynous wilfull perjurie and filthie whoredome are   245
In syght of God. The frentick fray betweene the Lapithes and
The Centaures is a note wherby is given to understand
The beastly rage of drunkennesse.

Book XIII

                                Ulysses dooth expresse
The image of discretion, wit, and great advisednesse.
And Ajax on the other syde doth represent a man   250
Stout, headie, irefull, hault of mynd, and such a one as can
Abyde to suffer no repulse. And both of them declare
How covetous of glorie and reward mens natures are.
And finally it sheweth playne that wisdome dooth prevayle
In all attempts and purposes when strength of hand dooth fayle.   255
The death of fayre Polyxena dooth shew a princely mynd
And firme regard of honor rare engraft in woman kynd.
And Polymnestor, king of Thrace, dooth shew himself to bee

230 *blabs:* babblers   251 *hault:* lofty, proud
239 *fayne:* glad, eager

A glasse for wretched covetous folke wherein themselves to see.
This storie further witnesseth that murther crieth ay   260
For vengeance, and itself one tyme or other dooth bewray.
The tale of Gyant Polypheme doth evidently prove
That nothing is so feerce and wyld, which yeeldeth not to love.
And in the person of the selfsame Gyant is set out
The rude and homely wooing of a country cloyne and lout.   265

Book XIV

The tale of Apes reproves the vyce of wilfull perjurie,
And willeth people to beware they use not for to lye.
Aeneas going downe to hell dooth shew that vertue may
In saufty travell where it will, and nothing can it stay.
The length of lyfe in Sybill dooth declare it is but vayne   270
To wish long lyfe, syth length of lyfe is also length of payne.
The Grecian Achemenides dooth lerne us how we ought
Bee thankfull for the benefits that any man hath wrought.
And in this Achemenides the Poet dooth expresse
The image of exceeding feare in daunger and distresse.   275
What else are Circes witchcrafts and enchauntments than the vyle
And filthy pleasures of the flesh which doo our soules defyle?
And what is else herbe Moly than the gift of stayednesse
And temperance which dooth all fowle concupiscence represse?
The tale of Anaxaretee willes dames of hygh degree   280
To use their lovers courteously how meane so ere they bee.
And Iphis lernes inferior folkes too fondly not to set
Their love on such as are too hygh for their estate to get.

Book XV

Alemons sonne declares that men should willingly obay
What God commaundes, and not uppon exceptions seeme to stay.   285
For he will find the meanes to bring the purpose well about,
And in their most necessitie dispatch them saufly out
Of daunger. The oration of Pithagoras implyes
A sum of all the former woorke. What person can devyse
A notabler example of true love and godlynesse   290
To ones owne natyve countryward than Cippus dooth expresse?
The turning to a blazing starre of Julius Cesar showes,

265 *cloyne:* clown, boor   279 *represse:* expel
271 *syth:* since   291 *To . . . countryward:* toward . . . country
278 *stayednesse:* restraint, sobriety

That fame and immortalitie of vertuous dooing growes.
And lastly by examples of Augustus and a few
Of other noble princes sonnes the author there dooth shew   295
That noblemen and gentlemen shoulde stryve to passe the fame
And vertues of their aunceters, or else to match the same.
　　Theis fables out of every booke I have interpreted,
　　To shew how they and all the rest may stand a man in sted.
Not adding over curiously the meaning of them all,   300
For that were labor infinite, and tediousnesse not small
Bothe unto your good Lordship and the rest that should them reede
Who well myght think I did the boundes of modestie exceede,
If I this one epistle should with matters overcharge
Which scarce a booke of many quyres can well conteyne at large.   305
And whereas in interpreting theis few I attribute
The things to one, which heathen men to many Gods impute,
Concerning mercy, wrath for sin, and other gifts of grace:
Described for examples sake in proper tyme and place,
Let no man marvell at the same. For though that they as blynd   310
Through unbeleefe, and led astray through error even of kynd,
Knew not the true eternall God, or if they did him know,
Yit did they not acknowledge him, but vaynly did bestow
The honor of the maker on the creature: yit it dooth
Behove all us (who ryghtly are instructed in the sooth)   315
To thinke and say that God alone is he that rules all things
And worketh all in all, as lord of lords and king of kings,
With whom there are none other Gods that any sway may beare,
No fatall law to bynd him by, no fortune for to feare.
For Gods, and fate, and fortune are the termes of heathennesse, 320
If men usurp them in the sense that Paynims doo expresse.
But if wee will reduce their sense to ryght of Christian law,
To signifie three other things theis termes wee well may draw.
By Gods wee understand all such as God hath plaast in cheef
Estate to punish sin, and for the godly folkes releef: 325
By fate the order which is set and stablished in things
By Gods eternall will and word, which in due season brings
All matters to their falling out. Which falling out or end
(Bicause our curious reason is too weake to comprehend
The cause and order of the same, and dooth behold it fall   330
Unwares to us) by name of chaunce or fortune wee it call.

<hr>

305 *quyres:* a quire is twenty-four sheets of　　321 *Paynims:* pagans
paper

If any man will say theis things may better lerned bee
Out of divine philosophie or scripture, I agree
That nothing may in worthinesse with holy writ compare.
Howbeeit so farre foorth as things no whit impeachment are   335
To vertue and to godlynesse but furtherers of the same,
I trust wee may them saufly use without desert of blame.
And yet there are (and those not of the rude and vulgar sort,
But such as have of godlynesse and lerning good report)
That thinke the Poets tooke their first occasion of theis things   340
From holy writ as from the well from whence all wisdome springs.
What man is he but would suppose the author of this booke
The first foundation of his woorke from Moyses wryghtings tooke?
Not only in effect he dooth with Genesis agree,
But also in the order of creation, save that hee   345
Makes no distinction of the dayes. For what is else at all
That shapelesse, rude, and pestred heape which Chaos he dooth call,
Than even that universall masse of things which God did make
In one whole lump before that ech their proper place did take.
Of which the Byble saith, that in the first beginning God   350
Made heaven and earth: the earth was waste, and darknesse yit abod
Uppon the deepe: which holy woordes declare unto us playne
That fyre, ayre, water, and the earth did undistinct remayne
In one grosse bodie at the first.
                        "For God the father that
Made all things, framing out the world according to the plat,   355
Conceyved everlastingly in mynd, made first of all
Both heaven and earth uncorporall and such as could not fall
As objects under sense of sight: and also aire lykewyse,
And emptynesse: and for theis twaine apt termes he did devyse.
He called ayer darknesse: for the ayre by kynd is darke.   360
And emptynesse by name of depth full aptly he did marke:
For emptynesse is deepe and waste by nature. Overmore
He formed also bodylesse (as other things before)
The natures both of water and of spirit. And in fyne
The lyght: which beeing made to bee a patterne most divine   365
Whereby to forme the fixed starres and wandring planets seven,
With all the lyghts that afterward should beawtifie the heaven,

335 *impeachment:* disparagement, discredit-   355 *plat:* plan, chart
  ing   362 *Overmore:* moreover
337 *desert of:* deserving   364 *in fyne:* finally
347 *pestred:* troubled

Was made by God both bodylesse and of so pure a kynd,
As that it could alonly bee perceyved by the mynd."
To thys effect are Philos words. And certainly this same   370
Is it that Poets in their worke confused Chaos name.
Not that Gods woorkes at any tyme were pact confusedly
Toogither: but bicause no place nor outward shape whereby
To shew them to the feeble sense of mans deceytfull syght
Was yit appointed unto things, untill that by his myght   375
And wondrous wisdome God in tyme set open to the eye
The things that he before all tyme had everlastingly
Decreed by his providence. But let us further see
How Ovids scantlings with the whole true patterne doo agree.
The first day by his mighty word (sayth Moyses) God made lyght,   380
The second day the firmament, which heaven or welkin hyght.
The third day he did part the earth from sea and made it drie,
Commaunding it to beare all kynd of frutes abundantly.
The fowrth day he did make the lyghts of heaven to shyne from hye,
And stablished a law in them to rule their courses by.   385
The fifth day he did make the whales and fishes of the deepe,
With all the birds and fethered fowles that in the aire doo keepe,
The sixth day God made every beast both wyld and tame, and woormes
That creept on ground according to their severall kynds and foormes.
And in the image of himself he formed man of clay   390
To bee the Lord of all his woorkes the very selfsame day.
This is the sum of Moyses woords. And Ovid (whether it were
By following of the text aright, or that his mynd did beare
Him witnesse that there are no Gods but one) dooth playne uphold
That God (although he knew him not) was he that did unfold   395
The former Chaos, putting it in forme and facion new,
As may appeere by theis his woordes which underneath ensew:
"This stryfe did God and nature breake and set in order dew.
The earth from heaven, the sea from earth he parted orderly,
And from the thicke and foggie aire he tooke the lyghtsome skye." 400
In theis few lynes he comprehends the whole effect of that
Which God did woork the first three dayes about this noble plat.
And then by distributions he entreateth by and by
More largely of the selfsame things, and paynts them out to eye
With all their bounds and furniture: and whereas wee doo fynd   405

[370] *Philo:* Philo Judaeus (c. 30 B.C.–A.D. 45) wrote both literal and allegorical commentaries on Genesis.   [379] *scantlings:* rough drafts, scanty portions   [405] *furniture:* accessories, appurtenances

The terme of nature joynd with God: (according to the mynd
Of lerned men) by joyning so, is ment none other thing,
But God the Lord of nature who did all in order bring.
The distributions beeing doone right lernedly, anon
To shew the other three dayes workes he thus proceedeth on: 410
"The heavenly soyle to Goddes and starres and planets first he gave
The waters next both fresh and salt he let the fishes have.
The suttle ayre to flickering fowles and birds he hath assignd,
The earth to beasts both wyld and tame of sundry sorts and kynd."
Thus partly in the outward phrase, but more in verie deede, 415
He seemes according to the sense of scripture to proceede.
And when he commes to speake of man, he dooth not vainly say
(As sum have written) that he was before all tyme for ay,
Ne mentioneth mo Gods than one in making him. But thus
He both in sentence and in sense his meening dooth discusse. 420
"Howbeeit yit of all this whyle the creature wanting was
Farre more divine, of nobler mynd, which should the resdew passe
In depth of knowledge, reason, wit and hygh capacitee,
And which of all the resdew should the Lord and ruler bee.
Then eyther he that made the world and things in order set, 425
Of heavenly seede engendred man: or else the earth as yet
Yoong, lusty, fresh, and in her flowre, and parted from the skye
But late before, the seedes thereof as yit hild inwardly.
The which Prometheus tempring streyght with water of the spring,
Did make in likenesse to the Goddes that governe every thing." 430
What other thing meenes Ovid heere by terme of heavenly seede,
Than mans immortall sowle, which is divine, and commes in deede
From heaven, and was inspyrde by God, as Moyses sheweth playne?
And whereas of Prometheus he seemes to adde a vayne
Devyce, as though he ment that he had formed man of clay, 435
Although it bee a tale put in for pleasure by the way:
Yit by th'interpretation of the name we well may gather,
He did include a misterie and secret meening rather.
This woord Prometheus signifies a person sage and wyse,
Of great foresyght, who headily will nothing enterpryse. 440
It was the name of one that first did images invent:
Of whom the Poets doo report that hee to heaven up went,
And there stole fyre, through which he made his images alyve:
And therfore that he formed men the Paynims did contryve.

---

419 *Ne:* nor
422 *resdew:* residue

435 *Devyce:* invention, fancy
440 *headily:* rashly, impetuously

Now when the Poet red perchaunce that God almyghty by   445
His providence and by his woord (which everlastingly
Is ay his wisdome) made the world, and also man to beare
His image, and to bee the lord of all the things that were
Erst made, and that he shaped him of earth or slymy clay:
Hee tooke occasion in the way of fabling for to say   450
That wyse Prometheus tempring earth with water of the spring,
Did forme it lyke the Gods above that governe every thing.
Thus may Prometheus seeme to bee th'eternall woord of God,
His wisdom, and his providence which formed man of clod.
"And where all other things behold the ground with groveling eye: 455
He gave to man a stately looke replete with majesty:
And willd him to behold the heaven with countnance cast on hye,
To mark and understand what things are in the starrie skye."
In theis same woordes, both parts of man the Poet dooth expresse
As in a glasse, and giveth us instruction to addresse   460
Our selves to know our owne estate: as that wee bee not borne
To follow lust, or serve the paunch lyke brutish beasts forlorne,
But for to lyft our eyes as well of body as of mynd
To heaven as to our native soyle from whence wee have by kynd
Our better part: and by the sight thereof to lerne to know   465
And knowledge him that dwelleth there: and wholly to bestow
Our care and travail to the prayse and glorie of his name
Who for the sakes of mortall men created first the same.
Moreover by the golden age what other thing is ment,
Than Adams tyme in Paradyse, who beeing innocent   470
Did lead a blist and happy lyfe untill that thurrough sin
He fell from God? From which tyme foorth all sorrow did begin.
The earth accursed for his sake, did never after more
Yeeld foode without great toyle. Both heate and cold did vexe him sore.
Disease of body, care of mynd, with hunger, thirst and neede,   475
Feare, hope, joy, greefe, and trouble, fell on him and on his seede.
And this is termd the silver age. Next which there did succeede
The brazen age, when malice first in peoples harts did breede,
Which never ceased growing till it did so farre outrage,
That nothing but destruction could the heate thereof asswage   480
For why mens stomackes wexing hard as steele ageinst their God,
Provoked him from day to day to strike them with his rod.
Prowd Gyants also did aryse that with presumptuous wills
Heapt wrong on wrong, and sin on sin lyke huge and lofty hilles

466 *knowledge:* acknowledge   481 *For why:* because

Whereby they strove to clymb to heaven and God from thence to
                                                            draw,   485
In scorning of his holy woord and breaking natures law.
For which anon ensewd the flood which overflowed all
The whole round earth and drowned quyght all creatures great and
                                                            smal,
Excepting feaw that God did save as seede wherof should grow
Another ofspring. All these things the Poet heere dooth show   490
In colour, altring both the names of persons, tyme and place.
For where according to the truth of scripture in this cace,
The universall flood did fall but sixteene hundred yeeres
And six and fifty after the creation (as appeeres
By reckening of the ages of the fathers) under Noy,   495
With whom seven other persons mo like saufgard did enjoy
Within the arke, which at the end of one whole yeere did stay
Uppon the hilles of Armenie: the Poet following ay
The fables of the glorying Greekes (who shamelessely did take
The prayse of all things to themselves) in fablying wyse dooth make   500
It happen in Deucalions tyme, who reignd in Thessaly
Eyght hundred winters since Noyes flood or thereupon well nye,
Bicause that in the reigne of him a myghty flood did fall,
That drownde the greater part of Greece, townes, cattell, folk, and all,
Save feaw that by the help of boats atteyned unto him   505
And to the highest of the forkt Parnasos top did swim.
And forbycause that hee and his were driven a whyle to dwell
Among the stonny hilles and rocks until the water fell,
The Poets hereupon did take occasion for to feyne,
That he and Pyrrha did repayre mankynd of stones ageyne.   510
So in the sixth booke afterward Amphions harp is sayd
The first foundation of the walles of Thebee to have layd,
Bycause that by his eloquence and justice (which are ment
By true accord of harmonie and musicall consent)
He gathered into Thebee towne, and in due order knit   515
The people that disperst and rude in hilles and rocks did sit.
So Orphey in the tenth booke is reported to delyght
The savage beasts, and for to hold the fleeting birds from flyght,
To move the senselesse stones, and stay swift rivers, and to make
The trees to follow after him and for his musick sake   520
To yeeld him shadow where he went. By which is signifyde

491 *colour:* rhetorical figures   510 *repayre:* restore, re-create
495 *Noy:* Noah

That in his doctrine such a force and sweetnesse was implyde,
That such as were most wyld, stowre, feerce, hard, witlesse, rude, and
                                                                    bent
Ageinst good order, were by him perswaded to relent,
And for to bee conformable to live in reverent awe   525
Like neybours in a common weale by justyce under law.
Considring then of things before reherst the whole effect,
I trust there is already shewd sufficient to detect
That Poets tooke the ground of all their cheefest fables out
Of scripture: which they shadowing with their gloses went about   530
To turne the truth to toyes and lyes. And of the selfsame rate
Are also theis: their Phlegeton, their Styx, their blisfull state
Of spirits in th'Elysian feelds. Of which the former twayne
Seeme counterfetted of the place where damned soules remaine,
Which wee call hell. The third dooth seeme to fetch his pedegree   535
From Paradyse which scripture shewes a place of blisse to bee.
If Poets then with leesings and with fables shadowed so
The certeine truth, what letteth us to plucke those visers fro
Their doings, and to bring ageine the darkened truth to lyght,
That all men may behold thereof the cleernesse shining bryght?   540
The readers therefore earnestly admonisht are to bee
To seeke a further meening than the letter gives to see.
The travail tane in that behalf although it have sum payne
Yit makes it double recompence with pleasure and with gayne.
With pleasure, for varietie and straungenesse of the things,   545
With gaine, for good instruction which the understanding brings.
And if they happening for to meete with any wanton woord
Or matter lewd, according as the person dooth avoord
In whom the evill is describde, doo feele their myndes thereby
Provokte to vyce and wantonnesse, (as nature commonly   550
Is prone to evill) let them thus imagin in their mynd:
Behold, by sent of reason and by perfect syght I fynd
A Panther heere, whose peinted cote with yellow spots like gold
And pleasant smell allure myne eyes and senses to behold.
But well I know his face is grim and feerce, which he dooth hyde   555
To this intent, that whyle I thus stand gazing on his hyde,
He may devour mee unbewares. Ne let them more offend

---

523 *stowre:* fierce, harsh   538 *letteth:* prevents; *visers:* masks
530 *gloses:* interpretations, explanations   548 *avoord:* afford
531 *toyes:* foolish or idle tales   552 *sent:* scent
537 *leesings:* lies

At vices in this present woork in lyvely colours pend,
Than if that in a chrystall glasse fowle images they found,
Resembling folkes fowle visages that stand about it round.   565
For sure theis fables are not put in wryghting to th'entent
To further or allure to vyce: but rather this is ment,
That men beholding what they bee when vyce dooth reigne in stead
Of vertue, should not let their lewd affections have the head.
For as there is no creature more divine than man as long   565
As reason hath the sovereintie and standeth firme and strong:
So is there none more beastly, vyle, and develish, than is hee,
If reason giving over, by affection mated bee.
The use of this same booke therfore is this: that every man
(Endevoring for to know himself as neerly as he can,)   570
(As though he in a chariot sate well ordered,) should direct
His mynd by reason in the way of vertue, and correct
His feerce affections with the bit of temprance, lest perchaunce
They taking bridle in the teeth lyke wilfull jades doo praunce
Away, and headlong carie him to every filthy pit   575
Of vyce, and drinking of the same defyle his soule with it:
Or else doo headlong harrie him uppon the rockes of sin,
And overthrowing forcibly the chariot he sits in,
Doo teare him woorse than ever was Hippolytus the sonne
Of Theseus when he went about his fathers wrath to shun.   580
This worthie worke in which of good examples are so many,
This Ortyard of Alcinous in which there wants not any
Herb, tree, or frute that may mans use for health or pleasure serve,
This plenteous horne of Acheloy which justly dooth deserve
To beare the name of treasorie of knowledge, I present   585
To your good Lordship once ageine not as a member rent
Or parted from the resdew of the body any more:
But fully now accomplished, desiring you therfore
To let your noble courtesie and favor countervayle
My faults where Art or eloquence on my behalf dooth fayle.   590
For sure the marke whereat I shoote is neyther wreathes of bay,
Nor name of Poet, no nor meede: but cheefly that it may
Bee lyked well of you and all the wise and lerned sort,
And next that every wyght that shall have pleasure for to sport
Him in this gardeine, may as well beare wholsome frute away   595.

568 *affection:* emotion; *mated:* overcome   577 *harrie:* drag
574 *jades:* vicious or worthless horses   592 *meede:* reward

As only on the pleasant flowres his rechlesse senses stay.
But why seeme I theis doubts to cast, as if that he who tooke
With favor and with gentlenesse a parcell of the booke
Would not likewyse accept the whole? Or even as if that they
Who doo excell in wisdome and in learning, would not wey   600
A wyse and lerned woorke aryght? Or else as if that I
Ought ay to have a speciall care how all men doo apply
My dooings to their owne behoof? As of the former twayne
I have great hope and confidence: so would I also fayne
The other should according to good meening find successe: 605
If other wyse, the fault is theyrs not myne they must confesse.
And therefore breefly to conclude, I turne ageine to thee,
O noble Erle of Leycester, whose lyfe God graunt may bee
As long in honor, helth and welth as auncient Nestors was,
Or rather as Tithonussis: that all such students as   610
Doo travell to enrich our toong with knowledge heretofore
Not common to our vulgar speech, may dayly more and more
Procede through thy good furtherance and favor in the same.
To all mens profit and delyght, and thy eternall fame.
And that (which is a greater thing) our natyve country may   615
Long tyme enjoy thy counsell and thy travail to her stay.

At Barwicke the xx. of Aprill. 1567
Your good L. most humbly to
commaund Arthur Golding.

596 *rechlesse:* heedless   611 *travell:* travail, labor
603 *behoof:* benefit   616 *stay:* support

TO THE READER

I would not wish the simple sort offended for to bee,
When in this booke the heathen names of feyned Godds they see.
The trewe and everliving God the Paynims did not knowe:
Which caused them the name of Godds on creatures to bestow.
For nature beeing once corrupt and knowledge blynded quyght   5
By Adams fall, those little seedes and sparkes of heavenly lyght
That did as yit remayne in man, endevering foorth to burst
And wanting grace and powre to growe to that they were at furst,
To superstition did decline: and drave the fearefull mynd,
Straunge woorshippes of the living God in creatures for to fynd.   10
The which by custome taking roote, and growing so to strength,
Through Sathans help possest the hartes of all the world at length.
Some woorshipt al the hoste of heaven: some deadmens ghostes and
                               bones:
Sum wicked feends: sum wormes and fowles, herbes, fishes, trees and
                               stones.
The fyre, the ayre, the sea, the land, and every roonning brooke,   15
Eche queachie grove, eche cragged cliffe the name of Godhead tooke.
The nyght and day, the fleeting howres, the seasons of the yeere,
And every straunge and monstruous thing, for Godds mistaken weere.
There was no vertue, no nor vice: there was no gift of mynd
Or bodye, but some God therto or Goddesse was assignde.   20
Of health and sicknesse, lyfe and death, of needinesse and wealth,
Of peace and warre, of love and hate, of murder, craft and stealth,
Of bread and wyne, of slouthfull sleepe, and of theyr solemne games,
And every other tryfling toy theyr Goddes did beare the names.
And looke, how every man was bent to goodnesse or to ill,   25
He did surmyse his foolish Goddes enclyning to his will.
For God perceyving mannes pervers and wicked will to sinne
Did give him over to his lust to sinke or swim therin.

3 *Paynims:* pagans   24 *toy:* caprice, trifle
8 *that:* what   26 *surmyse:* imagine
16 *queachie:* dense

By meanes wherof it came to passe (as in this booke yee see)
That all theyr Goddes with whoordome, theft, or murder blotted bee. ³⁰
Which argues them to bee no Goddes, but woorser in effect
Than they whoose open poonnishment theyr dooings dooth detect.
Whoo seeing Jove whom heathen folke doo arme with triple fyre
In shape of Eagle, bull or swan to winne his foule desyre,
Or grysly Mars theyr God of warre intangled in a net   ³⁵
By Venus husband purposely to trappe him warely set,
Whoo seeing Saturne eating up the children he begate
Or Venus dalying wantonly with every lustie mate,
Whoo seeing Juno play the scold, or Phoebus moorne and rew
For losse of her whom in his rage through jealous moode he slew,   ⁴⁰
Or else the suttle Mercurie that beares the charmed rod
Conveying neate and hyding them, would take him for a God?
For if theis faultes in mortall men doo justly merit blame,
What greater madnesse can there bee than to impute the same
To Goddes, whose natures ought to bee most perfect, pure and bright, ⁴⁵
Most vertuous, holly, chaast, and wyse, most full of grace and lyght?
But as there is no Christen man that can surmyse in mynd
That theis or other such are Goddes which are no Goddes by kynd:
So would to God there were not now of christen men profest,
That worshipt in theyr deedes theis Godds whose names they doo
                                                      detest.   ⁵⁰
Whoose lawes wee keepe his thralles wee bee, and he our God indeede.
So long is Christ our God as wee in christen lyfe proceede.
But if wee yeeld to fleshlye lust, to lucre, or to wrath,
Or if that Envy, Gluttony, or Pryde the maystry hath,
Or any other kynd of sinne, the thing the which wee serve   ⁵⁵
To bee accounted for our God most justly dooth deserve.
Then must wee thinke the learned men that did theis names frequent,
Some further things and purposes by those devises ment.
By Jove and Juno understand all states of princely port:
By Ops and Saturne auncient folke that are of elder sort: ⁶⁰
By Phoebus yoong and lusty brutes of hand and courage stout:
By Mars the valeant men of warre that love to feight it out:
By Pallas and the famous troupe of all the Muses nyne,
Such folke as in the sciences and vertuous artes doo shyne.
By Mercurie the suttle sort that use to filch and lye,   ⁶⁵

---

³⁵ *grysly:* horrible   ⁴⁸ *kynd:* nature
³⁶ *warely:* cunningly, alertly   ⁵⁹ *states:* rulers; *port:* station
⁴² *Conveying neate:* stealing cattle

With theeves, and Merchants whoo to gayne theyr travail doo applye.
By Bacchus all the meaner trades and handycraftes are ment:
By Venus such as of the fleshe to filthie lust are bent.
By Neptune such as keepe the seas: by Phebe maydens chast,
And Pilgrims such as wandringly theyr tyme in travell waste.   70
By Pluto such as delve in mynes, and Ghostes of persones dead:
By Vulcane smythes and such as woorke in yron, tynne or lead.
By Hecat witches, Conjurers, and Necromancers reede:
With all such vayne and devlish artes as superstition breede.
By Satyres, Sylvanes, Nymphes and Faunes with other such besyde,   75
The playne and simple country folke that every where abyde.
I know theis names to other thinges oft may and must agree
In declaration of the which I will not tedious bee.
But leave them to the Readers will to take in sundry wyse,
As matter rysing giveth cause constructions to devyse.   80
Now when thou readst of God or man, in stone, in beast, or tree
It is a myrrour for thy self thyne owne estate to see.
For under feyned names of Goddes it was the Poets guyse,
The vice and faultes of all estates to taunt in covert wyse.
And likewyse to extoll with prayse such things as doo deserve,   85
Observing alwayes comlynesse from which they doo not swerve.
And as the persone greater is of birth, renowne or fame,
The greater ever is his laud, or fouler is his shame,
For if the States that on the earth the roome of God supply,
Declyne from vertue unto vice and live disorderly,   90
To Eagles, Tygres, Bulles, and Beares, and other figures straunge
Bothe to theyr people and themselves most hurtfull doo they chaunge,
And when the people give themselves to filthie life and synne,
What other kinde of shape thereby than filthie can they winne?
So was Licaon made a Woolfe: and Jove became a Bull: 95
The t'one for using crueltie, the tother for his trull.
So was Elpenor and his mates transformed into swyne,
For following of theyr filthie lust in women and in wyne.
Not that they lost theyr manly shape as to the outward showe,
But for that in their brutish brestes most beastly lustes did growe.   100
For why this lumpe of flesh and bones, this bodie, is not wee.
Wee are a thing which earthly eyes denyed are to see.
Our soule is wee endewd by God with reason from above:
Our bodie is but as our house, in which wee woorke and move.

---

[83] *guyse:* way, manner   [86] *comlynesse:* the quality of being proper, becoming

T'one part is common to us all, with God of heaven himself: 105
The tother common with the beastes, a vyle and stinking pelf.
The t'one bedect with heavenly giftes and endlesse: tother grosse,
Frayle, filthie, weake, and borne to dye as made of earthly drosse.
Now looke how long this clod of clay to reason dooth obey,
So long for men by just desert account our selves wee may.   110
But if wee suffer fleshly lustes as lawlesse Lordes to reigne,
Than are we beastes, wee are no men, wee have our name in vaine.
And if wee be so drownd in vice that feeling once bee gone,
Then may it well of us bee sayd, wee are a block or stone.
This surely did the Poets meene when in such sundry wyse   115
The pleasant tales of turned shapes they studyed to devyse.
There purpose was to profite men, and also to delyght
And so to handle every thing as best might like the sight.
For as the Image portrayd out in simple whight and blacke
(Though well proportiond, trew and faire) if comly colours lacke,   120
Delyghteth not the eye so much, nor yet contentes the mynde
So much as that that shadowed is with colours in his kynde:
Even so a playne and naked tale or storie simply told
(Although the matter bee in deede of valewe more than gold)
Makes not the hearer so attent to print it in his hart,   125
As when the thing is well declarde, with pleasant termes and art.
All which the Poets knew right well: and for the greater grace,
As Persian kings did never go abrode with open face,
But with some lawne or silken skarf, for reverence of theyr state:
Even so they following in their woorkes the selfsame trade and rate,   130
Did under covert names and termes theyr doctrines so emplye,
As that it is ryght darke and hard theyr meening to espye.
But beeing found it is more sweete and makes the mynd more glad,
Than if a man of tryed gold a treasure gayned had.
For as the body hath his joy in pleasant smelles and syghts: 135
Even so in knowledge and in artes the mynd as much delights.
Wherof aboundant hoordes and heapes in Poets packed beene
So hid that (saving unto fewe) they are not to bee seene.
And therfore whooso dooth attempt the Poets woorkes to reede,
Must bring with him a stayed head and judgement to proceede.   140
For as there bee most wholsome hestes and precepts to bee found,

106 *pelf:* trash, refuse
125 *attent:* attentive, intent
129 *lawne:* fine linen
130 *trade:* path, course; *rate:* manner, style

134 *tryed:* refined, pure
140 *stayed:* settled, serious, controlled
141 *hestes:* commands

So are theyr rockes and shallowe shelves to ronne the ship aground.
Some naughtie persone seeing vyce shewd lyvely in his hew,
These persons overshoote themselves, and other folkes deceyve:
Dooth take occasion by and by like vices to ensew.
Another beeing more severe than wisdome dooth requyre,   145
Beeholding vice (to outward shewe) exalted in desyre,
Condemneth by and by the booke and him that did it make.
And willes it to be burnd with fyre for lewd example sake.
Not able of the authors mynd the meening to conceyve.   150
The Authors purpose is to paint and set before our eyes
The lyvely Image of the thoughts that in our stomackes ryse.
Eche vice and vertue seems to speake and argue to our face,
With such perswasions as they have theyr dooinges to embrace.
And if a wicked persone seeme his vices to exalt,   155
Esteeme not him that wrate the woorke in such defaultes to halt.
But rather with an upryght eye consyder well thy thought:
See if corrupted nature have the like within thee wrought.
Marke what affection dooth perswade in every kynd of matter.
Judge if that even in heynous crymes thy fancy doo not flatter.   160
And were it not for dread of lawe or dread of God above,
Most men (I feare) would doo the things that fond affections move.
Then take theis woorkes as fragrant flowers most full of pleasant juce,
The which the Bee conveying home may put to wholesome use:
And which the spyder sucking on to poyson may convert,   165
Through venym spred in all her limbes and native in her hart.
For to the pure and Godly mynd, are all things pure and cleene,
And unto such as are corrupt the best corrupted beene:
Lyke as the fynest meates and drinkes that can bee made by art
In sickly folkes to nourishment of sicknesse doo convert.   170
And therefore not regarding such whose dyet is so fyne
That nothing can digest with them onlesse it bee devine,
Nor such as to theyr proper harme doo wrest and wring awrye
The thinges that to a good intent are written pleasantly,
Through Ovids woorke of turned shapes I have with peinfull pace   175
Past on untill I had atteyned the end of all my race.
And now I have him made so well acquainted with our toong
As that he may in English verse as in his owne bee soong.
Wherein although for pleasant style, I cannot make account,
To match myne author, who in that all other dooth surmount: 180

144 *ensew:* follow · 152 *stomackes:* spirits
147 *by and by:* immediately 156 *halt:* limp, be at fault

Yit (gentle Reader) doo I trust my travail in this cace
May purchace favour in thy sight my dooings to embrace:
Considring what a sea of goodes and Jewelles thou shalt fynd,
Not more delyghtfull to the eare than frutefull to the mynd.
For this doo lerned persons deeme, of Ovids present woorke: 185
That in no one of all his bookes the which he wrate, doo lurke
Mo darke and secret misteries, mo counselles wyse and sage,
Mo good ensamples, mo reprooves of vyce in youth and age,
Mo fyne inventions to delight, mo matters clerkly knit,
No, nor more straunge varietie to shew a lerned wit.   190
The high, the lowe: the riche, the poore: the mayster, and the slave:
The mayd, the wife: the man, the chyld: the simple and the brave:
The yoong, the old: the good, the bad: the warriour strong and stout:
The wyse, the foole: the countrie cloyne: the lerned and the lout:
And every other living wight shall in this mirrour see   195
His whole estate, thoughtes, woordes and deedes expresly shewd to bee.
Whereof if more particular examples thou doo crave,
In reading the Epistle through thou shalt thy longing have.
Moreover thou mayst fynd herein descriptions of the tymes:
With constellacions of the starres and planettes in theyr clymes: 200
The Sites of Countries, Cities, hilles, seas, forestes, playnes and floods:
The natures both of fowles, beastes, wormes, herbes, mettals, stones and
                                                                  woods,
And finally what ever thing is straunge and delectable,
The same conveyed shall you fynd most featly in some fable.
And even as in a cheyne eche linke within another wynds,   205
And both with that that went before and that that followes binds:
So every tale within this booke dooth seeme to take his ground
Of that that was reherst before, and enters in the bound
Of that that folowes after it: and every one gives light
To other: so that whoo so meenes to understand them ryght,   210
Must have a care as well to know the thing that went before,
As that the which he presently desyres to see so sore.
Now to th'intent that none have cause heereafter to complaine
Of mee as setter out of things that are but light and vaine,
If any stomacke be so weake as that it cannot brooke,   215
The lively setting forth of things described in this booke,

---

189 *clerkly knit*: worked together with erudi-   204 *featly*: neatly, deftly
tion   208 *bound*: boundary, field
194 *cloyne*: clown, boor   215 *brooke*: endure
200 *clymes*: zones

I give him counsell to absteine untill he bee more strong,
And for to use Ulysses feat ageinst the Meremayds song.
Or if he needes will heere and see and wilfully agree
(Through cause misconstrued) unto vice allured for to bee,   220
Then let him also marke the peine that dooth therof ensue,
And hold himself content with that that to his fault is due.

FINIS

4B *The First Fower Bookes* . . . (1565).
E*1* The First Edition (1567). E*1* is used only where Rouse refers to it as the "first edition." Since his edition is "a reprint of a copy of the First Edition (1567) in the Cambridge University Library," it may be assumed that E*1* stands for that copy.
UI The University of Illinois copy of the First Edition.
E2 The Second Edition (1575).
R The edition by W. H. D. Rouse (1904).

I

116 R changes *things* (E*1*) to *thing* (E2). Yet *every* could be used with a plural noun: Shakespeare's "every . . . accidents." (*Tempest,* V, i, 249).
392 *cease* for *rease*
478 R reads *wax* for *warre*. But could *warre* be Golding's spelling of *wear*, "to pass gradually into (a condition, etc.)"?
633 Ovid's *certior* (520) supports R's *surer* for *sured*.
671 The *scarsly* of 4B and E2 for *scarce* corrects the meter (R).
685 *lockes* for *lookes*.
890 Misprint in R repeats *one that*.
909 *through* for *though*

II

51 *may* for *my*
88 R supplies *as* before *yse*.
187 R says E*1* has *I thus* for *that I*. UI, however, does have *that I*.
273 R is probably right in suggesting that the *Whole* of 4B (for *Whose* of E*1*) is the true reading: it translates *totas* (215).
386 *Stygian* for *Stygnan*
406 The *like to starre* of E*1* is unmetrical. R suggests *like to a Starre*.
459 *Stenels* for *Steucls* (R: for *Steuels*)
463 *along* for *alone*
548 R: *with* for *wich*. But UI has *with*.
626 R points out that E2 changed *God* to *Jove*.
653 R corrects the meter by supplying *other*.
676 *become* for *became*
692 R misprints *bodly* for *boldly*.

III

461 Narcissus for Narcists
690 R: Countrie for Countie.
724 R says E1 has froth for wroth. But UI has wroth.
762 R emends can to gan.

IV

256 daughter for daugher
335 Daphnyes for Daplynis (Ovid's Daphnidis, 277)
345 Smylax for Smylar
520 advaunst for advannst
525 R, citing Ovid, 423, emends thee to them.
615 fome for fame (for Ovid's spumas, 501)
633 chace for chach
644 R, citing Ovid's ferens (522), emends heares to beares.
653 headlong for healong
694 R says he changes chflde to childe. But it is childe in UI.
677 hir for his
754 disdaine for disdiane
802 and for add

V

196 R corrects the meter by writing than of a for than a.
543 take for eake (Ovid's prendere, 437)
723 it for is
794 In E1 the line is unmetrical: it has thereof twice. R corrects the line by omitting thereof after part.
821 grinnd for grind

VI

146 R is probably right in reading covering for hovering (though hovering can be transitive).
485 trunck for trunch

VII

318 R supplies tryple, missing in E1.
788 Astonied for Astnoied
831 on the same for on the the same
848 R reads ny for wy.
1003 off of for of of
1107 R: by the Love for by Love.
1110 The UI copy reads: This sed, she held hir peace, and I receyved the same—defective in sense and meter. R, without explanation, prints the line as in our text. It translates Ovid's Dixit et errorem tum denique nominis esse/Et sensi et docui (857-8).

VIII

68 R says *his* comes from E2. But it is in UI.
499 UI omits *goodly*, supplied without comment by R.
759 *maidhod* (?)

IX

43 R would read: *my pawing hands* for *my pawing armes*. He may be right: Ovid uses both *bracchia* and *manus* (33–4).
143 R: *uppon vaine hope* for *uppon a vaine hope*.
256 *to toe* for *too to*
569 R reads *awake* for *wake*.
579 *bee* for *mee*
695 *soft* for *oft* (Ovid's *vix . . . icto . . . aere*, 584)
749 R: *purpose of attempting* for *purpose attempting*.
784 R's suggestion of *turned* for *turnd* seems the simplest way of regularizing the meter.

X

67 *soft* for *oft*. She would hardly say her last farewell so *oft* that *scarse he heard the sound*. Ovid (62) has *quod iam* instead of *quodmia* as R gives it.
519 For *take*, bad at least metrically, R reads *taken*.
645 For the metrically defective *rest here* of E*1*, R supplies *us*.
660 R corrects the meter by adding *the* to *with sore*.
798 Probably the simplest way to correct the meter is to read, with R, *thinkest thou* for the final *thinks thou* of E*1*.
830. UI reads *Anemis least thy valeantnesse*. So R in his text, but he quotes in his notes the reading of E2, adopted here.

XI

59 R: the omission of the second *And* is a misprint.
83 *suttletye* for *suttlelye*
350 *were* for *where*
634 R: *then he* for *when he*.
734 *heaven* for *heave*
764 R thinks the second sentence of the line suspect as a translation of Ovid's *falso tibi me promittere noli* (662). He suggests *now* for *no*. But though the sentence in E*1* verges on a double negative, it seems possible: "Make no reckoning of my return! In vain!"
851 R: *if Ceyx* for *of Ceyx*.

XII

54 *or* for *are* (*qualemve*, Ovid, 51)
118 *Aetions* for *Axetions* (*Eetioneas*, Ovid, 110)
205 R: *mynd* for *myne*.

520 *thee give* for *the give*
664 R: *If any* for *It any.*

XIII

34 R corrects the meter by reading *Ajax third* for *Ajax the third.*
136 R: *those same* for *whose same.*
278 R misprints *As well others.*
352 R says E*1* reads *wha.* But U*I* has *what.*
659 *shee* for *see*
660 *hart* for *hard*
689 *Morning* for *morning* (Ovid's *Aurora*, 576)
706 *the* for *thee*
708 *Morning* for *morning*
1037 *it was* for *is was*
1073 *cleere* for *creere*

XIV

6 *And* for *An* (Ovid's *et,* 5)
266 R finds *thë* in E*1*. But U*I* has *the.*
332 *Eurilochus* for *Furilochus* (Ovid's *Eurulochum*, 287)
839 *by* for *bee*
980 R reads *ayre did up her* for *ayre p did vher.* In U*I*, the scrambled text seems *ayre did vher.*

XV

176 R changes *living* of E*1* to *leaving,* without comment. *Leaving* is correct: it translates Ovid's *relicta* (158).
219 R: *lesser* for *better.* But it is *lesser* in U*I*.
508 R's text reads *fowles* for *sowles,* corrected in his Textual Notes.
511 *spirits* for *sprits*
721 *Ambassadours* for *Ambassadour* (Ovid's *missi,* 644)
916 *bee quyght* for *beiquyght*
945 *cresset* for *cressed*

THE EPISTLE

582 *Alcinous* for *Alcimous*
606 R misprints as: *Theyrs not not myne.*

THE PREFACE

61 R says that in E*1* *lust* is misprinted for *lusty.* U*I*, however, has *lusty.*
108 *Frayle* for *Fraylie*
158 R's text reprints the misprinted *hane* of E*1* for *have;* corrected in his Textual Notes.
171 R's text reprints the misprinted *snch* of E*1* for *such;* corrected in his Textual Notes.

GLOSSARY OF NAMES AND PLACES

THIS LIST further identifies most of the persons and places mentioned. With the more important is given a reference to the point in the poem at which they make a significant appearance. Not every name Ovid uses will be found here: "Opheltes sayd (he was the Maysters Mate)" is not much clarified by an entry reading: "Opheltes: Master's Mate." Often what Ovid tells us about a person or place is all we know. Some names correspond to nothing historic or legendary: in the long battle scenes between Perseus and his enemies (V) or between the Lapithae and the Centaurs (XIII) Ovid, like the good storyteller he is, makes up names for many of the combatants and the casualties.

> *A wearie worke it were to tell you plaine*
> *The names of all the common sort.*

Abas: (1) King of Argos, father of Acrisius, grandfather of Perseus.
(2) Companion of Diomedes.
Acarnania: western province of Greece.
Acastus: son of Pelias; king of Thessaly.
Acestes: mythical king of Sicily.
Acetis: Acoetes, Lydian sailor, devotee of Bacchus. III, 739.
Achaia: Greece
Acheloe: Achelous, Greek river and its river-god, the father of the sirens. VIII, 708; IX, 1.
Archemenides: companion of Ulysses. XIV, 189.
Acheron: river of the underworld and its river-god.
Achylles: Achilles, heroic son of Peleus and Thetis.
Acis: river in Sicily and its river-god, child of Faunus and the nymph of the river Symaethus; loved by Galatea. XIII, 886.
Acrise: Acrisius, son of Abas, father of Danae; king of Argos.
Acrota: king of the Albani, brother of Romulus Silvius.
Acteon: Actaeon, son of Aristeus and Autonoe, grandson of Cadmus. III, 207.
Actium: promontory and town in Epirus, on the Ambracian Gulf.
Actor: father of Eurytus and Cleatus; king of Phthia.
Admetus: king of Pherae in Thessaly, husband of Alcestis.
Adonis: son of Cinyrus, king of Cyprus; loved by Venus. X, 614.
Aeacus: son of Jove by Europa, father of Peleus and Telamon; king of Aegina. VII, 649.

Aeacyds: descendants of Aeacus.

Aeeta: Aeetes, son of Sol and Persa; king of Colchis, father of Medea.

Aegeon: hundred-handed sea-god.

Aegeus: king of Athens, father of Theseus.

Aegina (Aegine): (1) daughter of Asopus, mother (by Jupiter) of Aeacus.
        (2) an island in the Saronic Gulf, struck by a famous
        plague. VII, 671.

Aello: a harpy.

Aemonian: of Thessaly. Sagittarius was thought of as one of the Centaurs, whose homeland was Thessaly.

Aeneas: son of Venus and Anchises; ancestor of the Romans. XIV, 95.

Aeolus: (1) god of the winds, son of Hippotas (or Jupiter) and Menalippa; ruler of the islands between Italy and Sicily.
    (2) a king in Thessaly, father of Sisyphus, Athamas, etc.

Aesacus: son of Priam, changed into a sea-bird. XI, 749.

Aesculapius: son of Apollo and Coronis. II, 792; XV, 599.

Aeserie: Aesar, river in lower Italy, near Crotona.

Aeson: brother of King Pelias of Thessaly, father of Jason. VII, 224.

Aethyop: Ethiopia.

Aetion: Eetion, father of Andromache; king of Thebe in Cilicia.

Aetna: Mt. Etna in Sicily.

Aetolia: province in middle Greece.

Agamemnon: king of Mycenae, son of Atreus and Aerope, husband of Clytemnestra, father of Orestes, Iphigenia, Electra; commander of the
  Greek forces at Troy.

Aganippe: fountain on Mt. Helicon, sacred to the Muses.

Agave: daughter of Cadmus, mother of Pentheus.

Agenor: Phoenician king, father of Europa.

Aglauros: daughter of Cecrops. II, 702, 923.

Agmon: Acmon, companion of Diomedes.

Aire: Aura, a supposed nymph. VII, 1066.

Ajax: (1) son of Oileus; king of the Locri.
    (2) son of Telamon. XIII, 3.

Alastor: companion of Sarpedon at Troy.

Alba: the mother-city of Rome, built by Ascanius.

Albula: earlier name for the Tiber.

Alcathoe: old name for Megara, Greek city.

Alcidamas: father of Ctesilla.

Alcinous: king of the Phaeacians.

Alcithoe: daughter of Minyas.

Alcmena: wife of Amphitryo, mother (by Jupiter) of Hercules, mother-in-law of Dejanira.

Alcon of Myle (or *Hyle?* disputed text): unknown artist. XIII, 812.

Alcyone: daughter of Aeolus, wife of Ceyx. XI, 479.

Alemon: father of Myscelus.

Alme: the Almo, small stream south of Rome.

Alphey: Alpheus, river in Elis and its river-god.

Althaea: wife of Oeneus, king of Calydonia; mother of Meleager. VII, 586.

Alyxothoe: for Alexirhoe, daughter of the river Granicus and mother of Aesa-
    cus. (Golding seems to have misread the lines about her.) XI, 879.

Amathus: town in Cyprus.

Amazons: warlike women of Thrace. (Pronounced Amázons.) XV, 621.

Ambrace: Ambracia, a town in southern Epirus.

Amesene: for Amenanus, a river in Sicily.

Amphion: son of Jove and Antiope, king of Thebes, whose walls were built by
    his music.

Amphissus: son of Apollo and Dryope.

Amphitrio: Amphitryo, king of Thebes, husband of Alcmene.

Amphitrytee: daughter of Ocean, wife of Neptune; the sea.

Amphrysus: Thessalian river.

Ampycus: father of the prophet Mopsus.

Amulius: son of Procas; king in Alba.

Amycly: Amyclas, ancestor of Hyacinth.

Anaphey: Anaphe, island in the Cretan sea.

Anapus: Anapis, a river in Sicily, and its river-god.

Anaxarete: disdainful beauty of Cyprus, loved by Iphis. XIV, 803.

Ancaeus: native of Parrhasia, in Arcadia.

Anchises: father of Aeneas, whose mother was Venus.

Ancon: Antium, town in Latium.

Anderland: Golding's name for Andros, one of the Cyclades.

Andraemon: husband of Dryope; changed into a lotus.

Andremon: father of Thoas; king of Lemnos.

Andrey: Andros, one of the Cyclades.

Andromad: Andromeda, daughter of Cepheus and Cassiope. IV, 823.

Anigrus: muddy and malodorous brook in Elis.

Anio: tributary of the Tiber.

Anius: priest-king of the island of Delos. XIII, 755.

Antaeus: African giant killed by Hercules.

Antandros: town on the shore of Mysia. (Golding calls it an isle.)

Antenor: Trojan in favor of returning Helen to the Greeks and making peace.

Anthedon: harbor in Boeotia, opposite Euboea; birthplace of Glaucus.

Antigone: proud daughter of the Trojan king Laomedon (not Sophocles'
    heroine). VI, 112.

Antiope: daughter of Nycteus, wife of Lycus, king of Thebes; mother of
    Amphion and Zethus.

Antiphates: cannibal king of the Laestrygones, in southwestern Italy and, later,
    Sicily. XIV, 270.

Antissa: town on the island of Lesbos.
Anubis: dog-headed Egyptian deity.
Aony: Aonia, a part of Boeotia.
Apharie: Aphareus, king of the Messenians, father of Lynceus and Idas.
Apidane: Apidanus, Thessalian river.
Apis: ox worshipped as a god by the Egyptians.
Apollo: the sun-god, son of Jove and Latona.
>   and Daphne, I, 545.
>   and Coronis, II, 677.
>   and Leucothoe, IV, 238.
>   and Hyacinth, X, 168.
Apulia: province in lower Italy.
Arachne: daughter of Idmon of Colophon, in Lydia. VI, 8.
Arcadia: mountainous province in the center of the Peloponnesus.
Arcas (Archas): (1) son of Callisto and Jove, eponymous hero of Arcadia.
>   II, 580.
>   (2) Arcadian. III, 250.
Arcesius: son of Jupiter, father of Laertes, grandfather of Ulysses.
Ardea: capital of the Rutuli.
Arethuse: Arethusa, a fountain near Syracuse in Sicily, thought to originate
>   in Pisa in Elis (the mother-city of the Italian Pisa). V, 605, 709.
Arge: Argos, the capital of Argolis in Greece.
Argus: hundred-eyed custodian of Io. I, 775.
Ariadne: daughter of Minos; deserted by Theseus, whom she loved. VIII, 231.
Aricine: of Aricia, ancient town near Rome.
Armen: Armenia.
Arne: woman changed into a jackdaw when she betrayed her home island of
>   Siphnos. VII, 597.
Ascalaphus: son of Acheron and Orphne. V, 669.
Ascanius: son of Aeneas and Creusa (some say, of Lavinia). (Also called
>   Iulus.)
Asop: Asopus, river in Boeotia and its river-god, the father of Aegina.
Assaracus: son of Tros, brother of Ilus and Ganymede, grandfather of Anchises.
Asteriee: Asteria, daughter of Coeus.
Astrey: (1) Astraea, daughter of Jove and Themis; goddess of justice.
>   (2) Astraeus, a Titan, husband of Aurora, father of the winds ("the
>   sonnes of Astrey").
>   (3) Astreus, companion of Phineus.
Astyanax: son of Hector and Andromache.
Astypaley: Astypalaea, island near Crete.
Atalant: Atalanta, daughter of King Schoeneus of Boeotia, or, some say, of
>   Iasus and Clyment. There may have been two girls of this name.
>   VIII, 427; X, 654.
Athamane: Athamania in Epirus.

438   GLOSSARY OF NAMES AND PLACES

Athamas: son of King Aeolus of Thessaly; father of Helle and Phrixus by Nephele, and of Melicerta (later called Palaemon) and Learchus by Ino. IV, 521.

Athe: Athos, mountain in Macedonia.

Atheney: for Ovid's "promunturium Mineruae," the Promontory of Minerva southeast of Sorrento. (Golding changes the Roman Minerva to the Greek Athena.) XV, 794.

Atlas: king of Mauretania, son of Iapetos and Clymene.

Atreus: son of Pelops and Hippodamia, brother of Thyestes, father of Agamemnon and Menelaus; king of Argos and Mycenae.

Atticke: Attica.

Atys: Attis, Phrygian youth, favorite of Cybele, who was changed into an almond tree.

Augie: Augias, king of Elis, whose stables, long neglected, were cleaned by Hercules.

August: Augustus Caesar.

Aurora: daughter of Hyperion, wife of Tithonus, mother of Memnon.

Auster: south wind.

Autonoe: daughter of Cadmus, aunt of Pentheus.

Aventine: (1) one of the seven hills of Rome.

(2) Alban king buried there.

Averne: Avernus, lake in Italy near Cumae. Also, the underworld, the entrance to which was thought to be in this vicinity.

Awlys: Aulis, seaport in Boeotia.

Awsonye: Ausonia, lower Italy, Italy.

Awtolychus: son of Mercury and Chione, father of Anticlea, grandfather of Ulysses, husband of Mestra, daughter of Erysichthon. A skillful robber, he could assume various shapes. XI, 360.

Bacchus: god of wine, son of Jove and Semele. (Cf. IV, 15 for his other names.) III, 316.

Barcey: for Bactria (now Balkh) in western Asia.

Battus: herdsman who tried to trick Mercury. II, 856.

Baucis: wife of Philemon. VIII, 807.

Beare: double constellation, Ursa Major and Minor.

Bele: Belus, legendary founder of Babylon.

Bellona: sister of Mars; goddess of war.

Biston: Bistonian, belonging to a Thracian people south of Mt. Rhodope.

Boebes: Lake Boebeis in Thessaly.

Bootes: constellation containing Arcturus.

Boreas: north wind; personified, the son of the river-god Strymon; father, by Orithyia, of Calais and Zetes. VI, 863.

Brauron: a village in Attica. (But Ovid, in VII, 487, apparently wrote Pleuron, a city in Aetolia.)

Bubasie: Bubasis, a town in Egypt, and the goddess worshipped there.

Burye: Buris, Achaian city.

Busiris: cruel king of Egypt, killed by Hercules.

Butes: son of Pallas the Athenian.

Buthrotos: town on the coast of Epirus.

Byblis: daughter of Miletus and Cyanee; brother of Caunus, whom she loved. IX, 540.

Cacus: giant bandit who lived on Mt. Aventine (Rome), killed by Hercules.

Cadmies: Cadmeides, the daughters of Cadmus. IV, 692.

Cadmus: son of the Phoenician king Agenor, brother of Europa, husband of Harmonia, father of Semele, Agave, Ino, and Autonoe. III, 5; IV, 694.

Caeny (Cene): Caeneus, originally a girl, Caenis, changed by Neptune into a boy. The father was Elatus. XII, 191, 458.

Caieta: (1) the nurse of Aeneas.

  (2) the town and harbor in Latium named for her. XV, 802.

Calabry: Calabria, region of southern Italy.

Calais: winged son of Boreas and Orithyia. VI, 900.

Calaurie: Calauria, an island on the eastern coast of Argolis.

Calchas: Greek prophet, son of Thestor.

Calliope: chief of the muses, goddess of epic poetry and other kinds as well.

Callirrhoee: Callirrhoe, daughter of Achelous, second wife of Alcmaeon.

Callisto: nymph loved by Jove, II, 513.

Calydna: in VIII, 298, for Ovid's "Calymne," an Aegean island near Rhodes.

Calydon: town in Aetolia, built by a hero of the same name. The boar hunt there, VIII, 359. The king of Calydon in XIV, 582, is Diomedes.

Camp: Castrum, a city of the Rutuli near Ardea, just south of Rome.

Campania: region in central Italy, south of Rome.

Canapey: sic for Capaneus, one of the seven against Thebes, slain by Jove. IX, 485.

Cancer: the Crab (Zodiac).

Candie: Candia, Heracleion, a city in northern Crete. However, Ovid's line (VIII, 43) reads "candida Dictaei . . . tentoria regis." It looks as if Golding has either mistranslated "candida," which means "bright, dazzling," or was working from a bad text. The adjective "Dictaei" means "of Dicte," a mountain in Crete.

Canop: Canopus, island-town in Lower Egypt. (Cleopatra is the "Queene of Aegypt" referred to, Antony the "Romane Capteyne." XV, 929.)

Capetus: fabulous king of Alba.

Capharey: Caphareus, promontory on the southern coast of Euboea.

Capreas: Caeprae, now Capri.

Capys: king of Alba.

Caria: province of Asia Minor, south of Lydia.

Carpathia: the Carpathian Sea, around the island of Carpathus in the Aegean. Proteus lived there.

Carthey: Carthaea, a town on Ceos.

Cassiope: mother of Andromeda.

Caucasus: mountain chain in Asia.

Caune: Caunus, son of Miletus; brother of Byblis. IX, 540.

Cawlon: Caulon, a city of the Brutii in southeastern Italy.

Caycus: river of Mysia (Teuthranie).

Cayster: river in Lydia, famous for its swans.

Cebrius: for Cebren, a river in the Troas, and its river-god, father of Oenone and Hesperie.

Cecrops: mythical founder of Athens and first king of Attica.

Celen: Celenna, city in Campania.

Celmus: Celmis, a priest of Cybele. IV, 341.

Cene: cf. Caeny.

Centaurs: wild Thessalian mountaineers, according to the fable half man, half horse. Sons of Ixion (some said) and a cloud in the shape of Juno. Battle with the Lapithae, XII, 236.

Cenye: Cenaeum, the northwest tip of Euboea.

Ceos: island off the promontory of Sunion, in Greece.

Cephalus: son of Deioneus or Pandion, grandson (not son, as Golding says) of Aeolus. Husband of Procris. VI, 861; VII, 630, 855.

Cephey: Cepheus, king of Ethiopia, husband of Cassiope, father of Andromeda.

Cephisus: river in Phocis and its river-god. The story of his niece is not known.

Ceramb: Cerambus, turned into a beetle for his assault on the nymphs. VII, 455.

Cerastes: Cerastae, a horned people in Cyprus, changed into bullocks by Venus. X, 237.

Cerberus: watchdog of the underworld.

Cercops: Cercopes, dwellers on the island of Pithecusa; because of their trickery, changed into monkeys. XIV, 108.

Cercyon: Attic robber slain by Theseus.

Ceres: daughter of Saturn and Ops, sister of Jove, goddess of agriculture, especially of fruit and corn. V, 434.

Ceyx: son of Lucifer; king of Trachis; husband of Alcyone. XI, 308.

Chaon: Chaonia, in northwest Epirus, where the famous oak forest of Dodona was.

Charon: ferryman in the underworld.

Charybdis: whirlpool between Italy and Sicily, personified as a female monster.

Choanie: region of Epirus.

Chryse: town in the Troad sacred to Apollo.

Chymera: Chimaera, a fire-breathing monster in Lycia, part lion, part dragon, part goat.

Chyone: Chione, daughter of Daedalion, mother of Autolycus by Mercury, of Philammon by Apollo. XI, 345.

Chyron: Chiron, a centaur, son of Saturn.

Ciconie: land of the Cicones, a Thracian people.

Cilicia: province in southern Asia Minor.

Cilla: town in the Troad, devoted to Apollo.

Cimmerians: (1) Thracian people in the Crimea.
　　　　　　　(2) fabulous race of cave dwellers between Baiae and Cumae, who lived in perpetual darkness.

Cinyras: king in Assyria, later in Cyprus. Father of Myrrha, and, by her, of Adonis. X, 325.

Cippus: Cipus, fabled Roman praetor. XV, 632.

Circe: daughter of Apollo and Perse (Perseis), sea nymph and enchantress. "Circes mountayne" (XV, 804) is the promontory of Circeii in Latium. XIV, 12.

Claros:.small town in Ionia famous for oracle of Apollo.

Cleona: Cleonae, small town in Argolis, in Greece.

Climene: Clymene, wife of Merops, mother (by Apollo) of Phaethon.

Clitor: town in Arcadia.

Clytie: (1) sea nymph, daughter of Oceanus, loved by Apollo. IV, 250.
　　　　　(2) Clytius, a companion of Phineus.

Clytus: son of Pallas (the Athenian).

Cocalus: mythical Sicilian king.

Colchis: province in Asia, east of the Black Sea.

Colophon: Ionian town in Lydia.

Combe: daughter of Ophius, mother of the Curetes.

Coronis: nymph loved by Apollo; mother of Aesculapius. II, 677.

Corycus: grot on Parnassus.

Corytus: Corythus, son of Paris and Oenone.

Cos: island in the Myrtoan Sea, off the coast of Caria in Asia Minor.

Crag: Cragos, a promontory and mountain chain in Lycia.

Crathe: Crathis, a river in lower Italy whose waters were said to redden the hair.

Cratye: Crataeis, mother of Scylla.

Cremyon: city near Corinth, harassed by a gigantic boar.

Creon: king of Corinth, whose daughter Creusa married Jason.

Crete: large island south of Greece.

Crocus: youth changed to a flower. IV, 345.

Croton: Croto, Crotona, town founded by Myscelus in southeastern Italy.

Cumes (Cumye): Cumae, town in Campania (southwestern Italy) famous for its Sibyl.

Cupid: son of Venus; god of love.

Curets: Curetes, Cretan priests of Jove.

Curie: Cures, chief town of the Sabines.

Cyane: (1) fountain near Syracuse, in Sicily, and the nymph transformed into it. V, 511.

(2) Cyanee, a nymph, daughter of Maeander, mother of Caunus and Byblis.

Cybaris: Sybaris in lower Italy.

Cybell: Cybele, a goddess, originally Phrygian, worshipped as the Great Mother.

Cyclades: islands around Delos in the Aegean Sea.

Cyclops: (1) race of giant one-eyed Sicilian shepherds, sons of heaven and earth.

(2) Polyphemus, a Cyclops. XIII, 880.

Cygnet: son of Neptune and Calyce; changed into a swan. XII, 79.

Cygnus: cousin of Phaethon. II, 459.

Cyllen: Cyllene, mountain in Arcadia. Mercury was called Cyllenius.

Cymoley: Cimolus, one of the Cyclades.

Cyniphis: Cinyps, river in Libya.

Cynth: Cynthus, a mountain on the island of Delos.

Cynthia: Diana.

Cyparissus: a youth changed to a cypress. X, 114.

Cythera: Aegean island famous for worship of Venus.

Cytheron: Cithaeron, mountain between Attica and Boeotia famous for Theban bacchic orgies.

Daedalion: son of Lucifer; brother of Ceyx. XI, 336.

Daedalus: father of Icarus; builder of the Cretan labyrinth. VIII, 211.

Damasene: for Tamasos, city in Cyprus.

Danae: daughter of Acrisius, mother (by Jupiter) of Perseus.

Danaus: son of Belus, father of fifty daughters, who—all but one—murdered their husbands at Danaus' command. IV, 573; X, 46.

Daphne: daughter of the river-god Peneus; loved by Apollo. I, 545.

Daphnye: Daphnis, shepherd on Mt. Ida. IV, 335.

Daunus: king of Calabria, father (or at least ancestor) of Turnus; father-in-law of Diomedes.

Dawlis: Daulis, a city of Phocis.

Deiphobus: son of Priam and Hecuba.

Delia: Diana, born on the island of Delos.

Delos: small Aegean island, birthplace of Apollo and Diana.

Delphos: Delphi, city in Phocis, famous for its oracle of Apollo.

Deucalion: son of Prometheus; husband of Pyrrha. I, 372.

Deyanyre: Dejanira, daughter of Oeneus, wife of Hercules. IX, 12.

Dia: older name of Naxos.

Diana: sister of Apollo, goddess of the hunt, the moon, virginity, etc.

Dictynna: Diana.

Didymey: Didyme, a group of islands on the coast of Lycia.

Dilos: Delos, the Aegean isle.

Dindymus: mountain in Phrygia.

Diomed: Diomedes, son of Tydeus; king of Aetolia. After the siege of Troy he settled in Italy, where he founded the city of Argyripa in Apulia.

Dircetes: Dercetis, a Syrian goddess corresponding to Aphrodite; mother of Semiramis.

Dis: Pluto.

Dodon: Dodona, city in Epirus, famous for its oracle of Jove in a grove of oaks.

Dolon: Trojan spy.

Doris: daughter of Ocean and Tethys, wife of Nereus, mother of the Nereids.

Drias: Dryas, a hunter; otherwise unknown.

Dryopee: Dryope, mother of Amphissus by Apollo.

Dulich: Dulichius, island near Ithaca, ruled over by Ulysses, who is therefore called Dulichius.

Dyctis: the region of Dicte, a mountain in Crete.

Dymant: Dymas, father of Hecuba.

Echidna: (lit., adder), a monster, half woman, half snake, the mother of Cerberus.

Echion: (1) follower of Cadmus.

(2) son of Mercury; an Argonaut.

(3) Orion (?). XIII, 823.

Echo: a wood nymph in love with Narcissus. III, 443.

Egeria (Aegeria): a nymph, wife and instructress of Numa. XV, 615.

Elatus: prince of the Lapithae, father of Caeneus.

Eleusis: city of Attica, famous for rites of Ceres.

Elpenor: companion of Ulysses; killed in a drunken fall. XIV, 290.

Ely: Elis, district and town in Greece.

Elysion: Elysium, the abode of the blessed in the underworld.

Emese: for Nemese, city of lower Italy.

Enipeus: river in Thessaly and its river-god.

Enna: Henna, city in the center of Sicily, near Lake Pergusa.

Envy: II, 949.

Epaphus: son of Jove and Io.

Eperie: for Hesperie, daughter of the river Cebren. XI, 885.

Epidaure: Epidaurus, city in Argolis.

Epit: Epytus, king of Alba.

Epyre: the province of Epirus, in northern Greece.

Erasine: Erasinus, a river of Argolis.

Erecthey: Erechtheus, legendary king of Athens, father of Procris.

Eribus: Erebus, god of darkness, son of Chaos, brother of Nox.

Erichthonius: child of Vulcan, born of the sun. II, 695.

Erigonee (Erygone): Erigone, daughter of Icarius of Sparta; she became the constellation Virgo.

Erisicthon: Erysichthon, son of Triopas, king of Thessaly. Father of Mestra. VIII, 924.

Erymanth: stream in Arcadia, near the city of Psophis.

Eryx: mountain in Sicily.

Euboea: island in the Aegean Sea off Boeotia.

Euenus: river of Aetolia.

Euip: Euippe, wife of Pieros; mother of the Pierides.

Eumelles: Eumelus (?).

Eumolphus: Eumolpus, Thracian singer and priest of Ceres; he brought to Attica the Eleusinian mysteries and the culture of the vine.

Eupalamon: apparently a misreading of Hippalmos, an otherwise unknown hunter.

Euphorbus: a brave Trojan, whose soul, thought Pythagoras, had transmigrated into his own.

Europa: daughter of Agenor. II, 1085; III, 1.

Eurotas: river in Laconia, near the promontory of Taenarus.

Eurus: east (or southeast) wind.

Eurydicee: wife of Orpheus. X, 32.

Eurylochus: companion of Ulysses; the only one to resist Circe.

Eurypil: Eurypylus, son of Hercules; king of the island of Cos.

Eurysthye: Eurystheus, king of Argos, who imposed on Hercules the twelve labors.

Eurytus (Ewryt): (1) king of Oechalia; father of Iole.
                    (2) a centaur. XII, 246.

Evander: Arcadian who, before the Trojan War, founded the city of Pallantium in Italy.

Ewrymed: for Eurymus, a seer, father of the seer Telemus.

Ewrypyle: Eurypylus, son of Euaemon of Thessaly, a Greek leader.

Fame (Fama): XII, 46.

Farfar: Farfarus or Fabaris, a tributary of the Tiber.

Formy: Formiae, ancient city of Latium.

Galantis: servant of Alcmene, changed by Lucina into a weasel. IX, 369.

Galat (Galate): Galatea, a sea nymph loved by Polyphemus, in love with Acis. XIII, 874.

Ganymed: son of Laomedon (or Troas), carried off by an eagle to become Jove's cup bearer. X, 161.

Garamant: one of a powerful African tribe.

Giant: one of the fabled sons of Earth and Tartarus, with snakes for legs. I, 210.

Glaucus: fisherman of Anthedon, changed into a sea-god. XIII, 1060; XIV, 13.

Gnossus: Knossos, capital of Crete.

Gnyde: Gnidus, Cnidus, Doric city in Caria, famous for Praxiteles' statue of
Venus.
Gorgee: Gorge, daughter of Oeneus; changed into a bird.
Gorgon: one of the three daughters of Phorcus; generally, Medusa.
Gotesea: Ovid's "Aegaeas . . . aquas," the Aegean Sea. Some derive the
name from the Greek word *aiges* (goats), which the many islands
were thought to resemble.
Grayes: Graii, the Greeks.
Gyaros: small Aegean island, one of the Cyclades.

Hammon: (1) Egyptian deity, worshipped in the form of a ram. V, 21.
(2) opponent of Phineus. V, 130.
Hebe: daughter of Juno; goddess of youth, cup bearer to the gods.
Hebrus: principal river in Thrace.
Hecat: Hecate, daughter of Perses (or Persaeus) and Asteria, sister of Latona;
goddess of enchantments, etc.; sometimes identified with Diana, Luna,
Proserpine.
Hector: son of Priam and Hecuba, husband of Andromache.
Hecubee: Hecuba, daughter of Dymas; wife of Priam. XIII, 489.
Helen: (1) Helenus, prophetic son of Priam and Hecuba.
(2) Helena, Helen, daughter of Jupiter (as swan) and Leda; wife of
Menelaus.
Helicee: Helice, town in Achaia swallowed up by the sea.
Helicon: mountain in Boeotia sacred to the muses.
Hellespontus: the Hellespont, the modern Dardanelles, the strait between
European and Asiatic Turkey.
Heme: Haemus, mountain range in Thrace, and the man whose body was
transformed into it.
Hercules, Hercle: son of Jove and Alcmena, husband of Dejanira. IX, 17; IX,
119; IX, 134. The "towne of Hercules" of XV, 796, is
Herculaneum at the foot of Mt. Vesuvius.
Hermaphroditus: son of Mercury and Venus, loved by Salmacis. IV, 352.
Hermes: Mercury.
Herse: daughter of Cecrops, loved by Mercury. II, 701, 898.
Hersilia: wife of Romulus. XIV, 958.
Hesion: Hesione, daughter of Laomedon, king of Troy; wife of Telamon. XI,
. 243.
Hesperids: Hesperides, the daughters of Hesperus, who were in charge of a
garden with golden apples on an island beyond Mt. Atlas.
Hill: Hyllus, son of Hercules by Dejanira; husband of Iole.
Hiperion: Hyperion, the sun-god.
Hippasus: son of Eurytus.
Hippocoon: native of Amyclae in Laconia; father of Enaesimus, Alcon, Dexip-
pus.

Hippodamas: father of Perimele, a nymph changed into an island.

Hippodame: daughter of Adrastus, wife of Pirithous. XII, 237.

Hippolytus: son of Theseus and Hippolyte, falsely accused by Phaedra, his step-mother, and destroyed by his father's curse. Brought back to life by Aesculapius, he was taken by Diana to a grove near Aricia for divine honors, under the name of Virbius. XV, 555.

Hippomenes: son of Megareus, husband of Atalanta. X, 669.

Hippothous: son of Cercyon.

Hyacinth: Spartan youth loved by Apollo. X, 168.

Hydra: water-snake with seven heads. When one head was cut off, two shot up in its place. Killed by Hercules.

Hyen: hyena.

Hyle: Hyleus, a hunter, else unknown.

Hymen: god of marriage.

Hymettus: mountain near Athens.

Hypanis: river in Scythia.

Hypep: Hypaepa, small town in Lydia.

Hypsiphile: daughter of Thoas, queen of Lemnos.

Hyrie: lady of Boeotia turned into a lake, and the name of the lake she became. VII, 476.

Ialyse: Ialysus, city on the island of Rhodes.

Ianthee: daughter of Telestes the Cretan. In love with Iphys. IX, 842.

Iasion: Iasius, son of Jove and Electra; loved by Ceres.

Iber: river Iberus (now Ebro) in Spain.

Icarus: (1) son of Daedalus. VIII, 264.

　　　　(2) (Icar) son of Oebalus, king of Sparta, father of Erigone and Penelope. He became the constellation Bootes.

Icelos: dream-producing son of Somnus. XI, 743.

Ida, Ide: (1) mountain in the Troad.

　　　　(2) mountain in Crete.

Idas: son of Aphareus, king of Messene.

Ide: Idas, companion of Diomedes.

Idominey: Idomeneus, leader of the Cretans against Troy.

Ilia: Rhea Silvia, daughter of Numitor, mother of Romulus and Remus.

Ilion: Ilium, Troy.

Ilithya: Ilithyia, Lucina, goddess of childbirth.

Illirie: Illyria, the modern Dalmatia and Albania.

Ilus: son of Tros, father of Laomedon; founder of Ilium.

Inachus: king of Argos, father of Io, and the river named for him.

Inarime: Tyrrhenian island, now Ischia.

Indiges: title of hero made a god after his death. Of Aeneas, XIV, 691.

Ine: Ino, daughter of Cadmus. IV, 515.

Io: daughter of Inachus. I, 722.

Iolay: Iolaus, son of Iphiclus; nephew and companion of Hercules. IX, 479.

Iolee: daughter of Eurytus, king of Oechalia. IX, 169.

Iphigen: Iphigenia, daughter of Agamemnon and Clytemnestra. XII, 33.

Iphis: young man of Cyprus, in love with Anaxarete. XIV, 802.

Iphys: Cretan girl changed into a boy. IX, 789.

Iris: goddess of the rainbow, messenger of the gods.

Isis: Egyptian goddess, wife of Osiris, mother of Horus.

Ismenos: river near Thebes.

Issa: Isse, daughter of the Lesbian king Macareus.

Istre: the Danube.

Ithaca: island in the Aeonian Sea, ruled over by Ulysses.

Itys: son of Tereus and Procne. VI, 560.

Ixion: king of the Lapithae, who murdered his father-in-law and attempted to assault Juno; father of Perithous. He begot the centaurs on a cloud. IV, 571; X, 47.

Janus: Italian deity with two faces in opposite directions, the god of doors, gates, etc.

Jason: son of the Thessalian prince Aeson; leader of the Argonauts. VII, 5.

Jove: Jupiter, Zeus, highest of the gods, son of Saturn and Rhea.
and Io, I, 727.
and Callisto, II, 512.
and Europa, II, 1058; III, 1.
and Semele, III, 316.
and Leda, Alcmene, Danae, and others, VI, 127.

Juba: king of Numidia, enemy of Caesar.

Julius Caesar: Roman Emperor. I, 235; XV, 840.

July: Iulus, another name for Ascanius, son of Aeneas.

Juno: daughter of Saturn and Rhea; wife and sister of Jove.

Kiddes: Haedi (the Kids) a double star in Auriga—called "rainy" by Vergil.

Lacine: Lacinium: promontory near Crotona in southeastern Italy.

Ladon: river in Arcadia.

Laelaps: "Hurricane," name of the dog that Procris gave to Cephalus.

Laert: Laertes, father of Ulysses.

Lampetie: one of the Heliades, daughters of Helius (the sun), sisters of Phaethon.

Lamye: Lamus, son of Neptune, founder of the town of Formiae in Italy. King of the Laestrygonians.

Laomedon: king of Troy, father of Priam and Ganymede. XI, 219.

Lapithae: mountaineer tribe in Thessaly who fought with the Centaurs at the wedding of Perithous, their king. XII, 236.

Larissa: city in Thessaly.

448   GLOSSARY OF NAMES AND PLACES

Latinus: (1) son of Faunus; king of Laurentium.

(2) son of Silvius; king of Alba.

Latium: the region about Rome.

Laton: Latona, daughter of Coeus and Phoebe, mother of Apollo and Diana. VI, 199.

Laurents: inhabitants of Laurentum, a town on the coast north of Rome.

Lavine: (1) Lavinia, daughter of Latinus, wife of Aeneas.

(2) Lavinium, a city in Latium.

Learchus: Laearchus, son of Athamas and Ino. IV, 637.

Lebinthos: one of the Sporadic Isles in the Aegean.

Leda: daughter of Thestius, wife of Tyndarus, mother (by Jupiter in the form of a swan) of Helen, Clytemnestra, Castor and Pollux. VI, 134.

Lelegs: a Pelasgic tribe.

Lelex: (1) a Locrian king.

(2) one of the Leleges, a Pelasgic tribe. Used as a proper name, VIII, 729.

Lemnos: island in the Aegean.

Lerna: forest and marsh near Argos, habitat of the Hydra.

Lesbos: island in the Aegean, off the coast of Troy and Mysia.

Lethaea: wife of Olenus.

Lethey: Lethe, underworld river whose waters induced forgetfulness in the drinker.

Leucothoe: (1) for Leuconoe, daughter of Minyas. IV, 203.

(2) daughter of Orchamus, king of Babylon, and Eurynome; loved by Apollo. IV, 238.

(3) Leucothea (or Leucothee), the name Ino took as a sea-goddess. IV, 670.

Leucyppus: Leucippus, father of Phoebe and Hilaira (?).

Lewcas: Leucas, a promontory (Golding says town) of the island of Leucadia.

Lewcosye: Leucosia, small island off the coast of Lucania, near Paestum.

Liber: Bacchus.

Limyre: Limyra, river and town in Lycia.

Lidia: country in Asia Minor.

Lincide: Lyncides, a descendant of Lynceus, one of the Argonauts.

Linterne: Liternum, city in Campania.

Lotos: Lotis, a nymph, daughter of Neptune, changed into a lotus tree. IX, 418.

Lucifer: (1) the morning star (the planet Venus).

(2) fabled son of Aurora and Cephalus; father of Ceyx and Daedalion.

Lucina: goddess of childbirth.

Lybicke: Libyan, African.

Lycaeon: impious king of Arcadia. I, 188.

Lyceus: mountain in Arcadia.

Lychas: Lichas, an attendant of Hercules. IX, 191.
Lycia: region in Asia Minor.
Lycormas: river in Aetolia.
Lyct (Lyctus): Ligdus, a Cretan, husband of Telethusa, father of Iphis.
Lycurgus: king of Thrace.
Lycus: (1) a companion of Diomedes.
　　　 (2) a Phrygian river.
Lymbo: Limbo, the underworld.
Lynce: son of Aphareus; king of the Messenians.
Lyncest: the Lyncestai, a people in a southwestern Macedonia.
Lyncus: Scythian king. V, 798.
Lyriop: Liriope, mother of Narcissus.
Lyrnessus: Lyrnesus, a town in the Troas.

Macare: Macareus, companion of Ulysses, and later of Aeneas in Italy.
Magnets: Magnetes, inhabitants of Magnesia in Thessaly.
Maia, May: one of the Pleiads, daughter of Atlas, mother of Mercury.
Manto: prophetess, daughter of Tiresias.
Maraeotis lake: the Mareotic lake, near Alexandria in lower Egypt.
Marathon: town in Attica.
Mars: god of war, son (in some versions of the myth) of Jove and Juno.
　　　 and Venus. IV, 208.
Marsias (Marsyas): (1) a satyr who challenged Apollo at flute playing. VI, 510.
　　　 (2) a river in Phrygia, formed by the tears of those who
　　　 wept the satyr's fate. V, 510.
Maydenwood: Parthenium Nemus, a grove near Mt. Parthenius in Arcadia
　　　 (Gk. *parthenos,* maiden).
Meander: river in Lydia.
Medea: daughter of Aeetes, king of Colchis; sorceress. VII, 10.
Medusa: snaky-haired daughter of Phorcus who turned beholders to stone.
　　　 IV, 953.
Megara: Greek city, between Attica and Phocis.
Megaree: son of Neptune; father of Hippomenes, who married Atalanta.
Melampus: physician and prophet, son of Amythaon.
Melantho: sea nymph, daughter of Neptune.
Melas: river in Thrace (where the Migdonians lived).
Meleager: son of Oeneus (king of Calydonia) and Althaea. VIII, 356.
Melicert: Melicerta (or Melicertes), son of Athamas and Ino who became the
　　　 sea-god Palaemon. IV, 644.
Memnon: son of Tithonus and Aurora; king of the Ethiopians, Trojan helper
　　　 in the war. XIII, 693.
Menalus: mountain in Arcadia.
Menelay: Menelaus, son of Atreus; brother of Agamemnon; husband of Helen.

Menephron: "the name of an immoral person" (Lewis and Short, *A Latin Dictionary*).

Meonie: (1) apparently for Ovid's "Mnemonides," daughters of Mnemosyne, the Muses.

(2) Lydia, VI, 185.

Meras: Maera, name of a woman changed into a dog. (Golding calls her "he" in VII, 464.)

Mercury: son of Jove and Maia, messenger of the gods.

and Battus, II, 853.

and Herse, II, 898.

Meremayds: the Sirens, whose "rocks" (XIV, 103) were three small islands off the southwest coast of Campania, in southern Italy. V, 689.

Meriones: charioteer and pilot of Idomeneus, the Cretan leader at Troy.

Merops: king of Ethiopia, husband of Clymene.

Messapie: Messapia, old name of Apulia and Calabria.

Messene: the capital of Messenia in Greece.

Methymnye: Methymna, city on the island of Lesbos.

Micole: Ionian promontory.

Midas: son of Gordius; king of Phrygia, given the power of turning what he touched into gold. XI, 102.

Migdonie: Mygdonia, name of several geographical regions. In VI, 55, Lydia.

Milet: son of Apollo and Deione, father of Caunus and Byblis.

Milo: famous athlete of Crotona.

Mime: Mimas, a mountain range in Ionia.

Minerva: daughter of Jove, goddess of arts and sciences. VI, 1.

Mineus: Minyas, king of Orchomenos in Thessaly.

Minos: (1) son of Zeus and Europa, king of Crete; after death a judge in the underworld.

(2) his grandson, king of Crete, husband of Pasiphae; builder of the labyrinth. VIII, 7.

Minotaur: monster with body of man, head of bull; born of Pasiphae and a bull. VIII, 230.

Minturne: Minturnae, a city of Latium.

Minyes: Minyae, the Minyans, Argonauts, companions of Jason; descended from Minyas, a Thessalian king.

Mnemosyne: the mother of the Muses.

Molossus: obscure king whose sons were changed into birds.

Moly: plant with magical powers.

Morph, Morphye: Morpheus, son of Somnus; god of dreams. XI, 736.

Mutinye: Mutinae in northern Italy (now Modena) where Octavian defeated Antony in 43 B.C.

Mycale: a witch, mother of the Lapith Orion.

Myconey: Myconos, one of the Cyclades.

Myrmidons: their origin, VII, 789.

Myrrha: daughter of Cinyras, in love with her father; changed into a myrrh tree. X, 327.

Myscelus: founder of Crotona, in Italy.

Mysen: Misenus, son of Aeolus, trumpeter of Aeneas, buried on the promontory of Misenum in Campania (southwestern Italy).

Mysia: country in Asia Minor.

Mythridate: Mithridates, king of Pontus, finally conquered by Pompey.

Nabathie: region in Arabia.

Nar: the Nar, river that flows into the Tiber.

Narcissus: son of the river-god Cephisus and Liriope. III, 431.

Narice, Narix: Narycia, Locri, a city in lower Italy founded by the Locrians under Ajax Oileus.

Narytium: Narycion, a Locrian city (in Greece).

Nasamone: a region of Libya.

Naxos: Aegean isle noted for the cult of Bacchus.

Neaeth Salentine: for Neretum, a city of the Salentini, a Calabrian people.

Nele: Neleus, father of Nestor, king of Pylos.

Nemea: a city in Argolis near which Hercules killed the famous lion.

Neoptolemus: Pyrrhus, son of Achilles.

Neptune: god of the sea, brother of Jove.

Nereus: son of Ocean, god of the sea.

Neritus: poetic for Ithaca.

Nesse: Nessus, a centaur killed by Hercules. IX, 119.

Nestor, Naestor: son of Neleus; king of Pylos, said to have lived through three lifetimes.

Niobe: daughter of Tantalus and Pleione (one of the Hyades), wife of Amphion, king of Thebes. VI, 184.

Nisus: king of Megara; father of Scylla.

Nonacris: city in northern Arcadia.

Noricum: country between the Danube and the Alps.

Noy: Noah.

Numa (Nume): Numa Pompilius, second king of Rome.

Numicke: Numicius, small river in Latium.

Numidy: Numidia, a country in northern Africa.

Numitor: king of Alba; grandfather of Romulus and Remus.

Nyct: Nycteus, companion of Diomedes.

Nyctyminee: girl of Lesbos punished for incest. II, 742.

Nysa: a town some said in Thrace, some in India.

Ocyroe: Ocyrhoe, prophetic daughter of Chiron and a nymph. II, 800.

Oechalia: city of Euboea.

Oeclie: Oecleus, father of Amphiaraus.

Oenie: Oeneus, king of Calydonia; husband of Althaea, father of Meleager, Tydeus, Gorge, Dejanira, etc., grandfather of Diomedes.

Oenope: island of Aegina.

Oeta: mountain in Thessaly.

Olenien: of the Greek city Olenus, where a goat nourished the young Jove.

Olenus: husband of Lethaea, changed with her into a stone because of pride.

Olyarey: Olearos, one of the Cyclades.

Olympus: mountain between Macedonia and Thessaly, believed the seat of the gods.

Onchestyes: of Onchestus, a city in Boeotia. (Golding seems to think it the name of a person.) X, 706.

Ops: wife of Saturn, goddess of plenty.

Ora: Hora, the deified Hersilia.

Orchomen: Orchomenos, city in Arcadia.

Orestes: son of Agamemnon and Clytemnestra.

Orion: (1) the constellation; in legend, a hunter transported to heaven.
(2) a Lapith, son of Mycale. XII, 291.

Orithya: (1) Orithyia, daughter of Erechtheus, king of Athens. VI, 864.
(2) So Golding renders "Eurytidae" in VIII, 497; it should refer to Hippasus (line 419), the son of Eurytus.

Orontes: river in Syria.

Orphey: Orpheus, son of Oeagrus and Calliope, husband of Eurydice. X, 2; XI, 1.

Orphne: "Darkness," a nymph of the underworld.

Ortygie: the island of Delos.

Ossa: mountain in Thessaly.

Osyris: Egyptian deity, husband of Isis.

Othrys: mountain in Thessaly.

Pachinnius: Pachynum, southeastern promontory of Sicily.

Pactolus: a Lydian river whose sands were said to be of gold.

Padus: the Po.

Paean: Paeas of Thessaly, father of Philoctetes.

Pagasa: town in Thessaly where the Argo was built.

Palamede: son of Nauplius, king of Euboea. XIII, 47.

Palatine: the Palatine, one of the seven hills of Rome.

Pale: Pales, goddess of shepherds and cattle.

Palemon: Palaemon, the name taken by Melicert, son of Athamas, when he became a sea-god. IV, 670.

Palik: of the Palici, sons of Jove and the nymph Aetna (or Thalia), worshipped at Palica in Sicily.

Palladye: image of Pallas in Troy, thought to protect the city, stolen by Ulysses and Diomede.

Pallant: Pallas, one of the giants, father of Aurora (Dawn), who was married to Tithonus.

Pallas: (1) Minerva.

(2) nephew of Aegeus, king of Athens.

Pallene: Phlegra, peninsula and town in Macedonia.

Pan: the goat-like Arcadian god of woods, music, etc. (also plural, XIV, 726). and Syrinx, I, 870.

Panchaya: rich and fabulous island east of Arabia.

Pandion: king of Athens, father of Procne and Philomela.

Pandrosos: daughter of Cecrops.

Panope: city in Phocis.

Panopie: Panopeus, a hunter, otherwise unknown.

Paphus: son (some say daughter) of Pygmalion and founder of Paphos on the island of Cyprus.

Paretonie: Paraetonium, north African town.

Parey: Paros, one of the Cyclades.

Paris: son of Priam and Hecuba, lover of Helen.

Parnasus: Parnassus, mountain in Phocis sacred to Apollo and the Muses.

Parrhasis: a name for Callisto, born in Parrhasia, a region of Arcadia.

Parthaon: king of Calydon, father of Oeneus.

Partrich: Perdix, partridge. VIII, 315.

Pasiphae: daughter of Helios, sister of Circe, wife of Minos, mother of Phaedra.

Patre: Patras, city in Greece.

Patroclus: son of Menoetius and Sthenele, friend of Achilles.

Pean: Paean, Apollo.

Pegasus: the winged horse of the Muses.

Pelagon: hunter, otherwise unknown.

Peley: Peleus, son of Aeacus, husband of Thetis, father of Achilles. XI, 258.

Pelias: king of Thessaly, uncle and guardian of Jason. VIII, 387.

Pelion: mountain in Thessaly.

Pelops: son of Tantalus; father of Atreus and Thyestes. VI, 515.

Pelorus: the promontory of northeastern Sicily (as Pachynus is on the southeast, and Lilybaeum—or Lilybe—on the south).

Peneis: Daphne, daughter of Peneus.

Penelope: wife of Ulysses, Laertes' son.

Peneus, Penew: god of the river of that name in Thessaly, father of Daphne.

Penthesilea: queen of the Amazons, who fought against the Greeks at Troy.

Penthey: Pentheus, king of Thebes, grandson of Cadmus; opponent of Bacchus. III, 645.

Peonie: Paeonia, a part of Macedonia.

Pepareth: Peparethus, small Aegean island.

Periclymen: son of Neleus, brother of Nestor. XII, 616.

Perimell: Perimele, a nymph, daughter of Hippodamas, changed into the island named for her. VIII, 757.

Periphas: king of Attica, turned into an eagle by Apollo.

Perrhebye: the country of the Perrhaebi, Thessalians who lived around Tempe and Mt. Olympus.

Persey: Perseus, son of Jove and Danae. IV, 750.

    and Andromeda, IV, 823.

    and Phineus, V, 1.

Persis: Persia.

Pest: Paestum, city in Lucania famous for its roses.

Phaeton: Phaethon, son of Apollo and Clymene. I, 944; II, 1.

Phaetuse: Phaethusa, one of the Heliades, daughters of Helios, the Sun, and sisters of Phaethon. II, 436.

Phantasos: son of Somnus. XI, 745.

Pharos: island near Alexandria with famous lighthouse.

Pharsaly: Pharsalos in Thessaly, where Caesar defeated Pompey in 48 B.C.

Pheaks: Phaeaces, the Phaeacians, inhabitants of the fabled isle of Scheria (Corcyra).

Phebe: Diana.

Phebus: Apollo.

Phegie: Phegius, king of Psofis, father of Alphesiboea.

Pheney: Pheneos, town and lake in Arcadia.

Pheret: Pheres, king of Pherae, father of Admetus.

Phestos: Phaestum, a town in Crete.

Philammon: musician son of Apollo and Chione.

Philemon: husband of Baucis. VIII, 808.

Philippos: Philippi, city in Macedonia where Octavian and Antony defeated Brutus and Cassius in 42 B.C.

Philomele: Philomela, daughter of Pandion, sister of Procne. VI, 578.

Phiney: Phene (Phoene), wife of Periphas; like him, turned into an eagle. (Cf. *Phyney.*)

Phlaegra: Phlegra, a region in Macedonia, where the giants were destroyed by the gods.

Phlegeton: Phlegethon, a fiery river of the underworld.

Phlegia: the country of the Phlegyae in Thrace (or Thessaly).

Phobetor: Nightmare, son of Morpheus. XI, 744.

Phocis: region in central Greece.

Phocus: son of Aeacus, slain by his brother Peleus.

Phoenix: (1) son of Amyntor, king of the Dolopians in Thessaly.

    (2) fabulous Arabian bird, from whose ashes, every five hundred years, a young Phoenix was thought to arise.

Phorbas: "the name of several mythic personages" (Lewis and Short, *A Latin Dictionary*).

Phorcis: Phorcys (or Phorcus), son of Neptune, father of Medusa, the Gorgons, and the Graeae. The latter as the "daughters" of, IV, 944.

Phoronew: Phoroneus, grandfather of Io.

Phryxus: son of Athamas and Nephele, who fled to Colchis on a golden ram whose fleece he hung in the grove of Ares there.

Phthya: city in Thessaliotis, birthplace of Achilles.

Phyle: Phyleus of Elis, otherwise unknown.

Phyllie: Phyllius, a Boeotian in love with Cycnus.

Phyney, Phineus: (1) brother of Cepheus. V, 8. (His companions in the battle, from various eastern regions, are mere names.)

(2) Thracian king and prophet, punished with blindness for blinding his sons. Calais and Zetes, sons of Boreas, delivered him from the Harpies, who had been stealing the food set before him. VII, 3.

Picus: prophet, son of Saturn, grandfather of Latinus (king of Laurentium), husband of Canens ("Singer"). XIV, 368.

Pieros: king of Emathia who named his daughters for the Muses. V, 383.

Pindus, Pind: Mountain in Thessaly.

Pirithous: son of Ixion; king of the Lapithae, friend of Theseus.

Pithey: Pittheus, king of Troezen; son of Pelops, father of Aethra, Theseus' mother.

Pleione: wife of Atlas, mother of the Pleiades (among them Maia, mother of Mercury).

Plexippus: son of Thestius, otherwise unknown.

Pleyades: Pleiades, the seven daughters of Atlas and Pleione; sisters of the Hyades.

Pluto: king of the underworld, brother of Jove. X, 50.

and Proserpine, V, 484.

Polemnestor: Polymnestor, king of Thrace, husband of Ilione, daughter of Priam.

Polydamas: son of Panthous; friend of Hector.

Polydect: Polydectes, king of the Aegean island of Seriphus. V, 305.

Polydore: son of Priam and Hecuba. XIII, 637.

Polypemon: grandfather of Alcione. She was turned into a kingfisher.

Polyphemus: Cyclops, son-in-law of Neptune, blinded by Ulysses. XIII, 892; XIV, 198.

Polyte: Polytes, companion of Ulysses.

Polyxene: Polyxena, daughter of Priam and Hecuba.

Pomona: goddess of fruit and fruit trees (from "pomum," fruit—a marginal note of Golding suggests that the name might be anglicized to "Applebee"). XIV, 709.

Pompeius: Golding supplies the name that Ovid hints at in "magnum . . . nomen." XV, 928.

Pons, Pontus: a region in Asia Minor around the Black Sea.

Praetus, Prete: Proetus, king of Tiryns, whose daughters were changed into cows by Juno because of their pride. V, 300.

Priam: king of Troy, husband of Hecuba.

Proca: Procas, king of Alba.

Prochite: small Italian island near Campania, now Procida.

Procris: daughter of Erechtheus, king of Athens, wife of Cephalus. VI, 861; VII, 890.

Procrustes: bandit famous for his Procrustean bed; slain by Theseus.

Progne: Procne, daughter of Pandion, sister of Philomela, wife of Tereus. VI, 547.

Prometheus: son of Iapetus, father of Deucalion. I, 95.

Propets: Propoetides, Cyprian girls turned to stone for denying the divinity of Venus. X, 221.

Proserpina: daughter of Ceres and Jove. V, 491.

Protesilay: Protesilaus, son of Iphicles, husband of Laodamia; leader of the Thessalians against Troy.

Protew: Proteus, the protean sea-god.

Pryap: Priapus, god of procreation, gardens, vineyards.

Psamathe: sea nymph, mother of Phocus.

Psophy: Psophis, city in Arcadia.

Puteoll: for Pucetia, a region in Apulia.

Pygmalion: grandson of Agenor; in love with a statue he made. X, 261.

Pyle: Pylos—name of three cities, one in Arcadia, one in Messenia, one in Elis. Nestor lived in the latter, sometimes confused with the second, where Neleus reigned. VI, 533.

Pyramus: Babylonian youth in love with Thisbe. IV, 71.

Pyren: Pyreneus, king of Thrace.

Pyrey: Piraeus, the port of Athens.

Pyrrha: wife of Deucalion. I, 372.

Pyrrhus: son of Achilles and Deidamia.

Pytanie: Pitane, city in Asia Minor.

Pythagoras: philosopher of Samos, c. 550 B.C., who taught at Crotona; founder of Pythagorean philosophy. XV, 66.

Python: serpent slain by Apollo, who was hence called the Pythian. I, 526.

Quirin: Quirinus, the deified Romulus. The Quirinal, one of the seven hills of Rome, was named after him.

Radamanth: Rhadamanthus, son of Jove and Europa, brother of Minos, a judge in the underworld.

Remulus: a king of Alba.

Rethenor: Rhexenor, companion of Diomedes.

Rhamnuse: Nemesis, the goddess of Vengeance.

Rhegion: Regium, city in southern Calabria, now Reggio.

Rhesus: Thracian king killed by Ulysses and Diomedes before Troy.

Rhetye: Rhoeteus, promontory and city on the Hellespont.

Rhodope: mountain range in Thrace, part of Haemus (q.v.).

Rhodos: nymph of the island of Rhodes.

Romeche: Rhomethium, a seaside city south of Squillace, not further identified.

Romulus: founder and first king of Rome, said to be the son of Mars and Rhea Silvia.

Rutills: the Rutuli, an ancient people of Latium.

Saba: largest town in ancient Arabia.

Sabine: the territory of the Sabines, neighbors of the people of Latium.

Salamin: city of Salamis in Cyprus, founded by Teucer from the island of Salamis.

Salmacis: a nymph in love with Hermaphroditus; and the spring in Caria she was changed into. IV, 347.

Same: Samos, island on the coast of Asia Minor near Ephesus.

Sardis: the capital of Lydia, on the Pactolus river.

Sarpedon: son of Jove and Europa; king of Lycia.

Saturnus: Saturn, Kronos, son of Heaven and Earth, father of Jove.

Schoenye: Schoeneus, king of Boeotia, father of Atalanta. VIII, 428.

Scio: Chios, Aegean island.

Scylla: (1) rock between Italy and Sicily, near Charybdis. Personified as daughter of Phorcys transformed by Circe into a sea-monster with dogs about the lower limbs. XIII, 867; XIV, 1.

(2) Daughter of Nisus, in love with Minos. VIII, 20.

Scyre: the Aegean island of Scyros. (Ovid wrote "Cythnos.") V, 321.

Scyron: famous robber slain by Theseus.

Scython: Sithon, a hermaphrodite. IV, 339.

Semele: daughter of Cadmus, mother of Bacchus (whose father was Jove). III, 316.

Semyramis: Semiramis, wife and successor of Ninus, king of Assyria.

Seriph, Seryphey: Seriphus, an island in the Aegean.

Sigaeum: promontory and town in the Troas.

Silenus: old tutor and attendant of Bacchus.

Silvius: the name of several Alban rulers.

Simethis: Ovid (XIII, 750) wrote "Symaethide," which refers to a nymph who was daughter of Symaethus, river and river-god in Sicily.

Simethus: Acis.

Simois: small river in the Troas.

Singer: Canens, daughter of Janus, wife of Picus. XIV, 387.

Sinis: Corinthian robber slain by Theseus.

Sinuesse: Sinuessa; a Latin colony in Campania.

Sipyle: Sipylus, mountain in Lydia.

Sirens: cf. Meremayds.

Sirts: sand banks in the sea, especially those on the northern coast of Africa.

Sisyphus: son of the Thessalian king Aeolus; punished for robbery and fraud. IV, 569; X, 47.

Sleep, House of: XI, 680.

Smylax: a girl changed to a flower. IV, 345.

Spart: Sparta.

Sperchius: river in Thessaly.

Stabye: Stabiae, small coastal town near Pompeii.

Strophad: Strophades, two islands off the coast of Messene, residence of the Harpies.

Stymphalus: district of Arcadia, plagued by foul birds of prey, killed by Hercules.

Styx: underworld river.

Surrent: Surrentum (now Sorrento) in Campania.

Swevite: from Syene (now Essouan) in Egypt.

Sybaris: the river on which the town of Sybaris was located, in lower Italy.

Sybill: prophetess, Sibyl. For Romans, the most famous was at Cumae. XIV, 123.

Symplegads: two islands in the Euxine Sea that (it was said) drifted about crashing into each other.

Syphney: Siphnus, one of the Cyclades.

Syrinx: Arcadian nymph loved by Pan. I, 858.

Sythney: Thrace (?).

Tacye: Tatius, a king of the Sabines.

Taenaris: promontory and town in Laconia; a cavern nearby was the fabled entrance to the underworld.

Tages: Etrurian divinity, grandson of Jove; taught divination to the Etrurians.

Tagus: a river in Spain, now the Tajo.

Tanais: the Don.

Tantalus: son of Jove, father of Pelops and Niobe. Punished for revealing the secrets of the gods. IV, 567; X, 45.

Tarent: Tarentum in lower Italy.

Tarpey: Tarpeia, a Roman girl who betrayed the Tarpeian citadel, on the Capitoline, to the Sabines. XIV, 898.

Taure: Taurus, a mountain in Cicilia in Asia Minor.

Taurica in Chersonese: Chersonesus Taurica, the Crimea.

Tegea: town in Arcadia near Mt. Lyceus.

Telamon: son of Aeacus, father of Ajax and Teucer.

Telchines: legendary family of priests in Rhodes, famous for magic.

Telemus: a soothsayer.

Telephus: king of Mysia, son of Hercules and the nymph Auge.

Telest: Telestes, father of Ianthe.

Telethusa: wife of Ligdus, mother of Iphis.

Temp, Timpe: (1) Tempe, valley in Thessaly.

(2) valley in Aetolia. VII, 474.

Tempsa: a town in the territory of the Brutii in southern Italy.

Tene: Tenos, one of the Cyclades.

Tenedos: island off the coast of Asia, near Troy.

Tereus: king of Thrace; husband of Procne, Philomela's sister. VI, 542.

Tethis: Tethys, daughter of Heaven and Earth, wife of Ocean.

Tewcer: son of Telamon, brother of Ajax; king of Samos.

Tewthranie: Teuthrania, region in Mysia ruled by Teuthras.

Thawmant: Thaumas, the father of Iris.

Thebe: small town in Mysia, destroyed by Achilles.

Themis: goddess of justice.

Theophane: daughter of Bisaltes.

Thermodon: river in Cappadocia, where the Amazons lived. Hercules conquered
their queen, who wore a golden belt given by Mars.

Thersites: Greek at Troy known for his ugliness and scurrilous tongue.

Thesey: Theseus, son of Aegeus and Aethra; king of Athens. VII, 404.

Thespian: of Thespiae in Boeotia, a town at the foot of Mt. Helicon.

Thestie: Thestius, king of Pleuron, father of Leda and Althaea, Plexippus and
Toxeus, who are called "the Thesties" in VIII, 569.

Thetis: sea nymph, daughter of Nereus and Doris, wife of Peleus, mother of
Achilles. XI, 270.

Thisbe: (1) Babylonian girl loved by Pyramus. IV, 71.

(2) little Boeotian town, famous for its wild doves.

Thoants: Thoas, king of Lemnos.

Thurine: belonging to Thurii, city in lower Italy.

Thyestes: son of Pelops, brother of Atreus, whose children he served as food to
their father.

Tirrhene: (1) Etruria.

(2) Etrurian, Tuscan.

Tisiphone: one of the Furies. IV, 587.

Titan: (1) one of a race of pre-Olympian gods, including Oceanus, Hyperion,
Rhea, Iapetos, etc.

(2) Epimetheus, son of Iapetos. I, 470.

(3) the sun-god.

Tithonus: son of Laomedon, consort of Aurora; given the privilege of immortality.

Titius: Tityos, a giant, son of Jove, punished by Apollo for attacking Latona.
IV, 565; X, 44.

Tlepolemus: son of Hercules; Rhodian leader at Troy.

Tmolus: mountain in Lydia.

Toxey: Toxeus, son of Thestius.

Trache: Trachas, Tarracina, a town in Latium, now Terracina.

Trachin: Trachis, town on Mt. Oeta in Thessaly.

Trinacris: Sicily.

Triop: Triopas, king of Thessaly, father of Erysichthon.

Triptolemus: king of Eleusis, inventor of agriculture. V, 792.

Tritonia: Minerva.

Triton lake: the Tritonian Sea near Pallene in Macedonia.

Troas: the region about Troy.

Troyzen: Troezen, a city in Argolis, ruled by Pittheus, the grandfather of Theseus.

Tryton: Triton, sea-god, Neptune's son and trumpeter.

Turne: Turnus, a king of the Rutuli, killed by Aeneas. XIV, 512.

Tyberine: a king of Alba.

Tyndarus: king of Sparta, husband of Leda, father (?) of Castor and Pollux, Helen and Clytemnestra.

Typho (Typhon): Typhoeus, giant struck by lightning and buried under Aetna.

Tyre: Phoenician city.

Tyresias: Tiresias, blind Theban prophet, father of Manto. III, 404.

Ulysses: Ulixes, Odysseus, king of Ithaca; son of Laertes and Anticlea, husband of Penelope. XIII, 7.

Uranie: Urania, the Muse of Astronomy.

Urchins: the Echinades, a small group of islands in the Ionian Sea. The Greek *echinos* meant a hedgehog (urchin).

Venilia: sea nymph, wife of Janus.

Venulus: Rutulian warrior, ambassador to Diomedes.

Venus: goddess of love; according to some legends the daughter of Jove and Dione, according to others, born of the sea foam.
  and Mars, IV, 208.
  and Adonis, X, 614.

Vertumnus: the god of the changing year (Golding suggests he be called "Turner"). XIV, 731.

Vesta: daughter of Saturn, goddess of the household.

Virbie: Virbius, the name of the resurrected Hippolytus (q.v.). (A marginal note of Golding explains it as "Twice-man.")

Vulcan: the fire-god, son of Jove and Juno, husband of Venus. His forges were under Mt. Etna, in Sicily.

Vulturne: Volturnus, a river in Campania.

Xanthus: (1) river near Troy.
  (2) mountain, river, and village in Lycia.

Zanclye: Messina, in Sicily.

Zephyr: the gentle western wind.

Zephyrion: for Ovid's "Amphrisia . . . saxa"—rocks of the promontory of Amphissa (*sic*) in the territory of the Locri Epizephyrii (whence Golding apparently gets his "Zephyrion") in lower Italy.

Zetes: winged son of Boreas and Orithyia. VI, 900.